THE
PUSHCART PRIZE, VI:
BEST OF THE
SMALL PRESSES

✹ ✹ ✹ THE PUSHCART PRIZE, VI:

An annual small press reader. Founding Editors Anaïs Nin (1903–1977), Buckminster Fuller, Charles Newman, Daniel Halpern, Gordon Lish, Harry Smith, H. L. Van Brunt, Hugh Fox, Ishmael Reed, Joyce Carol Oates, Len Fulton, Leonard Randolph, Leslie Fiedler, Nona Balakian, Paul Bowles, Paul Engle, Ralph Ellison, Reynolds Price, Rhoda Schwartz, Richard Morris, Ted Wilentz, Tom Montag, William Phillips. Assembled with the assistance of 147 staff and Special Contributing Editors for this edition, and with the cooperation of the many outstanding small presses whose names follow . . .

BEST OF THE SMALL PRESSES

BEST OF THE SMALL PRESSES

. . . WITH AN INDEX TO THE FIRST SIX VOLUMES

EDITED BY BILL HENDERSON

published by THE PUSHCART PRESS
1981—82 Edition

THE PUSHCART PRIZE, VI: 🔥 🔥 🔥

Library of Congress Card Number: 76-58675
ISBN 0–916366–12–X
ISSN: 0149–7863

First printing, May, 1981

Manufactured in The United States of America
by RAY FREIMAN and COMPANY, Stamford, Connecticut

Acknowledgements

The following works are reprinted by permission of the publishers and authors:

"The River Again and Again" © 1980 *Ironwood*
"After The Interrogation" © 1980 *Shankpainter*
"For Elizabeth Bishop" © 1980 *The American Poetry Review*
"Floor" © 1980 *The American Poetry Review*
"Return" © 1980 *The American Poetry Review*
"This Day" © 1980 *The Southwestern Review*
"The Widow's Yard" © 1980 BOA Editions
"World Breaking Apart" © 1980 *Water Table*
"Cantina Music" © 1980 *Antaeus*
"Weldon Kees in Mexico" © 1980 *Columbia*
"Silo Letters In The Dead of a Warm Winter" © 1980 *Massachusetts Review*
"Dying" © 1980 The Modern Poetry Association; reprinted by permission of the Editor of *Poetry*
"The Tomb of Stephan Mallarmé © 1980 *The Georgia Review*
"A Motel In Troy, N.Y." © 1980 The Modern Poetry Association, reprinted by permission of the Editor of *Poetry*
"Blame" © 1980 *Ploughshares*
"Three Studies for a Head of John The Baptist" © 1980 *Field*
"The Gentlemen In The U Boats" © 1980 *New Letters*
"Ode" © 1980 *The Kenyon Review*
"At the Far End of a Long Wharf" © 1980 *The Sonora Review*
"Scatsquall In Spring" © 1980 *The Kenyon Review*
"Dead Fish" © 1980 *The Iowa Review*
"When I Was A Child" © 1980 *Black Scholar*
"Leda" © 1980 *Field*
"Waiting In Line" © 1980 Barnwood Press
"Hunger" © 1980 *Ironwood*
"The Sadness of Brothers" © 1980 *The American Poetry Review*, © 1980 Galway Kinnell: From *Mortal Acts, Mortal Words*. Reprinted by permission of the publisher, Houghton Mifflin Co.
"Girl Talk" © 1980 *Shankpainter*
"In The Land of Plenty" © 1980 *The Iowa Review*
"Eclipse" © 1980 *Fiction International*
"Fionn In The Valley" © 1980 *Ploughshares*
"A Romantic Interlude. . ." © 1980 *Sun & Moon*
"Arthur Bond" © 1980 *Missouri Review*
"Woden's Day" © 1980 Farrar , Straus and Giroux
selections from *My Life* © 1980 Burning Deck Press
"Coyote Holds A Full House in His Hand" © 1980 *TriQuarterly*
"Dominion" © 1980 *The Iowa Review*
"Lost Time Accident" © 1980 *Massachusetts Review*
"The Flocculus" © 1980 *Paris Review*
"In Glory Land" © 1980 *Antaeus*
"What We Talk About When We Talk About Love" © 1980 *Antaeus*
"Why I Love Country Music" © 1980 *Threepenny Review*
"The General and The Small Town" © 1980 *October*
"New York City In 1979" © 1980 *Crawl Out Your Window*
"On The Contemporary Hunger for Wonders" © 1980 *Michigan Quarterly*
"The Archives of Eden" © 1980 *Salamagundi*
"Literature and Lucre" © 1980 *Genre*
"A Death In The Glitter Palace" © 1980 *North American Review*
"On The Metropol Almanac" © 1980 Amnesty International
"Interweavings. . ." © 1980 *Dreamworks*
"Experiment and Traditional Forms. . ." © 1980 *Sun & Moon*
"Four Ways of Computing Midnight" © 1980 *The Southern Review*
"Lagoon" from A PART OF SPEECH by Joseph Brodsky, translated by Anthony Hecht. Translation copyright © 1973, 1974, 1976, 1977, 1979, 1980 by Farrar Straus and Giroux, Inc. Reprinted by permission of Farrar, Straus and Giroux Inc.

This Book is For
Howard Galloway

🔥 🔥 🔥

INTRODUCTION:
About Pushcart Prize VI

EVERY OCTOBER, Pushcart Press begins the job of reading over 4,000 nominations for this annual anthology. These nominations of poetry and prose arrive from the editors of the 2,000 presses invited to participate, and from our many staff editors (who also give advice about the final selections). For this issue, Jon Galassi and Grace Schulman read the poetry and I packed up a huge suitcase and several large cardboard boxes with prose and headed into the cold of a mostly vacant Long Island resort town. I had rented a small apartment without a telephone.

Alone, and without the possibility of interruptions, I planned that I might somehow find a representative "best" in the suitcase and boxes.

But I hadn't figured on the persistence and dedication of a Pushcart staff editor, or the ingenuity of my landlord. One morning the landlord walked up the stairs to my apartment, knocked on the door and handed me a device that resembled the wireless toy walkie-talkies of childhood games. "Phone call for you," he said. After I figured out which end went where, I heard the voice of Ellen Wilbur from Cambridge, Massachusetts exclaiming to me about a story she had just read. I stood in my pyjamas, with the landlord hanging around for the return of his device, while Ellen went on and on about somebody called Gayle Whittier. Her voice faded, but finally I got it right: "Lost Time Accident, *Massachusetts Review*, just out!"

In the six years that I have been publishing *The Pushcart Prize*, I have heard many such promises of glory and have become wary, but Ellen's total commitment sent me off to the post office where I scribbled a card to *The Massachusetts Review* requesting a copy of the story.

Neither Ellen nor I had ever heard of Gayle Baney Whittier, and with good reason. She had published very little fiction before, concentrating instead on teaching French literature at The State University of New York.

This is the special joy of this task—to be knocked out of bed in the morning and to discover the love of one writer-editor for the work of a total unknown. Read Gayle Whittier's "Lost Time Accident"—our lead story. I think she will join Raymond Carver, Mary Gordon, John Irving, Tim O'Brien, Jayne Anne Phillips, Lynne Sharon Schwartz, Alexander Theroux and many others who gained wide recognition after appearing in our editions.

And don't miss the other new writers here: Denise Cassens for instance. An enthusiastic note from John Irving announced her "Girl Talk" from *Shankpainter* (A Provincetown, Massachusetts journal that is also making its first appearance here). "A lovely, lovely story . . . A *beauty!*" said John, author of "The Pension Grillparzer" (*Antaeus*), our lead story in *Pushcart Prize II*.

As usual most of the writers in *Pushcart Prize VI* appear here for the first time in the series. What's unusual about this edition is that three magazines that were themselves brand new in 1980 also are welcomed: Threepenny Review, Water Table, and The Sonora Review.

These new magazines are founded because of the vision and guts of their editors, who can't help but know at the onset that their chances of surviving past a few issues are minimal. Even the established quarterlies have trouble paying the bills. For example, *The North American Review* at The University of Northern Iowa, Cedar Falls, was rumored to be on the verge of folding. I thank the gods and the university accountant that the *Review* survived and gave us David Hellerstein's essay about a doctor's struggle to save a cancer patient. Read "A Death In The Glitter Palace." It had me crying out loud, and you won't be the same after reading it. By way of thanks to the author and to *The North American Review*, you might take out a subscription to that fine journal and you might write to the university's president asking for continued support of its publication.

Of course not everybody in this edition is as under-recognized as

Gayle Whittier, Denise Cassens and David Hellerstein. Even recognized writers had to turn to small presses for publication. We reprint prose by Raymond Carver, William Goyen, Leslie Fiedler, Theodore Roszak and George Steiner, plus Jean Stafford's last story, "Woden's Day".

Featured poets like Joseph Brodsky, Robert Creeley, Galway Kinnell and William Stafford often depend on small presses for publication. This is a situation documented in our first edition: Eugenio Montale had just won the 1975 Nobel Prize for Literature and nobody but New Directions and *Ploughshares* issued his work; in *Prize III*, Vicente Aleixandre had just won the 1977 Nobel Prize for Literature and only The Seventies Press and The Green Horse Press had him in print.

The *Pushcart Prize* series has been a publishing democracy. The 392 works by 367 authors from 212 presses in the first six volumes were picked with the advice of hundreds of staff editors, with new editors asked to serve for each edition. As we announced in the first *Pushcart Prize*, "no literary mafia has trafficked here."

We also encourage democracy elsewhere. In past issues we have honored poetry and prose from the Russian *samizdat* movement (*Chronicle of Current Events*), from Hungary (*American Poetry Review*), from Belgium (*Cross Currents*) and from Argentina (*Fiction*). In the current issue, we celebrate a glimmer of publishing freedom on mainland China with Chen Shixu's "The General and The Small Town" from *October,* an independent press attempting to survive in a political world entirely different from our own; we return to the *samizdat* movement with an account of the stifling of the *Metropol* Almanac; and we join Lawrence Kearney in his polemical outrage about South African justice, "After The Interrogation" (*Shankpainter*).

There is so much more to celebrate in *Pushcart Prize VI*, from the traditional to the experimental (Lyn Hejinian's selection from Burning Deck Press and Eleanor Antin's from *Sun & Moon*). And don't miss David Ohle's story "The Flocculus" (*Paris Review*) or Douglas Messerli's essay on experiment and traditional forms (*Sun & Moon*), or Kathy Acker's raw and real account "New York City in 1979" (*Crawl Out Your Window*).

In fact, try not to miss anything in *Prize VI*, starting with Gayle Whittier's "Lost Time Accident" and Derek Wolcott's poem "Cantina Music" (*Antaeus*) and David Hellerstein's "A Death In The

Glitter Palace"—all winners of the annual Lamport Foundation grant. Mrs. Harold Lamport, who for many years supported outstanding work in this series with her financial gifts, died of cancer recently. Each of these selections honors her as we never could, and she better than I would understand the meaning of David Hellerstein's essay.

Bill Henderson,
PUBLISHER

Note: nominations for this series are invited from any small, independent, literary book press or magazine in the world. Up to six nominations—tear sheets or copies selected from work published in that calendar year—are accepted by our October 15 deadline each year. Write to Pushcart Press, P.O. Box 380, Wainscott, N.Y. 11975 if you need more information.

THE

PEOPLE WHO HELPED

FOUNDING EDITORS— *Anaïs Nin (1903–1977), Buckminster Fuller, Charles Newman, Daniel Halpern, Gordon Lish, Harry Smith, Hugh Fox, Ishmael Reed, Joyce Carol Oates, Len Fulton, Leonard Randolph, Leslie Fiedler, Nona Balakian, Paul Bowles, Paul Engle, Ralph Ellison, Reynolds Price, Rhoda Schwartz, Richard Morris, Ted Wilentz, Tom Montag, William Phillips. Poetry editor: H. L. Van Brunt.*

EDITORS—*Walter Abish, Elliott Anderson, John Ashbery, Robert Boyers, Harold Brodkey, Wesley Brown, Hayden Carruth, Raymond Carver, Malcolm Cowley, Paula Deitz, Steve Dixon, M. D. Elevitch, Loris Essary, Raymond Federman, Ellen Ferber, Carolyn Forché, Stuart Friebert, Tess Gallagher, Louis Gallo, John Gardner, George Garrett, David Godine, Barbara Grossman, Harold Hayes, DeWitt Henry, Edward Hoagland, J. R. Humphreys, John Irving, June Jordan, Karen Kennerly, Mary Kinzie, Jerzy Kosinski, Richard Kostelanetz, Seymour Krim, Maxine Kumin, Stanley Kunitz, Seymour Lawrence, Naomi Lazard, Herb Leibowitz, Stanley Lindberg, Mary MacArthur, Frederick Morgan, Howard Moss, Cynthia Ozick, George Plimpton, Eugene Redmond, William Saroyan, Teo Savory, Harvey Shapiro, Bill and Pat Strachan, Ron Sukenick, Anne Tyler, Sam Vaughan, David Wilk, Yvonne, Bill Zavatsky.*

SPECIAL CONTRIBUTING EDITORS FOR THIS EDITION—
Michael Anania, Asa Baber, Bo Ball, Jim Barnes, Marvin Bell, Gina Berriault, Michael Blumenthal, David Bosworth, David Bromige, Michael Brondoli, Joseph Bruchac, Vlada Bulatovic-Vib, Kathy Callaway, Jan Carew, John Engels, Irving Feldman, Jane

Flanders, H. E. Francis, Marea Gordett, Jorie Graham, Allen Grossman, William Harmon, Seamus Heaney, George Hitchcock, John Hollander, Lewis Hyde, Janet Kauffman, Frank Kermode, W. P. Kinsella, William Kloefkorn, Romulus Linney, David Madden, Thomas McGrath, Sandra McPherson, Carol Muske, Cynthia Ozick, David Plante, David Perkins, Raphael Rudnik, Ed Sanders, Sherod Santos, Gerard Shyne, Charles Simic, Elizabeth Spencer, Gerald Stern, Pamela Stewart, John Taggart, Stephanie Vaughn, Richard Vine, Sara Vogan, Al Young, David Wagoner, Robert Penn Warren, Barbara Watkins, Bruce Weigl, Ellen Wilbur, Charles Wright, James Wright, Patricia Zelver

DESIGN AND PRODUCTION—*Ray Freiman*

EUROPEAN EDITORS—*Genie D. Chipps, Kirby and Liz Williams*

AUSTRALIAN EDITORS—*Tom and Wendy Whitton*

JACKET DESIGN—*Barbara Lish*

POETRY EDITORS FOR THIS EDITION—*Jon Galassi and Grace Schulman*

EDITOR AND PUBLISHER—*Bill Henderson*

PRESSES FEATURED IN THE FIRST SIX PUSHCART PRIZE EDITIONS

Agni Review
Ahsahta Press
Ailanthus Press
Alcheringa/Ethnopoetics
Alice James Books
American Literature
American Pen
American Poetry Review
Amnesty International
Anaesthesia Review
Antaeus
Antioch Review
Apalachee Quarterly
Aphra
The Ark
Assembling
Aspen Leaves
Aspen Poetry Anthology
Barlenmir House
Barnwood Press
Beliot Poetry Review
Bilingual Review
Bits Press
Black American Literature Forum

Black Rooster
Black Scholar
Black Sparrow
Black Warrior Review
Blue Cloud Quarterly
Blue Wind Press
BOA Editions
Boxspring
Burning Deck Press
Caliban
California Quarterly
Canto
Capra Press
Cedar Rock
Center
Chariton Review
Chicago Review
Chouteau Review
Chowder Review
Cimarron Review
Cincinnati Poetry Review
City Lights Books
Clown War
CoEvolution Quarterly
Cold Mountain Press
Columbia: A Magazine of Poetry and Prose
Confluence Press
Confrontation
Copper Canyon Press
Cosmic Information Agency
Crawl Out Your Window
Crazy Horse
Cross Cultural Communication
Cross Currents
Curbstone Press
Dacotah Territory
Decatur House
December
Dreamworks
Dryad Press

Duck Down Press
Durak
East River Anthology
Fiction
Fiction Collective
Fiction International
Field
Firelands Art Review
Five Trees Press
Gallimaufry
Genre
Georgia Review
Ghost Dance
Goddard Journal
The Godine Press
Graham House Press
Graywolf Press
Greensboro Review
Greenfield Review
Hard Pressed
Hills
Holmgangers Press
Holy Cow!
Hudson Review
Icarus
Indiana Writes
Inwood Press
Intermedia
Intro
Invisible City
Iowa Review
Ironwood
The Kanchenjunga Press
Kansas Quarterly
Kayak
Kenyon Review
Latitudes Press
L'Epervier Press
Liberation
Linquis

The Little Magazine
Living Hand Press
Living Poets Press
Lowlands Review
Lucille
Lynx House Press
Manroot
Magic Circle Press
Malahat Review
Massachusetts Review
Michigan Quarterly
Milk Quarterly
Montana Gothic
Montana Review
Missouri Review
Mississippi Review
Montemora
Mulch Press
Nada Press
New America
New England Review
New Letters
North American Review
North Atlantic Books
Northwest Review
Obsidian
Oconee Review
October
Ohio Review
Ontario Review
Open Places
Oyez Press
Painted Bride Quarterly
Paris Review
Parnassus: Poetry In Review
Partisan Review
Penca Books
Penumbra Press
Pentagram
Persea: An International Review

Pequod
Pitcairn Press
Ploughshares
Poetry
Poetry Northwest
Poetry Now
Prairie Schooner
Prescott Street Press
Promise of Learnings
Quarry West
Quarterly West
Rainbow Press
Red Cedar Review
Red Clay Books
Red Earth Press
Release Press
Russian *Samizdat*
Salmagundi
San Marcos Press
Seamark Press
Second Coming Press
The Seventies Press
Shankpainter
Shantih
Shenandoah
A Shout In The Street
Sibyl-Child Press
Small Moon
The Smith
The Spirit That Moves Us
Southern Poetry Review
Some
The Sonora Review
Southern Review
Southwestern Review
Spectrum
St. Andrews Press
Story Quarterly
Sun & Moon
Sun Press

Sunstone
Telephone Books
Texas Slough
THIS
Threepenny Review
13th Moon
Transatlantic Review
Three Rivers Press
Thorp Springs Press
Toothpaste Press
TriQuarterly
Truck Press
Tuumba Press
Undine
Unicorn Press
Unmuzzled Ox
Unspeakable Visions of the Individual
Vagabond
Virginia Quarterly
Water Table
Washington Writers Workshop
Western Humanities Review
Westigan Review
Willmore City
Word-Smith
Xanadu
Yardbird Reader
Y'Bird

CONTENTS

INTRODUCTION: ABOUT PUSHCART PRIZE VI   11
LOST TIME ACCIDENT
    Gayle Baney Whittier   29
CANTINA MUSIC
    Derek Walcott   50
A DEATH IN THE GLITTER PALACE
    David Hellerstein   53
LAGOON
    Joseph Brodsky   69
WAITING IN LINE
    William Stafford   73
RETURN
    Carolyn Forché   75
THE FLOCCULUS
    David Ohle   79
WHAT WE TALK ABOUT WHEN WE TALK ABOUT LOVE
    Raymond Carver   88
ON THE CONTEMPORARY HUNGER FOR WONDERS
    Theodore Roszak   101
LEDA
    Marilyn Krysl   119
THE TOMB OF STÉPHAN MALLARMÉ
    Charles Simic   121

WELDON KEES IN MEXICO, 1965
David Wojahn 124
IN GLORY LAND
Julia Thacker 126
COYOTE HOLDS A FULL HOUSE IN HIS HAND
Leslie Silko 142
SELECTIONS FROM *MY LIFE*
Lyn Hejinian 151
DOMINION
Barry Targan 154
THE ARCHIVES OF EDEN
George Steiner 177
FLOOR
C. K. Williams 213
WORLD BREAKING APART
Louise Glück 216
THE WIDOW'S YARD
Isabella Gardner 217
IN THE LAND OF PLENTY
Susan Engberg 219
ARTHUR BOND
William Goyen 242
WHY I LOVE COUNTRY MUSIC
Elizabeth Ann Tallent 247
INTERWEAVINGS: REFLECTIONS ON THE ROLE OF
DREAM IN THE MAKING OF POEMS
Denise Levertov 258
SCATSQUALL IN SPRING
Judith Moffett 273
AT THE FAR END OF A LONG WHARF
Thomas Lux 275
FIONN IN THE VALLEY
Benedict Kiely 276
A ROMANTIC INTERLUDE FROM *RECOLLECTIONS
OF MY LIFE WITH DIAGHILEV*
Eleanor(a) Antin(ova) 289
EXPERIMENT AND TRADITIONAL FORMS IN
CONTEMPORARY LITERATURE
Douglas Messerli 304

GIRL TALK
  Denise Cassens 325
THE SADNESS OF BROTHERS
  Galway Kinnell 329
DEAD FISH
  Daniel Halpern 334
A MOTEL IN TROY, N.Y.
  Josephine Jacobsen 336
FOUR WAYS OF COMPUTING MIDNIGHT
  Francis Phelan 338
ON THE *METROPOL* ALMANAC
  Russian *samizdat* 386
HUNGER
  Jack Gilbert 392
BLAME
  Elizabeth Spires 393
WHEN I WAS A CHILD
  S. Nourbese 395
NEW YORK CITY IN 1979
  Kathy Acker 396
ECLIPSE
  David Long 413
LITERATURE AND LUCRE: A MEDITATION
  Leslie Fiedler 429
THE RIVER AGAIN AND AGAIN
  Linda Gregg 441
FOR ELIZABETH BISHOP
  Sandra McPherson 442
AFTER THE INTERROGATION
  Lawrence Kearney 443
WODEN'S DAY
  Jean Stafford 447
ODE
  Philip Schultz 469
THREE STUDIES FOR A HEAD OF JOHN THE BAPTIST
  Chana Bloch 470
THE GENTLEMEN IN THE U-BOATS
  Sharon Olds 472
THE GENERAL AND THE SMALL TOWN
  Chen Shixu 473

DYING
    Robert Pinsky   487
SILO LETTER IN THE DEAD OF A WARM WINTER
    Michael McFee   489
THIS DAY
    Robert Creeley   492
CONTRIBUTORS' NOTES   493
OUTSTANDING WRITERS   497
OUTSTANDING SMALL PRESSES   506
INDEX TO THE SERIES   527

THE
PUSHCART PRIZE, VI:
BEST OF THE
SMALL PRESSES

LOST TIME ACCIDENT

fiction by GAYLE BANEY WHITTIER

from THE MASSACHUSETTS REVIEW

nominated by Ellen Wilbur

DON'T GET THAT STUFF near your mouth!"

"Why not? What'd happen?"

"It could kill you." But he deals this out easily, a man who moves daily among fatalities. My mother, fixing dinner, frowns: "I simply fail to see why you bring that poison home!"

He winks at me. "Why, that's not poison you're lookin' at, Lizzie, that's money."

"Oh, *sure*."

"Besides, Annie'll be the only kid in her class who's got *samples* for her project," he justifies. "Even Old Brown's daughter won't have nothin' like this!" A smile bonds him, the father, me the girlchild: Old Brown may be his boss's boss, but in school I get higher marks than Nancy Brown in every subject. In school, we get even. "Brown wouldn't even know where to *look for* samples," my father adds complacently.

"I still don't like it."

What she doesn't like lies in front of me: little vials of soft-looking abrasive dust, in various grinds like coffee or like spice; the lethal bead of mercury which, if smashed, reforms itself at once into a chain of smaller spheres; sharp green and black and rose-colored, manmade crystals, products of Diamonid, where my father works. A public relations booklet, "How Diamonid is Made," lies on the kitchen table too. But I already know that story.

"They heat up all them chemicals in furnaces—you know, you seen 'em—till it gets harder than diamonds. They even use this stuff to *cut* diamonds. What d'ya think of *that*?"

Reverently, my finger tries the needle tip of one of the crystals. It feels true: HARDER THAN DIAMONDS. That is the electric promise on a big sign between the factory's twin chimneys. Below it, a smaller legend swings in the cloudy wind along the riverfront:"— Days Since the Last LTA." LTA stands for "Lost Time Accident," my father says. As the crystal dimples my fingertip, imminent danger draws me nearer to my father and my father's world. I imagine how close to the surface our blood is.

He works in dangers, where a man should work, and wears the steel-toed "safety shoes" to prove it. So do my uncles and my male cousins, those who are old enough to quit school and get a job. "Wouldn't catch me in no office!" they all boast. Looking down now at the luminous bead of mercury, a bead pregnant with my own suddenly possible death, I feel the strict enchantment of my father's otherness; and I divine the high and final line where violence marries beauty. Risk is my father's legacy to me: my mother's will be different.

"Don't breathe!" she always cries out, in those nights when we drive homeward from a family party or a movie, following the ancient crescent of the Niagara River which will outlast us all. "Don't breathe it! Hold your breath!"—distrustful of the silicon and pungent air around the factories, blind to the terrible loveliness of their smoking, glowing slagheaps in our ordinary night. When the stench begins, my mother and father both take big, ostentatious breaths; he plants his foot down hard on the gas pedal;

the car jumps forward as if at the sound of a starting gun. A mile later, just beyond the row of factories, they surface, gasping. But although I always join them at the start, always draw my deep underwater-swimmer's breath too, I can't resist knowing what danger tastes like. Surreptitiously, I breathe them in: rancid, acid, strange odors that beg analysis even when they most disgust me. My throat is full of them, their sharpness and their exotic new complexities. Tasting them, I taste as well my coming sensuality, which will set experiment ahead of judgment, pleasure above safety, every time. That is why I disobey them both so secretly, seeming to gasp too, for the air which we pretend is safe again.

They would be worth a life or two, those alchemical fires glimpsed over my shoulder as we drive away. I try to read by colors what is smelted there: yellow for sulphur, framed in blue; the neon green, leafbright, to speak for copper; and a mysterious quiet mound, banked and smouldering pink as roses. Full of wonder, I feel myself moving towards a prayer in praise of my own human-kind, rash dreamers and builders of all that I behold. The words of awe rise upward on my young but going breath. In my mouth they turn back into air just as I start to speak them. Music, sometimes, even now, revives those visions and the troubling, stubborn vener-ation that I feel yet before the face of power.

Power is my native city's rightful name. The Power City. It rides on the neck of the rough white river, deadly too, like a leash on the leviathan. My father's maleness goes with it in its power, runs outward from the city's metal core into the country's infinite iron body. The river clasps Grand Island in a dread embrace, then parts like the branches of the human heart. But it feels nothing. America—this was my earliest lesson after God—is built on what he does.

But what exactly *does* he do? Like all my other childhood mysteries, this one will never yield its final name. "My husband works for the Diamonid," my mother merely says. Her brothers and his do, too—or for Hooker or Dupont or Olin. "He works at Olin." That's my Uncle Joe.

"What does he do?" I ask.

Her answer trades me word for unknown word. "He works in Shipping and Receiving. On the night shift now." Or, "Why, he makes *big money*. He's getting star rate now."

But what does he do? The proud-eyed men in my family come

back to mind: their serious, important look, the rare and hefty laughter salvaged when they "let themselves go": Thinking of their splendor, physical and brief, their dignity mined somehow from a day of taking orders—thinking of my childhood love which has outlasted them, I see that I am blessed not to know. They sold the only thing the poor have to sell, their breath and blood. And I confess the child I was. I would have loved my Uncle Casey, that night singer, less if I had known he spent the workday heaving sacks of concrete from a platform to a shed. And what if I had numbered, even once, my own father's compromises, counted out the daily spirit-killing facts behind his "steady job?" His pride is my pride too. If I had known, I could not have volunteered, when the teacher went around the room asking what all the fathers did, I could not have answered with such easy, innocent pride, "*My father works for Diamonid.*"

"That filthy place!"

Whenever the industrial stench, the greasy dust, invades our house, my mother curses and mourns her missed life elsewhere, with another sort of man, in another sort of place. "I could have married Leonard Price. My mother *begged* me to. And he's a lawyer now, he lives on the Escarpment. Oh, I was beautiful, just beautiful. . . ."

"Goddamighty," my father reminds her wearily, "that dust is what we live off, Lizzie. You can thank your lucky stars for it, if you got any sense." He has "seniority" now, then a promotion and another one. No longer paid from week to slender week, he gets his paycheck once a month, like the management. "Unless there's a big layoff," my father promises, he will always bring home his paycheck and his bonus at Christmas, every month, every year, for as long as I need him. Forever.

"Oh, they just give you a fancy title and less money," my mother sneers. "Why, my baby brother on the assembly line's earning more than you."

"Yeah, and doin' what?" he counters.

"Don't you insult my brother! Good honest work and nobody can say it ain't!" I listen to her slip back into the dialect she hoped to leave behind her.

"I'm sorry, Liz. By God, I'm sorry."

"I should hope so!" she tells him. "That filthy place. Why. . . ."

"Ahh, stop bitin' the hand that feeds you." He strides out of the room.

"Mr. High-and-Mighty," she mutters behind his back. Then she notices me. "Why, that man owes everything he is to me! When we got married, he couldn't even read. I used to teach him. Don't you ever tell him that I told you."

"I won't," I swear, I who will remember this forever.

Our day turns as evenly to the whistles of Diamonid as a monk's day to bells. It opens in my sleep. Sometimes I rouse myself dimly when my father leaves. The noise of his Studebaker unsettles my deep child's sleep long enough for me to feel and mourn his absence in the house. Later I wake up to find him gone. And until he comes home again, nothing sits in its right minute or right place.

"When's supper? What're we having?"

"Don't call it 'supper.' It's dinner; we aren't farmers."

No. Coal miners, my father's people were, used to laboring in blackness and in early deaths. Hers marched a safe and charted course as civil servants. The stamp of these ancestral trades imprints them both, but she has married him, drawn to that breakfree energy that sent him to Diamonid, that promoted him through the war, that brought him, finally, a crew of men.

Our family begins, then, only at four-fifteen in the afternoon, on the shrill distant note of the quitting whistle. My mother, newly fragrant with Friendship Garden, her pincurled hair unfurled around her solemn face, pretends to leisure, ties a ruffled apron over her clean dress. Then his car rushes into the driveway, the door's lock gives way with a click of metal like a broken bone. His footsteps. They are unique; the man himself is in them—a man no longer young, a man too old, really to have a child as small as I, an accidental blessing.

"*Was* I an accident?" I dare to ask my mother once.

"Who told you that?"

"Nobody. *Was* I?"

"You were a big *surprise*," she finally allows.

"Surprise!" my father shouts, bursting through the door. Behind it, almost flattened, we stand silently, SHHH, pantomimes my mother, raising a newly manicured finger to her lips. Something like an old, remembered joy brightens her features momentarily.

"Hey, anybody home?" he asks, pretending to look for us. "Hey, where is everybody? Ain't nobody here?" Mock worries. Then "BOO!" he's found us. And in his hand, a chocolate bar, a suitor's rose: for me, a sunset sheath of scrap papers, or carbons the color of midnight. Out of the giving and his old return, even my obdurate loneliness melts. "Daddy!" I shout, and we are home.

"Well, will you just look at my two beautiful ladies!" he lies. "Don't you look good enough to eat!"

"Oh, blarney," my mother says, but smiles a younger smile. I feel his lie, a long one by the time that I am born and stand beside her, sharing unevenly in all of his old compliments.

"Somethin' smells good! You got somethin' in the oven, Lizzie?" And he winks a broad vaudevillian wink.

"Herb!"

"Well, have ya?"

"Don't you hold your breath," she tells him, eyes snapping.

I understand them just enough to know that their teasing predates me, that they are remembering each other as they were alone. I am lonely again myself. What does he mean? What could be in the oven except one of my mother's thrifty casseroles, almost unsalted and tending towards one even color? Suspicious of daily pleasure, she cooks "plain." But we must be grateful for it because of all the children who are starving in Europe. Not even Grace can sweeten what she serves.

Now, "Don't get any of that filth on my clean floor!" she warns, as he pretends to lunge at her. "And don't get *near* that carpet! Why, it'd cut it all to pieces. Go wash up," she commands, turning into his mother too. And their flirtation is over for the day.

The Company follows him home. *Don't breathe it.* But the silent, ubiquitous black Diamonid dust collects invisibly in the folds of his clothing, sifts out unseen into a fine glittering shadow which outlines the place where he has stood. All at once you look down and see it there, pooled around his safety shoes with their steelcapped toes ("Company rule, cuts down on accidents") covering his own crooked, comical ones. Diamonid dust destroys whatever it touches; but every night my father comes back to us preserved, saved by his safety shoes and by his ready Irish wits. He comes home "on the dot," my mother boasts to her less-fortunately married friends, the wives of "ladies' men" or drunkards—which is the worst thing a man can be, because if he drinks he will not be a "good provider."

"I'd trust him anywhere," my mother sings. But she too clocks his fifteen minutes between the company gates and our back door. Suddenly, in the midst of one of their quarrels, I will hear her cry, "You work in a filthy place! Your secretary. . ." before his hand bruises her into silence. And I understand that there is moral filth, too, just outside her jurisdiction, in the subtle colors of the air where our livelihood inhales and exhales.

"Back in a jiffy," he tells us now, disappearing into the cellar. Bent over the washtub, he violently scrubs away the company dirt, puts on fresh clothes for the second half of his daily life.

Above him, just as energetically, my mother sweeps up the dark dust. It winks and glistens in her dustpan among our duller household kind. "I want to be sure I get it all," my mother says, as if acknowledging that it is aristocratic, powerful as if it had fallen from a magician's pack stamped with an open trademark diamond around the letter D.

"Diamonid," I try the latinate word, echoing an inventor who named, but did not make, that terrible powder with his own two hands, his nostrils, or his broken lungs. "Diamonid." I am softly in love with its strangeness. When I touch the dust my finger leaves its print, and the dust sets its shiny smudge against my skin.

He washes it away with a soap hard and yellow as a brick of amber. Coming back upstairs, he smells of the soap, acid and golden-brown and potent as the man himself. "Clean as a whistle," he supposes.

But in my father's lungs, invisibly, the black pollen settles, cutting and hardening into what will be his distant death. Some other day, coming back ashen from the doctor's office, "Oh, my God," he'll cry to us, "I got emphysema. Advanced, he says. Do you know what that is? That's just a new name for Black Lung, that's all. That's all." And he will recount, over and over, his grandfather's tortured death, the miner's death he thought he had outrun, until my mother ends it: "For the love of God, shut up! You think that you're the only one. . .?"

Now, that day unguessed, my mother serves dinner to us, I set the table, he lifts up his voice to tell us about Work. He spins stories out of it, takes male sustenance there, and somehow, miraculously, dreams a tall and fugitive pride in what he does. After the second story, or the third, I imagine that I stand in the stone and concrete of his masculine world. Sometimes, crushed, he seconds my mother's bitter knowledge: "Christ, what a hole that place is!" But, "You'll never have to work in a place like that, Annie," he promises us both. "You're real smart. Your teacher said. *You* won't end up in there."

It puzzles me. No other woman in my family works anywhere at all, except the wife of my uncle-the-gambler. *Men* work. Women marry them. Why would I ever have to work? Listening to my father, I suddenly guess that I am not pretty. I feel a confused shame, but he goes on: "You're college material. Get yourself a real good job," he is advising me. "Something clean. You got what it takes . . . I'd be right up there now, if I got an education."

Briefly, our lives ascend together. We exchange laurels. I recount the prizes that I win in school; he, a boss, tells stories about his men.

"What'd you do in school today? What's that you're reading?"

"French. I'm reading French."

"I'll be damned! Go on, say something in French for me."

"Ma plume est sur le bureau," I tell him, waiting until I make him ask for the translation, then: "My pen is on the desk."

"Me, I know some Polack and a lot of Eyetalian," he boasts. Then he says, "Eh! Ven'aca!" which means "Come over here," or "No capeesh?" for "Don't you get it?"

"You say it after me," he instructs, proud of my agile tongue and that textbook-stilted French, passwords into a world unlike his own, where he will not be welcome. Obeying him, I taste the flavor of my father's role at Work. The spoken phrases teach him to me. I see him merciful but just, commanding them in their homespoken tongues: *Come over here. Hey, buddy, don't you get it?*

"I got my men's respect," he always finishes.

They have simple, children's names, those men: Little, Big, Young, Old. Little Carl brings in the spring each Easter. He brings it tied up in a stout bag full of hard anise-seed cookies, the predictable chocolate rabbit that I am too old for now; a big bottle of bright red wine for my father, and a littler blue bottle of Evening in Paris perfume for my smiling mother. My father laughs, holding the wine up to the light. "Dago red!" And Little Carl laughs at himself, too, while my father claps him on his rounded back. "He's a pain in the ass, that guy," my father says, but says it chuckling.

"Why don't you fire him? *I* would," my mother vows.

"Ah, he's all right," my father redetermines.

Then the war lets go of us, and one day—no holiday at all—little Carl runs shouting and weeping towards our house, waving the first telegram from a brother he had thought was dead. In our staid Northern European neighborhood, people come defensively to the railings of their porches, grimace at him, and go back inside. Final judgment. But, "Hey, buddy! Eh, paysan!" my father is already running out to meet him, infected with his joy. They embrace, Italians together, in the back yard, while indoors my mother hardly needs to ask, but does, "What will people think?"

I watch them through the glass. They are clasping and dancing their fellowship. "You get damned close to guys, workin' with 'em," he has often said. But men don't hug each other like that, do they? Do they? I ask myself if what I see is love, workborn. My mother, as if she has heard my silent question, states, "Blood is stronger," looking at them too. Jealous now, "Blood can't be broken," she reminds us both. "*His* men indeed!"

She herself maintains a distance which my French lessons have not yet taught me to name *noblesse oblige.*

"Wouldn't you like a nice cup of coffee?" she asks, moving already towards the speckled coffee pot on a back burner. "It's only this morning's heated up, but I think it's still O.K."

A bearish blond giant stands shy and huge against our kitchen door. One black-mittened hand wrings another, warming him against the late November cold. He has just delivered our winter kindling.

"No, t'ank you, missus," he says roundly and severely.

"Oh, dear! Well, at least sit down for a minute. You look chilled to the bone!"

Wearing a darker shadow even than my father's, he maintains his statue's pose against the yellow door.

"No, t'ank you, I get your floor all dirty. Anyway, got to get to another job." Only, "chob" he says.

"They sure keep you busy, don't they? What's the next one?"

The silence lengthens. I wonder whether his language or his wits can run so slowly. At last, "We dump barrels in that old canal," he remembers.

"Oh? What're they dumping?"

"They don't tell *me*, missus."

"Well. Well, I guess you've got to run, then," she dismisses him. "Now you tell 'the boss,'" my mother winks, "I said, 'Hello there!'" She thinks it is a joke that both of them work for the same boss. He does not.

"Be seein' you, missus," he tells her. Then, still unsmiling, he lifts his denim cap, work-blackened, to make a courtly gesture that starts me laughing inwardly. But my laughter dies unborn. I take in the strip of forehead underneath the brim: pure and white as day. Beneath the dusty skin, the shadow of his livelihood, another man is hiding, a man all pale and gold: a Viking or a lion.

Only one of the men, Shorty, ever stays. Anomalously black as a junebug, delicate and maimed, with a glass eye to match his equally freakish blue one, and one elegant leg made out of wood, he calls my mother "Miz Elizabeth." His stump is aching, he tells her, as she pours her coffee in his cup; he thinks that it will rain or snow, that's how he knows.

My mother bends, easy in her sure superiority. From below the cupboard she lifts up an almost-full bottle of brandy for emergencies. She adds a dollop to the black coffee in his cup. "Don't you tell a soul!"

One September afternoon, while my mother was taking down her steel-colored hair, the telephone rang. "Your father!" she knew, although he never called home.

For once she loved him, she rushed so quickly to the telephone. But she let it ring one more shrill time, while her hand endorsed her breastbone with the sign of the cross, as if she were putting on perfume.

"I just knew it was you! What's happened?" she spilled into the receiver. ". . .Oh, *no*! Who is it? . . . No, I didn't, *don't* . . . Just where is he now? Is he still. . .? Oh, Oh. . . . I see. And when are you coming home?" Just as I thought she was about to hang up, she added gently, "Honey," as if her love must make some kind of difference now.

"What is it? Is there a strike?" I asked excitedly.

"No, there's been an accident at Work. Oh, your father's O.K.,
just shook up," she said. "But one of his men got badly hurt."

"Which one?" I warmed to the drama, selecting a victim in my
imagination. "Shorty? Little Carl?"

"No. His name is Stash, Stanley . . . Wuh . . . I don't know how
to say it," She added, "Be awful good to your father when he gets
home."

But I hardly had the chance. He walked in, giftless and mad,
deliberately striding right onto the forbidden linoleum with his
abrasive dust, then even into the hallway where my mother's
sacred expanse of new carpet started. He moved tight and fast,
dramatically ignoring us. Then, angrily too, he tore a number into
the telephone dial.

"Hello, is Mrs. Wyczolaski there? . . . Oh. Well, this here's
Herb O'Connor. I'm Stash's . . . Stash and me, we work together,"
he said. "You just tell Stella if there's anything she wants, *anything*, why, us boys'll give blood or whatever else. . .? I see. Yeah,
I understand. I'd feel the same damned way. Well, like I said,
anything. I'll call back later."

In the kitchen my mother was already sweeping up the fine black
silt behind his rage. But she swept slowly and gently, so as not to
anger him, I felt, or, perhaps, so as not to remind him that it was
there. It made a dark and gritty sound in her dustpan.

"There's dirt all over here!" I imitated her.

But, "Never mind," she said. And when he returned to the
kitchen, my mother did not mention it, only, "Tell me what
happened," and a moment later, "Your paper's over there on the
chair," as she always said, as it always was.

"Yes, tell us about it!" but I felt my enthusiasm for a story thrown
back at me by their silence. Ashamed, I stopped, and heard my
father speak only to my mother, to himself.

He documented it, how in the hot September afternoon, Stash
and the other men were out in the yard, "sweatin' like pigs," he
said. He would have called to them to quit work early, it was so
damned hot, only a bigger boss walked through, inspecting. Just as
the whistle blew, "Put 'er down!" he shouted. And Stash, tired, hot
himself, carelessly leaned over the pallet of the forklift and pushed
the release button. The whole load flattened him.

"Oh, Jesus," my father recalled. "Everybody's shoutin' and
yellin', nobody even remembered to get that fuckin' thing off of

him. 'Herb, help me!' he's screamin'. I push this button and it lifts up in the air, takin' part of him with it, I swear to God. Joe Vetucci, he fainted. And there's this sound out of him when I did it, like a crunch, only. . ."

"Oh, don't!" my mother cried. "No, no, that's all right. No. Tell me."

"Softer," he said. "Like a deep breath when it goes out." His face sealed itself over the trace of the mystery, the failure of his own description of it.

My mother's hand reached out for him as over greater space, but his words bore him away, back to the yard, miles from us, back to quitting time, centuries ago.

"You couldn't tell his shirt from his chest. Blood everywhere. Mrs. Prince, she's the company nurse, she come runnin' from the clinic with her bag and give him oxygen. They called the ambulance. Then she started cuttin' his shirt away, and he was screamin'. No. It wasn't a *scream*," he corrected. "He couldn't scream. It was more. . . ." And his voice left off in a chugging sound as his own mouth filled up with vomit. Keeping it back with an unwashed hand, he rushed into the bathroom. We could hear him vomiting there, wildly trying to get rid of what he had seen that day, or saying it.

"Shouldn't we go in?" I asked.

"No, leave him alone," my mother said.

After a while the vomiting dried off into sobs. The sobs stopped too. Finally, he came out angry.

"I'm gettin' the hell outta here! I'm goin' for a ride!" he shouted in my mother's direction, as if she meant to stop him.

"Herb, be careful! Please!" Futile. The door slammed; he punished the car, its parts shrieking and grinding against each other; it squealed down the street, him in it.

In the silence that gathered thickly where he had stood, I asked, "Can't that man get better? Can't they fix him?"

"Now, what do you *think*!" I heard my mother cry. Then, seeing that my question had for once been almost innocent, she added more kindly, "Oh, I doubt it." She took my father's plate away from the table, heaping it with portions of dinner, then putting it in the oven to keep it warm. She glanced at the kitchen clock, adjusted a dial, then moved our two remaining plates side by side. "Why, it would be a miracle if that man got well!" she afterthought.

But I lived then in a climate of miracles as of dust. First there were the stained-glass cures that had entertained my Sundays since my babyhood: "Take up thy bed and walk." These, however, I had recently understood to be ancient, outgrown events, mere precursors of the newer miracles, which my century's god, science, was dispensing. Through science—they told me so at school—we were getting an edge on death and illiteracy: also on other kinds of darknesses, bigotry, for example, and communism. Surely one of these hoarded miracles could save Stash.

Out of the clustered silence, my mother's voice awoke me. "Of course, *his* wife'll get a bundle."

"What? Oh."

"Because he died on the job," she explained. "That's why."

"Even if it was an accident?"

"Why, that's true," she considered. "He was *careless*, after all. Maybe she won't get anything." And now her voice took on vindication. "After all, it was his own fault, he didn't look what he was doing." *Careless*. I startled into shame, I who was accused daily of negligence and a child's innocent amnesia before the world. She had called me by my own secret name. Was death a kind of carelessness too?

Eight o'clock. Nine. The night went on without my being sent to bed. My mother turned on the radio, sat sewing against its background of ventriloquists and organ chords. I, defying sleep, lay listening, raised my head to see her golden thimble twinkle as she stitched, magically recalling my father, thread by thread. At last her simple magic worked, and he came home.

The car gently ("Don't wake the neighbors") in the driveway; the careful clasping of the garage doors; the snap of the familiar lock. His older, lonelier steps came towards us.

"Are you feeling any better, Herb?" she asked.

"Oh, shit," he said. "Shit. I seen him. I went to the hospital and seen him."

"How . . uh, what hospital is he in?"

"Memorial. It was nearest. She wanted St. Catherine's 'cause they're Catholics. But they can't move him anyplace, shape he's in. I seen him. He's so bad off they got him strapped to the bed, tubes goin' in and out. Givin' him blood. . . ." The uncaring tone began to take him away from us. Perhaps to prevent it, my mother cried too empathetically, *"Oh that poor man!"*

"He says to me, he says, 'Herb, I wanna die. Honest to God, I just wanna die,' is what he said. 'Just let me go.' Well, he mouthed it. I couldn't hardly make it out."

"Why, for heaven's sake!" My mother strung out her words like counted beads. "Didn't they give him something for the pain, those people?" An alert, outraged expression stuck to her face.

"Oh, sure, sure," my father answered bitterly. "But they can't give him enough, is all. I seen his doctor, I says to him, 'Doc, why the hell can't you people deaden this man's pain?' What were they there for, I asked him. And you know what? He told me they *would*, only that much pain-killer might kill Stash too. Dying anyway, I says. And the doctor just froze me out, said that's *different*, it's the *law*."

At the word "law" my mother faltered. "Well, maybe he's right, Herb. I mean, it probably *is* the law, isn't it?"

"The law can go fuck itself, far as I'm concerned."

"Now, Herb," my mother went on academically, "you have to see it from the doctor's side. . ."

"No, I don't. Why should I? Goddamned legalized thieves's all they are!"

My mother touched his arm. "Maybe he's got a chance, though . . . Stash, I mean."

"Oh, hell, Lizzie, you'd a seen him you wouldn't talk like that. The man's crushed to a pulp, that's what. A pulp." (The cliché tried to come alive in my mind, but didn't.) "And his wife's standin' out in the hall cryin', and his son . . . well, Jesus. 'I just wanna die,' he says to me."

"Son? I didn't know the . . . Wuh. . . ."

"Wyczolaski," he spat at her.

"I didn't know they had *two* children," my mother said almost brightly. "I thought there was only that one girl who goes to school with Annie. Annie, what's her name?"

"Wanda," I replied, disliking my mother. "Her name is Wanda."

"Of course," my mother acknowledged with the littlest of her smiles.

"Yeah, two kids. That poor woman. What's she gonna do now?"

My mother suppressed something sharper than she said. "Why, she's got Compensation coming, hasn't she? She'll do all right."

"Well, she gets it if I testify it happened on company time, before quitting," he said. "Or that the machine slipped."

In the length of silence my mother picked her way among the thickets where we lived. "A lot of people saw what happened, though," she finally ventured. "I mean, they'd know if you were lying, if you swore it happened on company time. Or was the equipment." His look, which I could not see from where I sat, must have embarrassed her. "Well, I *mean*, he *was* careless, really. It was his own fault."

"Own fault! Who the hell wouldn't get careless, all day in that heat?" He brought his fist down against the table. There was an interval of tiny chimes as her porcelain knick-knacks trembled against each other. "Anybody'd get 'careless,' that's all. That's *all.*"

"But suppose you lose *your* job? You're not even in the union any more. There's witnesses."

"Now, Lizzie. . ."

"What about us? Have you ever thought of that? Oh, no; not you. And there's *witnesses*," she repeated, her voice rising. Her finger rose too and pointed him out, one red nail gleaming blood-drop pure.

"You make a better lawyer than a wife, Lizzie. Now shut up. It was on company time, and that's that."

"But it wasn't. . . ."

"I said shut up, Lizzie, and I meant it," he commanded in a stonedust voice. Then my father's eye caught sight of me. "What the hell are *you* doin' up? Ain't you got school tomorrow?"

"It's not her fault."

"Well, go on. Scoot. Go get your beauty sleep," my father said. As I escaped the room, his large hand lightly told me of the shape of my child's head.

Through my door, half open to let in the whisper of the cooler early autumn night, a long finger of light crossed the thin yellow varnished floorboards and pillared up the wall. There a wallpaper lattice lifted up its repeated clusters of white roses, stale and old.

I slept a white sleep.

Later in the night, half conscious and alone, I heard the customary thunder of their household quarrel. It no longer frightened me. I could identify their cadences like phrases in a symphony. Sometimes I even fell asleep, while they still raged, as constant and as changing as the sea, beneath my painted bed. This time, sitting up alive, I sorted out new and different sounds.

Against the rocking of their human voices, he was throwing

things. Their dense thuds declared them heavy, breakable. They rang out dully. They reverberated against the floor. Once, I remembered, he had gotten angry at my mother and had thrown his breakfast at the wall. The plate splintered. But the fried egg slid slowly downward to the baseboard, a cartoon sun. Watching its descent, I held back my laughter, lest I disrespect the enchantment of my father's violence. But fear brought more laughter bubbling to my nervous lips. He had only broken the plate that one time, though. This breakage went on and on.

Where usually my mother's voice climbed, sickening, to half-evasive pleas, it kept instead a low and reasonable horizon note, a stranger's tone. They walked the circle of the rooms below, my father pacing heavily, erratically, my mother keeping up while he shouted: "That goddamn bastard! Polack son-of-a-bitch!" Crash—an object seconded his rage. "Stupid fucking idiot! If I told him once, I told him a hundred times: *One slip* and it's curtains, buddy! Yeah, I told him. . . ." Something struck the floor. "You, you gold-crowned son-of-a-bitch . . ." (even my mother's voice protested it) "Be-all, know-all fucker of the rest of us! . . . No, no, I won't, I won't . . ." And his body bore his words away, stepping through the stairwell to the kitchen to the dining room, almost never used, then the circuit of the downstairs floor. His muffled voice remained; against it, my mother's preserving obbligato. From time to time he climbed above language, and then I heard another heavy thud, and tried to imagine what it was he threw.

Slowly the intervals lengthened. At last, exhausting things to throw, he broke himself and cried. I lay in my changed bed, shocked in my hearing and my heart, while the night air carried up to me his foreign male weeping, wholly of this earth. I felt that my father's sobs would go on unbearably forever, but he was diminished too. In astonished meditation on the edge of sleep, I knew that he was less my father than he had been before. Aware of his abandonment, I abandoned myself to dreams.

There was a next day, and on it, everything resumed functionally but awkwardly, like a broken machine. Breakfast brought gluey oatmeal, acid orange juice, and lukewarm milk in the old chipped cup with a hair-thin crack through its pale wall. A lump of breakfast in me, I underwent my regimented schoolday. But through getting dressed and the roll call, through the Products of Peru and our spiritless public school singing of "The Volga Boatman," I waited. Something else must happen, I assumed. Nothing did.

When I got home from school, home was still there, a semaphore of well-known laundry strung behind it. My mother, newly powdered, wearing the set, severe expression of a woman living out a holy but mistaken life, ran her finger over a few inches of windowsill: "Just look at that! Third time today I dusted it!" she said. Then, at four o'clock exactly, she disappeared to put on a fresh dress, to brush out her cold hair. Even her face in the center of it all was her old face, rigid and alone, the face I remember her by, even now: my mother.

"Wash your hands, Annie," she commanded absently." And put on another blouse; that one's just covered with ink. How do you ever do it?"

Coming in to us, me with my clean hands, my mother in her unmarked apron, my father made no jokes at all that night, but went downstairs at once to scrub himself. I could hear the water rushing into the washtub, could sense his muted gestures as he changed into clean clothes. I felt his feet, my father's feet, measuring the steps deliberately as he climbed, purified, to the kitchen. Only then did my mother look at him questioningly, gently.

He shook his head. No. And again, as she asked, "Is he. . .?" No, but only with his eyes.

"Is Stash dead?" I asked, voicing what I knew must be her question too.

"Mr. Wyczolaski," he corrected me. "No."

"I suppose he's in a coma," my mother said.

"Still conscious."

"Oh, that's good," I tried.

"It isn't good at all! What do *you* know . . . !" my mother scowled.

"Somebody oughta do something," my father said only to her.

"Well, they won't," she answered him. "You know it and I know it. Your paper's over there on the chair," she said.

Proving what nobody would do, they separated their lives from the dying man's. Humming a little, even, she set out dinner plates in their three places; we thanked our same God for her utilitarian food, which was not really the same every night, but seemed so. Only our voices, by an unspoken accord, stayed deep inside us, and we did not talk.

After dinner, while I laid out my assignment book and papers to do homework, my parents briefly whispered together in the kitchen, murmuring low enough for mourning in our altered house. ". . . a collection?" I caught, and then my father said, "Oh, flowers, sure," loud enough to carry easily to me. "Hey, Lizzie, did you know they put coins on their eyes, them Polacks? Honest to God. It's to pay their way into heaven."

In the outer room, always my room, with my books and my unbidden fear spread out around me, I felt myself only fraudulently theirs: my untapped excitement, my young urgency against their casual resumption of our life. A man was dying. And it was their fault, I decided. Too easily, too carelessly, they had let go of him, just as if they had let go of my hand in a crowd and I was lost forever. They had not kept him in their minds, they had excluded him. I felt a spirit sympathy between the man and myself; but even more warmly, a learned and rancid sense of drama took possession of my imagination, phrase by rehearsed phrase, as I tried to encompass him. "He's in God's hands now." "His life is hanging by a thread!" Where had I heard those words, those keys to my unwritten drama? Which would work, would open it? "Nothing tried, nothing gained. . ." "Perseverance wins the crown" (my mother's favorite). And "if at first you don't succeed. . . ." So that was it. They hadn't cared to try for the magical third time. And that was why he was dying so invisibly.

"Somebody should do something," my father had admitted. *I* would, I answered to myself.

I did. Leaving my homework and my parents' voices in the rooms below, I put my own small upstairs bedroom in close to perfect order. The rug, a worn pink pile, I placed equidistant from the headboard and the footboard of my narrow bed. I spat on a turned-up corner of the chenille bedspread for luck, as if it were my skirt hem, and then I smoothed it into place. The window-shades, I saw, jogged awkwardly, one up, one down: I evened them.

Then I took up my last thing, my prayerbook, white leather stamped with a delicate gold cross. A recent Christmas present, it smelled like nothing else in the house, papery and new. Its thin pages clung to my clumsy fingers, and its scarlet bookmark lay silkenly against last Sunday's portion of the Psalter, accusing me of the early place where I had let my attention wander from the text. I was sorry now that I did not pray every day. I promised myself and God that, starting now, I would. I would read the Bible too, each morning, if only—but even I stopped sort of bribery.

Almost at once, I turned to the right prayer, but, like any browser, kept my finger there to scan the nearby titles. "For Social Justice," I read, "For the Navy," "For Rain." And I kept on reading, delaying as long as possible the moment of what I now suddenly saw to be a test. At last nothing but the moment of my trial remained, and I resorted to my destined prayer: "For a Sick Person." Briefly its Renaissance cadences helped me on, but then I stumbled from the archaic words, falling back into my century and my place. Perhaps, I reconsidered, spontaneous prayer would be better? Yes.

Still I had to find the name of God.

I meant to choose a title which best suited my petition and my own unaccustomed voice, used only to a bedside "Our-Father-who-art-in-heaven" run off proudly and not even consciously, the same way I recited muliplication tables or conjugated French verbs. But by now my knees reminded me of time, and all the names of God began to sound ponderous and strange. I could not even repeat some of them without hearing, over mine, the priest's majestic voice drawing out vowels and clicking consonants shut to speak God's grandeur—or his own.

"Most Gracious God," I imitated. But I felt at once remoter from Him than I had ever known myself to be. "Our Heavenly Father," then. No. I was only one abashed person speaking, no "we" at all; and anyway, "heavenly" felt too distant, and "father" too close in. "Lord" avoided these degrees, but struck me as bare and abrupt, almost rude. And I passed over "God Almighty" embarrassedly. Except when a priest said it, it was a curse. In our household, where everyone but me blasphemed with Celtic latitude, I had often heard that title eased into a punctuating "Goddamighty!" I could not now make my own tongue disobey these family cadences, replace them with the unctious elevation of the priest's. They were in me, my people's voices. Hearing them, the others, I stopped altogether, afraid that my mouth might name God wrongly and undo my prayer.

Finally, on my numb knees and exhausting God's known names, I shifted my felt weight and got familiar: "God," I said, "please. . ." (minding my manners), "please take care of, of. . ." But here again I hesitated like a child in a spelling bee. I practiced the word in my head, then spoke, "Mr. Wyczolaski," out loud, fast and right. Borne on my confidence in the victim's name, and in my own power to pronounce it, I next told God why he should save Stash, "*Stanley,*" I reminded God, although He would know a nickname, too, I reasoned to myself. "Save him for his daughter Wanda, who's the same age as me, and for his wife. . ." I had forgotten her name, but chanted bravely on, since God knew everything, "and for himself," I said. After a moment I added, "In Thy Infinite Mercy. . ." I felt the thrill of my translation. The extemporaneous prayer sounded almost like those in my book: I knew that it was good. But with this recognition of my composition's quality, I almost praised myself, the speaker: suddenly I knew that God must save Stash for my own sake most of all. It was for my words that I wanted the miracle to happen: to make them good. The prayer was for myself. Before this forbidden fact, I arrested: and the prayer's lost momentum fell away from me, inexorable as dust.

"Not just for *me,*" I tried to get it back. "For everyone, O God." But I doubted that He would be taken in by this patchwork charity: I did not believe it myself. It opened falsely onto my new world, which was flat, not round, no matter what they said, and had an edge where heaven ought to be, and big deaths even for its smallest, most accidental men.

Almost dumb with loss, I waited out my first time of nothing-ness. It felt like death, that space between the outgrown child who had dared to pray and this self-conscious stranger who suddenly could not. Then the image of the careless, crushed man formed itself in my mind, textbook clear. I knew he must lay smashed— "like an egg," my father had described him—beneath a hospital sheet; and so I started there. I envisioned it whiter and coarser than my mother's sheets, decently containing him. The room around him smelled of purity and pain.

I drew nearer to that invented bed. But I did not open his eyes. They closed on his unimaginable expression, which I did not know how to see. His iconic head, I saw, resembled my father's, was not a young man's head; and his imagined features came to view both personal and sure, as if I had seen him many times before.

Then—even now—I knew I really saw Stanley Wyczolaski's face. Safe white bandages held back his damage, like the swaddling on the porcelain Della Robbia in my new classroom.

I wanted to know more. In my mind's chamber still, I folded the silver bandages aside, neat as a lifted page. Underneath, everything showed itself smooth and charted, the proud high cage of ribs, the shadow of male hair. "There, there, you'll be all right," I comforted. Then, for the first time, I heard my own voice say, "Darling," in a whisper. At the word his body, a lattice in a birthday card, answered me by opening up. I saw all the mysteries that I had only read of: this, the four-chambered heart, but still, so still; here the arteries and veins running blue into it and red away; there the lungs, pink as shell. They lay as real as my eye, but unreal, too.

By now I had forgotten God. My dreaming hands moved in circles over the dying man, and in my vision they restored his life. Veins and arteries, collapsed, sprang full and fresh as stems after rainfall. I bent to kiss him better, and my borrowed breath lifted new roundness in his flattened lungs. I gave him my voice, too. "There, you see," I proved to him out loud.

Then my real hands began to move tenderly over the chenille ridges of my bed's coverlet. I breathed faster, conscious of a drum of pulse, my own, and of my will contracted tightly to a concrete thing meant to uphold him. The unguessed power of my life ran free, and with it, sadness older than the earth.

I could not know yet that my caresses, my reverence, and—when I moved—my newfound exactitude of care, made me a lover. But I knew that everything I did was futile, that I could not really mend: only I made the gestures of the healer all the same, defiantly. I felt my own bones age against the hardness of the floor, and, breathing for us both, for myself and for the dying man, I tasted my own mystery. In that dark way, among my vanquished gods, I began my work in the world.

CANTINA MUSIC

by DEREK WALCOTT

from ANTAEUS

nominated by ANTAEUS, *Robert Boyers, Stanley Lindberg, Howard Moss, Elizabeth Spencer and Sara Vogan*

A lilac sea between shacks,
and, at the Carenage overpass, the go-light
the exact hue of a firefly's faint emerald.
Coconuts, blasted with mildew,
rust between crusted roofs,
the pirogues seem soldered
to metal water, but, like paper lanterns,
rose, lilac, orange
the shacks shine through black hills like bullet holes.

Gauchos of the New World,
Rio, Buenos Aires,
the Wild West rumshops circling St. James,
your fantasies
thud to the rain's guitars
to the renegades whose names
darken on iron stallions,
directing traffic,
against a livid sunset whose palms droop,
morose moustaches of dead liberators,

50

as the foam's grey lather
shines like their horses.
Bandidos of the Old Republic,
your teeth flashed like daggers
your snarl like tom leather
you strode into the street
at the hour of the firefly
and, boots astride, facing the showdown,
you waltzed slowly to the dirt
to a flamenco from the tin cantinas.

Black hats of the double-feature,
Widmarks, Zapatistas, Djangos,
all revolution is rooted in crime.
Your dust is a cloud like a rose,
your hearts keep time
to the ruby beat of the jukebox
"adios muchachos,
compañeros de mi vida,"
from the grave of some boy shot by the police,
some wrong-sided leader
tenor-pan man from Renegades,
Gay Desperadoes.

When you fell there,
exactly as you had learnt to from the screen,
limp as a mountain lion
in whose glass amber eyes
there is no flickering question
about justice.

And the shot that flings
the bandit whirling
in perverse crucifixions
so that each frame, arrested,
repeats itself like a corrupt pietà
to the prodigal of The Mother of The World,
echoes as deep as any silver mine
from the rumshops,
from cantinas,

from the dark sky with a red flower in her hair,
from Rio, from Buenos Aires,
from Carenage,
from St. James,
and has more than they think to do with
the lilac sea between the shacks,
the highway overpass and the faint emerald
of the go-light
that unexpectedly
changes to red.

🔥 🔥 🔥

A DEATH IN
THE GLITTER PALACE

by DAVID HELLERSTEIN

from THE NORTH AMERICAN REVIEW

nominated by Mary Peterson

E VEN NOW, half a year after her death, I cannot entirely get Cha Nan Chen out of my mind. She was not family or a lover, this twenty-eight year old Vietnamese woman with a flat face and two lethal diseases racing to kill her, but instead a patient of mine, to whom I struggled to give good care under the hopeless circumstances. With Cha Nan Chen I shared the doctor's distant intimacy, even when I ordered the shots of morphine that let her die.

Her first malignancy, Hodgkin's Disease, a tumor of lymph nodes, had been cured by the time she came to the Medicine III Oncology Team at a major Medical Center, where, as a fourth year student, I was doing an advanced rotation. A combination of cell poisons and radiation therapy had melted it away. In its place, whether as a result of therapy or as an ironic natural evolution, mutant cells of Acute Myelogenous Leukemia (AML) began colonizing her decimated bone marrow and clogging her blood vessels. She had traded a cancer of the lymph nodes, with expected survival of perhaps three or four years, for a cancer of the blood cells that killed her in thirty days. The rationalization that such complications are uncommon, occurring in perhaps five percent of cases, and that the lifespan of cancer patients given such aggressive therapy is, on the average, lengthened, gives comfort only to the statistician. But Cha Nan Chen was my patient and I mourn her.

A physician writing in the *New England Journal of Medicine* this year describes the problem dispassionately:

> An increasing incidence of therapy-linked Acute Myelogenous Leukemia is being reported in patients who receive chemotherapy, radiation therapy or immunosuppressive drugs for neoplastic and non-neoplastic diseases, including Hodgkin's Disease, lymphoma, ovarian carcinoma and others. The response rate of these patients to chemotherapy is poor, with remission rates of less than ten per cent in most series.

Or, as Susan Sontag writes more succinctly in her recent book *Illness as Metaphor*: "The treatment meant to cure kills." The radiation and the poisonous drugs given to cancer patients, especially when given in combination, have a distressing tendency to create new, incurable disease. Cha Nan Chen had gotten both chemotherapy and radiation. Though I did not know it at the time, when she came to be my patient it was too late: she was good as dead.

On July 6, 1979 a young Vietnamese woman of Chinese extraction came to the Oncology Clinic at the University Medical Center. For the past three weeks she had felt tired and lethargic, and small red dots had appeared by the dozen on her lower legs, upper chest and back. On July 4th, at a fireworks display with her three year old daughter and her father who had recently arrived from Viet Nam via Hong Kong, she began coughing and shaking uncontrollably. At home, despite aspirins and cold washcloths to her forehead and chest, for a night and a day she burned with fever. In the morning of the 6th she found her way to our Oncology Clinic, to the doctor who had been following her progress after treatment for Hodgkin's Disease: He saw her in clinic, and had blood drawn, which, under the microscope, revealed a frightening scarcity of white blood cells and platelets. Even more disturbing, among the white corpuscles of her blood were peculiarly "young" forms, cells that normally are confined to the marrow until further development has occurred. He telephoned the Med III Resident, Larry, who sent me, his sub-intern, down to clinic to admit the patient.

Oncology is a star department in the glitter palace medicine of the University; unlike Pediatrics or Obstetrics, which attract the young and insolvent, Oncology counts among its patients professionals and businessmen and others whom large savings have not protected against malignancy. The clinic, located in the hospital basement, is luxuriously carpeted and wallpapered, all color-coordinated, and trays of fruit (apples, grapes, bananas, oranges) are provided for clinic physicians. Sitting in the Conference Room, I munched grapes while reviewing the new patient's records.

Two thick manila volumes told me this: three years ago this young woman, a recent immigrant to the U.S., had been swept with inexplicable fevers that came and went without cause. At night she would wake drenched in sweat. And though she did not at first notice them, rubber-hard bumps—lymph nodes—swelled in her neck. Her doctor did notice them, waited awhile to see if they would disappear, and when they did not, sent her to a surgeon who sliced one out. A pathologist "elsewhere" (as one refers to hospitals outside the academic medical center's "here") saw whorls of crazily proliferating cells, and diagnosed Hodgkin's Disease of the Nodular Sclerosing type. This is one of four types of the disease, having intermediate mortality, worse than Lymphocyte Predominant but nowhere near as lethal as Lymphocyte Depletion. She was sent "here," where similar hard nodes were noted in the folds of her groin, and a hard, enlarged spleen was felt to abdominal palpation, grown down below the margin of her left ribs.

Then the efficient machinery of the Medical Center's Hodgkin's Disease protocol was set into motion. It is a marvel of glitter palace medicine: costly, scientific, aggressive, requiring the cooperation of half a dozen different departments within the medical center, and achieving heretofore unexcelled results in the treatment of rare disease. Patients with Hodgkin's Disease flock to the area for treatment, much as prospective heart transplant recipients, drowning in the fluids of their own hearts' failure, wait in nearby motel rooms and apartments for motorcyclists to smash their brains out on state highways and provide new hearts for them.

Along with routine blood studies, chest x-rays and so forth, the young woman had another node, from her groin, taken for biopsy, which confirmed the findings in her neck; a bone biopsy; and a lymphangiogram, in which dye is injected into the tiny lymph vessels of the feet to illuminate to x-ray the lymph nodes that enwrap the descending aorta; then she was sliced wide open by surgeons who removed her spleen and took biopsies of her liver and abdominal cavity nodes to detect the spread of disease. This process of "staging" showed disease in her spleen but not her liver or bone. Her disease fit category PS-III-SB, pathological stage III disease ("B" meaning symptomatic in onset and "S" involving the spleen), and she was recommended for combination chemotherapy and radiotherapy. Radiotherapy came first: TNI, total nodal irradiation, which consisted in large doses of x-rays to an area of her body from neck to groin, a "mantle" of lymph node-bearing regions of her neck and chest, and an "inverted Y" from belly to hips. Her heart and lungs and ovaries were protected by "shields" from the decimating radiation. All this Cha Nan Chen tolerated well, or so I gathered from the records, as she did the ensuing chemotherapy, eight monthly courses of Bleo-MOPP, a combination of five drugs hopefully more poisonous to the cancer than to the patient. All treatment ended October 1976. Since then she had been well. The Oncology Clinic flow sheet listed her monthly blood counts, which were stable, and each visit's chest x-ray, weight and vital signs, showing no change. Until three weeks ago, Cha Nan Chen had been, in Oncology jargon, "NED," i.e. with no evidence of disease—a Glitter Palace cure.

The woman I saw lying on a clinic examining table was young, Oriental, with a broad and not particularly pretty face to which sweat had plastered strands of black hair. She had on a hospital gown and cheap clunky shoes and her arms were wrapped around herself to lessen her shaking and terror. I introduced myself.

"Why do I have to be in the hospital again? Why do I have to be sick?"

I was afraid she'd start crying. I stood awkwardly beside her, waiting for her to regain her composure.

"I am sorry," she said. "What do you want to know?"

I questioned her about the Hodgkin's and its cure and her new symptoms, then examined her, noticing the red spots like scattered flecks of blood across her back, down her chest almost to her breasts, along her shins. The roof of her mouth too was scattered with them. My stethoscope against flecked back transmitted the dry rubbings of collapsed lung. And her abdomen, though scarred with surgery and burnt with a permanent radiation tan, showed no clues to disease.

She wanted to know what I'd found.

"Well, red spots, of course," I said. "And you're hot, feverish, and you have a cough. I think you will have to be hospitalized."

"Oh," she said, looking down at her clunky shoes, absolutely desolate.

"But we'll try to get you home as soon as possible."

I was standing by the nursing station later that afternoon, finishing my note on Cha Nan, when Larry, my Resident, returned. He was supposed to supervise my every move but often disappeared for hours at a time, off running in the hills or weightlifting or eating dinner with his girlfriend. Short and topheavy with muscle, Larry leaned up against me to read my note:

28 y.o. f. NSHD CSIISB/PSIIISB 3 yr. hx., s/p TNI 4500 rads mantle/3500 rads inverted Y, last 4/76, s/p Bleo-MOPP, last 10/76 → now 3 wks. hx. fatigue, cough & fever, blasts on smear → ?? 2° AML

He borrowed my stethoscope and lumbered off, thick-necked as a minotaur, to examine her. Twenty minutes later he returned, slapping the stethoscope against his thigh.

"So you think it's AML?" he said.

"The smear sure looked like it. Blasts all over. I've got it here, in my pocket, if you want to see it."

He shrugged. "What have you done so far?"

"Cultured everything—blood, sputum, urine, throat. Chest

x-ray. All the usual bloods. Reverse isolation. Six units of platelets. Oh, also, I wrote for Hematology consult and scheduled a marrow for tomorrow. I didn't know whether to write for K, G and C."

"Let's wait on the antibiotics," he said. "Now, what do you want to do with her?"

"What do you mean? Treat her. Find out where the infection is. . . ."

"No, no, I mean the AML."

"I . . . I don't know. If it *is* AML, I guess, induce her. She's got a three year old daughter, she wants to get home to her."

"They don't respond, these AML's, to induction like the virgin ones do," he said. "Probably just end up killing her."

"The AML definitely will," I said. "She's already bleeding, febrile, probably septic. What choice do we have?"

"She's your patient."

The next morning, Cha Nan, lying on her belly, her flank scrubbed with iodine solution, draped with blue towels, anesthesized as well as can be done with xylocaine, screamed as I screwed a hollow metal bit into the bone of her hip. The bone marrow is one of medicine's most barbaric procedures, the exact technique one uses to drill a core from a tree to determine its age; for which one is most successful if speedy as a Civil War surgeon amputating a leg with only his sharp saw and bottle of whisky. My technique, though, lacking both brutality and speed, was immensely more painful. I could make her neither maple tree nor soldier: instead she remained a weeping Vietnamese woman who had lost her homeland and whose husband, an American once a soldier, had deserted her in the first illness, who was succumbing now to a second and worse disease we doctors had given her. Trembling, I screwed metal into bone. She writhed. I attached a syringe, tried to suck marrow out. She screamed. No marrow. "Just get the core," said Larry. I was drenched in sweat. I unscrewed the needle, hoping a red core of bone and marrow would stay caught in its hollowed center. But no—empty. "Have to do it again," said Larry, "We *need* the core." I stepped away from the bed, tore off my gloves. My bare hands shook. "I can't. You do it." Larry rolled up his sleeves, showing weightlifter's biceps, triceps, deltoids; he snapped on a pair of gloves and began.

Later, still sweating, I said, "I don't know *why* . . . I've done it

half-a-dozen times before . . . I just couldn't . . . couldn't get the
distance right."

He said, "You have to get *on* the bed, then bear down with every
ounce of your weight."

We ordered fresh frozen plasma and six units of platelets to help
her clotting, but when I left at nine that night, and indeed, when I
arrived the next morning, the bone marrow site in her hip was still
oozing blood.

2.

Treatment [of cancer] . . . has a military flavor. Radiotherapy
uses the metaphors of aerial warfare; patients are "bombarded" with toxic rays. And chemotherapy is chemical warfare, using poisons. Treatment aims to "kill" cancer cells
(without, it is hoped, killing the patient). Unpleasant side
effects of treatment are advertised, indeed over-advertised.
("The agony of chemotherapy" is a standard phrase.) It is
impossible to avoid damaging or destroying healthy cells . . .
but it is thought that nearly any damage to the body is justified
if it saves the patient's life. Often, of course, it doesn't work.
(As in: "We had to destroy Ben Suc in order to save it.") There
is everything but the body count.

Sontag, *Illness as Metaphor*

There is, with AML, the Blast Count: how many malignant cells
float through the blood, like mines in a harbor.

Over the next few days the Med III team had several discussions
about Cha Nan Chen. She was no more sick than half a dozen other
patients on the service, though she did continue to run high fevers,
to bleed from the marrow site and from her vagina (though her
period had ended ten days ago), and to break out late at night in
strange rashes that could only be controlled with large doses of
steroids. The two interns on the service complained she kept them
up all night. Her marrow biopsy was fixed and read: it was packed
tight with blasts. Myeloid type. Hematology came to consult on the
question of whether, and how, to treat what we now knew for
certain was Acute Myeloid Leukemia. They told us that the
ordinary patient with AML, if untreated, will die within two
months; if "induced" by intensive chemotherapy which essentially

wipes out the patient's bone marrow to allow the "good" cells to repopulate the areas where malignant cells have been killed, then the average patient may live a year or more. They laid emphasis on what we already knew: Cha Nan was not a typical patient and her disease was far less likely to respond. For treatment they recommended Ara-C and 6-TG which are in the class of "antimetabolite" drugs. In addition, they noted: "The patient will need to be supported with red cell, platelet and white cell transfusions through her period of aplasia." While her bombarded bone marrow was unable to produce normal blood cells, we had to replace them. Med III team, including our ward attendant, Dr. B., the two interns, and Larry and I, discussed what to do at morning rounds.

Larry said he was with me, he wanted to treat her. Especially since Hematology, despite the odds, wanted to. Dr. B., who has seen many of these patients in recent years, said, "I'm really not sure if it's worth it."

"But her white count's zero point seven with sixty blasts. She's not responding to antibiotics. Unless we do something," I said, "She'll be dead in a few weeks."

"I don't disagree with that," said Dr. B., "I'm just saying that in the past, no matter what we do, we haven't had good responses."

"Maybe you just haven't tried hard enough," said Larry.

After rounds I went to see Cha Nan. She lay in bed watching cartoons on the TV hanging from the wall. Her face was bloated. I put on a blue face mask, wiped my stethoscope with an alcohol swab and washed my hands before touching her. Listening to her lungs I discovered a new area of consolidation just below her left shoulderblade.

"Say EEEEE," I said.

"AAAAAA."

"EEEEEE."

"AAAAAA."

Infection had settled in her lung. Depressed, I said nothing.

"I had a terrible night," she said. "I could not sleep at all."

"I know, Cha Nan. The interns keep complaining. You just get too many fevers."

"Why is that, David? And why do I always keep bleeding?"

I sat on the bed beside her, and we talked for an hour about the Ara-C and 6-TG and the white cell transfusions. She had seen Hematology yesterday, and accepted their recommendations without hesitation. "It is like last time," she said, "It will be hard to be treated but I have to do it."

"We do want," I said, "to get you back to your daughter."

We talked about her daughter Charlotte, who had been born in the U.S. a few years after she left Vietnam with her husband, just before the Hodgkin's was discovered. She described the chaos of Saigon; the bombs and the refugees; the courtyard of a French hotel where she had stayed, where prostitutes sat for hours under umbrella tables, ordering nothing; the panic when the last planes were leaving; and the difficulty in getting her father out of the country after the collapse. Even now his status in the U.S. was uncertain.

"I have to get out of the hospital next week," she said, "for one day only. To go to the courthouse downtown and get him papers—permanent residency papers. . . ."

"I don't think you'll be able to," I said. "But I'll write a letter, saying you can't leave the hospital, and asking if they can send the papers here. Okay?"

"Can you do that?" Her hand touched mine momentarily, damp and ill, then pulled away. She said, "I should not touch you?"

"To protect you," I said.

6-TG and Ara-C began. I was On Call a few nights later when she got her first white blood cell transfusion. It was Passover, and I'd been invited out for Seder; but I just couldn't get away. The interns wanted tonight off too. I ate dinner alone in the almost deserted cafeteria, and everything seemed to be going well—the usual fevers, bleeding, cough, red spots, nothing more—when I went to bed around midnight. At two a.m. my phone rang. It was Maureen, the night nurse:

"I'm worried about Cha Nan. She's got a horrible rash all over her legs. And her temp's up."

"What to?"

"Forty-one four."

"Oh God. What is that in real degrees?"

"Over one oh six . . . I don't know . . . it's off the scale."

I lay in bed in my green scrub-suit, the thrum of the Pediatrics ICU air conditioner on the roof nearby vibrating my panic loose.

"I've started an alcohol sponge bath, cooling blanket, Tylenol. . . ."

"Is . . . is she having trouble breathing?"

"No."

"Well," I said, relieved, "I'll be there in a minute. You might call Larry too."

I put on shoes and white coat, and stumbled down to the ward, where, except for Cha Nan's, disease seemed to have abated this Passover night. Silent, empty except for the ward clerk with a cup of coffee, reading the *Chronicle*. I recalled what an English grad student friend asked: 'Do you get a sense of things like Lewis Thomas describes, of a wonderful and complex order to life? Do you get a sense of astonishment?' I told him I hadn't felt that, only the horror of fighting decay on multiple fronts; and the occasional victory attained only partial, a matter of delay. 'What is there but time?' I had answered him. 'If you can give a person that . . .'

In her room, Cha Nan lay in agony. Her legs were covered with a red confluent rash—maculopapular and erythematous, my chart note would say—but ugly, spreading, furious. She was coughing, sweating, holding her right side.

Maureen said, "Her right flank's started hurting all of a sudden. I don't know what it is."

I washed, masked up, overwhelmed by a vision of Cha Nan as battlefield—an image I only later found put into words by Sontag—as our burnt and blasted terrain, defoliated, napalmed, cratered. She coughed worse with the white cells, which "localize to the site of infection," clogging her lungs as they attacked the bugs within; she flared like an incendiary torch; she shivered uncontrollably; her flank was sprayed with fire. She had sprouted, I noticed now, viral ulcers on her mouth. Herpes . . . herpes encephalitis would be a miserable way to go. Better to die of any bacteria. I seemed to pull away from it all, to see her from a great distance—I thought of my father, a young soldier, a doctor, standing at the entrance of Bergen-Belsen on the eve of the concentration camp's liberation; the stacks of bodies he photographed; the tiny photographs I discovered in a rubberized canvas bag in the back corner of a desk drawer in the attic room of my Ohio childhood, photographs that awakened in me inexplicable memories of one war I had not experienced and the expectation of another coming, in which I would be a soldier. . . .

"How are you doing, Cha Nan?"

"Not too good," she said. "Cold."

"You've given Benadryl, right?" I asked Maureen. She nodded.

"A hundred of Solu-Medrol, then, that's what we want." Lateness buzzed in the air. "And for her side . . . Demerol, Dilaudid, whatever's ordered."

"I have to check with the Resident," she said.

"Fine," I said. To Cha Nan: "I know this is terrible. But your Blast Count *is* coming down. I think we're . . . you're making progress."

I went upstairs, wondering if any stem cells were left. If not, she might be getting from our treatment a third disease, aplastic anemia, worse than Hodgkin's and worse even than AML. Lying in bed unable to sleep, I couldn't help thinking of a tune from the *Haggadah*, sung tonight after a full, leisurely Passover meal:

> Then came the butcher and slaughtered the ox
> That drank the water
> That smothered the fire
> That burned the stick
> That beat the dog
> That bit the cat
> That ate the kid
> My father bought for two zuzim
> *Chad godya, Chad godya.*

I fell asleep hearing the tune, and worrying about Cha Nan.

Her Blast Count went down. 70, 50, 36, 27, 11, 4, 1 . . . then one day, zero.

"No blasts, Cha Nan! I think we're winning!" Said through blue paper masks, our white coats tenting around her so she entirely disappeared, as half a dozen stethoscopes clattered together on her sweaty back. "Listen!" said Larry. I listened. "You hear that? A new pleural rub." Her blasts were down but so were all her white cells. You or I have five or ten thousand floating through our vessels, squeezing through the sinusoids of our spleens, crawling among our bodily organs. She had six hundred, four hundred, three hundred. And platelets given her burst in her veins. Once half a million, now fifteen thousand was the best we could manage. She coughed more daily. On x-ray a white haze took refuge in the back gutter of her right lung. Not even the triple antibiotics— acronymically K, G & C—made it disappear, made her, talking about her father who was working illegally in the city making trousers, able to control the paroxysms of coughing. I felt helpless as a country doctor of the old days with his bleeding bowls and jars of leeches. Whenever I came in, Maureen or another nurse was trying to start an IV in Cha Nan's battered arms. Every vein-stick hurt, and every new IV blew under the corrosion of K, G & C or of 6-TG and Ara-C. The blood we dripped in could not replace what oozed out. Cardiac surgeons came to try placing a central line so Cha Nan would not have to get stuck so often for bloods and IV's But they failed. "Anomalous venous system," they wrote. "Will try other side next week." Cha Nan was always crying.

Then the husband showed up: a small, embarrased-looking ex-GI with a pointy chin and the look of a ferret or a weasel surprised at his kill. And with him he brought Charlotte, the little girl. Charlotte had Cha Nan's black hair, and an exquisite timidity. Passing the room I would see her, mask in hand, climbing on Cha Nan's belly. The room, when I entered it, which was more and more rarely, smelled vaguely rotten from the food her husband bought. I wondered just where he had been all this time.

I avoided her. Kübler-Ross may have an explanation of my conduct, in terms of an effort to minimize impending loss; all I know is that the second cycle of 6-TG and Ara-C ended, and Cha Nan looked worse than ever, and Med III team made briefer and more perfunctory rounds on her. And when alone, often I would just pass by the room, rather than poke my head inside with the latest white count or to ask about the letter for Cha Nan's father. I had dictated it: "To whom it may concern; Cha Nan Chen is a patient of ours at the University Medical Center, with the diagnosis of Acute Myelogenous Leukemia, and is unable to leave the hospital. . . ." Yet it had not arrived from Dictation. Somewhere on the way from telephone to typewriter to ward, those words for the old Chinese man had disappeared.

And so had her cells. Everything stayed down: blasts, white cells, red cells, platelets. I knew why I avoided her. There were no stem cells left.

3.

Now when I look back and try to unravel the events of those despairing days, I find somewhat clearer patterns. But still, fragments, confusions. The decision to treat her was, of course, not mine. I had some limited say in it. But I took on the burden for the whole Med III team and five consulting services as my own. As if I were responsible not only for the failure of her treatment but for the presence of her disease. I began to have the horrible suspicion that we were shortening her life, that our vigorous treatment was just killing her more quickly than her disease itself. The anguish of seeing her every day convinced me beyond suspicion, even beyond the facts. I worked harder on my other patients: a nineteen year old kid with testicular seminoma, a Mexican lady with ovarian cancer, a fifty-eight year old man who had sprayed asbestos in a World War II shipyard and now had mesothelioma, an old Swede with cancer of the prostate, a Greek surgeon, Dr. Odysseus, with non-Hodgkin's Lymphoma. All were ill, all but the nineteen year old would eventually die of their cancer, yet our work could give them something: time. But Cha Nan, no. And I avoided her.

Anyone who is sick or who treats sick patients today knows that the doctor is not a curer but an odds-player, trying to heal more disease than he causes. He is no longer the powerless observer; with the "big gun" antibiotics, anticancer drugs, and so on, which often have horrific side effects, he is inevitably made part of the disease. The doctor must maintain composure both against the knowledge that every treatment is to some degree Russian roulette, and against the patient's blind hope for cure. Each is dangerous. Insulin "saves" the diabetic from early death only to make crippled blind amputees on dialysis; phenothiazines alleviate schizophrenia but make some patients into writhing, wheelchair-bound freaks. Halothane for anesthesia, phenylbutazone for arthritis can kill your liver dead. There is no shortage of other examples for the cynical doctor, for the patient chary of treatment. The death of Cha Nan Chen is one small example of the paradox of medicine in twentieth century America: the doctor's helpless retreat from the effects of his own therapeutic "armamentarium." It is no accident that, as Sontag says, ". . . recently the fight against cancer has sounded like a colonial war. . . ." When and how do you pull out? And what of the ensuing collapse?

It was a relief to let her die.

She told me first, one Saturday morning when I came in to find her feverish as usual: "David, I don't want any more."

"Hematology wants to try once more," I said. "With the Ara-C and 6-TG." Though silently I doubted whether they had even seen her. For in their note they recommended another bone marrow too: "to assess our progress."

"*They* want," she said.

"They think that . . ."

"No."

The next day, Med III discussed her again, sitting in our conference room with her latest numbers up on the blackboard. Nobody had much to say.

"So we're pulling back?" I said at the end.

Dr. B. nodded. "She's finished," he said. "Up her morphine dose, stop her K, G and C, her blood products. If her IV falls out, keep it out. Agreed?"

Afterwards I went to see her. At the foot of the bed sat her father, a shrivelled Chinese with bushy gray hair. The letter that had gotten lost gnawed at me. Cha Nan's husband, unshaven, had the Sunday newspaper on his lap. Cha Nan lay in bed, eyes open enough only to show whites, and she breathed only every six or eight seconds, with shudders each time. Cheynes-Stokes respirations, a terminal pattern, evidence of brain damage . . . she was Cheynes-Stoking and they were sitting and watching her go. I called to her. She startled awake, wide-eyed, and stared at me.

"Go outside," she told her husband, "Go, go." And the same to her father in Chinese. She watched them leave before speaking again.

"I am tired," she said. "I want to go, David. Do you understand, I want to go?"

"To go, Cha Nan?"

"I am tired, so tired. Can you let me go?"

She was flushed, sweaty, in the close-aired room, with me and the newspapers and the IV bottles, and the heavy presence of death. It reminded me of nothing so much as a scene from a novel or a play, something one cannot believe could exist outside of art—the certainty of her desire for death, her impassioned clarity after days of somnolence and fever.

"All right, Cha Nan," I said. And her eyes closed.

At the nursing station, I was writing an order to increase her morphine to fifteen milligrams every two or three hours when Larry came by. He read over my shoulder.

"That isn't enough. Give her thirty."

I scratched out and rewrote.

He nudged me. "You're writing an order to kill that lady."

"I know."

"How's it feel?"

I looked at the order, in my crabbed handwriting. Larry pushed up against me, his weightlifter's bulk close.

"Lousy," I said. "Co-sign it."

"Give me your pen."

Later I came back into the room. It was the last day of my sub-internship, and I had been going around to my dozen patients, writing off-service notes and making sure all unfinished business would be followed up. Again I had dictated the letter for Cha Nan's father. I asked Maureen how Cha Nan was.

"I gave her thirty of morphine. Her family's in there again. She's talking with them."

"She's a brave lady," I said. "She knows, she really knows it's all over." I entered the room. Small dark people surrounded Cha Nan—her father, husband, three women I hadn't seen before. And she was Cheynes-Stoking with such shuddering finality that I was scared each breath would be her last one.

I touched her arm; she jolted awake.

"Oh! I feel so good!" Eyes wide open, staring black and unblinking, surveyed us.

"You were talking and fell asleep," said her husband.

"I thought . . . I thought I was dead," she said, in awe of us and herself. "I was dead—but look, I am not. I feel so good, so strong now. Oh I'm so happy, I'm not dead."

I told her about the letter, which had taken a peculiar importance to me, as if it were some sort of contract or waiver of responsibility; and it was a great relief to touch her hand, to hear: "Thank you, David."

Then she said, "I have to talk. Listen to what I have to say." And she spoke in Chinese to her family. I left her wide-eyed, unnaturally alert but opiated beyond pain. It was ten p.m. that Sunday night before I finished off-services notes and headed home.

The next morning, beginning my Hematology rotation, I was assigned two of my Oncology patients as consults: Dr. Odysseus, the Greek surgeon with lymphoma dying far from Athens, and Cha

Nan. When I came by the nursing station to check her chart, one of the nurses, not Maureen, told me Cha Nan had just died.

"That's good," I said.

I went down the hall. Perhaps she had just died, victim to her third disease contracted in treatment of the second, contracted in treatment of the first, a *Chad Godya* of illness begun with "one kid, one kid" of Hodgkin's Disease and culminating in a slow and agonized yielding to the Angel of Death (who had yet to yield to "the Holy One, blessed be He"). But already the low cart, disguised to look like a linen hamper, and the pointy-faced husband, and shrivelled father, and the three dark short women had gone. I headed toward the room of Dr. Odysseus, still living, still dying.

LAGOON

by JOSEPH BRODSKY

from THE PARIS REVIEW

nominated by THE PARIS REVIEW, *Walter Abish, and Daniel Halpern*

I

Down in the lobby three elderly women, bored,
Take up, with their knitting, the Passion of Our Lord
    As the universe and the tiny realm
Of the *pension "Accademia,"* side by side,
with TV blaring, sail into Christmastide,
    A look-out desk-clerk at the helm.

II

And a nameless lodger, a nobody, boards the boat,
A bottle of grappa concealed in his raincoat
    As he gains his shadowy room, bereaved
Of memory, homeland, son, with only the noise
Of distant forests to grieve for his former joys,
    If anyone is grieved.

III

Venetian churchbells, tea cups, mantle clocks,
Chime and confound themselves in this stale box
    Of assorted lives. The brazen, coiled
Octopus-chandelier appears to be licking,
In a triptych mirror, bedsheet and mattress ticking,
    Sodden with tears and passion-soiled.

IV

Blown by nightwinds, an Adriatic tide
Floods the canals, boats rock from side to side,
    Moored cradles, and the humble bream,
Not ass and oxen, guards the rented bed
Where the windowblind above your sleeping head
    Moves to the sea-star's guiding beam.

V

So this is how we cope, putting out the heat
Of grappa with nightstand water, carving the meat
    Of flounder instead of Christmas roast,
So that Thy earliest back-boned ancestor
Might feed and nourish us, O Savior,
    This winter night on a damp coast.

VI

A Christmas without snow, tinsel or tree,
At the edge of a map-and-land corseted sea;
    Having scuttled and sunk its scallop shell,
Concealing its face while flaunting its backside,
Time rises from the goddess's frothy tide,
    Yet changes nothing but clock-hand and bell.

VII

A drowning city, where suddenly the dry
Light of reason dissolves in the moisture of the eye;
    Its winged lion, that can read and write,
Southern kin of northern Sphinxes* of renown,
Won't drop his book and holler, but calmly drown
    In splinters of mirror, splashing light.

VIII

The gondola knocks against its moorings. Sound
Cancels itself, hearing and words are drowned,
    As is that nation where among

*Sculptured figures placed along the enbankments of the Neva River in Leningrad

Forests of hands the tyrant of the State
Is voted in, its only candidate,
    And spit goes ice-cold on the tongue.

IX

So let us place the left paw, sheathing its claws,
In the crook of the arm of the other one, because
    This makes a hammer-and-sickle sign
With which to salute our era and bestow
A mute *Up Yours Even Unto The Elbow*
    Upon the nightmares of our time.

X

The raincoated figure is settling into place
Where Sophia, Constance, Prudence, Faith and Grace
    Lack futures, the only tense that is
Is present, where either a goyish or Yiddish kiss
Tastes bitter, like the city, where footsteps fade
    Invisibly along the colonnade,

XI

Trackless and blank as a gondola's passage through
A water surface, smoothing out of view
    The measured wrinkles of its path,
Unmarked as a broad "So long!" like the wide piazza's
      space,
Or as a cramped "I love," like the narrow alleyways,
    Erased and without aftermath.

XII

Moldings and carvings, palaces and flights
Of stairs. Look up: the lion smiles from heights
    Of a tower wrapped as in a coat
Of wind, unbudged, determined not to yield,
Like a rank weed at the edge of a plowed field,
    And girdled round by Time's deep moat.

XIII

Night in St. Mark's piazza. A face as creased
As a finger from its fettering ring released,
    Biting a nail, is gazing high
Into that *nowhere* of pure thought, where sight
Is baffled by the bandages of night,
    Serene, beyond the naked eye,

XIV

Where, past all boundaries and all predicates,
Black, white or colorless, vague, volatile states,
    Something, some object, comes to mind.
Perhaps a body. In our dim days and few,
The speed of light equals a fleeting view,
    Even when blackout robs us blind.

Translated by Anthony Hecht

WAITING IN LINE

by WILLIAM STAFFORD

from BARNWOOD PRESS

nominated by BARNWOOD PRESS, *Louis Gallo and David Madden*

You the very old, I have come
to the edge of your country and looked across,
how your eyes warily look into mine
when we pass, how you hesitate when
we approach a door. Sometimes
I understand how steep your hills
are, and your way of seeing the madness
around you, the careless waste of the calendar,
the rush of people on buses. I have
studied how you carry packages,
balancing them better, giving them attention.

I have glimpsed from within the gray-eyed look
at those who push, and occasionally even I
can achieve your beautiful bleak perspective
on the loud, inattentive, shoving boors
jostling past you toward their doom.

With you, from the pavement I have watched
the nation of the young, like jungle birds
that scream as they pass, or gyrate on playgrounds,
their frenzied bodies jittering with the disease
of youth. Knowledge can cure them. But
not all at once. It will take time.

There have been evenings when the light
has turned everything silver, and like you
I have stopped at a corner and suddenly
staggered with the grace of it all: to have
inherited all this, or even the bereavement
of it and finally being cheated!—the chance
to stand on a corner and tell it goodby!
Every day, every evening, every
abject step or stumble, has become heroic:—

You others, we the very old have a country.
A passport costs everything there is.

RETURN

by CAROLYN FORCHÉ

from THE AMERICAN POETRY REVIEW

nominated by Laura Jensen and Bruce Weigl

FOR JOSEPHINE CRUM

Upon my return to America, Josephine:
the iced drinks and paper umbrellas, clean
toilets & Los Angeles palm trees moving
like lean women, I was afraid more than
I had been, so much so and even of motels
that for months every tire blow-out
was final, every strange car near the house
kept watch & I strained even to remember
things impossible to forget. You took
my stories apart for hours, sitting
on your sofa with your legs under you

& fifty years in your face. So you know
now, you said, what kind of money
is involved & that *campesinos* knife
one another & you know you can't trust
anyone & so you find a few people you can
trust. You know the mix of machetes
with whiskey, the slip of the tongue
& that it costs hundreds of deaths.
You've seen the pits where men and women
are kept the few days it takes without
food & water. You've heard the cocktail
conversation on which depends their release.
So you've come to understand that men & women
of goodwill read torture reports with fascination.
And such things as water pumps & co-op gardens
are of little importance & take years.
It is not Che Guevara, this struggle.
Camillo Torres is dead. Victor Jara
was rounded up with the others & Jose
Marti is a landing strip for planes
from Miami to Cuba. Go try on
Americans your long & dull story
of corruption, but better to give
them what they want: Lil Milagro Ramirez,
who after years of confinement did not
know what year it was, how she walked
with help & was forced to shit in public.
Tell them about the razor, the live wire,
dry ice & concrete, grey rats and above all
who fucked her, how many times and when.
Tell them about retaliation: Jose lying
on the flatbed truck, waving his stumps
in your face, his hands cut off by his
captors & thrown to the many *hectares*
of cotton, lost, still & holding
the last few lumps of leeched earth.
Tell them Jose in his last few hours
& later how, many months later, a labor
leader was cut to pieces & buried.
Tell them how his friends found

the soldiers & made them dig him up
& ask forgiveness of the corpse, once
it was assembled again on the ground
like a man. As for the cars, of course
they watch you & for this don't flatter
yourself. We are all watched. We are
all assembled. Josephine, I tell you
I have not slept, not since I drove
those streets with a gun in my lap,
not since all manner of speaking
has failed & the remnant of my life
continues onward. I go mad, for example,
in the Safeway, at the many heads
of lettuce, papayas & sugar, pineapples
& coffee, especially the coffee.
And I cannot speak with American men.
It is some absence of recognition:
their constant scotch & fine white
hands, many hours of business, penises
hardened to motor inns & a faint
resemblance to their wives. I cannot
keep going. I remember the ambassador
from America to that country: his tanks
of fish, his clicking pen, his rapt
devotion to reports. His wife wrote
his reports. She said as much as she
gathered him each day from the embassy
compound, that she was tired of covering
up, sick of his drink & the failure
of his last promotion. She was a woman
who flew her own plane, stalling out
after four martinis to taxi on an empty
field in the *campo* and to those men
& women announce she was there to help.
She flew where she pleased in that country
with her drunken kindness, while Marines
in white gloves were assigned to protect
her husband. It was difficult work, what
with the suspicion on the rise in smaller
countries that *gringos* die like other men.

I cannot, Josephine, talk to them.
And so you say, you've learned a little
about starvation: a child like a supper scrap
filling with worms, many children strung
together, as if they were cut from paper
& all in a delicate chain. And that people
who rescue physicists, lawyers & poets
lie in their beds at night with reports
of mice introduced into women, of men
whose testicles are crushed like *cojones*
like eggs. That they cup their own parts
with their bedsheets and move themselves
slowly, imagining bracelets affixing
their wrists to a wall where the naked
are pinned, where the naked are tied open
and left to the hands of those who erase
what they touch. We are all erased
by them. We no longer resemble decent
men. We no longer have the hearts,
the strength, the lives of women.
We do not hold this struggle in our hands
in the darkness but ourselves & what little
comes to the surface between our legs.
Your problem is not your life as it is
in America, not that your hands, as you
tell me, are tied to do something. It is
that you were born to an island of greed & grace
where you have this sense of yourself
as apart from others. It is not your right
to feel powerless. Better people than you
were powerless. You have not returned
to your country, but to a life you never left.

𝕭 𝕭 𝕭

THE FLOCCULUS

fiction by DAVID OHLE

from THE PARIS REVIEW

nominated by M. D. Elevitch

ONEBA TELLS OF AN OCCASION which found him riding the trench, pedaling himself, in his fabulous little pedalcar. As he went along, so the story goes, he was set upon by a band of *trochilics*, their attendant dogs, and their teetotums. They did nothing to him that would snuff his wick at once, and when he fainted from the awful agonies they inflicted upon him they would revive him with cups of cold trenchwater, befouled and stinky, and it seeped horribly through his wiry red beard, and then commence new and more ingenious tortures. When it seemed he could bear no more, the younger members of the band got about him, smoking pissweed in bamboo pipes, laughing at Oneba's apish shrieking, and fed pine needles and cones to a slow fire smouldering on his stomach.

The next day and the day after that Oneba supplied the fun for the camp. A comely young *trochilic* woman came to him and tried to make him open his mouth, as she unbuckled the straps of her khakies. Oneba realized her purpose was evil, and so refused. At this she took a half-brick lying by and one by one knocked his teeth in, smashing down the dentation of the upper jaw. Then she took a rough pair of wooden pincers, used them to grasp his tongue at the roots, dragged him about the place, convulsed with mirth at his torment and his attempts to scream out.

Another pleasantry was to amass a quantity of glowing charcoal on a strip of pony hide and bind it around his head. When he would swoon the coals were removed and he would recover, but in an instant a fresh lot was applied.

He made such sport for the women and children that his death was to be as long drawn out as possible. The children enjoyed breaking his feet in the fashion of bastinado. He was staked to the mudbank and the soles of his feet clubbed until every one of the innumerable small bones was broken and the flesh reduced to jelly.

Then he was tethered on a hill of fire ants and it seemed an eternity until he fainted.

The next day he was tortured further.

The third day signs indicated the *trochilics* were breaking camp. Oneba was stuck and trussed with aluminum rods sharpened to a pencil's point, in a way that they would not immediately wound him mortally. A flint arrowhead was used to pin his thigh to the dirt, and a *trochilic* woman cleft his chin with a skinning knife so he would remember her.

Shortly after they had broken camp and rode off on their scruffy ponies, one of them came back and shot him in the head, though not fatally.

Even now the bullet is lodged where it came to rest, and forms a great protuberance there.

If I open my window I smell the opprobrium of the City drifting in with the midday sun, my sad *nicotiana* dying in the window box.

Someone made the alarming statement to a *Halflife Times* reporter that a tamale man was making his hot meat rolls in the kitchen of a squalid house of the Eastside Historic Area, in which members of his family are suffering the ravages of diptheria.

On the backstreets of Halflife I've seen the new *trochilic* process artists spooning dogpats into the pale faces of Halflife's children, spinning teetotums and hooting at pedestrians, their goggles casting shimmering buttons on the banquette.

Remarkable illuminations were observed in the Northern heavens on Friday and Saturday nights. The bright, diffused, white and yellow lights continued through the night, fading at daybreak. Oneba claims the phenomenon may be connected with important changes on the sun's surface, causing electrical discharges. He mentions a similar occurrence in 1883, which was directly traceable to an outbreak of the Krakatoa volcano. Reports from Copenhagen and Koenigsberg tell of the same great lights being visible in those Cities, and it is presumed that they are seen throughout Northern Europe. Under this influence, he goes on, goats have been mauled, the lungs and hearts carted off mysteriously, and the udders of the she's clipped.

Eat at one of Mexico Lindo Cafe's next time you're pedaling through Halflife. We serve lambfries, chili hearts, swellfish, and skrada-kaka takeout.

A minister of the faith dances with an inflated companion, called *icies* here at Halflife, down the aisle of the Church of the Ark, Oneba's church, and people are sunning themselves by the millions, like turtles, all the way along the national trench.

Oneba says music is the fourth material want of our nature. First is food, raiment, then shelter, and finally music. He encourages us to play the short-horn, to whistle on the streets, to toot kazoos.

Here I am sitting in the squalid and closet-like kitchen of my trailer home, gumming a plug of D-meat, suffering a week of dry flatulence.

Come to the Dixie Peanut, Halflife's only tavern, enjoy any possible mixed drink. Pimm's Cup specials, the eagle flies on

Saturday, closed Sunday. We have peanuts every way—baked, boiled, raw, salted-in-the-shell. We feature Miss Derando and Little Toni doing their delicate short-horn work. They are true and pure styling.

Boiled the last of my D-meat pouches and made a bitter broth.

How sorry to hear it on the radio, Kenny Cubus is dead again, gone to sleep with the window open in the cool of the ides, and a grackle has flown in, and pecked at the lenses of his goggles.

Oneba is One. Celebrate National Week!

I've rolled my *Halflife Times* into a cone, I've looked out at things, clocked time, been on watch. It goes something like this: vintage, fog, sleet, snow, rain, wind, seed, blossom, pasture, harvest, heat, and then the fruiting, should the frost stay on the pumpkin long enough, and the possum piss crescents in the new-fallen snow. If the goats lie in the field, and if the chimney smoke sinks to the level of the rye, then a painful winter is afoot.

So many of us afraid to death of the flocculus, as we side-step those who have them, and wonder what their purpose is, hanging like a windsock, an elephant's trunk, in front of the face, at one glance seeming membranous and opaque, at another like canvas or cheesecloth.

I have a low stinkfire here, a screw of acrid smoke twisting from it, of shiplap and old newspaper, cooking a ball of D-meat on the end of a curtain rod, squatted in front of the Church of the Ark, saying my beads, mouthing a common prayer.

As you remember, reader, Kenny Cubus returned from the dead more than twenty years ago in the pages of *Halflife Times*, the first of the *trochilic* 'necronauts'. Today Kenny is as alive as you or me, busy jotting his impressions of the refrigerated rooms, the silent years of frosty discomfort, his breath gathered in a flocculus, like a hive of cotton candy, between his coonlike eyes and his automatic pencil.

Chewed off the head of a big devilhopper, let it sit like a hot pepper on my tongue, then washed it away with a bottle of La Perla.

A Kabuki star is dead here, *requiescat in pace*. Mitsuguro Bando, noted Kabuki actor, one of Halflife's most precious treasures, has died of swellfish poisoning at a restaurant in this City. After his performance he dined with fans on seafood at the Mexico Lindo and on remarking about particularly tasty puffer he collapsed, his cheeks engorged and pathologically distended. No doubt they'll perform a restoration and stuff him in a cubby at the City reliquary.

I jog the time away at Halflife, waterwell to waterwell, palmetto to palmetto, and do easy acrobatics, daily life a simple parcourse.

Water blister on the cock, another paralyzing Sunday.

Oneba is finally dead. Found moribund in his bedclothes, wrapped like a mummy. One of us will have to drape him with the flag and wake him, say the words, get the body ready. We'll need dung and pinestraw, palm oil and vinegar, a quart of Florida water, a bit of sawdust, according to his instructions.

Cricket fiddles under the loquat, a ring of dead fruit below the fig. Beyond the stone fence my hog, my goats, gaze stuporously at a hungry moon. Devilhoppers have eaten my iceberg, squash bugs cover my cantaloupes in a dark and seething envelope. Found a blue phosphorescent slime streaked the length of the trailer home.

Trochilics believe that eating a dog's heart, even goat or pony, will cause a child to grow up notably expulsive, phlegmatic, and given to hysteric depressions.

White worm in the morning stool.

The waterwells of Halflife reek of sulphur and rotted egg, but the day's eyes are all about, the wasps asleep in the legustrum, and *pannaeolus subbalteatus* strung beside the endless miles of pony roads.

The elevated railcars of the Historic Area, which at one time rolled in silence over the City on wide, soft wheels, now sit like the vacant husks of cicadas above our heads. Twenty-five thousand stand in the mud of an empty lot, awaiting a miracle, watching a nine-year-old boy, Kenny Cubus, pray at an improvised altar on the crest of a bluff. It is the sixteenth night Kenny has seen Oneba's head balloon up behind a row of sodden warehouses and in moments stretch formlessly across the Northern sky. At seven p.m. the boy rode through the waiting crowd on the shoulders of a neighbor, the ugly flocculus emerging like a snout, a feed bag, from his face. A soldier with his eyes blinded by flash, hysterics, a general swell of unfortunates and grotesques, were admitted through the crowd so they could stand nearest the altar, which was transformed from the pile of wooden crates, coffee cans, and scrap cardboard it had been, into a hill of flowers, statuettes, and dozens of candles. A whisper spread in the lot, "Look, he isn't getting wet, the rain does not touch him." But those who were closest could see the droplets glistening on his dark hair and blue sweater as he knelt in trance. We saw the boy shiver, his head dipping awkwardly forward, the flocculus bursting on contact with an altar crate, spilling out a pinkish jell, and a kind of yolk, which settled like a baseball in the mud. The gathering, which before this had been ahum with good feeling, was now perceptibly grave and still. We felt Oneba's hand buried in our cockles, opening like a rose, and we heard the familiar chopping litany of bony wings.

For some time past, a hut constructed of railroad ties, the crevices filled with old carpets, a roof of scrap tin, attracted the attention of pedestrians on American Street, in Halflife. The hut itself was not the only object of remark, but the fact that a crowd of *trochilics* daily held seances, clucking henlike in their fancy tongue, within its walls, and this excited workingmen in adjoining factories and mills. On June 3, Willy Spangenberg, a lad living on York Street, was killed in front of the place, a broken La Perla bottle pushed deeply into the throat, perhaps an accidental fall, more likely not. With this death the frequenters of the hut have dispersed and the structure razed to the ground. This reporter has seen four o'clocks sprouting up now, in the very spot where Willy lay, and tufts of rabbit grass surrounding it all.

Wilbur Wright, aeroplanist, selected Halflife for his experiments, now is injured, and will probably file civil complaint. He was painfully scalded on the chest and arms yesterday as a result of the bursting of a water tube while he was testing the mechanism of his aircraft. The boiling water scalded Wright, who fainted in pain. He recovered and walked to the Hotel La Coste on Cherry Avenue, where he drank La Perla and slept comfortably until awakened.

Hundreds of coot, what we call the trench duck, were found dead or dying along the levee of the trenchway. According to fishermen, the stricken birds, blood dripping from their beaks, crawled ashore or onto the decks of barges to die. Postmortems showed an absence of any visual organ damage, all the viscera being intact, except the lungs, which were puffy, fluid-filled, and eroded. In addition, the heart and major arteries showed a markable lack of blood.

Come to Halflife.

Celebrate National Week.

Oneba is One.

A young *trochilic* girl of Halflife is described in recent *Halflife Times* articles. She is Julienne H., from whose body dozens of needles are being extracted. The girl complained of considerable irritation of the skin, of itching rashes. A Halflife physician found a number of needles protruding from various parts of her body. He extracted them with pincers. The girl has, since that time, produced 143 needles from her arms, hands, breast, buttocks, feet, the lobe of the ear, her eyelids, and the corner of the right eye. This *trochilic* experiences no pain until she feels needles penetrating the epidermis. The needles emerge invariably thick-end-first, and unless immediately extracted, disappear again. Physicians say that needles inserted under the skin were known to have been borne through the muscles in many cases, to come to rest in distant parts from the place of origin, but there is no record of a needle introduced to the stomach, as they presume Julienne H.'s were, emerging from the ear, in a way that the needle must have traversed the skull, which is incomprehensible.

At Halflife we are shooting for an economic self-sufficiency and a healthy proportion of non-mechanical mobility. The general idea is to live as parasites on a herd of ponies and a pack of dogs and to get around either in our pedalcars or on pony backs. These are the easiest animals to handle in this way. The pony should be the size of the Indian and Mongol pony, about 13 hands, about 800 lbs. My family of six will need 12 mares and three or four geldings and stallions for heavy work. The ponies provide milk, meat and transport, and will take us through the backstreets, where a pedalcar won't go. These ponies provide cartage as well as hide for tents, harnesses, and ropes. The dogs provide meat and fur to make sleeping bags and warm winter clothing when we're on the road. Twelve mares should produce 12 colts a year. Butchered when they are nine months, at an average weight of 200 lbs., we have 2400 lbs. of meat to consume. We use a pressure cooker to reduce the bones and extra strips of hide, if any, down to an edible soup which we either feed to the dogs or eat ourselves if we have to. The most valuable part here is the living tissue locked into the mineral structure of the bone. Boiling down joints, hocks, hooves provides us with an oil to waterproof the 90-150 square feet of hide we get from 12 colts. We have nine ponies so far and we've named them after the Muses. We live as nomadic squatters and we do love our beasts, despite all. Oneba is.

Gloria Hurd, a 29-inch *trochilic* woman, has given birth to an 18-inch, five lb., nine oz. daughter, called Florinda, who physicians say is normal in every way. The mother and child are reported doing well, after birth by Cesarean section. Miss Hurd is called Tiny Tina in the band of familiars with which she travels. The father, she says, is a City man of average height and build.

We have forgotten the grand flocculus, Oneba's head rolling City to City, Muncie to Loma Linda, to so many like a medicine ball inflamed, to others a moon of Jupiter, his wide moronic smile the darkest feature, his radiance blinding to look at, and thus in his providence created the national trench, whose dim green water sustains us, in its way, though one man told this reporter that his frail daughter has come down with blisters of the mouth and lip after drinking a quaff of it.

A pony cart rattled on the brickwork of Cherry Avenue, a *trochilic* tooting a kazoo in the back of it, selling hot waffles. I bought two of them, served in a waxed paper bag, dripping with cane syrup and snowbound in generous amounts of powdered sugar. I sat on the stoop of a burned out curio shop and ate them. Their warmth radiated through my silver teeth. I happened to turn to look inside the shop, where I could see a rubber companion pallid and half deflated, hung by a clothespin from a nail in a cindered doorpost.

Normally I eat a cube of D-meat in the morning, or have a sliver of skrada-kaka, a bottle of La Perla, and then I sit in my deck chair on the trailer home's little porch and read my *Halflife Times*.

I see *trochilics* smoking birdwings over pinestraw in Centrola Park, fishing tainted carp from the trench, and otherwise strutting and fretting and firing their teetotums at our ankles, with a frightening suddenness, from the black alleyways, in the middle of these long, cool, Halflife nights.

Oneba is One. Celebrate National Week.

🔥 🔥 🔥

WHAT WE TALK ABOUT WHEN WE TALK ABOUT LOVE

fiction by RAYMOND CARVER

from ANTAEUS

nominated by Barbara Grossman, DeWitt Henry, Gordon Lish, Stephanie Vaughn, Sara Vogan, Bruce Weigl, and Patricia Zelver

M Y FRIEND MEL MCGINNIS was talking. Mel McGinnis is a cardiologist, and sometimes that gives him the right.

The four of us were sitting around his kitchen table drinking gin. Sunlight filled the kitchen from the big window behind the sink. There were Mel and I and his second wife, Teresa—Terri, we called her—and my wife, Laura. We lived in Albuquerque then, but we were all from somewhere else.

There was an ice bucket on the table. The gin and the tonic water kept going around, and we somehow got on the subject of love. Mel thought real love was nothing less than spiritual love. He said he'd spent five years in a seminary before quitting to go to

88

medical school. He said he still looked back on those years in the seminary as the most important in his life.

Terri said the man she lived with before she lived with Mel loved her so much he tried to kill her. Then Terri said, "He beat me up one night. He dragged me around the living room by my ankles. He kept saying, 'I love you, I love you, you bitch.' He went on dragging me around the living room. My head kept knocking on things." Terri looked around the table. "What do you do with love like that?" she said.

She was a bone-thin woman with a pretty face, dark eyes, and brown hair that hung down her back. She liked necklaces made of turquoise, and long pendant earrings.

"My God, don't be silly. That's not love, and you know it," Mel said. "I don't know what you'd call it, but I sure know you wouldn't call it love."

"Say what you want to, but I know it was," Terri said. "It may sound crazy to you, but it's true just the same. People are different, Mel. Sure, sometimes he may have acted crazy. Okay. But he loved me. In his own way, maybe, but he loved me. There was love there, Mel. Don't say there wasn't."

Mel let out his breath. He held his glass and turned to Laura and me. "The man threatened to kill me," Mel said. He finished his drink and reached for the gin bottle. "Terri's a romantic. Terri's of the kick-me-so-I'll-know-you-love-me school. Terri, hon, don't look that way." Mel reached across the table and touched Terri's cheek with his fingers. He grinned at her.

"Now he wants to make up," Terri said.

"Make up what?" Mel said. "What is there to make up? I know what I know. That's all."

"How'd we get started on this subject, anyway?" Terri said. She raised her glass and drank from it. "Mel always has love on his mind." she said. "Don't you, honey?" She smiled, and I thought that was the last of it.

"I just wouldn't call Ed's behavior love. That's all I'm saying, honey," Mel said. "What about you guys?" Mel said to Laura and me. "Does that sound like love to you?"

"I'm the wrong person to ask," I said. "I don't even know the man. I've only heard his name mentioned in passing. I wouldn't know. You'd have to know the particulars. But I think what you're saying is that love is an absolute."

Mel said, "The kind of love I'm talking about is. The kind of love I'm talking about, you don't try to kill people."

Laura said, "I don't know anything about Ed, or anything about the situation. But who can judge anyone else's situation?"

I touched the back of Laura's hand. She gave me a quick smile. I picked up Laura's hand. It was warm, the nails polished, perfectly manicured. I encircled the broad wrist with my fingers, and I held her.

"When I left, he drank rat poison." Terri said. She clasped her arms with her hands. "They took him to the hospital in Santa Fe. That's where we lived then, about ten miles out. They saved his life. But his gums went crazy from it. I mean they pulled away from his teeth. After that, his teeth stood out like fangs. My God," Terri said. She waited a minute, then let go of her arms and picked up her glass.

"What people won't do!" Laura said.

"He's out of the action now," Mel said. "He's dead."

Mel handed me the saucer of limes. I took a section of lime, squeezed it over my drink, and stirred the ice cubes with my finger.

"It gets worse," Terri said. "He shot himself in the mouth. But he bungled that too. Poor Ed," she said. Terri shook her head.

"Poor Ed nothing," Mel said. "He was dangerous."

Mel was forty-five years old. He was tall and rangy with curly gray hair. His face and arms were brown from the tennis he played. When he was sober, his gestures, all his movements, were precise, very careful.

"He did love me though. Mel. Grant me that," Terri said. "That's all I'm asking. He didn't love me the way you love me. I'm not saying that. But he loved me. You can grant me that, can't you?"

"What do you mean, he bungled it?" I said.

Laura leaned forward with her glass. She put her elbows on the table and held her glass in both hands. She glanced from Mel to Terri and waited with a look of bewilderment on her open face, as if amazed that such things happened to people you were friendly with.

"How'd he bungle it when he killed himself?" I said.

"I'll tell you what happened," Mel said. "He took this twenty-two pistol he'd bought to threaten Terri and me with. Oh, I'm serious, the man was always threatening. You should have seen the way we lived in those days. Like fugitives. I even bought a gun myself. Can you believe it? A guy like me? But I did. I bought one for self-defense and carried it in the glove compartment. Sometimes I'd have to leave the apartment in the middle of the night. To go to the hospital, you know? Terri and I weren't married then and my first wife had the house and kids, the dog, everything, and Terri and I were living in this apartment house. Sometimes, as I say, I'd get a call in the middle of the night and have to go in to the hospital at two or three in the morning. It'd be dark out there in the parking lot and I'd break into a sweat before I could even get to my car. I never knew if he was going to come up out of the shrubbery or from behind a car and start shooting. I mean, the man was crazy. He was capable of wiring a bomb, anything. He used to call my service at all hours and say he needed to talk to the doctor, and when I'd return the call, he'd say, 'Son of a bitch, your days are numbered.' Little things like that. It was scary, I'm telling you."

"I still feel sorry for him," Terri said.

"It sounds like a nightmare," Laura said. "But what exactly happened after he shot himself?"

Laura is a legal secretary. We'd met in a professional capacity. Before we knew it, it was a courtship. She's thirty-five, three years younger than I am. In addition to being in love, we like each other and enjoy one another's company. She's easy to be with.

"What happened?" Laura said.

Mel said. "He shot himself in the mouth in his room. Someone heard the shot and told the manager. They came in with a passkey, saw what had happened, and called an ambulance. I happened to be there when they brought him in, alive but past recall. The man lived for three days. His head swelled up to twice the size of a normal head. I'd never seen anything like it, and I hope I never do again. Terri wanted to go in and sit with him when she found out about it. We had a fight over it. I didn't think she should see him like that. I didn't think she should see him, and I still don't."

"Who won the fight?" Laura said.

"I was in the room with him when he died." Terri said. "He

never came up out of it. But I sat with him. He didn't have anyone else."

"He was dangerous." Mel said. "If you call that love, you can have it."

"It was love," Terri said. "Sure it's abnormal in most people's eyes. But he was willing to die for it. He did die for it."

"I sure as hell wouldn't call it love." Mel said. "I mean, no one knows what he did it for. I've seen a lot of suicides, and I couldn't say anyone ever knew what they did it for."

Mel put his hands behind his neck and tilted his chair back. "I'm not interested in that kind of love," Mel said. "If that's love, you can have it."

Terri said. "We were afraid. Mel even made a will out and wrote to his brother in California who used to be a Green Beret. Mel told him who to look for if something happened to him."

Terri drank from her glass. She said, "But Mel's right—we lived like fugitives. We were afraid. Mel was, weren't you, honey? I even called the police at one point, but they were no help. They said they couldn't do anything until Ed actually did something. Isn't that a laugh?" Terri said.

She poured the last of the gin into her glass and wagged the bottle. Mel got up from the table and went to the cupboard. He took down another bottle.

"Well, Nick and I know what love is," Laura said. "For us, I mean," Laura said. She bumped my knee with her knee. "You're supposed to say something now," Laura said, and turned her smile on me.

For an answer, I took Laura's hand and raised it to my lips. I made a big production out of kissing her hand. Everyone was amused.

"We're lucky," I said.

"You guys," Terri said. "Stop that now. You're making me sick. You're still on the honeymoon, for God's sake. You're still gaga, for crying out loud. Just wait. How long have you been together now? How long has it been? A year? Longer than a year?"

"Going on a year and a half," Laura said, flushed and smiling.

"Oh, now," Terri said. "Wait a while."

She held her drink and gazed at Laura.

"I'm only kidding," Terri said.

Mel opened the gin and went around the table with the bottle.

"Here, you guys," he said. "Let's have a toast. I want to propose a toast. A toast to love. To true love," Mel said.

We touched glasses.

"To love," we said.

Outside in the back yard, one of the dogs began to bark. The leaves of the aspen that leaned past the window ticked against the glass. The afternoon sun was like a presence in this room, the spacious light of ease and generosity. We could have been anywhere, somewhere enchanted. We raised our glasses again and grinned at each other like children who had agreed on something forbidden.

"I'll tell you what real love is," Mel said. "I mean, I'll give you a good example. And then you can draw your own conclusions." He poured more gin into his glass. He added an ice cube and a sliver of lime. We waited and sipped our drinks. Laura and I touched knees again. I put a hand on her warm thigh and left it there.

"What do any of us really know about love?" Mel said. "It seems to me we're just beginners at love. We say we love each other and we do. I don't doubt it. I love Terri and Terri loves me, and you guys love each other too. You know the kind of love I'm talking about now. Physical love, that impulse that drives you to someone special, as well as love of the other person's being, his or her essence, as it were. Carnal love and, well, call it sentimental love, the day-to-day caring about the other person. But sometimes I have a hard time accounting for the fact that I must have loved my first wife too. But I did. I know I did. So I suppose I am like Terri in that regard. Terri and Ed." He thought about it and then he went on. "There was a time when I thought I loved my first wife more than life itself. But now I hate her guts. I do. How do you explain that? What happened to that love? What happened to it, is what I'd like to know. I wish someone could tell me. Then there's Ed. Okay, we're back to Ed. He loves Terri so much he tries to kill her and he winds up killing himself." Mel stopped talking and swallowed from his glass. "You guys have been together eighteen months and you love each other. It shows all over you. You glow with it. But you both loved other people before you met each other. You've both been married before, just like us. And you probably loved other people before that too even. Terri and I have been together five years, been married for four. And the terrible thing, the terrible thing is, but the good thing, too, the saving grace, you might say, is that if something happened to one of us—excuse me for saying this—but if something happened to one of us tomorrow, I think the other one, the other person, would grieve for a while, you know, but then the surviving party would go out and love again, have someone else soon enough. All this, all of this love we're talking about, it would just be memory. Maybe not even a memory. Am I wrong? Am I way off base? Because I want you to set me straight if you think I'm wrong. I want to know. I mean, I don't know anything, and I'm the first one to admit it."

"Mel, for God's sake," Terri said. She reached out and took hold of his wrist. "Are you getting drunk? Honey? Are you drunk?"

"Honey, I'm just talking," Mel said. "All right? I don't have to be drunk to say what I think. I mean, we're all just talking, right?" Mel said. He fixed his eyes on her.

"Sweetie, I'm not criticizing," Terri said.

She picked up her glass.

"I'm not on call today," Mel said. "Let me remind you of that. I am not on call," he said.

"Mel, we love you," Laura said.

Mel looked at Laura. He looked at her as if he could not place her, as if she was not the woman she was.

"Love you too, Laura," Mel said. "And you, Nick, love you too. You know something?" Mel said. "You guys are our pals," Mel said.

He picked up his glass.

Mel said, "I was going to tell you about something. I mean, I was going to prove a point. You see, this happened a few months ago, but it's still going on right now, and it ought to make us feel ashamed when we talk like we know what we're talking about when we talk about love."

"Come on now," Terri said. "Don't talk like you're drunk if you're not drunk."

"Just shut up for once in your life," Mel said very quietly. "Will you do me a favor and do that for a minute? So as I was saying, there's this old couple who had this car wreck out on the interstate?

A kid hit them and they were all torn to shit and nobody was giving them much chance to pull through."

Terri looked at us and then back at Mel. She seemed anxious, or maybe that's too strong a word.

Mel was handing the bottle around the table.

"I was on call that night," Mel said. "It was May or maybe it was June. Terri and I had just sat down to dinner when the hospital called. There'd been this thing out on the interstate. Drunk kid, teen-ager, plowed his dad's pickup into this camper with this old couple in it. They were up in their mid-seventies, that couple. The kid—eighteen, nineteen, something— he was DOA. Taken the steering wheel through his sternum. The old couple, they were alive, you understand. I mean, just barely. But they had every-thing. Multiple fractures, internal injuries, hemorrhaging, contu-sions, lacerations, the works, and they each of them had them-selves concussions. They were in a bad way, believe me. And, of course, their age was two strikes against them. I'd say she was worse off than he was. Ruptured spleen along with everything else. Both kneecaps broken. But they'd been wearing their seatbelts and, God knows, that's what saved them for the time being."

"Folks, this is an advertisement for the National Safety Council." Terri said. "This is your spokesman, Dr. Melvin R. McGinnis, talking." Terri laughed. "Mel," she said, "sometimes you're just too much. But I love you, honey," she said.

"Honey, I love you," Mel said.

He leaned across the table. Terri met him halfway. They kissed.

"Terri's right," Mel said as he settled himself again. "Get those seatbelts on. But seriously, they were in some shape, those old-sters. By the time I got down there, the kid was dead, as I said. He was off in a corner, laid out on a gurney. I took one look at the old couple and told the ER nurse to get me a neurologist and an orthopedic man and a couple of surgeons down there right away."

He drank from his glass. "I'll try to keep this short," he said. "So we took the two of them up to the OR and worked like fuck on them most of the night. They had these incredible reserves, those two. You see that once in a while. So we did everything that could be done, and toward morning we're giving them a fifty-fifty chance, maybe less than that for her. So here they are, still alive the next morning. So, okay, we move them into the ICU, which is where they both kept plugging away at it for two weeks, hitting it better and better on all the scopes. So we transfer them out to their own room."

Mel stopped talking. "Here," he said, "let's drink this cheapo gin the hell up. Then we're going to dinner, right? Terri and I know a new place. That's where we'll go, to this new place we know about. But we're not going until we finish up this cheap lousy gin."

Terri said, "We haven't actually eaten there yet. But it looks good. From the outside, you know."

"I like food," Mel said. "If I had it to do all over again, I'd be a chef, you know? Right, Terri?" Mel said.

He laughed. He twirled the ice in his glass.

"Terri knows," he said. "Terri can tell you. But let me say this. If I could come back again in a different life, a different time and all, you know what? I'd like to come back as a knight. You were pretty safe wearing all that armor. It was all right being a knight until gunpowder and muskets and pistols came along."

"Mel would like to ride a horse and carry a lance," Terri said.

"Carry a woman's scarf with you everywhere," Laura said.

"Or just a woman," Mel said.

"Shame on you," Laura said.

Terri said, "Suppose you came back as a serf? The serfs didn't have it so good in those days," Terri said.

"The serfs never had it good," Mel said. "But I guess even the knights were vessels to someone. Isn't that the way it worked? But then everyone is always a vessel to someone. Isn't that right? Terri? But what I liked about knights, besides their ladies, was that they had that suit of armor, you know, and they couldn't get hurt very easy. No cars in those days, you know? No drunk teen-agers to tear into your ass."

"Vassals," Terri said.

"What?" Mel said.

"Vassals," Terri said. "They were called vassals, not vessels."

"Vassals, vessels," Mel said, "what the fuck's the difference? You knew what I meant anyway. All right," Mel said. "So I'm not educated. I learned my stuff. I'm a heart surgeon, sure, but I'm just a mechanic. I go in and I fuck around and I fix things. Shit," Mel said.

"Modesty doesn't become you," Terri said.

"He's just a humble sawbones," I said. "But sometimes they suffocated in all that armor, Mel. They'd even have heart attacks if it got too hot and they were too tired and worn out. I read somewhere that they'd fall off their horses and not be able to get up because they were too tired to stand with all that armor on them. They got trampled by their own horses sometimes."

"That's terrible," Mel said. "That's a terrible thing, Nicky. I guess they'd just lay there and wait until somebody came along and made a shish kabob out of them."

"Some other vassal," Terri said.

"That's right," Mel said. "Some vassal would come along and spear the bastard in the name of love. Or whatever the fuck it was they fought over in those days."

"Same things we fight over these days," Terri said.

"Politics," Laura said. "Nothing's changed."

The color was still high in Laura's cheeks. Her eyes were bright. She brought her glass to her lips.

Mel poured himself another drink. He looked at the label closely as if studying a long row of numbers. Then he slowly put the bottle down on the table and reached for the tonic water.

"What about the old couple?" Laura said. "You didn't finish that story you started."

Laura was having a hard time lighting her cigarette. Her matches kept going out.

The sunshine inside the room was different now, changing, getting thinner. But the leaves outside the window were still shimmering, and I stared at the pattern they made on the panes and on the formica counter. They weren't the same patterns, of course.

"What about the old couple?" I said.

"Older but wiser," Terri said.

Mel stared at her.

Terri said, "Go on with your story, hon. I was only kidding. Then what happened?"

"Terri, sometimes," Mel said.

"Please, Mel," Terri said. "Don't always be so serious, sweetie. Can't you take a joke?"

"This is nothing to joke about," Mel said.

He held his glass and gazed steadily at his wife.

"What happened?" Laura said.

Mel fastened his eyes on Laura. He said, "Laura, if I didn't have Terri and if I didn't love her so much, and if Nick wasn't my best friend, I'd fall in love with you. I'd carry you off, honey," he said.

"Tell your story," Terri said. "Then we'll go to that new place, okay?"

"Okay," Mel said. "Where was I?" he said. He stared at the table and then he began again.

"I dropped in to see each of them every day, sometimes twice a day if I was up doing other calls anyway. Casts and bandages, head to foot, the both of them. You know, you've seen it in the movies. That's just the way they looked, just like in the movies. Little eye holes and nose holes and mouth holes. And she had to have her legs slung up on top of it. Well, the husband was very depressed for the longest while. Even after he found out that his wife was going to pull through, he was still very depressed. Not about the accident, though. I mean, the accident was one thing, but it wasn't everything. I'd get up to his mouth hole, you know, and he'd say no, it wasn't the accident exactly but it was because he couldn't see her through his eye holes. He said that was what was making him feel so bad. Can you imagine? I'm telling you, the man's heart was breaking because he couldn't turn his goddamn head and *see* his wife."

Mel looked around the table and shook his head at what he was going to say.

"I mean, it was killing the old fart just because he couldn't *look* at the goddamn woman."

We all looked at Mel.

"Do you see what I'm saying?" he said.

Maybe we were a little drunk by then. I know it was hard keeping things in focus. The light was draining out of the room, going back through the window where it had come from. Yet nobody made a move to get up from the table to turn on the juice inside.

"Listen," Mel said. "Let's finish this fucking gin. There's about enough left here for one shooter all around. Then let's go eat. Let's go to the new place."

"He's depressed," Terri said. "Mel, why don't you take a pill?"

Mel shook his head. "I've taken everything there is."

"We all need a pill now and then," I said.

"Some people are born needing them," Terri said.

She was using her finger to rub at something on the table. Then she stopped rubbing.

"I think I want to call my kids," Mel said. "Is that all right with everybody? I'll call my kids," he said.

Terri said, "What if Marjorie answers the phone? You guys, you've heard us on the subject of Marjorie? Honey, you know you don't want to talk to her. It'll make you feel even worse."

"I don't want to talk to Marjorie," Mel said. "But I want to talk to my kids."

"There isn't a day goes by that Mel doesn't say he wishes she'd get married again. Or else die," Terri said. "For one thing," Terri said, "she's bankrupting us. Mel says it's just to spite him that she won't get married again. She has a boyfriend who lives with her and the kids, so Mel is supporting the boyfriend too."

"She's allergic to bees," Mel said. "If I'm not praying she'll get married again, I'm praying she'll get herself stung to death by a swarm of fucking bees."

"Shame on you," Laura said.

"Bzzzzzzz," Mel said, turning his fingers into bees and buzzing them at Terri's throat. Then he let his hands drop all the way to his sides.

"She's vicious," Mel said. "Sometimes I think I'll go up there dressed like a beekeeper. You know, that hat that's like a helmet with the plate that comes down over your face, the big gloves and the padded coat? I'll knock on the door and let loose a hive of bees in the house. But first I'd make sure the kids were out, of course."

He crossed one leg over the other. It seemed to take him a lot of time to do it. Then he put both feet on the floor and leaned forward, elbows on the table, his chin cupped in his hands.

"Maybe I won't call the kids, after all. Maybe it isn't such a hot idea. Maybe we'll just go eat. How does that sound?"

"Sounds fine to me," I said. "Eat or not eat. Or keep drinking. I could head right on out into the sunset."

"What does that mean, honey?" Laura said.

"It just means what I said, honey," I said. "It means I could just keep going. That's all it means."

"I could eat something myself," Laura said. "I don't think I've ever been so hungry in my life. Is there something to nibble on?"

"I'll put out some cheese and crackers," Terri said.

But Terri just sat there. She did not get up to get anything.
Mel turned his glass over. He spilled it out on the table.

"Gin's gone," Mel said.

Terri said, "Now what?"

I could hear my heart beating. I could hear everyone's heart. I could hear the human noise we sat there making, not a one of us moving, not even when the room went totally dark.

🔥 🔥 🔥

ON THE CONTEMPORARY HUNGER FOR WONDERS

by THEODORE ROSZAK

from THE MICHIGAN QUARTERLY REVIEW

nominated by Louis Gallo

THERE IS A MOMENT in Hermann Hesse's *Steppenwolf* when the hero is ushered down a dark alley into a "magic theater" where he will witness an esoteric ritual. Above the door through which he enters a sign reads:

NOT FOR EVERYBODY

But the novel which offers us this tantalizing glimpse of a forbidden rite is (as Hesse would never have guessed) a paperback bestseller available in drugstores and supermarkets across America, an assigned text for many thousands of college students each year.

101

The mysteries of redemption, the secrets of initiation: "not for everybody," but on display in every shop, for sale on every street corner. It is an apt and ironic summary of the strange cultural condition in which this generation finds itself as the public fascination with transcendent experience intensifies on all sides.

Until the end of the second world war, even a passing acquaintance with the spiritual crisis of modern Western society might have been labeled "not for everybody." The age of longing was not presumed to be a democratic fact. The stuff of high art and difficult literature, it was the elite concern of tormented poets, anguished philosophers: the soulful few sensitive enough to suffer the pangs of metaphysical dislocation. The philistine bourgeoisie—what more could one expect them to have on their shallow minds except money and new clothes? Their religious attention was wholly invested in the gospel of wealth. As for the woebegone masses at the bottom of the social order . . . their heads were filled to distraction with hunger and hard times. If they were also in search of a soul, surely the effort would lead them no further than Dostoyevsky's Grand Inquisitor or various ideologies of social revolution.

But by the time I reached college—in the mid-Fifties—the death of God had become the stuff of undergraduate survey courses, even in a state university like UCLA vastly enrolled with middle and working-class students. The standard reading list must be familiar to all of us: Kafka's *Trial*, Eliot's *Waste Land*, Auden's *Age of Anxiety*, Russell's *Free Man's Worship*, Mann's *Magic Mountain*, Camus' *Stranger*, Colin Wilson's *Outsider*, Beckett's *Waiting for Godot*, a dash of Kierkegaard and Heidegger, snippets of Nietzsche and Sartre. The elite concern had become three units of freshman humanities. We learned the existential abyss, the cosmic abandonment of man like so many data points in the history of the modern world; we took essay exams on "contrasting concepts of the absurd in human existence—time limit 30 minutes."

Perhaps these grave matters are still handled in the same pedantic way in the universities. But something has clearly shifted in the surrounding society. The longing has gotten around; the sense of absurdity and alienation, now widely publicized, has invaded the popular culture of our day, suddenly and massively. Weekly news magazines run slick features on crisis theology and the death of God; a clever comic like Woody Allen confabulates with existentialist clichés, finessing the heavy angst into successful film satire. But as the experience of spiritual crisis enters the popular mind, it is significantly transformed. The tragic sense of life becomes a temporary discomfort; the dilemma becomes a problem. And like all problems that appear in the public realm, this too is presumed to have a solution . . . somewhere, somehow. A technique, a medicine, a cure-all that will bring fast relief.

Does such vulgar optimism cheapen the experience? Or does it introduce a certain brash and healthy resiliency into what too often becomes, in more complex minds, a morbid fascination with despair? It may, after all, be the bad habit of creative talents to invest themselves in pathological extremes that yield remarkable insights, but no durable way of life for those who cannot translate their psychic wounds into significant art or thought.

Over the past several years, in the opportunities I have had to travel and speak, I have become acutely aware of this restless spiritual need in the audiences I meet. They wonder: Have I a vision, an epiphany, an uncanny tale to relate? A moment of illumination or unearthly dread, a close encounter with arcane powers . . .? It is a need, I hasten to add, which I have never sought to or been able to gratify. This hunger for wonders powerfully engages my sympathetic concern, but utterly outruns my knowledge and skill. I have, however, seen it fasten upon others about me in ways that often leave me sad or fearful. Because the appetite can be so indiscriminately eager, so mindlessly willing to be fed on banalities and poor improvisations—on anything that purports to be an experience of the extraordinary. And at that point, I realize that the eclipse of God in our time has never been the exclusive anguish of an intellectual and artistic few, except in its more articulate forms. As a nameless moral anxiety, a quiet desperation, it has been festering in the deep consciousness of people everywhere, and at last it has erupted into the totalitarian mass movements of our century. Self-enslavement to easy absolutes and mad political messiahs: that is the poison tree which flourishes peculiarly in the Waste Land.

Mercifully, the metaphysical insecurity of our time does not always reach out toward such vicious manifestations. Currently, its foremost expression in the industrial societies is the rapid spread of evangelical and charismatic forms of Christianity, faiths that teach the immediate inspiration of the Holy Spirit. These highly personal, emotionally electrifying versions of Christianity are now the most burgeoning congregations of our day and growing apace. In America they are fast developing an alternative educational establishment and their own mass media, which now rival the outreach of the major broadcasting networks.

Beyond such formal, religious affiliations, the hunger for wonders expresses itself in countless forms of pop psychiatry and lumpen occultism which thinly disguise the same impetuous quest for personal salvation. The most widely read newspapers in the United States—weekly gossip and scandal sheets like *The National Enquirer* which sell at supermarket checkout stands everywhere—carry steady coverage of UFO cults and ESP, spiritualism, reincarnation, and faith cures. Esoteric forms of oriental meditation have been opened to the public by university extensions and the YMCA; they have even been organized into successful franchise businesses that promise tranquility and enlightenment to anyone who can spare twenty minutes a day. At the other extreme from transcendental calm, there is the undiminished popular fascination with Gothic horror which makes Satanism, demonic possession, supernatural thrills and chills one of the film industry's most reliable attractions. Very likely a reader of this journal would never guess that there exists a busy trade in mystical comic books in our society: *Dr Strange, The Eternals, The New Gods, The First Kingdom,* a pulp-paper folklore of sorcery and psychic phenomena whose avid readership is by no means restricted to mindless adolescents.

One might conclude that at the popular cultural level such preternatural curiosities have always been incorrigibly and insatiably with us, from the mystery cults of the ancient world to the table-tilting spiritualism of the late nineteenth century. That would be true, and all the more to be pondered that they should survive and even flourish as a feature of modern industrial life. But more significant is the fact that the allure of psychic and spiritual prodigies has lately traveled well up the cultural scale, and not only, as at the turn of the century, in the form of clandestine fraternities like the Order of the Golden Dawn. We might say it has "come out of the closet" among academics and professionals who have been touched by the same metaphysical yearnings as the public at large, and who have simply stopped defending against them as if they were some form of unmentionable sexual perversion. They make up the principal audience for the human potential therapies, the main membership of the Associations of Humanistic and Transpersonal Psychology, organizations which offer a professional shelter where psychiatry, eastern religions, etherealized healing, and the exploration of altered states of consciousness may freely cohabit. Far and away the largest number of students who have gravitated to Zen and Tibetan Buddhism, and to spiritual masters like Swami Muktananda, Bhagwan Shree Rajneesh, and the lama Chögyam Trungpa are maverick or dropped-out academics. Intellectuals constitute the largest public for such developments as Elizabeth Kubler-Ross' investigations of immortality, and the remarkably successful Course on Miracles (a new Christian mystical discipline revealed by way of "channeled messages" to a New York University clinical psychologist). There are also the many study centers—the Institute for Noetic Sciences, the Parapsychology Department at the University of Virginia Medical School, the Kundalini Research Foundation—which serve to draw academic talent into the realm of the extraordinary.

I cannot vouch for the depth or quality of these efforts; what I do know is that more and more frequently I find myself at conferences and gatherings in the company of learned and professional people who are deliberately and unabashedly dabbling in a sort of higher gullibility, an assertive readiness to give all things astonishing, mind-boggling, and outrageous the chance to prove themselves true . . . or true enough. Among these academic colleagues, as among my undergraduate students, the most prominent laudatory expletives of the day are "Incredible!" "Fantastic!" "O, wow!"

Let me mention only a few of the "incredible" breakthroughs and "fantastic" possibilities that have come my way lately.

A prominent psychotherapist remarks to me over lunch that people sleep and die only because they have been mistakenly "programmed" to believe they have to . . . and goes on to suggest how this erroneous programming might be therapeutically undone. A neurophysiologist tells me of her research in liberating latent mental controls over pain, infection, and aging. A psychologist shows me photos of himself being operated on by Philippine psychic surgeons whom he has seen penetrate his body with their bare hands to remove cartilege and tissue. I attend a lecture where another psychologist tells of his promising experimentation with out-of-the-body phenomena. I come upon a physicist writing in

Physics Today about "imaginary energy" and the supposedly proven possibilities of telepathic communication and precognition. I find myself in a discussion with a group of academics who are deeply involved in Edgar Cayce's trance explorations of past and future, which they accept as indisputably valid. A historian tells me of his belief that we can, by altering consciousness, plug into the power points of the Earth's etheric field and by so doing move matter and control evolution. An engineer I meet at a party explains how we might influence the Earth's geomantic centers and telluric currents by mental manipulations, which he believes to be the technology that built Stonehenge and the pyramids.

In the presence of such dazzling speculation, I find myself of two minds. These are hardly such things as I would believe at second or third hand; and in so far as they involve physical or historical events, I am inclined to hold that standard rules of verification should apply in distinguishing fact from fallacy. I tend to welcome the clarity that a decent respect for logic and evidence brings to such matters.

On the other hand, I can so clearly hear the restless spiritual longings behind the reports, the urgent need to free the fettered imagination from a Reality Principle that brings no grace or enchantment to one's life, that I usually listen sympathetically, unresistingly . . . though seldom creduously. This is not the course I would follow, but perhaps these unauthorized speculations can also lead to a Renaissance of wonder. In any case, I am dealing here with people who learned all the objections I might raise—as I did—in their undergraduate years. This is clearly a post-skeptical intellectual exercise for them, requiring a critical response that is more than simple doubt and denial.

What impresses me especially about these strange metaphysical fevers is the way they blithely appropriate the authority of the hard sciences. In these circles, far from being rejected, science enjoys (or suffers) a smothering embrace. There is a certain broad license that has been borrowed from theoretical physics—especially by nonphysicists in the academic world—which leads even well-educated minds to believe that, since the fifth Solvay Conference a half century ago, all standards of verification and falsification have been indefinitely suspended in the scientific community, and anything goes. For, after all, if matter is energy and time is space, then all things are one, as the Upanishads taught. And if the observer jostles the infinitesimal observed, then the world is our will and idea, and one paradigm is as good as the next. Accordingly, the revolution in modern physics is freely interpreted as having abolished the objective reality of nature and sanctioned all forms of paranormal and mystical experience. Einstein is understood to have established that "everything is relative"; Bell's theorem and the uncertainty principle are invoked as a defense of unrestrained subjectivity; split-brain research is said to validate the status of metaphysical intuition; Kirlian photography is cited as evidence of auras and astral bodies; holograms are construed as proof of extrasensory perception, synchronicity, and transcendental realities. In recent days, I have had students spin me tales about "charmed quarks" rather as if these might be characters invented by Tolkien.

Robert Walgate, discussing books like Lyall Watson's *Supernature*, John Gribbins' *Timewarps*, Gary Zukov's *The Dancing Wuli Masters*, and the science fact and fiction magazine *Omni*, has made an interesting distinction. Such literature, he suggests, is not "popularized science, but a truly *popular* science, transformed by the interests of the readers it serves. . . . Like science fiction, it is much better supplied with speculation and myth than the dry, exclusive world of science that feeds it."

Popular science in this vein is not much to my taste. I sometimes enjoy its freewheeling and fanciful brainstorming, but I back off rapidly as it approaches a scientized mysticism. By my lights at least, that is a fruitless confusion of categories. Still, it is hardly within my province to censor these rhapsodic variations on scientific, or quasi-scientific themes. The positivists among us, however, would seem to have a tricky new problem on their hands: *scientific superstitions*, the loose use of scientific ideas to appease an essentially religious appetite.

What I offer here is only a brief sketch of a post-Christian, post-industrial society in search of the miraculous. I believe that search could be documented at great length and at many social levels—from teen-age acid rock to the painstaking labors of scholars and philosophers to salvage the teachings of the world's endangered spiritual traditions. But even this impressionistic survey points to a significant conclusion. If we can agree that Western society's most distinctive cultural project over the last three centuries has been to win the world over to an exclusively science-based Reality Principle, then we have good reason to believe that, for better or worse, the campaign has stalled and may even be losing ground in the urban-industrial heartland. Though it continues to dominate our economic and political life, in the deep allegiance of people, in the secret crises of decision and commitment, the scientific worldview simply has not taken. Our culture remains as divided as ever—top from bottom—in its metaphysical convictions. Now, as at the dawn of the Age of Reason, the commanding intellectual heights are held by a secular humanist establishment devoted to the skeptical, the empirical, the scientifically demonstrable. That viewpoint may admit a sizeable range of subtle variations; but, taken as a whole, as a matter of stubborn ethical principle, it refuses rational status to religious experience, it withholds moral sanction from the transcendent needs.

But meanwhile, in the plains a thousand miles below that austere high ground, there sprawls a vast popular culture that is still deeply entangled with piety, mystery, miracle, the search for personal salvation—as much so today as the pious many were when the Cartesian chasm between mind and matter was first opened out by the scientific revolution. If anything has changed about this cultural dichotomy, it would be, as I have suggested, that the membership of the humanist elite has lately been suffering a significant and open defection as academics, intellectuals, and artists take off in pursuit of various strange visionary and therapeutic adventures. It would be my conclusion that the great cultural synthesis of the Enlightenment—Reason, Science, Progress—is much less securely positioned today than in the heyday of crusading positivism . . . say, in the time of Darwin and Marx, Freud and Comte. (On the other hand, as I have indicated, the democratic values of that synthesis are very much with us now as a brash demand for access to the mysteries and wonders.) It may be that the only substantial popular support the ideals of the Enlightenment and the scientific revolution still enjoy stems from their lingering promise of material abundance . . . and how heavily will we be able to lean on that expectation in the years ahead?

Now, what is one to make of this schizoid state of affairs? There are two major interpretations open to us.

The first—I would call it the secular humanist orthodoxy—would be to regard the hunger for wonders as a continuing symptom of incurable human frailty, an incapacity to grow up and grow rational that is as much with us today as in the Stone Age past. Sadly, one would have to conclude that the masses have not yet matured enough to give up their infantile fantasies, which are, as Freud once designated religion, illusions that have no future. As for the intellectuals who surrender to that illusion, their choice would have to be regarded as a lamentable failure of nerve. They betray the defense of reason, the cause of progress.

Once memorable example of this position: at the end of his highly successful television series *The Ascent of Man*, Jacob Bronowski—who had laboriously defined that ascent as man's struggle toward scientific knowledge—deplored the new climate of irrationality he saw growing up around him. He offered a short bill of particulars: "ESP, mystery, Zen Buddhism."

It is important to recognize that this interpretation of religious need as neurosis or moral weakness is deeply rooted in humanitarian values. Any criticism it may merit must begin by acknowledging its essential ethical nobility, or we will fail to do justice to a central truth of contemporary history: namely, that the rejection of religion in modern society is an act of conscience and has functioned as a liberating force in a world long darkened by superstition and ecclesiastical oppression. There should be no question but that the service done by secular humanism in this regard is to be respected and preserved.

Then, there is the second interpretation of our society's undiminished transcendent longings. It accepts that need as a constant of the human condition inseparably entwined with our creative and moral powers: a guiding vision of the Good that may often be blurred, but which is as real as the perception of light when it first pierced the primordial blindness of our evolutionary ancestors. In this interpretation, it is not transcendent aspiration that needs critical attention, but the repressive role of secular humanism in modern culture, which may be seen as a tragic overreaction to the obscurantism and corruption of the European ecclesiastical establishment: a justified anti-clericalism which has hardened into a fanatical, anti-religious crusade.

In following out this second line of interpretation, I have found the work of William Blake especially valuable. Because he was gifted with an extraordinary visionary power, Blake was among the first to perceive clearly the way in which a psychology of willful alientation had fastened itself upon the ideals of the Enlightenment and the world view of science. Hence his prayer:

> May God us keep
> From single vision and Newton's sleep.

"Single vision" would be Blake's term for secular humanism in its alienative mode. In his prophetic epics, he embodies this sensibility in the mythic figure of Urizen, an awesome and dynamic titan who turns against the other energies of the personality—the "Zoas," as Blake called them: the sensuous, the compassionate, the visionary. The result is a cruel censorship of human experience in body, emotion, and mind. Urizen is "Your Reason," acting as a repressive power in the personality, tyrannically closing the doors of perception until only a narrow range of scientifically productive objectivity is left to occupy the mind—and carrying out this psychic mutilation as the agent of high moral duty. Curious, is it not, that in modern Western society alone "Enlightenment" with a Capital E came to mean the repression of transcendent aspiration, the destruction of religious experience.

Here we have the secret psychological warfare that has underlain the tumultuous history of industrial society since the advent of the "dark satanic mills." In the depths of the psyche, a brutal politics of consciousness has been played out which pits critical intellect against the innate human need for transcendence. Because both parties to the struggle are welded into the foundations of our full humanity, neither can finally be cast out. But the personality—torn between them—can be disfigured to the point of insanity and self-destruction. Steadily, as the best minds of our society have been drawn into the service of Urizen's withering skepticism, the human will to transcendence, especially at the popular level, has been left without counsel or guidance. Untutored, it runs off into many deadends and detours. It easily mistakes the sensational for the spiritual, the merely obscure for the authentically mysterious. Dominated by the technological ethos of single vision, it strives to outdo the technicians at their own game by identifying psychic stunts (ESP, levitation, spirit readings, etc.) with enlightenment. It may reach out toward emotionally charged, born-again religions that generally weaken toward smugness, intolerance, and reactionary politics. It may blunder into occult follies and sheer gullibility, discrediting itself at every step. At last, it falls into the vicious circle: as spiritual need becomes more desperate for gratification, it rebels against intellect and moral discernment, losing all clear distinction between the demonic and the transcendent. Accordingly, the secular humanist establishment is confirmed in its hostility and proceeds to scorn and scold, debunk and denigrate more fiercely. But, indeed, this is like scolding starving people for eating out of garbage cans, while providing them with no more wholesome food. Of course, they will finally refuse to listen and become more rebellious. Under severe critical pressure, the transcendent energies may be bent, twisted, distorted; but Blake's dictum finally holds true: "Man must and will have some religion," even if it has to be "the Religion of Satan."

The wisdom of Blake's diagnosis lies in its honest attempt to integrate the splintered faculties of the psyche. He recognized that the "mental fight" within the self cannot be brought to peace by choosing sides between the antagonists. To choose sides is not to win, but to repress—and only for the time being. Our course is not to strengthen half the dichotomy against the other, because *the dichotomy is the problem*. It must be healed, made whole.

In the most general terms, what we face in the tragic stand-off between single vision and spiritual need is the place of experience in the life of the mind—a problem that has not been adequately addressed by the religion, philosophy, or science of Western society.

"Experience" is not an easy word to use here; I take it up for lack of any better term, recognizing that it sprawls troublesomely toward ubiquity. What *isn't* an experience, after all? In a sense, *everything* is an experience of some order. We experience words and ideas as meanings that stir the mind to thought. We experience another's report of experience. Let me, arbitrarily then, delimit experience here to that which is *not* a report, but knowledge before it is reflected in words or ideas: immediate contact, direct impact, knowledge at its most personal level as it is lived.

In the growing popular hunger for wonders, what we confront is an effort to experience the transcendent energies of the mind as directly as possible, to find one's way back through other people's reports to the source and bedrock of conviction. Charismatic faith, mystical religion, oriental meditation, humanistic and transpersonal psychotherapy, altered states of consciousness . . . there are obviously many differences between these varied routes. Yet, I would argue that they point in a common direction—toward a passionate desire to break through the barriers of single vision into the personal knowledge of the extraordinary. At one extreme, this surely accounts for the obsession with psychedelic drugs that has gripped our society during the past generation. That fascination arises from a craving for transcendent experience, a willingness to try anything that might jar, jolt, shock, batter, blast the benumbed mind into some heightened state of awareness resembling the reported ecstasies of the saints and sages. It is a risky form of neurophysical alchemy.

All this must be seen against the background of an extraordinary historical fact: that ours is a society which has been peculiarly starved for experience as I speak of it here. It is the uncanny characteristic of Western society that so much of our high culture—religion, philosophy, science—has been based on what contemporary therapists would call "head trips": that is, on reports, deductions, book learning, argument, verbal manipulations, intellectual authority. The religious life of the Christian world has always had a fanatical investment in belief and doctrine: in creeds dogmas, articles of faith, theological disputation, catechism lessons . . . the Word that too often becomes mere words. In contrast to pagan and primitive societies with their participative rituals, and to the oriental cultures which possess a rich repertory of contemplative techniques, getting saved in the Christian churches has always been understood to be a matter of learning correct beliefs as handed down by authorities in the interpretation of scripture.

Philosophy has shared this same literal bias. True, Descartes, at the outset of the modern period, developed his influential method by way of attentive introspection. Even so, his approach is a set of logical deductions intended for publication. Philosophy has not gone on from there to create systematic disciplines that seek to lead the student through a similar process. Instead, one works logically and critically from Descartes' argument, or from that of other philosophers, writing books out of other books. As philosophy flows into its modern mainstream, it invests its attention more and more exclusively in language: in the minute analysis of reports, concepts, definitions, arguments. The English positivist Michael Dummett, in a recent work, offers the following revealing definition of philosophy:

> The goal of philosophy is the analysis of the structure of thought which is to be sharply distinguished from the study of the psychological process of *thinking*. And the only proper method for analyzing thought consists in the analysis of language.

I do not question the value of such a project. I only observe that it is, like the theological approach to religion, a "head trip." Its virtue may be the utmost critical clarity, but, as the literature of linguistic and logical analysis grows, we are left to wonder: Is there anybody out there still experiencing anything besides somebody else's book commenting on somebody else's book? Where do we turn to find the experience—preverbal, nonverbal, subverbal, transverbal—on which the books and reports must finally be based? If we follow Dummett's program, such "psychological processes" are driven out of philosophy. Where? Presumably, into psychiatry, psychotherapy, meditation—which is exactly where we find so many people in our day turning to have their untapped capacity for experience authorized and explored.

If Existentialist philosophy has found its way to a larger public in our day than the various linguistic and analytical schools, it is doubtlessly because the Existentialists ground their thought in vivid, even anguished experience: moral crisis, dread, the fear of death, even the nausea of hopeless despair. There is the high drama here of "real life," the urgent vitality that allows philosophy to flow into art and so reach a wide audience. But there are strict limits to what Existentialism can contribute to the transcendent need of our society. Excepting the Christian Existentialists, the range of experience that dominates the movement is restricted almost dogmatically to the dark and terrible end of the psychological spectrum. The terrors of alienation we find there are posited as the defining qualities of the human condition. This is, in fact, the bleak underside of single vision employed rather like a scriptural text for endless, painstaking exegesis. Paradoxically, we are offered a minute examination of such experience as is left over for us after the experience of transcendence has been exiled from our lives. We are left to explore a psychological Inferno, with no Purgatory or Paradise in sight beyond.

It may seem strange to include science among the nonexperiential head trips of our culture. Isn't science grounded in physical experimentation and empirical method? Yes, it is. But as science has matured across the centuries, its experiments and methods have become ever more subtle and technical, ever more medicated by ingenious instruments whose readings must be filtered through intricate theories and mathematical formulations. As scientific techniques of observation grow steadily more remote from the naked senses, they require the intervention of more intricate apparatus between knower and known. Whoever may be doing the "experiencing" in modern science, it is not the untutored public. Here, indeed, is a body of knowledge, supposedly our only valid knowledge of the universe, which is "not for everybody"—except by way of second-hand accounts. We are a long way off from the day of the gentleman scientist, figures like Benjamin Franklin and Thomas Young, who might keep up with the professional literature and even make significant contributions to basic research in their spare time.

There is a special irony to this development in the history of science. As the field has moved toward professionalization, it has become more and more involved with subliminal realities, entities or theoretical structures which, while understood to be in some sense "physical" (surely the word has been strained to its limit) are yet "occult" in much the same sense in which Newton understood the force of gravitation to be occult: known only by the mathematical expression of its visible effects. Particle physics is obviously such a science of the subliminal; microbiology is only a shade less so in its dependence on techniques like x-ray crystallography. Astronomy, in its use of radio wave, x-ray, and gamma ray observation, in its reliance on advanced physical theory, becomes ever more preoccupied with bodies, vibrations, processes beyond the range of direct visibility. These are no longer fields of study that can be explored by those lacking special training and elaborate apparatus; often even ordinary language will not cope with their subtleties.

For that matter, much the same tendency toward the subliminal can be seen in psychology and the newer human sciences like semiotics, or structural linguistics and anthropology, or highly statistical forms of sociology. These too tend to locate their realities in exotic theoretical realms that defy common sense and the evidence of ordinary experience. In search of the foundations of human conduct, they burrow into unconscious instincts, into hidden structures of language and the brain. Currently, the sociobiologists are busy tracing human motivations to the subliminal influence of as yet undiscovered (and perhaps undiscoverable) behavioral genes. In all these cases, the surface of life is understood to be underlain by deep structures which cannot be fathomed by untrained minds and which are envisaged as being of a wholly different order from surface phenomena. I grant that all these entities and forces are still dealt with by scientists as objective and physical; but from the view of the unschooled public, nature— including human nature—seems to recede into a phantom province that is nothing like the everyday world of appearances. The visible and tangible stuff around us becomes a Maya-like shadow-show; nothing that happens there is the "real" nature of things. Only trained minds can penetrate this veil of illusions to grasp the occult realities beyond.

And here is the irony of the matter. Psychologically speaking, the relationship this creates between scientist and public cannot be widely different from that between priesthood and believers in more traditional societies. It might even be seen as a secularized transformation of the age-old religious distinction between the esoteric and the exoteric. And in modern science as in religion, much that crosses the line between the priestly and public realms becomes garbled in the mind of the laity. Hence, the "scientific superstitions" I alluded to earlier—essentially attempts, as in all religious superstitions, to wring some hint of the extraordinary from reports and verbal formulations imperfectly understood.

If I interpret the contemporary hunger for wonders correctly, it is at once a profoundly religious and a profoundly democratic movement. Its rejection of single vision is a rejection of the peculiar literalism of Western culture, and of the elitism that has dominated almost every culture of the past. It is a demand for mass access to sacramental experiences that have traditionally been the province of a select spiritual minority, and which have been "retailed" to the populace by way of prescribed rites under priestly guidance. I will not presume to judge every culture of the past that dealt with the mysteries in this way; perhaps not all were plagued with corrupted mystagoguery and caste privilege. But most were, surely within the civilized period, where, again and again, we find priest and king, church and state interlocked as an exploitative power elite grounded in obfuscation and brutal dominion. They betrayed and discredited the natural authority that may properly belong to spiritual instruction. So today we are faced with an unprecedented demand for popular access to the temple, a demand that could arise only in a society deeply imbued with democratic values. That, in turn, could happen only in a society that had passed through a secular humanist phase in which all hierarchical structures had been called into question.

We might see this as a dialectical process which progresses by way of contradiction. The theological literalism of Western religion makes its doctrines vulnerable to the skeptical thrust of single vision. Thus, single vision undercuts the religious establishment of its society and projects a revolutionary, humanitarian ethic into the world. In its turn, single vision produces a new scientific and technocratic elite that betrays its democratic commitment; at the same time, it inflicts an even more oppressive, because wholly secularized literalism upon its culture. As a result, it leaves the transcendent longings of the populace unsatisfied. So we have the insurgent contemporary demand that sacramental experience cease to be labeled "not for everybody," that the esoteric be demystified and democratized.

Perhaps that is an impossible demand . . . perhaps. If that is so, then we may see our society settle for a dismal and degrading compromise. The familiar pattern of priestly authority will regenerate itself, only now it would most likely organize itself around the sort of ersatz religion that Naziism and Bolshevism have represented, with priestly authority vested in the state, the party, the leader; and the mass rituals of the totalitarian cult would be vicious celebrations of collective power. So our industrial culture in its time of troubles might lurch from one "Religion of Satan" to another. We have had more than enough signs to warn us that such forms of self-enslavement remain an ever-present temptation for desperate people.

But there is a happier possibility: that we will indeed find ways to democratize the esoteric that are morally becoming and life-enhancing. And here philosophy might find a guiding ideal in its own history: the image of Socrates in the marketplace, among the populace, practising his vocation as an act of citizenship.

We know that Socrates went among the ordinary people—tradesmen, merchants, athletes, politicans—and brought into their lives a critical clarity that only a persistent gadfly might achieve. It is this element of intellectual rigor that distinguishes Socrates from prophet, messiah, mystagogue. There is the willingness to put the uncomfortable question—to oneself and others—which separates philosophy from faith. But why was the populace willing to come to Socrates? Why were these ordinary citizens willing to face his hard critical edge? I suggest it was because this gadfly was also something of a guru: both at once at the expense of neither. Socrates placed personal experience at the center of philosophy; he used deep introspection as his primary tool of inquiry. There was that quality of personal attention, even loving concern about his work that we might today associate with psychotherapy or spiritual counseling.

More than this, Socrates himself embodied the promise of transcendence at the end of the dialogue. For him, criticism and analysis were not ends in themselves; there was something beyond the head trip, a realm of redeeming silence where the mysteries held sway. Socrates had been there and returned many times. So he was often found by his students standing entranced, caught up in his private vision. He had escaped from the cave of shadows; he had seen the Good. Something of the old Orphic mysteries clung to this philosopher and saved his critical powers from skeptical sterility. I suspect it was because he offered this affirmative spiritual dimension that Socrates found affectionate and attentive company in the agora—though, of course, finally martyrdom as well.

Just as he had borrowed his fragile balance of intellect and vision from Pythagoras, so Socrates bequeathed it to his pupil Plato. But neither Pythagoras nor Plato were daring enough (or mad enough) to follow Socrates into the streets in search of wisdom. Instead, the one sequestered philosophy in a secret fraternity; the other retreated to the academy. As these two options come down to us today, they have fallen disastrously out of touch with one another. The academy has come to specialize in a sheerly critical function; the spiritual fraternity—any that survive—has concentrated upon techniques and disciplines of illumination that are no longer on speaking terms with critical intellect.

Can these two be brought together once again in their proper Socratic unity as an ideal of rhapsodic intellect: the critical mind open to transcendent energy? More challenging still, can that balance of intellect and vision once more be taken into the public realm, to meet the spiritual need that has arisen there? Or will philosophy shrink back from the importunate vulgarity, the citizenly burden of the task?

This much is certain: we will not find what we refuse to seek; we will not do what we refuse to dare.

LEDA

by MARILYN KRYSL

from FIELD

nominated by FIELD

A man
isn't
a swan. A man isn't a calculator
either, even if he does make phone calls and memos
at a desk. A man isn't a man at a
desk and a man at a desk isn't a father,
the broken lake isn't his daughter,
and the only woman in a cluster of men
isn't a man.
              When the maps
are finished, she won't tell you what to do.
He's not your keeper. This isn't a halfway

house, a home, a security blanket or a kettle
of fish. Mary isn't his mother, Shakespeare
isn't a man. This isn't a manual. A woman
isn't a mixing vessel, and he isn't outside
looking in. This isn't a sonnet and it isn't
easy. You're not a fake and I'm not
faking. Tasting alone won't tell us
if the water's pure.
                I can't be
                    encouraging.
I won't urge you to make yourself useful.
The artist isn't an answering service, and
she's not a physical therapist. A behaviorist
isn't a man, God isn't a woman. I didn't
install the electric fence, you didn't invent
the cattle prod. God
isn't black either. He didn't deliver the missing
piece, instructions for dismantling
didn't come with it, and while you were out
there was no mail. She didn't come. A cow
isn't a woman. This isn't the letter she
didn't leave, or a red flag. A man's not a bull
or a goat. Or a sheep. We're not lambs, this
isn't the slaughterhouse. If you need directions
to the party, make them up. This isn't Hollywood
calling. I didn't answer the phone. Hollywood
isn't calling, the phone didn't ring. And the
phone isn't ringing now. Why are you waiting,
why are you still expecting a phonecall.

THE TOMB OF STÉPHAN MALLARMÉ

by CHARLES SIMIC

from THE GEORGIA REVIEW

nominated by THE GEORGIA REVIEW, *Jim Barnes, Louis Gallo and Daniel Halpern*

Beginning to know
  how the die
navigates
  how it makes
its fateful decisions
  in eternal circumstances
what it feels like
  to be held tight
between the thumb
  and the forefinger
to be hexed
  and prayed over

to wake up lucid
  at the heart of the shipwreck
a dark pilot's cabin
  of the die on the move
to have the earth and heaven
  repeatedly reversed
to have the mirror and the razor
  momentarily aligned
only to fall
  head over heels
to be set adrift
  in the middle of
nowhere

  the die
worn clean
  by endless conjectures
my die
  perfectly illegible
white
  as a milk tooth
the perfect die
  rolling
picking up speed
  how delightful
this new contingency
  occupancy
both inside and outside of
  the unthinkable

the blindman's die
  free of
the divinatory urge
  the Number
even if it existed
  the death-defying
somersault
  beating the supreme odds

two by two
    along for the ride
only
    the roller-coaster
endlessly changing directions
    and mind
in a state of blessed
    uncertainty

cast
    on the great improbable
table
    among the ghostly saltcellars
bones
    breadcrumbs that say
there goes:
    Cerberus' new toy
Death's great amateur
    night
the childhood of Parmenides

oh yeah

WELDON KEES IN MEXICO, 1965

by DAVID WOJAHN

from COLUMBIA

nominated by COLUMBIA *and Tess Gallagher*

Evenings below my window
the Sisters of the convent of Saint Teresa
carry brown jugs of water from a well
beyond a dry wash called *Mostrenco*.
Today it was hard to waken
and I've been dead to the world for ten years.
They tread the narrow footbridge
made of vines and wooden planks, sandals clicking:
brown beads and white crosses
between hands that are also brown.
Over the bridge they travel in a white-robed line
like innocent nurses to a field hospital.

Exactly ten. I've marked it on the calendar.
Maria, who speaks no English,
is soaping her dark breasts by the washstand.
Yesterday she said
she'd like to be a painter and sketched
on the back of a soiled napkin,
a rendition of a cholla—
with her lipstick. And laughed,
then drew below each nipple
a smudged rose. Weldon

would have been repelled
and fascinated, but Weldon is dead;
I watched him fall to the waves
of the bay, the twelfth suicide that summer.
He would have been fifty-one this year,
my age exactly, and an aging man.
Still, he would not be a fool
in a poor adobe house, unwinding
a spool of flypaper from a hook
above the head of his child bride.

When she asks my name, I tell her
I am Richard, a good Midwestern sound.
She thinks Nebraska is a kingdom
near Peru, and I
the exiled Crown Prince of Omaha.
I've promised to buy her a box of paints
in a shop by my palace in Lincoln.
We'll go back, Maria and I,
with the little Sisters of Saint Teresa
who are just now walking across the bridge
for water to be blessed at vespers.

❦ ❦ ❦

IN GLORY LAND

fiction by JULIA THACKER

from ANTAEUS

nominated by Marea Gordett, Joyce Carol Oates, and Richard B. Smith

> *The wind bloweth where it listeth, and thou hearest the sound thereof, but canst not tell whence it cometh, and whither it goeth.* JOHN 3:8

ONE OF LIFE'S POIGNANCIES is that we cannot know our parents and grandparents in their youth. But my grandfather's house is full of stories and story tellers—stories of and by his daughters: Edna Beatrice, Margie Rose, Flora Pauline, Mary Lucille, Juanita Lily (still-born), June, Roxie Anita (dead at two), and Margaret Sue. The two babies are buried in the cemetery of an abandoned mining camp grown over with vines. Every few years, when two or more of "the girls," as the Douglas sisters are known, are home, they climb over the rusty wire fence surrounding the graveyard and cut through the bramble to clean off the granite lambs which sit on top of the two small graves. "We put a spray of flowers on the babies'

126

graves," they report to Fatdaddy. "What kind?" he wants to know. "Mixed: six four o'clocks for Anita, six roses for Juanita." And he nods solemnly.

"I can't figure which these Douglases like to do more, eat or talk," a new in-law once exclaimed. At any gathering of the clan you'll find most of the girls in the kitchen around a table of fried chicken, gravy, shuck beans, tomatoes from the garden, lettuce and onions "killed" in bacon grease, applesauce cake, and other dishes warming on the stove, having kicked off their high heels, feet in one another's laps, lipstick-stained cornbread on small luncheon plates. Aunt Pollye's theory is that you think you're eating more than you actually do if you eat off a luncheon plate. Food is urged on any man who strays into the kitchen: "Herman, try some of this corn salad. It's out of this world." Fatdaddy stops in to refill his plate and announce, "Lucille, you're going to look like Aunt Lizzie if you don't get away from that table." Lizzie is one of Fatdaddy's sisters, who could get a job as The Fat Lady in a circus. "*That*," Aunt Pollye says, "is what has kept us all a size nine."

So we smoke and drink coffee, ashes falling into our half-full plates. Aunt Pollye, who hides her cigarette under the table while Fatdaddy is in the room, though she is in her early fifties, may take one of us into the bathroom to smoke and talk, and one by one, the other girls knock on the door and are admitted to pee, while the rest of us make room on the edge of the bathtub or clothes hamper, or fix our hair in the mirror. Sometimes there is an empty corner where I show Aunt Sue the Latin Hustle or another new step.

"Honey," Aunt Margie says, "did your mother ever tell you about when your Fatdaddy was young and propped a ladder against his sisters' bedroom window to sneak them out to square dances? Poor old Ma Douglas was as holy roller as they come and those girls weren't allowed to cut their hair, wear rouge, nor nothing. I'm telling you, when we get together with that branch of the family it looks like Before and After."

"That's the truth," Aunt Pollye says. "I told Herman, 'When Rebecca and her family come to visit, it's just like somebody left the gates to the zoo open.' That's the ugliest one group of people I ever saw." She flicks her ashes into the bathtub. "But, you know, Daddy acts like he loves them."

Roscoe Daniel Douglas was a red-haired young mine foreman, a

well-paying position in the Harlan County of 1916, when he met
my grandmother, a devout woman whose no-good husband had
abandoned her and a baby daughter. Fatdaddy married Ethel
Envy Davis and gave her child his name. Over the next twenty
years Grandma produced seven more daughters. When his girls
were little, Fatdaddy told, he felt the Lord calling him to the
ministry, but mining camps could not pay a preacher much, so he
ignored the call. Neighbors stood on their porches listening to
Fatdaddy pray aloud as he walked home on the tram road.
Grandma said in those days he came in from the mines, laid down
his cap with the light attached, and turned the gramophone up to
full volume, afraid that in silence the Holy Spirit might touch him.
Then Anita, his favorite, became ill with colitis. She languished for
two days. Anita's big white cat, Fluffy, striking in a mining camp
where even tables and chairs were covered with black dust, pined
under her bed and would not take food, while Fatdaddy paced and
prayed in her room, offering the Lord his life if He would spare his
girl. His daughter's death was my grandfather's burden to bear.
"Daddy always said God took Anita because he refused The Call,"
my mother said. The stained-glass windows of the church were
open on the following Sunday, the muggy August day of my
grandfather's first sermon. Before he could begin, the wind lifted
his prepared text from the pulpit, scattering white sheets across the
plank floor. This, Fatdaddy took as a sign he should preach from
the heart, and thereafter he did.

Some of my first memories are of watching my grandfather move
congregations to tears. A great stylist in the pulpit, red-faced,
Scotch-Irish, he looked like a beardless Santa Claus. "Preacher
Douglas has saved half the souls in Harlan County," his church
members claimed. Fatdaddy contended that churches were made
of wood and spirit, and he built many a church in small hollows and
mining camps. There were tales of him rushing to the bedside of a
dying miner to save him from eternal damnation. Fatdaddy was in
demand for revivals and funerals in Kentucky, Tennessee, and
West Virginia. His every gesture was grand, so his daughters, and,
later, his granddaughters, seemed always waiting to be touched by
him. Of twelve grandchildren, eight are female. "Boys," he would
brag, "my house is always full of pretty women."

When my mother brought us to visit, we drove for twelve hours
from Ohio, usually arriving late Saturday night after my brother

and I had fallen asleep in the car. Because Fatdaddy left the house at daybreak on Sunday to pray, I wouldn't see him until church. On the Christmas when I was two he appeared in the aisle carrying a staff, a towel wrapped around his head for a turban—Joseph in a living Nativity. "Well, Fatdaddy," I called in the reverent silence, "where you got your hat?" He winked and laughed in the procession. But soon I realized my family's position and behaved accordingly: number one was to outdress everybody else. Our mothers dressed us in lace-trimmed anklets and velvet, lace-up vests. Grandma leaned from her pew to whisper of one lady's outfit, "Children, I wouldn't be caught dead in the woods with that on." Around us were men with missing fingers and toes, lost in mining accidents, men whose greased faces had taken on the permanent darkness of coal, never to be washed away, not even in the river baptism for which they put on white robes, men who, during the service, coughed coal dust into their wives' handkerchiefs, embroidered with lilies and violets, the blooms that lasted in their yards only a season. There were also a few on whose small parcels of land coal had been discovered, like Mr. Buttermore, who, Mother whispered to me, had added two marble columns to the porch of his shack and owned three washer-dryer combinations in mint-green, flamingo-pink, and sunrise-gold. There were little girls in feedsack dresses on whose feet was the dust of miles, dust of furrowed mountains, dust of the lonely hollows. And we all cooled ourselves with paper fans on sticks decorated with pictures of The Garden of Gethsemane and The Last Supper.

"Now I want to introduce some of my family here today," Fatdaddy announced. That was the signal for my brother and me to stand up in our pew until everyone had a good look at us.

"This morning we take our scripture from John," he began gravely. " 'For God so loved the world, that He gave His only begotten Son . . .' "

It was our family's duty to remain dry-eyed during the invitation to the alter. "Come up," Fatdaddy said, extending his hands. "Come up and say, 'Preacher I want to live with the Lord,' or say, 'Preacher, I'm a Christian and I haven't been living right.' "

"That Harry Parrot rededicates his life every other Sunday," Aunt Pollye ventured. "By Tuesday dinner time he'll be drunker than a monkey."

Those saved or rededicated stayed on their knees until church was over, then stood in a reception line with their loved ones to shake our hands. "Pray for me sister," they said to me.

In the spring of the year of the flood, when I was fifteen, I had an emotional collapse. I was put on a Greyhound bus and sent to Fatdaddy's, past the bluegrass and genteel church steeples into the mountains where wooden crosses along the road promised salvation. Flood waters had left mud in the shops and on the streets of Harlan, had carried gold watches and doll-babies with real, blinking eyelashes into the basements of strangers. Already there were snapshots of wooden rowboats filled with rescuers tacked above the pay phone in Grayson's Drug Store, which would remain until they yellowed. And even while the filthy, rushing water still touched the second-story shutters of lowland houses, the flood had become a way of measuring time and distance; old men in the obituaries that spring and summer were remembered in watermark dreams. "When did she take sick?" a neighbor asked my aunt about me. "About three weeks after the flood," my aunt said.

Glass light fixtures on the ceiling of the bus station were caked with grime, casting a pallor over the long benches, the iron grille of the ticket window, the ribbed leather stools at the soda fountain, and an old black man in a rumpled fedora, chewing tobacco. Fatdaddy met me with galoshes over his oxfords, a poncho over his suit and tie. During the year I had gained fifty pounds and lost my fluid speech. Each word was like a heavy stone for me, and I stumbled over anything but the shortest sentences. My grandfather, searching for a laughing, cute little girl, glanced at me, looked away, then my bloated frame registered and he called my name. I nodded and he took my bags.

Driving through town, Fatdaddy kept a hand out the window in response to "Howdy, Preacher" from men shoveling mud. When we reached the mountain roads he told me the flood had risen within feet of his house on the hill, but the Lord had kept the water back. It never surprised me that people with mountains outside their front doors, heavy with trees in spring, dwarfing their houses, their cars, could believe in God so easily. Now Fatdaddy wanted to know what was the matter with me. Did my stepfather beat me?

"No," I answered, although he had made the threat. Even my mother was afraid of the man she had married after he had made her pregnant with her third child. Unwilling to fail in the eyes of her father, Mother had kept the details of the past few years of our lives from Fatdaddy. Barely able to carry on a conversation, how could I make him understand our world?

"Up there people from Kentucky are just briars," I said.

The slur-word made Fatdaddy angry. "A briar is what you prick your finger on when you're picking raspberries. If anyone calls you that, you tell them a *briar* was what made the crown for Jesus on the cross."

How could I tell him that briars were little boys in the back of the classroom with oily burr haircuts, their daddies' nylon shirts tucked snugly into their overalls, hair stiff like brushes that might prick or sting if they were included in games, who had flat, mountain accents, whose daddies played "Don't Touch Me" on the car radio and crowded Highway 25 South on weekends to go home for one day. When I quit high school a counselor waved high test scores and said it was a shame. He was surprised to find out I was from one of those briar families, oh, excuse him, he meant: to find out that my family was from out of state.

"What about your daddy," Fatdaddy asked: "he comes to see you, he looks after you, doesn't he?"

"Yes," I said.

I lived in an industrial city of smokestacks that produced cash registers and soap, where Southerners, black and white, had come after the war to escape the coal mines. My father's life was as unclear to my brother and me as the sooty windows we shined with our elbows to try and look through. He lived in a single room, because, although he could afford more, a rented room does not invite visitors. Other facts: as a country boy of eighteen he was drafted, and after hand-to-hand combat in Germany was given an honorable discharge for a "nervous disorder." While he was married to my mother he accused her of spying on him and kicked my toys across the room. I could not remember him ever touching me, although he paid us regular visits. He never came in, but waited in front of our house with the motor running until we came out at the appointed time. There were two safe topics: the weather, and how Doug and I were doing in school. Any personal question —"Daddy, what is your job like?" or "Daddy, how did you get the bruise on your arm?"—would send him into a black rage. He'd spin the car, speed recklessly, and yell, "Why do you want to know?" terrifying us. But without visits, we would not receive the

weekly child-support checks that my stepfather pocketed. My
mother, silent in guilt, was concerned with talcum for her new
baby. So I learned to talk about the weather, the snow on the hood,
and to distinguish shades of gray in the horizon. It was my job to
poke my little brother in the ribs if he said the wrong line. My
stomach hurt after these visits, when we were deposited on the
sidewalk. One visitation day I was playing and forgot the time.
When I went to the window, Daddy was sitting in the car, the
motor off, two hours past our appointed meeting, his face con-
torted, and I thought he might kill me; but he drove us to a
shopping center and yelled at me in a department store.

All this I could not tell my grandfather, so he knew only that I
was crushed, like the brown corsage he had come upon, pressed in
one of his theology books, a flower he didn't know the story of.

He said, "Your mother is taking you-all to church, isn't she? You
can talk to the Lord."

"Yes," I said, because it was easier than explaining. In the bleak
north my mother had stopped going to church and learned to
clutch her open coat against the wind.

My Aunt Bea was in my grandfather's house that year to cook
and wash and iron. Aunt Pollye and Uncle Herman lived down the
road, so Aunt Pollye visited daily to make flower arrangements of
pine cones and Queen Anne's lace for my dying grandmother.
Fatdaddy said to his daughters, "Girls, we don't love your mother
for what she is now, but for our memory of her." Grandma was
frail, in a wheelchair, and I was speechless. So Grandma was
wheeled into the kitchen, where Aunt Pollye used a curling iron
on her white hair, tinted blue; and Aunt Bea showed me how to
mix cornbread and brown the edges in an iron skillet. My aunts
took to speaking about me as if I weren't there.

"That child doesn't have a stitch to her name," Aunt Pollye said.
"What could June be thinking of, letting Julie go around like that?"

"When you were a baby," Aunt Bea told me, "your mother
polished your little white shoes every morning. If there ever was a
wanted child, you were it. June just thought the moon rose and set
in you."

"Honey," Aunt Pollye said, "June was scared to death when she
was pregnant with Julie, after watching Cille carry that dead baby
for two months. When Cille was in her seventh month, the doctor
told her there was no heartbeat."

"Well, sometimes that's a blessing. Remember when Verda O'Hara gave birth to that albino child? Everybody else in her family had a whole head full of red hair. That albino is thirty-seven now. Verda keeps her dressed in blue, so her eyes will look blue. Or take Preacher Bill Follit from Loyall. His boy is thirteen and can't walk nor talk. He carries him everywhere he goes. When Bill brings him over and sets him down in the floor, the boys spreads out like some old rag doll," Aunt Bea said.

"The longer you have a child," Grandma rasped, "the harder it is to give one up."

"Bill Follit comes to Daddy for guidance about that boy," Aunt Bea said. "They shut the living room door, and Daddy will just counsel with him, about the will of God."

"I'll tell you what," Aunt Pollye said, "if it wasn't for leaving Susan and Herman, I'd say, 'Lord, just come and get me and take me on to heaven, away from this grief.'"

"Why, Pollye," Aunt Bea said, "they've got special schools in New York I bet could teach that boy to paint with his teeth. He could paint trees and flowers."

"Well," Aunt Pollye said, "they sent cousin Joyce's two little blind boys to a school in Knoxville and they read with their fingers. Honey, can you beat that, having one little blind baby right after another? Her husband owns that furniture store up Pansy. Last time I went in to see Joyce there were little hand prints in the dust on the furniture where the boys had walked through."

Fatdaddy was often away comforting flood victims, helping pump water out of basements, holding services for people with last night's toil in their eyes. On Sundays his sermons were often aimed at me. There was never much doubt about who he was aiming at, whether at a deacon who had the gall to smoke on the church steps, or at those Fatdaddy called "the clock-watchers."

"Now, you-all better turn your faces up this way," he shouted. "I'm a-trying to save your soul, and *I'll* tell you what time it is: one minute closer to Judgment Day." The clock-watchers blushed. He leveled at me, then, the cold, blue-eyed stare his congregation dreaded. "We may ask, 'Lord, why do you let our loved ones suffer?' But faith means accepting, faith means there's a plan. I don't care what kind of lashing you take," he thundered. "God said, 'Out of these stripes, I will make you whole.' I will make you whole," he repeated gently.

And each Sunday I became more stoic in my anger, because I needed help Fatdaddy couldn't give. He pranced and whispered and shouted in a cadence brought from the shores of Ireland. "Take one step to the altar. Say, 'Lord, I can't walk no more. I'm tired.' And He'll help you. 'Come unto me all that labor and are heavy laden and I will give you rest,' " But I would not take a step or bow my head to pray. I would not give up my last dignity, which was my hurt, to fit into one of God's plans. So I stood like Lot's wife turned to salt. He would not save me.

I don't know if I understood then why Fatdaddy did not pet and tease me the way he had once. Now I know that to acknowledge me meant acknowledging his helplessness. Yet in the evenings, in the smoke of his cherry pipe tobacco, when I brought him a cup of coffee, he sometimes put his hand absently around my waist, and I would be very still to make it last, until he remembered. There were occasional questions he might address to a stranger, "What are those books you read?"

"Nothing, just books."

So I was surprised one day when he stormed into the house and clapped his hands. "Get dressed up; we're going to town."

I put on a flannel shirt and jeans that dared him to say anything.

He drove over the mountain at a speed that once made my cousins and me squeal as we peered over the steep drops into hollows. But this time I pretended not to notice.

"You know that nice young couple I married last evening?" Fatdaddy asked.

He had been weeding cabbage when a girl and boy got out of a pickup truck and came to the door shyly. "Daddy," Aunt Bea called out to the garden, "there's a couple here want you to marry them." He put on a suit and tie and performed the ceremony in the living room by his glass-paned bookshelves, as he had done so many times before, dirt still under his fingernails. My aunts and I huddled with Grandma in the kitchen and she shushed them, "Quiet, children, someone's getting married in there."

"Well, that boy was a Bailey from Cattern's Creek," Fatdaddy explained now. "He said, 'Preacher, you saved my daddy last winter and he had been drunk for most of my life. I told Patty no one is marrying us but Preacher Douglas.' When they left he slipped this in my pocket." It was a twenty-dollar bill. "Now we'll go to Belks and doll you up."

But when we arrived among the racks of cottons and chiffons, I knew most of those clothes were too small for me. I was ashamed and longed to get away from the press of people.

"There's here nothing . . . there's n-nothing . . ." I tried to say that there was nothing I wanted.

"We'll get one of these gals to help us pick something out," Fatdaddy said. "Anything in the store you want." He made an expansive gesture, taking in mannequins, cash registers, and shoppers.

"I don't think clothes are important," I said, and went to the car to fold my arms until he took me home.

"Where's your pretty clothes?" Aunt Bea asked. There were Aunt Pollye, Uncle Herman, and his sister, Pearl, in the living room.

"Didn't get any."

"And where's your Fatdaddy?"

"Gone to prayer meeting early," I said, and escaped into my bedroom.

Aunt Bea followed, closing the door behind her. "Honey, there's something I've been meaning to show you." She opened the bureau and took out a handkerchief. Wrapped inside was a coin layered with dirt. "It's a penny," she said, "muddy from the flood. I found it in front of Dora's Beauty Shop and I'm never going to wash it." She placed it deep in a drawer and guided me back into the living room. "Well, they didn't have a thing at Belks," she said.

"Then take a look in that Sears catalogue and see if there's anything you want, honey," Aunt Pollye offered. "Remember, Bea, when we were little we'd pick us something in the catalogue and Momma would just lay some newspaper on the floor and cut us out a pattern?"

"Certain people don't care how they look. Do you know the last time Cille's Kitty was down here, she wanted me to make her a dress out of some old blacksmith's apron," Aunt Bea said.

"She shows up looking any old way," Aunt Pollye said. "When she comes in, she may have cow shit on her shoes and she may not. And, honey, that long-haired boy she brings with her . . . you name it and I'll feed it."

"Oh, God," I screamed, "why don't we talk about something important. Clothes, clothes, that's all I hear. I don't even believe in God. You might as well know I'm an atheist."

Aunt Bea put her hand to her throat. "Lord, have mercy. Honey, you're scaring me to death."

"Now, hush," Aunt Pollye said. "Momma's asleep in there. That would kill your grandma, sure enough."

I ran to my bedroom and slammed the door. It was the first time in a year I had raised my voice and the first time I had cried.

When Fatdaddy took me to the bus station, it was an admission that we lived in different worlds; whatever I was going to do, however I was going to struggle, this was not the place for it. *And Job said: Therefore have I understood not . . . wherefore I abhor myself, and repent in dust and ashes.* I would have to return to my smoky city, and by this time I wanted to begin living again. He sat with his arm around my shoulder. There was an abyss between us, as if I were going to a foreign country for which he did not know the language or customs, so he offered me no advice, and we were mostly silent. But he gave me the twenty-dollar bill I had refused with my name and the date inscribed in red ink on the corner.

"You know," he said, "I would never marry any of my girls. When Lucille married Carl, she begged me to perform the ceremony, but I said, 'No, that would be too much like giving one of mine away and that I'll not do.' So I can't ever officiate the ceremony for you. Don't ask me."

"Okay," I said.

He looked small to me as he handed the bus driver my ticket—he was, after all, only five feet eight. He waved until I was out of sight.

Fatdaddy kept correspondence from children and grandchildren in an antique coal bucket with a scalloped spout, like a sea shell, beside his reclining chair. There was nothing in my letters of the lover with whom I regained a voice, or of the shabby room with peeling wallpaper and a neon light blinking on and off in the window, a room that said, "My people are also among the disinherited, have also been misplaced and misused," where in langurous and entwining ways we told each other: "I am one of the injured." Nor did I write about my feelings toward God and church, and when Fatdaddy's voice crackled over long-distance wires, he did not ask, because he knew I would tell him the truth. Perhaps more than I knew, my life was revealed in my stationery, which went from notebook paper, to Hallmark cards, to psychedelic hand-printed notes, to heavy, brown bond; the splashing stamps and distant postmarks; the traces of perfume, chalk, and sand. He reread my letters in the evenings, his feet, swollen with water, up in the hassock, his pipe smoldering in the ash tray. Something in my life must have been expressed, too, in the presents I brought him on holiday visits, exotic teas and tobacco blends from across the ocean.

"What did you think of the Earl Grey, Fatdaddy?" I asked.

"Well, honey, I didn't think it was much good."

Once I brought a friend from college with me, a Jew from New York, and as Uncle Herman brought out his guitar and we began to harmonize on hymns for Fatdaddy, Jane looked more and more stricken. "All these songs are about blood," she said.

Fatdaddy roared.

Certainly, each time he saw me, I was happier and thinner, and he kidded me, "Left some of yourself behind, didn't you, doll baby?" So I suppose it was clear to him that all traces of the year of the flood had vanished, except regret, like the mud on my aunt's flood penny, persists.

When an illness struck Fatdaddy, he struck right back. When his neck stiffened, he ordered a visiting daughter to go out and point his baby-blue Eldorado in the right direction, and he sped away. Each year he traded his last-year's car for the latest model; a member of his church was a car dealer, so he also enjoyed a silver Continental with red corduroy interior at one time. Eventually, of course, his body just wore down. He recovered from one disease, only to be felled by another: heart, prostate, kidneys. I heard the first rumor of senility in a telephone call to my mother.

"Honey, I just talked to Pollye," she said, "and Fatdaddy's worse. They took him to the hospital for tests and he was out of his head. He worked his hands all day, like he was building something; he'd drive a nail, then hammer some. 'What are you building, Daddy?' Pollye asked him. He said a bridge. A minister visiting in the room said, 'A bridge to Jordan, Preacher?' Daddy said, 'If you were truly a man of the Lord, you would know that bridge was built for us long ago by Jesus Christ. I'm just building a bridge so my girls can cross the river.' "

"Good," I said. "They'd better keep whoever that minister is away from me." I could witness Fatdaddy's physical pain, but to watch him lose his dignity, his mind, I doubted I could bear. If he didn't recognize me, then neither would I know myself.

The next weekend I went to Harlan. I flung my arms open in entrance at the front door, "Look who's here."

"Well, there's my baby," Fatdaddy said, and I breathed again at seeing him clear and lucid in yellow pajamas, his false teeth in a swan ash tray on the coffee table, a clear plastic urine bag attached to his body. Surrounded by six conversations at once, I sat on the free arm of his chair and talked. Then I went to the bathroom, turned on the tap, and cried into a towel; returned, and talked some more.

"That woman, Clara. . ." Fatdaddy began.

"She's one of the women we hired to help take care of Daddy," Aunt Pollye explained.

"Pauline, *I'm* telling this. That Clara just about had a cow when she saw this," he laughed, pointing to the bag of urine, which had turned bright red from medication. "She thought I was hemorrhaging, and was getting ready to call me an ambulance. She said, 'You poor, old thing.' I said, 'You're the poor, old thing. You're the one preparing to have a heart attack.' "

Fatdaddy now spent most of the day in bed; so I went out with my cousin on errands. I was surprised to see, for the first time, shopping centers and quick-food chains in place of general stores. I had to get a check cashed and pulled into a shopping complex between a bank and a Pinball Haven, dreading the trouble of out-of-town identification. As we stood in the line of harried shoppers, I dug for my driver's license and old student I.D.

"Do you have anything else?" The teller, whose name tag said Vernetta, eyed me dubiously.

"My grandfather has an account in town," I said, and handed her his checkbook, which he had given me to buy groceries.

"You're Preacher Douglas's granddaughter? Harold Lee," she called to the other teller, "this is Preacher Douglas's granddaughter."

Harold left his line of customers to come over and inspect me through the bars. "Is? Which one do you belong to?" he asked me.

"June," I said.

He peered closer. "Yup. I see some of June in those dimples and that dark, curly hair. Your mother used to sit in my back yard and eat tommy toes, long before you was ever thought of."

"Yes," Vernetta said, "June loves those tommy toes."

And although our family now dots the map from Detroit to Houston, and along both coasts, there are other recognizable similarities. We are all good dancers, most of us to the distraction of whatever we are trying to accomplish at the moment, or, as Fatdaddy used to say to my mother, "You're up there to iron, June, not jitterbug around the ironing board."

The house was so crowded on this visit, we decided to eat in shifts. Fatdaddy came to the table carrying his urine bag. "Just let me get my purse here, girls," he said. I had never seen him sit down to dinner in his pajamas. Word went through the house, "Shh, Fatdaddy's about to pray." Babies were shifted on hips, and Cokes stilled in their glasses.

"Our Heavenly Father, bless the food we are about to receive to the nourishment of our bodies. Bless and keep our family on the highways as they journey home." He paused. "Guide these young people, Lord, as they take their places in the world, which belongs to them now. In Jesus' name we pray. Amen."

The grace I heard was a dying man's voice as he sat at the table in his night clothes, holding a plastic apparatus to relieve himself, giving up his place in the world.

Each of us has a moment when the person we love dies for us, sometimes through hatred or loss of stature; expiration doesn't always take place when breath leaves the body. I gave up my Fatdaddy on that afternoon when it was my turn to sit with him. Because it could be cranked upright, he lay in a hospital bed adjacent to the four-poster oak he had shared with my grandmother. On the wall above were pictures of baby girls in lace bonnets, the center photos in sepia, the ones below in color, including one of me. On the opposite wall hung his Kentucky Colonel Commission, his Mountain Preacher of the Year Award, a Douglas coat of arms, and a framed letter of condolence on the loss of my grandmother. On his night table an artificial rose in glass weighted his papers and letters; beside them was a pipe and a Burgundy leather Bible, on which I set a glass of water.

"Is that how you treat the Lord's book?" he asked sharply.

"No, sir." I removed the glass, leaving a round water mark. *As the hart panteth after the water brooks, so panteth my soul after thee.*

On the nightstand also was an enlarged tintype of Grandma and Fatdaddy, recently tinted in pinks and reds, as if to say, "We are alive and fresh and young." His room was yellow with sunlight and chintz curtains, starched to cut. Even the weather denied his suffering, and it seemed to me if there were a natural order, the weeping willows in the yard would be weighted with rain until they scratched against the window panes. But the day was going on in its pleasant, sunny way and only we were left to interrupt our lives, to try and still time and sit with him. As I watched his troubled breathing, the words of a hymn came to me, "The fields are white/ And the reapers are few / We children are willing / But what can we do?"

"That Lucille kept me up all night," he laughed.

He knew I was aware the opposite was true, that Aunt Cille had tried to sleep in the oak bed, and he had talked into the morning in the natural pull from the dark; but he liked to poke fun at himself.

"She did? I don't where she gets that gift of gab, do you?"

The light was so pure in the room we spoke directly. Fatdaddy told me he loved me, and I hated the knowledge of death that made him say it outright.

"I'm real proud of you," I told him.

"Honey, I'm proud of you." And he pointed to one of my poems, which he had shellacked to a piece of wood. "There's something I want to ask you." He shut his eyes and lay very still. "Have you accepted the Lord as your Savior? Have you ever been saved?"

And this was the moment when I became the adult who would lie to him, as to a child, the moment from which he would never return, and there was no funeral, no raised hand at the door in good-bye. I wanted to cry, "Help me. I'm afraid for you to die. I believe in nothing, except you. I believe that when you die, there will be nothing." But I said, "Yes, I have been."

"Where's your church membership?" he asked, testing me.

"It's still at Northridge, Mother's church. There was never a Baptist church close enough to college for me to move it; but I'm all right with the Lord. You don't have to worry about that."

He raised his head off the pillow and looked straight into me. "If you tell me I don't have to worry, then I won't."

"Well, you don't," I said, without blinking.

The weight with which he sank onto the bed startled me, and I saw the burden of my soul had been lifted from him, my spirit cleansed.

"Fatdaddy, one of the girls told me you played the banjo when you were young, did you?" One of the questions I always meant to ask.

"Lord, honey, I wouldn't have been worth my salt if I had, that, and had me a coon dog."

"Had you a coon dog," I repeated, not understanding the connection. Suddenly I was afraid that his mind was clouding. All right, I thought, I can stand this. Then he grinned.

"Aunt Margie," I called from the door, "Fatdaddy says he wouldn't have been worth his salt if he'd played the banjo and had him a coon dog."

She came running, wiping her hands on a floral apron. "Oh, back in the old days," she said, "all the bums would hunt raccoon and squirrel all day, then sit by the river bank and pick all night."

"What do city girls know? Fatdaddy asked.

I heard his belly-laugh from the bed. And I understood from his laughter that I was to forgive the willows their uprightness; the photographer, his red and pink tints; the day, its sunlight.

🔥 🔥 🔥

COYOTE HOLDS A FULL HOUSE IN HIS HAND

fiction by LESLIE MARMON SILKO

from TRIQUARTERLY

nominated by Joseph Bruchac, DeWitt Henry, William Strachan and Stephanie Vaughn

HE WASN'T GETTING ANY PLACE with Mrs. Sekakaku. He could see that. She was warming up leftover chili beans for lunch, and when her niece came over, they left him alone on the red plastic sofa and talked at the kitchen table. Aunt Mamie was still sick, her niece was telling her, and they were all so worried because the doctors at Keams Canyon said they'd tried everything already and old man Ko'ite had come over from Oraibi and still Aunt Mamie was having dizzy spells and couldn't get out of bed. He was looking at the same *Life* magazine he'd already looked at before, and it didn't have any pictures of high school girls twirling batons, or plane crashes, or anything he wanted to look at more than twice,

142

but he didn't want to listen to them because then he'd know just what kind of gossip Mrs. Sekakaku found more important than him and his visit.

He set the magazine down on his lap and traced his finger over the horse's head embossed on the plastic cushion. It was always like that. When he didn't expect it, it always came to him, but when he wanted something to happen, like with Mrs. Sekakaku, then it shied away.

Mrs. Sekakaku's letters had made the corner of the trading post where the mailboxes were smell like the perfume counter at Woolworth's. The Mexican woman with the fat arms was the postmaster and ran the trading post. She didn't approve of perfumed letters and she used to pretend the letters weren't there, even when he could smell them and see their pastel edges sticking out of the pile in the general delivery slot. The Mexican woman thought Pueblo men were great lovers. He knew this because he heard her say so to another Mexican woman one day while he was finishing his strawberry soda on the other side of the dry-goods section. In the summer he spent a good number of hours there watching her because she wore sleeveless blouses that revealed her fat upper arms, full and round, and the tender underarm creases curving to her breasts. They had not noticed he was still there, leaning on the counter behind a pile of overalls. " . . . The size of a horse" was all that he had heard, but he knew what she was talking about. They were all like that, those Mexican women. That was all they talked about when they were alone. "As big as a horse"—he knew that much Spanish and more too, but she had never treated him nice, not even when he brought her the heart-shaped box of candy, having carried it on the bus all the way from Albuquerque. He didn't think it was his being older than her; she was over thirty herself. It was because she didn't approve of men who drank. That was the last thing he did before he left town; he did it because he had to. Liquor was illegal on the reservation, so the last thing he did was have a few drinks to carry home with him, the same way other people stocked up on lamb nipples or extra matches. She must have smelled it on his breath when he handed her the candy because she didn't say anything and she left the box under the counter by the old newspapers and balls of string. The cellophane was never opened, and the fine gray dust that covered everything in the store finally settled on the pink satin bow. The postmaster was jealous of the letters that were coming, but she was the one who had sent him into the arms of Mrs. Sekakaku.

In her last two letters Mrs. Sekakaku had been hinting around for him to come see her at Bean Dance time. That was after Christmas when he had sent a big poinsettia plant all the way to Second Mesa on the mail bus. Up until then she had never answered the parts in his letters where he said he wished he could see the beautiful Hopi mesas with snow on them. But that had been the first time a potted plant ever rode into Hopi on the mail bus, and Mrs. Sekakaku finally realized the kind of man he was. All along, that had been the trouble at Laguna: nobody understood just what kind of man he was. They thought he was sort of good-for-nothing, he knew that, but for a long time he kept telling himself to keep on trying and trying.

But it seemed like people would never forget the time the whole village was called out to clean up for feast day and he sent his mother to tell them he was sick with liver trouble. He was still hurt because they didn't understand that with liver trouble you can walk around and sometimes even ride the bus to Albuquerque. Everyone was jealous of him and they didn't stop to think how much it meant to his mother to have someone living with her in her old age. All they could talk about was the big COD that came to the post office in his name and she cashed her pension check to pay for it. But she was the one who had told him, "Sonny Boy, if you want that jacket, you go ahead and order it." It was made out of brown vinyl, resembling leather, and he still wore it whenever he went to town. Even on the day she had the last stroke, his two older brothers had been telling her to quit paying his bills for him and to make him get out and live on his own. But she always stood up for him in front of the others, even if she did complain privately at times to her nieces, who then scolded him about the bills from the record club and the correspondence school. He always knew he could be a lawyer; he had listened to the lawyers in the courtrooms of the Federal Building on those hot summer afternoons when he needed a cool place to sit while he waited for the bus to Laguna. He listened and he knew he could be a lawyer because he was so good at making up stories to justify why things happened the way they did. He thought correspondence school would be different from Indian school, which had given him stomachaches and made him run away all through his seventh-grade year. Right after that he had cut his foot pretty bad, chopping wood for his older brother's wife—the one who kept brushing her arms across his shoulders whenever she poured coffee at the supper table. The foot had taken so long to heal that his mother agreed he shouldn't go back to Indian school or chop wood any more. A few months after that, they were all swimming at the river and he hurt his back in a dive off the old wooden bridge, so it was no wonder he couldn't do the same work as the other young men.

When Mildred told him she was marrying that Hopi, he didn't try to stop her, although she stood for a long time like she was waiting for him to say something. He liked things just the way they were down along the river after dark. Her mother and aunts owned so many fields they expected a husband to hoe them, and he had already promised his mother he wouldn't leave her alone in her old age. He thought it would be easier this way, but after Mildred's wedding, people who had seen him and Mildred together started joking about how he had lost out to a Hopi.

Hopi men were famous for their fast hands and the way they could go on all night. But some of the jokes hinted that he himself was as lazy at lovemaking as he was with his shovel during spring ditch cleaning, and that he would take a girlfriend to the deep sand along the river so he could lie on the bottom while she worked on top. Later on, some of the old men took him aside and said he shouldn't feel bad about Mildred, and told him about women they'd lost to Hopis when they were all working on the railroad together in Winslow. Women believed the stories about Hopi men, they told him, because women liked the sound of those stories, and the women didn't care if it was the Hopi men who were making up the stories in the first place. So when he finally found himself riding the Greyhound bus into Winslow on his way to see Mrs. Sekakaku and the Bean Dance he got to thinking about those stories about Hopi men. It had been years since Mildred had married that Hopi, and her aunts and her mother kept the man working in their fields all year round. Even Laguna people said "Poor thing" whenever they saw the Hopi man walking past with a shovel on his shoulder. So he knew he wasn't going because of that—he was going because of Mrs. Sekakaku's letters and because it was lonely living in a place where no one appreciates you even

when you keep trying and trying. At Hopi he could get a fresh
start; he could tell people about himself while they looked at the
photos in the plastic pages of his wallet.

He waited for the mail bus and drank a cup of coffee in the cafe
across the street from the pink stucco motel with a cowboy on its
neon sign. He had a feeling that something was about to change
because of his trip, but he didn't know if it would be good for him
or bad. Sometimes he was able to look at what he was doing and to
see himself clearly two or three weeks into the future. But this time
when he looked, he only saw himself getting off the bus on the
sandy shoulder of the highway below Second Mesa. He stared up
at the Hopi town on the sand rock and thought that probably he'd
get married.

The last hundred feet up the wagon trail seemed the greatest
distance to him and he felt an unaccustomed tightness in his lungs.
He knew it wasn't old age—it was something—something that
wanted him to work for it. A short distance past the outside toilets
at the edge of the mesa top, he got his breath back and their
familiar thick odor reassured him. He saw that one of the old toilets
had tipped over and rolled down the side of the mesa to the piles of
stove ashes, broken bottles, and corn shucks on the slope below.
He'd get along all right. Like a lot of people, at one time he
believed Hopi magic could outdo all the other Pueblos, but now he
saw that it was all the same from time to time and place to place.
When Hopi men got tired of telling stories about all-nighters in
Winslow motels, then probably the old men brought it around to
magic and how they rigged the Navajo tribal elections one year just
by hiding some little painted sticks over near Window Rock.
Whatever it was he was ready for it.

He checked his reflection in the window glass of Mrs. Sekakaku's
front door before he knocked. Gray hair made him look dignified;
that was what she had written after he sent her the photographs.
He believed in photographs, to show to people as you were telling
them about yourself and the things you'd done and the places you'd
been. He always carried a pocket camera and asked people passing
by to snap him outside the fancy bars and restaurants in the
Heights, where he walked after he had had a few drinks in the
Indian bars downtown. He didn't tell her he'd never been inside
those places, that he didn't think Indians were welcome there.

Behind him he could hear a dog barking. It sounded like a small dog but it also sounded very upset and little dogs were the first ones to bite. So he turned, and at first he thought it was a big rat crawling out the door of Mrs. Sekakaku's bread oven, but it was a small, gray wirehaired dog that wouldn't step out any farther. It must have known it was about to be replaced because it almost choked on its own barking. Only lonely widows let their dogs sleep in the bread oven, although they always pretended otherwise and scolded their little dogs whenever relatives or guests came. "Not much longer, little doggy," he was saying softly while he knocked on the door. He was beginning to wonder if she had forgotten he was coming, and he could feel his confidence lose its footing just a little. She walked up from behind while he was knocking; that was something he always dreaded because it made the person knocking look so foolish—knocking and waiting while the one you wanted wasn't inside the house at all but was standing right behind you. The way the little dog was barking, probably all the neighbors had seen him and were laughing. He managed to smile and would have shaken hands, but she was bending over petting the little dog running around and around her ankles. "I hope you haven't been waiting too long! My poor Aunt Mamie had one of her dizzy spells and I was over helping." She was looking down at the dog while she said this and he noticed she wasn't wearing her perfume. At first he thought his understanding of the English language must be failing—that she had really only invited him over to the Bean Dance, that he had misread her letters when she said that a big house like hers was lonely and that she did not like walking home alone in the evenings from the water faucet outside the village. Maybe all this had only meant she was afraid a bunch of Navajos might jump out from the shadows of the mesa rocks to take turns on top of her. But when she warmed up the leftover chili beans and went on talking to her niece about the dizzy spells, he began to suspect what was going on. She was one of those women who wore Evening in Paris to Laguna feast and sprinkled it on letters, but back at Hopi she pretended she was somebody else. She had lured him into sending his letters and snapshots and the big poinsettia plant to show off to her sisters and aunts—and now his visit, so she could pretend he had come uninvited, overcome with desire for her. He should have seen it all along, but the first time he met her at Laguna feast, a gust of wind had showed him the little roll of fat

above her garter and left him dreaming of a plunge deep into the
crease at the edge of the silk stocking. The old auntie and the dizzy
spells gave her the perfect excuse and a story to protect her
respectability. It was only two-thirty, but already she was folding a
flannel nightgown while she talked to her niece. And here the
whole bus ride from Laguna he had been imagining the night
together—fingering the creases and folds and the little rolls while
she squeezed him with both hands. He felt it lift off and up like a
butterfly moving away from him, and the breathlessness he had felt
coming up the mesa returned. He was feeling bitter—that if that's
all it took, then he'd find a way to get that old woman out of bed.

He said it without thinking—the words just found his mouth and
he said, "Excuse me, ladies," straightening his belt buckle as he
walked across the room, "but it sounds to me like your poor auntie
is in bad shape." Mrs. Sekakaku's niece looked at him for the first
time all afternoon. "Is he a medicine man?" she asked her aunt,
and for an instant he could see Mrs. Sekakaku hesitate and he knew
he had to say, "Yes, it's something I don't usually mention myself.
Too many of those guys just talk about it to attract women. But this
is a serious case." It was sounding so good that he was afraid he
would start thinking again about the space between the cheeks of
the niece's ass and be unable to go on. But the next thing he said
was they had a cure that they did at Laguna for dizzy spells like
Aunt Mamie was having. He could feel a momentum somewhere
inside himself. It wasn't hope because he knew Mrs. Sekakaku had
tricked him, but whatever it was, it was going for broke. He
imagined the feel of grabbing hold of the tops of the niece's thighs,
which were almost as fat and would feel almost as good as the tops
of Mrs. Sekakaku's thighs. "There would be no charge; this is
something I want to do especially for you." That was all it took
because these Hopi ladies were like all the other Pueblo women he
ever knew—always worrying about saving money, and nothing
made them enemies for longer than selling them the melon or
mutton leg they felt they should get for free as a love gift because
all of them, even the thin ones and the old ones, believed he was
after them. "Oh, that would be so kind of you! We are so worried
about her!" "Well, not so fast," he said, even though his heart was
racing. "It won't work unless everything is just so. All her clanswomen must come to her house, but there can't be any men there,
not even outside." He paused. He knew exactly what to say. "This

is very important. Otherwise the cure won't work." Mrs. Sekakaku
let out her breath suddenly and tightened her lips, and he knew
that any men or boys not in the kivas preparing for Bean Dance
would be sent far away from Aunt Mamie's house. He looked over
at the big loaf of fresh oven bread the niece had brought when she
came; they hadn't offered him any before, but now, after she
served him a big bowl of chili beans, she cut him a thick slice. It
was all coming back to him now, about how good medicine men get
treated, and he wasn't surprised at himself any more. Once he got
started he knew just how it should go. It was just getting it started
that gave him trouble sometimes.

Mrs. Sekakaku and her niece hurried out to contact all the
women of the Snow Clan to bring them to Aunt Mamie's for the
cure. There were so many of them sitting in rows facing the sick
bed—on folding chairs and little canvas stools they'd brought just
like they did for a kiva ceremony or a summer dance. He had never
stopped to think how many Snow Clan women there might be, and
as he walked across the room he wondered if he should have made
some kind of age limit. Some of the women sitting there were
pretty old and bony, but then there were all those little girls; one
squatted down in front of him to play jacks and he could see the
creases and dimples of her legs below her panties. The initiated
girls and the women sat serious and quiet with the ceremonial
presence the Hopis are famous for. Their eyes were full of the
power the clanswomen shared whenever they gathered together.
He saw it clearly and he never doubted its strength. Whatever he
took, he'd have to run with it, but the women would come out on
top like they usually did.

He sat on the floor by the fireplace and asked them to line up.
He reached into the cold, white juniper ashes and took a handful,
and told the woman standing in front of him to raise her skirt above
her knees. The ashes were slippery and they carried his hands up
and around each curve, each fold, each roll of flesh on her thighs.
He reached high, but his fingers never strayed above the edge of
the panty leg. They stepped in front of him one after the other, and
he worked painstakingly with each one, the silvery white ashes
billowing up like clouds above the skin they dusted like early snow
on brown hills—and he lost all track of time. He closed his eyes so
he could feel them better—the folds of skin and flesh, the little
crevices and creases—as a hawk must feel canyons and arroyos

while he is soaring. Some thighs he gripped as if they were something wild and fleet like antelope and rabbits, and the women never flinched or hesitated because they believed the recovery of their clan sister depended on them. The dimple and pucker at the edge of the garter and silk stocking brought him back and he gave special attention to Mrs. Sekakaku, the last one before Aunt Mamie. He traced the ledges and slopes with all his fingers pressing in the ashes. He was out of breath and he knew he could not stand up to get to Aunt Mamie's bed; so he bowed his head and pretended he was praying. "I feel better already. I'm not dizzy," the old woman said, not letting anyone help her out of bed or walk with her to the fireplace. He rubbed her thighs as carefully as he had the rest, and he could tell by the feel that she'd probably live a long time.

The sun was low in the sky and the bus would be stopping for the outgoing mail pretty soon. He was quitting while he was ahead, while the Hopi men were still in the kivas for the Bean Dance. He graciously declined any payment, but the women insisted they wanted to do something, so he unzipped his jacket pocket and brought out his little pocket camera and a flash cube. As many as could squeeze together stood with him in front of the fireplace and someone snapped the picture. By the time he left Aunt Mamie's house he had two shopping bags full of pies and piki bread.

Mrs. Sekakaku was acting very different now: when they got back to her house she kicked the little gray dog and blocked up the oven hole with an orange crate. But he told her he had to get back to Laguna right away because he had something important to tell the old men. It was something they'd been trying and trying to do for a long time. At sundown the mail bus pulled onto the highway below Second Mesa, but he was tasting one of the pumpkin pies and forgot to look back. He set aside a fine-looking cherry pie to give to the postmaster. Now that they were even again with the Hopi men, maybe this Laguna luck would hold out a little while longer.

SELECTIONS

by LYN HEJINIAN

from *MY LIFE* (Burning Deck Press)

nominated by David Bromige and Loris Essary

A pause, a rose,
something on paper
A moment yellow, just as four years later, when my father returned home from the war, the moment of greeting him, as he stood at the bottom of the stairs, younger, thinner than when he had left, was purple—though moments are no longer so colored. Somewhere, in the background, rooms share a pattern of small roses. Pretty is as pretty does. The better things were gathered in a pen. The windows were narrowed by white gauze curtains which were never loosened. Hence, repetitions, free from all ambition. The shadow of the redwood trees, she said, was oppressive. The plush must be worn away. On her walks she stepped into people's gardens to pinch off cuttings from their geraniums and succulents. An occasional sunset is reflected on the windows. A little puddle is

151

overcast. If only you could touch, or, even, catch those gray great creatures. I was afraid of my uncle with the wart on his nose, or of his jokes at our expense which were beyond me, and I was shy of my aunt's deafness who was his sister-in-law and who had years earlier fallen into the habit of nodding, agreeably. Wool station. See lightning, wait for thunder. Quite mistakenly, as it happened. The afternoon happens, crowded and therefore endless. Thicker, she agreed. It was a tic, she had the habit, and now she bobbed like my toy plastic bird on the edge of its glass, dipping into and recoiling from the water. But a word is a bottomless pit. It became magically pregnant and one day split open, giving birth to a stone egg, about as big as a football. In May when the lizards emerge from the stones, the stones turn gray, from green. When daylight moves, we delight in distance. The waves rolled over our stomachs, like spring rain over an orchard slope. Rubber bumpers on rubber cars. In every country is a word which attempts the sound of cats. "Everything is a question of sleep," says Cocteau, but he forgets the shark, which does not. Find a drawer that's not filled up. That we sleep plunges our work into the dark. The ball was lost in a bank of myrtle. I was in a room with the particulars of which a later nostalgia might be formed, an indulged childhood. They are sitting in wicker chairs, the legs of which have sunk unevenly into the ground, so that each is sitting slightly tilted and their postures make adjustment for that. The cows warm their own barn. I look at them fast and it gives the illusion that they're moving. An "oral history" on paper. That morning this morning. The overtones are a denser shadow in the room characterized by its habitual readiness, a form of charged waiting, a perpetual atten-dance, of which I was thinking when I began the paragraph, "So much of childhood is spent in a manner of waiting."

As for we who "love   You spill the sugar when you lift the spoon.
to be astonished"   My father had filled an old apothecary jar
with what he called "sea glass," bits of old
bottles rounded and textured by the sea, so
abundant on beaches. There is no solitude.
It is as if one splashed in the water lost by one's tears. My mother had climbed into the garbage can in order to stamp down the accumulated trash, but the can was knocked off balance, and when she fell she broke her arm. She could only give a little shrug. The

family had little money but plenty of food. At the circus only the elephants were greater than anything I could have imagined. The egg of Columbus. She wanted one where the playground was dirt, with grass, shaded by a tree, from which would hang a rubber tire as a swing, and when she found it she sent me. These creatures are compound and nothing they do should surprise us. I don't mind, or I won't mind, where the verb "to care" might multiply. The pilot of the little airplane had forgotten to notify the airport of his approach, so that when the lights of the plane in the night were first spotted, the air raid sirens went off, and the entire city on that coast went dark. He was taking a drink of water and the light was growing dim. My mother stood at the window watching the only lights that were visible, circling over the darkened city in search of the hidden airport. Whether breathing or holding the breath, it was the same thing, driving through the tunnel from one sun to the next under a hot brown hill. She sunned the baby for sixty seconds, leaving him naked except for a blue cotton sunbonnet. At night, to close off the window from view of the street, my grandmother pulled down the window shades, never loosening the curtains, a gauze starched too stiff to hang properly down. I sat on the windowsill singing sunny, lunny, teena; ding-dang-dong. He broke the radio silence. Why would anyone find astrology interesting when it is possible to learn about astronomy. What one passes in the Plymouth. It is the wind slamming the doors. All that is nearly incommunicable to my friends. Were we seeing a pattern or merely an appearance of small white sailboats on the bay, floating at such a distance from the hill that they appeared to be making no progress. And for once to a country that did not speak another language. To follow the progress of ideas, or that particular line of reasoning, so full of surprises and unexpected correlations, was somehow to take a vacation. Still, you had to wonder where they had gone, since you could speak of reappearance. A blue room is always dark. Everything on the boardwalk was shooting toward the sky. It was not specific to any year, but very early. A German goldsmith covered a bit of metal with cloth in the 14th century and gave mankind its first button. There is something still surprising when the green emerges. The blue fox has ducked its head. Where is my honey running. You cannot linger "on the lamb." You cannot determine the nature of progress until you assemble all of the relatives.

🔥 🔥 🔥

DOMINION

fiction by BARRY TARGAN

from THE IOWA REVIEW

nominated by Robert Boyers, Joseph Bruchac, and Stephanie Vaughn

In a moment, in the twinkling of an eye, at the last trump: for the trumpet shall sound, and the dead shall be raised incorruptible, and we shall be changed.

I Corinthians 15:52

HE PLAYED ABSENTLY with the tiny party hat in his hand, a hat such as a leprechaun in a movie cartoon might wear, a truncated cone of metallic green paper board with a flat silver brim and a black paper buckle. He pulled at the thin rubber band that would hold the hat in place and listened carefully to what the men were explaining. Sometimes he would nod in comprehension. Last night he and Sandra had gone to the Balmuth's New Year's Eve party. And now, January the first, suddenly a lifetime later, he listened to the two men, the accountant and the lawyer, explain what had happened.

What had happened was that Poverman and Charney, a small

manufacturer of lightweight women's clothing, was ruined, embez-
zled into insolvency by Charney, who even now sat in Florida in
the noonday sun. Morton Poverman sat here, at his chilling dining
room table cloaked with the fabric of his loss, the neat stacks of
paper—bills, letters, invoices, bank statements, memoranda, and
packets of canceled checks—that chronicled Charney's wretched
course, his wicked testament.

Poverman said, "And all this could have happened without my
knowing? Amazing."

In a corner off from the table, Poverman's wife, Sandra, sat in a
stuffed chair with her right leg raised up on an ottoman. Her leg,
up to the middle of the calf, was in a cast, her ankle broken. "Oh,"
she said like a moan, a curse, a threat. "Oh God." It was all she
could say now, though later, Poverman knew, she would say more,
her vehemence strident, hot, and deep. For twenty years she had
disliked Paul Charney, distrusted him always, his flamboyance, his
fancy women and his fancy ways, the frivolous instability of his
unmarried state. And now to be right! To be helplessly confirmed!
She put her head back against the chair and closed her eyes as she
clogged with rage nearly to fainting. "Oh God."

"Not so amazing," Friedsen, the accountant snapped. "You
never looked at the books. You never asked a question." He
slapped at some figures on a pad before him. "Five thousand
dollars for the material for the chemises? When is the last time you
made a chemise? Who buys chemises any more? And this?" He
looked down at the pad. "The bias tape? Forty cases? and here," he
jabbed at the entry with his finger, his nail piercing at the numbers
like the beak of a ravening bird. "The printing bill on the new
boxes? You weren't suspicious of that?" Friedsen was angry. He
had done their books from the start, had managed them well. And
now he held them in his hands like smudged ashes. Like dirt. Like
an affront. If one was a thief, then the other was a fool.

"I never looked at the books," Poverman told him, though
Friedsen knew that already, knew everything. "If I had looked, so
what would I have known? I did the selling, Philly did the rest. For
twenty-five years it worked okay."

"The bastard," Friedsen said.

Poverman could not find his own anger. Perhaps he was still too
startled. What Phil Charney had done, he had done quickly, in less
than a year altogether, but conclusively in the last quarter before

the Christmas season, when their money moved about most rapidly and in the largest amounts. Friedsen, for his own orderly reasons, liked to see his client's fiscal shape at the end of the calendar year. He had gotten to Poverman and Charney two days ago and, hour by hour, he had tumbled ever more quickly through the shreds that Charney had made of the once solid company. Friedsen had gone to no New Year's Eve party. And this morning he had pulled the lawyer, Kuhn, to this dreadful meeting. It had not taken him long to explain and demonstrate the bankruptcy and its cause. Now Kuhn explained the rest, the mechanism of foreclosure and collection, the actual bankruptcy petition to the courts, the appointment of the referee, the slim possibility of criminal action against Charney. He went on, but to Poverman, the intricacies of his disaster like the details of his success were equally abstractions. He could not contain them. He could understand the results, of course. He could understand purposes and conclusions. Consequences. But he had always been the man in front, the one to whom you spoke when you called Poverman and Charney. Morton Poverman, a man of good will and even humor who had put in his working years directly, flesh on flesh, voice against voice, eye to eye. Let Friedsen and Kuhn do what must be done in their rigorous and judicial way. But let him do what he could do in his.

"So what's left?" he asked, first to one then the other. "Anything?"

Of the business there was not much. He would lose the factory and everything in it and connected to it, including the dresses, housecoats, and nightgowns already on the racks. There were two outlet stores, the largest, the newer store in Fairlawn Shopping Mall he would have to close. The older store in the business strip just off of North Broadway, he could probably keep. Where he and Phil had begun.

Personally, there was the paid-up life insurance, fifty-thousand. That was safe. There was also about twenty thousand in cash. There were things like the cars and all that was in the house. The house itself might be a question. Kuhn said the house would depend on too many variables to discuss now. And there was the trust fund for Robert's education. Twenty-five thousand dollars. Nothing could touch that. There were some small investments, mostly stocks. Those would probably have to be called in, for one reason or

another. For one bill or another, like Friedsen's perhaps, or
Kuhn's. Or merchandise for the store. At this point who could say?

"So? That's it?"

"That's about it," Kuhn said.

"Well, it's not nothing, is it?" Poverman said.

"No," Kuhn said. "It's not nothing."

Sandra Poverman sobbed high and quietly at the top of her
voice, still unable to open her eyes to what she would have to look
at forever after.

When the men left he did some small figuring of his own.
Immediately there would be no Florida vacation this winter.
Perhaps he would sell one car. The membership in the country
club? What did he need that for, he didn't even play golf? He
started to write down numbers—mortgage payment, property tax,
homeowner's insurance, the car payments, but after these he could
not say. He did not know what his heating bill was, his electricity,
food, clothing. And the rest. Did Sandra? Did anyone in this house
know such things? Probably not. He had earned, each year a little
more, and in the last five years nearly, though not quite, a lot.
Yesterday the future was all before him various with pleasures just
about to come within his grasp, the long-planned trips to Europe,
to South America the year after that, Hawaii. The house in the
semi-retirement village at Seadale, a hundred miles north of
Miami. Gone. Today only the future itself was waiting, empty and
dangerous. The little store on North Broadway with the old
lighting fixtures and the cracked linoleum flooring from twenty five
years ago. That was waiting.

He had earned and they all had spent what they needed, and
each year they had needed a little more. So now they would need
less. They would make an accommodation. Tomorrow he would go
to the outlet store and take stock and make arrangements. Begin.
He was fifty-three.

The phone rang. It was Phil Charney calling from Miami. He
knew that Friedsen would find him in the year-end audit.

"Morty, this is Phil. You know why I'm calling?"

"Friedsen was here. Just now. And Kuhn. They just left."

"Morty, this is so terrible, I can't say how terrible."

Sandra stiffened. "That's him?" she hissed. He nodded. "Give
me." She motioned the phone to her. "Give me. I'll tell him
something. I'll tell that filth something. Give me. Give me." She

waved for the phone, her voice rising. He covered the mouthpiece. She tried to stand up.

"Morty, I'm sitting here weeping. I didn't sleep all night. Not for two nights. Not for three nights. I couldn't help it. I still can't. She wants and wants and I must give. *Must!* Who knows where it ends. There's not so much money I can go on like this. Then what? But what can I do? *Morty,* what can I do, kill myself?"

"No, no, of course not."

He scrambled for his outrage like a weapon, but a weapon with which to defend himself and not attack. He was embarrassed for the man sobbing at the other end of the line, his agony. He summoned his hatred for protection, but it would not come. But he had always lacked sufficient imagination, and what he felt now was more the loss of his life-long friend, the swoop and gaiety of his presence as he would click about the factory, kidding the women on the machines, hassling in mocking fights the blacks on the loading platforms. He had even picked up enough Spanish to jabber back at the volatile Puerto Ricans. Even the Puerto Ricans Phil could make laugh and work.

That would be gone. And the flitting elegance, the Cadillacs and the women. The clothing and the jewelry. The flights to anywhere, to Timbuktu. He would miss the women. They were an excitement, these strenuous pursuits of Phil Charney's, these expensive pursuits. He was a tone, an exuberant vibrato that pushed into and fluttered the lives of anyone near him. Battered floozies or sometimes women much younger, but often enough recently divorced or widowed women ready at last for madder music, headier wine. Sandra Poverman condemned it, but her husband could afford his own small envy, safe enough within his wife's slowly thickening arms to tease her with his short-reined lust. That would be gone. Tomorrow he would go to work as he had known he would even before Friedsen, but now in silence with no edge of scandal or tightly-fleshed surprise.

"Filth. Murderer," Sandra shouted into the phone. She had gotten up and hobbled over to him. "Liar. Dog."

"She's right, Morty. She's right. I'm no better than a murderer."

"No. Stop this, Phil. Get a hold."

"Die," Sandra screamed. "Die in hell. Bastard. Scum." She pulled at the phone in his hand but he forced it back.

"Oh Morty, Morty, what I've done to you! Oh Morty, forgive me."

"Yes, Phil. OK. I do." He hung up before either could say more.

What more? That time had come to take away their life together, abandoning Phil Charney more severely than himself? But if had said that, would he be certain enough himself what he meant? That only the sorrow was left, enough of that to go around for them all, so what did the rest of anything else matter?

"What?" Sandra demanded. "What did he want? 'I do' you said. You 'do' what?" He told her. And then she screamed, raised her fists to her ears to block his words, but too late. She fell against him, staggered by the shaking that was bringing down upon her the castles they had built. And now he had even taken from her the solid and pure energy of revenge.

The large, good, sustaining thing that happened in January was that his son, Robert, received the report of his Scholastic Aptitude Tests: 690 in Verbal, 710 in Math. In the achievement tests he did comparably well. The rest of the month, however, was not unexpected as what he had come to do grew clearer. The store had made economic sense as an outlet for the factory, a nice way of taking some retail profit right off the top. But without the factory as the primary supplier, the store was just another women's clothing store, in competition everywhere. That situation would be impossible. But Morton Poverman had his accrued advantages from twenty-five years in both ends of the business. He knew enough to know where he could get over-runs, returns, seconds from other manufacturers, small producers such as he had been. What credit he needed, at least with some cash down, he could still get from them.

By the end of January he could at least begin to think seriously about his spring line; various enough and inexpensive as it was, he had a chance to exist. Not much more. But already the stock was coming into the storeroom in the back faster then he could handle it. Still, that was not so bad. Better more than not enough. He would put in the time to inventory and price and mark it all.

In January he had let go all the workers in the store, three of them, and handled the front himself. Only on Saturday, dashing back and forth from customer to cash register, was it too difficult. The stock he worked on at night. At first until nine o'clock and now until midnight. But it was coming together, the store brightening with variety and loading up with goods. And people were still shopping downtown, he could tell. He would get by on his low pricing and his long hours. And now he was bringing in a whole line of Playtex girdles and bras, all kinds of pantyhose and lingerie. In a year maybe he would bring in sewing articles, fabrics, patterns. In a year. Or two.

It was easier to say that twenty-five years ago when there was still a year or two or three or five to invest. And two of them to do it. But he could say it now, nonetheless, again and alone. His flame burned, steadily if low, even by the end of January when, like fuel for the flame, Bobby's SAT's had arrived. 690/710. Fuel enough. Then Morton Poverman would crush back in the large cardboard boxes under the dim, bare-bulbed lighting of the storeroom with his supper sandwich and the last of his thermos of coffee and think that though he was bone-weary and hard-pressed, he was not without intelligent purpose and a decent man's hope. More he did not ask. Or need.

February, March—a time for clinging to the steep, roughly-grained rock face of his endeavor, seeking the small, icy hand-holds, the cracks and fissures of little victories to gain a purchase on, by which to lever himself up an inch: he picked up one hundred assorted dusters for nearly nothing, garbage from South Korea with half their buttons gone. He would replace the buttons. Kurtlanger's, the largest women's clothing store in the area, was dropping its entire line of women's nylons. It was not worth the bother to Kurtlanger's to supply the relatively few women who still wore separate stockings. It was all pantyhose now. For Poverman the bother could become his business. He stocked the nylons and put an ad in the newspaper saying so. Seeds for springtime. He put money into a new floor, found bags in Waltham, Massachusetts, at a ten percent saving, joined the Downtown Merchants Association protesting for increased side-street lighting and greater police surveillance. He checked three times a day the long-range weather reports. Would winter freeze him shut, March blow his straw house down?

At first Sandra had gone mad with anger calling everyone to behold her suffering. She called her friends and relatives, *Charney's* friends and relatives, the police. Worse than the stunning death of a loved one in a car crash or by the quick, violent blooming of a cancer in the lymph, where you could curse God and be done with it, this that Charney had done to her was an unshared burden, separate from life and others' fate, and unsupportable for being so. If we all owe life a death and perhaps even pain, certainly we do not owe it bankruptcy and humiliation. She cried out, howled, keening in the ancient way of grief and lamentation.

And then she dropped into silence like a stone.

She would hardly speak to him, as if his failure to share her intensity of anger had separated them. Or to speak to anyone. She grew hard and dense with her misery, imploded beneath the gravity of her fury and chagrin. At first she had fought with her simple terrifying questions: Who could she face? What was the rest of her life to be like? But then, far beyond her questions, she grew smaller yet until at the last she atomized into the vast unspecific sea of justice and worth, and there she floated like zero.

Late at night Poverman would come home and get into bed beside her and chafe her arms and rub her back. Sometimes he would kiss her gently on the neck as she had always liked. But she was wood. Still, he would talk to her, tell her the good things that were happening, his incremental progress, prepare her for the future. But she would not go with him. The future, like her past, had betrayed her, had disintegrated. She would trust in no future again.

Robert Poverman said to his father, "I'll come in after school. You'll show me how to mark the clothing, and that will be a help."

"No," his father said. "By the time you come in after school, get downtown, it would already be late. What could you do in an hour?"

"What do you mean, 'an hour'? I'd work with you at night. I'd come home with you. If I helped, then we'd both get home earlier."

"No. Absolutely not. You're in school. You do the school, I'll do the business. In the summer, we'll see. Not now, Sonny. Not now."

"Are you kidding, Dad? School's over. I'm a second semester senior. It's all fun and games, messing around. It's nothing."

"So do fun and games. Mess around. That's part of school, too. Next year you'll be in college, with no messing around. And what about your activities, the Photography Club, the Chess Club,

Current Events Club, Student Council, French Club, the math team. Your guitar. And soon it's track season. So what about track?" Poverman knew it all, remembered everything.

"Dad, listen. I'm a third string miler. Sometimes they don't even run me. I struggle to break six minutes. And the clubs are strictly baloney. Nothing. Believe me, *nothing*. Let me help you, please. Let me *do* something."

"No. NO. If you want to do something, Sonny, do school, *all* of it just the way you always did. Do it the way you would have before . . . *this*." He smeared his hand in the air.

His son took his hand out of the air and kissed it. "Ok, Daddy," he said softly. "Ok. And I'll pray for you, too."

That night, turning the handle of the machine that ground out the gummed pricing tags, Poverman recalled what his son had said, that he would pray for him. The machine clicked on: size, stock number, price. What could that mean? But Poverman had enough to think about without adding prayer. He had ten crates of L'Eggs to unpack by morning, two dozen bathrobes that had arrived that day without belts, and all the leather accessories that he still had to stick these tags on. He turned the crank faster.

February, March, and now, somehow, April. Already the first wavelets of Easter buying had lapped at his shore, eroded slightly the cloth of his island. Good. Let it all be washed away in a flood of gold. Poverman walked about. He was working harder than ever, but accomplishing more. The hard, heaving work was mostly done, and there was a shape to everything now, his possibilities limited but definite, and definite perhaps because they were limited. So be it. He had started in quicksand and had built this island. The rest now was mostly up to the weather and the caprice of the economy. At least it was out of the hands of men like Phil Charney.

Poverman seldom thought of him even though he had to meet often enough with Friedsen and Kuhn. He had even made a joke once that he had to work for Charney twice, before and after. Friedsen had not laughed. But what did it matter? What mattered was what *could* matter.

It was six o'clock. He walked about in the crisp store, straightening a few boxes, clothes loosely strewn in bins, the merchandise hanging on the racks. Tonight, for the first time in months, he was closing now. Tonight he was going home early. To celebrate. Let the three hundred pairs of slaps from the Philippines wait. Let the gross of white gloves wait. Tonight he was going home to celebrate. Today, all on the same day, Robert Poverman had been accepted at Yale, Cornell, and the State University of New York at Binghamton, a university center. He had until May fifteenth to make his decision and send in his deposit. They would talk about it tonight. And everything.

Poverman turned out all the lights after checking the locks on the back door. He walked out of the store pulling the door to and double locking it. He looked up at the sign recently painted on the door, the new name he had decided upon: The Fashion Center. Nothing too fancy. Nothing too smart. But what did he need with fancy or smart? He had Robert Poverman of Yale or Cornell. *That* was fancy. *That* was smart.

After supper Poverman spread out on the diningroom table the various catalogues and forms and descriptive literature from the three colleges. He had also added to that, clippings from magazines and newspapers. They had seen most of it all before, when Robert had applied, but now it was to be examined differently as one seriously considered the tangibilities of life in Harkness Memorial Hall or Mary Donlon Hall. Here, this material, was what they had from which to read the auguries of Robert Poverman's future. Even Sandra leavened as they discussed (As always. Again.) what he would study. Which school might be best for what. Neither Poverman nor his wife knew how to make their comparisons. It would, now as before, be their son's choice. But who could refrain from the talking? The saying of such things as law or medicine or physics or international relations? Poverman again looked up the size of the libraries. Yale: 6,518,848. Cornell: 4,272,959. SUNY at Binghamton: 729,000. 6,518,848 books. How could he imagine that? Still, it was one measure. But what did Robert Poverman want? His interests were so wide, his accomplishments so great, what could he *not* decide for? What could he not illimitably cast for and catch?

They drank tea and talked. In two days Sandra would go for a small operation on the ankle to adjust a bone that had drifted slightly. Even with his medical coverage it would cost him a thousand dollars. But okay. Of course. Let her walk straight. Let her life go on. He had hoped that she would be able to help him in the store now that the Easter push was happening, but instead he had hired someone part time.

He looked at the pictures in the college catalogues, the jungle of glass tubes in the laboratories, the pretty girls intensely painting things on large canvases, the professor standing at the blackboard filled with lines and numbers and signs like a magical incantation, smiling young men like Robert flinging frisbees across the wide Commons, the view of Cayuga Lake, the wonderous glowing cube of the Beinecke Library at Yale (*another* library, a *special* library for the rare books alone). Yale. Yale began to creep into Morton Poverman's heart. He would say nothing. What did he know? It was up to Robert. But he hoped for Yale. 6,518,848 books.

"I don't know," Robert said. "What's the rush?" He turned to Sandra.

"This is an important decision, right? And he's got a mouth. Think about it, that's the smart thing," he said to his son. "Sure. Don't jump before you look." He gathered up the evidence of what was to come, the scattered materials about one of Robert Poverman's schools, and put it all back into the reddish brown paper portfolio. He took the letters of acceptance and the letters to be returned with the deposit and put them elsewhere. He wished that he could have sent one back in the morning with a check enclosed, a down payment on his son's happiness, a bond, a covenant.

That night in bed he held his wife's hand.

"Which do you like?" he asked.

"Cornell, I think."

"Not Yale? Why not Yale?"

"The bulldog," she said. "It's so ugly. What kind of animal is that for a school?"

The weather was warm and balmy. Good for light cotton prints. Easter did well by him and spring, too. Business was beating through the veins of the store. Sandra's ankle was fixed for good now, mending correctly, though she would still need more weeks of resting it. This Sunday he had asked Robert to come to the store with him to help him catch up on some stock work. Also he wanted to describe what Robert would do in the store that summer, his job. Robert would work in the store and his pay, except for some spending money, would be put into a bank account for his use in college. And today Poverman would push his son, slightly, toward his decision. Time was now growing short. Ten days till the deadline. He would like to have this settled.

At three o'clock they sat down to some sandwiches that Sandra had packed for them.

"So? What do you think?" he asked his son. "Do you think you can last the summer? Listen, this is the easy part. The stock don't talk back. The stock don't complain. You think you can explain to a size twelve lady why she don't fit into a size ten dress? Hah? Let me tell you sweetheart, everything to know is not in books." Then he reached across and stroked his son's softly stubbled cheek. His oldest gesture. "But Sonny, all of this is nothing to know. What you're going to learn, compared to this, you could put all this into a little nut shell." Then, "Did you choose a college yet?"

Robert Poverman said, "I don't know."

"There's only ten days," his father said. "What can you know in ten more days that you don't know already?" What do you want to know? Who can you ask? Sonny, maybe you think you have to be certain. Well let me tell you, you can't be certain of nothing. And with any one of these schools, you can't go so far wrong. You can't lose anyway."

"It's about college," Robert Poverman said. "I'm not so sure about that."

His father did not understand.

"Maybe college isn't for me. Just yet, anyway. I don't know."

"Know?" his father said. "Know what? What is there to know? You think you want *this?* he indicated the store around them. "Maybe you want to go into the Army? Shoot guns? Maybe you want to be a fireman and ride on a red truck?" He was filling out.

"Don't be angry, Dad. Please." But it wasn't anger ballooning in Morton Poverman now, it was panic.

"Then what are you talking about? *What* don't you know? You go to college to find out what you don't know. Ah," it occurred to him, "it's the money. Is that it? You're worried about the money, about me and your mother. But I told you, the money is already there. Twenty-five thousand and that will make interest. Plus a little more I've got. Plus what you'll earn. Don't worry about the money, Bobby, please. I swear to you, your mother and I are going to be okay that way. Look, look. The store is working out, Sonny."

"Daddy, it's not that. Maybe there's another way." They were silent.

"So?" Poverman finally asked. "What other way?"

"I've been thinking about religion." He looked at his father evenly. "There's a religious retreat down at this place in Nyack this summer, from the middle of July to the middle of August. I think maybe I should go there." He looked down away from his reflection in his father's brightening eyes.

"Why?"

"Yes, *why*. I need to find out the meaning of things. Not *what* I want to do or where I want to go to college, but *why*. Is that unreasonable?"

But what did Morton Poverman know about reasonableness? What he knew about was hanging on, like a boxer after he has been hit very hard.

"So what has this to do with college? Why can't I send in the deposit?"

"I might not go to college right away. I can't honestly say now. Or I might not want to go to one of those colleges. Where I was accepted. I might find out that I want to go to a . . . a religious type of college. I just don't know. I've got to think about it. I don't want you wasting the money. If I change my mind, I can probably still get into a good college somewhere."

"Money again," Poverman roared. He stood. "I'm telling you, money is shit. I know. I've lost money before. That's nothing."

Driving home from the store Robert told his father that for the past six months he had been attending weekly meetings organized by the Society of the Holy Word for high school age people. Driving down Pearl Street, he pointed to a store with many books in the window and the name of the organization neatly lettered on the panes of glass.

"So everybody's in business," Poverman said as he drove by. "Do they belong to the Downtown Businessmen's Association?"

"They're not selling," his son said.

"Oh no? Aren't they? So what's that, a church?"

"No, Dad. It isn't a business and it isn't a church. It's a place for people to meet to discuss things."

"Yeah? Like what?"

"Religion, meaning of life, ethical conduct. The Bible, mostly. The Bible as the word of God."

"Is that right? The Bible tells you what college to go to? Yale or Cornell? Amazing. I never knew. But then, there's so much I don't know."

"Daddy, please don't be angry. Don't be bitter."

"No? So what should I be, happy? For eighteen years I'm thinking Chief Justice of the Supreme Court and now my son tells me he's thinking of becoming a monk. Wonderful. Terrific." He drove faster.

"Ah Daddy, come on. It's not that way at all. We sit and talk about how religion can give a full and wonderful meaning to our lives. It's raised some important questions for me about my future. And it's offered some possible answers and solutions."

"Solutions? Why? You've got problems?"

"We've all got problems, Daddy."

"Like?"

"Like our souls," Robert Poverman said. "Like the fate of our immortal souls."

"Souls? *Souls?* You're eighteen and you're worried about your soul? What about your body?"

But his son closed down then, as did he, each caught in the other's orbit as they would ever be, but as silent now and awesomely distant as Venus to Pluto. And what could the earthbound Morton Poverman breathe in such empty space?

"Yes? Can I help you?" the tall man asked. He was very clean, scrubbed so that he was pink and white. He did not seem to need to shave, his skin as smooth as thin polished stone, nearly translucent. His steel gray hair was combed straight back over his head. He wore small octagonal rimless glasses.

"Just looking," Poverman said. He walked about in the converted store. Converted to what? All he saw were arrangements of books with such titles as *Satan in the Sanctuary* and *Which Will You Believe.* There were piles of small folded tracts and pamphlets on different color paper, pink, green, blue. Newspapers called the *New Word Times* and *Revelation Tribune.* On the walls were large, poster-sized photographs of people, mostly healthy young people, working at good deeds in foreign countries, in ghettos, in hospitals, in old folks homes. Even Poverman could quickly see that the young people in the photographs were shining with pleasure in the midst of the misery and needs they were serving, gleaming and casting light so that, behold, their light warmed and illuminated the rheumy-eyed old woman in the wheelchair smiling toothlessly;

the bloated-bellied excema-scabbed children in the jungle clear-
ing; the slit-eyed hoodlum sucking deeply on his joint of dope. All
down the wall—growing, building, feeding, helping. Hallelujah.

Past the main room, behind a partition, was another room. He
turned and walked back to the pink and white man.

"I'm Morton Poverman," he said, and put out his hand.

"I'm George Fetler," the pink and white man said, and took the
hand.

"I've got a son, Robert Poverman. He comes here."

"Oh yes. Robert. A wonderful boy. Brilliant. Absolutely brilliant. I'm very pleased to meet you. You must be very proud of
such a son."

But Poverman did not have time for this playing. Even now, four
blocks away in his own store, United Parcel trucks would be
arriving with goods he must pay for and he had not yet made the
deposit in the bank that would cover them, and Francine Feynmen
(now working fulltime) would be on two customers at once (or
worse, none), and the phone would ring with the call from
Philadelphia about the slightly faded orlon sweaters. And what had
he come here for, this man's opinions?

"Yes," Poverman said. "Proud." But he did not know what to
say, nor what to do. What he *wanted* to do was dump five gallons of
gasoline over everything—the books, the newspapers, the green
pamphlets—and put a match to it. But there were too many other
empty store fronts downtown for that to matter. So he was stuck.

George Fetler said, "You're probably here because you're worried about Robert."

"Yes. That's right. Exactly." Poverman beat down the small loop
of gratitude.

"Robert's such a thoughtful fellow. He's quite uncertain about
college now, about his future. I suppose you and Mrs. Poverman
must be concerned."

"Yes," Poverman said again, eagerly, even before he could stop
himself. Oh this guy was smooth. He was a salesman, all right, as
soft as Poverman was hard.

"You're probably upset with the Society of the Holy Word, too."

Poverman clamped his lips but nodded.

"You must think that we've probably poisoned your son's mind."

Poverman nodded again. What else?

"Let's sit down, Mr. Poverman, and let me tell you about us. Briefly. You're probably anxious to get back to your business."

Oh good, good. Oh terrific. All his life Morton Poverman wished he could have been so smooth with customers—buying, selling, complaints, but with him it had always been a frontal attack. A joke, a little screaming or a quick retreat into a deal for twenty percent off. But never like this, quiet, slick as oil, full of probabilities, the ways so easily greased. Yes yes yes where do I sign?

He took Poverman into the back room. Half the room was set up like a small class, rows of metal chairs facing a small table and blackboard. The other half of the room was soft chairs drawn around in a circle. They sat there.

George Fetler described simply and directly what the Society of the Holy Word did as far as Robert Poverman was concerned. On Thursday evening it conducted, right here, right in these soft chairs, discussions about religion generally, Christianity specifically, and most of all the idea that the Bible was the exact word of God.

"That's it?" Poverman asked.

"Let's be frank. Let *me* be frank. If you believe that the Bible is the exact word of God, then that can certainly raise some important questions about how you lead your life henceforth. I think this is what has happened to Robert. He came to us six months ago with two friends. I'm sure he came because his two friends, already Christians, wanted him to come. Like many before him, he came more as a lark, skeptical and doubting. But he read the Bible and he discussed what he read and the questions arose, Mr. Poverman, they just arose. And Mr. Poverman, I just wish you could see him, his openness, his honesty, his intelligence. It is very gratifying. Very." Fetler sat back and locked his hands together in front of him.

"You'll pardon me for asking," Poverman asked anyway, "but how does this all get paid for?"

George Fetler smiled, unlocked his hands, and stood up. "Here. This will explain it in detail." He went out to the tables in the front and returned with a booklet. "This will tell you what you probably want to know, including a financial statement. The Society of the Holy Word is but one arm of the Church of the Resurrection, Incorporated. We're based in Chicago. We've got our printing operation there and headquarters for our evangelical units. The Church also has two colleges, one in San Diego, the other . . ."

"In Nyack?"

"Yes. Has Robert mentioned that? He's thinking of going on our summer retreat there."

"But sooner or later, it all comes down to them—what do you call it?—coming out for Jesus? Right?"

"One need not declare for Christ, but that is what we hope will happen." George Fetler and Morton Poverman were coming closer now to what they thought of the other. "Yes. That is what we hope and pray for."

"Why?"

"It is," George Fetler said, not such a soft guy anymore (no sale here), "the only way to avoid the everlasting torments of Hell."

Morton Poverman had never been able to handle the Christian's Hell. It looked to him like the answer to everything and to nothing. And what did they need it for, this endless knife at the throat? Besides, about Hell—here, now, right away—he had his own ideas. No. Not ideas. Necessities.

His week went on, all his life became a tactical adventure now, no crease in it without its further unexpected bend, no crack that might not open up suddenly into an abyss from which he could not scramble back. This is what he slept with now. Battle. War.

On Thursday evening at seven o'clock he went to the discussion meeting at 183 Pearl Street, to the Society of the Holy Word. And he had studied. From the array of pamphlets and tracts on the tables in the Society's store he had taken copiously. And he had read them, late at night in the back of the store, later than ever, he had read slowly in the bad light, bent to this new labor as the unopened cartons piled up on each other and each morning Francine Feynman would complain of empty this and replaced that.

THE BIBLE SAYS YOU HAVE SINNED!

For all have sinned, and come short of the glory of God (*Rom. 3:23*)

THE BIBLE SAYS YOU DESERVE HELL!

For the wages of sin is death: but the gift of God is eternal life through Jesus Christ our Lord (*Rom. 6:23*)

THE BIBLE SAYS YOU HAVE A CHOICE!

And if it seem evil unto you to serve the Lord, choose you this day whom ye will serve . . . (Joshua 24:15)

THE BIBLE SAYS JESUS DIED FOR YOU!

But God commendeth his love toward us, in that while we were yet sinners, Christ died for us (Rom. 5:8)

THE BIBLE SAYS YOU MUST BELIEVE JESUS!

For whosoever shall call upon the name of the Lord shall be saved (Rom. 10:13)

THE BIBLE SAYS YOU HAVE ETERNAL LIFE!

And this is the record, that God hath given to us eternal life, and this life is in his Son. He that hath the Son hath life. (I John 5:11)

Poverman got himself a Bible and checked it out. It was all there.

There were ten people at the Tuesday night meeting, all as young as Robert or a little older, all regulars, except for the new member, Morton Poverman, who was introduced all around. Also attending were George Fetler and the Reverend Julius Meadly, who more or less conducted things.

It went well enough. After Poverman explained to them that he had come out of interest in his son's interest and his talk with Mr. Fetler, the discussion picked up where, apparently, it had left off last week.

The point of concern, always a tough one Reverend Meadly told them, was whether those born before Christ, before, that is, the opportunity to receive Christ, would go to Hell. The Reverend drew the distinction between Pagans, who had not had the chance to embrace Christ, and the Heathens, those born since Christ who did and do have the opportunity but reject it. Heathens were unquestionably doomed to Hell, but about Pagans there was still some serious debate, for surely Abraham and the Prophets were in Heaven already, and Moses as well as Adam.

They all discussed at length the fairness of this, that those who had had no choice should be so grievously punished. The Reverend said that indeed the ways of the Lord were not always apparent to Man, and they were certainly unfathomable, but it did no good to question what was *not* going to happen to the Pagans, and one should concentrate instead on the glory of what *was* going to happen to the Saved. And he concluded, "You know, sometimes I think that the last chapter and verse isn't completed. That on

Judgment Day, God in his infinite wisdom and mercy will raise up even the unfortunate Pagans." They closed on that high note. Through the evening Robert Poverman had said nothing.

Driving home he said, "What are you doing?"

"What do you mean?" his father said.

"You know what I mean. Why did you come tonight?"

"What's the matter, suddenly it's not a free country. A man can't worship how he wants anymore?"

"Cut it out, Dad. You know what I mean."

"You go to this place because you've got questions, right?" Poverman said. "Well, I've got questions too."

"Like what?"

"Like have you declared for Jesus, or whatever you call it?"

"No."

"Are you going to?"

"I don't know. I can't say."

"Do you believe in all that . . . stuff?"

"I think about it." They drove on in silence. "Are you going back? To another meeting?" Robert asked.

"Yeah. Sure. I still got my questions. What about you? Are you going back?"

Robert did not answer that. "You're not sincere," he said.

But there, Morton Poverman knew, without any doubt at all, his son was wrong.

He hacked at his store and grew bleary with fatigue. What he sold in front he brought in through the back and touched everything once, twice, thrice in its passage. Slips, underwear, dresses, bandanas, now bathing suits and beach or pool ensembles. From passing over all that plastic, his fingertips were sanded as smooth as a safecracker's. And doggedly he studied the Word of the Lord. Bore up his wife. Bore his son.

At the second meeting that Poverman attended, Fetler understood. Robert Poverman, once so animated and involved, would not participate, not in the presence of his father. And the blunt intensity of his father's questions caused the Reverend Meadly to veer about, put his helm over frequently to avoid the jutting rocks of Morton Poverman's intent, not that he was making an argument. He was polite enough, whatever that cost him. But his questions, they were so fundamental.

Almost all of the group had been together for months and had already covered the ecclesiastical ground that was new to him. It was not fair to the group to have to pause so often while the Reverend Meadly (the soul of patience) answered in detail what they all had heard and discussed before. This is what Fetler explained to Poverman after the meeting.

"You're throwing me out?" Poverman said. "You're telling me to go elsewhere with my soul in danger of eternal perdition?" He had studied well. He had the lingo, like in every line of work.

"No no no," Fetler said, growing more pink than ever. Close to him, Poverman could see the blue fretwork of his veining. His whole face was like a stained-glass window. "That would be unthinkable, of course. What I had in mind was our Sunday afternoon group for older people." Poverman shook his head at Sunday afternoon. "Or private instruction," Fetler followed up. Perhaps you could come to us, the Reverend Meadly or me, on another evening? Then we could give you a 'cram course,' so to speak?"

"Ok," Poverman said. They agreed on Tuesday night.

On Tuesday night Poverman met with Reverend Meadly and after two hours of explaining—starting with Genesis (oh it would be a long time before he would be able to rejoin the young group already well into Corinthians), Poverman leaned back and said.

"But it's all faith, isn't it? All this reasoning, all this explaining, if you've got the faith that's all that matters."

"Yes," the Reverend said. "Faith more than anything else."

"And if you get the faith, then what?"

"You must declare it. You must stand forth and join God through His Son, Jesus Christ."

"Yes, but how? I mean could I just say it to you now? Is that enough? Would God know?"

"If you declare yourself through us, the Church of the Resurrection, there are certain formalities."

"A ceremony?"

"Yes, that's right. You must answer certain questions, take certain vows before a congregation."

"What about this?" Poverman produced one of the pamphlets that the Society of the Holy Word published. "Wherever I look, I'm always on trial. Some trial. Listen." He read the fiery, imprescriptible indictment through to the end. "Verdict: Guilty as charged. Appeal: None. Sentence: Immediately eternal, conscious, tormenting, separational death in a burning lake of fire and brimstone.' "

"Well?" Reverend Meadly asked. Nothing else.

"So that's it for me? For Robert?"

"Unless you embrace the Lord Jesus as your Savior, that is your fate and Robert's fate, yes."

"No either/or huh?"

"Either Love or Damnation," Reverend Meadly said. Kindly.

On Thursday Poverman showed up at the meeting. Fetler called him aside. "I thought we agreed that you would work privately?"

"I wouldn't say a single word," Poverman promised. "I'll listen. I'll watch. I can learn a lot that way, and I won't interrupt. Not one word."

But there were no longer any words to say, for Morton Poverman had decided that at long last the time and event had come for God to stand forth and defend Himself, make good his terrible threat and vaunt or scram. He had paid enough with good faith and would not bargain now. He had reached his sticking price. Take it or leave it. What was his, was his, and what belonged to his son, the legacy of his life, for all his—Poverman's—own clumsiness on this earth, *that* he would not let be stolen easily. And whatsoever should raise his hand or voice against his son must answer for that to him.

Thus girded, midway through the meeting Poverman suddenly stood up. The Reverend Meadly had just finished an intricate restatement of Paul's words:

In a moment, in the twinkling of an eye, at the last trump: for the trumpet shall sound, and the dead shall be raised incorruptible, and we shall be changed.

Poverman stood up and said:

"Me too. I have seen the way and the light. I want to declare for Jesus." There was commotion.

"Mr. Poverman!" George Fetler said, standing too, quickly in his alarm.

"Now," Poverman said. "Right now. The spirit is in me." He stepped away from the group of seated young people and then turned to them. "Be ye followers of me, even as I also am of Christ' " he intoned, trying to get it right. One of the group clapped. "I've been thinking and so this is what I want to do, thanks to Reverend Meadly." Reverend Meadly smiled, but Fetler curdled, his pink now blotched redness.

"So what's next?" Poverman asked. "What do I got to do?"

There was a happy excitement in the young people at this immanence of spirit, all the thick words of the past months came true like a miracle. Fetler urged a later time, a more appropriate time for the declaration, but "Now," Poverman insisted. "Between now and later, who knows what could happen? And *then* what about my soul?" He looked at Fetler. "Now."

Robert Poverman, stiff and frozen, watched his father don white robes (cotton/polyester—60/40, not silk) that drooped to the floor and take in either hand a large Bible and a heavy brass crucifix. The classroom was turned into a chapel, the lights dimmed. The Reverend Meadly took his place behind the table. From a drawer in the table he took out a paper.

"Wait," Poverman said. "I want my son Robert to stand next to me. He should see this up close." He motioned Robert to him.

The Reverend said, "You must be delivered to Christ by one who has already received Him. Robert has not yet."

"That's okay," Poverman said. "Let Mr. Fetler deliver me. I just want my son to stand by. This is a big thing for me." And so it was arranged, George Fetler, crimson and his eyes like thin slivers, on Poverman's right, Robert Poverman, cast into numb darkness, on his father's left. "Okay," Poverman said. "Let's go."

It was simple enough. The Reverend would read statements that Poverman would repeat. After a brief preamble in which Reverend Meadly explained the beauty and importance of this glorious step toward Salvation, the ceremony began.

"Oh Lord I have offended thee mightily," Poverman echoed the Reverend Meadly flatly.

"Oh Lord I am an infection of evil that I ask you to heal and make clean," he went on.

"Oh Lord I ask you to break open my hard and selfish heart to allow your mercy into it that I might learn love."

"Oh Lord I have made the world foul with my pride."

"Oh Lord I am a bad man and stained with sin."

"No," Robert Poverman said out of his darkness.

"Sha," his father said. He motioned for the Reverend Meadly with his cross to go on.

"Daddy, please. Stop this. Don't." He wept.

"I am an abomination in Your eyes," the Reverend read from his paper.

"I am an abomination in Your eyes," Poverman said after him.

"NO!" Robert Poverman shouted. Demanded. "NO!" He stepped forward, but his father held out his Bible-loaded hand like a rod.

"Don't you be afraid," he said to his son. "Don't you worry *now*, Sonny," he said. "I'm here." And unsheathing the great sword of his love, he waved it about his balding, sweaty head and advanced upon his Hosts in dubious battle. And fought.

Not without glory.

🔥 🔥 🔥

THE ARCHIVES

OF EDEN

by GEORGE STEINER

from SALMAGUNDI

nominated by SALMAGUNDI *and Louis Gallo*

Preface

by Robert Boyers, editor of Salmagundi

In "The Function of the Little Magazine," an essay first published more than thirty years ago, Lionel Trilling wrote that nothing was more necessary for educated people than "to organize a new union between our political ideas and our imagination." Contemporary liberalism had produced what was in some respects a satisfactory literature of social protest and analysis, a literature "earnest, sincere, solemn," though without those qualities of imagination properly associated with the best literary minds—the minds of Joyce, Lawrence, Yeats, Mann, Eliot, Kafka and a few other writers. To those writers, as Trilling argued elsewhere, the concerns promoted by liberal social critics were decidedly marginal. Students who were taught to read the works of the great modernist masters would be taught implicitly to draw a line around their literary experience, to protect against the contagion that might be spread by permitting their decent political and social views to be unduly affected by the ideas freely circulating in Kafka's Penal Colony or Gide's Immoralist.

In later years, Trilling himself came to be more wary of the peculiar contagion associated with "subversive" ideas, particularly as those ideas became accredited by people who

EDITOR'S NOTE: *This essay was delivered as part of a symposium at Skidmore College. Mr. Steiner's views were disputed by other speakers at that symposium.*

177

espoused them without really taking them seriously. But Trilling never gave up his belief that we needed a fresh "union between our political ideas and our imagination." He did not, perhaps, sufficiently indicate in so many words what that union would bring to pass, and more than one contemporary critic has complained of Trilling's failure to spell out his political convictions. But these critics are best characterized as people for whom the great and necessary task described by Trilling is not a living option, people for whom culture is clearly subordinate to politics. The imagination to which Trilling looked will always seem, to his more virulent critics, a fact best acknowledged and kept out of the way. His idea that a serious intelligence would in some degree submit to the experience recommended by a Yeats or a Kafka—whatever the resistance properly thrown up and maintained—ensured that Trilling would stand a little to the side of his more activist contemporaries who knew better than to have their heads turned by the obsessive ravings of "Genius."

In recent years, it seems to me, a good many Anglo-American intellectuals have addressed themselves to the task Trilling assigned in his early essay. In Salmagundi we have tried to publish chiefly the writings of people who believe that the essential task has yet to be accomplished, that the modernist legacy remains as important as it seemed to Trilling, and that intellectuals can sustain and fruitfully extend the modernist tradition only by refusing to settle for a managed political consensus and the illusion of technological progress. Among those who have stood firm against that illusion and others like it, no one has more strenuously insisted upon the prerogatives of imagination than George Steiner. No one has argued more consistently against the idea that common sense is sufficient to answer every question or to propose ideals on behalf of which people may organize their resources. No one has demonstrated more vividly the way in which a fine mind may be, in his own words, "infected with the leprosy of abstract thought" and yet driven to discover ample ways of keeping faith with the imperatives of sanity and reason. Less wary than Trilling of the subversive ideas associated with high modernist literature and art, he has routinely challenged the established wisdom of the liberal majority, asking unpleasant questions not only about mass culture in general but about the scandal of higher education in America, about the relation between pornography and the language of recent fiction, and about the disaffection of contemporary intellectuals from the values that might make them a significant counter-force in American political life. Deeply unpopular with those who envy the range of his competencies and resent the sometimes sharp insistence of his criticism of modern civilization, he has persisted in putting himself on the line in a way routinely urged upon younger writers by earnest liberals most of whom would never think to try out an "unthinkable" proposition themselves. In so persisting, Steiner has also called into question the validity of certain literary values to which most successful critics and journalists show unwavering allegiance. As—in Donald Davie's words—"an eloquent, ornate and driving writer, above all a copious one," Steiner has had to put up with the contempt of a long line of journalistic and academic hacks whose only claim to literary "mastery" is that they manage to write—again in Davie's terms—with "a dry or casual tone" and with "a conversational or colloquial vocabulary." The fact that such a prose would not have seemed impressive to a Mann or a Lawrence or a Joyce cannot be said to have given even a moment's pause to most of Steiner's detractors.

But the issue for us is not, cannot be, Steiner's prose. What matters is that he has prepared for Salmagundi a long paper on the state of art and intellect in America. The paper repeats and extends what Steiner has been saying in one book after another for twenty years, and breaks new ground mainly in suggesting that American culture, more than any other, must be held accountable for much that we find distressing in the modern world. In the extended comparison Steiner draws between the United States and Europe, readers will inevitably find much that they approve and disapprove. No reader will fail to see that Steiner has gone a long way towards effecting a union between political ideas and qualities of imagination not often found in the precincts of recent social thought. . . .

"The Lord has brought us hither through the swelling seas, through perills of Pyrats, tempests, leakes, fyres, Rocks, sands, diseases, starvings: and has here preserved us these many yeares from the displeasure of Princes, the envy and Rage of Prelats, the malignant Plotts of Jesuits, the mutinous contentions of discontented persons, the open and secret Attempts of Barbarous Indians, the seditious and undermining practices of heretical false brethren." Thus John Winthrop in 1643. This 'bringing hither', this Great Migration, in Puritan parlance, was no common fact of history. Thomas Hooker, back in England, had speculated whether the establishment of the New England polity was not a signal of the end of secular time, for this was the *ne plus ultra* of mundane innovation. Any ulterior discovery and instauration would exceed terrestrial possibilities and herald the beginning of the reign of everlastingness as foretold in Revelation. But the ambiguities in the trope of final renovation, in the theology and sociology of the Edenic, were formidable from the outset.

If New England was the enactment of a fresh Covenant of Grace (Cotton Mather's constant term), if the members of this Covenant benefited from the greatest opportunity of salvation granted to any people since the birth of Christ, were they, in some real sense, 'new men', analogues to Adam? Vexatious, almost socially destructive, controversies over the need and quality of baptism in the new world, over the operative transfer of original sin in the new community and individual, bear witness to the literal, yet opaque, character of the Adamic model. And if the newfound lands of the Covenant of Grace were indeed, as Peter Bulkeley had proclaimed, "as a City set upon an hill, in the open view of all the earth . . . because we profess ourselves to be a people in Covenant of God," and the *only* such people to be found on a lapsed planet— what then of the 'mutinous contentions' and the 'heretical false brethren' cited by Winthrop? What then of the 'barbarous Indians' and the plagues of drought and sickness visited upon the new Jerusalem?

No less ambiguous was the question of the relations to the old world. Perry Miller summarizes one main current of thought (*The New England Mind: The Seventeenth Century*, p. 470): the Puritans "did not, at least in the first settlements, regard themselves as fleeing from Europe but as participating to the full in the great issues of European life; they did not set out to become provincial

communities on the edge of civilization but to execute a flanking
manoeuvre in the all-engrossing struggle of the civilized world."
But a more radical current of severance was also at work. By the
1630s, it was manifest that neither Geneva, nor Amsterdam, nor
Edinburgh had been able to bring to ailing Christendom the light
of enduring rebirth and true Congregation. Soon prelacy and worse
would reassert themselves in the English realm. Episcopacy and
Popery were the universal portents of a nearing apocalypse. The
new Israel must leave behind the places and legacy of damnation.
Thus New England was not only the precise analogue to the
Promised Land, but the Noah's ark in a period of deluge. To look
back would be suicidal. This doctrine of divorcement could,
moreover, justify the problematic harshness of the western Eden:
had the children of Abraham not had to dwell in the desert and
suffer affliction and attack on their journey? The collision between
these two currents or, more accurately, the intricate hybrids and
compromises between them, made the problem of cultural heritage acute. In one sense, the intellectual baggage brought by the
Puritans, the language and the logic of all articulate awareness,
were those of post-Renaissance Europe, with their evident foundations in pagan classicism and Christian humanism. How could it
have been otherwise? Yet in another sense, this legacy carried with
it the very seeds of error and corruption, the histories of scission
and heresy, which had edged man towards ruin. If the Great
Migration was to escape from the blackness of Goshen and take
possession of the New Canaan, it could only do so in the (literal)
light of a newborn knowledge, of an innocence of intellect and
sensibility. Adam's pre-lapsarian wisdom gave warrant for such a
concept of knowledge purged of knowingness, of perfect *natural*
wisdom.

All these antinomies, and the spectrum of intermediate positions
between them, turn on the primary trope of 'felt time', of the
chronological. Was America 'young' or 'old'? Was America the
mundus novus promised by St. John and proclaimed by Spanish
ecclesiastical chroniclers almost immediately after Columbus's
journey? Was it an authentic vestige of the Garden set aside for the
re-entry of the new Adam? In which case, it had no 'history'. Or
was it, on the contrary, an ancient world, no more intemporal and
immune from the inheritance of the Fall than were the lands from
which the Pilgrims came? And what of these new Israelites them-

selves? Some held the Covenant of Grace to be, concretely as it were, regenerative. In the new world man was made new, the vestments of his fallen state stripped from him. Others were less sanguine. Even if this was, or was to be, 'earth's other Eden', it was the Old Adam who had come to it 'through the swelling seas'. Inevitably, he carried with him the contagion of history.

The options, the conflicts of vision implicit in these contrasting suppositions, extend to the whole fabric of American sensibility. They have largely determined the course of American religious and political development, the politics and sociology of American self-definition, the psychological diversities in American public and private conduct. In essence, pragmatic agencies prevailed. The 'City set upon a hill' did not found a new language. It spoke its message of renovation in European tongues and via the logic of Aristotle, of Ramus and, after the 1670s, in that of Descartes. Unlike the Jacobin utopians of September 1792, the men of the new world did not begin a new calendar, a Year One of messianic inception: Yet impulses towards apocalyptic novelty continued to press on the fabric of American institutions and challenges. Utopian communities and movements were a recurrent phenomenon. The Mormons moved on in search of the new and the real Zion. Indeed, the mechanism of the Adamic is one of the fundamental aspects of American history: in the face of political-social atrophy or corruption, the claims of the ideal, of the Covenant of Grace, seen now as a non- or post-theological contract with history, are reaffirmed. Time and again, American consciousness would turn its back on the blighted past; the restlessness of hope points west. The conflict is unresolved. From it springs much of the creative wealth of the American temper. From it, as well, spring essential uncertainties and frustrations in respect of 'culture', of the life of the mind in society as this life has, *mutatis mutandis,* been construed and experienced in the 'old west' since Hellenistic times.

To consider these uncertainties, simply to view them as potentially negative, is to choose, almost unawares, between the two polarities of 'young' and 'old', of the Adamic and the historical. It is to set aside, even if only provisionally and in the service of a working hypothesis, the claim that it is far too soon to attempt any balance-sheet of the American intellectual or artistic achievement. It is to dissent from the belief that we are, substantively, dealing with a 'young culture' some three brief centuries old and that any judgment of its harvest of thought and of its literacies in the perspective of more ancient models is futile and unfair. One's choice in regard to these alternatives is, finally, a matter of instinct, a deep-seated hunch. *It may well be erroneous;* it may well be of a kind which future events or a re-ordering of the intractably manifold evidence will refute. But whoever engages—and this mere engagement may be fatuous—concepts as inchoate, as recalcitrant to agreed definition and transcription, as 'culture', as 'spiritual values', will have to start from instinct, from persuaded arbitrariness if he is to proceed at all.

I take it that American culture has no extraterritoriality to time; that it is not a 'young' culture in any but the most banal and localized sense (i.e. that the institutions in, through which this culture is expressed and disseminated were founded at a later date than their European counterparts and in a physically undeveloped or underdeveloped setting). I am positing that the great conceit of the Edenic, of the American Adam, whatever its manifest theological-political force, whatever its continued translation into later radical and messianic theories and practices of society, is not culturally determinant. The begetters and first organizers of American cultural affairs, in education, in the arts, in the pure and applied sciences, were Europeans whose equipment, whose modes of understanding and argument, were as 'old' as those of the neighbours they left behind. I am assuming that none of the great American re-negotiations of the contract between society and history—be it in the promise of happiness in the Bill of Rights, in the *catharsis* of Jacksonian populism, be it in Woodrow Wilson's New Freedom or Franklin Delano Roosevelt's New Deal—differs, ontologically, from similar renovations in European social history and that none constitutes a *novum* in the sense attached by the Puritans to the covenant with Abraham or the instauration of Mosaic Law. In short: the Puritan programme of a break with the 'corrupt ancientness' and hereditary taint of European history, the great hunger of successive waves of immigrants for a new dispensation free of the terrors and injustice which had marked their communal past, have played a central role in the American imagination and in the rhetoric of American identity. But they do not afford the actual products of American culture a calendar of Arcadian youth, a time of special grace. On the contrary. American culture has stood, from its outset, on giant shoulders. Behind Puritan style lay the sinew of English Tudor, Elizabethan and Jacobean prose. Behind the foundation of American universities lay the experience of Oxford and Cambridge, Aristotelian logic and the mathematics of Galileo and Newton. British empiricism and the world of the *philosophes* underwrite the Jeffersonian vision of an American enlightenment. Goethe stands behind Emerson as Shakespeare and Milton do behind Melville. It may be, as D. H. Lawrence found, that American culture is 'very old' precisely because it has been heir to so much. The New England divines would concur. By the early eighteenth century, William Cooper testified to "God's withdrawal" from a new world whose conditions of spirit and civil practise were no better than in the old. The idiom of his testimony was that of Jeremiah and the Cataline orations, of Juvenal and the Aesopian satirists of the European reformation.

If 'American culture', so far as any meaning worth disagreeing about can be attached to so general a notion, is not *sui generis*, if it is a branch of the classical-Christian aggregate of European civilization, it may be legitimate to ask what its relations to Europe are and where the present centres of gravity lie.

Methodologically, such questions are indefensible. 'American culture(s)' is a pluralistic concept whose diverse components are themselves very nearly as diffuse as their aggregate. No individual can provide anything but the most intuitively vague, partial account of any one aspect of American intellectual-artistic-scientific activity. The notion that one can say anything responsible about the whole construct is patently absurd. There have been histories and analytic deliniations of 'the American mind' at one or another period and attempts at a summarizing profile. Invariably, these have fallen short of the complex and amorphous data. At the very best, one will generalize and drop names in an impressionistic register of guesswork and prejudice. This is exactly what I shall do: to generalize, to drop names. But what other method is there? How else does any critique or inventory of values proceed? The necessary scruple is that of self-irony, of the hope that one's 'indefensible' asking will elicit not so much F. R. Leavis's famous response 'Yes, but' as it will that even more fertile instigation to understanding, 'No, but'.

American philosophy has been thin stuff. There have been

psychologists of undoubted penetration and stylishness, notably William James. There is, certainly since the 1940s, a distinguished school of analytic logic (from Quine, say, to Kripke). American jurisprudence and theory of contract, in the social and ethical sense, has made useful contributions to the general current of western liberal thought. But it is doubtful whether there has been on native ground a major philosophic presence with the possible exception—the work is still, in large measure, unavailable—of C. S. Peirce. And even in this fascinating instance, it is difficult to make out a metaphysics, an attempt at a philosophic discourse from the centre. But it is metaphysics and a central discourse on values which constitute the quality of western philosophy from the Pre-Socratics to the present. It is the endeavor of successive philosophers and schools of reflection, from the Ionian to the existentialist, to 'think being' as a manifold totality and to extend this ontological act to every principal category of human behaviour, which has largely informed the inward history of man and society in the west. Such ontological centrality and continuity has been either derivative in or, indeed, absent from the climate of American feeling. There are, therefore, regards in which the tenor of American feeling is closer to the bias for magic, for pragmatic *bricolage*, current in non-western traditions than it is to the world of Plato and of Kant (one can invoke the singular here because the unitary fabric of western metaphysics has been so striking). The twentieth century offers graphic evidence: there is, quite simply, no American metaphysician, no 'thinker on being', no enquirer into the meaning of meaning to set beside Heidegger or Wittgenstein or Sartre. There is no phenomenology of American provenance comparable to that of Husserl and Merleau-Ponty. No philosophic theology of the order of radical challenge proposed by Bultmann or by Barth. The inheritance of ontological astonishment (*thaumazein*) and systematic response remains unbroken from Heraclitus to Sartre's *Les Mots*. It runs through Aquinas, Descartes, Hume, Kant, Hegel and Nietzsche. There is no American membership in that list. And what I am trying to spell out is not a technical consideration: it is a constant in Hellenic and European existence. The major philosopher is one whose discourse, as it were, successive generations carry on their person. Platonism, Cartesianism, the idealism and moral imperatives of Kant, the historicism of Hegel and Marx, existentialism after Kierkegaard and Nietzsche, have been ways of life, landscapes of private and public motion, for countless men and women entirely innocent of any formal philosophic schooling or specialized interest. Philosophic debate, between Platonists and Aristotelians, between Thomists and Cartesians, between logical positivists and Heideggerians or Sartrians or Bergsonian vitalists, are emphatic elements of political and generational identity. Just now, a fair number of my students carry Gramsci's prison-texts in their left pocket. A fair number carry the prison-writings of Bonhoeffer in their right (the two books being dialectically cognate). The best will carry both. It is 'the book in the pocket' which matters, the espousal of a text as radical and pivotal to private impulse and social stance. It is the Socratic conviction that a community of rational men is one pervaded by explicit philosophic argument and that abstract thought is the true motor of felt life. This conviction is, on the American scene, 'academic' in a sense which I hope to make usefully arguable.

Roger Sessions, Elliott Carter are composers of undoubted stature. Charles Ives is a most intriguing 'original'. Up to this point in its history, however, American music has been of an essentially provincial character. The great symphony of 'the new world' is by Dvorak. It is Varese's *Amériques* which comes nearest to a musical transposition of its spacious subject. Again, limiting oneself to the twentieth century—a limitation inherently weighted in America's favour—it is obvious that there are in American music no names to set beside those of Stravinsky, of Schoenberg, of Bartók, of Alban Berg and Anton von Webern, that the *oeuvre* of a Prokofiev, of a Shostakovich, perhaps even of a Benjamin Britten represents an executive 'density' and imaginative continuity strikingly absent from the work of American composers. And even if the Stockhausen-Boulez era is now passing, its role, its formal and substantive logic in the history of western music, are on a level which, until now, American composers have rarely challenged, let alone matched.

It is, at this point, incumbent on the brief to say something of the development of mathematics in the new world. For me to do so is merely to dramatize incompetence. Anyone with even the most amateurish interest in the field will be able to cite a score of American names close to or at the top of the pyramid. There have been in this century, there continue to be, classic American achievements in every branch of analysis, of algebraic topology, of group theory, of measure theory and stochastics, of number theory. Yet, looked at closely, the roster shows that much of the pre-eminent work has been done *in* America by mathematicians and mathematical thinkers of a foreign origin and schooling (Gödel, von Neumann, Weyl, Bochner, Milner, etc.). And although it is absurd for a layman even to conjecture along these arcane lines, it looks as if much of the fundamental progress, notably in topology and number theory, this is to say in the high reaches of pure rather than applied mathematics, is being made in France, in Russia, in the British school of mathematics, to be taken up thereafter on American ground. (This, at least, is the impression of one who has been a mute witness to the proceedings and recruitment of the Institute for Advanced Study in Princeton.)

The triad metaphysics-music-(pure) mathematics is, of course, purposed. It crystallizes, since Pythagoras and Plato, the singular bent of western sensibility towards abstraction, towards the wholly disinterested, non-utilitarian, non-productive (in any literal sense) play of the mind. It crystallizes the singular western obsession with the creation of sensory "monuments of unageing intellect." The pursuit, even at the risk of personal existence or of the survival of the *polis*, of speculative thought; the invention and development of melody, *mystère suprème des sciences de l'homme* (Lévi-Strauss); the proposal and proof of theorems in pure mathematics—these define, quintessentially, the cancer of the transcendent in western man. It is they, it is the place which education and society afford them, which make of western spiritual history a legacy of Greece.

It is they which, in short-hand, allow, indeed compel a working definition of the concept of a 'high culture'. Why it should be that Thales of Miletus was so absorbed in the predictive calculation of an eclipse that he fell down a well or that Archimedes should, in his garden at Syracuse, have chosen to continue his work on conic sections rather than flee for his life from invading enemies—these remain enigmas of genetics, of climatic and economic environment, of pathological good luck which historians and sociologists of science continue to debate. But the fact is plain enough: the hunter's cry when an abstract verity is cornered, the commitment of personal life to perfectly 'useless' metaphysical or mathematical concerns, the range and formal complexity of music in the west, have their specific source in the Greek 'mental set', have been the basis for our theory and practise of excellence. Personally, I would go further. The evolution of the species has given little ground for comfort. We are, on the whole, a cowardly, murderous bundle of appetites endowed with seemingly limitless instincts of destruction and self-destruction. We are the wasters of the planet and the builders of the death-camps. Ninety-nine percent of humanity conducts lives either of severe deprivation—physical, emotional, cerebral—or contributes nothing to the sum of insight, of beauty, of moral trial in our civil condition. It is a Socrates, a Mozart, a Gauss or a Galileo who, in some degree, compensate for man. It is they who, on fragile occasion, redeem the murderous, imbecile mess which we dignify with the name of history. To be in some touch, however modest, with the motions of spirit and soul in metaphysics and the abstract sciences, to apprehend, however indistinctly, what is meant by the 'music in' and 'of thought', is to attempt some collaboration in the tortuous, always threatened, progress of the human animal (biological progress being on a time-scale which escapes both our understanding and significant intervention). To grasp, to be able to transmit to others some modest paraphrase of the beauty in a Fermat equation or a Bach canon, to hear the hunter's halloo after truth as Plato heard it, is to give life some excuse. This is, I repeat, my own absolute conviction. As such, it is without any general interest. But the fact that such a conviction will strike the vast majority of *educated* Americans as effete or even (politically, socially) dangerous nonsense, may not be without relevance. As may not be irrelevant to the heart of our subject—the state of 'American culture', the relations of this culture to Europe—the fact that American philosophy and music remain of a distinctly secondary order and that much of what is stellar in American mathematics is of a foreign source. Aquinas, Spinoza, Kant have their statues in European cities; my own childhood transpired between the Rue Descartes and the Rue Auguste Comte, between a square dedicated to Pascal and a statue of Diderot. The most voluptuous of central European chocolates is named after Mozart, the most seductive of steak-dishes after Chateaubriand and Rossini. Such *kitsch* pays tribute to a formidable recognition. Why are American streets so silent to the remembrance of thought?

Argument by head-count is tedious. All one wants to indicate are some rubrics for discussion by more competent critics and historians. American painting has been explicitly imitative of European conventions and models until the close of what is now called 'post-Impressionism'. American abstract expressionism, action painting, the parodistic genres of Jasper Johns, of Warhol, of Lichtenstein, the work of de Kooning and of Rothko, point to a veritable explosion of talent and influence. It was plausible to argue, from the mid 1950s to ca. 1975, that the mastering energies in painting and the graphic arts had emigrated from Paris or London to New York. This is no longer the case. It now looks as if much of American art after the second world-war pressed to a conclusion *in extremis* instigations, formal suggestions, contradictions inherent and articulate in the great currents of Russian and west-European abstraction, constructivism, collage, and so on. For all its wit and incandescence, the American scene was one of the epilogues to modernism. This impression may well be myopic. What does seem dubious is that any modern American painter will emerge as possessing a stature, an innovative or recreative strength comparable to that of Marcel Duchamp (perhaps *the* artist-programmer of our century), Braque, Kandinsky and Picasso. It could well be that in the fine and applied arts there are only two fields in which the American performance, to this date, gives unambiguous evidence of innovative genius. These would be architecture, with its obvious links with technology and engineering, and modern dance. It is when a Balanchine or Cunningham ballet is being danced, or when the eye seeks to take in the tower-friez of lower Park Avenue or Pei's addition to the National Gallery in Washington, that the sense of America's 'making it new' is unquestionable. But again, on a continental scale, in terms of a history which has behind it the classical and the European past, this is not an overwhelming harvest.

It is in no Adamic or Pentecostal tongue, such as the Puritans lovingly pondered, that American writers write: it is in English. This banality may well render intractable, if not spurious, the question of 'the Americanness' of American literature. Strictly regarded, American English and the literature it produces is one of the branches, if statistically the most forceful, of the prodigal ramifications of the mother-tongue. Like the language and literature of Canada, Australia, New Zealand, of the Anglo-Indian community, of the West Indies or of the English-speaking nations of Africa, American speech defines itself in interactive terms of dynamic autonomy and of dependence upon the eroded but still canonic primacy of the motherland. In this planetary perspective, American literature is at once dialectal and regional in respect of the source-centre, a formal and structural relation unaltered by the fact that the 'American dialect' is now more and more dominant throughout the English-speaking and, what matters even more, the English-learning world. This 'continentally regional' literature is itself composed of regional elements in the more natural sense of the word. Indeed, the strengths of American literature have, characteristically, revealed themselves in regional clusters and local constellations. The Hawthorne-Melville-Emerson-James grouping in New England, the regionalism of Faulkner, the urban-Jewish and even Yiddish aggregate of Bellow-Mailer-Malamud-Roth-Heller are obvious cases in point. A wary gregariousness, even in expatriation, has marked American literary talent. If the history of American drama has been, in the main, provincial (consider the parochial rhetoric, the crankiness of O'Neill's late plays which, in many respects, represent the decisive achievement in American playwriting), that of American poetry and, pre-eminently, of the American prose novel, has been exhilarating. The decades after the second world war witnessed a general western turn towards the examples and authority of the American novel (*c'est l'heure de roman americain,* proclaimed French critics who had been among the first to spot the seminal role of Dos Passos, Hemingway and Faulkner). The summits are *not* American: they are Thomas Mann, Kakfa, Joyce and Proust. But the general terrain of the novel in the mid-twentieth century has been widely governed and, at vital points, redrawn by American novelists and masters of the short story. The contrast with the palsied state of fiction in England after D. H. Lawrence is drastic. The state of American poetry solicits more tentative, qualified placement. Here the landscape is strewn with critical hyperbole and modishness. How much is there of continuing life in Frost? To what degree will the presence of Wallace Stevens depend on astringent anthologizing? How brief was the period of Robert Lowell's shaping trust in his own considerable but fitful powers? These are unstable areas. One is bound to get magnitudes and relations wrong. The self-evident point is this: in distinction from American philosophy or music, American literature has claims to classic occasion. The 'deep-breathing' necessities of executive form and voice which it manifests (to adapt a phrase from Henry James) are indisputable. The question I want to come back to is a different one: what are the relations between literature and society on American ground (for it is these relations which enter crucially into the notion of 'culture')? How much does American poetry and fiction, even or particularly when it is of major seriousness, matter in America?

If these cursory questions have been worth putting, if there is anything but ignorance or short-sightedness to the observations from which they derive (a likelihood of which I am acutely aware), a paradox should spring to view.

As he takes notice of and part in American daily life, even the most jaundiced of observers will be literally overwhelmed by the scope, generosity, technical brilliance and public prestige of the American cultural enterprise. Museums dot the land. There is scarcely a town or city, however isolated, which does not boast its art gallery, its academy and collection of painting and sculpture. For the American these are no mausolea. No country, with the exception of the Soviet Union, can match the civic, didactic energies and imaginative largesse of the American museum-world. Via lectures, mobile exhibitions, workshops, the dissemination of its holdings through reproductions, the plain fact remains: millions of young and not-so-young Americans (consider night-schools, centres of continuing education, community colleges of every kind) are engaged in the systematic study of the arts and the sciences on a time-scale, in a context of public fiscal support, with access to libraries and laboratories, studios and planetaria, picture-galleries and concert-halls, undreamt-of in history. In short: Americans are engaged, like no other society, in a general pursuit of intellectual and artistic attainment in establishments of tertiary education. Nor does any other society rival the continuity of impulse which reaches out from these establishments into the life of the adult. The alumnus, with his financial, but also intellectual and heuristic stake in the forward-life of the college or university which he has attended, is a singularly American phenomenon. It has been said that Oxford and Cambridge colleges own land whereas American colleges own loyalties. In recent years, in midst of a recession, such institutions as Stanford and Princeton have raised capital from their alumni on a scale which equals the entire budget for higher education in a number of European countries.

Given the institutional eminence and diversity, given the economics of American cultural enterprise—the museums and the symphony halls, the natural history emporia and the pillared 'Athenaeums', the colleges and the universities (is there now a Californian community without one or both?)—can one honestly query the dynamism, the future hopes of the American 'motion of spirit' (*moto spirituale* is Dante's perfectly concrete but resistant tag)? Seen from the gray and ennervation of the European condition, is American culture not precisely what Puritan theodicy and Jeffersonian meliorism saw it to be: a 'City upon a hill', a second wind for the spent runner? The answer is, I think, 'Yes', but it is 'Yes' in a peculiarly paradoxical, even retrograde sense.

The vital clue lies, of course, with that prodigality of conservation and re-transmission to which I have pointed. American museums and art collections are brimfull of classical and European art. European and antique edifices have been brought to the new world stone by literal stone or mimed to the inch. American appetites for the treasures and bric-a-brac of the medieval, the Renaissance or the eighteenth-century past remain devouring. Scarcely a day passes without the translation westward of some further artefact of European glory. American orchestras, chamber groups, opera companies, perform European music. The resistance to new American compositions on the part of impresarios, conductors and, presumably, their audiences, is notorious. As is the massive conservatism of the symphonic and operatic repertoire. More new or experimental operas are produced in the opera houses of provincial Germany in a year than in the Metropolitan in a decade. The commissioning and performance of new music by the BBC in Britain, by the Cologne and South-West German Rundfunk broadcasting networks, by the research-centres for music at Beaubourg or in Milan, have no real parallel in the Victoriana of the American operatic-orchestral and classical-music establishment. New York has yet to hear Schoenberg's greatest opera, and when this 'revolutionary' event will take place, it will, naturally, have a European cause and substance. American libraries are the manifold Alexandria of western civilization. In them are to be found the accumulated treasures and trivia of the European millennia, the Shakespeare folios and the ephemera of a hundred languages. Communities with no tolerable bookstore— Bloomington, Indiana, Austin, Texas, Palo Alto, California—

enshrine the incomparable archives of the literatures of Europe in the nineteenth and twentieth centuries or the documents, periodicals, personal memoirs, graphic memorabilia of whole decades of European thought and calamity. It is to Widener Library that Soviet scholars must travel in search of the pre-October and Leninist past; it is to Rice University in Texas that English bookmen must journey if they wish to explore in depth the Brontës and their background; it is to the Folger in Washington, to the Huntingdon in Pasadena that the Shakespeare-editor proceeds for his collations. If Europe was to be laid waste again, if the wolves, as a chronicler of the Thirty Years' War put it, were to take lodging in its cities, very nearly the sum total of its literatures, of its historical archives, together with a major and representative portion of its art, would survive in America's safe-keeping. It was as if the American Adam, on re-entering the Garden, had brought with him the enormous lumber of his passage through history.

This, then, is my surmise: the dominant apparatus of American high culture *is that of custody.* The institutions of learning and of the arts constitute the great archive, inventory, catalogue, storehouse, rummage-room of western civilization. American curators purchase, restore, exhibit the arts of Europe. American editors and bibliographers annotate, emend, collate, the European classics and the moderns. American musicians perform, often incomparably, the music which has poured out of Europe from Guillaume de Machaut to Mahler and Stravinsky. Together, curators, restorers, librarians, thesis-writers, performing artists in America underwrite, reinsure the imperilled products of the ancient Mediterranean and the European spirit. America is, on a scale of unprecedented energy and munificence, the Alexandria, the Byzantium of the 'middle kingdom' (that proud Chinese term) of thought and of art which is Europe, and which is Europe still. Again and again, the impetus of American modernism, most particularly in poetry, has been paradoxically antiquarian. T. S. Eliot and Ezra Pound, Robert Lowell in *History*, have laboured to re-assemble into comely order, to inventorize and anthologize by inspired quotation, the whole of the European past.These poet-critics are erudite tourists racing through the museum galleries and libraries of Europe on a mission of inventory and rescue before closing time. And if the *American Poetry Review* is anything to go by, the change since Lowell is only this: it is not the British Museum, the Uffizzi or the Louvre which is seminal today, but the National Museum of Amerindian Art and Archaeology in Mexico. Thus it is that American museums stage sovereign shows of Picasso or of Henry Moore, but that American painting and sculpture do not generate canvases or statues which would make for a comparable *oeuvre;* that American orchestras play Schoenberg and Bartók rather than American composers whom, reasonably I think, they deem of distinctly lesser stature; that American philosophers edit, translate, comment upon and teach Heidegger, Wittgenstein or Sartre but do not put forth a major metaphysics; that the pressure of presence throughout the world of the mind and of moral feeling exercised on civilization by a Marx, a Freud, even a Lévi-Strauss, is of a calibre which American culture does not produce. That this disparity continues in a century in which America has achieved unprecedented economic prosperity while Europe has twice lurched to the brink of suicide, seems to me to point to fundamental differences in value-structure (some of which I will touch on briefly). If these differences are indeed fundamental, and if we are looking not at a 'young' culture yet to find its own life-forces but an 'old' and a 'museum-culture', then it may follow that, in some cardinal domains at least, America will not produce first rate contributions.

This is both a desolate and impudent supposition. One must, of course, resist it. It does, however, press on me in what is one of the high places in the American pantheon: the Coolidge room in the Library of Congress. Here hang the finest Stradivarius violins, violas, cellos on earth. They hang lustrous, each milimeter restored, analysed, recorded. They hang safe from the vandalism of the Red Brigades, from the avarice or cynical indifference of dying Cremona. Once a year, unless I am mistaken, they are taken from their cases and lent for performance to an eminent quartet. Haydn, Mozart, Beethoven, Bartók fill the room. Then back to their sanctuary of silent preservation. Americans come to gaze at them in pride; Europeans in awed envy or gratitude. The instruments are made immortal. And stone dead.

Suppose these hunches or provocations to be worth disagreeing with. How, then, is one to 'think the contradiction'? On the one hand, there is America, 'the morning star of the spirit', as Blake saw it. On the other, in the words of that influential poet from St. Louis and the Maine coast, a culture principally engaged in 'shoring up (European) fragments to set against its ruin'. What dialectic will relate the frontier and the archive, the Adamic and the antiquarian?

Cogent answers go back at least as far as de Tocqueville. But the libertarian cant which now inflects political and social discourse in the United States does not make it easy to touch frankly on their demographic components. Like the trope of the new Eden, that of the 'pioneer' comports an unexamined force of vitalism. Implicit in it is the presumption of élan, of a westward ho of men and women resolute, equipped to brave the fearful perils of the voyage and of the wilderness in order to build the new Jerusalem. There *were* such men and women, beyond doubt. There were pilgrims and frontiersmen who would, had they remained in 'the old country', have risen to the top. But the great mass of emigrants were not pioneers; they were fugitives, they were the hounded and defeated of Russian and of European history. If there is any common denominator to their manifold flight, it is precisely this: the determination to opt out of history in its classical and European vein, to abdicate from the historicity of injustice, of suffering, of material and psychological deprivation. It is in this regard that the recurrent analogy between Zionism, as it reaches back into the claustrophobic fantasies of the ghetto, and the 'Zionism' of the Puritan or the Mormon, is wholly deceptive. The return to Israel is a willed re-entry into tragic history. The march to New Canaan or Mount Sion in Utah is a negation of history. In this sense, it may well be that the ethnic-demographic elements in the successive waves of American settlement are 'Darwinian negative', that they embody the brilliant survival of an anti-historical species, where 'anti-historicism' would entail an abdication from those adaptive mechanisms of tragic intellectuality, of ideological 'caring' (Kierkegaard's, Heidegger's word *Sorge*) which are indispensable to cultural creation of the first rank. Those who abandoned the various infernos of social discrimination and tyrannical rule in Europe were not, perhaps, the bold and shaping spirits, but very ordinary human beings who could 'no longer take it'. Those who saw in the Russian, Balkan, Mediterranean and west European condition nothing but a dead end were, perhaps, not the great forward dreamers of 1789, 1848, 1870, or 1917, but the carriers of the gene of tired common sense. Send me "The wretched refuse of your teeming shore," urges the Statue of Liberty. Could it be that Europe did just that?

The counter-examples are so dramatic as to make the argument almost unassailable. The obvious exceptions to the intellectual, cultural norm of immigration are the Puritan in seventeenth-century New England and the Jewish refugee of the 1930s and 40s. Both represent an élite whose impact proved to be overwhelmingly greater than its numbers. The latter case has been studied in detail. It is scarcely an exaggeration to say that the explosive excellence of American pure and natural sciences (notably physics) between, say, 1938 and the 1970s is the direct consequence of Nazi and fascist persecution. This persecution brought to America what is almost undoubtedly the intellectually most gifted community since fifth-century Athens and Renaissance Florence, that of the post-ghetto middle-class Jews of Russia, Central Europe, Germany and Italy. It is the community of Einstein and of Fermi, of von Neumann and of Teller, of Gödel and of Bethe. American Nobel Prizes in the sciences have been its address-book. But this formidably selected immigration animated far more than the sciences. Intellectual and art-history, the classics, musicology, *Gestalt* psychology and social theory, jurisprudence and econometrics, as they flourish in American colleges, universities and research-institutes during and after world war two, are the immediate product of the Central European and Slavic *diaspora*. As is the *floreat* of art-galleries and of symphonic orchestras, of intellectual journalism and of quality publishing in that nerve-centre of the mid-century we call Manhattan. Think away the arrival of the Jewish *intelligentsia*, think away the genius of Leningrad-Prague-Budapest-Vienna and Frankfurt in American culture of the past decades, and what have you left? For the very concept of an *intelligentsia*, of an élite minority infected with the leprosy of abstract thought, is radically alien to the essential American circumstance. Till the current recession bit hard, American institutions of higher learning, American orchestras and museums, publishers in search of senior editors or the *New Yorker* looking for critics, have been able to bid for European talent. Refugees, emigrants, guests by choice have continued to arrive, though in relatively small numbers. The Vietnam war and economic crisis have very nearly halted the 'brain-drain'. In numerous quarters, the cheerful undergrowths of mediocrity and of the provincial are already encroaching on the inspired clearings made in the 1940s and 50s. What if there is no further *diaspora* of excellence? The question is not hypothetical. Oppenheimer posed it starkly the last time I saw him. He had been, both at Los Alamos and at the Institute in Princeton, the shepherd of the prize European flock. Where, he asked, were the American successors to Bohr and von Neumann, to Szilard and to Fermi, to Panofsky and to Kantorowicz, to Auerbach and to Kelsen? The appointments Oppenheimer made at the end are eloquent: a Frenchman and an Englishman in pure mathematics, a somewhat younger member of the refugee galaxy in art history, an historian from London. Can such importation continue?

After de Tocqueville, the pertinent headings could be those argued by Veblen and Adorno. In the Puritan scheme, secular culture was ancillary to, instrumental towards the theological centre. Successive generations of immigrants and settlers might bring with them a cultural inheritance but had to establish *de novo* its institutional media. Such instauration was, necessarily, a by-product of more primary disciplines of survival and social-political consolidation. From the outset, the secular arts and sciences, the constructs of speculative thought and of the imaginary had, in America, an unavoidable strain of artifice, of willed implantation. To reverse Ezra Pound's famous phrase, it was the Muses' diadem itself which was "an adjunct". This, together with an instinct for palpable organisation which informs both the American political and industrial-technological performance, led to the development of culture as craft, as specialization. Adorno's mordant term is *Kulturproduktion*, the application to cultural values and embodiments of intense professionalism, of manufacturing practises and packaging. 'Culture', the arts, literature, can be set high, can be monumentalized. But the resultant phenomenology is immediately reflective of the division of labour, of the ideals of efficacy, crucial to the American ethos. It is a 'thing out there', to be brought into and maintained in being by specialists (the academic, the curator, the impresario, the performing artist). Its interactions with the community at large are those of ostensible presentment, of contractual occasion rather than of anarchic and subversive pervasiveness.

Perhaps the distinction can best be made this way: the main enactments of American cultural life are organised (superbly so) rather than organic. Inevitably also, this organisation will take on the prevailing cast of economic valuation. The cultural, in Veblen's idiom, becomes a part of the overall dynamics of conspicuous consumption. There is not only *Kulturproduktion*, but a competitive marketing of the achieved product. Almost before it enters into the disinterested, if always problematic, zone of art, the American aesthetic, intellectual, literary product is made artifact. The energies against solitude, against the mystery of neglect on which the deployment and subterranean daemon of education in great art seems to depend, are compelling. A *bourse* of unequalled hunger and competitive largesse waits daily for new issues. Its investment in the artist or thinker is, quite literally, a trading in 'futures'. Successful issues rise to dizzying heights of display and reward; bankruptcy is no less swift. Master-critics or brokers of the value-market have been known to 'make or break' playwrights, novelists, composers, painters. The media, the clients follow their markings. There is not, or only rarely, that private rebellion of judgment, that prodigality and incoherence of critical debate which, given much humbler and decentralized economic conditions, enables a play in London or Paris, a painter in Newcastle or Barcelona, a publishing house in Sheffield or Bari, not only to endure in the face of metropolitan repudiation, but to generate (to 'invent', as it were) its own public. The which 'invention' is a decisive element in the penetration of artistic, philosophic, literary 'issues'—allowing both the technical and the general sense of the word—into the ordinary, quotidian awareness of a society. These are not points which it is easy to put concisely and transparently. They implicate the deep layers of social history. They are made manifest, if at all, in tidal motions across centuries. But, nevertheless, it may be worth supposing that the twofold impetus of 'cultural production' and of 'conspicuous consumption', an impetus immediately related to the initial planning and technical apartness of the life of intellect in the new world, does provide some explanation for the *conservative exhibitionism* to which I have pointed. *Kulturproduktion* and investment in competitive display would, indeed, help to account for a culture of museums, academies, libraries, institutes of advanced study. The name of a recent addendum to this list, Research Park in North Carolina, is compact with connotations of both the Adamic and the mummified.

The riposte is self-evident. The pervasive density, the organicism of high culture in Europe is or was, until very recently, illusory. Those freely involved were a small caste, a more or less mandarin élite which happened to possess the instruments of articulate political and pedagogic enforcement. If European streets and squares are studded with the monumental vestiges of art and intellect, if debates on abstruse points in political theory (Aron *contra* Sartre) or Byzantine issues in the theory of culture (Leavis *contra* Snow) are front-page and even television news, if one's lobster is called by the name of Robespierre's red and fatal month of Thermidor, if examination questions in European schools and universities are published and argued nationally—all this is simply because the bureaucratic shamans of high literacy have, for essentially strategic purposes, imposed their (often hypocritical) sublimity on a numbed, indifferent or basically recalcitrant lower class. If they have any substance whatever, the handicaps or dilemmas which I have suggested in reference to artistic reaction and philosophic thought of the first rank in America, are inseparable from the democratic ideals and populist proceedings of the new world.

Often invoked, this argument is intuitively satisfying. In fact, it demands careful handling. The Periclean vision of the essential worth of a society in terms of its intellectual, spiritual, artistic radiance, the Socratic-Platonic criterion of the philosophically-examined individual life and of a hierarchy of civic merit in which intellect stood supreme were, presumably, formulated and codified 'from above'. But collective accord in this vision, whether spontaneous or conventional, *is* an authentic feature in classical and European social history. What we can reconstruct of communal participation in medieval art and architecture, of the passionate outpouring of popular interest in the often competitive, agonistic achievements of Renaissance artists and men of learning, of the complex manifold of adherence which made possible the Elizabethan theatre audience, is not nostalgic fiction. Nor is the witness borne today by the thousands and ten thousands who come to look on the most demanding of modern arts at Beaubourg. In other words: the notion that artistic-intellectual creation is the crown of a city or of a nation, that 'immortality' is in the hands of the poet, the composer, the philosopher, the man or woman infected with transcendence and *le dur désir de durer* (a phrase coined, as it h?ppens, by a marxist and 'populist' poet), is inwoven in the fabric of Hellenic, of Russian, of European values, public styles and, above all, educational practises. I repeat: there may well be in this inweaving a large part of hierarchic imposition, and it may well be that acceptance by the mass of the population has been conventional or halfhearted. But this acceptance is made manifest, it is *taught*. The American commitment to an existential, to a declaredly open economic value-system is unprecedented. The adoption, on a continental scale, of an eschatology of monetary-material success represents a radical cut in regard to the Periclean-Florentine typology of social meaning. The central and categorical imperative that to make money is not only the custom-ary and socially most useful way in which a man can spend his earthly life—an imperative for which there is, certainly, precedent in the European mercantile and pre-capitalist ethos—is one thing. The eloquent conviction that to make money is also the most *interesting* thing he can do, is quite another. And it is precisely this conviction which is singularly American (the only culture, correla-tively, in which the beggar carries no aura of sanctity or prophecy). The consequences are, literally, incommensurable. The ascription of monetary worth defines and democratizes every aspect of profes-sional status. The lower-paid—the teacher, the artist out of the limelight, the scholar—are the object of subtle courtesies of con-descension not, or not primarily, because of their failure to earn well, but because this failure makes them less *interesting* to the body politic. They are more or less massively, more or less consciously patronized, because the 'claims of the ideal' (Ibsen's expression) are, in the American grain, those of material progress and recompense. *Fortuna* is fortune. That there should be Halls of Fame for baseball-players but no complete editions of classic American authors; that an American university of accredited standing should, very recently, have dismissed thirty tenured teachers on grounds of utmost fiscal crisis while flying its football squads to Hawaii for a single game; that the athlete and the broker, the plumber and the pop-star, should earn far more than the pedagogue—these are facts of life for which we can cite parallels in other societies, even in Periclean Athens or the Florence of Galileo. What we cannot parallel is the American resolve to proclaim and to institutionalize the valuations which underlie such facts. It is the sovereign candour of American philistinism which numbs a European sensibility; it is the frank and sometimes sophisticated articulation of a fundamentally, of an ontologically *immanent* economy of human purpose. That just this 'immanence' and ravenous appetite for material reward is inherent in the vast majority of the human species; that we are a poor beast compounded of banality and greed; that it is not the spiky fruits of the spirit but creature comforts we lunge for—all this looks more than likely. The current 'Americanization' of much of the globe, the modulation from the sacramental to the cargo-cult whether it be in the jungles of New Guinea or the hamburger-joints, laundromats and supermarkets of Europe, points to this conclusion. *It may be that America has quite simply been more truthful about human nature than any previous society. If this is so, it will have been the evasion of such truth, the imposition of arbitrary dreams and ideals from above, which has made possible the high places and moments of civilization.* Civilization will have endured after Pericles by virtue, to quote Ibsen again, of a 'life-lie'. Russian or European power-relations and institutions have laboured to enforce this 'lie'. America has exposed it or, pragmatically, passed it by. The difference is cardinal.

But let us assume that the 'élite model' is correct. Let us assume that the "touchstones" (Matthew Arnold) of human excellence in the arts, in the life of intellect, in the pure and exact sciences are, at any given time, the product of the very few—this, surely, is almost a tautology—and that the context of echo, of valuation and transmission which these products require in order to endure and to energize culture—what F. R. Leavis designated, in a somewhat deceptive phrase, as "the common pursuit"—is, in turn, in the custody of a minority. The evidence points, very nearly overwhelmingly, to just such an assumption. The number of men and women capable of painting a major canvas, of composing a lasting symphony, of postulating and proving a fundamental theorem, of presenting a metaphysical system or of writing a classic poem, is, even on the millennial scale, very restricted indeed. Again, the current ecumenism of liberal hopes (or bad conscience) makes it difficult to discuss the vital issue of the sources of high art and intellect. But that these sources are 'genetic', though, very possibly, in a sense subtler and more resistant to biological-social analysis than nineteenth-century positivism supposed, that they are, in some way, 'prepared-for mutations' within very special hereditary and environmental matrices, is eminently probable. One says: 'and environmental', because there can be no doubt that environmental factors *are* significant, notably in respect of inhibition, of the blockage of a latent vocation. But this significance can be, has often been, vastly overstated in the perspective of egalitarian myths and ideals. The curve of genius, even of high talent is, most likely, inelastic. Environmental support might add to the distribution at this or that point; it might have filled one or another gap in the line. But there is no evidence whatever that the multiplication of piano lessons throughout the community will generate one additional Bach, Mozart or Wagner. It is at the absolutely indispensable but, of course, secondary level of understanding, executive performance and transmission that the argument becomes more elusive. Here it is plausible to contend that better schooling, a wider spectrum of leisure, a general elevation in the material condition of private and public life, do matter. It seems almost self-evident that the appreciation of serious art, literature or music, a more general awareness of philosophic debate and scientific discovery and a willingness to respond actively to the instigations of meaning and of beauty, can be markedly augmented or curtailed by the economic and social context. I would not quarrel with this truism; only sound a cautionary note. The effects of environmental amelioration on the prevailing level of aesthetic, philosophic, scientific literacy and 'response-threshold' seem to be slow, diffuse and, rigorously considered, marginal. It does look, and this is a somewhat perplexing phenomenon, as if the number of human beings capable of responding intelligently, with any genuine commitment of sensibility, to, say, a Mozart sonata, a Gauss theorem, a sonnet by Dante, a drawing by Ingres or a Kantian proposition and deductive chain, is, in any given time and community, very restricted. It is, obviously, much larger than that of the creators and begetters themselves. But it is not exponentially larger. And, what is even more puzzling, its increase by means of educational and environmental support, though material, is not exponential either. (Somewhere in this opaque area may lie the explanation for the often-noticed fact that great critics—and a great critic is nothing but a loving, clairvoyant parasite feeding on the life of art—are so rare.) In brief: no amount of democratization will multiply creative genius or the incidence of truly great thought.

And although democratization, i.e. the extension of better education, of more leisure, of a more liberal space of personal existence, to a greater number will add to the 'supporting cast' in civilization, it will not add massively, let alone without limit.

So be it. A number of corollaries follow. To generalise the Periclean or Socratic formula, man's often undone, generally fractional advance from animality can be measured, if at all, in terms of his artistic, philosophic, scientific creations and conjectures. We are the creatures of the bingo hall and the concentration camp. But we are also the species from which Plato and Mozart sprang (or broke loose). If man's condition, if man's bestial history has any meaning whatever it lies, quite simply, in trying to shift, however minutely, the two halves of the equation, in trying, as it were, to add an occasional factor to the 'Plato-Mozart' end. The first thing a coherent culture will do, therefore, is to maximalize the chances for the quantum leap, for the positive mutation which is genius. It will try to keep its educational-performative-social institutions open-ended, vulnerable to the anarchic shock of excellence. As I have emphasized, such open-endedness, such alertness to the sudden track of the supremely-charged particle in the cloud-chamber of society, will not, materially, increase the percentage of artistic, philosophic greatness. But it may do something towards lessening the inhibitions, the densities of obtuseness, which can stifle greatness or deflect it from its full course. A coherent culture will do a second and much more important thing. It will construe its public value-scale and its school-system, its distribution of prestige and of economic reward, so as to maximalize the 'resonant surface', the supporting context for the major work of the spirit. It will do its utmost to educate and establish a vital audience for the poet and composer, a community of critical echo for the metaphysician, an apparatus of responsible vulgarization for the scientist. In other words, an authentic culture is one in which there is an explicit pursuit of a literacy itself focused on the understanding, the enjoyment, the transmission forward, of the best that reasons and imagination have brought forth in the past and are producing now. An authentic culture is one which makes of this order of response a primary moral and political function. It makes 'response' 'responsibility', it makes echo 'answerable to' the high occasions of the mind. I have said that such pursuit, through education and improved environment, does not have a boundless yield. The number of true 'respondents' will remain fairly small. The conclusion—as Athens and the European *polis* after Athens have drawn it—seems ineluctable. A culture, in the precise sense of the word, is one in which the small number of effective receivers and transmitters of art and of intellect will be placed to greatest advantage, in which they will be given the means to extend what they can of their obsession with transcendence to the community at large. To divorce the springs of civilization from the concept of a minority is either self-deception or a barren lie.

Yet it is on this divorce that the theory and practise of American secondary education in the twentieth century are founded. Whereas European meritocracy, open-ended at the base, sharply narrowed at the apex, seeks to select and recruit a minority capable of serving excellence, the American pyramid is, as it were, inverted. It would make excellence fully accessible to the vulgate. This desideratum is inherently antinomian. It labours to correct the oversight or snobbery of God, the failure of nature to disseminate generally and equitably among men the potential for response to the disinterested, the abstract, the transcendent. This correction can only be undertaken at the cultural end of the stick. One cannot, beyond a severely limited and superficial degree, inject sensibility and intellectual rigour into the mass of society. One can, instead, trivialize, water down, package mundanely, the cultural values and products towards which the common man is being directed. The specific result is the disaster of pseudo-literacy and pseudo-numeracy in the American high school and in much of what passes for so-called 'higher education'. The scale and reach of this disaster have become a commonplace of desperate or resigned commentary. The pre-digested trivia, the prolix and pompous didacticism, the sheer dishonesty of presentation which characterize the curriculum, the teaching, the administrative politics of daily life in the high-school, in the junior college, in the open-admission 'university' (how drastically America has devalued this proud term), constitute the fundamental scandal in American culture. A fair measure of what is taught, be it in mathematics, be it in history, be it in foreign languages, indeed with regard to native speech, is, in the words of the President of Johns Hopkins, "worse than nothing." It has produced what he calls "America's international illiteracy" or what Quentin Anderson entitles "the awful state of intellectual affairs in this country."

Does this 'awfulness' not run counter to the widespread and public support for the arts and music which I have referred to earlier? I think not. But the point is one that needs to be made accurately. In the American élite such support embodies authentic response and involvement. In the great mass of cultural fellow-travellers—they are a great mass precisely because of the pseudo-values instilled in them by a totally superficial and mendacious populist ideal of general education—this support signifies only passivity, 'conspicuous consumption', the treatment of the cultural as a unit of economic-social display. Here there is no "common pursuit" but, to reverse Leavis's phrase, a "common flight", an evasion from the political connotations and intellectual discomforts inseparable from major art and thought. The conjunction of an élite profoundly ill at ease in respect of its own status and function in a mass-consumer Eden together with a *profanum vulgus* numerically enormous and committed to self-flattering passivity in the face of excellence is, precisely, that which would generate the 'exhibitionist conservatism', the archival ostentation, of American cultural emporia. The incunabula and first editions shimmer inert in the hushed sanctuary of the Beinecke Library in New Haven, untouched by human hands (as is most of American bread). The Stradivarius hangs mute in the electronically-guarded case.

An élite "profoundly ill at ease": why should it be? Those Americans who have troubled to consider the matter at all have entertained the shrewd suspicion that high culture and the hierarchic structure of artistic-intellectual values on the European model are not an unmixed blessing. From Thoreau to Trilling, there has been in the sensibility of the American *intelligentsia* a nagging doubt about the relations between the humanities and the humane, between institutions of intellect and the quality of political-social practices. It is not only (a point made emphatically in Whitman) that such institutions are exclusive, that they select against the common man in an inevitable subversion of genuine democracy. This would be damaging enough, given the American experiment in equal human worth. It is that the fabric of high literacy in the Periclean and European vein offers little protection against political oppression and folly. Civilization, in the elevated and formal sense, does not guarantee civility, does not inhibit social violence and waste. No mob, no storm-troop has ever hesitated to come down the Rue Descartes. It is from exquisite

Renaissance loggias that totalitarian hooligans proclaim their will. Great meta-physicians can become rectors of ancient universities in, at least, the early days of the Reich. Indeed, the relations between evaluative appreciation of serious music, the fine arts, serious literature on the one hand and political behaviour on the other are so oblique that they invite the suspicion that high culture, far from arresting barbarism, can give to barbarism a peculiar zest and veneer. American thinkers on the theory and practice of culture have long sensed this paradox. The price which the Athenian oligarchy, the Florentine city-regime, the France of Louis XIV or the Germany of Heidegger and Furtwängler have paid for their aesthetic-intellectual brilliance is too steep. The sacrifice of social justice, of distributive equity, of sheer decency of political usage implicit in this price is simply too great. If a choice must be made, let humane mediocrity prevail. Feeling the manifest force of this line of insight, having articulated this force within its own expressive means, the American cultural establishment is sceptical of itself and apologetic towards the community at large. This self-doubt and defensiveness have produced a subtle range of attitudes all the way from mandarin withdrawal to public penitence. It is the latter, with its embarrassing rhetoric of radical *angst*, with its attempts to obtain forgiveness and even approval from the young, which has been particularly prominent during and since the start of the civil rights movements and the Vietnam war. It is not merely that there has been, exactly along the lines of Benda's prophetic analysis, a "treason of the clerics": the clerics have sought pardon and rejuvenation by seeking to strip themselves of their own calling. One need hardly add that this masochist exhibitionism is often dramatized by the inherent malaise of the Jewish intellectual and middle-man of ideas in an essentially gentile setting. But let me repeat: whatever the unappetizing, risible currency of scholars or teachers seeking to howl with the wolves of the so-called 'counter-culture', the roots of their anguish reach deep and to a valid centre. The correlations between classic literacy and political justice, between the civic institutionalization of intellectual excellence and the general tenor of social decency, between a meritocracy of the mind and the overall chances for common progress, *are* indirect and, it may well be, *negative*. It is this latter possibility, with all that it comports of paradox and suffering, that I want to turn to in the final motion of my argument.

That the "touchstones" of human genius are the products of the very few, that the number of those truly equipped to recognise, experience existentially and then transmit these "touchstones" is also limited are, I submit, self-evident truths, almost banalities. The genesis of supreme art or thought or mathematical imagining resists adequate analysis, let alone predictive or experimental control. But historical record does suggest something of the matrix of creation, of the individual and contextual elements in, through which the alchemy of great art or philosophy operates. One element seems to be that of privacy *in extremis*, of a cultivation of solitude verging on the pathological (Montaigne's tower, Kierkegaard's room, Nietzsche's clandestine peregrinations). Or to put it contrastively: absolute thought is antisocial, resistant to gregariousness, perhaps autistic. It is a leprosy which seeks apartness. Now there is in American history and consciousness a recurrent motif of solitude. But it is *not* the solitude of Diogenes or of Descartes. To enforce the difference, to show how profoundly civic and neighbourly was Thoreau's stay at Walden Pond, would need careful documentation. But the fact is there, I think. And in the American grain, as a whole, it is gregariousness, suspicion of privacy, a therapeutic distaste in the face of personal apartness and self-exile, which are dominant. In the new Eden, God's creatures move in herds. The therapeutic primal impulse, as Rieff has argued, extends further. The American instinct is one of succour, privately and socially, of companionable cure for the infections of body and soul. In America epilepsy is no holier than beggary. Where body or soul sicken, medication is the categorical imperative of personal decency and political hope. But one need not mouth romantic platitudes on art and infirmity, on genius and madness, on creativity and suffering, in order to suppose that absolute thought, the commitment of one's life to a gamble on transcendence, the destruction of domestic and social relations in the name of art and 'useless' speculation, are part of a phenomenology which is, in respect of the utilitarian, social norm, pathological. There *is* a strategy of chosen illness in Archimedes' decision to die rather than relinquish a geometric deduction (this gesture being the talisman of a true clerisy). And there *are* contiguities, too manifold, too binding for doubt between the acceptance, indeed the nurture of physical and emotional singularity on the one hand and the production of classic art and reflection on the other. The inhibitions, the cruel handicaps imposed upon, available to a Pascal, a Mozart, a Van Gogh, a Galois (the begetter of modern algebraic topology done to deliberate death at the age of twenty-one), the *cordon sanitaire* which a Wittgenstein could draw around himself in order to secure minimal physical survival and total autonomy of spirit—these are not only hard to come by in the teeming benevolence of the new world, they are actively countered. It is almost a definition of America to say that it is a *Prinzip Hoffnung* (Ernst Bloch's famous term for the institutionalized, programmatic eschatology of hope) in which a psychiatric social worker waits on Oedipus, in which a family counselling service attends on Lear. 'And there are, my dear Dostoevsky, cures for epilepsy.'

The point has been made often (most acutely in James's *Golden Bowl* and in Henry Adam's *Education*). American history is replete with tragic occasion. But such occasion is precisely that: a contingent disaster, a failing to be amended, the fault of circumstances which are to be altered or avoided. The American Adam is not an innocent—far from it. But he is a corrector of errors. He has, after its brief and creative role in the New England temper, all but abandoned even the metaphor of original sin. The notion that the human condition is, ontologically, one of 'dis-grace', that cruelty and social injustice are not mechanical defects but 'primaries' or 'elementals' in history, will seem to him defeatist mysticism. No less so the hunch that there are between tragic historicism, between the concept of 'fallen man' and the generation of the unageing monuments of intellect and of art instrumental affinities. It may be that these monuments, born of autistic vision, are counter-statements to a world felt, known to be 'fallen'. There is in eminent art and thought a manichaean rebellion. "A veritable soul," taught Alain, the French *maître de pensèe* (itself a phrase significantly untranslatable), "is the refusal of a body." There can be no didactic sophistry more un-American, no ideal more alien to the pragmatic immanence of "the pursuit of happiness."

The upshot is this. There is little evidence that civilization civilizes any but a small minority or that its deployment is effective outside the elusive domain of enhanced private sensibility. The relations of such enhancement to civic standards of behaviour, to political good sense, are, at best tangential. There is, on the other hand, substantial evidence to suggest that the generation and full valuation of eminent art and thought will come to pass (preferrentially, it seems) under conditions of individual *anomie*, of anarchic or even pathological unsociability and in contexts of political autocracy—be it oligarchic *ancien regime* or totalitarian in the modern cast. "Censorship is the mother of metaphor," notes Borges; "we artists are olives," says Joyce, "squeeze us." Czarist and post-1917 Russian is the acid test. From Pushkin to Alexander Zinoviev, the central fact of Russian poetry, drama, fiction, literary theory, music has been that of official repression and Aesopian or clandestine response. The lineage of genius is utterly unbroken. Stalinism and the feline bureaucracies of blackmail after Stalin have witnessed, are witnessing at this very moment, a literary output which is truly fantastic in its formal virtuosity and compulsion of spirit. To cite Mandelstam, Akhmatova, Tsvetayeva, Pasternak, Brodsky is to refer, with almost careless selectivity, to an incomparable breadth and depth of poetic presence. This breadth and presence have been matched, perhaps even excelled, in the fiction of Pasternak, Bulgakov, Siniavsky, V. Iskander, Zinoviev, G. Vladimirov and literally a score of other masters much of whose writing is not yet available in English. To set against Nadezhda Mandelstam's memoires, against Solzhenitsyn's first novels, against the philosophic-Rabelaisian leviathans of Zinoviev, against Natalie Ginzbourg's autobiography, against *Zhivago* and Pasternak's translations even the most powerful of modern American narrative or personal statement, is to court a bewildering sense of disproportion. The specific gravities, the authorities and necessities of felt life, the boldness of stylistic experiment, the urgent humanity in Russian literature probably constitute what claim there is to redemption in the modern dark ages—and have done so since Tolstoy, since Dostoevsky. By such steady light, this month's 'great American novel' is merely embarrassing. The exemplary implications, moreover, seem to extend to eastern Europe as a whole. It is one of the current characteristics of Anglo-American literacy, even in alert circles, to have almost no knowledge of the lives of the mind and of the arts between East Berlin and Leningrad, between Kiev and Prague. The volume and standard of poetry, of parable, of philosophic speculation and artistic device are inspiring. It is not the 'creative writing centres', the 'poetry workshops', the 'humanities research institutes', the foundation-financed hives for deep thinkers amid the splendours of Colorado, the Pacific coast or the New England woods we must look to for what is most compelling and far-reaching in art and ideas. It is to the studios, cafés, seminars, *samizdat* magazines and publishing houses, chamber-music groups, itinerant theatres, of Krakow and of Budapest, of Prague and of Dresden. Here, I am soberly convinced, is a reservoir of talent, of unquestioning adherence to the risks and functions of art and original thought on which generations to come will feed.

If this is so, if the correlations between extreme creativity (literally, concretely, creativity *in extremis*) and political justice are, to a significant degree at least, negative, then the American choice makes abundant sense. The flowering of the humanities is not worth the circumstance of the inhuman. No play by Racine is worth a Bastille, no Mandelstam poem an hour of Stalinism. If one intuits, believes and comes to institutionalize this credo of social decency and democratic hope, it must follow that utmost thought and art will have to be imported from outside. The bacteria of personal anarchy, of tragic pessimism, of elective affinity with and against political violence or authoritarian control which western art and thought have carried with them from their inception, must be made sterile. As are the curare tips on the Amerindian arrow-heads in our museums of ethnography or natural science. The fundamental, if subconscious, strategy of American culture is that of an immaculate astrodome enveloping, making transparent to a mass audience, preserving from corruption and misuse, the cancerous and daemonic pressures of antique, of European, of Russian invention and tragic being ("destroyer of cities . . . anarchic Aphrodite" said Auden). Here lie the archives of Eden.

Which brings up a final point. The preference of democratic endeavor over authoritarian caprice, of an open society over one of creative hermeticism and censorship, of a general dignity of mass status over the perpetuation of an élite (often inhumane in its style and concerns), is, I repeat, a thoroughly justifiable choice. It very likely represents what meagre chances there are for social progress and a more bearable distribution of resources. He who makes this choice and lives accordingly deserves nothing but attentive respect. What is puerile hypocrisy and opportunism is the stance, the rhetoric, the professional practice of those—and they have been legion in American academe or the media—*who want it both ways*.

Of those who profess to experience, to value, to transmit authentically the contagious mystery of great intellect and art while they are in fact dismembering it or packaging it to death. For the exigent truth is this: a genuine teacher, editor, critic, art historian, musical performer or musicologist, is one who has committed his existence to a consuming passion, who cultivates in himself, to the very limits of his secondary skills, those autistic absolutes of possession and of self-possession which produce an Archimedaean theorem or a Rembrandt canvas. He is a man or woman gratefully, proudly sick with thought, hooked, past cure, on the drug of knowledge, of critical perception, of transference to the future. He knows that ninety-nine percent of humanity in the developed west may aspire to only one vestige of immortality: an entry in the telephone book; but he knows also that there is one per cent, perhaps less, whose written word alters history, whose paintings change the light and the landscape, whose music takes immortal root in the ear of the mind, whose ability to put in the speech of mathematics coherent worlds wholly outside sensual reach, make up the dignity of the species. He himself is not of this one per cent. He is, as Pushkin calls him, the 'necessary courrier' or, as I have called him in this paper, a loving, a clairvoyant parasite. He is an obsessed servant of the text, of the musical score, of the metaphysical proof, of the painting. This obsession overrides the claims of social justice. It abides the hideous fact that hundreds of thousands could be fed on the price a museum pays for one Raphael or Picasso. It is an obsession which registers, in some way, the possibility that the neutron bomb (destroyer of nameless peoples, preserver of libraries, museums, archives, book-stores) may be the final weapon of the intellect.

I have said 'obsession', 'contagion', even 'craziness', for such is the condition of the cleric. Of the master teacher. Of the virtuoso executant. Of the unappeased bibliographer. Of the translator literally devoured by his mastering original. By all means, let such a condition be ridiculed and resisted in the name of common sense, civics, and political humanity. But it is not *we* (a category which includes *you* by virtue of the simple fact that you are reading this essay, that you possess the vocabulary, codes of reference, leisure and *interest* needed to read it) who can mask, water down or even deny our calling. It is for, through the great philosophic texts, musical compositions, works of art, poems, theorems that we conduct our ecstatic lives. To espouse—a justly sacramental verb—these objects while seeking to deny the conditions of person and of society from which they have come to us, from which they continue to come, *this* is treason and mendacious schizophrenia. As one Kierkegaard put it: Either/Or.

The choice is not a comfortable one. But perhaps the concept of choice is itself a fallacy. As I have implied throughout, the intellectual, the inebriate of thought is, like the artist or philosopher, though to a lesser degree, born and not made (*nascitur non fit*, as every school boy used to know). He has no choice except to be himself or to betray himself. If 'happiness' in the definitions central to the theory and practice of "the American way of life" seems to him the greater good, if he does not suspect 'happiness' in almost any guise of being the despotism of the ordinary, he is in the wrong business. They order these matters better in the world of the Gulag. Artists, thinkers, writers receive the unwavering tribute of political scrutiny and repression. The KGB and the serious writer are in total accord when both know, when both *act on the knowledge* that a sonnet (Pasternak simply citing the first line of a Shakespeare sonnet in the venomous presence of Zhdanov), a novel, a scene from a play can be the power-house of human affairs, that there is nothing more charged with the detonators of dreams and action than the word, particularly the word known by heart. (It is striking and perfectly consequent that America, the final archive, should also be the land whose schooling has all but eradicated memorization. In the microfiche, the poem lies embalmed; recited inwardly, it is terribly alive.) The scholar in the Soviet Union understands precisely what the KGB censor is after when he seizes and minutely scans his article on Hegel. It is in such articles, in the debates they unleash, that lie the motor forces of social crisis. The abstract painter, the composer in the perennial twilight of the Soviet setting know that there is in serious art and music no such thing as inapplicable formality or technical neutrality. A technique, says Sartre, is already a metaphysic. From a Kandinsky, from a Bach canon can stream the subterranean impulses towards political and social metamorphosis. These impulses reach only the few (or at first), but in authoritarian societies, in societies where the word and the idea have *auctoritas*, meaning and action work from the top. To imprison a man because he quotes *Richard III* during the 1937 purges, to arrest him in Prague today because he is giving a seminar on Kant, is to gauge accurately the status of great literature and philosophy. It is to honour perversely, but to honour nevertheless, the obsession that is truth.

What text, what painting, what symphony could shake the edifice of American politics? What act of abstract thought really matters at all? Who *cares*?

Today, the question is this: which carries the greater threat to the conception of literature and intellectual argument of the first order—the apparatus of political oppression in Russia and in Latin America (currently the most brilliant ground for the novelist), the sclerosis in the meritocracy and 'classicism' of old Europe *or* a consensus of spiritual-social values in which the television showing of "Holocaust" is interrupted every fourteen minutes by commercials, in which gas-oven sequences are interspersed and financed by ads for panty-hose and deodorants?

The question is overwrought and unappetizing. It contains over-simplification, of course. But it is a question which those of us who are by infirmity and summons accomplices to the life of the mind must ask ourselves. It is, I suspect, a question which that antique ironist, history, will force us to answer. In Archimedes' garden, barbarism and the theorem were interwoven. That garden may have been a 'counter-Eden'; but it happens to be the one in which you and I must continue our labour. My hunch is that it lies in Syracuse still—Sicily, that is, rather than New York.

FLOOR

by C. K. WILLIAMS

from THE AMERICAN POETRY REVIEW

nominated by Ai, Kathy Callaway, Lewis Hyde, and Cleopatra Mathis

A dirty picture, a photograph, possibly a tintype, from the turn of
    the century, even before that:
the woman is obese, gigantic; a broad, black corset cuts from
    under her breasts to the top of her hips,
her hair is crimped, wiry, fastened demurely back with a bow one
    incongruous wing of which shows.
Her eyebrows are straight and heavy, emphasizing her frank,
    unintrospective plainness
and she looks directly, easily into the camera, her expression
    somewhere between play and scorn,
as though the activities of the photographer were ridiculous or
    beneath her contempt, or,

213

rather, as though the unfamiliar camera were actually the much more interesting presence here
and how absurd it is that the lens be turned toward her and her partner and not back on itself.
One sees the same look—pride, for some reason, is in it, and a surprisingly sophisticated self-distancing—
in the snaps anthropologists took in backwaters during those first, politically pre-conscious,
golden days of culture-hopping, and, as Goffman notes, in certain advertisements, now.

The man is younger than the woman. Standing, he wears what looks like a bathing costume,
black and white tank-top, heavy trousers bunched in an ungainly heap over his shoes, which are still on.
He has an immigrant's mustache he's a year or two too callow for, but, thick and dark, it will fit him.
He doesn't, like the woman, watch the camera, but stares ahead, not at the woman but slightly over and past,
and there's a kind of withdrawn, almost vulnerable thoughtfulness or preoccupation about him
despite the gross thighs cast on his waist and the awkward, surely bothersome twist
his body has been forced to assume to more clearly exhibit the genital penetration.
He seems, in fact, deeply abstracted—oblivious wouldn't be too strong a word—as though, possibly,
as unlikely as it would seem, he had been a virgin until now and was trying amid all this unholy confusion—
the hooded figure, the black box with its eye—trying, and from the looks of it even succeeding
in obliterating everything from his consciousness but the thing itself, the act itself,
so as, one would hope, to redeem the doubtlessly endless nights of the long Victorian adolescence.

The background is a painted screen: ivy, columns, clouds, some muse or grace or other,
heavy-buttocked, whorey, flaunts her gauze and clodhops with a half-demented leer.

The whole thing's oddly poignant somehow; almost, like an
    antique wedding picture, comforting:
the past is sending out a tendril to us, poses, attitudes of stillness
    we've lost or given back.
Also there's no shame in watching them, in being in the tacit
    commerce of having, like it or not,
received the business in one's hand: there's no titillation either,
    not a tangle, not a throb,
probably because the woman offers none of the normal symptoms,
    even if minimal, even if contrived— ⸄
the tongue, say, wandering from the corner of the mouth, a glint
    of extra brilliance at the lash—
we associate to even the most innocuous, undramatic, parental
    sorts of passion, and the boy,
well, dragged in out of history, off of Broome or South Street, all
    he is is grandpa;
he'll go back into whatever hole he's found to camp in, those
    higher contrast tenements
with their rows of rank, forbidding beds, or not even beds, rags
    on a floor, or floor.
On the way there, there'll be policemen breaking strikers' heads,
    or Micks' or Sheenies',
there'll be war somewhere, in the sweatshops girls will turn to
    stone over their Singers.
Here, at least, peace. Here, one might imagine, after he
    withdraws, a kind of manly focus taking him,
the glance he shoots to her is hard and sure, and, to her, a
    tenderness might come,
she might reach a hand—Sweet Prince—to touch his cheek, or
    might—who can understand these things?—
avert her face and pull him to her for a time before she squats to
    flush him out.

🔥 🔥 🔥

WORLD BREAKING APART

by LOUISE GLÜCK

from WATER TABLE

nominated by WATER TABLE, *Jorie Graham, Daniel Halpern, Cleopatra Mathis, Stanley Lindberg and Charles Simic*

I look out over the sterile snow.
Under the white birch tree, a wheelbarrow.
The fence behind it mended. On the picnic table,
mounded snow, like the inverted contents of a bowl
whose dome the wind shapes. The wind,
with its impulse to build. And under my fingers,
the square white keys, each stamped
with its single character. I believed
a mind's shattering released
the objects of its scrutiny: trees, blue plums in a bowl,
a man reaching for his wife's hand
across a slatted table, and quietly covering it,
as though his will enclosed it in that gesture.
I saw them come apart, the glazed clay begin
dividing endlessly, dispersing incoherent particles
that went on shining forever. I dreamed of watching that
the way we watched the stars on summer evenings,
my hand on your chest, the wine
holding the chill of the river. There is no such light.
And pain, the free hand, changes almost nothing.
Like the winter wind, it leaves
settled forms in the snow. Known, identifiable—
except there are no uses for them.

THE WIDOW'S YARD

by ISABELLA GARDNER

from THAT WAS THEN: NEW AND SELECTED POEMS

(BOA Editions)

nominated by BOA EDITIONS

For Myra

"Snails lead slow idyllic lives . . ."
The rose and the laurel leaves
in the raw young widow's yard
were littered with silver. Hardly a leaf lacked the decimal scale
of the self of a snail. Frail
in friendship I observed with care
these creatures (meaning to spare
the widow's vulnerable eyes
the hurting pity in my gaze).

Snails, I said, are tender skinned.
Excess in nature . . . sun rain wind
are killers. To save themselves
snails shrink to shelter in their shells
where they wait safe and patient
until the elements are gent-
ler. And do they not have other foes?
the widow asked. Turtles crows
foxes rats, I replied, and canned
heat that picnickers abandon. Also parasites invade

their flesh and alien eggs are laid
inside their skins. Their mating
too is perilous. The meeting
turns their faces blue with bliss
and consummation of this
absolute embrace is so
extravagantly slow
in coming that love begun
at dawn may end in fatal sun.

The widow told me that her
husband knew snails' ways and his garden had been Eden for them. He
said the timid snail could lift three
times his weight straight up and haul
a wagon toy loaded with a whole
two hundred times his body's burden.
Then as we left the garden
she said that at the first faint chill
the first premonition of fall
the snails go straight to earth . . . excrete
the lime with which they then secrete
the opening in their shells . . . and wait for spring.
It is those little doors which sing,
she said, when they are boiled.
She smiled at me when I recoiled.

🔥 🔥 🔥

IN THE LAND
OF PLENTY

fiction by SUSAN ENGBERG

from THE IOWA REVIEW

nominated by Jon Galassi and DeWitt Henry

M ARGARET HAD BEEN WORKING nine months at the New Life
Food Cooperative when her husband came back to town. She
hadn't been expecting him; she had been trying not to expect
anything from anyone. Simplicity was her desire now: to care for
her two children, to get enough sleep, to pay the rent. Her present
life was such a surprise to her, so unimagined, that in her abash-
ment she felt ignorant, remote from her own future. Many dozens
of faces came up the stairs to the store each day, and it was her job
to stay still and let their needs flow through her mind and into her

fingertips; when she went to pick up her children each afternoon, joining these streams of people, she tried to keep herself compact, her own needs minimal. She felt peaceful on nights when she was able to go to bed at the same time as her children, especially when she might wake up at midnight and understand that she had already slept for three or four hours and that a full passage of rest remained. As she went back to sleep, the undemanding night would seem to be caring for her, perceptibly, but beyond her knowledge.

The afternoon that Sloan came up the stairs of the co-op, reports had been blowing in with customers of a bitter shift in the weather, a temperature drop of at least twenty degrees and stupefying icy wind. Margaret had been listening to Mimi and John joking as they stacked away produce in the walk-in cooler about the coming of another ice age, not two thousand years hence, but now, brothers and sisters. Mimi, dressed in her usual plaid flannel shirt, her long hair braided, had been throwing twenty-five pound bags of organic carrots through the doorway to the lanky, down-vested figure of John, astride crates of lettuce and broccoli in the cooler's interior, and in their exuberance they seemed to Margaret exempt from catastrophe. She herself was at least ten years older than either of them, she had children, her father was dead, her education incomplete, her marriage a bewildering disappointment, yet she listened to them companionably. Never, before this job at the New Life, had she felt so comfortable and accepted. She liked the large upper room with its bins of grains and seeds, its shelves of herbs and spices and coolers of dairy products and fresh produce, she liked the section of useful, invigorating books, and she liked the people, Mimi and John, and Carl.

"Yes, it's coming," said John. "This here cooler is nothing compared to what's coming."

"Do you know what's really going to happen?" laughed Mimi. "We're all going to learn to lower our body temperatures and live forever."

"Naw, we'll just change into something else," called John.

Margaret rang up a customer and went back to stocking the herb jars. She heard Sloan's drawl before she saw him.

"Is Margaret around?" he was asking.

"Margaret the True is yonder with the herbs," said John's voice.

She tightened the lid on a jar of anise stars and put it back on the shelf before she turned around.

"Hello, Sloan."

"Stump said I'd find you here." He glanced around the store, and when he turned back to her, Margaret noticed the network of bright red blood vessels on his cheeks and nose, like frail explosions. He smelled of cigarettes. "How's business?"

"Very good," she made herself answer casually. "We're going to open up a bakery." Sloan looked sickly. At the thought of what he might have been eating and doing to himself, she took down a jar of peppermint tea and began refilling it carefully from a large plastic bag.

"Working hard?" asked Sloan.

"That's right. How have you been, Sloan? Stump told me about California. That's too bad."

"Yeah, well, that's just one of quite a few that didn't work out." He pulled out a cigarette.

"No smoking here," she said briskly.

He looked at her hard, and his skin seemed to flare out at her. His blue eyes were watery and bloodshot. Then he eased away the cigarette and looked around again. "Not bad up here. It's pretty damn cold outside."

"That's what we've been hearing," she said. She took down a depleted jar of cinnamon quills with unsteady hands.

"How are the girls?" asked Sloan.

"They're all right. They're in school, of course." She tipped the jar to keep the cinnamon vertical. The quills looked like rolls of brown parchment, curled around secrets.

"I'd like to see them," said Sloan. "I'd like to spend some time with them." His voice had risen slightly.

"When would that be? It's the middle of the week, and they have to have their sleep or they'll get sick. You could have written ahead." She bit down on her lip and lowered her eyes. It was the eldest girl, Helen, who missed her father the most. They had been pals, of sorts; he had taken her places. He was fond of saying that his daughter had saved his life once, when she was only five and he was as low as he had ever been. She had held his hand all night, he said, until the drug wore off, and what a miracle it had been, the touch of that child. It was a story Margaret always heard with a tight heart, for she had never been able to tell what a nighmare it had been to her not to know where her child was, for four hours, six hours, twelve hours.

"I could stop by tonight," said Sloan. "I'll pick up a pizza or something."

Margaret shuddered. "That's all right," she said quickly. "I'll feed them. You could come by around six-thirty. But they've got to be in bed by eight."

"Hey, look, what is this? I haven't seen my girls for over a year." He spread out his hands and drew out the words as if he had rehearsed them. "All of them," he added.

The jar of cinnamon slipped from her hands and shattered on the floor, quills rolling under the weighing table and against the base of the shelves. *Coriander*, said a jar near her eyes as she bent to pick up one of the larger pieces of glass.

She wasn't sure if Sloan helped clean up the mess or not. John appeared with a broom and dust pan. Several more customers came in, and an elderly woman asked her where to find the bran.

"I'll be around then," she heard Sloan saying, and he was gone.

She looked up and saw the wooden ceiling fan at the head of the stairs wheeling slightly.

"So that's the old man?" asked John as he gave a last sweep.

"Flesh and blood," she answered and held out her hands for the broom and dust pan and bag of glass. "I'll put these away if you'll mind the register for a few minutes."

"Take what you need," he answered.

In the partitioned office at the back of the stock room, high above the sloping alley, Carl was still working on the books as Margaret slid into the old school desk by the corner window. A gull rode by on a blast of wind. Roof tops down the hill and towards the center of town seemed in this weather to be turning human life in upon itself. The fear of what she might have done or was still doing to deserve her husband bore down on her. She lowered her eyes to the scarred surface of the desk.

Carl turned a page and she felt his eyes on her. "You're quiet." he said.

"Speechless," she agreed.

"And you look a little peaked."

"My husband was just here."

"You didn't know he was coming?"

"No, I've been trying not to think about him at all. He never writes, I've told you that." She looked across the shabby room at Carl, upright now above the ledger book, his eyes intent on her.

"Why aren't you divorced?"

"I'm not sure how to go about it. I haven't any money. I thought maybe he'd never come back.

"You're afraid of him."

"What do you know!" she suddenly exclaimed. He sat composed and solitary in the grey light; he lived in two rooms; he had no responsibilities other than to himself, and these he took seriously indeed: he was going to medical school; he was going to transform the profession with ancient wisdom; he was going to teach people how to eat, how to exercise, how to be quiet. He glided in and out of the co-op, performing his job, helping with policy decisions. "What do you know?" she repeated, but less angrily. She felt her spirit draining into the afternoon's bluster.

"Not too much," he said finally.

She drew an uneven breath and looked out again over the town. "I'm tired," she said. "One of my children had bad dreams last night. I was up more than down." Then she was silent, because what she was not saying was that she herself had also dreamt, had wakened from the dream, and had not been able to sleep again: she had been nursing a child, a baby adept and ravenous in suckling, and her milk had been instantaneous, prodigal, a miracle of abundance. When she had wakened, and the pleasurable flush of the dream had given way to the realities of her life, she had sat up with confusion in the cold room, wondering who in the wanton recesses of her mind could have been the father of this child. Its infant desire had been so strong and so easily fulfilled by her! The action had been so simple!

"Why don't you go home then?" asked Carl.

"No, I've got to wait until my children are out of school anyway."

"So. What about your husband? Does he stay with you?" Carl had taken an almond from a bowl on the desk and was cracking it with his teeth. He lifted out the kernel and chewed thoughtfully.

"No," she said firmly. "No, he does not."

He will not, she repeated to herself later that afternoon as she pushed her way through the weather to the grade school where Helen and Sarah were waiting inside the glass doors, behind circles of breath frost.

"I have a stomachache," complained Helen.

Thoroughly chilled, Margaret stood for a moment inside the door, working her feet up and down on the rubber mat and shaking life into her hands.

"Can you walk home?" she asked her eldest daughter.

"I'll try, but why does it have to be so cold?"

"I wish I knew," answered Margaret as she bent to tie little Sarah's scarf.

"How bad is your stomachache, Helen?"

"I just don't feel good."

"Well, let's get on home. You might just be hungry."

The wind drove against them a biting, granular snow. Bending into it, Margaret felt her energy reaching out to encircle her children. She wanted to gather them to her, to spread her arms and sweep them home, to have them instantly warmed and fed and safely at rest. The cold on her forehead was like a mark; she bore it; she was their mother, she told herself, their mother. Then she remembered that she hadn't told them about Sloan. The mark of cold seemed to concentrate itself, to radiate from her head into a zone of defiance. When men like Sloan chose to default in the care of their children, then there had to be certain forfeitures; there had to be.

Her fingers were so numb she was barely able to unlock the door. The children collapsed onto the couch. "Get your boots off," she said. "Here, wrap up in this blanket until the place warms up." Her own voice returned to her in the sparsely furnished room. She went to turn up the heat. She hung up her coat and put on an old sweater, and then she came back to the couch and began rubbing the girls' cold feet.

"Your father is in town," she said.

"Daddy!" shouted Sarah.

"Yes, he'll be stopping by tonight to see you."

It was almost too much, she saw, for Helen especially. She sat silently, her eyes full of tears, looking at her mother, and then she overlapped her coat carefully on her knees; she knotted her fingers; she pressed her lips together in an expression so unchildlike that it frightened Margaret.

"How long is he going to be here?"

"I don't know. I only saw him for a few minutes this afternoon."

"Mother, are you going to get a divorce?" the child's body remained rigid.

"I don't know that, Helen." She tried to speak soothingly. She tucked the blanket around them. "Now I'm going to get supper started. We'll see if that doesn't help how you feel."

"I want Daddy to stay home," said Sarah as she burrowed deeper into the blanket.

Kneeling before them, Margaret looked uncertainly at the package she had made of them, tucked up, mothered. She turned on a light beside the couch and without a word went down the hallway to the kitchen. How had Sloan done it? Without lifting a finger he had their love.

In the kitchen she breathed deeply, measuring her strength. The old alarm clock on the counter ticked metallically; five, perhaps six hours stretched between herself and the release of sleep. She turned on the red-shaded lamp on the table and the light above the stove. She rinsed the alfalfa sprouts and watered the fern above the sink. Gently she shook its fronds. This was her room. Small triumphs bloomed in this kitchen. There were curtains; the cupboards had been painted brick red; more plants grew on the window sill; there was a new toaster; there was Black Cat, who jumped down from the chair beside the radiator and placed himself in her path. Margaret fed the cat. She stood in the middle of the room, staring at his body crouched over the bowl and thinking about the number of hours in each twenty-four that this animal slept.

Sloan was unbelievable. What did he expect of her? She felt confounded by memories.

She cooked an omelet for the girls and carrots and whole wheat noodles, food that they liked. She gave them slices of homemade bread and quartered apples for them and poured their milk and watched them eat. What she longed for were actions simple or humble enough to cleanse away the taint of having lived with Sloan, of having chosen to live with Sloan, of being connected to him still and not knowing what to do about it. Her mother had warned her, but Margaret had taken a last look at that pinched, anxious face and gone away. These days her mother sighed to Margaret on the long distance telephone, or wept; life was out of control, she said, but at least she and Margaret were finally reconciled, there was that, though how it was all to end, who could possibly tell? And those poor fatherless girls, she had added.

Margaret ate a little of the supper. "Can't you eat more, Helen?" she asked, but the child shook her head.

"How long until Daddy comes?" she asked.

"Half an hour or so," Margaret answered. "Why don't you get ready for bed now so you won't have to spend time on that while he's here?"

"I don't want to. Maybe he'll take us somewhere."

"Not tonight!" Margaret swooped upon the words. "It's bitter, bitter cold. You can't possibly go out tonight. You, Sarah, don't you want to get cozy in your pajamas? I'll read to you while you're waiting."

"No," said Sarah as she pushed a last slice of carrot through the butter on her plate. "I want to do cartwheels."

Margaret got up and cleared away the plates. She flooded them with water. She scoured the table with her dish rag and slammed shut the cupboards. She swept the floors. "Out!" she said to Black Cat, "out of the way!" and she swatted him with her broom.

"Mad Meg," her father used to call her with amusement when she was angry, and simply knowing that he was thinking about her, even through the artificial sympathies of alcohol, she would feel some of her frustrations dissipating.

Margaret put away the broom. Wind whistled in the back door. Downstairs was the furnace; upstairs two medical students slept in the rare hours when they were at home; outside stretched a nondescript vista of frame duplexes, a featureless corridor along which the wind had been whirling hollowly when they walked home. Twenty years her father had been dead. She put water on the stove for tea, took her books from the top of the refrigerator and sat down at the table. The idea of death ballooned in her mind.

She could hear Sarah thudding now and then in the living room with her cartwheels. Helen she imagined to be lying on the couch, with a library book, perhaps, nursing images of the reunion with her father. Margaret opened her book deliberately and ran her hand over the smooth pages. This time she was not going to allow herself to be angry with Sloan. When she looked at him, she was going to remember that this year she had found out what it was like to go to bed with a feeling of innocence, with no regrets for the day;

to be on speaking terms with oneself; to close one's eyes like a child.

She bent her eyes to the book. She was reading about the life cycles of ferns, and next fall she was going to take a few classes. Why shouldn't she, Carl had said, since she was always reading anyway. Pressing her breasts against the edge of the table, she examined the circular diagram that was the journey of a fern. Last night in her dream her breasts had been translucent, and she had been able to see the milk streaming down to the child. She had been sitting in a tub of warm water while she nursed the baby, a stout wooden tub in the middle of a warm room, and she had been holding the child securely against her bare body, just above the level of the water.

It had been three o'clock when she woke up from the exotic fullness of the dream into the starkness of her room. In spite of the cold, she had been damp with sweat. She had put on a dry nightgown and gone to cover the girls, stepping over ghostly toys in the night light, bending low over their beds, but the ususal reassurance to her of this motherly action was missing. Something seemed to have been cut loose, a connection. Back in bed, she huddled alone, adrift and sleepless on a night that had lost its effortless and soothing progression. Who was this strange child? Where was the source of her abundant milk?

Folding her arms over the biology book, she laid down her head, close to the smells of wool and paper.

Startling sounds woke her, shouts, the kettle's whistle, footsteps. Leaden, she dragged her head up. It was all happening. Slouched in the doorway, Sloan had already insinuated himself into the heart of the house. The children tugged at his old leather jacket, begging to be lifted up. She saw it obliquely, dimly; she had the sensation of being unable to straighten up or move; her hair straggled against her cheeks; her jaw felt slack, dream-weighted.

"Your kettle's going off, Margaret," he drawled.

She swung her eyes to the stove.

"Helen," she said, "can you get the stove?"

Sloan had entered the room. His eyes roved, taking stock. Sarah jumped up and down at his elbow.

"Not now, babe," he said, blowing into his hands. "Give me a minute to warm up."

Slowly Margaret straightened her back and leaned her head against the wall, her hands folded over her book. She saw him flick the fern and run a forefinger over the new toaster.

"Looks like you're getting a little ahead," he commented. He rocked on his heels. "Looks real homey here." He pulled one of Helen's braids. "You know how to make coffee yet?"

She shook her head. "I can make scrambled eggs."

Helen looked challengingly at her mother. It was all happening. "Go ahead," said Margaret, "we've got eggs." She made herself stand up and go to the stove. She measured tea into the pot. "We don't have coffee, Sloan. Do you want to sit down?"

He hung his jacket on the back of a chair and picked up Sarah. "You're getting big, babe, you know that?"

"I know that," said Sarah. "And guess what!"

"What!" said Sloan.

The child's six-year-old voice giggled, halted, and began again, "You know what?"

"Do you want toast, Daddy?" asked Helen. Her cheeks were flushed.

"Watch the heat under that butter," said Margaret. She turned to the table with the teapot. It was ten minutes to seven.

"You know what?" said Sarah.

"What!" repeated Sloan, leaning back and bouncing her on his thigh. He looked amused, and Margaret felt her own face to be flat, exhausted. Sloan had on a clean, checked shirt.

"What kind of witch rides on a gold broom?"

"Dummy!" cried Helen bossily from the stove. "You've said it wrong."

"No, I haven't."

"Yes, you have. You gave it away. You say, 'who rides on a gold broom.'" She brought a plate of eggs to the table. She fetched salt and pepper, toast and butter and sat down importantly.

"Helen," said Margaret, "that wasn't necessary."

Sarah had hung her head. Now she climbed off Sloan's lap and came to hide her face against Margaret.

"Well, she always gets them wrong," said Helen, shrugging her shoulders and smiling self-consciously.

Margaret felt a panic rising in her. She took a sip of tea and stroked Sarah's head.

"Tell us again," she said. "Who rides what?"

Sarah shook her head and pressed harder against Margaret.

"What's the answer?" asked Sloan, his mouth full of eggs. "Somebody tell me."

"Well," said Helen, "the person is supposed to ask who rides a gold broom, and the answer is—"

"Stop it!" screamed Sarah. "That's my joke."

"Well, tell it then," said the older child.

"No." She was crying now. Margaret gathered her up. She felt helpless, bound to her children, yet ineffectual.

Sloan pulled out a cigarette. "What are you doing these days?" he asked Helen.

"Reading," returned Helen quickly. "I read lots of books from the library."

"You do, huh?" Sloan was squinting at her over his smoke. "You going to grow up to be a reader?"

"I'm going to write movies, like you."

Sloan snorted. He poured himself more tea and glanced briefly at Margaret. Then he took a dollar from his pocket and tickled Sarah behind the ear. "Come here, babe," he said, "I've got a trick with this dollar. Let me see if I can get it right. Come on, get your face out of your mommy so you can see George Washington here. Ok, you see this dollar? Now, I'm going to fold it over once, lengthwise."

Helen leaned close to her father, following his hands. Sarah was watching sidelong, snuffling against Margaret.

"Ok now, you fold it again. Let's see, am I doing it right? Now, what's going to happen to old George is that he's going to turn upside down. See that?"

"Let me try!" shrieked Helen.

Sloan looked again at Margaret.

"You've learned a few new tricks?" she asked.

"That's an old one," he said. "And yourself?"

"No tricks," she answered.

"Ah yes," he said, stretching back, "still the same."

Restless, he surveyed the kitchen again, and Margaret felt her life diminishing.

"What are you reading?" he asked, nodding at her book.

"Introduction to Biology."

"That's a new one, isn't it?"

She shrugged. "I liked biology before I even knew you, Sloan."

"Ah yes," he said carefully.

"Show me again," said Helen, as she held out the dollar.

"Let's go spend it, girl," Sloan said suddenly. He put the dollar in his shirt pocket and slapped a hand over it. "Go get your coat and you can help me spend it."

"Sloan, please, no, don't take her out tonight. It's much too cold. She had a stomachache this afternoon. You can't do it. Look, it's almost her bedtime." Then she looked at her daughter's face and fell silent.

"Simmer down, Meg. One ice cream with her old pa isn't going to kill her. How about you babe?" he asked Sarah. "You going to make up to me? You want an ice cream?"

"She does not," Margaret said quickly, holding her youngest child closely on her lap. "She had an ear infection last week, and you're not going to take her out."

Sloan whistled dramatically and shrugged into his jacket.

"Mama, please," begged Helen.

Margaret pressed her lips together and closed her eyes. She was in a corridor; she was being dragged along a corridor of whirling voices, and wind, death-cold. An icy defiance gathered behind her eyes. The stiffened membrane of her lids opened and she looked fixedly at Sloan.

"How long are you going to be in town, Sloan?" she said coldly.

Sloan whistled again and stared at her.

"I said how long," she repeated harshly.

Sarah had begun whimpering again.

"I'm going to get my coat," said Helen desperately. She looked from one parent to the other. "Don't yell at each other. Daddy, don't get mad." She tugged at his hand.

"All right, all right," he said, pulling out another cigarette. "Now go get your coat."

"You can't keep on doing what you're doing to that child," said Margaret in a low voice when Helen had gone down the hall.

"I'm not doing anything to her. I'm still her father. She understands me."

"She does not. She's a child, with the needs of a child."

"Well, what do you want me to do?" He gestured broadly. He dismissed the kitchen with a single fling of his arm. "I couldn't possibly work in a place like this. I can't play your little games. That kid understands me better than you ever will."

"I told you I play no games," said Margaret, her voice rising. "I'm simply trying to raise my children."

She felt Sarah's body tighten in her arms.

"You want me to apologize, is that it? You want me to say I'm sorry I didn't get the money to you? Look, I didn't have a cent, I didn't have enough to eat myself."

"I don't care about the money anymore," said Margaret wearily. Her moment of angry energy had passed and she looked dully across the room at the person she had once willingly followed two thousand miles from her childhood home into a day to day excessiveness that had become more alarming and enervating than any of the strictures from which she had escaped.

"What do you want me to do?" Sloan repeated in a loud voice.

"I don't know." A blankness was passing before her eyes. She thought of sleeping; she thought of being in her bed, with none of this happening, the night unfolding gently, everyone safe, everyone good.

"You could get her home by eight o'clock," she said finally.

Helen was standing in the doorway. She had remembered her boots and scarf. Her bluejeans and coat were too short, her mittens unmatched. She wore the red hood that Margaret had knitted at Christmas.

"Eight o'clock," enunciated Sloan, snapping his heels together.

Margaret saw Helen put her hand in Sloan's as they disappeared down the hallway. The house shook with the closing door, and Margaret shivered, as if she herself were facing the wind.

Sarah's body had slumped over in her lap. Margaret lightly touched her lips to the soft center of skin and neck curls between her braids. Lifting up the child's face, she kissed her cheek; she kissed the tearful eyes; she pressed her lips against her hair.

"I wanted to go," cried Sarah. "I wanted an ice cream. Daddy likes Helen best. He didn't want me to go."

"There, there, you can blame me about the ice cream because I didn't want you out in that wind. Now come on, let's get you to bed. I'll read to you."

"He does, he likes Helen best. I can't stand it any more. I can't stand being a little sister."

Margaret lifted her up. "You'll feel better when you've slept."

Sarah was almost too big to carry. The motions of putting her to bed seemed to contain all that Margaret had ever done for the children, the countless garments that had passed through her hands, and the dishes of food, the weights that she had carried, the nights alone when she had bent over their beds, constrained by Sloan's vagaries to an austere constancy that she had gradually begun to embrace gladly, as a possible means of separating herself from him, of redeeming herself from her own follies.

"There now," she said, pulling the covers over Sarah. "Shall I read to you? Shall I finish the one about the king and the princess?"

"No," said Sarah, her voice still catching from her tears, "tell me about when you were a little girl."

"I think I've told you all there is to tell."

"Then tell me again." She clutched at her blanket.

Margaret sat down on the edge of the bed in silence. She rested a hand on Sarah's knee. Across the room the covers on Helen's unmade bed were twisted and empty. Margaret had taped many of the children's drawings to the walls. She remembered the Saturday she had done it, how she had been making soup, how she had washed the girls' hair, how together they had made a board and brick bookcase and straightened up the room.

"I used to say my prayers every night," she said unexpectedly to Sarah. "I used to put my head under the pillow and pray to God to be with me."

"When you were a little girl?"

"Yes. I don't know how old I was, nine or ten, I suppose."

"Like Helen."

"Or maybe I was six." Margaret leaned close to her daughter. Two of her teeth were missing, another half grown in. Her face was quieter now; it looked as if a hand had passed over it and smoothed out the contortions of sadness.

"Did God come under your pillow?" she asked sleepily.

"I don't know."

"Tell me more."

"Close your eyes."

"Tell me about when you were six."

"Every winter my legs got chapped and they burned when I got into the bath water."

"Just like mine. What happened?"

"Someone would put cream on them."

"Your mother or your father?"

"I don't remember. Now go to sleep. You're almost asleep."

"Stay here with me."

"I'll stay until you're asleep."

"Go get Black Cat. Please. Make him sleep with me."

"I don't know where he is. I'll look for him in a little while and bring him in."

Margaret turned out the light and sat for a long time on the end of the bed, listening to the wind outside and the sheltered breathing of her child. Where was Black Cat, she wondered. She had hit him with the broom, and where had he gone? Her face tightened with the pain of her own weakness, her mistakes. Noiselessly she began to get up from the bed, but Sarah said, "Stay," from a deep layer of her sinking consciousness and so Margaret felt herself assuming again the shape of a mother, waiting. The image soothed her a little.

Once at the age of twelve or thirteen she had had a friend whose mother she had loved. This woman had passed into her like a light, sometimes over the years forgotten, brightly to reappear and remind her of a value possible perhaps even for herself. As a girl, locked in the bathroom, she had caught her own profile in two mirrors and pondered the seldom-seen contours, looking for a similar distinction.

"It's that damn way you hold your head," Sloan had gibed one night with his hands around her neck and his thumbs overlapped lightly on her throat. "Don't tell me you're not like the rest of them," he had said.

Margaret knotted her hands. The room was growing colder. This time when she stood up, Sarah was silent. Out in the hall she blinked. "Black Cat?" she said at the door of her own room. She snapped on the light, but bed and chair were empty. In the living room she pulled the make-shift drape, a bed spread, across the street window and folded the blanket on the couch.

Sometimes he slept on the rug in front of the bathroom radiator, sometimes he went to the furnace room and scratched in the dirt where the old well had been filled in.

At the head of the basement stairs she called his name again, and her voice met the low breathiness of the furnace that was like a faint, steady underground wind. "Black Cat?" She went halfway down the stairs. The furnace labored hypnotically inside its box. "Here, kitty, kitty," she said, sitting down and resting her forehead against the railing.

"You can't tell me anything," Sloan had said. "I know you too well."

She seemed to hear his voice laughing in the upstairs hallway, as if it were all happening again. "Good girl," he was taunting, "good girl, good girl, good girl," and she hadn't known whether to laugh or cry because the worst part hadn't come yet, the worst nights were still to come, and she had let him push her up against the wall because she was still listening for something else, a softening from bravado, an inflection she could trust, a moment of clarity that would explain the power he had over her.

Without sound or color the cat came to her out of the darkness and jumped into her lap. "Here you are," she said vaguely. She put a hand around him and felt the way his breath swelled and sank.

Upstairs a door seemed to blow open, but there were no footsteps. "Helen?" she called. "Sloan?" She ran up the steps and through the kitchen. It was nine o'clock. Wind cut along the hallway. The front door was open, and in the light from the street a million brilliant particles of snow swarmed expansively. Gripping her sweater over her throat, Margaret looked up and down the vast night before shutting the door.

In the freezing cold of the hallway she covered her face with her hands and was startled by her own substantiality. Sloan was uncanny. Like a shadow he had returned and in a moment the walls of her life had been displaced. What was she doing wrong that she should be so far from home?

At ten o'clock she rose numbly from the couch and walked the strange spaces to the telephone in the kitchen and dialed Stump's number. She knotted and unknotted the cord as she waited for his inscrutable, wheezing, corpulent voice. The phone rang again and again. Sloan had no other friends. Finally she put down the receiver and whirled around to face her own vacuous kitchen and gaping hallway.

Once before she had called Carl about a meeting at the co-op, and now she found his number without trouble. His voice answered immediately, a full, intimate vibration near her ear.

Not to worry, he answered. He'd take a look downtown. They were probably in the Pizza Palace or someplace like that. Red hat? All right. Yes, he knew what she looked like.

She thanked him in a deadened voice. She thought of his rooms where she had gone once with Mimi, their spareness and order, the bowl of oranges.

Hey, he said, hey, she was to take it easy, all right?

All right, she heard herself answer. Her shaking hand clattered down the receiver.

A moment later the front door opened, and Helen came in alone, muffled, frosted, her face barely visible.

"You walked!" Margaret rushed to her. "Where is Sloan? You're frozen! Where is he? Come to the kitchen."

Margaret led her along the passageway. She turned on the oven, and before its open door unwound the child's scarf and began to peel the stiffened garments from her.

"Helen, Helen, where did you walk from?"

"From the drugstore." She was crying. Tears had frozen to her cheeks. Her lashes were hoary.

"But where is Sloan? Why isn't he with you?"

"He was."

"But where is he now?"

"I don't know."

"What do you mean you don't know!"

"I don't know!" the child wailed.

Margaret said nothing more. She fetched a blanket. She warmed a cup of milk. She took her daughter into her lap and sat until her shaking had subsided.

"Can you sleep now?" she asked.

Helen shrugged.

"Do you want to tell me more?" Margaret pressed, frightened by the child's downcast silence.

"I don't want to talk about it," she answered theatrically, and Margaret winced. She shuddered with an unspeakable impulse to hit her child; instead she picked her up, long legs dangling, and carried her to the bedroom, where in silence she helped her into pajamas and tucked her in.

"Helen," she began, sitting on the edge of the bed, but she found no words.

Across the room Sarah sighed in sleep. Margaret bowed her head with her own fatigue. Helen had turned her face to the wall. "May I lie down with you?" she asked.

Within her embracing arm, Helen's body felt elongated,

stretched far beyond its solid babyhood into a new condition of bones and hollows. The bed was close to an outside wall against which the wind continued to moan and thud. Margaret pulled the covers higher and lay breathing on the pillow close to Helen's hair. There had been other nights when she had slept with her children, in one narrow bed or another, when their bodies had seemed like islands of comfort and goodness in the turbulence of her marriage, nights too awful even for anger, when she had locked herself in the nursery and laid down her own destiny alongside those of her children, wherever it was that they slept cradled, and she had dreamt of beginning again, herself rich, abundant, at peace. Some nights she had almost stopped being afraid.

Helen's breathing was gradually slowing. Margaret felt herself loosening into sleep; she felt pieces of her mind returning home, sinking down.

There were footsteps, and she dreamt of being asleep and trying to wake. She heard voices. The door might or might not be closed. She was slobbering. Dragging herself up, she explained in a drugged voice that she could barely see her visitor because her eyes were still sleeping. In response, a wave of joy engulfed her, then another and another. A presence was appreciating her; miracle of miracles, she was loved. Everywhere there was dimness and snow, and now she was searching for a place to sink down with this new presence in the light of an eternal understanding, almost within reach. You can do it, said the voice, come where I am, and for an instant she did, weightless, bathed in an expanding stillness of delight. And then she had to go hurriedly down some wooden steps to slog through a heavy snow. The truck was leaving.

When the doorbell rang, she started up instantly from the bed, her body pulsing with alarm.

"Yes!" she cried, "yes, who is it?" She ran in stockinged feet down the hall. The lamp still burned in the living room. She had no idea of the time.

The door was opening.

"Any luck here?" asked Carl's voice.

"Carl!"

"I've looked in the most likely places." He kicked his boots against the sill and stepped into the gloomy hall. Inside the hood of his parka his face was barely visible.

"She came home."

"That's good! No worries then?"

"I've troubled you." She peered into his face. "I'm confused tonight. I fell asleep just now."

"That's good. Go back to sleep, that's what you need."

"I don't know where Sloan is."

"Where he's staying?"

"He didn't bring her home. I don't know where he is."

"Wait a minute. What does the kid say?"

"Nothing. She couldn't talk. She was crying, and then she turned stony."

Carl loosened his hood and drew her into the light. "Now step by step," he said, but there was little more that she could tell. She huddled ashamedly inside her baggy sweater.

Carl was silent a moment and then he began to unlace his boots. "I'll sit a little while and warm up, if you don't mind."

"I'm sorry to be troubling you!"

He shrugged. "You've got some idea that you're not worth it, don't you?" He shed his parka and began blowing into his hands. His eyes were on her.

"It's just that all of this, tonight, before, it's not the way I want to be living."

"I know that." His eyes seemed to be taking her in.

She straightened up. "I'll make some tea," she said and motioned him towards the kitchen.

It was a quarter to twelve. He stood beside the stove and held his hands close to the kettle.

Would she tell him about her husband, he asked.

What about? His past? Their marriage?

Anything.

Carefully she was warming the teapot and readying the mugs. She felt a need to be deliberate, accurate, to think about what she was doing. Heat for this water came from the gas that also fed the furnace that warmed the water that coursed through the two apartments that were formed of walls, separating outside from inside.

Her husband was not easy to talk about, she answered. What he said, what he did, what he appeared, were not the same. He hated domestic life. He had had two complete families, two wives, two sets of children, both abandoned now. He was suspicious of anybody whose life wasn't at least half sordid. Oh, what could she say? She measured the herbs precisely and set the tea to steep, keeping her hands around its warm belly. Persuasive, that's what he was, amazingly persuasive. He was very good at getting you just where he wanted, and you never realized what pressures there had been until afterwards. And he liked to experiment with himself. He couldn't stand for things to be the same. What more could she say? He was almost completely unreliable, that went without saying. He was cruel. He was kind. He was very good with children, when he wanted to be. He hated women, probably, she wasn't sure.

Her eyes were staring into the slow emission of steam from the pottery spout, and then she shifted quickly to Carl.

Well, she asked him with a strained laugh, was she a fool?

He had no answer beyond his steadfast gaze, and her voice rushed on as she carried the honey pot and tea to the table. She wasn't used to talking like this, she said, he shouldn't let her go on because then there'd be no stopping her. A couple of years ago in Texas she had had a girlfriend and she had been able to talk to her about all sorts of things, it had been such a relief, but Sloan had put an end to that; he had done that friend, sure enough.

"Done her?" asked Carl.

"So that she hadn't the face to come back," Margaret rushed on. "He hated to see women together. Witches, he called us. He never let me answer the telephone first when he was at home."

She stopped, exhausted, and dropped her forehead to her arms. "Have you heard enough?" she asked.

"Have your tea," he said, pushing the mug close to her hand.

"You haven't heard the worst part," she broke out. There was no holding back now this cataract of words. "The first time was after Helen was born and I was sitting in the bed nursing her and he brought this guy in—he said he was an old friend, but I had never seen him before—and he sat on the edge of the bed talking to me and then Sloan went out and left us, and the whole time the baby was beside me on the bed." Her head dropped again to her arms. She rolled her forehead against her sweater. "There was another time, too," she cried. "And what could I have done? Who was I to tell? I had no strength."

And then her voice changed. She heard its stridency but was unable to stop. "Aren't you sick?" she asked fiercely. "Aren't you sorry you've come this far? Aren't you just sick? Don't you want to walk right out of here?"

"Hey," he said, "hey, I'm here because I want to be."

"I'm sorry," she said. She brought the mug of tea to her lips with both hands. Her body was sustaining deep, internal twitches, as if nerves were being jammed. Now and then she shuddered. "I don't think I was brought up very well," she said shakily. "Sometimes I look at people who know how to act, and I feel so desperate, I can't tell you. I've kept thinking all this year that maybe if I could just stay quiet long enough, I might learn how to live."

"That's a possibility," he answered.

"Talk to me," she implored. "Why do you just sit there letting me make a fool of myself? Tell me something. Where were you born? Did you have parents? What are you really interested in? Let me hear the sound of your voice."

He laughed. "What am I really interested in?" He poured more tea for both of them and slowly spun a spoon of honey for himself, and then he looked at her directly. "What I'm interested in is perfection. Perfectability."

"Perfection?"

"That's right. The richness of us all. We don't know it yet."

"Some people are richer than others."

"No, not absolutely." He smiled at her, and she felt suddenly cleansed by a gush of relaxation. The warmth of the tea had spread to her cheeks.

"I've had the strangest dreams the last few nights," she murmured. "But you keep on talking. I like hearing your voice."

"You're getting tired, I can see it."

"That's the doctor in you."

"Anybody could see it."

"I've got one more thing to tell you. Something just made me think of it," she said. "Once when I was about twelve I got sick at a friend's house in the middle of the night. My fever went terribly high," Margaret continued dreamily. "My neck was so stiff I couldn't move. It was pneumonia. All the rest of the night the mother of my friend sat beside my bed. She had turned on a little light, and she sat in a chair close beside me until it got light. My parents were gone somewhere, I don't know, maybe my mother had to drive my father to the hospital again. Every time I came to myself and opened my eyes, there was my friend's mother. I was very frightened of my delirium, but I could always come back to her face. It was a life line, it was, I can't tell you what it meant to me. I felt as if no one had ever been so good to me." Margaret rested her jaw in her hands. Her eyes were beginning to close.

"She kept watch," said Carl.

"Yes, she kept watch. I'd never had a gift like that before, at least it seemed that way."

"That's a beautiful story," said Carl. He finished drinking his tea in silence.

"I'll tell you what," he said, fitting the lid back on the honey pot, "you go on in and go to bed—you're halfway there already—and I'll stay a bit in the living room. I'll stay all night if you like."

"That's too much for you. You've got classes tomorrow."

"Never mind. I want to see what it feels like to be the mother of your friend. Now go ahead, I'll turn out these lights."

All her weariness was rushing to its conclusion. "All right," she consented, "I don't know what else to say."

"Nothing more now."

He led her down the hall and left her at the door of her room. She heard him running water in the kitchen. She heard the basement door closing. She heard the footsteps of the upstairs dwellers, coming home. She got in between the covers and lay floating downstream in the half-light from the hall. A shadow layered her course. "I forgot to cover the girls," she said aloud. "And I promised Sarah she could sleep with the cat."

"I'll do it," said Carl from the doorway, and the shadow moved.

Then it passed over her again and Carl came in and sat down beside her.

"They're covered," he said. "Do you want anything? A drink of water?"

"No. Thank you."

"I'm going to pull up that chair and sit for a little while."

She acquiesced, already asleep, and then she swam back and opened her eyes. He was sitting with his legs outstretched, his arms folded over his chest. The light was on his forehead.

"Carl?" she said heavily.

"Yes?"

"I want to say something."

"All right."

"I hope nothing has happened to Sloan."

She saw him nod reflectively and lower his gaze, and then she was given the blessedness of rest.

ARTHUR BOND

fiction by WILLIAM GOYEN

from THE MISSOURI REVIEW

nominated by Bo Ball, Louis Gallo, and Robert Phillips

REMEMBER MAN named Arthur Bond had a worm in his thigh. Had it for years, got it in the swampland of Louisiana when he was a young man working in the swampland. Carried that worm for all his life in his right thigh. Sometimes for quite a spell Arthur Bond said it stayed peaceful, other times twas angry in him and raised hell in him, twas mean then and on some kind of a rampage Arthur Bond said, stung him and bit him and burnt him, Arthur Bond said, and itched and tickled and tormented him. Arthur Bond himself told us that he was a crazy man then.

He was sick a lot from the worm. Nest was in the sweetest part of the thigh, if you will look there on yourself and feel of it, there where the leg gets the softest and holds the warmth of the loin, halfway between the knee and the crouch, where it's mellow and full and so soft, like a woman's breast if you catch hold of it. (I have noticed that the parts of a man and a woman are a lot alike and feel the same, and why not? One God made them both, settled that in the Garden, *Man and Woman created He them,* though God knows it still don't seem to be settled in some, but don't want to get into that).

One time worm begun to try to come out his knee, Arthur Bond said, said saw its head in a hole that had opened up in his knee. Doctors tried to pull the worm out but it broke off and drew itself back into Arthur Bond's thigh and lived on—without a head, Arthur Bond said. Jesus Christ a headless worm. Doctors saved the head, put it in a bottle of fluid and the face was pretty, face of the worm when you looked in and saw it looking at you lolling in its fluid was like a little doll's. Nobody, no doctor anywhere could kill out that infernal worm from the swampland of Louisiana living without a head in Arthur Bond's pale thigh, (he died with the worm,) old and vile and aflourishin, in his thigh. Poor Arthur Bond, how that worm of the swampland tormented him all his life since he was eighteen and went into the ground with Arthur Bond when he was sixty-six. But the head of the worm with its pretty doll's face still bobbles in a bottle where Arthur Bond left it when he died, to Science, at the University. Yet Arthur Bond hisself never even got to high school, idn't that funny? Went to work in the swampland when he was fourteen. If he hadn't gone to work in the swampland, wonder what his life would have been? Without the curse of the worm, I mean.

Anyway, what I'm thinking is that we can't all see in a bottle the face of our buried torment. Arthur Bond was lucky? Worm made him drink until he was sodden on the ground or a lunatic in a brothel. Was Arthur Bond lucky? Worm made him vicious, wild amok in bars, beat up women. Worm took over his life, command-ed his life, he had a devil in him, a rank, vile headless devil in him, directing his life. Arthur Bond, older he grew, was at the mercy of the worm, slave of the slightest wish of the worm. Let me tell you two examples. Worm seemed to take it out on women worst of all. Heat of a woman sent that thing into a crazed-out fit. Got to where women wouldn't get close to poor Arthur Bond, they certainly didn't want to be mashed and rolled on like a steam-roller, not to mention choked to death, or twisted like an insane chiropractor was a-handlin 'em, worm'd get aholt of that leg of Arthur Bond and jerk it like a crazy dancer. Course somebody that ud a-wanted that kind of a thing, that kind of a fightin thing, ud a called the leg of Arthur Bond a leg of gold and sought it out; but wasn't nobody like that come to him and guess Arthur Bond ought to have thanked God for it, he'd a died a horrible death of convulsions and probly a broken neck; people stayed away from Arthur Bond. This made Arthur Bond even more lonely and naturally led him to drink more whiskey. Whiskey was puredee wildfire to the worm. Then Arthur Bond would knock down people and break up chairs and bash a man's head in with a bottle. When he killed a man in an alley, where he said the man accosted him to rob him and in self-defense cut half his face off with the butt of a beer bottle he begged the doctor again to do anything, to even cut off his leg, for when he sobered up he was horrified at what the worm had done, killed a man, and he didn't know what the thing would do next. But the doctor wouldn't amputate. He said he wasn't sure where the worm had his hind part, his vile tail, whether maybe twas in the very groin of Arthur Bond, maybe even in his sack and curled around his balls. Naturally the next thought was was it in his member, my God was his member now a part of the worm, it was too much to suffer and seeing that the worm could possibly take over his body, his whole flesh and body and Lord God with Arthur Bond's head, Arthur Bond's own head of yellow hair and green eyes, that he could finally be just the walkin worm itself with head of yellow hair and green eyes, Arthur Bond went crazy and tried to kill hisself and the worm by drinking a glass of rat poison. He was not successful and lay choking in his own bile, though it was hoped for awhile that the worm was poisoned dead until it began to rustle and twinge and tingle in his thigh again, as if to say hello Arthur Bond you fool; so both lived on.

Now the worm struck in vengeance at him. Crazed by the poison it whipped him to the ground. And he died rank green and foaming. People said that in the casket the body of Arthur Bond was in such a sudden trembling from time to time under the continued whippings of the worm that the casket holding Arthur Bond rocked and jumped so much funeral home had to fasten it down to the floor with strong ropes, man'd come in from the woods with his wife to pay his two dollars a month on his Funeral Layaway

Plan that the Funeral Home gives, said now what's Arthur Bond
trying to do now, crazy drunk, trying to ascend up like the Savior
so they have to tie him down? Man'd had a few drinks himself and
said if Savior takes up Arthur Bond what'll he do with the rest of us
in Sands County tried to live like Christians? Must surely be end of
the world, 's wife said if violent men are taken. Worm had
triumphed so and had shrunken the body of Arthur Bond so much
to skin and bones looked like it'd sucked his flesh away. Twas like
they was a-burying the worm that was dressed up to look like a
nightmare Arthur Bond, like they was a-buryin a worm a-wearin
Arthur Bond's body like a costume for a man.

One more thing more and I'm done talkin about it. Often
wondered if the worm lives on in the man's grave or died with him;
but didn't matter did it? somebody said. If it's not one worm in the
grave it's another, isn't it? somebody said. But wait a minute, I
said. Heard tell of another man had a berry in his brain. Grew out
from his vein like a berry on a vine, in's brain. And a thoughts'
been in my mind, like that man's berry in my mind, that won't
vanish, and tis the following, that worms in the grave are worms of
death in the dark, and the worm in Arthur Bond was a wild live
thing among us all, in the light, we all seen its workings in the
daylight, now that I see more about it, oh a very special fearsome
thing of our life, very unusual, can't get the word for what it seems
to me it twas, can't get it out of my mind, some days in there like a
hard berry on a vine, and especially nights; in my mind come to me
that maybe twas put in Arthur Bond by the very hand of God, it
will seem to me in my thinking then when I can't get it out of my
mind almost like, my God, almost like the worm of Arthur Bond's
got into my mind, God help me a worm in your *mind*, worse ten
times than one in your thigh, and I was one that lessened him the
most and yet seems like am now the most taken over by thoughts of
him, perplexed and restless and confounded; living power of
Arthur Bond living on in my mind has begun to make me wonder
something about him, something sweet about him, like he is a kind
of a Saint in my mind, kind of an angel; maybe twas hand of God
put a struggle in Arthur Bond to pull him and throw him and lay
him down, to show His mighty works like the Scriptures say, and
finally let him go on, free, finally, to a new life hereafter and a
better one; had to be better, couldn't be worse'n what he had, pore
Arthur Bond, was kind of a Saint; was worm God's worm? Did God

put a worm in a man's thigh to show me something, used a worm to show me something and to win eternal life for a man in the hereafter, to be a Saint, to be an Angel, my God the workings of Jehovah's ways, a worm to make an Angel, oh Lord why is there so much darkness in this life before we see the light of things your ways are strange your ways are dark before we see the light.

WHY I LOVE
COUNTRY MUSIC

fiction by ELIZABETH ANN TALLENT

from THE THREEPENNY REVIEW

nominated by THE THREEPENNY REVIEW *and Pat Strachan*

Nₒᴅ ɪs ᴀ ᴍɪɴᴇʀ. He has long dark hair and owns probably a hundred different pairs of overalls; he likes to go dancing in cowboy bars. Because he weighs about two hundred pounds and is no taller than I am—about 5′4″ in my bare feet—the sight of Nod, dancing, has been known to arouse the kind of indignation in the hearts of cowboys which, in New Mexico, can be dangerous to the arouser. Cowboys in slanting hats—not only their Stetsons, in fact, but often their eyes are slanting, and the dark cigarettes stuck in one corner of their mouths, the ash lighting only with the brief, formal intake of each breath—watch Nod dancing with the slight contemptuous smiles with which they slice off a bull calf's genitals on hot afternoons in July. The genitals themselves are plums buried in soft pouches made of cat's fur; if you are not quick with the small curved knife the scrotum slides between your fingers, contracting against the calf's ermine-slick black belly, the whites of its eyes almost phosphorescent with fear. The cowboys—with what seems to me an unnecessary lack of tact—often feed the remains to the chickens. Sometimes, living in the desert, you understand the need for an elaborate code of ritual laws; without them, the desert makes you an accomplice in all kinds of graceless crimes. They are not even crimes of passion—they are crimes of expediency, small reckonings made in the spur of the moment before the white chickens boil around the rim of the bloody, dented bucket.

"Want to go dancing?" Nod says. It is still early and he has just called. I stare at the picture on the wall by the phone: my ex-husband, standing up to his knees in a stream, holding a trout. In the picture my husband is wearing a dark t-shirt, and the water in the stream is the color of iodine. Only the trout is silver. "That job came through," Nod says. "The one in Texas, you remember? It put me in a bad mood. I want to go sweat out my anguish in a dim-lit bar. And it's Saturday night and you're a lonely woman with love on her mind. Come with me. You've got nothing else to do."

I paused. It was true, I wasn't doing anything else: on the television in the other room a long-haired muppet with a quizzical expression was banging on a black toy piano with a toy hammer. My ex-husband was in Oregon. The trout, when he had opened it, was full of beautiful parallel bones. I was amazed by the transparency of the bones, and the fact that they had been laid down so perfectly inside the fish, lining the silvery gash of its intestines. My husband was pleased that I was taking such an interest in the trout; "This is an art," he said. He showed me the tiny minnow he had found, perfectly whole, inside the belly cavity. The minnow had tiny, astonished eyes. I wanted to put it in water. He refused. He wrapped it in a scrap of newspaper and threw it away. "It was *dead*," he told me. When he finally called me from Oregon, I could hear a woman singing in the background. My husband pretended it was the radio.

Nod waits a moment longer. "Come on," he said. "I already told you I'm in a bad mood. I don't want to wait around on the phone all night."

"Why are you in a bad mood?" I countered. "Most people would be in a good mood if their job had just come through."

"Coal mining always puts me in a bad mood," Nod said. "Now get dressed and let's go to the Line Camp. I'll be at your house in twenty minutes."

I hung up the phone and went into the other room to get dressed, pulling on my Calvin Klein jeans while the long-haired muppet sang "The Circle Song."

The cowboys, leaning against the left-hand wall as you go in, look you over with the barest movement of the eye, the eyelid not even contracting, the pupil dark through the haze of cigarette smoke, the mouth downcurved, the silent shifting of the pelvis against the wall by which one signals a distant quickening of erotic possibility. The band is playing "Whiskey River." My white buckskin cowboy boots—I painted the roses myself, tracing the petals from a library book—earn me a measure of serious consideration, the row of Levi-shaded pelvises against the wall swiveling slightly (they can swagger standing still, for these are the highest of their art, O men) as I go by, the line of cigarettes flicking like the ears of horses left standing in the rain, movement for the sake of movement only. The cowboys stand, smoking, staring out at the dance floor. Everyone who comes in has to pass by them. My hair has been brushed until it gleams, my lips are dark with costly gels. I pay my five dollars. Nod follows me. He pays his five dollars. The man at the card table, collecting the money, has curly sideburns which nearly meet under his chin. He whistles under his breath, so softly I can't tell whether it is "Whiskey River" or something else. He keeps the money in a fishing tackle box, quarters and dimes in the metal compartments which should have held coiled line, tiny amber flies. The cowboys shift uneasily against the wall. Nod graces them with a funereal sideways miner's glance, the front of his overalls decorated with an iron-on sticker of Mickey Mouse, giving the peace sign. There is one like it on the dashboard of his jeep. Nod is nostalgic for Mickey Mouse cartoons, which I do not remember. Fingers in their jeans, the cowboys watch us like the apostles confronted with the bloody, slender wrists: horror, the shyest crease of admiration, hope.

In Nod's arms I feel, finally, safe: a twig carried by lava, a moth clinging to the horn of a bull buffalo. Nod, you see, thinks I am beautiful—a beautiful woman—and that in itself is an uplifting experience. Nod is, for the most part, oddly successful with women; he has been married twice, both times to women you would think, if not beautiful, at least strikingly good-looking. Nod faltered through his second divorce, eking out his unemployment with food stamps, too depressed to look for work. He listened to Emmylou Harris records day and night in his bare apartment; his second wife had taken everything, even the aloe vera. In the end, Nod says, it was "Defying Gravity" that saved him. He had the sudden revelation that there were always other women, deeper mines; he got dressed for the first time in months and sent a resume to Peabody Coal. Peabody Coal, Nod claims, knows how to appreciate a man who has a way with plastic explosives. Don't they use dynamite anymore? I asked him. Nod grinned. Dynamite, he said, is the missionary position of industrial explosives; some men won't try anything else. He described the way explosives are placed against a rock face; in the end it often comes down to a matter of intuition, he said. You just *know* where it should go. Now, in the half-dark of the Line Camp dance floor, Nod is not unattractive. I imagine him closing his eyes, counting. (Do they still count?) No matter how many times you have seen it before, Nod says, when you see rock explode it still surprises you.

He holds me tightly, we move around the floor. Night washes the Tesuque valley in cold shadow, the moon rises, the eyes of the men along the wall glint seductively behind their Camels. In the mountains the last snow of the year is falling. On the stage, the harmonica player's left hand flutters irritably, as if he were fanning smoke from his eyes; his mouth puckers and jumps along the perforated silver, anemone flow of sound rising and falling above the whine of the pedal steel. The lead singer is blond and holds the microphone close to her teeth. She is wearing a blue satin shirt, the beaded fringe above the breasts causing her nipples to rise expectantly in dark ovals the size of wedding rings.

"Aren't they fine?" Nod says. He is pleased. He sweeps me around in a tight, stylish circle, my boots barely touching the floor. Around us women dance with their eyes closed, their fingernails curving against plaid or embroidered cowboy shirts, their thoughts—who can have thoughts, in this music?—barely whispered. At the end of the set couples separate from each other slowly. There is a smattering of applause. Everyone's face looks pale and slightly shocked. A couple in a corner near the band's platform continue dancing as if nothing had happened. The woman is several inches taller than the man, who is wearing, above his black bolo tie, a hugh turquoise cut in the shape of Texas. The woman stares straight ahead into the air above the man's slick black hair. It is very quiet. Around us people are moving away, to tables, to the bar against the far wall. Nod takes me by the hand. Someone unplugs the cord of the microphone. The harmonica player is left standing alone in the light, talking to himself. He cleans the spit from his instrument with a white handkerchief so old it is nearly transparent.

In the parking lot Nod lets go of my hand. Around us headlights are coming on like the lamps of a search party—dust rising from white gravel, the sound of many car doors slamming in pairs. Nod turns me around, kissing me. Ahead of us a tall girl in a white skirt patterned with flamingoes is walking awkwardly on pink platform shoes, singing to herself in a voice blurred with fatigue. The skirt blows apart around her thighs; she stumbles. Nod takes her gently by the elbow. The three of us walk together to the end of the parking lot, where there is a black van with the words "Midnight Rider" painted in silver cross the doors. The windows are round, and seem to be made of black glass; there is a sound of muffled drumming from within. When Nod knocks a man gets out of the van, taking hold of the tall girl—she is still singing, her head thrown back, her eyes now tightly closed. She seems indifferent to his grasp. The man nods to us; he has a light scar across one corner of his mouth which makes him seem to be smiling slightly, ironically. He balances against the van, shifting the weight of the girl against him so that she falls inside. The floor of the interior is covered with a dark red-and-black rug. The girl lies on her side; her voice is muffled by the blond hair which has fallen across her face. The man shuts the door. He looks at us and touches the scar absent-mindedly, with one finger. "She knows the song," he says, "but not the words."

The cowboys had seen us leave together. There was this, which might have been considered an incident: a blond cowboy with a narrow mustache—it seemed to be slightly longer on one side of his mouth than the other—kissed me on the nape of the neck as I went by him on my way to the bathroom. It was a very fast kiss, and his expression never changed; it left a faint circle of evaporation on my skin, cold as a snowflake. It was, I understood, an experiment. In the other room, far away, the guitarist rasped out a few chords, tightened his strings, rasped again, fell silent. He seemed to be taking a long while tuning his guitar. The blond hummed comforting sounds into the microphone: one, two, three foah—

We stood for a moment, staring at each other. This always happens to me when I am confronted with a cowboy in a shadowed hallway; it has to do with having watched too many Lone Ranger matinees during a long and otherwise uninteresting midwestern adolescence. I thought of those Saturday afternoons, looking at him; I thought of the long white mane foaming against those gleaming black gloves, the eyes barely visible behind the mask, the steely composure in the face of evil and uncertainty. I tried for a few moments to summon my own steely composure. The cowboy leaned against the wall, cocking one shoulder jauntily. My steely composure had been abandoned somewhere between the second tequila sunrise and the third, and now it was hopelessly lost. The cowboy stared at me; I hoped that I emanated a kind of cool innocence. I understood that cool innocence ran a poor second to steely composure. His eyes were gray, his fingers in his jeans, knuckles riding the ridge of the hip bone, no wedding ring (good sign). Coors belt buckle (bad sign; cliché). Boots of dark suede with tall slanting heels (good sign). Blue eyes (neutral). Slight smile (very good sign: he is not pressing the issue, neither is he willing just to let it drop). I stood there, thinking about it.

He looked at me. I looked at him. My shoulders—one shoulder only if I am to be utterly truthful—lifted of its own accord: a shrug.

He watched me as I walked away. Out of the corner of my eye I could still see him; he shook his head vaguely, stood and strolled down to the end of the hall, walking with real grace on his tall, scuffed heels. The jukebox was indigo and silver and there was a framed photograph of Loretta Lynn on the wall above it. He stood and looked at Loretta Lynn for a few moments, cocking his head like a bank clerk trying to decipher a blurred check. Loretta Lynn, it was clear, would not have refused him. He eased a quarter from his pocket, pressed several of the numbered buttons, and paused. When nothing happened, he leaned slightly forward and nudged the jukebox suddenly with his hip. I could hear the coin drop from where I stood.

The door to the women's room says "Fillies." Inside there was a fat lady powdering her nose; the powder in her tortoise-shell compact was the color of band-aids. She watched me from the corner of her eye. Tonight, I thought, everyone is watching everyone from the corners of their eyes. I closed the door and latched it. I could hear the fat woman sigh deeply as she clicked her compact shut. As I sat down, I neighed.

Nod would have been a diamond miner if there had been any diamonds in New Mexico: he only missed it by a continent. He could have been in South Africa, supervising the long-fingered black men in the dank caverns, if his father hadn't been a physicist in Los Alamos. But he was, and Nod regrets it. Diamonds, he says, think of that, coming out of the earth, thinking hard, now that would be *something*, the first human being to touch a *diamond*. Of course they don't look like diamonds right away, but you can tell. In South Africa the men dig hunched over—it is "uneconomic," in the words of the mining companies, to dig away enough earth for the men to stand upright, the traditional vertical posture of *Homo sapiens*, but not, it seems, of miners. So the miners of diamonds remain for years in their position of enforced reverence, on their knees. The depths of the earth are open to them, the glinting, ancient lights buried within are retrieved and sold, only to end up on the fingers of virgins in fraternity house basements, turn the lights down and kiss her with your tongue between her teeth, she don't say anything that means she must *like* it.

The night had clouded over, leaving only the moon which followed us from behind. Nod was driving. The Toyota jeep bucked in second gear over the narrow, stony road. Below us on the left was an abyss filled with the looming, lightning-struck tips of ponderosa, wind stroking through the heavy branches until they roared. Occasionally a single branch glittered in the moonlight. I stared down at my boots. I had placed them carefully, toe by toe, out of the way of the gear shift: now the toes seemed remote, indifferent as the pointed skulls of lizards. I was very tired. "No," Nod said, rubbing a clear space in the mist which covered the windshield. "That light you see over there, *that's* the moon." I looked. It was light as a flying saucer, cold and white, full of intelligent life.

When we got to the end of the road Nod parked the jeep, pulling out the handbrake. He stood at the entrance to the mine, his hands thrust into the pockets of his overalls, looking down. "This whole mountain is honey-combed with mines," he said. I did not feel reassured. He bent and threw a small stone into the interior. It made a very small chink, like a ring tapped against a mirror. "This is one of the oldest," Nod said. "Look how they cut the wood from those braces: look at the craftsmanship in those notches. Those fuckers are going to last a thousand years." I looked: I could see nothing except darkness.

"Smell the coal," Nod said.

He went back to the jeep for a light. Nod always carries rare and useful things in his jeep: a bottle of Algerian wine, a blanket, a light. He drove the jeep a few more feet forward so that the headlights glared down into the entrance of the mine: this was so we could find our way out. The light grew hazy only a few feet from the front of the jeep. The jeep itself seemed mystically beautiful: a lost island, an airplane after you have just jumped out.

"Minotaur," I sang out. "Come home. Ally-ally-ox-in-free." Nod laughed. I was more than a little drunk. "We always said it different," he said. "We always used to say, 'Ally-ally-in-come-free.'" He ran the light down the curved walls. The walls were dark and seemed to have been chiseled; the light barely touched them. We did not go far. "Here," Nod said. He got down on his knees. The earth at the floor of the shaft seemed raw and gemmy, as if it had never quite healed. Nod's shadow swept along the walls. He took off his overalls and stepped away from them lightly. Barefoot, he swung the beam of the flashlight in my direction.

"Nod," I said. "Take the damn light out of my eyes."

"I love you," he said. He turned the light off. I could hear nothing. No sound from Nod. No matches in the pockets of my jeans. I cursed heatedly: the cowboy, Nod, the darkness, the mine, Algerian wine, the full moon, Calvin Klein.

"Find me," he said, out of the darkness.

I wished for a long moment that I was with the cowboy, fucking in the back of his International on an old Mexican blanket smelling of dog hair, between bales of pink-yellow hay.

"Nod," I said. "It's dark, it's cold. I'm tired. Do you want to make love or do you want to fuck around all night?"

(The idea suddenly of his agile two-hundred-pound mass moving naked down the gleam-wet corridors forever and ever.)

I lay down on the blanket. I took off my boots. "Ally-ally-income-free," I said. He was very drunk: suppose he got lost, how would I ever find him? "Ally-ally-come-home-free," I called. The wine bottled tipped cool against my spine, I lifted it, held it against my cheek for the comfort of a solid object in the darkness. "You damn well better get your ass *over* here," I screamed. I waited. If he was anywhere near at all he could hear my crying.

When he came from the darkness he was different: he had small curved horns, yellow tipped with ebony, and his eyes were dark in the centers, ringed all the way around with startled white, his forehead covered with ringlets damp as a rock star's. He stared at me. I stared at him.

For a long while neither of us moved. In the light from the headlights small motes of dust danced around his motionless horns.

"It's a lovely trick, Nod," I said. "How long have you had that thing hidden down here?"

I stood up and pulled down my jeans, tripping slightly in the process. I laid them in the corner of the blanket near my cowboy boots, feeling for the bottle again in the darkness. I held it up for him to see. He stood with his mouth half open.

"What the hell is the matter with you?" I said. "Haven't you ever seen a naked woman before?"

He took a small step toward me. I undid my shirt, one button at a time. "I want you, okay?" I said. "Nod, is that what you wanted me to say? I want you. Come over here, Nod. I want you right now." He came toward me, lowering his head. He was not clumsy: miners never are, in the dark.

Nod, like all true heroes, left in the morning for Austin. He had written down my address on the side of a carton packed full of old copies of *National Geographic*. His cat, asleep on a pile of dirty overalls in the back of the jeep, opened one eye and stared at me coldly. She was not jealous, Nod said. She just disliked being looked at while she was trying to sleep; anyone would. Nod had on a pair of immaculate white overalls over a striped t-shirt; there was a red ceramic heart pinned to the front of the overalls. He had curled the *Rand McNally Road Atlas* into a narrow tube in his left hand, and now he swung it idly as if it were a baseball bat. His eyes were veiled.

"I'll bring you a diamond," Nod said. "If I find any."

Of course, I thought he was lying.

I told this story to my analyst. Her hair is thick and curly and she sits in a white wicker chair in a sunny front room, listening to God knows what and nodding her head. In one corner of the room there is an old wooden carousel horse. When she first started practicing in her own house, she thought of moving the horse into another room. The horse had faded blue eyes, a pure, vacant stare, small curved ears. Think of the dizzying moments that horse has known: small girls kissing its ears, caramel vomited across its flanks, a distant smell of mountains. Every single one of her clients protested when she moved the horse. She had to bring it back. These are crazy people? I thought. Once, when she thought I could not hear, she made a phone call. The conversation concerned another client. The session she had had with this client must have disturbed her. She whispered into the telephone.

"What is the professional term for someone who eats dirt?" she whispered. She writes the word down on a small yellow pad.

She must have know it, and forgotten. Here is someone, telling her the story of how, as a child, he had eaten dirt, and here she is, in her white wicker chair, nodding gently, knowing she can't think of the word. When my husband calls from Oregon, the static sounds like sand blowing across glass; against the static I can make out a baby's crying. He asks how I am. I ask how he is. We are both fine. I count how many months it is that he has been gone; he pretends the baby crying is a Pamper's commercial.

A small brown paper box from Austin. The UPS man who handed it to me looked at me queerly, because my face was painted. The neighbor's children had been here, and we all painted our faces together. Mine is gorgeous: dark gold, indigo. Silver false eyelashes. The little girl next door has promised to invest her allowance in a box of Fake Nails. The UPS man does not know what to say, handing me his slate. The pencil is attached to the slate by a small beaded chain. His truck—the same color as his uniform— ticks distantly in my driveway.

"Is it going to go off?" I asked.

He pretends not to get it. His name is stitched over his pocket, approximately where his left nipple would be, and below that, his heart. Alan. Alan leaves me the box. He shifts the gears in his truck and drives slowly away.

I open the box.

The earth inside smells dusky, rich. There is no message. I lift it, sifting the dirt between my fingers, sniffing. I even taste a little, hoping it will taste foreign and rare, like imported chocolate. It is only faintly sour. Perhaps a square foot of dirt. It will take me all night, I think. I dig through it softly, trying to feel with the insides of my fingers as well as the tips, the way I imagine a mole feels things with the damp pink skin of its nose, its body cloistered, remote. Certain nuns are not even allowed to see the priest, they receive the sacraments through tiny jeweled windows, in darkness. Only the hand, the whisper, the little piece of bread. "Nod," I whisper. The name goes no farther than the smoke from a match. The dirt feels good, it crusts against my fingers beneath the nails. I rub a small clod against my teeth, like a child toying with an aspirin, letting it dissolve into separate bitter grains. I lift two handfuls and finger the dry clumps, breaking the soft clods apart, watching them fall.

INTERWEAVINGS:

REFLECTIONS ON THE

ROLE

OF DREAM IN

THE MAKING OF POEMS

by DENISE LEVERTOV

from DREAMWORKS

nominated by Joyce Carol Oates

CAN I DISTINGUISH between dreaming and writing—that is, between dream images and those which come into being while I am in the poem-making state? I'm not sure.

I began writing at a very early age, but the two childhood dreams I remember were beyond my powers to articulate. One of them was a kind of nightmare; and after it had recurred a couple of times I found I could summon it at will—which I did, in much the same spirit, I suppose, as that in which people watch horror movies. Retrospectively, I see it as a mythic vision of Eden and the Fall: the scene is a barn, wooden and pleasantly—not scarily—dark, in which the golden hay and straw are illumined by a glow as of candlelight. And all around the room of the barn are seated various animals—cows, sheep, horses, dogs, and cats. They all sit somewhat the way dogs do, with their front legs straight and their back ones curved to one side, and they look comfortable, relaxed. There's an atmosphere of great peace and well-being and camaraderie. But suddenly—without a minute's transition—all is changed: all blackens, crinkles, and corrugates like burnt paper. There's a sense of horror.

I was not more than six when I first dreamed this, and it frightens me still; can it (I think to myself) have been a prophetic dream about the nuclear holocaust we live our lives in fear of? Then I console myself a bit with the knowledge that it didn't have to be so; I'd already long since been terrified several times by the sight of the newspaper my mother, with astounding rashness, would wrap around the metal-mesh fireguard to make the new-lit coals draw, catching on fire, the charred tatters of it flying up the chimney like flimsy bats. Someone had accidentally dropped a sheet of newspaper over my face when I was in the cradle and apparently I went into convulsions from the fright of it. I seem to remember it, in fact, though I was only a few months old; and this connected itself to the way a page of the *Times* would burst into a sheet of flame and so quickly blacken. In my dream there were no flames, only the switch from the soft glow in which all the friendly beasts (and I among them) basked and were at peace, to the horror of irreversible destruction, of ruin.

The other dream came when I was eight. I used as a child to love reading the descriptions (often accompanied by small photographs) of country houses for sale which at that time occupied the back page of the *London Times*. They ranged from cottages to castles, and I was not only fascinated by their varied architecture but also by their names. I would furnish each with inhabitants and make up "pretend games" (long, mainly unwritten serial stories within which I moved not so much *doing* anything as *being* one of the people in them—another form of dreaming). Another source of these daydreams was the sample notepaper, embossed or printed with the names of persons or places I presume were made up by the stationer, which my father, as a clergyman, used to receive from time to time. He would give me these advertisements to play with; and from a letterhead such as

Colonel & Mrs. Ashley Fiennes
The Manor House
Rowanbeck,
Westmoreland

I could create not the *plot* of a story—I've never been good at
that—but a situation and its shadowy children. So—this dream was
of a house. When I first dreamed it there were some scenes,
events, something of a story or situation in the dream; but those
soon faded, and what I remembered (and now still either remember, or remember remembering, so that the picture still has
clarity) was the vision of the house itself. It is seen from a hillside
perhaps a quarter of a mile away, and it's a Jacobean house with
two projecting wings. The stone it's made of is a most lovely warm
peach-pink; and the English county it's in is Somerset—lovely
name! The mood or atmosphere of this dream is as harmonious and
delightful as that of the barn, but this time there's no disaster; it
just goes on glowing, beaming, filling the self who gazes from the
hillside with ineffable pleasure. Not long ago I realized that the
reason I always give my present address as *West* Somerville, which
though correct is not necessary for postal purposes, is not from
some snobbish concern (East Somerville, like East Cambridge, is a
poorer, uglier neighborhood) but because Somerville sounds like
Somerset and Somerset is in the West Country. The associations
are pleasant; when I say "West Somerville" I evoke for myself the
old-rose color of the house in my dream, though plain "Somerville"
makes me think of Union Square and its traffic jams. The house of
the dream had a name too: Mazinger Hall; and I dreamed it on a
Midsummer's Eve. For many years just to think of it could give me
a sense of peace and satisfaction. What connection do these two
early dreams, which never became poems, have with the images of
poetry or with my later activity as a writer? The powerful first one
perhaps embodies some basic later themes, of joy and fear, joy and
loss. But it's the second one, because of its verbal element—the
house *having* a name and an awareness of the sounds and associations of *Somerset, West Country,* being implicit—that links
itself to the writing of poems.

Although my first book, *The Double Image,* is full of the words
dream and *dreamer,* it is daydreaming and the idea of dreaming
that really prevail in it. It was some years later that I began to write

directly from real dreams; "The Girlhood of Jane Harrison,"[1] for instance. I had been reading J.H.'s *Prolegomena to the Study of Greek Religion* and some of her other work, but had not then read her charming autobiographical memoir, later given me by Adrienne Rich because I'd written the poem. My dream is *described* in the poem, but I don't know that the sense, in the dream and in the wake of it, of the symbolic value of the window, indoor and garden darknesses, the sweetness of marzipan, the naming of roses, the diagram ("like the pan for starcake") of the dance in which Jane Harrison and her *semblances* moved from the central point out towards and beyond the dissolving boundaries of youth's garden, is adequately presented in the text. "Marzipan" is an especially unrealized reference; I myself can only dimly recall what part it played in the dream, and I don't see how anyone else could derive its significance from the poem unaided by any trace of memory. I think it was a word that the figure in the dream murmurs to herself as if its sound and the sweetness and dense texture of the substance so named expressed the feeling of the summer night and its roses. Also it was linked with the "star cake." The garden was a nineteenth century English one, with ample lawns and rosebeds, the surrounding shrubbery backed by taller trees, and a great cedar in the middle distance. Jane leans out of a groundfloor window at first; then she steps into the outdoor space. Though it's dark there's some moonlight, or possibly a glow from the house behind her—enough for trees and bushes to cast shadow. Starting from near the cedar, she begins to dance; and in forming the star figure of the dance, which is a ritual to welcome the autumn that is soon to begin, she multiplies, as if reflected in many mirrors or as if a cluster of identical dancers spread out to the points of a compass rose. She's moved out of the house of childhood, recognized the end of summer, saluted the fall (The Fall from innocence into the vast adventure of Knowledge?) to which her own grown-up life corresponds. Something like that. But as a poem it may be incompletely evolved, or partially unborn. And this is the great danger of dream poems: that they remain subjective, private, inaccessible without the author's gloss. Not only dream material presents this danger, of course; one of the most typical failures of student poetry is the writer's failure to recognize

1. Levertov, Denise. *With Eyes at the Back of Our Heads*, New York: New Directions, 1959, p. 25.

what has actually emerged into the poem and what remains available only to the poet or through explications that are not incorporated in the work. Such non-articulated material may originate in all kinds of experience; but dream experiences are particularly likely to be insufficiently transmuted into art unless the writer is sensitive to the problem and to its solution.

"Relative Figures Reappear"[2] is another dream-poem I seldom read to audiences. I feel it *describes* a dream but does not evoke it vividly enough for it to stir in others feelings analogous to those it gave to me; and because of this descriptive, rather than evocative, quality its *significances* remain unshared in much the same way as those in the Jane Harrison poem. "The Park,"[3] on the other hand, in which persons and places of my own life also appear, seems somewhat more evocative—its images have more feeling-tone— and ends with a rather clear statement of intent, specifying the park as the

> country of open secrets where the elm
> shelters the construction of gods
> and true magic exceeds all design.

The dream (and I hope, the poem) gave a sense of the way in which "real magic" may be arrived at by means of illusive modes; or rather that it transcends the trickery or sleight-of-hand it may condescend to utilize. The elm (real, natural, an "open secret") may indeed shelter the construction, by carpenters, of wooden "gods"—but they are real gods! Magic is *happening*, a multi-layered paradox.

Many of my poems of the fifties and early sixties—"Nice House," "Scenes from the Life of the Pepper Trees," "The Springtime," "The Departure,"[4] for example—may seem to have been dream-derived, but they were not. Rather they are typical examples of the poetic imagination's way of throwing off analogues as it moves through, or plays over, the writer's life. I see a difference between these poems and those of a still earlier period, however: being more concrete and more genuinely related as analogies,

2. ———. *Collected Earlier Poems 1940-1960*. New York: New Directions, 1979, p. 124.
3. *Ibid.* p. 127.
4. *Ibid.* p. 69, p. 72., p. 82, p. 87.

metaphors, images, to that life-experience—more rooted, in a word—they are truly poems in a degree that the stanzas of vague talk, unfounded either in actual dreams or in daily waking life, which filled *The Double Image*, were not. One poem from the early sixties which might easily be mistaken for dream account is "A Happening;"[5] here a metaphor that expressed for me the trauma of returning to the city after two years in Mexico, proved to be meaningful to many readers. For me it was New York City that was the intractably alien and terrifying place, despite years of residence there and attempts to love it; for others it may have been any other great metropolis. However, the poem includes a conscious irony that I now think is a flaw because of its peculiar obscurity: one of the protagonists (a stranger bird who turns into a paper sack and then "resumes its human shape" when it touches down in the streets of the city) goes uptown to seek the source of "the Broadway river." Now, only someone familiar with New York would know, first, that Broadway does have a river-like meandering course, and second, that in fact it *begins* downtown, where Manhattan's earliest buildings were constructed near the harbor. So the stranger is looking in the wrong direction. That's part of the "plot" of the poem, but it's not fully accessible, and even to a New Yorker can too easily seem merely a mistake on the part of a writer who was, at the time, a fairly recent immigrant. (I had come to the U.S. at the end of 1949, but had spent almost four years out of the country during the fifties.)

In dreams, of course, just such "mistakes" do occur; but the dream *atmosphere* of a poem must be as strongly convincing as a Magritte painting to ensure the reader's not being distracted by its peculiarities from the dynamics of the poem itself. When the images of certain poems (dream derived or not) make one feel one is entering a real dream, it is a sign of their strength, their power. We are convinced, just as, ourselves dreaming, we accept without question situations and juxtapositions our waking reason finds illogical or "weird." Poems "about" dreams which are not well written are as boring or depressing as other shoddy work; and poems which (like my own early work) make constant reference to the dream state but provide no concrete evidence of its existence are at best vaguely pleasant in a melancholy, misty way. When a poem "feels like a dream" it does so by virtue of the *clearness* of its

5. *Ibid.* p. 97.

terms (however irrational they may be). When we wake from actual dreams, isn't it precisely the powerful clarity, not any so-called "dreaminess," that speaks to us? It is true that sometimes dream episodes, and figures in them, dissolve or melt into one another and that this witnessed metamorphic process forms part of the dream-drama; but we are not commonly brought to question it while dreaming, any more than we question the transitions of place, mood, and persons we experience while waking.

In the early sixties my husband began working with a Jungian therapist who encouraged him to talk over his dreams with me; and this stimulated me to remember and think about many more of my own dreams than hitherto, both because of our discussions and his account of the therapist's interpretations and because I began to make a practice of writing down what I remembered, and of participating to some extent in the emotional effect of Mitch's dreams as well as my own. Thus, in "A Ring of Changes,"[6] I wrote,

> I look among your papers
> for something that will give you to me
> until you come back;
> and find: "Where are my dreams?"

> Your dreams! Have they not nourished my life?
> Didn't I poach among them, as now on your desk?
> My cheeks grown red and my hair curly
> as I roasted your pheasants by my night fire!
>   My dreams are gone off to hunt yours,
> I won't take them back unless they find yours,
> they must return torn by your forests. . .

It was a time of great pain and a lot of growth for us; looking back I see that the sharing of our dream-life, and of what we were learning about how to *think* about dreams, was what kept us going and held us to one another in those years more than anything else. Whatever conflicts we endured, we nevertheless found ourselves linked in the unconscious; not that, as some have done, we dreamed the same dream or answered dream with dream: yet our common intense interest in our own and each other's nightly adventures in the inner world acted as a powerful bond. After a while I too began

6. *Ibid.* p. 106.

to see a therapist and to work more methodically in trying to comprehend the symbolic language. Specifically dream-originated poems of this time are part IV of "A Ring of Changes," "The Dog of Art," the prose story about Antonio and Sabrinus (A Dream)[7] and To the Snake,[8] as well as some of those previously mentioned: but not The Goddess,[9] though people have thought so. The daisy-eyes, worked in wool, of the Dog of Art are the "lazy-daisy" embroidered eyes my mother (and later I, myself, when my son was little) used to substitute for the dangerous button-eyes on wire pins with which stuffed toy animals used to be furnished. The dream-images, and consequently the poem, imply relationships between the embroiderer's practical creative imagination and the child's imagination that infuses still more life into the toy; the functioning of imagination in dream, and the way it incorporates memory; and the way in which artists (of any kind) draw upon all of these things. Daisies suggest the "innocent eye" of art.

Something the Antonio and Sabrinus dream made even clearer for me than it had been before was the urgent tendency of some material toward its medium—in this case prose, not verse. I began telling the story as a poem, but it had been a dream with a very distinct tone or style, a *tale told*; and the slightly archaic diction which was virtually "given," or at least which the dream lay on the very brink of, sounded stilted in verse. (It was in conversation with Robert Bly that the possibility of capturing the tone better in prose rhythms emerged, I remember—unlikely as that seems, for Bly has never, in my opinion, really understood the sonic aspects of poetry, which is why, focusing almost exclusively on the image, he has felt free to translate such various poets. Had he been concerned with ear and voice he would have been daunted by auditory problems he has simply ignored.) The stanzas of verse which conclude "A Dream" began, I think, as the opening of the subsequently abandoned first version. I had a similar experience of material "wanting to be" prose in writing the non-dream experience of a tree-felling, the story "Say the Word."[11] One must learn to listen to the form-needs of events; and dream material often seems to make this necessity specially clear.

7. *Ibid.* p. 118.
8. *Ibid.*
9. *Ibid.* p. 131.
10. *Ibid.* p. 110.
11. ———. *O Taste and See*, New York: New Directions, 1964, p. 41.

This retrospective evaluation of my own relation to dreams as a poet reveals so far two main points. One is the difficulty of adequately conveying not only the mood of the dream, and of not only describing or presenting its facts, but also—along with mood and facts combined—of capturing within the poem itself a sense of its significance. For the poem to work, this significance may be narrowly personal only if a sufficient context is provided for that personal meaning to justify itself as a dramatic component. For example, in "A Sequence"[12] it is possible that the tense situation presented in the first four parts of the sequence provides a sufficiently novelistic context for the dream references of part five, tenuous though their meaning may be, to have some impact. One can at least comprehend that the dream joke (which, as often happens, doesn't really seem all that funny when one wakes and looks for the point of it) does in fact give a crucial moment of relief to the protagonists. And perhaps this puts it on a less narrow, more universal level: one accepts the laughter and relief (I speak now as reader, not writer, for the poem was written so long ago) not because one shares the joke but because one has witnessed the characters' previous misery, and also because one is probably familiar with the way in which such tension can at last be broken by something simply silly.

The other point revealed is that the attempt to render dream into poem is potentially an excellent way to learn one's craft, for if the difficulties inherent in that process can be surmounted, those attendant upon the articulation of other experience seem less great. Moreover—and this perhaps is a third and separate point—consideration of dream-images, in which the imagination has free play, or at least less censored and inhibited play, than it has in the waking mind, provides valuable models of possibility for the too-deliberate, cautious, and thus "uninspired" writer. (Or perhaps I should say, for the writer temporarily in an uninspired, over-intentional phase; for if a poet's sole experience of being taken over by the imagination took place in dreaming, could one consider him a poet at all?)

There is a certain kind of dream in which it is not the visual and its associations which are paramount in impact and significance, but rather an actual verbal message, though a visual context and the identity of the speaker may be important factors. The first

12. ———. *The Jacob's Ladder*, New York: New Directions, 1965, p. 8.

dream I can recall having written into a poem ("The Night," *Collected Earlier Poems 1940-1960,* p. 34) was dreamed in London in 1945 but not composed until several years later, probably in New York. The encounter with William Blake—who was sitting on the floor, his back against a wall and his knees drawn up, and who looked at me with his prominent, unmistakable eyes as he spoke— was so memorable that the lapse of time has scarcely blurred it. And it coincided with the "real life" fact of a bird's getting caught in my room that night and at dawn, when I pushed down the top half of the sash window, shooting unhesitatingly out, calmed by the sleep into which it had sunk when I turned out the light. But it was the extraordinary Blakean words, "The will is given us that we may know the delights of surrender," that made the dream an artistic whole which seemed to ask only for transcription. Yet if I'd tried to write the poem at the time of dreaming I would not have had the craftsmanship to accomplish it, and it would have been lost to me, because once crystallized in an inadequate form, it would almost inevitably have become inaccessible to another attempt.

Then there are verbal dreams whose visual context vanishes on waking, or never appeared at all, the dream having consisted purely of words. The context may arrive later, in the world of external events. "In Memory of Boris Pasternak"[13] exemplifies this latter eventuality. In its second section I wrote about the way in which a great writer can impart to scenes of one's own world a character they would not otherwise have had—in other words, can give one new or changed eyes to see through. While I was working on the poem, I looked at the barn and woods and clouds and buried the dead fledglings among wild strawberries, a dream I'd lost track of re-entered my consciousness, and though at the time, two nights before, I'd not associated it with the recently-dead poet, the lines a disembodied voice had spoken, "The artist must create himself or be born again," came clearly into the constellation of images and experiences clustered around my feeling for Pasternak, so that the dictum seemed not only directive but also a comment on how, for the poet, "self–creation" consists in attaining, in a lifetime's practice of the art, the ability to reveal the world, or a world, to others. The dream words are syntactically ambiguous; do they mean, "If the artist fails to give birth to himself (to his creative potential) he

13. *Ibid.* p. 32.

must undergo reincarnation until he does so"? Or is the syntax appositive, i.e., "The artist must create himself, *or in other words, be born anew in each work of his art,* as in Christian theology the New Adam takes the place of the Old"? As the dreamer, my sense is that both meanings are implicit. Indeed, this leads me to note one of the most important lessons a poet can learn from dreaming—namely, that just as in dreams we effortlessly receive, rather than force into being by a process of will, images and their significances, including double images and complimentary double meanings, so in writing (from dream or non-dream sources) the process is rather one of recognizing and absorbing the given than of willing something into existence. But this "given" is not the taken-for-granted reality of superficial, inattentive moving through life, but the often disregarded reality that lies just beyond or within it.

A dream that exemplifies the verbal message without visual or other sensuous context is this one, in which the following proposition was presented to the intellect (presumably in much the same way as solutions to mathematical problems have occurred to people during sleep):

$$\text{"Trauerzucker} = \text{Zauberzucker"}$$

The dream consisted of these equated German words (which meant "mourning sugar" and "magic sugar") and of the awareness (a) that (in the dream world) there exists a funeral rite in which lumps of sugar are distributed to guests at a wake, and (b) that this was understood to signify "out of sorrow comes joy." Thus, a ritual of sorrow and death, in which sugar is handed out to sweeten the bitterness, turns out to have an intimate connection with or even to be identical with (as shown by the equal sign) the rituals of (favorable, "white," or "good") magic—so that (it was implied) the sugar cubes don't just alleviate, but *transform* the sorrow (into joy).

A curious point was that the word "trauer" was misspelled, so to speak, in this non-visual dream, as "trauber," a word that doesn't exist; however, the word "traube," meaning a bunch of grapes, does, so that "traubenzucker" would be "grape-sugar" (as in Trauben-saft, grape-juice).

Often a dream presents a ring from which to hang the latent questions of that moment in one's life. "The Broken Sandal"[14] was

14. ———. *Relearning the Alphabet.* New York: New Directions, 1970, p. 3.

such a one. As it states, I "dreamed the thong of my sandal broke." The questions that follow—from the most literally practical ones about how I'm going to walk on without it over sharp dirty stones, to the more abstract ones:

Where was I going?
Where was I going I can't go to now, unless hurting?
Where am I standing, if I'm to stand still now?

arise (gradually waking) from the initial event. The dream demanded of the dreamer that some basic life-questions be asked. That was its function. In becoming poem, the organic process begun in dream continued, statement and questions giving the poem its necessarily terse form; and the mode of the questions was provided by the dream's sandal-thong metaphor, so that "Where am I (is my life) going?" is given concrete context, a matter of bare feet, of hobbling, of hurting. Finally the dreamer-writer is brought to enquire the nature of the place that is the poem's present. This type of dream experience and poem experience is not hampered by the intrusion of the ego and its so often untransferable trappings, but translates seamlessly into the reader's own "I". I wish that happened oftener. Yet perhaps a poetry devoid of the peculiarities of a less universal experience might seem bland; an occasional such poem may have some degree of stark force precisely because it is unusually simple, whereas a whole book of such poems might make one suspect the author of deliberately aiming at universality in the manner of gurus and greeting-card rhymesters. The hope is always that, when autobiographical images occur in a poem, readers will respond with the same combination of empathy and of a recognition of their own equivalents with which they would receive a novel, a play, a film. For instance, in "Don't You Hear That Whistle Blowin. . .,"[15] the "Middle Door" and the personages named—Steve, Richard, Bo, Mitch—are unknown to the reader, but the theme of the poem is loss and change, and my hope is that the poem clearly expresses this and (because of the givens of the dream source) reinforces that theme with the folkloric, nostalgic associations of railroad trains.

There is a type of dream that, like the simple image of the broken sandal, virtually writes itself: the kind whose very terms are

15. ———. *Freeing the Dust*. New York: New Directions, 1975, p. 64.

those of the myth or fairy tale. "The Well,"[16] about which I've written elsewhere, is an instance. More recently the nature of a close relationship was dreamed in what felt like mythic terms, the resulting poem ("A Pilgrim Dreaming"[17]) having its rhythms and diction deriving partly from the feeling-tone of the dream itself and partly of my waking feelings—rather awestruck—about having dreamed something seemingly from my friend's point of view rather than my own, almost as if I had dreamed his dream. Again, one of the friends of whom I'd written twenty-five years before in "The Earthwoman and the Waterwoman"[18] (not a dream-derived poem) was visiting me one day in 1978, and after she left I dreamed about her as "The Dragonfly Mother,"[19] the long-ago images of water and blueness reappearing in a metamorphosis that expressed the growth and change in her and also in my response to her personality. Thus the sequence was, *impression, first poem, passage of time, new impressions, dream, second poem.* And in addition (as recounted in the second poem) her visit affected my actions on that day, making me forego doing something I'd thought it was my duty to do (but which as a matter of fact wasn't important, since it was only a matter of speaking for two minutes at a big outdoor rally, at which I would not really be missed). Instead, I slept, dreamed, wrote a poem I like, and recognized how often the fear of displeasing masks itself as a sense of obligation.

Perhaps it is when dreaming and waking life thus interweave themselves *actively* that we experience both most intensely. When such interaction takes place for someone who is not an artist in any medium, the recognition of its power remains restricted to that individual. But the poet or other artist may sometimes experience the primary interweaving in the very doing of the poem, painting, dance, or whatever. It is then more than recapitulation, it is of one substance with the dream; and its power has a chance to extend beyond the limits of the artist's own life.

Appendix

Some dreams contain a great quantity of narrative detail than seems manageable in a poem. An example would be the following (which I can hardly believe occurred as long ago as 1963, it is so vivid to me: that is, its orientation—the placement of doors or rooms to the right or left in relation to the beholder—is so clear in my mind). I am visiting a mental hospital, or

16. *Op. cit. The Jacob's Ladder*, p. 37.
17. ———. *Life in the Forest*, New York: New Directions, 1978, p. 124.
18. *Op. cit. Collected Earlier*, p. 31.
19. Levertov, Denise, *The Nantucket Review*, Summer 1978, p. 74.

rather a *residential clinic* in search of a woman who works there in some more or less menial capacity, and whom I have agreed to help move into a new apartment. She is in fact moving into my building but I'd promised to assist her before I knew that, and she still doesn't know—I'm going to surprise her with the information later. I find that this place she works in is so interesting that I want to look at everything for its own sake. I more or less forget about looking for her, the people in her office know I'm doing so, anyway.

It's an old building without "grounds," right in the city, a mixture of City and Country School (a private elementary school in New York City) and the Judson Health Center (a neighborhood clinic in New York City). It works on the principle of keeping promises and of lots of creative occupational therapy. The O.T. rooms occupy almost all the space, unlike the situation in most hospitals. On a woman's floor I learn that troubled housewives can come for short periods (e.g., a week) and immerse themselves in doing painting or sculpture or whatever. On a door is a sign about "perpetual counsel"—I open it, not expecting to find anyone there during the lunch hour, but sure enough, there is: promise kept. Likewise on the children's floor is a door saying "The Friendly Lady" will be there at all times: and I look in, and she is.

Also on the children's floor is a special quiet library-room, quite small, rounded or vaulted in shape, in which there are four mural panels—silvery-white designs on milky-pale-blue background—of subjects "from the Zohar,"[20] showing constellations and kingly figures on horseback rising from, *and composed of,* stars; all prophetically tending towards the Stable of Bethlehem which can be seen afar as if amid the nebulae. A theme here is of reassurance—promises are kept, the "Friendly Lady" is actually there, "counsel" really is perpetual. There is a sense of consolation and grace akin to that in the idea of the Madonna, the Holy Mother. And the final scene, with the magical starry mural has its own evident symbolism, with powers and principalities moving towards the humble stable. (That the Zohar enters into this can be variously interpreted.)

Another dream "told itself" in the immediate writing down in what, with a little crafting, might approximate to the style of the Grimms' *Household Tales*. It's only an amusing anecdote, however; I enjoyed dreaming it but it could not impel me into trying to make a work of art of it: A little girl had longed, as many do (I did, passionately) for the inanimate to speak. To find one of her dolls actually addressing her one day! But as she grew older she of course became more and more aware it probably wouldn't happen. Then one day, when she was about ten years old, it *did* happen!—though it was not a doll that spoke. This is what occurred: Her parents took two newspapers, one conservative, one radical; latter was lying on a couch or bed when, as she looked at it, it raised itself up n to speak, and began to address her. In delight and excitement she exclaimed wanted this to happen!—And before, it never did, no matter how mu I "Ah," said the newspaper (whose name was *The Emancipator*), "I'll tell you the secret of how to get us Things to speak—" And just then I woke up.

Yet another type of dream, verbal but not poetic, is illustrated by the following:

I am at Yale for a reading. A professor points out how many Black college Fellows (as the term is used at Oxford, or in Harvard's "Society of Fellows") are in the hall. I say, ironically, "Oh yes—angels on the point of a needle, right?"

The dream that follows suggests to me two literary possibilities: one would be, to re-enter the dream imaginatively and draw forth from it some further elements of story—this would tend to become prose fiction. The other possibility is that since the dream-experience becomes as much a part of one's memory-bank as any other, its images (rather than the fictional situation) may come into play unbidden in the course of some later poem. With another girl (Jean Rankin, my childhood friend) I come to the edge of the sea. (We are about eleven and twelve years old.) There seem to be shelves, or levels, of sea, and the whole expanse is cluttered with wrecked tankers, some floating, some half-beached, as far as the eye can see. It's a dank, dark-green, eerie seascape but the water's not cold and we have come to swim. We swim aboard the decks of the nearest wreck—stanchions and bits of companion-way all awash and covered with eely seaweeds. We have fun swimming in and out of it all; we don't scrape or hit against anything. There is absolutely no living creature in sight and the shore is a vague sedgy marsh. After a long time, though, we realize that the boat is free of the bottom (and of the ridges or reefs of dark tufa-like rock) and has drifted out with the tide.

20. A group of Jewish Cabalistic texts.

We become troubled and decide to make our way (wading along the half-submerged decks to the end nearest land) back as far as we can without swimming, and then swim to shore before we get carried out any further. But even then it looks like a long swim—can we make it? Jean thinks we *must;* I am hesitant, thinking it might be better to risk staying on board the many hours till the next high tide washes us inshore again. We are perplexed—especially since it's so hard to judge the distance and the variable depth. Looking out to sea, the other levels stretch away and away, faintly gleaming, thick with wrecks. We might get wedged so that our particular wreck would *not* wash in with the next tide—or, half submerged as it was, it might sink, further out than we were already. On the other hand, the distance we were already out at sea looked greater than any we had ever tried to swim. No one to whom to signal. Woke in perplexity.

SCATSQUALL IN SPRING

by JUDITH MOFFETT

from THE KENYON REVIEW

nominated by THE KENYON REVIEW

What salt sprinkled over half a ripe tomato
does to acid and red—
what sandpaper rasped over fingertips
does to the tumblers—

this squall of rain
swept like a sprinkling can
over fields and pastures has done
to the smells of cut grass, riverwater, weedflowers,
turned clods and foddercrops, and to the superior
dung of graminivore:

on the paved footpath, bountiful green amoeba-splashes
(messy, though not offensive) of beefcow;
from the deep brown paddock,
intoxicating cloud of pony.

We Sunday ramblers,
canine and human, who watch our step
among these creatures now with pleasurably
twitching nostrils and no conscience to speak of,
might well feel mortified. We've dined,
and will again, upon the grass-gross haunches of their kind,
and know the muck they make of grass
is out of comparison nicer than the muck we make
of them,
of grass-in-them.

Like a slipped hound
a question circles, nose to the ground.
Ponder the rabbit-pellet whitetail,
the "flower-fed buffalo" with his fuel chips,
wildebeest, wapiti, wild ass; rehearse the natural habits of
the zebra, the slim pronghorn, the eland and the ibex,
and of the kudu.

Think how they live,
the ones you've seen—about the Zoo:
those dirt enclosures lacking one green blade,
that haybale diet (not Asian or African hay
even), and yet recall
how happily far
their dense organic odors are
above the stifling cathouse or
the house of apes and monkeys. There was a man ate grass
once, in the Bible, but it was madness.

A little tax
on brainpower? A little joke
at wits' expense?

Upside down in the gleaming river now
the elderly white pony, the chestnut, the roan,
gleam and crop grass.
A fresh breeze dries the fragrances
pouring off turf and blossom; and beyond the last stile
forty lowing Herefords with but a single thought
between them lope on joints of wood
to the pasture's watered lower end. As one
they lower ponderous heads
to graze. Stiffly, one by one, they raise
tails of frayed rope.

AT THE FAR END OF A LONG WHARF

by THOMAS LUX

from THE SONORA REVIEW

nominated by THE SONORA REVIEW, *Kathy Callaway, Carolyn Forché, Louis Gallo, Charles Simic, and Pamela Stewart*

At the far end of a long wharf
a deaf child, while fishing, hauls in
a large eel and—not
because it is ugly—she bashes its brains
out of eeldom on the hot
planks—*whamp whamp whamp,* a sound
she does not hear. It's the distance
and the heat which abstracts
the image for me. She also does not hear,
nor do I, the splash the eel makes
when she tosses it in her bucket,
nor do we hear the new bait
pierced by the clean hook nor
its lowering into the water again.
Nobody could. I watch her
all afternoon until, catching nothing
else, she walks the wharf towards
me, her cousin, thinking
with a thousand fingers. Pointing
to our boat she tells me
to drag it to the water. She wants me to row
her out to the deep lanes of fish.
Poetry is a menial task.

🔥 🔥 🔥

FIONN IN THE VALLEY

fiction by BENEDICT KIELY

from PLOUGHSHARES

nominated by Nona Balakian, Carolyn Forché, DeWitt Henry, and Teo Savory

BELOW THEM is the sweep of the valley, widening from nothing in the grey-brown mountains down to deep green pasture-land. The river winds in the most approved style. The farmhouses are square and white and solid. No poverty in this part of the world.

Never in my life nor in my nightmares have I heard so many sheep. Heard rather than seen. Thousands of them. Say a million, for the sake of easy accounting. Their mouth-noises after a while seem to disturb the primeval peace more than the noise of engines. Bleats and meh-meh-mehs by the million while, in the sky, the larks, still gaily singing, fly, scarce heard amid the sheep below.

They park the car, sit on the roadside, meditate on the price and succulence of mutton and on the obvious advantages of being a sheep-farmer in a wild, beautiful valley. Deborah asks them to think of what they'd pay for a plate of that in the Hibernian or the Shelbourne or in Simpson's on the Strand.

—Not to talk, says Killoran, of the price of wool. They're secure in this valley.

—Listening to the bleats of the bloody things, says Jeremiah, might be the hardest part of it.

For a full five minutes they listen to the bleats. The sound is a continuing pattern, or a line on a graph, rising and falling but never breaking. There is never a moment when twenty or more sheep are not simultaneously speaking. Killoran says: That's his house, the long one, where the river makes the double bend. He was one of the world's greatest guerillas, this man we're going to see.

—Of course I've heard of him, Deborah says, he fought for Ireland.

—Jeremiah bleats back at the sheep: But tell me, madam, what has he done since then.

—You tell me, smartass.

She likes Jeremiah.

—Easy in the telling. Talk. That's what he's done. Talk. We've come to listen to him. Old hero in the inglenook. Oisin after the Fenians. Killoran loves it. Killoran worships him. How many men had the British there? And we shot them in pairs coming up the stairs in the valley of Knockanure. . . .

Jeremiah sings that sentence in Galli-Curci bel-canto.

. . . What Michael Collins said to him the time he met Collins in the snug of a pub in Gardiner Street, Dublin. What Tom Barry, the greatest guerilla, said to him two days after the ambush at Crossbarry. The number of commemorations and unveilings he has attended since 1922. We're great at the commemorating. We commemorate Wolfe Tone, father of the Republic, that blue baby, that mongoloid child, four times on the one day by four opposing groups. Under the clay at Bodenstown in Kildare the poor bastard must be as confused as Jesus. And Jesus, they say, had the wit and ability to get out of the grave and up and away.

Deborah says: Are you an Irishman at all?

Yet it is still obvious that she likes Jeremiah. Possibly because he makes a vocation of not being taken in. Killoran pays little attention to his brother-in-law. He must have heard it all before. From the car he takes a massive pair of Japanese binoculars, then walks to a low wall at the roadside and surveys the valley. He says: I see him. He's up the slope two fields away from the house. Walking like a young fellow. Crossing a stile. God, he's a wonder for his age. Come and have a look.

Out of courtesy, Deborah is given the first chance. She wrestles with the focussing and can see nothing but the sky above which is darkening for rain. Jeremiah deliberately puts the wrong end to his eyes because that, he says, is the way he prefers to see Ireland. Mervyn slowly focusses and surveys, first, the empyrean, rain is coming and heavy rain, then the ridge of the mountains, smooth in places, jagged in others: then the higher slopes where even sheep are few and where dry gullies gape for torrents, then down through the bleating thousands to the oblong, well-kept fields, the fine farmhouses, the winding river. In a field above the house at the double bend a tall man is standing quite still. He is wearing corduroy knee-breeches, white woolen stockings, a green zipper-jacket. His hair is white and copious. He shades his eyes with his left hand and looks up towards them. From the binoculars he may catch reflected the last glimpse of the smothering sun. Old Hawk-eye himself. Scanning the horizon for Britannia's Huns with their tanks and their long-range guns.

Mervyn feels himself outstared. He waits almost for the man to talk to him, right into his ear. Then, disconcerted, he hands the binoculars to Jeremiah. Who, this time, gets them right way round and sweeps the valley as if he were a field marshal. Killoran is back at the station-wagon, holding the door for Deborah. Jeremiah shouts: She's a beauty, that's what she is, a beauty.

—Not you, Deborah, he says as they go down towards the house of the hero. Although that's true, too. But I saw a sheep there and I never saw the like of her before.

—Are you fond of mutton?

—No, it's not that, but a fellow I know was a secret agent or something in Greece told me never have a sheep. He did once, he says, in Crete, nothing else being available, and the silly thing, he says, got so fond of him she used to follow him around.

Then, after a pause while they manage a steep tricky series of descending bends: This valley must be a paradise for the bucolic bachelor man.

Killoran makes no comment. The larks are above them, the

bleating choirs of sheep all around them. They are on the floor of the valley.

When they come to the house the old man is no longer standing in the field. He has quite clearly seen them and has gone to his throne-room to receive them in proper style. It is a large, square, low-raftered room down two steps to the left of an oval entrance-hall. The steps and the floor are of grey flagstones. There is a wide, open hearth with whitewashed brace ornamented with the stars and stripes and the green, white and orange of the Irish Republic. In spite of the summer outside there's a blazing turf-fire. To the right of the fire, his back to a closed latticed window, the old man sits, his left elbow on a long oaken table, his right hand holding a book. They are led into the room by a tall, middle-aged, greyheaded woman dressed in widow's black, her hair in a net: one of the two daughters the hero lives with: and they are down the steps and well into the room before he takes his eyes from the book and acknowledges their presences. He doesn't close the book. He says: You're welcome, Killoran, you and your friends. Margaret, the other girl, got your message below in the post office. We wouldn't have a telephone in the house. We value our peace. We fought hard for it.

He holds up the book. He says: The young fellow who wrote this is either ignorant or a damned liar. He says there were only thirty five British military lorries at the ambush. Ergo: only three fifty British troops. When every dog, goat and divil knows there were at least thirteen hundred, at most fifteen hundred.

—Next Tuesday, says Killoran, there'll be a debate about it on the radio.

Softly Jeremiah hums about shooting them in pairs coming up the stairs, but nobody pays any attention to him. Mervyn says to the old man that his valley is very beautiful. He has his doubts about heroes but, unlike Jeremiah, he has no intention of farting in the cave of the oracle.

—Beautiful it is, the old man says. And Irish it is. And the Irish is still spoken here from the bridge below to the highest house on the mountain. And the fuchsia, *na deora Dé*, the tears of God, scarlet for blood, purple for kingliness, do you see the way it grows? The fuchsia and the Irish language, all the way from Dingle to Donegal, go together.

—As in Japan, says Jeremiah.

Mervyn is alarmed but the old man is only amused and he is quite pleasant when he laughs, dentures dancing and shining, great oblong face corrugated with what seems to be genuine kindliness, eyes a bright seacold blue: Jeremiah Gilsenan will have his little joke. Up in Dublin, as a high-up civil servant, they pay him well for it.

Jeremiah says he is not complaining.

—Polsh, the bottle, the old man says. And glasses for Killoran and his good friends and the lady with them. 'Tis an historic valley moreover. Didn't the great O'Sullivan, chieftain of Beare, lead his people through this valley in the end of the wars with Elizabeth of England, Wilmot waiting for him there, Carew pursuing him here. That was after the heroic defense and tragic fall of the fort of Dunboy on Bantry Bay. And Carew's men after the siege ran their swords to the hilt through the babe and mother and paraded before their comrades with children writhing and convulsed on their spears, and the survivors of the gallant garrison they threw over the cliffs and showered on them shot and stones.

The walls of the house must be thick like the walls of a fortress. In the square room the bleating of the sheep cannot be heard. The old man broods. Jeremiah, for the moment, leaves well enough alone. Killoran says: It was the end of the sixteenth century. Wars were rough.

—War is hell, the old man says. Sherman said. But sometimes there's no way but war. Some authorities say that O'Sullivan Beare went up the Pass of Kimaneigh to the northeast to pray at the shrine of St. Finbarr in Gougane Barra. But I know he came up this valley. The old people said so. And over the point you were all standing on a while ago.

He had seen them, he had stared Mervyn in the eyes.

It is winter in this valley three hundred and seventy years ago. Crooked Domhnall O'Sullivan, one shoulder lower than the other, and Latin and English and Spanish and Irish easy on his tongue, leads the remnant of his broken people on that marathon northward march to O'Rourke's country: not all that far from Carmincross.

Jeremiah breaks the spell: This away, that away, all we know is that he never came back.

—But his spirit, Jeremiah Gilsenan, still lives on in the men of today. Ireland is Ireland through joy and through tears. Hope never dies through the long weary years.

—A lot of other people die, says Jeremiah. Kill now, live later.

Rising wind shakes the fuchsia bushes outside the latticed bay-window behind them. The first heavy drops of rain strike separately, sullenly on the panes. The whiskey-bottle circulates, or Jeremiah does, carrying the bottle and a glass water-jug, a coloured handkerchief draped like a waiter's napkin over one elbow, bowing and scraping and covering-up for the sourness of his last remark, finally giving himself a triple helping, unwatered, and relaxing into a low couch beside the tall stiff daughter.

—Show them the albums, Polsh, show the strangers the albums.

Then the storm is around them, darkening the room, battering at the windows, leaping over the high ridges, rushing into and swamping the valleys. The tall woman rises, lights two oil lamps that hang from the low brown ceiling and have tall flower-patterned globes. By the warm mellow light she brings for examination two huge, old-fashioned photograph albums which she takes reverently from the lower portion of a mahogany bookcase. The hero says: If my memory ever fails me it's all there, caught by the camera.

—Your memory will never fail you, father.

That seems to be the first time the daughter has spoken. She sits down again beside Jeremiah. She smiles at her hands, locked together in her lap. Jeremiah cups his hands around his whiskey, looks into its depths as if he is seeing the sunken towers of the past in the waters of the great lake in the heart of Ulster but he is sharply conscious, as he afterwards tells Mervyn, of the clean hotpress odour of the woman, of her fine long thighs, not as young as they once were but, Lord God, have they ever been parted in fun, escaping from the surveillance of that eagle father into some unsanctified hedgerow or some hotel bedroom in city or seaside resort? For her widow's black mourns not a husband but a mother. Or has she all her life done nothing but look after Fionn Mac-Cumhaill here and listen to his hero-talk about scuffles on Munster roads with British soldiers: the gutters of London, he keeps saying. These photographs and the commentary that goes with them, over and over again, shouldered his crutch and showed how fields were won, only he needs no crutch, and without looking at either album he can tell which photograph is being, at any moment, inspected.

Behind him the wind threatens to uproot the fuchsia bushes. He raises his voice to conquer the storm. For emphasis he hammers his left fist into his right palm. He has the look of a man who, when not otherwise engaged, has been making that gesture all his life.

—That there's Tom Barry himself, the prince of them all, a natural soldier. He went with the British to the big war not to uphold the empire but to get a gun in his fist, to see other countries and to feel like a grown man. Those there are the officers of the fourth and fifth battalions of the third Tipperary brigade in training-camp in 1921. The good old days. That's an enlargement there on the wall beside the printed declaration of the Irish Republic, Irishman and Irish women in the name of God and of the dead generations, nobler words were never spoken not even by Lincoln at Gettysburg.

Four young men tailor-squat, four more kneel behind them, seven more stand in the backrow, all clutching rifles, wearing big boots and leggings, knee-breeches, cloth peaked-caps back to front, and stare into the room over the heads of Jeremiah and the tall woman: and through a space in time of more than fifty years. They seem pleased with themselves and their regalia. Some of them are even happily smiling. Jeremiah hums: Forget not the boys of the heather where marshalled our bravest and best, when Ireland lay broken and bleeding. . . .

—That's the crowd there outside Mountjoy jail in Dublin the night before Tom Trainor was hanged and he the father of a large family. But we held District Inspector Potter hostage and when the British hanged Trainor we shot Potter.

—Oh fair play all round, says Jeremiah, hang one, potshot another. Was Trainor hanged for being the father of a large family? Did Potter have any little Potters?

—It was war and an eye for an eye, Gilsenan, not just sitting on your arse in the civil service.

—Father, Polsh says. Language.

—Sit on my arse for fifty years, Jeremiah says, and hang my hat on a pension. As the poet says.

—In a land, says the hero, made safe for you by the blood and sacrifice of the heroic dead. The dead generations.

The hero seems peeved. Killoran polishes the fingernails of his right hand on the lapel of his jacket, then studies them as if they

were interesting and, surprisingly, smiles: and now I know where
I've seen him before, in Madame Tussaud's, that well-dressed,
amiable, charming, smiling, English businessman, John George
Haigh who used to chat up aged ladies in private hotels in London,
persuade them to invest in his industrial enterprises, bring them
along to inspect his plant, tap them on the head and put them to
sleep in baths of sulphuric acid. Did he smile above the Lethean
pools? In wax he smiles forever.

Deborah walks to the bay-window and looks out at the storm.
Mervyn studies his album and wishes he were somewhere else.
The old man rises out of his chair and stands behind Mervyn. The
album rests on the table. The wind is easing. The movement of the
fuchsias is now only a coloured summer dance. The two lamps are
irrelevant. The crowd around that jail, fifty-odd years ago, is,
young and old, a most decorous crowd. Killoran comments on that.
An effort to make the peace. The hero agrees: None of the dirty,
longhaired louts you see today on television throwing stones at the
Garda Siochana, the natural guardians of the people.

Jeremiah is also peeved: Behold I come to thee that dwellest
in a valley upon a rock above a plain: who shall strike us, who
shall enter into our houses?

Nobody bothers to ask him what in hell he's mumbling about.

The two albums do add up to an elaborate picture-gallery.
Mervyn is reminded of a photograph album he once saw in an
English countryhouse, a record of shoots made by parties at
countryhouses all over these islands, pictures of elegant long-
skirted women and powerful hairyfaced men, glosses giving extravagant statistics of slaughtered wildfowl, the air stifling with feathers. Jeremiah grumbles: We must have had the most photographed
small army in the world. Our memories and military records are
superb.

The hero says nothing. Mervyn, feeling his tenseness above him
and behind him, turns the pages, slowly so as to simulate an
interest he scarcely feels. Deborah stands beside the hero. Her
odour comfortingly reminds Mervyn of other matters.

Dan Breen, a happy warrior who stole the first move in a war by
shooting two policemen in the back, smiles at them from one page.
He wears breeches and kneeboots, a Sam Brown and an enormous
holster. He digs, for the fun of it by his smile, and for the sake of

the picture, in a Tipperary field. The year is 1921. At the time of the taking of the picture the British, who over the centuries have done their share of dirty shooting, are offering ten thousand pounds, a lot of money in 1921, for this Tipperary farm-boy whom they describe so villainously on the reward notice that he has only to smile and not even Sherlock Holmes would recognise him.

Here on another page and by way of contrast (to put it mildly) is Field Marshal Lord French, spurred feet steady on the ground, riding crop in hands, survivor of all the attempts the patriots made to shoot him. Once, it is rumoured, they came close to decimating his female entourage: he had a marquee tent full of the old hoohah at the western front. There by his side, but in another picture, stands a thin ascetic boy who was eliminated while trying to eliminate Lord French and preserve the purity of nations.

Here, backs to the wall, is a round dozen of Black-and-Tans vainglorious enough to pose for a photograph, and somewhere in the County Limerick where Black-and-Tans were not the social success of that season. The camera then was still a bit of a novelty. The thugs who bodyguard film-actors had not yet started knocking photographers down. Criminals leaving courthouses had not yet taken to hiding their heads in bags. A vain and flattered world smiled back at the camera: watch the little birdie. Yet that photograph had fallen into patriot hands and some of the dozen were x-marked for identification and elimination.

Here's a slew of Tipperary fighters overflowing a charabanc: and here's a crowd in a Dublin street around the dead body of the guerrilla, Sean Tracy: and here's a governmental murder gang all in caps and mufflers and looking murderous, and x-marked and numbered on the picture by the patriots so that they, the murder gang, may the better be murdered. Here's the crowd outside the gate of the ancient fortress of Dublin Castle waiting to hear that the truce has been declared between Great Britain and Ireland: and here's the corpse of the hero, General Liam Lynch, after the treaty has been signed and the Irish have gone on murdering each other for the principle of the thing: and here is the house that Jack built.

So Mervyn thinks, and says nothing. Jeremiah says: It's a wonder to Jasus none of them were photographed after exhumation.

This could end bad. The old man is back in his chair knitting his fingers until the knuckles crack. Behind him, like stage-lighting, the window is bright with sunshine on the glistening rain. He's in

the pulpit and ready to preach. He says: It was well said by a good
man that the highest expression of our nationhood was the flying
column of the army of the people.

—The man that said it, says Jeremiah, was running a flying
column.

—Irish towns, villages, factories, creameries and homes had
been burned-out or blown-up by the high explosives of the British.

—Home industry can do it all nowadays. Sinn Féin Abú or Up
Ourselves and up the lot of them.

National institutions were banned or declared illegal. Farm
implements and the wheels of carts were taken by the enemy so
that the land could not be worked. The use of motorcars and
pedal-cycles was not allowed except under permit. In the town of
Bandon you weren't even allowed to walk with your hands in your
pockets.

—So that you couldn't, says Jeremiah, even scratch yourself in
comfort.

—But begod we fought fire with fire.

Fionn, the hero, and Conan the Bald, the mocker of heroes, are
off like two galloping horses. Killoran, respectable in dark pin-
striped suit, is struck dumb. Deborah makes the gestures and
twittering noises than can mean only one thing, and is led away by
the tall daughter.

—But tell us, says Jeremiah, about the Auxiliaries, Britain's
fighting best. Daddio, it always blows my mind to hear about the
Auxiliaries. Come tell us all about the war and what they fought
each other for.

—Then Gilsenan you'll hear, begod, that other times may hear
and know. The worst flesh and blood that ever walked on Ireland's
ground. Officer class they called themselves. Looters, murderers
and maltreaters of women and children. Each man with two
revolvers and a rifle, and two bombs hanging from his belt.

—Ready to fight, sings Jeremiah gurgling softly into his glass,
ready to die for fatherland.

—They took a village prisoner once, parish priest and all, and
stripped the men naked and bate them black and blue before the
women.

—Rest is pleasant after toil as hard as ours beneath a wild and
stranger sun.

—These things happened, says Killoran.

—Oh Killoran, dear brother-in-law, so did the Fomorians, each man with one eye, one leg and one tooth. So did Genghis Khan. Today we have other problems.

—It's a poor day, Killoran, that I should be mocked in my own house by a relation of yours.

—He's not a blood relation. His sister's a good woman. He may be a relation of mine but there are times when I'm no relation of his.

Killoran, Mervyn realizes, is a man to be reckoned with. His smiling composure soothes the old man for a moment, gives Jeremiah a chance to steady himself, to slither soft-footedly across the room, to tinkle at a grand piano that supports yet another gallery of portraits, family and patriotic, men in uniform, men and women in graduation gowns. He is a glib pianist. He hammers out a patriotic marching-tune: An outlawed man in a land forlorn, he scorned to turn and fly, but kept the flag of freedom safe upon the mountains high.

—It's a rousing tune, the old man says, and Gilsenan you play it well. Bad as you are. We marched to it in our youth.

Killoran sings, surprisingly, for the slow self-possessed smile of Mr. Haigh putting the ladies to sleep in the acid bath does not go with enthusiastic patriotic songs: Oh, leave your cruel kiss and come when the lark is in the sky, and it's with my gun I'll guard you on the mountains of Pomeroy.

—Pomeroy, Killoran. A magic name. That's in the fighting North. If I wasn't so old I'd make the journey up there to see how the boys are doing in O'Neill's Tyrone.

Jeremiah has stopped playing. Pray Jesus he keeps his drunken mouth shut. Mervyn says: I'm heading north myself. To a wedding. That's why I came home from the States. In a place called Carmincross.

The old man says: It's good to be home, even in troubled times. There's no place like Ireland. The exile's burden is a heavy one to carry. Four years myself, after the Treaty and the civil war, I spent in Chicago. There was no welcome in Ireland for the likes of me in those days. But this time, please God, we may see the end of the struggle with the hereditary enemy, the fulfillment of the hopes of the dead generations.

—The dead have no hopes.

That was Jeremiah speaking. But as he continues to play the piano nobody pays much attention to him. He tinkles and hums, his singing voice has no harshness: Come back to Erin, mavourneen, mavourneen, come back, aroon, to the land of thy birth.

The room is suddenly amber with sentiment. The old man wipes an eye with a stiff hand. The tall woman and Deborah have returned, chatting and laughing down the steps from the hallway, then falling silent and listening and standing close to Jeremiah. He turns and rises and slithers towards them and the door. He says: Polsh, sound the loud timbrel in my stead. I go away to meditate.

As he passes he hums to Deborah: Bless you for being an angel.

Her blonde wrinkles are soft and curved with good humour: Heaven is not for you.

He stands on top of the three steps and raises his arms for his curtain speech: Meletus says I am an inventor of gods. And it is precisely because I invent new gods and do not acknowledge the old ones that he has brought this action against me.

Polsh sits and plays fragments of old operas, the heart bowed down and marble halls and the moon hath raised her lamp above. Jeremiah does not return. Killoran goes looking for him but comes back, smiling over the sulphuric pool, hands depreciatingly extended: We'll find him in the pub at the crossroads. He had the sense and decency not to take the car. . . .

. . . Holding his daughter's arm, the old man walks with them to the door. In the bright evening the floor of the valley is a sparkling green, beyond comprehension. The sound of the river is twice as loud as it was. The calling of a million sheep comes from a world that has nothing to do with old men's dreams. Mervyn knows that he is very hungry. All that mutton around him, he supposes, and the drop of hospitable whiskey. The old man wishes him luck on the journey to the north. After the rain the birds are as loud and plentiful as the sheep. To assuage the hero Mervyn reminds him that the birds do whistle and sweetly sing, changing their notes from tree to tree, and the song they sing is old Ireland free.

Jeremiah is waiting for them in the pub at the crossroads. Or not exactly waiting. Just there. And singing. But not like the birds. What he is singing is: Just a lad of fourteen summers, but there's no one can deny that in Belfast one sunny morning he shot a peeler in the eye.

The wisp of a girl behind the counter wipes glasses and pretends not to hear him. . . .

. . . The sun is out again. Their road out of the glen repasses the hero's house. In the glass porch, a miniature conservatory, he is standing between two tall women, one of them dressed in green slacks and a red pullover, the daughter they have not met. Killoran hoots the horn. The old man salutes.

—Le rouge et le noir, Deborah says.

Mervyn is surprised, until it dawns on him that she means gambling and not French novels. Killoran says that the red-and-green one is a widow: She doesn't meet people much. She's a dipso.

Relentless Jeremiah says she was driven to it, listening to that day in and day out, and her husband dead and she with nowhere to go, and the whole country crazy listening to the like of that for centuries.

—Oh God, says Killoran, give it a miss, we've had our share for one day.

South of the highest mountains they drive through magic, sun-slit, drifting mist. But over the ridge the southwest wind is behind them, the mist dispersed, the evening sun glorious over the plains of Limerick, the Galtee mountains clear in the distance. An animal's body, shining silver in the sun in the middle of the road, halts them: a dead badger struck down by a passing car. With an ashplant torn from the hedgerow Mervyn, for the sake of safety, pokes the corpse: telling Deborah that in Baton Rouge, Louisiana, a man, walking on a river-bank, saw a recumbent alligator on the grass and, thinking it was dead, kicked it, and the alligator wasn't dead. But this badger is, blood still oozing from his snout, blood spattered on his fine fur. So Mervyn lifts him by the brush and lays him to rest on the grass margin, knowing nobody who would stuff him for immortality or skin him for the sake of his coat.

They drive on and leave him. The sunlight fades. Jeremiah sulks and sleeps all the way home. . . .

A ROMANTIC INTERLUDE FROM *RECOLLECTIONS OF MY LIFE WITH DIAGHILEV*

fiction by ELEANORA ANTINOVA

from SUN & MOON

nominated by SUN & MOON, *Walter Abish and M.D. Elevitch*

THERE ARE MANY FANTASTIC STORIES about how I became a soloist after 3 years in the back row of the Corps. How somehow I made water on stage so that when Vera Petrovna did her *fouettes* she slipped and crushed her kneecap. Or, how because my room was next to hers in the *pension*, I kept her awake all night singing love songs. Naturally, these made her cry bitterly, so that by the end of the week she was so tired she fell asleep on stage in the middle of an *adage*. It has even been said that I slipped castor oil into her vodka after a matinee and she soiled her evening tutu and couldn't go on.

It was the Russians who passed these stories around. They made

up stories like devils. They rolled their eyes and whispered so loud
you could hear them out front and they beat their chests and
groaned and told you terrible things. They themselves thought
nothing of scattering broken glass around the floor to steal a rival
dancer's part. Everybody knows how at the Maryinsky, Kches-
sinska's dresser searched the floor before she went on—to make
sure it was powdered with resin and not glass. They say the Grand
Duke Andrei, when he was her lover, enjoyed crawling around on
his hands and knees, getting rosin all over his clothes and face,
while she encouraged him from the wings. It was only because
Sergei Pavlovitch knew what they were like and wouldn't stand for
it, that we had so little of that. Still—the time the trap door opened
under Bohlm during the *Polovetsian Dances* and he fell through
and was out for the rest of the season. . . .

It was Boris danced the part after that!

The real story is that Vera Petrovna was 8 months pregnant and
couldn't get away with dancing any longer. She took to her bed and
tried peasant remedies to bring the baby out early; but nothing
worked, and she had to stay put for a while. That was the day Lydia
took to elope with the English Lord, and Sokolova was still ill in
Monte Carlo, and Alicia already had more parts than she could
handle at her age.

The rumours were fantastic!

Grigoriev was trying to get Karsavina back out of retirement.
They even wired Pavlova in Argentina to beg her to come. As if she
would even answer their cables!

There was nothing for it but for Sergei Pavlovitch to call us all
together in the rehearsal room. He sat surrounded by the Maestro,
Grigoriev and Kochno, while we stood at the *barre* shivering with
nerves. Dounya bit her lip so hard, it bled. The old man tapped his
cane and stood up. He looked around the room very slowly. I,
myself, was perfectly unconcerned. There was no chance for me.
My luck with the company had been running too bad. I was
thinking of quitting and seeking my fortune in London Music
Halls. Surely Sergei Pavlovitch would not choose an American,
and a black one at that.

It must have been 5 minutes before his eyes settled on Little
Maria. He offered her his hand. She moaned softly and fell over in
a faint hitting her head on the *barre*. She was unconscious and
everybody ran around in hysterics not knowing what to do, until

Patrick took the Maestro's bottle of mineral water and poured it over her. She got up looking dazed, stepped forward and fell over my foot.

I didn't ask her to fall over me. I was merely doing some *battements tendus* to work out the cramp in my instep. So now she had a sprained ankle and everybody got hysterical again. Kochno was jumping up and down. Katya started to scream and the Maestro began playing his violin to calm everybody down. I went up to Sergei Pavlovitch who was hunched over his cane, an unbelieving look on his face.

"Can't we have some peace and quiet, Sergei Pavlovitch," I asked.

"How can we work with such children?"

The old man looked at me as if he didn't understand what I was saying. Then he smiled.

"Eleanora," he sighed. "That is what we need. A practical American." Signalling Kochno to follow, he walked to the door.

"Eleanora, be at rehearsal promptly at 1:00. Grigoriev, you will begin coaching her in Vera Petrovna's roles."

He paused at the door.

"And fine Little Maria 2 francs for disturbing the peace!" We broke for lunch. I ran home.

"Mitya, Mitya, I am to have Vera Petrovna's roles. Our fortune is made."

There was only a crowd of fat drunken flies sucking the mouth of yesterday's wine bottle. A torn sheet, tangled tights, soiled shorts—the floor was like a memory of a day old mistral. In the blazing afternoon sun the room had the weatherbeaten look of barns back home. We should paper the walls. Cheer the place up. Maybe now we could move to a larger room—with a toilet, perhaps . . . But I had forgotten to ask about my new salary.

Coward!

You didn't forget. You were afraid of the withering looks, the aggrieved tone.

"We have done so much for you. You are our child. We have adopted you, a poor orphan."

"I am not an orphan. I have 2 parents, 3 brothers, 1 sister . . ."

"They might as well be in Russia. They are 10,000 miles away, Here you are an orphan. If you should sicken and die—God Forbid!—it is we who will sit with you, pray for you."

"But it isn't fitting that a soloist of the Ballets-Russes should wear only rags upon her back. I need a new trunk. Mine was given me by a music hall dancer. It isn't fitting."

"Look!"

He will sit down and show me the soles of his shoes. They will have big holes in them the size of nickels.

"Is this fitting for the greatest impressario in the world? Alas, it is the price of Art. For myself, I must suffer. But you—you are young. An artiste. It is easy for you. Do as the others do. Find a patron. You will have a trunk with a lining of silk from the Avenue de l'Opera. You will travel like an Assoluta."

"But I am an American. We are clumsy. We do not have a knack for such things. And I am hungry." I will stare at his portly belly.

"You, at least, do not deny yourself."

Like a rug merchant from the Caucassus, his eyes narrow into slits.

"So! Thus do you repay me! How will it look—tell me—a mahogany Sugar Plum Fairy? Can this be Sylphides? A black face in a snowbank? The critics will denounce me. I will become a laughing stock. Thus do you repay my sacrifices . . . But what does one expect of Americans? Savages! Half-breeds! Gangsters! Go back, go back! Capone! He will love you! Dance for Capone! He will applaud you with machine guns!"

. . . But now time was passing. Soon I must return for the afternoon rehearsal . . .

I ran down to the market without much confidence. Every morning when I left for class I used to see the cooks from the big villas with immense baskets over their arms. Within an hour they would have cleaned out the stalls of the reddest cherries, the straightest asparagus, the blackest truffles. Sure enough, the locusts had come and gone. Picked the street clean. The stalls were closed.

"Here, ma petite, over here," a bossy voice called out. "Why do you stand there in the empty street like a plucked pullet? Take my cut of veal. It's all you'll get now. God knows. Serves you right, too. Sinning all night. Sleeping all day. I shouldn't even help you, such a sinner."

She began to roll a suspiciously dark cut of veal into a newspaper.

"Ah, I am a fool, a fool. I have always been a fool."

"It is the only calf who died of old age," I marvelled. "You should frame it and place it in a museum."

"What do you know? You know nothing. A good beating and it will serve you like an angel. Here. 3 francs. My feet hurt. I want to get out of this sun. I am an old woman. If I stay out any longer, I shall begin to look like you." She cackled loudly at her joke.

"You are a nasty old woman," I said, giving her 2 francs. "That is all you deserve."

A good pounding along with some lemon and butter, a dish of dandelion greens . . . My veal would grow young again.

"Au revoir, ma petite."

"Au revoir."

When I came home that night after the performance, his voice roared out from under the kitchen table.

"I will never show my face again. I will eat here, sleep here. I will die here. Send for my blanket, my poor torn pillow. I will live here with my chamber pot. My pen. I am a poet."

Like a distraught Ouija board, the table jumped up and down. The marinading veal was certainly having a hard time of it.

"But, Mitya, dear, even poets must eat and you are endangering your dinner."

As if in answer, the dish slid off the top and crashed to the floor. I screamed and tried to save the meat but his hand reached out and grabbed my ankle. He twisted so hard, I fell and slipped on the wet floor.

"Mitya," I begged. "Please do not do this. You do not understand. We are supposed to celebrate. I am to dance Vera Petrovna's roles. I have been chosen by Sergei Pavlovitch, himself."

"You should be ashamed," he shouted. "You call that dancing? For Czars, that is dancing. For perverts. Neurasthenics. With water in their veins."

"We shall be rich," I lied.

"I do not need you, dark witch. Hard like a brick sidewalk . . . Ah, Maxim . . . Essenine, my beloved . . . Where are my friends? How we would drink together, eh, my beauties? We were giants then . . . Poets all . . . food of my soul . . ." His voice roared out. "Not this band of bloated fish!"

I lost my temper then.

"This band of bloated fish feeds you. You haven't a sou. You are helpless like a count. You can do nothing. I hate you. You are an ungrateful wretch. You have ruined my triumph." The new wine slid dangerously along the rim of the table.

"A friendly Bourdeaux," Fat Jules had confided. "From the town of my brother-in-law. He is a miserable miser and only brought me one barrel." His great red paw stroked my arm. "Take it to your poet, *my petite chocolate*. It will bring you happiness."

But a broken ankle cost a dancer more than spilt wine. I was afraid to come closer.

"Evil blackamoor. What do you know. I have other fish. A young lady is coming. She will lie down with me in my coffin under the table. We will curl up and you will see nothing, you menacing darkness. You will bend low to spy, to pull our toes, cruel Egyptian Princess, Voodoo Spirit, Abyssinian Witch, but you will see nothing for we will curl into a ball of dust, a mite in your eye, and fly away. Free as the dust. Light as the air. Tonight, I will be in Petrograd."

I shut my eyes as the bottle smashed to the floor, spraying a warm velvet liquid on my legs.

"12, 13 hours of dancing that cost," I wailed. "You are devouring my life."

"Swolitch! Take back your life! What are you, a stinking watchmaker? Here, I return your life! I spit upon your life! Ho! A gift! A gift from Dimitri! Fortunate woman!"

He lived under the table singing and crying for 3 days and nights, barricading himself behind the growing number of empty vodka bottles. He shouted that I was trying to kill him, "a poor exile, a wanderer," forcing himself to stay awake nights when I was home by crooning lullabies, rocking the table like a cradle . . .

> nothing is the same
> my shoes are made of leather . . .
> I have walked for seven years

When I left for class in the morning he was snoring peacefully.

When I returned home after the evening performance the pile of papers around his quarters had grown. "He's getting a lot of poems written," I thought grimly. "Doing better than me, for sure!"

"You are distracted," the old man scolded. "Have you been gallivanting with that moujhik poet of yours? You must rest nights. You are a ballerina, not a flapper."

"I am sorry, Sergei Pavlovitch. There are so many new steps. It's hard to keep up . . ."

"You prefer old steps?" he muttered. "Soon you will dance in tango contests at the Casino." He turned away in disgust. He hated ballroom dancing.

"The price of living with a genius," Tania whispered consolingly in the wings, *pas de boureeing* past me onto the stage. What did she know? What did any of them know? I wept each night at the injustice of life.

On the 4th night, after a performance that had been plagued by endless delays and accidents, he was waiting at the door, bathed, shaved, a laundered shirt open at the neck.

"You look dashing!"

He kissed my hands.

"I have written a mountain of poems. I am content." The next few days he couldn't do enough for me. He bathed my feet in soda water floating herbs along the top and then painstakingly removed the bunions and callouses caused by the additional hours of re-hearsing the new roles. He read his new poems to me, carefully translating the Russian into French, so I could understand the most subtle nuances. When I feel asleep he sat up beside me reading quietly into the night.

I was always the last to leave after the evening performance. I liked the silence of the deserted theatre. It was a good time to take stock of things.

One night, I was alone in the dressing room darning a pair of rehearsal tights which had more holes than threads when one of the supers shuffled in.

"A gentleman is here and wishes to see you."

"Please send him away."

Half an hour later he shuffled back.

"The gentleman is waiting for you. He asks what you would like to drink."

"What would *you* like to drink?" I asked.

He gave me a broad toothless smile.

"Champagne."

"Tell him champagne and go drink it yourself."

"And make sure he sees you," I called after him.

The small round gentleman with the cane limped towards me out of the shadows. For several weeks we had observed him in faultless evening clothes standing apart from the usual motley crowd of friends and family waiting at the stage door. "He has a history, that one," the girls agreed, wondering who had excited the interest of such a distinguished "and rich" gentleman. Franca, who was part Italian and very daring, grew impatient and threatened to speak to him. "But what is he then, a mute? We shall grow old. He must declare himself."

"I am sorry about the champagne," he murmured.

"I'm tired," I explained sharply. "I have been working since 8 o'clock this morning. It is now almost midnight."

"But I thought perhaps a *chocolate* at Chez Pasquier. I have seen many of the Russian dancers there."

"Don't you understand? I must be back in class again tomorrow morning at 8 o'clock."

He gripped my arm with the surprising strength lame men often have.

"It has taken me weeks to get up the nerve to speak with you. Tonight, I am mad with courage. It will be gone tomorrow. I beg of you . . ."

"It is your problem . . ."

"You are cruel . . . You . . . an artist . . ."

"Art is cruel . . ."

"And love? . . ."

I looked into his large dark eyes. He was short like me and they were on a level with my own.

"No," I relented. "Love is not cruel. It has no class at 8 o'clock in the morning."

There were very few people still up at that hour and we easily found a corner table out on the terrace where we could listen to the distant sounds of waltzes from the casino orchestra.

Since I was a guest I ordered *tartelette, gateau anglais, tablette de chocolat* and a tray full of *buiscuits des fourrages.*

"I am a Scott," he introduced himself in English. "Bobby Duff,

8th Earl of Fife. They call me Gray Bobby. I have lived a very lonely life."

He began escorting me home every night.

We fell into the habit of first stopping at Chez Pasquier. My boorishness amused him and he encouraged me to wolf down successive quantities of *gateaux, cremes, petits fours, chocolates, glaces* . . .

"I am like an old woman who has lost all other pleasures in life," I confessed to Tania. "I am ashamed."

Whereupon she exclaimed, "Qu'est-ce que vous voulez, ma petite? On se volupte comme on peut."

No doubt about it, my voluptuous life was beginning to tell. Mitya took to pinching me when I passed close to him. "Like grapefruits," he shouted, lunging for my breasts.

Only my patron took no notice of the changes in me. It was enough for him to enjoy the pleasures of feeding me while sharing the experiences of my day. He revelled in backstage intrigue, pestered me to remember facial expressions, pondered the meaning behind simple words.

"And what do you suppose she means by that," he would often say.

"Not much, I expect, Russians have bad memories. They forget tomorrow what they raved about today."

But he was a Scotsman and wasted nothing. He spent hours trying to convince me of the depths lurking beneath the simplest events. A shrug of a shoulder was enough to set him fabricating for the rest of the night. His connections were very ingenious. Fortunately, they weren't true but I don't think truth had anything to do with it.

"*Could* this be the case," he insisted.

"It *could* be, Gray Bobby, but it *isn't.*"

He shook his head sadly.

"Poor Eleanora. A lamb among wolves. You will never get anywhere in this world."

"You have taken my advice. You have a patron," the old man nodded approvingly. "They say he is a Scotch Earl. The Scots are all rich. It is a well-known fact. He must give you many presents."

"Look at my new diamond!"

The girls buzzed admiringly around Choura trying to touch the sparkling stone on her short stubby fingers.

"Who gave it to you, you little demon? The one with the fat nose or the little red one?" They pestered her with questions. "Will you keep it or sell it?"

"I would keep it . . . even if I were starving. I would keep it . . ."

"Me, I would rather have fillet every night for a year. For that I would sell my diamond."

"You do not have a diamond. With your common character, you never will."

"What do you know? I have had 10 diamonds in my time. But I have preferred a good meal, a good bed . . ."

"I won't argue that one!"

Giggling and back slaps . . .

That night for the first time I noticed Gray Bobby's hands.

"You don't wear many rings," I said. "The gentlemen in Sergei Pavlovitch's circle wear many rings. It's the thing."

His voice was brusque, angry.

"What with so many thieves running around looking like gentlemen?"

But at the theatre the next night he carried a large box with a silver wrapper.

"A present." He blushed.

It looked awfully large for a ring.

Could it be a fur coat?

Lydia always swore they were the best. "With a cold finger you can dance, ma petite. But with a cold *cul?*"

At our table at Chez Pasquier he drank a toast to my future and I unwrapped my present. It was a red wool sweater.

"From my factory," he beamed proudly. "The neck, the sleeves, are hand fashioned."

It really was a very nice sweater. I put it on and puffed out my chest. He applauded, ordered more wine and cried with pleasure at his success.

"What's that?" Mitya muttered sourly when I pranced in. "You look like a *concierge*."

"A present from Gray Bobby," I announced proudly.

"Well tell him I need one, too," he growled. "It has been getting cold at night. But tell him a big size. I don't want to wear a glove around my neck."

The next night I told Gray Bobby of Mitya's request.

"But, of course, I love poets, too. I would like nothing better than to present him with a token of my handiwork. Perhaps he could present me one of his, as well? An autographed copy of his book? Do you think it is possible?" His voice sounded wistful.

Naturally, Mitya agreed. He had hundreds of copies of his book stacked under the bed. They held up the sagging mattress.

"And tell the old capon he can have copies of my other books as well. One for each sweater. I'll send them to my mother and sisters back home. That will give them something to howl about all right."

Soon I was requesting sweaters for everybody. The studios were filled with sweaters of all colors and sizes. It looked like all of Russia would be warmed by Scotch wool since after getting several for themselves the requests came in for a poor old mother freezing in Moscow, and a young sister without a stitch for her trousseau, the old dancer with crippling arthritis freezing in the bed he would never leave.

"But, of course, poor things. Dear, dear people. Of course, I am honoured to help the Russian dancers. Such great artistes. Perhaps an old slipper? The discarded costume from Les Biches? May I be the fortunate recipient of the glories of the old one?"

Etc. Etc.

Soon dancers were running up to ask whether I thought "his Lordship" would prefer a torn slipper or a shredded tutu. These were always in terrible shape since we continued to repair and mend our worn dance clothes until there was just no fabric left to sew two torn parts together. It was unimaginable that anybody would want them and certainly not in exchange for new wool sweaters. Once I came upon the girls talking about a man who collected the cut hair from dancer's heads and at night did something with the strands but I didn't catch what it was because when they saw me they changed the subject. When we met any of them in the cafes or on the boardwalk wearing their new sweaters, they would stroke their brightly clad breasts with one hand and giggle behind the other like peasants.

"*Charmante, charmante,*" Gray Bobby would murmur, doffing his hat and bowing.

Once I stuck out my tongue at the false Grushinkas behind his back and they cracked up with laughter.

Katya wondered whether "his Lordship" would be interested in some snapshots she had collected over the years. She had a very "artistic" one of herself and Sokolova doing arabesques on Idzikowski's shoulders on the beach at Cannes, and several unfortunately blurry ones of the American tour—even one of Nijinsky and Romola sitting on the deck of the boat. When it got about that she exchanged her box of photographs for three sweaters there was a run on old souvenirs. Virginia came up with some letters the Maestro had written to her when she was in the children's class back in London when she would sit in his lap after class and eat chocolates while he pinched her lightly on the arms and legs. She got a yellow sweater for those.

Whether the exchange was arranged directly with him or through me, Gray Bobby was very meticulous about writing my name in his careful, florid script on the gift cards. He never referred to the exchanges as anything but gifts.

"You are the Lady Bountiful," he smiled graciously at me. "Now what else can they do but love you?"

"Thief! Thief!"

The unaccustommed words rang out through the dressing rooms. Doors slammed. People started running.

"It is Stefan. They say it is Stefan."

"I have stolen nothing," shouted Stefan. "I am innocent. Call Grigoriev before it is too late. The Russians are attacking me."

"Help," Dounya wailed. "The Russians are attacking Stefan."

"He stole my sweater, he did," Franca screamed.

"How can a man steal his own sweater? It is mine. It came this morning in a white box."

They crowded through the door into my dressing room. I surveyed them cooly from my mirror where I had been painting my lips.

"I know nothing about any sweaters," I said.

"What do you mean you know nothing? Your name is on this card."

"You are Antinova—the giver of sweaters—who else if not you?" Dounya waved her finger accusingly at me.

"It is my patron. I am a miser. I do not give presents. Ask Tania. She knows I am a miser."

"It is true," Tania defended me. "A terrible miser."

"A man will go to jail. You must lift a finger." Dounya began to cry.

"Idiot! One does not go to jail for stealing a sweater."

"How do you know? You are not a judge. My grandfather went to Siberia."

"This is France."

"I have not stolen any sweaters. It is my property. It came in a white box."

"Stop shouting, you nasty Hungarian! Who cares about your dirty sweaters."

Everyday, messengers delivered gaily wrapped boxes to the *pension*. The small rooms filled with sweaters and I began to despair of keeping the place clean. Afraid I would complain to my benefactor, Mitya took to whisking them away before I returned from the theatre. I suppose he sold them in the cafes because I began to see bright blue and yellow sweaters on the boardwalk in the evenings. Mitya, himself, began to sport fancy ties, spats, a dandy straw hat, a new fountain pen. I never saw a penny from his new business. Not even a silk scarf. He could at least have bought me a silk scarf.

"How is the little capon, lately?" he asked anxiously. "You were early last night. Didn't he feed you?"

"I was tired last night, Mitya. Have you forgotten that I am dancing the new roles? I wanted to sleep."

"These aristocrats want to be led." He pulled the end of his nose. "Whet his appetite. He'll snap to, all right."

He uncurled a large scented handkerchief from the breast pocket of his new silk suit and blew his nose.

"Tell him I need more sweaters with turtle necks. They are very popular."

I grabbed my practise clothes and slammed the door behind me. My only peaceful moments were in class where everybody agreed my dancing grew richer, deeper.

"You are maturing," the girls said. "Your *adage* breathes, the poses melt like butter into each other. Such *epaulement!* Choura looked at you from under her eyelids today. She is worried."

"But I suffer, so." I confided to Tania. "Men are such bores. They think only of themselves."

"Alas, with women, it is always so. So long as you are not beaten you can count yourself lucky."

"Karsavina is not beaten. Pavlova is not beaten."

"But you are not Karsavina. You are not Pavlova."

"How do you know I am not? I am young yet."

"Hush! Be thankful. You are dancing principal roles. Sergei Pavlovitch has plans for you. Two men love you."

"Who needs them? One robs me and the other is so complicated! I shall collapse with weariness."

"Foolish girl! You are fortunate."

"But I do not feel fortunate," I wailed.

"You Americans are spoiled. Life is so!"

"But I don't like it!"

"Who asked your opinion? One lives the best one can. It is bad business all around."

"Gray Bobby," I begged one night. "Please do not give us any more sweaters."

His eyes grew big like saucers.

"But my product is good. I thought you appreciated my sweaters."

"I love them, dear Gray Bobby. But couldn't you give me another present? A ruby, maybe? Or a diamond? The girls all say that when a diamond merchant gives a dancer diamonds she knows what he wants, but when a sweater manufacturer gives her sweaters who can know what he wants?"

"Who has said this?" He began to weep. "Who has turned you against me?"

"Oh, stop it, please. I am not against you. I am just bored with your absurd sweaters."

He pressed by fingers passionately to his lips.

"Eleanora, you are a brave, generous, passionate creature. But then you are a great artist. I, alas, am a miserable cripple, good only for carrying your shawl, your fan, running after you with scent bottles when you are faint, gazing in ecstasy at your pirouettes."

He thrust his arms straight up above his head.

"Whereas horse's legs have long been the ruin of my family, I wish only to devote myself to the support and well-being of yours."

"You are doing it again, Gray Bobby. Making mountains out of molehills."

"You do not know. I am afflicted."

Leaning over the table, our faces touching, he whispered of his hopes "this time around," his dreams. "I like to think that you alone can save me. An American. A black woman. I could lose myself. I would be born again."

He sounded ominous. Were the girls right, after all, with their dark looks and secret whisperings?

"Now look here, Gray Bobby. This is getting out of hand. You'd better explain yourself."

He groaned.

"More than anything I would be brave, generous, passionate. That is why I love artists. Have you ever heard of a stingy artist? But I cannot help myself. I despise myself. Yet I suffer even more when I go against my nature."

He began kissing my hand, my wrist, my forearm, my elbow . . .

"If I should give you a ring, now . . . and how I have dreamed of this . . . your wicked little face looks mysteriously up at me. I tremble . . . your fingers move toward the pretty little Tiffany box I hold out to you . . . but my passionate dream always breaks off here. It is my disease. . . ."

He hid his face in his hands.

"I can not suffer to see you open it. 1000 cannon pointed directly at me could not force me to look into that little box . . . . We are frozen there, you and I, forever. . . ."

He hid his face in his hands.

"My darling, if I should give you a ring now I would suffer the pangs of fierce regret and morbid miseries. I should torment you with entreaties to return it to me if but for a moment. I would cajole you to loan it to me for an evening. I would offer to repair an imperfection I had noticed in the setting and steal it from you.

There is no hope for me. Have pity. . . ."

That night I wrote to my sister.

"Dear Marcia,
   I am still unlucky. I have always been unlucky.
Please accept this lovely green sweater as a present
            from your loving and very tired sister
                     Eleanora
P.S. Next week I will send you a yellow one and perhaps also a brown.

EXPERIMENT AND TRADITIONAL FORMS IN CONTEMPORARY LITERATURE

by DOUGLAS MESSERLI

from SUN & MOON

nominated by SUN & MOON *and M.D. Elevitch*

ONE GENERALLY does not associate contemporary literature and art with the use of forms, either traditional or newly invented. Within the context of the high-spirited eclecticism of the writing and visual art that has come to be described as Postmodern, the contemporary arts patently represent a renunciation of formalist principles—whether they be those of Clement Greenberg or of Robert Penn Warren and Cleanth Brooks. After all, if Modernism often demanded "pure" expression and absolutist thinking, its antithesis (if Postmodernism *is* its antithesis) obliges the artist to be self-consciously syncretic. Contemporary literary works such as Bruce Andrews, Charles Bernstein, Ray DiPalma, Steve McCaffery, and Ron Silliman's collaboratively composed *Legend,* in

304

their mix of poetry, prose, linguistic games, and babble, are anything—perhaps *everything*—but formal. Rather, they dramatize a tendency in contemporary literature towards what Jonathan Culler has described as the "non-generic," writings so eclectic in their sources and styles that they transcend or evade generic classification.[1] By contrast, poetic forms and genres bring to mind the concerns of many Moderns, and their continuing dominance in the academy, effected, in part, by critics such as Donald Davie and Harold Bloom, whose theories and criticism are grounded in writers of traditional forms such as Emerson, Hardy, and Frost. And, accordingly, for a great many less academically-oriented writers and readers, an interest in issues of form and prosody suggests a kind of nostalgia, a longing to return to the formal systems so apparent in the works of Hardy, Yeats, Eliot, and Frost, as manifested in the contemporary poetry of Richard Wilbur, Robert Penn Warren, Howard Nemerov, and the early works of Donald Hall and W. S. Merwin.

But, of course, the very definition of form—particularly as it applies to poetry—is a relative matter. Throughout history, one century's poetic forms often have been the previous century's experiments, the constrictions of the next. And in our own accelerated century each literary generation has reused, rejected, or invented new formal systems according to social, political, and personal expedients. Entire genres have risen and fallen in the span of a few decades: the "confessional" mode of poetry of the 1950's and 60's appears not to have survived a third decade; the concretist experiments of the 1960's today look almost like ancient hieroglyphs. And new forms and genres continue to evolve; recently, Ron Silliman has implied that works of his and fellow Californians Barrett Watten, Bob Perelman, Carla Harryman, Lyn Hejinian, David Bromige, and Steve Benson function to create a new prose poem genre focused on what he calls "the new sentence," works in which "actual elements of poetic structure" enter "into the interiors of sentence structure itself."[2] In other words, genres and forms really have not disappeared from even the most seemingly "avant-garde" of poetics; it is only that in the context of a protean literature, one may have difficulty in recognizing them.

[1]Jonathan Culler, "Towards a Theory of Non-Genre Literature," in Raymond Federman, ed., *Surfiction: Fiction Now . . . and Tomorrow* (Chicago: Swallow Press, 1975), pp. 19-33.

[2]Ron Silliman, in an interview with Vicki Hudspith, *Poetry Project Newsletter*, no. 72 (February 1980), non-paginated (8).

However, along with this inevitable establishment of new genres by some contemporary poets, and the return to traditional forms by more academically-aligned ones, a substantial number of writers who would have to be described as Postmodern in sensibility,[3] consciously use traditional forms in new ways, and/or work in traditional genres that were less suited to Modern ideas of structure. Indeed, these writer's works—in which form or genre often is used as a foundation or base which frees the author to experiment with or even subvert the form itself—may provide one with a clearer picture of contemporary poetics than either the formal strictures of Richard Wilbur's poetry or the emphatic shapelessness of *Legend.

Clearly, the "remaking" or "reconstructing" of forms is nothing revolutionary. In this century, one thinks immediately of Ezra Pound and his employment of traditional forms in his attempt to bring new life to poetry and ultimately to language, to "make it new." Pound's continued interest in forms such as the sestina, villanelle, and ode, in fact, is directly or indirectly reflected in the contemporary experiments with form. For Pound form is more a tool to teach the poet, than it is a container within which to create a poem. "The artist should master all known forms and systems of metrics," he argues; and, indeed, "most symmetrical forms" have "certain uses"; but the vast number of subjects, he concludes, cannot be rendered in a formal manner.[4] Pound's idea of a poem obviously is one in which structure is more open: poetry is to be built "tower by tower," "the plan/follow(ing) the builder's whim."[5] And, in that sense, Pound's theory initiated the constructionist view of poetry that underlies so much of contemporary poetics, the idea that poetry should be a thing of linguistic process as opposed to representing a set of preconceived ideas and images bound to convention. Nonetheless, if such a poem results in a "rag bag" for the modern world to "stuff all its thought in," the skein from which it is wove is form itself; if the poet/builder creates his towers according to whim, in Pound's thinking they stand on the solid foundation of formal traditions.[6]

---

[3]Although several definitions of Postmodernism have been argued in the last few years, Charles Altieri's "From Symbolist Thought to Immanence: The Ground of Postmodern Poetics," *Boundary 2*, I (Spring 1973), 605-641, is still the most coherent and suggestive. I also refer the reader to my own study of Postmodern fiction, "Modern Postmodern Fiction: Toward a Formal and Historical Understanding of Postmodern Literature," an unpublished dissertation, The University of Maryland, 1979.

[4]Ezra Pound, "A Retrospect," in *Literary Essays* (Norfolk, Conn.: New Directions, 1954), pp. 9-10.

[5]Pound, "Three Cantos," *Poetry*, X (June 1917), 113-114.

[6]*Ibid.*

This idea of form as a foundation or base for the poem made its way quite directly into the poetry of the New York writers in the 1950's and early 60's through the influence and poetry of Frank O'Hara. Marjorie Perloff points out in her book, *Frank O'Hara: Poet Among Painters,* that

> One of the special pleasures of reading O'Hara's poetry is to see how the poet reanimates traditional genres. Ode, elegy, pastoral, autobiographical poem, occasional verse, love song, litany—all these turn up in O'Hara's poetry. . . ."[7]

That is not to say that O'Hara's commitment to the tradition is the same as Pound's. Speaking on his "Ode to Lust" O'Hara remarked in 1964: "I wrote it because the ode is so formidable to write. I thought if I call it an ode it will work out."[8] Beyond the facetiousness of such a statement, O'Hara suggests that the genre here is not something which controls his poem, but rather an attitude that helps to shape it; the poem is not written to *be* an ode, but is written with the idea that it will be *called* an ode. Clearly, that incorporates the knowledge of how an ode works, an awareness of its form; and, as Perloff points out, many of O'Hara's *Odes* have "traces of the Greater or Pindaric Ode."[9] And, in that sense, for O'Hara as for Pound the genre is not an enclosure but a starting point, a kind of impetus which sets the process of the poem in motion. Nevertheless, O'Hara's statement *is* ironic, and that reveals his basic attitude. Although O'Hara uses forms, as Perloff notes, "his tendency is to parody the model or at least to subvert its 'normal' conventions."[10]

This "subversion of normal conventions" was especially attractive to many writers of the so-called "New York School," in part because of the Dadaist spirit which imbued their work, and, perhaps to a lesser degree, because of their inherent anti-academicisim. And at one time or another each of the New York poets has employed traditional genres in parody. However, their self-conscious attitude towards the tradition often has led them to more sustained and serious formal experiments. John Ashbery's

[7]Marjorie Perloff, *Frank O'Hara: Poet Among Painters* (New York: George Braziller, 1977), p. 139.
[8]Frank O'Hara, as quoted in Perloff, pp. 152-153.
[9]Perloff, p. 153.
[10]*Ibid.,* p. 139.

several meditations, sestinas, and sonnets, Kenneth Koch's comic epic *Ko,* and Ted Berrigan's *The Sonnets* all exemplify a usage of traditional forms closer to Pound's avowal of the tradition than to O'Hara's subversion of it.

Ted Berrigan's description—in an interview with Barry Alpert—of how he came to write *The Sonnets,* summarizes, it seems to me, the attitudes of some of the New York writers, and points to the way in which forms are perceived by many younger poets today.

> TB: I was very interested in the sonnet—I had been for a number of years, actually, because it seemed to me like a dynamic and exciting form. I guess I was stimulated by the fact that nobody was writing them. Literally you weren't supposed to write them and everybody was down on them. . . . So I was very excited by the form yet every time I tried to write one it was true that the form sort of stultified the whole process. Then sometime later after I had gone through Pound very much in my own manner but very extensively and gotten a certain sense of structure that was like form turned inside out . . .
>
> BA: You mean using the old forms and making them new?
>
> TB: Yeah, but really the way he did it with *The Cantos* rather than when he wrote imitations. But I mean I went through the imitative process—I imitated certain poems of John Ashbery that are in his book *Some Trees.* And one night I was looking at those imitations; I had about six or seven of them. They were a little too stiff and rigid for me. I seemed to be coming close, yet I had a brick wall all around me. I was reading John Cage and Marcel Duchamp and I was familiar with William Burroughs, but it occurred to me to go back through them and take out lines by a sort of automatic process and just be the typist. I had the poems right next to me and I decided to take one line from each page until I had six lines. Then go back through backwards and take one more line from each page until I had six more. That was twelve. By then

I could see that I would know what the final couplet would be.[11]

The differences between what Berrigan is saying here and what O'Hara does in his pastorals and odes, although subtle, are important to note. Both, obviously, are using forms very loosely, and neither is interested in remaining faithful to the sentiments that their forms have by tradition expressed. If O'Hara mocks the pastoral notions by locating the action of his poem in the middle of Manhattan, through his "automatic" process Berrigan utterly ignores the conventional topics of the sonnet. And like O'Hara, Berrigan's attraction to the form stems partly from the fact that it is "out of fashion"—what O'Hara meant, one imagines, by saying that the ode was "formidable." In short, the *idea* of the form is more important to both poets than are the actual formal strictures; Berrigan, like O'Hara and Pound, uses the form as a foundation or base upon which to build, upon which to express the process. Nonetheless, in Berrigan's case the form at poem's end has not been parodied or subverted, but has been *re*created. *The Sonnets*, no matter how different in subject matter from conventional sonnets, are formally sonnets[12]; they do not merely contain traces of the form, they *are*. And, in that respect, Berrigan has *remade* the form, has brought the form new expression. As he puts it, he has turned form "inside out." By beginning with the idea of the form, and yet allowing the poem to create itself, Berrigan has given new dimension to the form; and, in that regard, he has *re*constructed it almost as the first sonneteer would have had to construct his sonnet.

Accordingly, in works such as *The Sonnets* one can observe a gradual shifting away from the use of traditional forms for parodistic purposes towards a serious *re*creation or *re*construction of the poetic genres. In Michael Palmer's *The Circular Gates*, David Antin's *Meditations*, Peter Frank's *The Travelogues*, Terence Winch's *The Attachment Sonnets*, Robert Long's *The Sonnets*, Bernadette Mayer's many autobiographical poems and sestinas (such as "The Aeschyleans" and "The People Who Like Aeschylus"), Barbara Guest's odes, Anne Waldman's new formally

[11]Ted Berrigan and Barry Alpert, "Ted Berrigan—An Interview Conducted by Barry Alpert, Chicago, May 9, 1972," *Vort*, no. 2 (Winter 1972), 39-40.

[12]Berrigan's sonnets, however, are generally neither Italian nor English in form.

structured poems, and works by many others one witnesses this same, "turning of the form inside out," the poet permitting the poem to create the form, rather than the form to create the poem. As Michael Davidson has expressed it, "many recent poets (use) a formal convention as a way to extend and play with its limitations: incurring them, varying them and opening them into the "genius," to use Robert Duncan's term, of their complexity."[13]

Between Pound and O'Hara, of course, there are other poets, some of whom I have mentioned, who abjured free verse and the general abandonment of traditional forms. But their reasons for doing so were quite different from those of O'Hara and these contemporaries.[14] If for poets such as Berrigan, Mayer, and Palmer one can say that form is something from which the poem opens out, for poets such as Robert Frost and Richard Wilbur—two modern poets most associated with the use of traditional forms—form is something that closes the poem in, that serves as a boundary, as a protection. In his recent study of Robert Frost, Richard Poirier observes that for Frost (as for William James) "Form is a gratifying act of will and also a protective one in a universe where we are otherwise fully exposed to chaos. . . ."[15] Questioned by John Ciardi regarding his attitude toward the structure of the total poem, Richard Wilbur phrased this idea in a somewhat different manner:

> . . . The use of strict forms, traditional or invented, is like the use of framing and composition in painting: both serve to limit the work art, and to declare its artificiality: they say, "This is not the world, but a pattern imposed upon the world or found in it; this is a partial and provisional attempt to establish relations between things.[16]

For Frost and Wilbur, in other words, the form is a container, something that encloses or frames the language of the poem, and in so doing, separates and protects writer and reader—momentarily at least—from the flux of life. It is through creating or reading the

[13]Michael Davidson, "Advancing Measures: Conceptual Quantities and Open Forms," a paper delivered at the Modern Language Association's Convention in San Francisco, 1979.

[14]There are, of course, several exceptions to this generalization. Robert Duncan and Helen Adam, some of whose works fall into this period, are more akin to Pound and O'Hara than to Frost and Wilbur.

[15]Richard Poirier, Robert Frost: The Work of Knowing (New York: Oxford University Press, 1977), p. 24.

[16]Richard Wilbur, interviewed by John Ciardi, as quoted in Donald L. Hill, Richard Wilbur (New York: Twayne Publishers, 1967) p. 90.

poem—or involvement in any such creative act—that imagination, that Romantic repository of correspondences, is freed, as Wilbur puts it, to "establish relations between things," the "things" axiomatically being "out there" in "real" life. For the contemporary poets such as Berrigan and Mayer, however, the in/out dichotomy is inoperative. Influenced by the current semiotic and structuralist environment, these writers conceive language to be less a "signature" of reality than a "sign"—a conception akin to what Richard Palmer describes as the pre-modern notion of language as a "man-invented designation which can be changed at will."[17] Thus, the poem no longer holds the world-of-flux at bay. Immediately upon being said or put to paper the words, concretized as things in space, become as subject to flux—what Frost calls "the chaos"—as all other objects. For the contemporary, as for Wilbur, the poem is "artificial"—is grounded in artifice—but, unlike Wilbur's poem, the contemporary poem does not retain an organic link with what it names. The poem is not a sanctuary, but a "convention" of words that have their own existence in space. The language of the poem does not *correspond* to life because it *is* a reality in its own right. And, in this regard experiments in traditional forms by poets such as Berrigan, Mayer, and Palmer reflect not only a different methodology, but a changed poetics.

When one suggests, therefore, that living poets such as Wilbur and Warren are nostalgic in their use of forms, it is less a judgment than a distinction that when blurred helps to obscure the fact that contemporary poetry is as involved—one might easily argue it is more involved—with traditional forms than was Modernism.

This is even more true of prose fiction; but, the context here is much different. If a substantial number of Modern poets have continued to practice the traditional poetic genres and forms, few Modern novelists have demonstrated any interest in genres outside of the tradition beginning with Cervantes of the prose romance. And for the majority of Modern fictionists the prose romance has been seen less as a genre with certain strictures than as a stage for intense experimentation. When one thinks of Modern fiction it is inevitably its experimentors—James, Proust, Woolf, Joyce, Faulk-

[17]Richard Palmer, "Toward a Postmodern Hermeneutics of Performance," in Michel Benamou and Charles Caramello, eds., *Performance in Postmodern Culture* (Milwaukee and Madison: Center for Twentieth Century Studies/Coda Press, 1977), p. 25. This and other distinctions that Palmer makes between Modern and Premodern attitudes are based on his reading of Jean Gebser's *Ursprung und Gegemoart*.

ner, Kafka, and Gide—who first come to mind. Certainly there are exceptions: Ivy Compton-Burnett, Ronald Firbank, Henry Green, and other British narrativists worked in the genre of the dialogue novel, related to the Socratic dialogues; Gertrude Stein, Djuna Barnes, Wyndham Lewis, Aldous Huxley, and Norman Douglas all attempted anatomies or Menippean satires; and Stein, Barnes, Lewis, Joyce, and Williams experimented in genres and modes as diverse as the almanac, monologue, *tableaux vivants*, picaresque, travel guide, and encyclopedia. But these forays into other genres generally have been regarded as oddities, viewed in the context of eccentricism. Indeed, fictionists such as Compton-Burnett, Barnes, Firbank, Stein, and Lewis *are* eccentrics—with respect to the prose romance.

However, if the prose romance has long appeared to be a genre with nearly limitless structural potential, the organicism which most Moderns have required of it has made it as constricting for several younger authors as a Richard Wilbur stanza. From Percy Lubbock's insistence that "The well-made book is the book in which the subject and the form coincide and are indistinguishable—the book in which the matter is all used up in the form, in which the form expresses all the matter,"[18] to Brooks and Warren's claim that "a story is successful— . . . it has achieved form—when all the elements are functionally related to each other, when each part contributes to the intended effect,"[19] Modern critics and authors in large have argued for the novel what Wilbur and Frost have for poetry: that narrative art requires a closure, a frame which separates—thus allowing a correspondence between—expression and life.

Predictably—in fact contemporaneously with O'Hara's experimentation with poetic forms—several narrativists, most notably Ralph Ellison and John Barth, sought narrative alternatives to the prose romance. Ellison's choice of the picaresque genre for *Invisible Man,* one suspects, was a necessary abandonment of a form so long dominated by white society and its values. But, just as importantly, in such a pseudoautobiographical form wherein a radically undefined hero generally encounters a random and chaotic series of events,[20] Ellison found a near perfect metaphor for the

[18]Percy Lubbock, *The Craft of Fiction* (New York: Viking Press, 1957), p. 40.

[19]Cleanth Brooks and Robert Penn Warren, *Understanding Fiction* (New York: Appleton-Century-Crofts, 1959), p. 684.

[20]These qualities of the picaresque are taken from those described by Stuart Miller, *The Picaresque Novel* (Cleveland: Case Reserve University Press, 1967), p. 70.

circumstance of the contemporary Black. However, in that fact one must presume at the very least, that Ellison's attitude toward the picaresque as a viable literary form is ambivalent. And one cannot help wondering if the American Black were less subject to social and political oppression, whether Ellison might not have chosen the prose romance. It is likely, in other words, that Ellison's choice of another genre came about more as a strategem to express his theme than as a genuine interest in the form itself.

Similarly, Barth's imitation of traditional genres in works such as *The Sot-Weed Factor* and *Giles Goat Boy*—which Robert Scholes has described respectively as an "historical novel" and a "mock epic allegory"[21]—and in his recent epistolary work, *Letters*, is less an affirmation of alternative forms than a commentary on the exhaustion of serious fiction in general—including the works themselves. Leslie Fiedler summaries this attitude:

> We may begin . . . by thinking that *Giles Goat Boy* is a comic novel, a satire intended to mock everything which comes before it from *Oedipus the King* to the fairy tale of the Three Billy Goats Gruff. But before we are through, we realize it is itself it mocks, along with the writer capable of producing one more example of so obsolescent a form, and especially us who are foolish enough to be reading it. It is as if the Art Novel, aware that it must die, has determined to die laughing.[22]

Barth's repeated emphasis on the "exhaustion of literature"[23] places his use of traditional genres in a context not unlike that of the New York poets, wherein the artist employs forms he perceives to be ridiculously obsolescent in order to mock the works of his predessors while mocking himself.

However, as with poetry, such a self-consciously defensive stance has led several contemporary fictionists into new rapport with older genres. In his 1958 fiction, *Alfred & Guinevere* James Schuyler began experimenting with the dialogue novel, which in *A Nest of Ninnies* (written in collaboration with John Ashbery) and *What's for Dinner?* achieves as consummate expression as the

[21]Robert Scholes, *Fabulation and Metafiction* (Urbana: University of Illinois Press, 1979), pp. 75 and 207.

[22]Leslie Fiedler, "The Death and Rebirth of the Novel," in John Halperin, ed., *The Theory of the Novel* (New York: Oxford University Press, 1974), p. 200.

[23]John Barth, "The Literature of Exhaustion," in Raymond Federman, ed., *Surfiction: Fiction Now . . . and Tomorrow* (Chicago: Swallow Press, 1975), pp. 19-33.

fictions in the genre by Henry Green and Anthony Powell—if not those of Compton-Burnett. Schyler's intentions, like Barth's, are parodistic; in his relinquishment of the greater part of his fiction to the inanities of stereotypical suburban Americans he has given himself little choice. But in that very relinquishment the form opens up; by using the genre as a base rather than a mold for his satire Schuyler, like Berrigan, accords it different qualities. The wit and intelligence that pervade the British dialogues—inherited from the philosophical cunning of Socrates—in Schuyler's fictions become cliche and near idiocy. Indeed, the conversations of Schulyer and Ashbery's "ninnies" are about as mundane as the discourse's of Compton-Burnett's figures are complex; the compelled machinations of Compton-Burnett's figures are little more than whimsical choices for Schuyler's suburbanites. The genre as reconstructed by Schuyler, in short, has been turned inside out: the form is no longer matrix but matter, is no longer a structure which defines the fiction, but one from which the fiction is propelled into new possibilities, into its own life. Nonetheless, the form here remains intact; and in that fact the genre is enriched rather than merely mocked. In Schuyler and Ashbery's hands the dialogue novel suddenly becomes a dynamic expression of the effects of suburban culture on language and thought, which the more realistic presentations of writers such as John Cheever and John Updike—in their careful use of symbols, metaphors, and analogies antithetical to the lives of the character's they present— have been less successful in capturing. The characters of Schuyler's fiction may be fools, but the works themselves are brilliant satires of contemporary American life.

Marvin Cohen is another writer who uses dialogue to probe contemporary thought. But Cohen's model clearly is Plato rather than the British, and, accordingly, in works such as "On the Clock's Business and the Cloud's Nature" and "Rain's Influence on Man's Attitude to Art," his dialogues, at least superficially, appear to function as gnomic philosophical encounters. Yet, here too the genre is turned on its head: in Cohen's commentaries rational logic is demolished as interrogater and respondent surrender rational thinking to puns, malapropisms, cliches, corn-ball jokes, and irrelevant questions and answers. If a sort of logic eventually *is* established, it reminds one less of Socrates than of Gertrude Stein.

Stein, in fact, has had the same relation to the experiments in forms in contemporary fiction as Pound has had to its poetry. As Pound did with poetic forms, Stein began to experiment very early in her career with the constituent elements of narrative form, the sentence and the paragraph, in an attempt to find "a whole thing" "created by something moving as moving is not as moving should be."[24] Stein's idea of narrative form implicitly is not that of the sequence as in counting one, two, three, four, but of the sequence in which each element—be it clause, sentence, or paragraph—is given new potential, as in counting one and one and one and one."[25] Accordingly, Stein rejects the prose romance—which requires the sequence of addition for its organcism—in favor of older genres such as the anatomy and picaresque, in which narrative is noncumulative, in which count is lost rather than kept. Indeed, beyond the apparent radicalness of her clauses, sentences, and paragraphs, Stein's fictions are generally grounded in traditional genres. *The Making of Americans* and *A Long Gay Book* have close affinities with the anatomy; *Ida* is a picaresque[26]; *Lucy Church Amiably*, as Donald Sutherland indicates, is a pastoral[27]; *The Geographical History of America* is both a treatise on the relationship between history and geography and is a fictional history and geography of American thought[28]; *Brewsie and Willie* contains elements of the dialogue; *To Do* is an alphabetically structured litany of birthdays; and *The Autobiography of Alice B. Toklas* and *Everybody's Autobiography* are "fictional" autobiographies. In short, like Pound, Stein uses the traditional genres as a base from which language creates a reality-in-flux.

Stein's influence has been far-reaching, and extends beyond the confines of narrative and fiction into poetry, drama, and non-literary modes of expression. But Stein's particular interest in the interrelationship between language, performance, and life has had the greatest impact, perhaps, upon contemporary experiments in traditional genres of narrative. Nearly all of Stein's works are focused upon the way in which language creates reality—or, as I expressed it earlier in this essay, the way in which words said or put to paper suddenly become "things" which are subject to the

[24]Gertrude Stein, "Poetry and Grammar," in *Lectures in America* (New York: Vintage, 1975), p. 225

[25]*Ibid.*, p. 227.

[26]See my discussion of *Ida* in "Modern Postmodern Fiction: Toward a Formal and Historical Understanding of Postmodern Literature."

[27]Donald Sutherland, *Gertrude Stein: A Biography of Her Work* (New Haven, Conn.: Yale University Press, 1951), p. 140.

flux of life. However, in several of her works Stein further explores how those literary expressions affect real life experiences in the lives of reader and creator. What some critics have interpreted as the mythologizing of an egocentrist, arguably is an active investigation of the limits of language and the individual. Especially in her portraits, lectures, and autobiographies Stein, through the personae of others such as Picasso, James, and Toklas, seeks to know whether language (the expression of her personae), rather than merely coexisting in reality, can actually remake the individual's life—whether language defines *a* reality or *all* reality. Thus, in these works language is far more than a "analogue of experience"—which William Gass has argued it is for Stein[28]: it is experience itself.

Stein's quest is reflected in many intermedia works of contemporary literature, music, and art. But in terms of the contemporary work in traditional genres, it has had a special impact on performance fictionists such as Norma Jean Deak and Eleanor Antin. Deak also uses the genre of the dialogue as the base of her short "fictions." Her "Dialogues for Woman," however, share little in common with either the British dialoguists or Socrates, but are closer to the dialogues of the Middle Ages between body and soul. Just like the body and soul dialogues, Deak's conversations between two women are represented as emanating from the same consciousness; as Deak notes, "The original idea behind the dialogues was to create a theatre of mind. In the performance I wanted to retain this idea."[29] Thus, the women's voices (her voice on tape) are generally neutral in tone; neither is given dominance. But here the analogy seems to end. Deak's conversations seldom contain any apparent "encounter" of ideas or emotions; in fact, extrinsically they communicate very little of anything: a glass of water, a slight tremor, a broken vase—such are the apparent focuses of these works. It is only because one has been trained to see art within a frame, however, that the conversations appear to be so mundane. The real focus of Deak's art is not on the dialogue between the women—those two projections of her imagination—but on the dialogue between those projections and herself as she performs them. Deak writes of her performances:

[28]See William Gass, "Introduction," Gertrude Stein, *The Geographical History of America or The Relation of Human Nature to the Human Mind* (New York: Vintage, 1973), pp. 24-25.
[29]*Ibid.*

While I was rehearsing, I noticed that I repeated particular gestures—for example, scratching the left side of my head or pushing my hair out of my eyes. I wrote some of these gestures into the stage directions. As a result, what was first perceived to be an unconscious gesture on the part of the performer was later identified as belonging to one of the characters. At other moments I assumed the character of one of the women and made a gesture immediately following its indication in the stage direction. As I made the movement, I said the same text line at the moment it was said by the taped voice.[30]

In other words, as in Stein's portraits and autobiographies, Deak's dialogues present a constant interaction between personae and author, between language and act. In the end these *are* dialogues between body and soul, not as in the literary dialectics of the Middle Ages, but in a more profound sense; underlying each of Deak's performances is an almost palpable tension between her own physical being and the substantiation through language of her intellect. The body and soul encounter is not between two characters, but between what one calls "reality" and what one calls "fiction," between life and the word make flesh.

Similarly, through various media Eleanor Antin explores the relationship between personae and self. Hers is not a dialogue, however, but a near-complete immersion of self in four personae—the Nurse, the King, the Black Movie Actress, and the Ballerina—each of which manifests itself in what Howard N. Fox has described as work that "is autobiographical in the way that any fantasy or any fiction may be an autobiographical work of art."[31] Yet, of course, these fictions when enacted become historical facts in effect. The whole of Antin's oevre, accordingly, is tied up with issues of autobiography and biography. But particularly in *Recollections of My Life with Diaghilev*, the memoirs of the Ballerina, in which the issues of traditional genre, language, performance, and "real" experience are linked, one can observe an inextricable relationship between the self-as-fiction and fiction-as-self.

Real autobiography—that is the genre as it has defined itself—

[30]Norma Jean Deak, "Dialogues for Two Women," *Sun & Moon*, nos. 9/10 (Summer 1980), 178.

[31]Howard N. Fox, *Directions* (Washington, D.C.: Smithsonian Institution Press, 1979), p. 27.

Antin argues, "makes a powerful claim to truth."[32] And, in that sense, Antinova's memoirs are "merely" fiction. Indeed, in that Antinova, as a member of Diaghilev's Ballet Russe, is a university educated American Black, and in that throughout the *Recollections* Antin brilliantly mimics the style of late-nineteenth and early-twentieth century memoirs, one easily might argue that the form is used primarily for parody. But as scholars of autobiography such as Robert F. Sayre have pointed out, although the traditional autobiographer ". . . is not passing off the imaginary as actual or willfully falsifying important facts," in his very selection of incidents, and in the tone and manner of personality (the masks) in which he presents them, autobiography has far more to do with fiction than one might suspect.[33] If, as Sayre suggests, autobiography is something in which a "life . . . is made over in a discovery of the present by means of rediscovering the past,"[34] one might question what role does memory play? Can one "mis-remember, make mistakes," even "lie?" Antin asks.[35] The problem is further complicated by desire; desire may not only color the autobiographer's version of reality, Antin implies, it may be so powerful that it surfaces as a major factor in the autobiographer's life.[36] Even if it does not, Antin might argue that no self-examination can afford to ignore the effects of desire and fantasy upon a life.

In this respect, Antin's writings and performances do not undermine the genre, but extend it. Antinova's *Recollections* do not merely reflect a consciousness in the present remaking a past, but, as Antin puts it, "a present trying to produce the past to take possession of the future."[37] Through her readings of the *Recollections* and performances language does, in fact, *re*make life—just as Stein suspected. After nearly every reading of her memoirs, David Antin reports, people have naively asked Eleanor when she performed with the Ballet Russe and/or to share stories of Nijinsky, Diaghilev, and Pavlova.[38] Such improbable belief in Antinova's memoirs (in order for Antin to have performed with the Ballet

[32]Eleanor Antin, "Some Thoughts on Autobiography," *Sun & Moon*, nos. 6/7 (Winter 1978-79), 81

[33]Robert F. Sayre, *The Examined Self: Benjamin Franklin, Henry Adams, Henry James* (Princeton, N.J.: Princeton University Press, 1964), p. 7. In equating autobiography and memoirs, however, I am glossing over important distinctions between the two made by Sayre and by Roy Pascal in *Design and Truth in Autobiography*. I do so because I am interested less in defining these specific forms than I am in pointing to their convergence in contemporary literature. Certainly, I encourage the reader to examine those general distinctions made by Pascal and Sayre.

[34]*Ibid.*, p. 33.

[35]Antin, "Some Thoughts on Autobiography," 81.

[36]*Ibid.*, 82.

[37]*Ibid.*, 81.

[38]From a telephone conversation between David Antin and the author, April 1980.

Russe she would have to be at least eighty years old) is a testament to both the genius of Antin's reconstruction of the autobiographical genre and to the dynamism of all language; it represents what Antin describes as the credibility or "credit" that reality requires between word and being, between name and body. In her performance of the ballet, *Before The Revolution*, Antinova observes:

> Sometimes there is a space between a person and her name. I can't always reach my name. Between me and Eleanor Antin sometimes there is a space. No, that's not true. Between me and Eleanor Antin there is always a space. I act as if there isn't. I make believe it isn't there. Recently, the Bank of America refused to cash one of my checks. My signature was unreadable, the bank manager said. "It is the signature of an important person," I shouted. "You do not read the signature of an important person, you recognize it." That's as close as I can get to my name. And I was right, too. Because the bank continues to cash my checks. That idiosyncratic and illegible scrawl has credit there. This space between me and my name has to be filled with credit.[39]

In Antinova's *Recollections*, in short, one again observes a traditional fictional genre being utilized as a foundation or ground for a remaking of the genre and of life itself. Not all contemporary fictionists take traditional forms as far as does Antin, but a great many writers employ the autobiography and related genres such as letters, journals, and confessions in an attempt to explore the boundaries of fiction. From Toby Olson's *The Life of Jesus*—which Olson describes as "an autobiographical novel" told in terms of Jesus' life[40]—to Kathy Acker's *Kathy Goes to Haiti*, Lynne Dreyer's letters and journals, and Nathaniel Mackey's epistolary *From a Broken Bottle Traces of Perfume Still Emanate*, contemporary writers have experimented with autobiographically related genres in an attempt to return what Jean-Luc Nancy describes as the "pure I," the "I who utters myself uttering" *into* (as opposed to *upon* or *beside*) fiction.[41]

[39]Antin, "Before the Revolution," in *Dialogue/Discourse/Research* (Santa Barbara, Ca.: Santa Barbara Museum of Art, 1979), nonpaginated (30).

[40]Toby Olson, *The Life of Jesus* (New York: New Directions, 1976), inside front cover.

[41]Jean-Luc Nancy, "Mundus est Fabula," *Modern Language Notes*, XCIII (1978), 638.

Underlying this remaking of the self, moreover, is a reconstructing of the world, of the universe. Accordingly, contemporary fictionists have also been attracted to more inclusive forms such as the travel guide, picaresque, anatomy, and encyclopedia. Before her current involvement with personae, Antin experimented with the travel guide in *100 Boots*, subtitled an "Epistolary Novel" less because of its form, than because the travels of the boots were documented as picture postcards, mailed to various art journals, newspapers, and friends. Clearly, the journey of one hundred empty boots across the United States belies a parodistic, if not Dadaist spirit. But a true commitment to the travel guide genre as established by Defoe, Sterne, and Swift is evidenced in the fact that, absurd as they are, the boots do undergo a fictional voyage in which the world is revealed as it is remade. The boots' travels are visually depicted in terms of "real" places—Niagara Falls, the Western desert, the Pacific Ocean, indeed, nearly all the typical tourists stops. But Antin's photographs of these places as invaded by boots makes for a new landscape, a new world never seen before.

Such a visual transformation of the world is achieved linguistically in travel guides such as Walter Abish's *Alphabetical Africa*—in which journey and journeyers are generated and deconstructed by alphabetical accretion and subtraction—in Italo Calvino's *Invisible Cities*—in which Marco Polo, through "memory, desire, and signs," tries to describe his several journeys to a disbelieving Kublai Khan—and in my own *Letters from Hanusse*—which, like Antin's early work, uses the letter as a means to relate the nature of a world in the process of being recreated.

Moreover, in Abish's newest fiction, *How German Is It*, and in my own fiction the I and the world are brought together in a structure that bears some resemblence to the picaresque. Neither of these fictions is a true picaresque: in each the consciousness of the narrator controls and shapes the work too strongly to permit it the episodic form of the traditional picaresque. But such works do indicate a tendency in the contemporary fictionist to reconstruct a self and world against the backdrop of an ever changing time and space. In the hands of a writer like Kathy Acker, indeed, character, scene, and circumstance shift in a kaliedoscopic rapidity that brings to mind the picaresques of Grimmelhausen and Nash. In her fictions such as *The Adult Life of Toulouse Latrec, The Childlike*

Life of the Black Tarantula, and *Girl Gangs Take over the World,* self and world are not merely transformed, but are continually rebuilt before the reader's eyes. Form and language is in near-perpetual motion as Acker, having raided sources as diverse as detective stories, political tracts, and pornographic novels, opens her tale to the barrage of experience facing any contemporary picaro(a).

Ultimately, this interest in traditional forms as a base from which to remake the self and the world is reflected in an interest in restructuring the universe, in reinterpreting and remaking its metaphysics. And if the picaresque combines the self and the world in its structure, it is the anatomy, with its mix of prose and poetry, of philosophy, fact, and fiction, of catalogue, monologue, and dialogue which is most suited for such a discovery. Two contemporary works stand out as conscious uses of the anatomy genre: *Seeking Air* by Barbara Guest and *Mulligan Stew* by Gilbert Sorrentino.

Guest's work—like Joyce's great anatomy-encyclopedia, *Finnegans Wake*—is focused on the issues of artifice and reality. The central narrator of her work, in fact, begins as merely a literary figure, surrounded by other such figures, several of whom, like Clarissa Harlowe, make specific reference to fictions of the past. What Guest explores through her use of such artifice is whether or not the contemporary author, faced with an inescapable awareness of the literary and art traditions from Swift to Harry Matthews, from Ingres to Tony Smith, can create a character that is anything beyond—to steal William Carlos Williams' description of his poems—a "machine of words." Accordingly, the chapters of Guest's fiction represent different strategies, various literary episodes in the history of narrative art. If her character, Morgan Flew, eventually does "find the way," as Guest puts it, to come to life, it is not because the fiction culminates in realism, but because Guest has had such utter faith in the tradition, in the multitude of linguistic experiments of the past. Her character does not come to life as flesh—or what the imagination conjures up as flesh—but as words in space, the very same space in which man breathes his air.

Sorrentino's anatomy also calls up the presence of Joyce. But while paying homage to Joyce—Joyce even appears as one of the fiction's characters—*Mulligan Stew* is basically a reaction against the whole avant-grade tradition that Joyce and his peers begat. And in his attempt to satirize what he clearly sees as the degenerate condition of contemporary literature, Sorrentino is much closer to Flaubert, who in his anatomy, *Bouvard et Pecuchet*, attacked the *petit bourgeois* attitudes of the whole nineteenth century.

As in Guest's work, several of Sorrentino's characters bear literary names, and a couple of them, metaphorically speaking, "come to life." But unlike *Seeking Air*, these figures of langauge remain bound within the confines of *Mulligan Stew* because their creator purportedly is not Sorrentino, but Sorrentino's character, Antony Lamont, an author who has little facility with language, and who continually binds his characters to narrative plot. The whole of *Mulligan Stew*, in fact, dissects and analyzes the ways in which twentieth-century literature has failed to create a dynamic art. And, in that sense, Sorrentino's anatomy does not really rebuild a self, a world, or a universe, but, rather, takes all three apart. Opposed to this dissection, however, is Sorrentino's own play with language, the countless puns, metaphors, leaps of logic, lists, litanies, imitations, and literary references, all of which impose a linguistic vitality upon what is otherwise *de*constructed, collapsed. Accordingly, Sorrentino becomes his own hero, so to speak. Instead of his fiction coming to life through language, through his linguistic energy Sorrentino transforms life into fiction.

The idea of life transformed into fiction is an ancient one, and has been central to a great many Modern fictions—the works of Proust, Hemingway, Lowry, and Mailer immediately come to mind. But once again the contemporary work such as *Mulligan Stew* reflects a far different relationship between lived experience and fiction than one observes at work in *The Sun Rises* or *Under the Volcano*. For the Moderns like Hemingway and Lowry life experiences as transformed into the prose romance are necessarily objectified because the artifact is conceived as being temporarily static, a frame. The life presented thus becomes a thing of memory, of the past. For Sorrentino, on the other hand, memory has little to do with it; there is no attempt to recall life, only to express it in the action of writing, what Derrida would call *trace*. [42] Thus, there is no objectification of experience in *Mulligan Stew*; Sorrentino directly enters into the fiction through the play of words. His fiction does

[42]Jacques Derrida, *Of Grammatology*, trans. by Gayatri Chakravorty Spivak (Baltimore: Johns Hopkins University Press, 1976).

not present a life as lived, but a life as it is being lived in linguistic presentism.

Many contemporary writers interested in this sort of "deconstruction" of experience through language, write what one tentatively would have to call non-fiction. Yet, interestingly enough, these authors also often use traditional forms, especially autobiography, letters, and journals. Here too Stein has been influential; the same autobiographies in which Stein takes on other personae, causing the works to be fictions, simultaneously express what are supposedly "true" events. Therefore, the same techniques are often used in these prose works as in the poetic and narrative experiments in traditional genres. Ray DiPalma's *The Birthday Notations,* for example, ostensibly is a mere collation of passages from actual eighteenth, nineteenth, and twentieth century journals; however, in the context of these passages, all being dated the same month and day as DiPalma's birthday, they link to create a kind of fiction in which the hero is bibliographer. Hannah Weiner's *Clairvoyant Journal* is made up of what she declares are "real" events, but for the non-believer the words she sees written on objects, on the foreheads of friends, and in the air, might certainly be perceived as fiction. Bernadette Mayer's *Eruditio ex Memoria* appears to be a kind of confession, a "memory of knowledge"; but, in its mix of metaphysical statement and authorial intrusion, the work has similarities with the anatomy; indeed, the work has been described by Mayer as being taken "from random pages of school notebooks at a moment when I had to throw them all away and couldn't bear not to save some kind of part of them"—a description which supports the feeling that one has of this work being a "cutting up," a "dissection."[43] Similarly, Ronald Vance's *Canoe,* a collation of notes and papers that survived a fire, has many parallels with the anatomy and journal. And what David Antin calls "talk poems"—oral works usually centering around his personal experiences and ideas, are structured according to the classical rhetorical strategies of synedoche, metonymy, antithesis, and hyperbole. In short, it is not that these works have no genre, but that they cross boundaries between prose, poetry, and fiction. And along with more definitively prose works such as John Ashbery's *The Vermont Notebooks,* Lewis Warsh's autobiography,

[43]From a letter from Bernadette Mayer to the author, dated April 27, 1979.

Earth Angel and the letters of friends, *The Maharajah's Son*, Bernadette Mayer's autobiographical novel, *Memory*, Tom Clark's metaphysical speculations, "Some Thoughts on the Subject," and Bill Berkson's epigrammatic "50 Great Essays," these works reflect a contemporary fascination with traditional prose forms.

What one quickly perceives in the light of so much experimentation with older forms and genres is that contemporary literature not only has "continuity with its literary antecedents"—as Robert Alter has argued for contemporary fiction[44]—but that it represents an active seeking out and utilizing of pre-Modern forms and genres as a ground from which language opens the work to new dimensions. In such a perspective it even may be valuable to question whether what is generally called Modernism is actually "the tradition," or a diversion from it.[45]

---

[44]Robert Alter, "The Self-Conscious Moment: Reflections on the Aftermath of Modernism," *TriQuarterly, no. 33* (Spring 1975), 218.

[45]From a letter from Charles Bernstein to the author, dated April 28, 1980. Bernstein is not making a distinction here between Post-modernism and Modernism, nor between poets who use formal structures and those who do not. Rather, his distinction is between writers who use language that "in its syntax & vocabulary controls/mediates/circumscribes what can be thought/seen" and others. Bernstein writes: "I absolutely do believe that "we" are the tradition—in a sense the "high modern" poets like Eliot or Lowell or Auden (are) really a diversion from that more central poetic project going back to Dickinson or Thoreau or Blake or whatever overblown list I'd throw out—Campion!"

GIRL TALK

fiction by DENISE CASSENS

from SHANKPAINTER

nominated by John Irving

Aʟʟ ᴛʜᴇ ɢɪʀʟs who come to my house are beautiful; all have a parade of lovers in all shapes, sizes, with all colors of hair, eyes, teeth. . .they talk about these lovers in the evening by the radiator as it toots and wheezes; all these boys who are tall, short, straight, stooped, gaga-eyed, rat-eyed, butchers, bakers, candlestick-makers; silk-skinned like transparent slices of ham they float over our heads, yelling, laughing, playing poker in thin air.

"There's the Saga of Sam the Sailor," said Lou Anne, for example, one night in front of the radiator.

We burst out. This is very funny, funnier than banana peels, runaway Fords, sprung pianos.

"Sam was the first boy who ever told me he wanted me," said Lou Anne.

"Mmmm," we said.

"He really became a sailor, long after he left me. He joined the Navy, the big Navy that skirts the globe."

"Oh boy do they skirt the globe," we said.

"I can't remember what I looked like then. But this is what he told me: Oh Girlie, Girlie, your tits are mangos and your eyes are Sin, your kitten wants breakfast and I want in."

Our hands flew to our mouths. Our seats creaked.

"A sedan. He had some sort of old sedan, tan, with gumdrop windows in the back, pink stuffing balled up out the seats. 'Where do you want to go, Baby?' he said. 'This Dreamobile will take you anywhere you want to go.' "

"What did you tell him?" we said.

"I made a face like *I don't care.*"

"Ah," we said.

"We drove a ways down the road and he started to sing. It was an old ballad." She leaned close. "It's about a Scottish boy who ran away from home and fell in love and jumped into the sea and was rescued by an oriental merchant who took him to Singapore and gave him a houseboat where he could live off goldfish under a tree of nightingales."

"Ah, that one," we said.

"He took me to the state park. In the dark we saw redwood tables, GO SLOW signs, litter bins."

"What did you tell him then?" we said.

"I made a face like *out here?*"

"Were there stars?" we said.

"Oh yes. We crawled under a table, but my head stuck out. I remember the stars because I was on my back. I felt sorry for him because, being on his stomach, he missed everything. He was stuck rubbing his knees and palms in the dirt, like he lost a contact lens."

"How did he get inside you?"

"He took that Little Fish right out and stuck it under my nose. It winked in the dark. 'Kiss it, kiss it, oh kiss it,' he said."

"What did you say?"

"I made faces like *what do we do?*" She rubbed her tummy and rolled her eyes. "Then he came in my mouth. 'Does it taste good?' he said. He was yelling. 'Tell me it tastes good.' "

"What did you tell him it tasted like?" We sat up and listened. We wanted to learn something.

"Clouds," she said.

"Hmmm," we said. "Did he come inside you after he came in your mouth?"

"He fell down on his knees then. I threw my arms around him and made all kinds of faces to let him know I was sorry if I bit him. 'Oh rub me and get me hard again,' he said. 'I don't want you to go away and not feel anything.' "

"*Did* you feel anything?" We hung our heads. We were instantly ashamed, of ignorance, or longing, or both.

"I felt something. You always do. Not what *they* think, of course."

None of us knew but we nodded.

"First he said, 'Do I fit?' Then he said, 'What size am I?' "

"And you said?"

"I had to do a lot of fast talking. I said, oh you're about porpoise size."

" 'What am I like?' he said. 'What do I remind you of?' So I said, 'It feels like I went out camping with my pants off and something like a weasel burrowed inside me.' "

" 'Oh Sugar,' he said, breathing hard. 'What do you feel *down there*?' "

"What did you say?"

"Well of course I was stuck," she said. "I knew he meant *in* there, what he felt on his own skin, did I feel anything like that, bells, water, thrills, the pitter-patter of little feet, on the inside, not the outside. I couldn't tell him the truth—you all know the truth."

We nodded anyway.

"The truth, which is, in there right at the end you feel nothing. It would drive you crazy to feel anything there, where you can't get to it yourself. Plus which, how could you have babies if you felt anything there?"

Now we saw her point.

"So he shoved as hard as he could and said, 'Can't you feel anything right here, where I *am*?' 'Ugh,' I said. 'Yes.' 'Well, what, for God's sake, what?' 'I don't know,' I said. 'I never know what I feel down there.' "

This is one thing we all have in common, we never know what we feel down there. Medical science doesn't even know what we feel down there. Lou Anne tells me her doctor says it ends in a nose. Can you believe it? A nose. You can touch it if you bend forward.

Of course, anyway, what does it matter if you have a nose inside you? This is all just girl talk: all about love. Boys don't care, they stand on streetcorners and laugh it off. There's no such thing as boy talk, only girl talk. And I'm full of it, girl talk, giggled in a shell's ear. That's how I think of us, talking into things—shells, phones, our hands. And what do we say? Over and over, I love you.

THE SADNESS OF BROTHERS

by GALWAY KINNELL

from THE AMERICAN POETRY REVIEW

nominated by Ai and Gerald Stern

1

He comes to me like a mouth
speaking from under several inches of water.
I can no longer understand what he is saying.
He has become one
who never belonged among us, someone
it is useless to think about or remember.

But this morning, I don't know why,
twenty-one years too late,
I imagine him back: his beauty

of feature wastreled down
to chin and wattles, his eyes
ratty, liver-lighted, he stands
at the door, and we face each other, each of us
suddenly knowing the lost brother.

2

I found a photograph
of a tractor ploughing a field—the ploughman
twisted in his iron seat
looking behind him at the turned-up earth—among
the photographs and drawings he hoarded up
of all the aircraft in the sky—Heinkel HE70s, Dewoitine D333
    "Antares," Loire-et-Olivier H24-2—
and the fighting aircraft especially—Gloster Gauntlet, Fairey
    Battle I, Vickers Vildebeest Mark VII—
each shown crookedly
climbing an empty sky
the killer's blue of blue eyes
into which all his life he dreamed
he would fly; until pilot training, 1943,
when original fear
washed out
all the flyingness in him; leaving
a man who only wandered
from then on; on roads
which ended twelve years later
in Wyoming, when he raced his big car
through the desert night, under
the Dipper
or Great Windshield Wiper
which, turning, squeegee-ed existence everywhere,
even in Wyoming, of its damaged dream life;
leaving only
old goods, few possessions,
matter which ceased to matter; and among the detritus,
the photographs of airplanes; and crawling
with negative force among these,
a tractor, in its iron
seat a farmer half turned, watching without expression
as the earth flattened away
into nowhere,
into the memory of a dead man's brother.

3

In this brother
I remember back, I see the father
I had so often seen in him . . . and known
in my own bones, too: the serene-
seeming, sea-going gait
which took him down Oswald Street in dark of each morning
and up Oswald Street in dark of each night . . .
this small, well-wandered Scotsman
who appears now in memory's memory,
in light of last days, jiggling
his knees as he used to do—
get out of here, I knew
they were telling him, *get out of here, Scotty*–
control he couldn't control
thwarting his desires down
into knees which could only jiggle
the one bit of advice least useful
to this man who had dragged himself to the earth's ends
so he could end up
in the ravaged ending-earth
of Pawtucket, Rhode Island; where the Irish wife willed
the bourgeois illusion all of us dreamed
we lived, even he, who disgorged
divine capitalist law
out of his starved craw
that we might succeed though he had failed
at every enterprise but war,
and perhaps at war,
for what tales we eked from his reluctance
those Sunday mornings when six of us
hugged sideways in the double bed—
when father turned we all turned—revealed not much
of cowardice or courage: only medium mal
peered through pupils
screwed down very tiny, like a hunter's.

4

I think he's going to ask
for beer for breakfast, sooner
or later he'll start making obnoxious
remarks about race or sex
and criticize our loose ways
of raising children, while his eyes
grow more slick, his puritan heart more pure
by virtue of sins sinned
against the Irish mother, who used to sit up
crying for the lost Ireland
of no American sons,
no pimpled, surly fourteen-year-olds
who would slip out at night, blackjack
in pocket, .22 pistol in homemade armpit holster,
to make out with rich men's wives
at the Narragansett Track now vanished,
on the back stretch of which horses ran
down the runway of the even more vanished
What Cheer Airport, where a Waco biplane
flew up for a joyride in 1931
with him waving from the rear cockpit,
metamorphosed at age six;
and who would stagger home
near dawn, snarl to reproaches, silence to tears.

5

But no, that's fear's reading.
We embrace in the doorway,
in the frailty of large,
fifty-odd-year-old bodies   .
of brothers only one of whom has imagined
those we love, who go away,
among them this brother,
stopping suddenly
as a feeling comes over them
that just now we remember
and miss them, and then turning

as though to make their own
even more vivid memories
known across to us—if it's true,
of love, only what
the flesh can bear surrenders to time.

Past all that, we stand
in the memory that came to me this day
of a man twenty-one years strange to me,
tired, vulnerable, half the world old; and in large,
fat-gathering bodies, with sore, well or badly spent,
but spent, hearts, we hold each other, friends to reality,
knowing the ordinary sadness of brothers.

DEAD FISH

by DANIEL HALPERN

from THE IOWA REVIEW

nominated by Jim Barnes and Marvin Bell

The pale arc of line feeds
into the green of the bank
and drops its fly into the shallows
of the stream in shadow
without sound. The line floats down
onto water and the current
takes it on, deeper.
Cast after cast the fly moves
in the afternoon
from one edge of the stream
to the other, snapped into place
as I move downstream, replacing
cast with the imagined weight
of a feeder trout unseen in current.
Shadows wobble the stream.
I see a fish hung
near the bank, gills at rest,
life only in buoyancy,
its resistance against current.
I move close, drop the fly
upstream so it floats back
over the dull eyes of the sleeper
fish. The fly floats past.
It won't move. It won't move
as I move closer. It hangs there
and won't move as I bring down the rock
with terrified force. In the explosion

334

of water I see the white fungus
it has grown, the sucker-mouth
and its full fish-body not trout.

It is imperfection I hate,
the age, the gamelessness of immobility,
the sudden decision to live.
When it floats to me
later, having fought to free itself
from branches of the stream trees,
I need its dead weight against my leg
to know ambition and its net, how it turns
on the object pursued,
dead now and my prize
as I cast in pale light,
the evening
pulled in on a fly.

A MOTEL IN TROY, N.Y.

by JOSEPHINE JACOBSEN

from POETRY

nominated by Bo Ball

A shadow falls
on our cribbage. The motel window
is a glass wall down to grass.

A huge swan
is looking in: cumulus-cloud body,
thunder-cloud dirty neck

that hoists the painted face
coral and black. Inky eyes
stare at our lives.

It cannot clean its strong
snake-neck. It stands
squat on its yellow webs

splayed to hold
scarcely up the heavy
feathered dazzle.

All of us stare. Then
in a lurch it turns
and waddles rocking,

presses the stubble, to the tip
of the blue pond. Sets sail
in one pure motion

and is received by distance
and the shadowy girl
across the water.

FOUR WAYS
OF COMPUTING
MIDNIGHT

Fiction by FRANCIS PHELAN

from THE SOUTHERN REVIEW

nominated by THE SOUTHERN REVIEW, *Elizabeth Spencer and Ellen Wilbur*

JUDAS PRIEST! said Billy Simons, hanging on to the back of the cattle truck and kicking his cowboy boots excitedly, "*Ju–das–K–Priest!*" Every time the truck rounded a bend and gave us a glimpse of where we were going he repeated it: "*Judas Priest!*" he would say, darting a wild look at me, and then he would say "*Judas Priest!*" again.

I smiled, as I often did when he talked like that, and I looked away, off into the distance, for I was excited too. All twenty of us on the back of the truck were joyful, for it was transporting us past fields of ripening corn and wheat to the one place we wanted to be: the Novitiate of the Holy Cross, in Rolling Prairie, Indiana.

It was a strange time, however, for a group of young men to be on a truck bound for anything other than military service, for the year was 1944. We were aware of the strangeness, of course, and most of us felt uncomfortable in our black clerical suits.

My black suit, at least, felt very uncomfortable on me. I had grown up fascinated with the world of the thirties, preparing itself for war. I spent my childhood on the North Side of Pittsburgh dreaming about becoming a fighter pilot. I covered my schoolbooks with drawings of Spitfires and Hurricanes and Messerschmitts, and with Stukas, dive-bombing tanks. With my friends in the streets I collected the "War Cards" that came with bubble gum. We would divide up the gum as we came out of what we called "the Jew Store" on Perrysville Avenue and then look feverishly at scenes of war in places like China and Spain and Ethiopia. We played games with the cards, flipping them against walls and people's front steps and talking about what we wanted to be when we grew up. I let everyone else talk, for I wanted to be the grandest thing of all. And when they were finished and asked me what I wanted to be, I said I would be a Navy fighter pilot, who took off from catapults over the waves and had to land his plane on the deck of the carrier which was the size of a football field but which looked from the air no larger than a postage stamp in the ocean. Then everybody else would saw "Wow!" and for a while, they wanted to be that too.

And yet, as I grew older, I became somehow blessed with what was known as a Vocation. A Vocation was something that came quietly, for it was really the voice of God. It called you when you were young, to give your life to God in His priesthood. You heard it in the strangest places—when you were playing in the streets, or talking with friends, or turning over at night in your bed. I talked with my Confessor about it in the darkened Confessional up in Nativity Church on Saturday afternoons—old Father O'Connor. I explained things to him over and over, trying to settle it, trying, in a way, to get rid of it, but trying to be fair: for I knew—every Catholic boy knew—that a Vocation was a wonderful thing, undoubtedly the most wonderful thing in all the world; to neglect the signs of possessing one was the most terrible of failures. But no matter how many times I explained to the priest that I really was not all that anxious to go to the seminary, the answer was always the same: all signs pointed to my having been called; I must test my Vocation, to see whether it was genuine; and the only way to do that was to enter a seminary and see, once and for all, if I had not been privileged by the grace of God to spend my life as a priest.

As I grew, it grew with me; it grew stronger, if anything, rather than weaker. I remember thinking up schemes by which I might manage to be both a priest and a fighter pilot at the same time. Eventually, however, I recognized the truth; I could not say I liked it, but my Vocation was there, and there was only one thing I could do about it. I got a black suit, with my parents' help, and a steamer trunk at Boggs and Buhl's Department Store (difficult items to find in wartime). I got on a train, which was really a troop train, and went off to the preparatory seminary at Notre Dame, Indiana. By that August I had been prepared, and so I got on the truck with the others, to help save the world and to give my life to God in what was referred to by spiritual authorities as the Holocaust of Divine Love.

That was why I smiled at Billy Simmons. He was ridiculously young; they said he had come to the seminary at the age of twelve, having gotten a dispensation from Rome to come so early. He was precociously bright, able to read Greek and Latin. He knew everything about the Religious Life and the Church and Canon Law and Breviaries and the Novitiate and the order and the priesthood, and he so instructed me. He knew nothing about the war or what was going on in the world, and I instructed him. He had a beautiful high voice which led us in the Sacred Liturgy. His little black suit seemed the perfect uniform, and even the fact that he insisted on wearing cowboy boots with it did not destroy the impression. And yet I could sense as we drew nearer to the Novitiate that Billy, though he was happy, was frightened too. That was the reason for his darting looks at me, and that was the reason for all his Judas Priests. In a way, we were very much the same.

On the back of the truck we sang. Billy led us, mostly in cowboy songs. We sang about the streets of Laredo and the wind blowing free and the Red River Valley and a lot about "little dogies" (Billy, though he was from Ohio, had always wanted to be a cowboy). Then as the truck left South Bend we sang about the Halls of Montezuma and the field artillery and trampling out the vineyards. We began calling one another "Mister," for that was how we would have to talk for the next twelve months. Mister Hanratty and Mister Skeffington argued theology on the floor of the truck, while Mister Kaminsky amused himself by being tail-gunner out the back: each time a car passed he would gun it down as though it were a Jap Zero or a German Messerschmitt, shouting "Doo-Doom!" as though it had exploded; then he would mark down an invisible Rising Sun or Swastika on the railing of the truck. Finally, at the outskirts of the town of Rolling Prairie, in the middle of "Praise the Lord and Pass the Ammunition" we knew we were coming to the end of our journey and we stopped singing.

Suddenly Billy touched his hand on my shoulder."Listen, Mister!" he said. I listened but didn't hear anything and asked him what we were listening for. "Can't you hear it?" he asked. "It's the big bell in the Novitiate tower. *Judas Priest!*" he said, shuddering with excitement. He explained to me that everything in the Novitiate was kept strictly under control of the sound of that bell. Whether you ate or drank or woke or slept, everything was done precisely to its sound. Bells were baptized, like people, he said, and were actually given names. The huge one in the Novitiate tower was from Oberammergau in Bavaria, and was called "Augustine"—it could be heard twenty miles. I listened but could hear nothing.

Brother Meinrad Kriegspeiler slowed the truck down and turned into a long lane lined with barbed wire fences, and we knew we were on the grounds of the Novitiate cattle farm, though the building itself was two miles farther. I strained with Billy to see what it was like. "There it is!" he said, and the huge structure rose up over us, dominating everything. The first thing I noticed were the swallows flying endlessly in and out of the bell tower against the blue August sky. When I looked at the building itself I thought it was beautiful, of course, but even darker and more severe than I had been prepared for.

In the last few moments in which we were allowed to speak, Billy told me as much as he could. We would be taken to our rooms or "cells," and later in the evening we would go to Chapel, where Father Master would instruct us on the topic of Vocation. But first, in the courtyard, Brother Meinrad would read off the list of jobs or "obediences" each one of us would have for the year. The most important was the job of Cantor, for he led everybody in the daily singing of the Divine Office. We both knew that Billy would have that. The next most important was the job of being "Regulator," for whoever was given that spent all his time ringing the bell and looking at the clock. He had to get up in the morning to wake everybody at five o'clock, and it was very difficult. Nobody wanted it, for to tell the truth, nobody really *liked* whoever was Regulator.

In the last seconds, Billy turned and looked at me intensely. I knew he wanted to say something important to me and was wondering how far I might be trusted. Finally he said, "We are friends—at least you know me better than anyone else. Promise me. If I weaken, do not let me give in. I've got to make it. No matter what I do or say, don't listen to me. *Don't help me quit.* I will not be able to go on living if it is not as a priest." Then with a sweeping gesture that took in, I thought, the vows, the priesthood, and a good deal of the prairie itself, he said, "This is the one thing I want."

He looked at me. I understood perfectly, and I nodded. "Same with me. Of course, I would want you to treat me exactly the same." We shook on it, swearing a kind of eternal allegiance to one another. We would be priests together.

"Now watch what happens," he said quickly as the truck stopped. "Brother Kriegspeiler is a little bit . . . strange. There's something wrong with him—that's why he's out here. He's always doing funny things, but it's meant in kindness, to help you get through the year. Make friends with him—you'll eat lots of extra desserts."

Brother Meinrad jumped from the cab, drawing himself up into an exaggerated attitude of "attention," pretending to be a German officer. I had heard about it; it was his one great joke, and he played it over and over: we were the Jews, you see, and Brother Meinrad was everything from *Herr Kommandant* to *Der Führer* himself. Sometimes, they said, he could be quite funny about it and made you laugh, because, after all, it was only a joke.

"*Choos!*" I heard him shout, in a ridiculous accent. "*Choos! Line up!*"

Rather sheepishly, for though it was a joke we were not sure how far it extended, we began getting off the truck. A piece of fencing that formed the tailgate of the truck was lowered to form a ladder, and as we got off we formed two rows. First, Brother Meinrad strode down the two lines passing out little strips of linen cloth with numbers on them. It turned out they were our laundry tags: each novice was given a number, to be sewn on everything we wore. I looked down at mine: 421, with a little plus sign in front of it. For the rest of the Novitiate, for the rest of my religious life, I would be +421. It would be inside the collars of my shirts, and on my shorts and socks; and even when I took out my handkerchief to sneeze or blow my nose it would be there: You are 421, it would say. I looked over at Billy: his number was 30.

Brother Meinrad then took out a piece of paper and began reading out the list of assignments or obediences for the year. Mister Zimmer was given the cow barn, and Mister Coon and Mister Reedy got the pig barn. Mister Dark got chickens. Finally, Mister Simmons, as we all expected, was named Cantor, and a very great tension built up over the group: Brother Kriegspeiler had saved the best for last.

It was then I noticed that he held a bell in his hands, a bronze bell that he had been concealing all the while behind his back. He pulled it out to let us see it and then like a magician concealed it once more. He started slowly down the rows; he was *Herr Kommandant* again, inspecting the troops. He savored the moment, stopping first at little Mister Sorin from New Orleans and frightening him that *he* might be the Regulator; then he went to Mister Jenkins, who had trouble to keep from laughing. When he came to Mister Kaminsky and paused, Mister Kaminsky pointed his finger at him and said, "Doo-*Doom!*", pretending to have a gun. Brother Meinrad scowled—that was breaking silence—and moved on, past Mister Simmons. He stopped at me, smiled, and handed me the bell. I was Regulator.

A great roar of laughter went up. I was famous for being late; I never owned a watch and usually did not know what time it was. In the prep seminary I had been continually reprimanded by Father Grimm and Father Fiedler and warned that if I did not improve, I would have to leave, that I would be dismissed, and that I could never be a priest, for a priest had to know what time it was.

I tried to smile back as I took the bell. Brother Meinrad beckoned me up to take his place in front of the men; I did so and waited to be told what to do next. He said something in German which I did not understand, but it contained the word *arbeit* (work), which we all knew was his favorite word. "*Machs schnell,*" he said quietly, and indicated that I should ring the bell and lead the men into the interior of the Novitiate. I managed to give it a few clangs, and then I led my brothers into the dark old building.

Over the door was carved the words *Crux Spes Unica,* the order's motto: "The Cross, Our Only Hope." After we passed under it, each man was led to his cell. The Novitiate had begun.

"You are a chosen people, a priesthood set apart!" said Father Master in his opening talk, later that evening. "This was rightly said of old," he continued, "to the Children of Israel, through their prophets. It is rightly said now, once again, even more rightly, to you, to every man taken from among men to be ordained in the things of God, for it is told you through the divine wisdom and authority of Holy Mother the Church and is therefore infallible.

"Sacred Scripture tells us. Some men there are who are eunuchs. Some men are eunuchs from their mother's womb. Some are made eunuchs by their fellow man. I would not have you ignorant," Father Master added by way of parenthesis. "I would have no person under my care ignorant; but in the corrupt days of the Middle Ages certain misguided people actually had operations performed—*i castrati* they are called in the Italian language—whereby their singing voices would be enhanced. This is of no concern to us for we are in the twentieth century. And finally, some men make themselves eunuchs for the Kingdom of Heaven's sake!

"It is the one thing that is necessary, my dear young men, the *Unum Necessarium.* In that splendid passage wherein Vocation is described, where Our Lord quintessentially told the Rich Young Man—who was rich in the things of this world, who had many things to live for—what it meant to have a Vocation. He said to the young man, who would be perfect, 'There is still one thing that is necessary: give up all things, and come, follow me'. And you know what happened. That young man—that *good* young man—it is said, in Sacred Scripture, that he turned away, *'for he had many possessions!'*

"The Apostles came to Jesus and said that we must give up our freedom, and all things to follow you, it is a hard saying. And you know what Christ said? In the splendid Latin of the Vulgate it reads *'Qui potest capere, capeat!* He who is able to take, let him take!' "

These last words were delivered with a tremendous effect; you could hear them echoing down the main corridor after he said them. *"Qui potest capere, capeat!"* he said again: "To the world, this is foolishness. It is foolish to give up human love, ownership, and most important of all, our freedom. *Astiterunt Reges terrae,* says the psalm that you will sing: See how the Gentiles devise vain things, and the nations unite against God's Annointed! Make no mistake; you are assuming a heavy burden. You have come here in response to the call of God; you come to answer nothing less than Christ's command, Be ye perfect, as your Heavenly Father is perfect. You come to this Novitiate for nothing less than to seek perfection itself."

We had many aids to do this. The Rule of Silence, by which we did not speak; the Rule of Recollection, by which we shut out everything and did not think except to think about the one thing that was necessary; the Rule of Obedience, by which we desired nothing except the will of God manifested to us by the orders of the legitimate Superior. The movements of the body were taken care of by the Rule of Regular Discipline. ("If a man's trouble is below his belt," Father Master added in a sardonic tone, "he has no business, of course, being here; novices should be beyond that.")

Father Master now came to his main point of the evening. It was the matter of time, and promptness, and exactitude in the answering of the bell: this more than anything else would assure that we would have a successful Novitiate year, and become candidates for Profession. "*A man must learn to tell time,*" said Father Master, almost shouting at us. "It is no exaggeration to say that the religious life consists essentially in being in the right place at the right time. It is the one thing in your life that you can be infallibly certain about. When you hear the sound of the bell, my young men, it is God Himself speaking to you, and the bell is rightly called *Vox Dei*, the Voice of God. When you answer it, promptly and precisely, you know that you are being pleasing to God as no man is, for each of you is giving up his own free will and making of his life a holocaust. God is no longer God of the Jews, to be pleased by burnt offering. *That was the Old Testament.* No! He is your God now, and it is through the devout self-immolation of young people like yourselves that He chooses to be honored.

"Learn, therefore, my dear novices, what time it is. Set your watches by the great Oberammergau Bell in the Chapel tower; it is never wrong. Be wise virgins, ready for the Bridegroom, for it is late, always much later than when you first heard the good tidings of Redemption: 'For ye know not the day nor the hour.' "

Father Master then went on to tell us something that was very interesting, something that I had never heard about before, nor indeed had dreamed existed. He explained to us that, so important in the Economy of Salvation was the element of Time that the Church taught, not one, but *four* different ways of telling it. The hour of midnight, for example, was extremely important in the life of the Church, for so many grave obligations either began or terminated on the stroke of midnight. He quickly went through four types, and showed us the four ways of computing midnight.

The first kind of Time, Sidereal or Celestial, he said, did not concern us, it concerned only astronomers. The second, Standard Time, might seem to us to be True Time, but it was not, for it was of course arbitrarily divided up by man for his own use into time zones; to find True Time, you had in fact to add or subtract minutes and seconds, depending upon where in the time zone you were located. It was useless to us, too, during the Novitiate year, since Rolling Prairie was situated eleven minutes to the east of the center of its zone. For us to calculate True Midnight, for example, we would have to subtract eleven minutes from the clock, which would of course be useless, for in Rolling Prairie when the clocks showed eleven minutes to twelve, True Midnight had already occurred! He went on to tell us about True or Sun Time, and about special types, such as Daylight Saving, and, of course, what actually was being observed by the nation, War Time.

After he concluded the matter, he remarked that it all might seem irrelevant to us, but it was not. "My dear young men, a year is made up of weeks and months and days and hours. At the end of eight days, your initial Retreat, you will receive the Holy Habit. It will, fittingly enough, be the Feast of the Transfiguration of Christ; later on that same morning, you will be witnesses to the First Profession of Vows by the members of this year's class. The seasons will then turn. Summer will become autumn, and autumn, winter; the Church's Liturgy will sing you through Advent, to Christmas, into the new year, and the year of Our Lord 1944 will become the Year of Our Lord 1945. Lent will come, with its fast, and Holy Week, and you will die with Christ, only to rise with Him again on Easter morning. And at last, in God's good time, if you are worthy, you will in that year of Our Lord 1945, on the Feast of the Transfiguration of Our Lord, August the sixth, you too will profess your vows, and in so doing make of your life a perfect holocaust for God."

Father Master concluded his talk with a warning. It would not be easy. There would be times during our Novitiate year when we would be tempted to give up, to seek permission to leave, to escape the heavy obligations of the religious life, to return to families and friends and to the world and its lesser concerns. There would be times when even the best of us would then feel that he was throwing away his young life for nothing; we would then feel that we were going through what the spiritual writers called the Dark Night of the Soul, and that God had abandoned us. "Make no mistake," he said sharply, "God will not abandon you, no more than He abandoned His Chosen People, for God never abandons those who place their trust in Him.

"Begin, then, tonight," he concluded. "When the bell has sounded initiating this first of all the nightly Grand Silences of your Novitiate, beg, pray, beseech Almighty God that all these things may come to pass."

After he had finished, Father Master rose, went to the center of the sanctuary, genuflected solemnly before the Tabernacle, and returned to his pew in the back of Chapel. Mister Simmons put away a notebook (in which he had fiercely been writing down what Father Master had said, for later study), came to his feet, and led us in the singing of Vespers: "Blessed is the Lord Our God," he sang, "for He has visited us and come at last, to save His People, Israel." Finally, Complin, the Night Prayer of the Church, was sung, and Billy sang to God for us about the swift departing light, asking for peace in sleep, and ending with Christ's last prayer on the cross: "Father, into Thy hands I commend my spirit."

When the last words of the beautiful Gregorian plainchant were sung, I picked up my bell and rang it one clang, as I had been carefully instructed to. With that began the Grand Silence, which was to last all night.

Before going up to my cell, in a final meditation in the Chapel, I prayed as I had been told to: I begged and beseeched Almighty God that it would happen—that I would have a successful Novitiate, that I would prove equal to the task of making my life a holocaust for God, and that, a year to the day, I would be found worthy to pronounce my vows.

In my cell, however, after I had, in effect, put everyone else to bed, I found that I could not sleep. In reality, I was afraid to sleep for fear I would not wake in the morning to get everyone else up at five o'clock. Besides, it had been a hectic day, a day in which there had been no time to think. I tried to fall asleep—even in private, alone where only God could see me, I knew that I was under the obligation to sleep, and so I tried. I was unsuccessful; songs kept coming back into my head, especially one from the back of the truck, that Billy had sung, a cowboy song, about a calf being led to market:

> Calves are easily bound and slaughtered
> Never knowing the reason why
> But whoever treasures freedom
> Like the swallow has learned to fly.

It went on about the winds blowing free in the chorus, and as I lay awake trying to sleep, the thin little voice of Billy kept coming back to me, keeping me awake.

I came to a rather startling thought: I did not like the Novitiate. I hesitated to admit it, but eventually, in the night, I had to. I more than did not like it, I feared it; and in a way, I detested it. I wished I could run away to the war and become a carrier pilot, or maybe join the Marines and fight in places like the island of Saipan or Guadalcanal. Unfortunately, however, there was little I could do about it. I had to test my Vocation and this was the only way to do it. At least I was certain of one thing. I would do it well, even though I disliked it. I would seek perfection, as God and the Church demanded. With a twinge of guilt I recalled that I had not taken notes as Billy had; I was not even off to a good beginning. I would get a notebook at once; I would take down everything that was told me; I would meditate on those thoughts, and use them to learn the Practice of the Presence of God. And in the end, with God's grace, I would become perfect and pleasing to Him.

I turned over and went to sleep. The alarm sounded and I thought I had made a mistake setting it, for it was still dark; but the clock was right—the time was 4:45 A.M. I jumped into my robe, with its 421 already sewn neatly into its collar, and went down into the cold main corridor and waited for Augustine in the tower to sound. For a moment I was afraid to ring the bell. The huge place seemed so silent and so dark that I wondered if I might not be dreaming, that I might not really be supposed to wake anybody. But Augustine sounded, and I thought of the will of God; I swallowed hard, took a deep breath, and started to ring my smaller bell. At first it made a ridiculous sound—the clapper slithered around the side, not making a true ring; but I began to catch on to it, and by the time I reached the Professed Corridor, it sounded right. I stopped, and shouted out as loud as I could, *"Benedicamus Domino!"* and here and there, in sleepy voices, I heard the words *Deo Gratias*, my brothers in Christ thanking God for being awakened. I went on to wake the rest of the house, and was relieved that I had, at least, begun correctly.

I became a good bell ringer after that. I became a fine, rigorous person, indeed, conscious of the clock, and on time, always. I rang my brothers to everything—to prayer and meals and choir and recreation. But most of all it was to the barns I rang them—to the pig barn and to the horse barn and to the dairy barn, and of course to the greatest barn of all, the slaughterhouse itself, for the Novitiate farm, more than anything else, consisted in that kind of operation. I knew that it did not make me popular—that as soon as people saw me coming they thought of unpleasant things. Only Mister Simmons seemed not to mind. He had warned me; but I reasoned that it was my sacred obedience, that it was the will of God, and that it was my special test in the Novitiate.

At the end of the Retreat, on the Feast of Transfiguration of Our Lord, on August the sixth, I was invested in the holy habit, and my entire class became true novices. Later in the morning, I was appointed to stand at Father Master's side during the vow ceremonies for the departing class, and tie up the cinctures for the new *professori*.

"Gloria et honore coronasti eum!" intoned Mister Simmons from the choir loft; but I had the more solemn duty: as each man came up the aisle carrying his Vow Formula and knelt down before the huge old Missal Book in Father Master's lap to freely promise his life in dedication to the highest good of all, I stood ready at hand, first with a pen for him to sign with, and then to help tie the cincture around the waist as each one finished, for the knot was difficult to make. They all had trouble pronouncing the words for the year 1944 in Latin: *Millesimo, nongentesimo, quadragesimo quarto*. And each time, after each one had gotten out his *quadragesimo quarto*, I held out to him and helped fashion around his waist the heavy, silken, almost velvet cord. And as I did so I found

myself devoutly wishing that I could be in his place, that it would already be next year, with some other new young novice doing exactly the same for me.

The departure on the truck of the newly professed to study Dogmatic Theology, the next stage of training for the priesthood, left the Novitiate empty and lonely, for we had made friends with them. We had lapses, too, in keeping some of the rules. At first, when the Novitiate was still new, we amused ourselves. For a while, during Recreation in the hour after supper, when we were allowed to speak, we went through a spell of calling one another by number instead of names. "Mister 421!" I would hear Mister Kaminsky call out, "Mister 421!" "Yes, Mister 83, what is it?" I would answer, and so on. We asked Billy what his number was, and he announced solemnly, "Thirty," and we all laughed—it seemed so short, and such a good number for him.

But later that evening word came down from Father Master's office that we were breaking the Rule of Address, that we were to stop referring to one another as numbers.

And very early, we were loaned out as a group to a nearby orchard farmer at Williams Orchards. He had a full crop of peaches, and, his own sons gone off to war, had no one to harvest them. He was our neighbor, and so we helped him. All twenty of us were sent over, on the back of the truck again, and were shown the proper way to pick peaches. You were to fill up your fruit bucket, carefully; you were to walk over to the bushel basket, and then gently—very, very gently—so as not to damage the tender fruit, you were to release the little ropes that held the canvas bottom of the bucket, allowing the peaches to roll, *undamaged,* into the bushel basket.

Billy and I (or that is, Mister Simmons and I, of course) got ourselves assigned to the same row of trees. It was beautiful summery weather. Hour after hour we would climb the ladder up into the laden peach trees, looking out over the countryside and up into the clear air, and then descend to carefully deposit our burden in the baskets on the ground. We worked hard, for the glory of God and for our neighbor; we kept the Rule of Silence and the Rule of Recollection, so that we should be able to pray while we worked, and most of all, above all, practice the Presence of God.

That afternoon I had been especially successful in retaining custody of the eyes and ears, refusing to pay heed to distractions, concentrating on the peaches, and practicing the Presence of God by frequent aspirations such as "My Jesus, mercy!" and "Lord have mercy on us!" and many others. I found myself at the very top of the tree, looking up into the sky when I noticed something— something, with all due respect for recollection, that I could not help noticing the previous few days. It was an airplane, high up in the sky, flying westward. I knew a lot about planes: this was a bomber, and it was a new kind. It was, I knew, not just an old "Flying Fortress"—those I had seen all through my childhood. This I recognized as something new, and much larger, with a tremendous deadly snout on it and a high, high tail. The planes flew very high, and always westward as they passed over the Novitiate: they were obviously headed for the Pacific Theater. What were they? I wondered. What gigantic new weapon had my country created? I descended and walked over, past Mister Simmons, to the bushel basket.

I stood there looking downward for a moment. Then, *"Bombs away!"* I shouted, breaking silence, and letting the peaches fall violently and bruisingly into the bushel basket below.

Mister Coon from the next row over heard me and laughed delightedly. Mister Simmons looked at me, startled. He may have wanted to say "Judas Priest!" a few times, but if he did, he controlled the urge. Instead he walked calmly over to the receptacle and poured his own peaches, gently and properly, into it. I felt corrected. He really was perfect, impossibly so; already he had transformed himself into such a perfect novice that no Rule could ask more from a human being.

All the same, I was not the worst. There was one novice, Mister Eddie O'Donnell, who lived totally in his imagination. For him the war was omnipresent and he made it so to everyone around him. He sounded like a war movie, for his talk was full of "Krauts" and "Heinies." Instead of working, he spent whole work periods sneaking up on "Japs" through the bean rows and the strawberry patches, and turned his part of the farm into Guadalcanal or Normandy. His favorite trick was to shout (in the solemn silence), "Hand-grenade! Fall on it!" Then he would dive to the ground, clutching it to his breast, to save the rest of us—his buddies. His last words were always "The Krauts got me!"

One September afternoon as he pulled his routine, Brother Meinrad stepped out of the bushes and said, "Mister O'Donnell, come with me," and took him up to Father Master's office. Eddie left four days later, to join the Marines.

Our mood changed as we became more aware of the heavy reality of the Novitiate year. On Sunday afternoons, the only time we were allowed out, off the grounds, on the weekly Community Walk, some people like Mister Conroy or Mister Knous still managed a frolicsome attitude, for a while, at least until we got down to the stockyards of LaPorte, where we would have to turn around to come back. But that stopped, too, and the bleak and wintry dark late afternoons, along endless cornfields and sow pens, with the barbed wire fences that stretched to the horizons and beyond that to infinity, made each of us think over and over about such things as why he was there and how long he would last.

There were occasional diversions, but very few. I discovered that Brother Meinrad had another side to him. When he came in from work and went to his room I would hear his phonograph playing music endlessly. It was all German music, usually Bach and Wagner and Beethoven. His favorite was Beethoven's Ninth, the Choral Symphony, and when he played that, Brother would lift his voice and join in the splendid German, and the Professed Corridor would be filled with *Gotterfunken's* and *Feuertrunken's* and *Alle Menschen's*. Whenever that happened, or whenever I heard the great opening four notes of the Fifth—the "dot-dot-dot-dash" of Churchill's "V for Victory" speech—I would run and get Billy, and, without breaking the Rule of Silence, or at least, breaking it only as little as was necessary, we would together go up outside Brother's door and listen. "What's he singing?" I would ask, and Billy would explain the German of Schiller's "Ode to Joy": how *Freude* was Joy—The Daughter of Elysium, and that all men became brothers under her starry wings. We kept ourselves ready to walk off in different directions if anyone came, as though nothing was happening, but when we were very brave and no one interrupted us, as the words came up to *Gepruft im Tod* we found ourselves singing, to the music coming through the door, about how there must be something—*some*thing—faithful unto death, how there must be something—One—above the starry heavens of the night, that would last forever and remain faithful to the end. It moved me deeply, and for the rest of the Novitiate, and indeed for the rest of my life, I came to hear myself, while I was working, shouting meaninglessly words like *Bruder!* or *Welt!*, only in my mind, where no one could hear me.

But one day, when I was standing outside the door alone, not having been able to find Mister Simmons, Brother opened the door suddenly and found me. He looked at me, surprised, and was about to berate me. But then he only nodded, and we both walked away.

It became very hard. As Regulator, because I had to keep close to the bell, I had to remain in the house in the afternoons while everyone else went out to work. I was assigned, like all Regulators, to sweeping the Basement Chapel. This was a complex of basement corridors and side altars hidden away in the subterranean darkness beneath the Main Chapel. It was referred to as "the Polish Corridor" because in the past so many novices with Polish names had been assigned there. It was a place to which few people ever came, for it was dark and totally without daylight. Yet, for some reason I could not figure out, it required sweeping every day—careful, methodical sweeping with a big broom and buckets of dampened sawdust. It was not really enough work to occupy the whole two and a half hours of work period, and time became very tedious. I mentioned this to Father Master during Spiritual Directions, but he only smiled and pointed out that it had unparalleled opportunity for Meditation, and that a man was very close to God down there.

I had just turned eighteen. And as I walked out of Father Master's office I reflected that, whatever other young men of my age were doing, it was clear that I was going to spend the eighteenth year of my life down in that place, with the faded aroma of church linens and of incense and, of course, the eternal smell of dampened sawdust on the floor.

And so the life of the farm, with all its interesting activity, was kept far from me. I thought often of the happy day out in the peach orchard with Billy, but as fall came that memory faded. I struggled manfully to practice the Presence of God; I knew that obedience—the one thing that was necessary—was all that mattered; I was in the Novitiate, after all, to perfect myself. Yet it was awful; and it was very difficult sometimes, down there in the darkness, in spite of all I had been told, to keep from wondering if I was not a young man entering into some form of the Dark Night of the Soul.

I lost track of Billy ("Old Mister Thirty," he now called himself); indeed, it might almost be said that I lost track of my fellow man. I only heard him; he became a voice singing out the Church's Liturgy: all those prayers, promises, arguments, failures, shouts, cries for help, hymns of victory, of comfort and affliction which together tell the story of mankind's endless search for a redeemer, for someone to come and save him. *"O Adonai!"* he would cry out, or *"O, Oriens!"* in the Great Antiphons of Advent, or *"Pange Lingua"* during Holy Hours, or *"Vindica Sanguinem!"* during Solemn High Mass. His voice, though it was beautiful, seemed increasingly sad and distant, although I wondered if it were not my imagination—if it was not *I* who was the one going through something, and that he was all right.

One morning in Conference, however, something happened which, for the first time, gave me reason to think that my friend's condition might well be worse than my own.

Father Master had been giving us our first conference on ownership, as preparation for the Vow of Poverty. He had explained how we really were not capable of possessing anything, once we had made our vows—that we were *incapax,* as he called it—that we had given up ownership entirely, and that the *ad usum* mark we were to put on books above our name and on anything else we were tempted to call our own meant simply "for the use of," not "for the possession of." It was good training for the kind of life we would lead; we were to think little of the things of this world and place our whole concern on that other world yet to come.

After he had finished the rather technical lecture detailing all the possible ways of owning, Father Master asked, as he always did, whether anybody had any questions. Very rarely did anybody take him up on this; it was generally acknowledged that Father Master really did not see why there should be many questions after his very thorough way of explaining things, and the few times a novice did gain the courage, in the heavy silence which followed the talks, to ask how or why a certain thing should be so, we all watched for Father Master's famous temper to manifest itself.

That morning, however, after the Poverty lecture, there was a little stir behind me and to the left; I was afraid to turn my head to look, but I had found out that by staring intensely off into the distance in front of me I could often in a way see what was going on around me without appearing to. That morning by looking very hard I was able to see one small part of the mass of black behind me detach itself a little from the rest. Mister Simmons had stood up; he had no doubt been writing notes intently on what had been said, and now he wanted to clarify something.

"Yes, Mister?" Father Master said.

"Father Master," said Billy in a thoughtful voice, "I have a question about Poverty, but first I would like to ask about Time. We sing Matins, the Morning Song of the Church, at five o'clock in the evening, then we sing Little Hours—which should be in the afternoon—in the morning, and that leaves Vespers and Complin, the Night Prayer of the Church, to be done at one-thirty. It seems off, all the words about being asleep are during the day, and the ones about being awake are at night!"

Father Master enjoyed the way the question was put. "The reason for that, Mister," he replied, smiling, "is simply the importance of midnight. So grave is the obligation to complete the office of the day that we anticipate, we say it ahead of time, so that we are never caught by the hour of midnight, which would be unthinkable. What is your other question?"

Billy sounded even more thoughtful this time. "I was just wondering, Father—you have explained ownership in all its ramifications; but I was wondering—who owns our bodies? Who do *we* belong to?"

He should not have asked it; I knew that at once. There was something wrong with that kind of question in the particular context, though I could not say just what; I shuddered a bit, though I would not be able to say why.

The question struck Father Master in a certain way, too; he began to get angry; I could see his skin starting to get red around his Roman collar and his face strain with the effort to hold his temper; the fact that it was Mister Simmons who had asked the question did not help. Finally, he could not control it any more and he burst out in the voice we all knew he used when he had lost his temper, almost screaming: *"God* owns your bodies! Mister, *you belong to God!"* And with that he gathered his books and strode out of the room as though we were all impossibly stupid, the best of us little less dumb than the very beasts of the field.

After that Billy asked no more questions, nor, for a very long time, did anyone else; if anyone had any questions, they tended very much to keep them to themselves. I worried about Mister Simmons after that; he seemed to be going off on a direction by himself that might bring harm; but, of course, it would be his misfortune—I had my own problems.

Lost in the darkness of the Basement Chapel I played games, so that Time, dreadful, empty, silent Time would pass on—so that the awful, terrible year of 1944 would move on, would hurry on, and become glorious, joyful 1945, so that the month of August 1945 would finally come with all it signified, that my time of trial would be over, and that I would win my fight with myself.

To help Time along, however, I played games. One dark afternoon that was proving especially dreary, when I seemed to be moving the sawdust around to no particular purpose, and the basement corridor seemed awfully far removed from the Presence of God, so that I was even beginning to really doubt that it could be pleasing to Him to have me down there sweeping something that obviously did not need sweeping, I noticed something: the three bronze access panels in the floor. It was not the first time I noticed them—they were the only bright things in the basement and I had swept around and over them every dreadful work period from the beginning of my Novitiate; no, what I noticed was their particular positioning: a person with any kind of eye for such things could easily see that the entire layout of the floor strongly resembled the map of Europe, if you thought of the three panels as the cities of Rome, Paris, and Berlin. I stopped to consider what Rule I could possibly be breaking if, instead of sweeping the floor in the usual boring, straightforward manner, I actually made it all mean something. I decided that by turning the piles of sawdust into moving armies I could parallel exactly what was going on at that moment in Europe, one bronze circle representing Rome, one for Paris, and one for Berlin.

I did so. Each day after that I assembled the armies so as to represent the Allies coming from one direction past Paris, and General Clark's Eighth Army going up the center past Rome, and the Russians coming from the other side to close in on Berlin. The game varied as each day I changed the scenario. From my meager, and mostly illicit, sources of information about what was going on in the world, I knew that Eisenhower and Patton had already freed Paris and that Rome had been taken, too (we had prayed for the safety of the Holy Father in Chapel); the real excitement was who would take Berlin? Some days I let the Russians get awfully close, but in the end, of course, the Americans always ended up the victors. When that happened I had to move awfully fast—if Father Master, or *anyone* noticed the huge pile of sawdust in front of the altar rail they would certainly wonder what was going on.

One afternoon, in fact, I thought I heard someone in the Sacristy. Nothing happened, but a week later, just as I was closing in on Berlin with the Russians, Brother Meinrad strode out into the Chapel and asked me what I was doing, playing? Being a novice, I had to respond with the truth when asked; I was humiliated, but told him that the bronze panel represented Berlin; he snarled in delighted laughter, but when he saw that the Russians were winning, Brother Meinrad ripped the broom out of my hands and pushed that pile of sawdust back where it came from. *"Heraus mit du!"* he shouted. Then he turned to me.

"You are much too old a fellow to be playing games," he said, with a smile, handing me back my broom. "Tomorrow report to the barns, and I will give you a man's work!" With that he stepped down the center aisle over the sawdust and out of the Chapel.

I had heard that the Novitiate farm was really a complete cattle slaughtering operation, and that the Professed Brothers had all the equipment of a great meat-packing plant. But I was not prepared for what I saw the first time I walked out into the great slaughterhouse. The first thing I saw were men standing ankle deep in blood. Other men were sharpening knives. There were huge clamps being used to rip off the hides of steers. One man, presumably a Brother, was standing in the midst of a mass of intestines while he slitted each animal from gut to groin. I heard the insistent, grating whine of a buzz saw someplace, and looked over: it was slicing off hooves.

I had been prepared for blood, but not that much. Every worker was covered with it. There were endless instruments of torment, too: knives, axes, saws, forceps, grindstones, cleavers, pliers, hammers, and drills. But most of all, there were hooks. A conveyor belt endlessly full of them passed right by me: it came up to my face, and then passed above me, hook after hook, each one bearing the head of a lamb, which looked at me, wide-eyed in death. And of course there were the great hoses, to wash away the blood.

I wanted to get back outside, for I was afraid I would be sick. A man came up to me, laughing; he too was covered with blood, at least his rubbery uniform was. He was being friendly: "Your first time," he said, "—you'll get used to it." He made a movement as if to put his rubber-covered arm around my shoulders and I remembered the blood, so I made a ducking movement. He laughed; it was Brother Meinrad. I managed not to throw up. "You'll be a smart old buck yet," he said, "—you'll get used to it."

You did have to get used to it; we all knew that you had to become a man. That was what the Novitiate was all about. And yet it took me a long time, and some things I never did get used to.

The slaughter of a calf, for instance. Brother took care of each one of those himself. They never seemed to sense the presence of death. Each calf invariably allowed itself to be led into the slaughter pen by what was called the Judas Goat, which then of course departed safely. The calf would be left looking straight at Brother Meinrad, who was always strained and nervous. I could see his knuckles white on the shaft of the sledgehammer. I had not known exactly how it was done. The calf's meditative head was held; Meinrad's whole form tensed with anticipation of what he was about to do. Then he hit the forehead of the animal, and the calf went down with its two forelegs splayed out ridiculously, as though the whole thing were an animated cartoon. At once Meinrad leapt from the hammer to the knife and quickly—mercifully, perhaps, as he would claim—slit the animal's throat to let the blood out. We novices, cumbersomely, and pretending that it did not bother us, hooked the carcass up by the heels and hung it on a meat hook. Then we got ready for the next calf.

I was learning, I suppose. But it never seemed to get any better. Always there was some new surprise, some harshness I had not known about. One time Brother sent me to the pig barn with four other novices. When I found out what we had to do I was quite frightened: Brother wanted to do something to Chester, the huge boar. He needed us to hold Chester in his sty. Five of us leaned against the boar and held him against the side of his pen: Chester had been breaking out of it, escaping by lifting up the fence with his powerful snout, and now Brother was going to put metal clips into his nose to discourage him from rooting. While we had the huge boar immobilized (watch your feet, someone said, he can cut right through a boot), Meinrad planted the clips, to the agonized shrieks of Chester. Then, grinning, Brother seized the opportunity to do something else he had wanted to do for a long time: to break back the huge saber teeth. It was awful; he took a large pliers and simply broke poor Chester's great eyeteeth out of the corners of his mouth. Then he let him go, and I saw Chester feeling the empty places with his tongue, like a child after the dentist. I was glad to be through with it.

But I was not through with it. Brother Meinrad was making good his word. Next day they needed novices to hold the four legs of each of the males of the sow's new litter: they were to have an operation performed on them so that they would produce more meat. I hated it, for I could feel each little animal's terror and the pain through his legs so that it almost turned my stomach. During the surgery itself the little pigs were too frightened to squeal, but when Brother applied a bluish antiseptic to the cut, it cauterized them, and they screamed all afternoon, and on into the evening, so that other novices could hear it all through the whole Novitiate. And Mister Simmons, who had replaced me at my endless task of sweeping the basement, said at the supper table where we were given a *Deo Gratias* and allowed to speak, "I could hear it all the way down in the Basement Chapel. What were you doing to them?"

The whole table looked at me; some already knew of course, but others around the table looked at me with blank, ignorant stares. I became a bit embarrassed, picked up the bread dish, and almost did not say anything; instead, I turned my lips into a smile and looked away, as though I were a seasoned cowhand. "We were de-balling them, Mister Simmons," I said, and laughed, the way I had seen Meinrad laugh all afternoon.

Poor Billy. He had come to the Novitiate thinking he was a cowboy, singing all those songs about coyotes and dogies and buckos and broncos, all that about "a-walkin" and "a-ridin." In the end he had been sent inside, to sweep and do his choir practice. I smiled; he was no more a cowboy than I was a fighter pilot.

And he was in trouble.

One day after a hard afternoon's work, just before I was to go up and ring the bell, Brother Meinrad motioned me over to a little cubbyhole of an office off the side of the barn. He had a coffee pot there with some doughnuts. Incredibly, he offered me one and a cup of coffee.

I suppose we novices that year were very immature young men in our love of food, but things like ice cream or Coke or pie were terribly high in our scheme of things. When Brother Meinrad asked me to come in, sit down with him and have a doughnut, it was the most delicious thing that could have happened. I felt very respectful.

"Would you like to hear about the war, Mister?" he asked. I nodded; it had been six months since I had heard anything from the world. "It is very bad," he said, shaking his head. "It's all over on the Eastern Front. This country should stop fighting Hitler and help him against the Russians. He never was our enemy anyway."

I nodded, absently. I had really not heard what he said properly, for munching on the doughnut. Anyway, I had heard it all before. Everyone in the Novitiate knew that Meinrad believed the war to be an unjust one. Over and over he told everybody that the Treaty of Versailles had created it—the International Bankers and the Jews had placed Germany in an intolerable position. They had *created* Hitler themselves. And as far as the many things the newspapers said that he did wrong, why that was pure propaganda, ordered by Mister Roosevelt. "And they say Goebbels is a propagandist!" Brother shouted, "why, compared to the New York *Times* he is a *kinderling*! I am tired of it!"

"Where is the front now?" I asked, eagerly; I thirsted for this kind of information. "Where is General Patton?"

"They've taken Rome and Paris, as you probably know (I wondered if he thought back to my panels on the floor, among the sawdust)—Patton? He is almost to the Rhine. If something isn't done he will be in Germany."

The coffee was finished, and the doughnut gone. I looked at my watch and felt strangely uncomfortable. I got up, fearful of over-doing my stay. But as I did so, Brother Meinrad motioned me to remain where I was. I sat back down.

"Tell me, Mister," Brother asked, "how is your friend doing? Is he all right?"

I looked at him with some fear, "My friend? Which novice do you mean?" I asked.

Brother Meinrad smiled. *"Der Voegelsinger. Kikey.* Mister Simmons, the Ohio Cowboy."

"Mister Simmons? He's doing all right, isn't he? He keeps the Rule perfectly."

Meinrad looked directly into my eyes, smiling a very knowledgeable smile. "Mister, take my advice: keep away from him. He is in trouble. He is full of questions, and he *worries* too much. *Keep away from anybody you see like that!*" He hissed this out quietly, intensely. That was what the coffee and doughnut had been for; Brother Meinrad was warning me of something; he was telling me to become wiser in some way, as if he was almost telling me that Billy's way would not work, that that way could only lead to disaster.

"And now, *Heraus mit du!*" he said, making a shoveling, scooping gesture, the way we did when shooing some farm animal up the chute, and he added, laughing, "You better get out of here or the other novices will start to call you the Judas Goat. *Der Judas-Zeigen!*"

Mister Jenkins, whose chief fault was his inability to control his laughter, was standing inside the harness shop when I came out, in a state of recollection, doubtless trying to practice the Presence of God while he waited for the end of work period. He was in a position, however, to hear perfectly the last words Brother had uttered. "*Der Judas-Zeigen. . .*" he started to giggle. "*Der Judas-Zeigen!*" he said, between gasps for breath. He laughed and laughed, leaning back against the wall, trying to control himself.

So that was it? I was embarrassed, first by Meinrad's comment and then by the unending ridicule of the laughter of Mister Jenkins, which followed me outside, and my skin felt that it was burning. Then my feeling changed to anger. Before starting up the hill to the Novitiate building, I deliberately and purposefully strode over to look at the Judas Goat in his pen. He was staring, glassy-eyed, on some distant prospect; he looked peculiarly absent-minded, for he was chewing, ruminating on some fodder. The bell around his neck made a soft tinkle when he moved, and he looked for all the world as though he were trying to think of something, something which eluded him, something that was ever on the verge of his memory, but which, no matter how long he thought, he could not quite recall.

He looked so foolish and so human that I forgot my annoyance. I looked around, and since there was no one to hear but me, I said something. "You bloody, fucking bastard, you!" I said to him. It made me feel better getting the words out; I had not talked that way in six months, and I laughed quietly as I walked off—because there wasn't any Rule against talking to goats. I mounted the hill and rang the bell on time to end the work period. Then I headed for the showers.

And so, somehow, Christmas was coming on. As a result of my relationship with Meinrad, which I was careful to preserve without overdoing it in any way, I remained among those novices privileged to see nature in all its aspects. I saw the year go round in seasons. First the hay creaking into the barns in late summer, and the spiders in their parachutes flying from tree to tree in September. I awoke one day to the swallows gone from their tower, where old Augustine still called out that it was late, late, much later than when first we saw them, swooping in and out around him, from the back of the truck. I saw the stalks of corn shredded and sent into the silo as fodder, and we novices, much free labor, sent to tramp it down with our feet, round and round in circles, and in the enforced silence of work heard my mind bring up snatches from the Psalms and the Divine Office (the only language, increasingly, that ears heard and memory stored): "Thou shalt not muzzle the ox that threshes the grain," my feet would say as I tramped, or "*Venite Fillii audite me,*" or "*Jam sol recedit igneus,*"—"Now fades the light of the setting sun." I saw the leaves turn first and then fall, and so I rang myself and the men from summer to autumn into winter.

When the first almost liturgical snows fell, the *O Antiphons* were sung, Billy's voice lifted in the great cries of mankind waiting for a Saviour: "*O Adonai!*" he sang, or "O Scepter of Israel and Key to the House of David!" or "*O Oriens!*"—Bright Star of Day. And we responded, to a man, praying ardently that God would come and dwell among men, and take us all from the torment of here below.

I wondered, of course, how Billy was doing; his chant was perfect and impersonal; and yet when he shouted man's cries to Heaven for help, I could not keep from feeling that it was from the depths of his own heart that he was shouting.

Things were not all that bad with me. As Christmas approached, I felt satisfied; I had survived. I had rung them, rung them all, with very few mistakes, to the mid-point of the Novitiate year. I was proud, justifiably; in a way it was consoling to be Regulator, for during the long hours I had spent in the basement corridor I had had time to think. I came to the conclusion that if it was true that the sound of the bell was the Voice of God and that you knew infallibly when you obeyed its sound that you were being pleasing to God by being in the right place at the right time, why then it followed that the person who rang it, the Regulator himself, was, in the very act of ringing it, and obeying, also certain that he too was being pleasing to God. It was good to be infallible about *something;* I was amazed at how far I had come.

On Christmas Eve everyone had to retire early, so as to be up for Midnight Mass. Only instead of waking to the bell, the house was gently aroused by some of us in choir singing Christmas carols—"Adeste Fideles" and of course "Silent Night." The most touching moment came when we went up to old Father Mathias Oswald's room and gently sang outside his door (something we had prepared at length for) "Silent Night" in German: *"Stillige Nacht! Heilige Nacht!"* so that he would awaken to the sounds that he had known as a boy, back in Bavaria, over eighty years ago.

At Midnight Mass, Father Master was vested in seemingly solid gold vestments. The *Consolamini* was sung: "Be consoled, O my people, be consoled, for behold, I am come, and am with you!"

And after reading the simple Gospel of the birth of Christ ("In the dark eternal night, O Lord, the night in the midst of its course, Thy Word came down to us, and the earth blossomed forth a Savior"), Father Master in his sermon announced to all the world the good news that salvation had come: "Tonight, in this winter of the Year of Our Lord 1944—a blessed year in which the life of the Supreme Pontiff has been spared and the sacred character of the City of Rome respected—much good has been accomplished. Men have reason to know that God has kept His Word, God has again kept His Promise, and once again His Chosen People are comforted by His Coming. Make no mistake: *He is among us! He has not delayed!*

"And you my dear young novices, is there a man among you that does not have reason to look forward with confidence to the year of Our Lord 1945? No man can tell ahead of time what that year will bring to the world, but you among all men have reason to find yourselves blessed in it: you are here hidden away with Christ—and Christ is God's! Do not be concerned with the world, for you have given up the world. Complete your part of the bargain: God has kept His. Look forward in 1945 to the perfection of your life, so that in the Holocaust of Divine Love you may seal it, on that bright day in August, with the victory that awaits you, the profession of your Vows of Poverty, Chastity, and Obedience."

For that brief while, on Christmas Eve of 1944, I could honestly say that I felt happy. As I clanged the bell and led the rest of the men out of their pews, I looked at my friend, Mister Simmons, to see if he was happy. I looked at his face; he was tired and indescribably weary from it all, perhaps from all that singing. He seemed almost not to notice anything that was going on, and seemed driven along by some private misfortune that I knew nothing about. I wondered, to tell the truth, if he knew what time of year it was, or if he really cared.

And so the new year came.

One night late in January, long after Augustine had tolled eleven, I was startled by a knock at my cell door. My first thought was that it would be Brother Meinrad telling me about what kind of work I would do in the barns next day, or Father Master making a change in schedule. I quickly jumped into my robe, pulled the belt tight around me, and opened the door. It was my neighbor from across the hall; it was Mister Simmons.

No novice was ever to visit the room of another novice, day or night, under any circumstances whatever; that was the strictest rule in the Novitiate. To break that rule and be discovered meant that you would be dismissed at once and lose everything that you had come for—the vows, life in a religious order, even the priesthood itself. To me that was unthinkable.

I stood there looking at him. I stepped back, and more or less led him into my room. I did not know what to do, but I certainly did not want to keep my door open at that hour of the night.

"I have to talk to someone," he said. "You are my friend. I think I am going mad."

I had never heard anyone talk that way before.

"Father Master called me in today. He said that I had problems. I exhibited such anxiety over fundamental matters that it did not bode well for the future. He said he had been observing me, that I had a look on my face during lectures that made him feel I was not accepting things. Then he asked me what was I having difficulty with.

"I told him. I said that it was the Problem of Evil. That so many cruel things happened, on the farm, in the Novitiate, and in the world itself that I had trouble believing in an Infinitely Good God. I said that I was praying over it, and that I was reading in the library to help me solve it.

"He hit the ceiling. '*The library!*' he shouted, 'The *library?* Mister, you are not competent to solve such problems! You have not even had Philosophy yet, and you are far away from Sacred Theology. You are not trained to deal with such things as the Problem of Evil.' "

Mister Simmons was silent for a moment, and I became aware that I had not yet said anything; I decided to speak. "What did he tell you that you *should* do?" I asked, as a kind of politeness, under the circumstances.

"He told me that I should stop 'rooting and delving' among the 'tomes in the library.' He said that on the contrary my duty was to flee, to flee such thoughts when they occurred. 'Pray to God to resist such temptations. Should you not, should you on the contrary continue to entertain them, I shall have no other recourse than to consult the House Council, and to have you sent home.'

"He told me that it would be a sin against the Light, that it was the sin against the Holy Spirit. . ."

Billy stopped and looked at me. "I can't even sleep. You are my friend. What is your opinion? What do you say?"

I let him be, in silence. I was agitated myself, and really did not know what I was supposed to do. *Here is your fellow man*, I remember saying to myself; *treat him as you would be treated*. I wondered how that was. I tried desperately to remember all that Father Master had taught us, all that I had read and taken notes on from the beginning of the Novitiate year. Here is your first Soul, I heard myself saying. He is the first of all those who will ever come to you for aid. May God help you to do the right thing.

And so I told him, simply and honestly, what I hoped that anyone would tell me in such a situation: that, having consulted competent spiritual authority, having talked things over with his Director, and having been reassured that his soul still possessed the marks of a genuine Vocation, that he should calm himself, that he was sure in fact he was still one of the People of God, one of God's own elect, actually, indeed, that he could now consider himself all but infallibly certain that he would be pleasing to God by remaining a novice and continuing the fight; furthermore, that he could be sure that God would not abandon him, for God never abandoned anyone, He only hid His face occasionally in the Dark Night of the Soul, which some were privileged to endure. We would all undergo it sooner or later, I suggested, and I would wish that he, Mister Simmons, would say the same things to me, if I came to him, in other circumstances. I reminded him of our pledge to one another on the back of the truck that had brought us there: with God's help we would both survive such difficulties, and later on, in the glorious month of August, on the Feast of the Transfiguration, August 6, 1945, we would both make vows together. We would both be happy once again.

Billy just looked at me and nodded; he remembered the back of the truck; it was what he had come expecting to hear; it was quite a sermon, my first.

I helped him back to his cell; but before I closed the door, I warned him that, for both our sakes, he should never visit my room again. I said good night and closed the door on him quietly. I had of course been severe. But on the whole I had done just fine. Instead of returning directly to my room, however, I made a trip to the john; that way, if anyone noticed I was up, they would expect it to be normal, and not at all suspect that I had been talking with a fellow novice in the middle of the night.

It was a hard time apparently; Mister Flint left us the next day during work period; we checked, and sure enough, his trunk was gone from the basement. And Mister Kaminsky left a few days later; it was said that he had joined the Marines.

And yet spring did come. I doubt if anywhere in the world there was a more appreciated early spring than that which occurred at Rolling Prairie in 1945: everything burst into green and the prairie came alive with color. The lambs, let out, frolicked, and even old McTavish, the Black Angus bull, when he was let out into the north pasture, as soon as he was free of the five terrified novices who had herded him across the fields, rolled and rubbed himself in the bushes as though he were rolling out of him all the cold confines of the barns and of winter. "He'll have a ball now," said one of the Professed, who was free to speak.

The swallows appeared up in the tower once again; I didn't notice them coming, they were just there one day, having in them their own good sense of what time of year it was. And we began to feel that we had made it—those of us who were left—that we had survived, and that it would soon be all over. Except for Mister

Simmons, of course, poor old Mister Thirty; yet he, too, was still among us, his voice even more beautiful as he sang us on from Ash Wednesday through Lent and up to Holy Week. And I wondered: had I helped him? Had my words of advice and my loyalty helped him be what he wanted to be? I wondered very much—for by this time everyone seemed to be aware that he was having trouble.

I certainly took things better; nothing on the farm—stenches or sights or the feel of the innards of animals made me want to retch anymore. I was able to laugh at my earlier queasiness; you did get used to everything. Even when Brother Meinrad told me about something called "broadtail lamb" I was not as upset or annoyed as I would have been six months earlier. He called me over to him one afternoon in late February, holding something up that seemed even brighter than the last of the snow which gleamed in the sunlight behind him.

"Look at this, Mister," he said. "Touch it."

I felt it; it seemed incredibly soft, the softest thing I had ever felt. "It's nice," I said. "What is it? Is it fur?"

"It's called broadtail lamb. The reason it's so soft is that the lamb is not allowed to be born. It's taken out of the mother ahead of time, just after it has developed its skin. The Russians started it with a breed of Angora sheep called Carakul. We are trying to do it here with our own breed, trying to get a broadtail operation going."

I stared at him. "You mean people actually have a little animal ripped out and killed just for its fleece? I never heard of such a thing!"

Brother Meinrad laughed amiably; he was continuing my education. "I thought you'd like it," he said, "—it is rather hard on the mother—actually it's a bloody mess. But people use it for gloves and things, it's really high fashion. It could mean a lot for the Novitiate, especially during wartime. There is money in it."

I waited to go; I knew by this time that when Brother Meinrad called me over he always had something else to say that was not connected with what he first spoke about. What was the latest in the war? I wanted to know.

"They've crossed the Rhine into Germany, a place called Remagen. Some traitors didn't blow the bridge up. *Die Verrat!*" he said disgustedly.

Then he said, "Hey—we got our own *Kike!*"

I thought for a moment he was speaking again about Mister Simmons, or about Mister Hanratty, for Meinrad had been angry with him the previous day for going to the infirmary during work period without getting permission. Brother Meinrad had an endless series of Jewish and Yiddish terms—he was really quite educated on the subject—for referring to people he did not like as if they were Jews. "Mister Hanratty?" I asked.

He was annoyed. "*No*, I mean a real Jew. We have a visitor! He was a prisoner in Germany and escaped. You should hear the things he says, I don't believe a word. I'll tell you more later."

The visitor turned out to be Father George Severne, a military chaplain from the British Army. Rumors about him—incredible rumors—swept the Novitiate. It was variously reported that he had been parachuted into Germany in a commando raid, that he had been in on the plot to assassinate Hitler, and that he had had to breathe through a reed underneath the water while the Nazis searched for him.

None of these turned out to be true, yet the reality of the man when we finally perceived it was more effective than if they were. I could not wait to hear him but, because it was Lent, we would have to wait until Holy Saturday evening for this sort of diversion. Each novice knew to the moment when such things happened—that the long fast and abstinence of Lent were over at noon of Holy Saturday, that the "Corbonam" or candy press would be thrown open that afternoon, and that the earliest time for a welcoming soiree and a talk in Chapel from Father George would be after supper. But first, all the grand and triumphant events of Holy Week must take place.

"*Tenebrae Factae Sunt!*" the choir shouted out that Good Friday evening in the great Feast of Darkness. Everything else was forgotten in the stupendous service with its incomparable music which recapitulated the entire story of mankind, from the very beginning even into the night of the death of the Savior, the voice of God crying out, "My People, My People! What is there that I could do that I have not done for you? Like a chosen vineyard I have planted you and watered you, but Thou wouldst not! *Responde Mihi!*" Billy was especially moved by the music which he sang: I could see his face, singing so that he almost became the words; it became almost unbearable when the lights were put out, and each candle of the seven-branched candlestick was put out by

Brother Sacristan, who mounted the altar steps to douse it, to the words of the *Benedictus*, until there was one solitary candle left lighting the entire Chapel, so that it seemed the last flickering light left on earth, and then in that dramatic Good Friday gesture, it too was taken by Brother Sacristan back away behind the altar, so that we novices, now a little group of only thirteen young men lost away in the darkness in that tiny place called Rolling Prairie, in that burgeoning spring of 1945, felt that we were all left totally in gloom, without light, without Christ, without God, it seemed, as indeed it was supposed to seem, it was as if Billy was singing us all away, far away from the world; it was as though the voice of Billy had become the flickering tongue of flame, so that I actually felt apprehension when it disappeared behind the altar that it had gone out, that Billy himself had met his end.

"Illumine those who sit in darkness, and in the shadow of death," the psalm concluded, the choir shouting to a crescendo, "—and direct instead their feet into the way of peace!" The candle was brought back, in silence, and the tension was over; suddenly a wild explosion of noise thundered through the Chapel as though a bomb had gone off: it was only the choir slamming their books shut, as monks have done from time immemorial, but the huge tomes closing upon themselves, sounding like the clap of doom and the bursting of the earth open, left us all giggling and snickering embarrassedly when the lights were turned on. The novices were astonished; but the wise old ones among us, the Professed, were left smiling in their knowledge of how things were done.

And so on Good Friday there was death; everything died with Christ. All and each of us felt death in us. The statues were covered with purple cloth and had been since Palm Sunday. No bell or musical instrument was sounded from Maundy Thursday on—the piano lid in the recreation room was put down over the keys, and Mister Coon, the organist, quietly folded down the cover over the great Chapel organ. For the only time in the year even old Augustine was silenced and stopped ringing out to us how late the hour was and how much later it was than when we first believed.

I, too, as Regulator ceased ringing life on; my small bell was silenced: instead I was given a ridiculous wooden clapper that everybody snickered at when I first tried to use it. All other sound had gone out except the sound of human voices mourning to God over death. Nowhere was death more evident than in the Chapel itself. The Tabernacle door lay open: there was nothing in it. The Tabernacle—the tent, literally, that God had pitched among us, in which the manna from heaven had been stored, the memory of the Paschal Lamb had been preserved—the sacred Last Supper that God ate with Man, the Eucharist of Divine Love for poor humans, all was gone and departed utterly, just like the Veil of the Temple rent from top to bottom, as though God had left His Temple, as though God had abandoned His Chosen People, and as though God had abandoned Man.

We lived the events of Holy Week more than sang them; we had prepared many months for it, so that the Last Supper and the Washing of the Feet and the kiss of Judas and the cutting off of the ear of the high priest's servant all became more real than the events of the day; the ordinary actual happenings of the week of March 25, 1945, in the rest of the world, and the life of the farm, were by contrast somehow less real. We were exhausted from it, and our Roman collars hung on us like the harnesses that you saw on the great dray animals in the barns.

And yet it was not all finished. That year Father Master granted permission for a liturgical experiment. Instead of the Blessing of the New Fire as it was traditionally done at dawn of Holy Saturday, we were to have it as a late night vigil for Easter.

Thus we celebrated the end of Lent earlier in the evening, with a full meal—the first since Ash Wednesday. Afterward, at a soiree, the Corbonam was opened and we were given candy, too, for the first time in six weeks. For all our self-control and pursuit of perfection, we were still young men, and whatever immaturity we possessed came out on such occasions. Mister Reedy, who remained large and fat in spite of all his fasting, asked us ahead of time to keep him from "making a pig" of himself; nevertheless he had to be physically restrained by his friend Mister Carsten, to the inevitable amused cries of "Greedy Reedy!" from all over the recreation room.

It was into this mood of celebration that Father George Severne came. When it was explained to him what was happening, he laughed politely and said in a pronounced British accent, "The Corbonam? Well, you young men have got quite a novel name for your candy press, I must say!"

As things quieted, and the candy disappeared, Father George

was introduced. Father Master began by saying that he would not have us ignorant, that he was not known to let young men pass out from his tutelage "wet behind the ears"; consequently, when the opportunity arose to have someone such as Father George speak to us of the experience of the Church and its priesthood in difficult areas, he felt it incumbent upon him to invite the visitor to address us and to share with us some of his wisdom and experience. He then yielded to Father George.

Father George thanked him, remarked that any comments of his would possess more experience than any wisdom that he was aware of, and he asked us what it was we were most interested in hearing.

Some wanted to hear about the war, and when it would end, but Father George said he did not know when it would end and that the only part he had been in had been North Africa, which was now part of history. Mister Knous then shouted, "Your escape, tell us about your escape!"

"I had best tell you something about life in the camps, first. Lindenfels is in the Schwartzewald," he said. "It is on the Romantischestrasse—the Route of the Old German Heroes. Siegfried passed that way on his Rhineland journeys." Father George immediately struck me as an educated man, one who perhaps had read history and attended great operas; a vague yearning to be such a man tinged my spirit as he spoke. "Lindenfels, in fact, in more than one way reminds me of your place here, for though it is certainly more hilly than Rolling Prairie, still the pine forest you have up on your Hill of Calvary makes it seem the same. But the air is much cleaner here . . ." He looked at us for a moment, as though he might be wondering how much and what of his experience it would be good for us to hear. He turned to Father Master and asked, "Father Master, perhaps there are some things you would prefer the novices should not hear? Perhaps I ought not to tell too much about life or death in the camps?"

Father Master bridled; we all knew that one of his main themes was how we were all developing into mature adults. Moreover, from my talks with Meinrad I knew what his views were on the war; they were the views of the Reverend Charles Coughlin, the ones that I had been raised on: that the war was brought about by the International Bankers and the Jews, and that America had no business being involved with foreign entanglements.

Instead of losing his temper, however, Father Master simply

turned to Father George and said, "These men know what time of day it is," nodding in our direction. "It is unlikely anything you have to say will shock them. Proceed."

Father Severne shook his head thoughtfully. Then he began. "They're burning people, you know. The main difference between Lindenfels, as I have said, and your lovely place here is the quality of the air: at Lindenfels the sky during the day has a sickly brown pallor hanging over it, depending on which way the wind is blowing. At night, there is always an overcast which lights up from time to time from the constantly burning furnaces. And every day, as you grow weaker at work and have less to eat, you know that you are closer and closer to the furnace yourself and that one day you will be gone up the chimney or lighting the night sky. It is difficult to be charitable, or to regard *anyone* as your neighbor under such circumstances.

"Nevertheless, I did find one man who was a neighbor in that hell, one man who still managed to be kind. His name was Mordecai—I never got his last name—he was a Jew, from Poland, I think. People are numbers in the camps, not names, and he wore a number and *Der Gelbe Sterne*—the yellow star of David—always over the right back shoulder. The SS pinned it on prisoners as though they were animals stamped for meat approval.

"It was terrible. The dogs went for the genitals if you tried to escape. Women with child coming into the camps were shot, the child dying in the womb unborn. The Germans were getting short on things, you know, and a pregnant woman is just a burden, they cannot work, and they take up food. All children under a certain age were marched right off the trains to grave ditches in the forest; we knew it; they had to dig their own graves first, take off their clothes, and then fall, naked, into the earth. Most of them were Jews, though some were "slave nationalities" from the rest of Europe also. I was captured as a legitimate prisoner of war in North Africa in 1941, and for a while was treated as a prisoner of war according to the rules of Geneva. But after a while, because I did not answer questions properly or perhaps asked too many, I ended up in the camps like everybody else, and for all practical purposes was treated as a Jew myself."

As I listened, I became conscious of mutterings or mumblings behind me several pews back. At first I thought someone might be having trouble holding back laughter about some irrelevancy and was afraid that Mister Jenkins' inevitable nervous guffaw might break loose, but the disturbance was coming from too far back in the Chapel for that and I realized it was from among the Professed Brothers, and then of course I knew what was going on: Brother Meinrad would be making a running commentary on everything the English priest was saying. I knew by heart what it would include—that the war was England's war, that Hitler had been forced into it, that the Treaty of Versailles was unjust, and so on. Ever so often in his delivery Father George would look up and pause, until he turned to Father Master and said, "Someone seems to be having some sort of difficulty—I wonder if there is a question I might answer?"

At once Brother Meinrad shot to his feet. I could see him out of the corner of my eye. He was standing with his hands on the pew in front of him like some American patriot from a painting, a "Give Me Liberty or Give Me Death" stance, or like a prisoner at the dock about to make a heroic last speech.

"Yes, Brother?" Father Master asked.

Indignantly Brother asked what truth there could possibly be in the assertions that the Germans had committed anything worse than what was common to all wars, and that the British and the Americans were in reality doing the same things and worse, only Churchill and Roosevelt did not let us know. Brother Meinrad asked Father George (for a question it was more like a speech) for specifics, what precisely did the Nazis do that was any worse than what the Russian Communists were doing to German boys on the Eastern Front? And what of Mister Roosevelt's cooperating with them in foreign meeting after foreign meeting? What was it that they did, he screamed, that made them so bad?

For a long time Father George did not speak. Then he said simply, "They used people like meat—the SS hung them up on hooks while they were still alive and their hearts still pounding."

Brother Meinrad was briefly taken aback, but only briefly. He paused, and took a deeper breath. "What I want to know is, is this something you *heard* about and are now telling us like it was the gospel truth or is this something you saw and were present for? *All I ask is to know:* to understand what it is that has been done wrong? What did they do?"

There was so much confusion at this point that a guffaw came from Mister Jenkins, which we all knew by this late date in the year he only did at moments of extreme tension, that he was not really laughing at all, and yet when he did it it made others want to laugh in spite of themselves, and I was afraid that uncontrolled giggling might occur.

Father George controlled the situation. "Brother," he said in a kind voice, "I know that as you are a Religious it may be impossible to believe that mankind would act this way. And I know that as you are obviously German and I am English it may be equally as difficult to believe that I am being objective about things. And so I will simply tell you one incident—which I was present for—and I was *indeed* present for it, which should be sufficient.

"The man in charge of Lindenfels was Felix Fromm, a general of the SS, and a staunch Roman Catholic. But he was mad; he was insane—or perhaps deliberately appeared to be—on the subject of butterflies."

There was another pause, and I cringed in my pew lest someone would titter.

" 'Butterfly collecting is not slight!' he would shout at us, as though we cared. He must have been a professor in civilian life, or else that is what he wanted to be. He would stand us up and give us long lectures—after work when we were exhausted—about how all things could be seen even in the small wings of a butterfly were we but sensitive enough to observe. 'Man is not worthy of the butterfly,' he would shout, '*Die Schmetterling!*' He would tell us this in German, and then in English, and in a half a dozen other languages, for he was fluent. 'My friends,' he would say, 'observe them when they fly through our camp: in the fall they are— *peregrinus*—how do you say, pilgrims?—to the far and distant deserts of Africa, across the Mittlesee. Then in spring, like the birds, they fly, across the Pyrenees, the Alps, through here, on the way to La Manche, to England, and to the Hebrides.'

"He was entranced, captivated; even in our exhausted state we knew that he knew his business, that he was intoxicated with his subject, totally entranced by it. And so he would make us stand, hour after hour, for his lectures. He told us everything, better I am sure than many university professors, and I am certain that had I been in something approaching a human condition I would have been enlightened by wisdom concerning one of God's lesser creatures, the entire genus of Lepidoptera.

"But, my dear men, we were not—we were most horrendously

not—in a state remotely resembling a human condition, or what you hear these days referred to as 'a proper learning environment.' Fromm was sick; he was sicker than we were. He kept us standing there in the hot sun or the cold rain or, often, snow, telling us about butterflies, their wings and their habits—to us who cared for nothing but to get inside and stop standing and gain some nourishment.

"Why? For one reason: it all had to do with escaping. The man's mad mind was filled with only one thought, that we would escape, that even one of us would get away, away from the dogs, past the barbed wire and the searchlights. He was Felix Fromm, you see, general of the Third Reich and of the SS, and the security of Lindenfels was his grave responsibility. All the talk about butterflies was to torment us into a perpetual, final and frozen fear, to keep us from ever even thinking about escape.

"And yet, Mordecai—my friend—did, or, that is, he tried.

"Mordecai was a sensitive, kind person, even in the hideousness of the camp. I greatly admired his religious faith, his sense of humor, even in all the happenings of Lindenfels. Instead of shoes, he wore a pair of rubbers which he had saved from somewhere, and though he joked about them, they were actually his prize possessions for they protected him against the slush and offal that was everywhere. He once pulled me aside and told me that if anything ever happened to him, I should consider them his gift to me. When I protested and asked why he was so thoughtful, Mordecai whispered simply, in his broken way of speaking English, 'I try to help my next.' I had to ask him to repeat it before I realized he meant he tried to help his neighbor—I was his next.

"He used to pray at night. I could not understand the mixture of language that he spoke, but I knew the Scripture well enough to catch snatches of Isaiah, Elias, Jeremiah. The one I always knew, for I felt like saying it with him, was Elias's great complaint about God. 'You have duped me, O Lord; I am become an object of laughter, all the day the word of the Lord has brought me reproach. I say to myself, I will not mention Him, I will speak His name no more.'

"Poor Mordecai! They were among the last words out of him. He was caught trying to escape in the night.

"Next morning, Fromm announced a lecture of supreme importance: we were to see our first Red Butterfly! One had been caught, in camp! The collection would be enriched by a most exquisite specimen."

Father George stopped, clearly considering one more time if he should go on. "Look here—I did not come to intrude upon your beautiful celebration here, the observance of Holy Week which you are all doing so well; I hesitate to mention what happened within the walls of a Novitiate. Moreover, many of you are young people, deserving of special consideration.

"And yet you also deserve to hear, and the world deserves to hear, the worst. You cannot shut your ears, no man can, and still call himself a man, cannot shut your ears to what has happened among us. The thing must be said by somebody, must be listened to by someone—if not an infinite merciful God, then at least by poor, fallible, frightened man."

Father Master nodded, to something of what had been said.

"We were hauled out after work period; *nothing* was sacred enough to excuse us from work period. Fromm was there as Herr Professor with all his talk about *Kunst, die Aufgabe,* and *der Nachtfalter, die Raupe.* Mordecai, caught, was brought out and held between two SS men like some guilty student standing in front of the classroom about to be made a dunce in the corner. After what seemed about two hours of endless chatter and non-sense about how fine the collection was, including doubtless some very real and valuable knowledge about the genus Lepidoptera which, had we been anything but starving, exhausted prisoners, might have interested us, Fromm rapped his baton sharply on his lectern. He flipped it like a wand in the direction of the prisoner and four more SS came up, armed with equipment.

"It was . . . odd equipment. There were ropes and various irons—a buzz saw which I took to be for putting up a scaffolding, so that for a moment I thought there was going to be a hanging or even that we were to witness a crucifixion scene.

"It was worse.

"I will get this over as quickly as possible. What was done was that the prisoner was spread-eagled, roughly and very tautly, his arms pulled and pinioned to stakes, his legs to other stakes, until his body was taut and he could not move. An SS made two cuts in his back beneath the two shoulder blades. Another SS came up with the cutting saw. He then cut through the bones, several ribs on each side, as though the human being in front of him were some farm animal instead of a man. I still could not conceive of what they were up to; how could anyone have thought in that direction. A third SS man, a butcher of a person, then reached in with the aid of cruel grappling instruments and extracted each of the prisoner's lungs, so that, still breathing, still functioning, they lay out flat upon the back. Then, under Fromm's scrupulous scrutiny, they were carefully arranged out into their full form.

"At last he was satisfied. 'The Red Butterfly, my friends,' Fromm said. 'It is very rare, I am sure you will have to admit. I want you to look at it closely. Study it, the movement of its wings. *Die Schmetterling!*"

"For hours, how many, I do not know, we were compelled to stand at attention. I do not know whether Mordecai was conscious or not, or whether he had been unconscious from the beginning. He did live for some time though; the cruel evidence of his waning life was terribly clear. I felt that he died sometime within the first half hour. I wondered what he thought now, or if he was capable of thought. And standing there, his last words kept repeating themselves in my brain: 'I say to myself I will not mention Him, I will speak his name no more . . .'

" 'My next,' I thought. 'My poor next.'

"After it got dark—it must have been well past eleven at night—Fromm returned, spoke some more of *Die Aufgabe,* and released us. As we broke ranks to return to barracks, on legs that could hardly move, I managed to pass close by the dead body of my friend. I saw his two rubbers strewn beneath him where they had fallen when they had raised him. I reached down, with terrible pain; I picked them up, his last heritage to me.

"The next day, weak as I was, I escaped. I saw a chance, and slipped under the electrified wire at the ditch near the septic tanks at the end of the camp, wearing my friend's rubbers—they were better than what I had on my feet; and, you know, I think I may have owed my life to them: the bloodhounds were out, I heard them often during my trip, but they never came close to me, and I think maybe they were following the wrong scent, that the rubbers were not what they had been set to follow.

"I succeeded in leaving the Lindenfels area. I ate acorns and certain small clumps of vegetation. I got sick on food often, and yet it was better than in camp. Once I stole some eggs from a German farm. I headed south, toward what I hoped was the Swiss border. Over the next forty days I wandered: I climbed first through the Odenwald; I remember places with names like Sternenfels, Todtmoos, Schöunau. I actually crossed over into Switzerland apparently above a place called Sackingen, and did not know I was free, and was afraid to ask. I only felt that I must head for the Alps, and the biggest line of mountains I could see were of course the Jura, but I had no maps.

"I felt very much at home in the Jura. The plant life reminded me of my native England—Saxifrage, Bedstraws, and Speedwells looked out at me from the rocks. But most of all, I saw flying rapidly that most British of butterflies, the Painted Lady! I knew all about them, from Fromm—even their Latin name: *Vanessa Cardui*. I knew they bred on the edges of the Sahara, and that they would be flying north at that time of year, coming down from the Alpine passes, to find their way to England—only, of course, they were going backward, for my purposes, toward Lindenfels! I even found time to laugh at them, for they seemed as anxious to get to Fromm's butterfly farm as I was to leave it. I used to lecture them, while following their path, the other way, in my rubbers: 'Be careful, Vanessa!' I would say, 'Be careful, little one—you will end up in the Commander's collection!'

"By following them, I actually climbed over the Schwieze Jura, through one of the lower passes; I collapsed by a road outside the town of Aarburg, and awoke in a Swiss hospital.

"That was only one year ago."

After Father Severne got to that point he decided to stop, as though he had gone on long enough. Father Master seemed pleased that the talk was over; he asked if anyone had any questions. I turned in my seat and looked at Brother Meinrad; he looked weary, as though exhausted in the effort to communicate with this Englishman. He arose, and in that patient tone some people use when talking to children he said, "The Germans are a loving people. Do you know the word *Gemütlichkeit?* There is no word for it in the English language. It means a feeling of humanity, of the Soul. Schiller had it. Brahms and Beethoven had it. That is why the Germans love music. '*Seid umschlangen, Millionene!* You Millions, I embrace you!' they sing. Now how can they be so bad!"

Father Severne said something to the effect that he could not answer that, that he could only tell what he had seen.

"Then they were betrayed," Brother said, and sat sadly back in his seat.

I began to fear it would all be over before I understood it. I felt myself rising, and I heard my voice, hoarse as it usually was when I am nervous, speaking. "Father Severne," I heard it say, "why did you risk such a terrible death by trying to escape? How could you possibly have the courage to even think of such a thing?"

The answer was simple and matter of fact: "It is the duty of a British officer to escape in time of war; it is written into the Manual of Arms."

I was astonished by the answer, but there was no more time for questions; the Easter Vigil was about to begin, and Father Master urged us all to move quickly to the Chapel for it.

The Feast of Light is really the high point of the Church's liturgy. Light is kindled from flint sparks upon strands of flax, and the lighted candle signifying Christ the Savior is brought up the darkened main aisle. The celebrant calls out three times the words *"Lumen Christi!"*; the congregation genuflects in adoration and calls back *"Deo Gratias!"*

The *Exultet* follows, springing from the mind of mighty Augustine of Hippo, and put to plainchant by the High Middle Ages; in it, creation itself is said to exult that the long night of sin and darkness is over, that mankind's loneliness of enmity with God and with himself is at last finished, ended by the arrival at last of the long-awaited Redeemer. "This is the night," it shouts. "This then is the night of the ancient paschal rites, wherein the true Lamb is slain, with whose blood the doorposts of the People of God are consecrated. This is the night, on which Thou didst cause our fathers, the Children of Israel, to cross dry-shod the Red Sea, leading them out of the bondage of the Land of Egypt. This then is the night which has purged away the darkness of sins with the illumination of the Pillar of Fire. . . . O Wondrous Condescension! O inestimable affection! Oh, *happy* fault, which brought about so glorious a Savior!"

Mister Simmons sang the words remarkably well: *"O vere beata nox, quae exspoliavit Aegyptios, ditavit Hebraeos!"* He more than sang them, he became them, to such an extent that, knowing what

I did about his problems, I wondered where it would end with him.

It is a strange thing; many people cannot say exactly where they were on a given date, in World War II or anywhere else, once the moment has receded from memory; but for some of us, certain dates will never be forgotten; they refuse to recede from memory. I know where I was on the night of March 31: I was with my brothers, at Rolling Prairie, Indiana, singing the Easter Vigil. It was the night my friend died.

After that, however, my memory is not a reliable record. I have some memory, or is it imagination, that Billy came to me again, speaking Latin. He was full of *"Hora venits"* and *"Quare fremuits"* and *"sunt inanias"* and other things which I did not understand. The hour was late and I was asleep. "Go back to bed, I will speak to you in the morning," I said drowsily but firmly and closed the door.

My sleep was vexed to nightmare and sickness, and I was in the infirmary up next to the Chapel tower; I must have passed in and out of consciousness, the big bell interfering with my rest. I heard it saying all sorts of things to me: that Billy was dead and that others were dead, that it was late and that it was night and that I was sleeping when I should be awake and that I should get up to awaken the others and that I had failed and that my faith was vain and that the Tabernacle was empty and that Father George was escaping and that God had lied.

All day long in the bright sunshine of the infirmary bed, I up closer to Augustine in the hot warming days of that spring of 1945, all through the bright day the huge voice boomed out above me that it was night, and I who had eyes to see the bright light of day with, I looked out and could not see, for the voice kept telling me it was night and that True Midnight had already occurred and oh it was terrible and that the swallows were gone and that Father George had escaped and did not believe and going out he hanged himself and it was he that put his hand with me in the dish and the great vats steaming and the entrails and the blood, how you had to toughen yourself up for everything and be a priest forever, deliriums and temperature 104 in the heat outside the empty Tabernacle in the desert with Bedouins and camels and who owns our bodies and the flutterwings of the butterfly, the Red Butterfly, the *Schmetterling*, he called it, crucified spread-eagled out above them and an escape in rubbers over the mountains to Switzerland, and it stopped. But then it would start again and I heard the great clanking chain mechanisms of Augustine winding up to tell me again the day and the hour.

Sometimes, too, there were funeral bells and the *Chorus Angelorum* and the *Ego Sum* of Job of the march to the cemetery, and the hump of sod in the soil of the prairie, the clay. Adam, clay: man, all humans, death and work and bells and time. And I asleep and it started over again, that it was *millesimo*, that it was *nongentesimo*, that it was *quadragesimo*, that it was *quarto. Quarto?* No, what came after *quarto* was *quinto*, the Year of Our Lord, and my year, too.

"Good morning, Mister!" It was the sternly happy voice of Mister Skeffington, the infirmarian, with a breakfast of tea and toast. I was better. Better of something that I had had. I was getting well. I was no longer Regulator, that job had been thought too demanding for someone in my condition. Father Master had indicated instead a little rest was necessary and soon I would be all right.

Father George was all right, too, I slowly learned, only he was someplace else. But it was some time before I learned that Billy was not all right and that that part of my dreams was true, that he was dead, and that Father Master had publicly announced that it was not suicide because the man was in no condition to be responsible for his own death, that he had been overwrought. But it was a very long time later that anyone would tell me anything about how he died: that he had hanged himself on Holy Saturday night out in the barn. I had slept in the next morning and for the first time all year had failed to wake the house up on time, and it was then they discovered something wrong with me and sent me to the infirmary to rest.

"You gave us quite a time of it," said Mister Skeffington smiling. "One morning you went running through the main corridor ringing the bell and shouting, 'It is midnight! It is midnight! True Midnight has already occurred!' You were right, too, of course; it was two o'clock in the morning!"

I do remember some things. The death of President Roosevelt; the deaths of Mussolini and Hitler and prayers of thanksgiving that the city of Rome and the life of the Holy Father had been spared in the war. Then VE Day, and the war over in Europe, at least.

After that, the spring hurried by and turned quickly into summer. I was allowed out to work again, only in the fields now, doing good hard work that repaired me. For a while I worried whether I would be allowed to be professed on time, but Father Master told me that I worried about too many things; he pronounced me fine and a perfect candidate for the religious life and the vows. By June it was as though nothing had happened, and my life at the Novitiate had returned to normal. Father Master called me in for Monitions in early July and told me I should prepare myself to take vows on August 6, the Feast of the Transfiguration of Our Lord, with the other members of my class, who now numbered eleven, the others having departed.

Profession Day finally did arrive. The day dawned with a brightness the world had never seen. Looking out my window I saw that the prairie was beautiful, and off toward the west rose little fluffy clouds—fair weather clouds, I knew, far, far beyond the town of Rolling Prairie; it would be a good day.

Later, I recited my vows. I was nervous and could not at first sign my name, my hand was shaking so. And I needed help with the cincture; Mister Lawson kindly helped tie me. The Latin was difficult, but eventually I, too, along with eleven others, I too got to my ending, to the "*Millesimo nongentesimo quadragesimo quinto*" of August 6 of the Year of Our Lord 1945. After it was over, Father Master in the sacristy reached over and our hands grasped in a firm, manly gesture of fraternal unity.

There is not much more to say. We spent, as was the custom, one week more at the Novitiate to lead the next class into their year. And during the week we worked, on silence, at the same old jobs we had done before we were professed. One afternoon during the week, however, as I was reporting into the subkitchen to help can tomatoes and other fruits in season, Brother Just pulled me over to the side to tell me something. "They've dropped a big bomb on Japan. It's called an atom bomb. My brother sent me a card: he said the heat from the bomb was so great it seared the bottom of the plane, and it flipped the plane over three times!"

So that was it. That was the reason for the big bombers, the B29s I had noticed flying over the Novitiate during the entire Novitiate

year, with their high, high tails and long, deadly noses. So much
had happened in the world while we were on the prairie. "The war
will soon be over," Brother Just continued. "They probably have
more of them." I nodded and turned to the vegetables with a
feeling of guilt—for having broken silence with a fellow novice.

The last day was August 14, the eve of the Feast of the Assumption of Our Blessed Lady as Queen of Heaven. Father Mulloughney, a noted liturgist, took as his texts for a lengthy talk, a
collage of quotations from the liturgy both for the Feast of the
Assumption of the Blessed Virgin as Queen of Heaven and quotes
from the Feast of the Transfiguration of Jesus a week earlier, whose
octave we were celebrating. He ingeniously wove them together
with the history of the day, in such a way that the Sacred Scriptures
themselves seemed to have foretold what had happened in the
skies over Hiroshima eight days before: "And He was transfigured
before them," Father Mulloughney quoted. "His face shone as the
Sun, and His vestments were as white as snow. A blinding flash
illuminated the East, and the Earth shook in its tracks!" he
shouted. Then he moved on to the day's feast: "Who is this that
ascends like the dawn into the heavens? Beautiful as the moon,
shining as the sun, terrible as an army in battle array?" He went on
to show that the world was in its latter days, that there were
unmistakable signs upon the heavens that Christ's Second Coming
was imminent.

Knowing our ignorance, Father Mulloughney brought us up to
date with things. A powerful bomb, called an atomic bomb, had
been dropped on Japan, at a place called Hiroshima, something
more powerful than the world had ever seen. It had turned that
city into a pyre of immense magnitude. Half a million people had
been estimated dead. Reports emanating from the doomed country
of the enemy described people losing their eyes in the first fraction
of a second. Some, closer to what was called "Zero Point," were
totally vaporized in the terrible fiery holocaust. Outlines of human
beings—what were once human beings—were visible, it was said,
in the sidewalks where they had been standing. There was no
question that the world had entered upon a new age, and little
question that man was in the final stages of human history.

He closed by congratulating the newly professed, and urged us
to develop a life of dedication to the Queen of Heaven, in order to

bring God's mercy to the People of God. I thought the talk remarkable, but wished that I could get more information on the subject than was possible through a sermon.

Later in the morning of August 14, my last day, toward high noon, in fact, I went up to Calvary for one last look out over the prairie and all that it had meant to me, and all that had happened while I had been there. I felt exuberant, a quiet sense that I had conquered myself and had won out in the end. I stood there looking out upon God's world with a sense of hard-won peace. I prayed for different things, looking out into the distance, remembering especially all those who had vowed their lives with me that day, and trying to remember all those who were no longer with us. I could hear the sounds of the farm and could see everything. Brother Meinrad was bringing the truck up to the Novitiate building, and the men were assembling to get on. Suddenly there was a sound of another engine, louder than the truck, and I looked up to see a fighter plane rapidly approaching. The sound became exciting and rising in pitch as it got closer, and I recognized it as a P-47 Thunderbolt. The pilot must have caught sight of the solitary figure in black upon the little hillock, and he came roaring down right over me, so near that I could even see his grinning face, his two fingers pointing up in Churchill's "V for Victory," and two long rows of Swastikas painted underneath the cockpit window: he was an "ace"—he had clearly shot down enough in combat for that.

Now, years later, I know what I did not know then: that that morning the world was celebrating "VJ Day," that the war was over, not only in Europe but in Japan. The young man was celebrating, with Rolling Prairie and anybody else who wanted to, the victory of freedom.

I alone seemed not to know, and not even to surmise what was happening. I went down the hill toward the truck to get in line with those who were waiting. I looked up at the tower and saw Old Augustine, without the swallows. After I got in line, I whispered something to the man standing next to me. "Judas Priest," I said, "—Judas K. Priest." But he was staring off into the distance and either did not hear me or did not want to. *"Bruder!"* I heard the voice inside me saying, and *"Welt!"* for no apparent reason. The truck was ready, to take us closer to priesthood, closer to the white linen binding annointed hands, closer to being hidden with Christ, to the one thing that was necessary. First our suitcases were tossed onto the truck and tied securely with heavy farm ropes so that they could not escape; then we got on ourselves, all that was left of us, the other eleven and I; the piece of fencing that served as a tailgate was lifted into position and fastened. There were some cheers, and Brother Meinrad turned the heavy wheels out into the farm lane, down past the various barns, which were busy as usual, between fields of ripening grain, and finally out, beyond the last of the barbed wire fences to the highway, the open road, taking us on to what came next: to the House of Dogmatic Theology, where we would learn the Sacred Dogma of the Church, study the ways of God with Man, and make of our lives a Holocaust of Divine Love.

ON THE

METROPOL ALMANAC

by Russian *samizdat* authors

from A CHRONICLE OF CURRENT EVENTS, 52 (Amnesty International)

nominated by AMNESTY INTERNATIONAL

(EDITOR'S NOTE: *The following account of the Russian government's action against the literary almanac,* Metropol, *was circulated by underground samizdat in Russia and published in England by Amnesty International in 1980.*)

Towards the end of 1978 some members of the USSR Writers Union—Vasily Aksyonov, Andrei Bitov, Viktor Erofeyev, Fazil Iskander and Evgeny Popov—compiled a literary almanac entitled *Metropol*. It contained poems by Evgeny Rein, Inna Lisnyanskaya, Semyon Lipkin, Andrei Voznesensky, Genrikh Sapgir, Yury Karabchiyevsky and Yury Kublanovsky; poems and songs by Vladimir Vysotsky and Yuzef Aleshkovsky; prose works by Bella Akhmadulina, Pyotr Kozhevnikov, Evgeny Popov, Fridrikh Gorenshtein, Andrei Bitov, Fazil Iskander, Boris Bakhtin, Arkady Arkanov and Viktor Erofeyev; an extract from a new novel by John Updike, a 'guest of the almanac'; a play by Vasily Aksyonov; and essays by Mark Rozovsky, Vasily Rakitin, Viktor Trostnikov and Leonid Batkin on various aspects of culture. A significant number of these works had been rejected by Soviet publishing-houses. The first 'edition' of the almanac was prepared by the Artists David Borovsky and Boris Messerer: each copy is a large file containing Whatman paper, each sheet of which has four sheets of ordinary typing paper fixed to it; there are altogether 500 sheets.

The literary material is preceded by a notice which states:

The *Metropol* almanac represents all its authors to an equal extent. All the authors represent the *Metropol* almanac to an equal extent. The *Metropol* almanac, which is issued in manu-script form, may be published in printed form only if the original composition is preserved. The works of each author may be published separately with the permission of the par-ticular author, but no earlier than one year after the almanac is first issued. Reference to the almanac is obligatory.

This notice is followed by a copyright symbol and 'METROPOL 1979'.

A foreward states the principle of the authors' personal responsi-bility for their own work.

The compilers decided to hold a 'preview' on 23 January 1979 in a Moscow café called 'Metropol', where the almanac would be 'presented' to specially invited guests: representatives of the press; well-known figures from literature (including V. Kaverin, G. Vla-dimov, V. Kornilov, B. Okudzhava), the theatre (A. Efros, O. Efremov, Yu. Lyubimov, O. Tabakov, M. Kozakov) and the sci-entific world (Academicians M. Leontovich, V. Engelgardt and others). On 12 January V. Erofeyev and E. Popov were summoned to the Secretariat of the Moscow Writers Organization to see F. Kuznetsov, First Secretary of the Board of the RSFSR Writers Union Moscow Office. Together with Kobenko, the Secretary of Organizational Matters, Kuznetsov conducted a formal questioning (at first, they had tried to interrogate the two men individually, suggesting that the other 'wait in the corridor'). In the days which followed the compilers of the almanac were summoned one by one for similar treatment: questioning, threats, and attempts to per-suade them 'not to do anything foolish' and to set them against each other (Aksyonov, Bitov and Iskander were asked: 'Why do you, famous people, get yourselves mixed up with a load of drips?'; Erofeyev and Popov were asked: 'What are you doing running after them?! What has Aksyonov got to lose—he's got half a million in American banks . . .', etc).

On 22 January all five compilers were 'slated' for four hours at a joint session of the Secretariat and the Party Committee of the Moscow Writers Union presided over by F. Kuznetsov (those taking part included N. Gribachev, A. Sofronov, M. Alekseyev, Yu. Gribov, M. Prilezhayeva, S. Kunyayev and others—over 50 participants in all). The beginning was relatively 'calm', but after only half an hour there was a loud chorus of 'lack of ideological content', 'low level', 'unintelligibility', and 'pornography' with regard to the almanac; and the 'preview' set for the following day was described as a 'political provocation' and an attempt to undermine détente designed—according to the compilers' malicious aims—to incur millions upon millions of losses for the USSR (their scheme was that with all this we would have to expel a few people from the Union; that will arouse protests, followed by a malicious slander campaign; and the US Congress is just waiting for a pretext not to ratify the SALT 2 agreement).

The compilers, who had five days earlier presented Kuznetsov with a copy of the almanac, insisted on the need for an objective analysis of it, on their right to freedom of publication, and on the absence of any covert political motivation whatsoever behind the almanac or the 'preview', to which all those present were invited.

By this time, however, the compilers had already decided to cancel the 'preview', as it might have served as a pretext for provocations against those involved in producing the almanac. Nonetheless, the café 'Rhythm' (on Gotvaid Street), where a room had already been booked with the management, was closed 'for a cleaning day' just in case, and surrounded by reinforced squads of police.

After 22 January the almanac compilers received no more summonses. But all the writers were subjected to persistent, repeated threats and to attempts to extract public repentance and renunciations from them. 'Sanctions' followed. Contracts which have already been made are not being broken, but sources of income are being cut off. The publication of Aksyonov's book by 'Soviet Writer' has been stopped, a film for which he had written the screenplay has been taken off release, and a publication in the journal *Daugava* has been stopped. A contract which had been planned between Akmadulina and the Kishinev publishing house has not been concluded and all her advertised performances in Minsk were cancelled (one did, however, take place; the chairman of a collective farm was very keen for a real poet to appear at his farm, and took the responsibility for the evening on himself). Bitov's screenplay for the film 'On Thursday for the Last Time', which was already on release, was taken off general release (it has been shown in clubs), his seminar engagements in the Literary Institute have been cancelled and his participation in the 'Green Lamp' association stopped. The publication by 'Soviet Writer' of a book by Iskander has been stopped and his publications in *Country Youth* suspended. The publication of a book by Popov by the Krasnoyarsk Publishing-House has been held up. Lipkin's foreword to a translation of the 'Shah-Name' by Firdousi has been deleted, and his access to translation contracts cut off. Translations which Lisnyanskaya had already prepared were not accepted (the work was reallocated to other translators). Arkanov's screenplay for 'Mosfilm' has been 'closed', and his television broadcasts stopped. Rozovsky was taken off the production team at Mosfilm and his theatre shows stopped. All Messerer's orders for book-illustrations and lay-outs have been cancelled. The publication of a book by Batkin for the 'Knowledge' publishing house has been postponed (so far 'for a year') and all references to him in another writer's book removed; the Writers Union has not reissued Erofeyev and Popov with membership cards. The one single, but very notable exception is the non-cancellation of Voznesensky's appearances in America, which had received extensive advance publicity.

On 7 February *Moscow Litterateur*, the newspaper of the Board and Party Committee of the Moscow Writers Organization, published an article by F. Kuznetsov in which those involved in the almanac were accused of playing 'a filthy political game which has nothing to do with literature'.

On 23 February *Moscow Litterateur* reported:

On 20 February a conference took place to which members of the Moscow Writers Organization who had studied the type-written almanac *Metropol* talked about their impressions and

conclusions. More than 100 writers had studied the almanac
. . . In his summing-up remarks to the conference . . . Felix
Kuznetsov thanked all the writers who had been forced to tear
themselves away from their work and waste their time reading
and discussing such artistically worthless, cheerless and tedious material as the collection contained. Not one of the writers
who had read the almanac expressed the slightest doubt as to
its very poor aesthetic and moral quality. They all agreed on
one point: the extremely low artistic level of most of the
collection pointed quite clearly to the fact that its organizers
did not have literary aims. They had set themselves quite
different tasks, far removed from those of literature, art and
morality.

The paper cited 30 excerpts from the 'speeches and comments':

Representatives of national literatures whose epics used to be
translated by Lipkin are now wondering whether to wait until
another Lipkin is found' (S. Mikhalkov); 'What a betrayal of
patriotic feeling, of feelings for our Motherland' (M.
Prilezhayeva); 'The strategists of ideological warfare . . . will
try to use this so-called 'purely literary venture' for provoca-
tional purposes' (N. Shundik); 'In my opinion, not even a
microscope could succeed in detecting any literature in it.
Political aims, on the other hand, are clearly visible' (V.
Karpov); 'The very idea of such a publication cannot but incur
professional and moral censure' (P. Nikolayev); 'Sexopathology
. . . the literature of the small shopkeeper. We cannot allow
this, you have to go to America for this' (R. Kazakova).

The compilers of the almanac, and also Akhmadulina, declared
that if a single writer were excluded from the Writers Union they
would leave it themselves. After all the 'slatings' they wrote a
number of letters: to Brezhnev and Zimyanin, a secretary of the
CPSU Central Committee, enumerating the ensuing repressive
actions (they received no reply); to the State Press Committee
requesting the publication of the almanac in the USSR (the reaction on the telephone was: 'We do not actually publish. Give it to
'Soviet Writer'); and to the All-Union Copyright Agency, request-

ing that it defend the copyrights (the oral reply was: 'If it's published, then we will defend it.').

Meanwhile the 'Ardis' Publishing-House in the USA is preparing the almanac for publication.

In a letter to Academician G. E. Clancier, President of the French PEN Club, George Vladimov writes:

This almanac . . . is a remarkable phenomenon of present-day social life and, in my opinion, merits a place in history on two counts: as the first instance of the large-scale exercise of uncensored literary freedom, and also as an example of rare unity by the participants in rebuffing all attempts to make them retreat.

HUNGER

by JACK GILBERT

from IRONWOOD

*nominated by Jane Flanders, David Madden, Sherod Santos and Gerald
Stern*

Digging into the apple
with my thumbs.
Scraping out the clogged nails
and digging deeper.
Refusing the moon color.
Refusing the smell and memories.
Digging in with the sweet juice
running along my hands unpleasantly.
Refusing the sweetness.
Turning my hands to gouge out chunks.
Feeling the juice get sticky
on my wrists.
The skin itching.
Getting to the wooden part.
Getting to the seeds.
Going on.
Not taking anybody's word for it.
Getting beyond the seeds.

BLAME

by ELIZABETH SPIRES

from PLOUGHSHARES

nominated by PLOUGHSHARES, *Kristine Batey, and David St. John*

I do not believe the ancients—
the constellations look like nothing at all.

See how their light scatters itself
across the sky, not bright

enough to guide us anywhere?
And the avenues of trees, leaking

their dark inks, are shapes I can't identify.
The night is too inconstant, a constant
injury, alchemical moonlight
changing my body from lead to silver,

silver to lead. I lie
uncovered on the bed, unmoved

by the love you left, bad dreams,
bad night ahead. All summer

you held me to your chest:
It's the heat, you said, accounting

for our sleeplessness, so that
touch became metaphor for what kept us

separate. Our lives construct
themselves out of the lie of pain.

I lied when I sent you away.
To call your name would be another lie.

WHEN I WAS A CHILD...

by S. NOURBESE

from THE BLACK SCHOLAR

nominated by Eugene Redmond

Lamplight, fireflight, soft lies
and rounded eyes a listening table;
floating fiery tales of socouyants
lacing the edge of night with
lamplight, softlight and fireflies;
worms of delight tickle,
curls of toes rooted in safety large laps
secure from little dwens with feet turned
backwards, and la diablesse
the cloven footed siren
far from the soft light, lamplight and
    fireflight;
waking child to sunbaked days
on an island greening of cracked hopes,
decorated with coconuts candied
in delicious names of tulum bum bum,
kazer balled cheeks bursting, splattering
blooded spit balls of sweetened saliva
through Queens English, pappyshow and
    mama guy
as we simmy dimmied and sold
breeze bottled sea water mottled green
untouched as by brown warmed hands
    hypnotizing
hot laced milk filigreed in froth
from cup to cup,
and salted dreams shuffle back and forth
in the soft lies, lamplight and fireflight.

NEW YORK CITY IN 1979

fiction by KATHY ACKER

from CRAWL OUT YOUR WINDOW

nominated by CRAWL OUT YOUR WINDOW

to Jeanne's insulted beauty

SOME PEOPLE SAY New York City is evil and they wouldn't live there for all the money in the world.

These are the same people who elected Johnson, Nixon, Carter President and Koch mayor of New York.

THE WHORES IN JAIL AT NIGHT

—Well, my man's gonna get me out of here as soon as he can.

—When's that gonna be, honey?

—So what? Your man pays so he can put you back on the street as soon as possible.

—Well, what if he wants me back on the street? That's where I belong. I make him good money, don't I? He knows that I'm a good girl.

—Your man ain't anything! Johnny says that if I don't work my ass off for him, he's not going to let me back in the house.

—I have to earn two hundred before I can go back.

—Two hundred? That ain't shit! You can earn two hundred in less than a night. I have to earn four hundred or I might just as well forget sleeping, and there's no running away from Him. My baby is the toughest there is.

—Well, shit girl, if I don't come back with eight hundred I get my ass whupped off.

—That's cause you're junk.

—I ain't no stiff! All of you are junkies. I know what you do!

—What's the matter, honey?

—You've been sitting on that thing for an hour.

—The pains're getting bad. OOgh. I've been bleeding two days now.

OOgh Oogh OOGH.

—She's gonna bang her head off. She needs a shot.

—Tie a sweater around her head. She's gonna break her head open.

—You should see a doctor, honey.

—The doctor told me I'm having an abortion.

—Matron. Goddamnit. Get your ass over here matron!

—I haven't been bleeding this bad. Maybe this is the real abortion.

—Matron! This little girl is having an abortion! You do something. Where the hell is that asshole woman? (The matron throws an open piece of Kotex to the girl.) The service here is getting worse and worse!

—You're not in a hotel, honey.

—It used to be better than this. There's not even any goddamn food. This place is definitely going downhill.

—Oh, shutup. I'm trying to sleep. I need my sleep, unlike you girls, cause I'm going back to work tomorrow.

—Now what the hell do you need sleep for? This is a party. You sleep on your job.

—I sure know this is the only time I get any rest. Tomorrow it's back on the street again.

—If we're lucky.

LESBIANS are women who prefer their own ways to male ways.

LESBIANS prefer the convoluting halls of sensuality to direct goal-pursuing mores.

LESBIANS have made a small world deep within and separated from the world. What has usually been called the world is the male world.

Convoluting halls of sensuality lead to depend on illusions. Lies and silence are realer than truth.

Either you're in love with someone or you're not. The one thing about being in love with someone is you know you're in love: You're either flying or you're about to kill yourself.

I don't know anyone I'm in love with or I don't know if I'm in love. I have all these memories. I remember that as soon as I've gotten fucked, like a dog I no longer care about the man who just fucked me who I was madly in love with.

So why should I spend a hundred dollars to fly to Toronto to get laid by someone I don't know if I love I don't know if I can love I'm an abortion? I mean a hundred dollars and once I get laid, I'll be in agony: I won't be doing exactly what I want. I can't live normally i.e. with love so: there is no more life.

The world is gray afterbirth. Fake. All of New York City is fake is going to go all my friends are going crazy all my friends know they're going crazy disaster is the only event people get off on more and more disaster cause that's the only thing that's happening.

Suddenly these outbursts in the fake, cause they're so open, spawn a new growth. I'm waiting to see this growth.

I want more and more horrible disaster in New York cause I desperately want to see that new thing that is going to happen this year.

JANEY is a woman who has sexually hurt and been sexually hurt so much she's now frigid.

She doesn't want to see her husband anymore. There's nothing between them.

Her husband agrees with her that there's nothing more between them.

But there's no such thing as nothingness. Not here. Only death whatever that is nothing. All the ways people are talking to her now mean nothing to Janey. Most of the words she reads mean nothing. She doesn't want to speak words that are meaningless.

Janey doesn't want to see her husband again.

The quality of life in this city stinks. Is almost nothing. Most people are now deaf-mutes only inside they're screaming. BLOOD. A lot of blood inside is going to fall. MORE and MORE because inside is outside.

New York City will become alive again when the people begin to speak to each other again not information but real emotion. A grave is spreading its legs and BEGGING FOR LOVE.

Robert, Janey's husband, is almost a zombie.

He walks talks plays his saxophone pays for groceries almost like every other human. There's no past. The last six years didn't exist. Janey hates him. He made her a hole. He blasted into her. He has no feelings. The light blue eyes he gave her; the gentle hands; the adoration: AREN'T. NO CRIME. NO BLOOD. THE NEW CITY. Like in Fritz Lang's METROPOLIS.

This year suffering has so blasted all feelings out of her she's become a person. Janey believes it's necessary to blast open her mind constantly and destroy EVERY PARTICLE OF MEMORY THAT SHE LIKES.

A sleeveless black T-shirt binds Janey's breasts. Pleated black fake-leather pants hide her cocklessness. A thin leopard tie winds around her neck. One gold-plated watch, the only remembrance of the dead mother, binds one wrist. A thin black leather band binds the other. The head is almost shaved. Two round prescription mirrors mask the eyes.

Johnny is a man who don't want to be living so he doesn't appear to be a man. All his life everyone wanted him to be something. His Jewish mother wanted him to be famous so he wouldn't live the life she was living. The two main girlfriends he has had wanted him to support them in the manner to which they certainly weren't accustomed even though he couldn't put his flabby hands on a penny. His father wanted him to shut up.

All Johnny wants to do is make music. He wants to keep

everyone and everything who takes him away from his music off him. Since he can't afford human contact, he can't afford desire. Therefore he hangs around with rich zombies who never have anything to do with feelings. This is a typical New York artist attitude.

New York City is a pit-hole: Since the United States government, having decided that New York City is no longer part of the United States of America, is dumping all the laws the rich people want such as anti-rent-control laws and all the people they don't want (artists, poor minorities, and the media in general) on the city and refusing the city Federal funds; the American bourgeoisie has left. Only the poor: artists, Puerto Ricans who can't afford to move . . . and rich Europeans who fleeing the terrorists don't give a shit about New York . . . inhabit this city.

Meanwhile the temperature is getting hotter and hotter so no one can think clearly. No one perceives. No one cares. Insane madness comes out like life is a terrific party.

IN FRONT OF THE MUDD CLUB, WHITE STREET

Two rich couples drop out of a limousine. The women are wearing outfits the poor people who were in ten years ago wore ten years ago. All the poor people who're making this club fashionable so the rich want to hang out here, even though the poor still never make a buck off the rich pleasure, are sitting on cars, watching the rich people walk up to the club.

Some creeps around the club's entrance. An open-shirted skinny guy who says he's just an artist is choosing who he'll let into the club. Since it's 3:30 A.M. there aren't many creeps. The artist won't let the rich hippies into the club.

—Look at that car.

—Jesus. It's those rich hippies' car.

—Let's take it.

—That's the chauffeur over there.

—Let's kidnap him.

—Let's knock him over the head with a bottle.

—I don't want no terrorism. I wanna go for a ride.

—That's right. We've got nothing to do with terrorism. We'll just explain we want to borrow the car for an hour.

—Maybe he'll lend us the car if we explain we're terrorists-in-training. We want to use that car to try out terrorist tricks.

After 45 minutes the rich people climb back into their limousine and their chauffeur drives them away.

A girl who has gobs of brown hair like the foam on a cappucino in Little Italy, black patent leather S&M heels, two fashionable tits stuffed into a pale green corset, and extremely fashionable black fake leather tights heaves her large self off a car top. She's holding an empty bottle.

Diego senses there's going to be trouble. He gets off his car top. Is walking slowly towards the girl.

The bottle keeps waving. Finally the girl finds some courage heaves the bottle at the skinny entrance artist.

The girl and the artist battle it out up the street. Some of the people who are sitting on cars separate them. We see the girl throw herself back on a car top. Her tits are bouncing so hard she must want our attention and she's getting insecure, maybe violent, cause she isn't getting enough. Better give us a better show. She sticks her middle finger into the air as far as she can. She writhes around on the top of the car. Her movements are so spasmatic she must be nuts.

A yellow taxi cab is slowly making its way to the club. On one side of this taxi cab's the club entrance. The other side is the girl writhing away on the black car. Three girls who are pretending to be transvestites are lifting themselves out of the cab elegantly around the big girl's body. The first body is encased into a translucent white girdle. A series of diagonal panels leads directly to her cunt. The other two dresses are tight and white. They are wriggling their way toward the club. The big girl, whom the taxi driver refused to let in his cab, wriggling because she's been rejected but not wriggling as much, is bumping into them. They're tottering away from her because she has syphilis.

Now the big girl is unsuccessfully trying to climb through a private white car's window now she's running hips hooking even faster into an alleyway taxi whose driver is locking his doors and windows against her. She's offering him a blow-job. Now an ugly boy with a huge safety pin stuck through his upper lip, walking up and down the street, is shooting at us with his watergun.

The dyke sitting next to me is saying earlier in the evening she pulled at this safety pin.

It's four o'clock A.M. It's still too hot. Wet heat's squeezing this city. The air's mist. The liquid that's seeping out of human flesh pores is gonna harden into a smooth shiny shell so we're going to become reptiles.

No one wants to move anymore. No one wants to be in a body. Physical possessions can go to hell even in this night.

Johnny like all the other New York inhabitants doesn't want anything to do with sex. He hates sex because this air's hot, because feelings are dull, and because humans are repulsive.

Like all the other New Yorkers he's telling females he's strictly gay and males all faggots ought to burn in hell and they are. He's doing this because when he was sixteen years old his parents who wanted him to die stuck him in the Merchant Marine and all the marines cause this is always what they do raped his ass off with many doses of coke.

Baudelaire doesn't go directly toward self-satisfaction cause of the following mechanism: X wants Y and, for whatever reasons, thinks it shouldn't want Y. X thinks it is BAD because it wants Y. What X wants is Y and to be GOOD.

Baudelaire does the following to solve this dilemma: He understands that some agency (his parents, his mistress, etc.) is saying that wanting Y is BAD. This agency is authority is right. The authority will punish him because he's BAD. The authority will punish him as much as possible, punish me punish me, more than is necessary till it has to be obvious to everyone that the punishment is unjust. Punishers are unjust. All authority right now stinks to high hell. Therefore there is no GOOD and BAD. X cannot be BAD.

It's necessary to go to as many extremes as possible.

As soon as Johnny sees Janey he wants to have sex with her.

Johnny takes out his cock and rubs it. He walks over to Janey, puts his arms around her shoulders so he's pinning her against a concrete wall.

Johnny says, "You're always talking about sex. Are you going to spread your legs for me like you spread your legs all the time for any guy you don't know?"

Janey replies, "I'm not fucking anymore cause sex is a prison: it's become a support of this post-capitalist system like art. Businessmen who want to make money have to turn up a product that people'll buy and want to keep buying. Since American consumers now own every object there is plus they don't have any money anyway cause they're being squeezed between inflation and depression, just like fucking, these businessmen have to discover products that obvious necessity sells. Sex is such a product. Just get rid of the puritanism sweetheart your parents spoonfed you in between materialism which the sexual revolution did thanks to free love and hippies sex is a terrific hook. Sexual desire is a naturally fluctuating phenomena. The sex product presents a naturally expanding market. Now capitalists are doing everything they can to bring world sexual desire to an unbearable edge."

"I don't want to be hurt again. Getting hurt or rejected is more dangerous than I know because now everytime I get sexually rejected I get dangerously physically sick. I don't want to hurt again. Everytime I hurt I feel so disgusted with myself—that by following some stupid body desire I didn't HAVE to follow, I killed the tender nerves of someone else. I retreat into myself. I again become frigid."

"I never have fun."

Johnny says, "You want to be as desperate as possible but you don't have to be desperate. You're going to be a success. Everybody knows you're going to be a success. Wouldn't you like to give up this artistic life which you know isn't rewarding cause artists to survive as artists now have to turn their work/selves into market objects/fluctuating, images/fashion to competitively knife each other in the back because we're not people, can't treat each other like people, no feelings, loneliness comes from the world of rationality, robots, every thing one as objects separate from each other? The whole impetus for art in the first place is gone bye-bye? You know you want to get away from this media world."

Janey replies, "I don't know what I want now. I know the New York City world is more complex and desirable even though everything you're saying's true. I don't know what my heart is cause I'm corrupted."

"Become pure again. Love. You have to will. You can do what you will. Then love'll enter your heart."

"I'm not capable of loving anyone. I'm a freak. Love's an obsession that only weird people have. I'm going to be a robot for the rest of my life. This is confusing to a human being, but robotism is what's present."

"It's unnatural to be sexless. You eat alone and that's freaky."

"I am lonely out of my mind. I am miserable out of my mind. Open open what are you touching me. Touching me. Now I'm going into the state where desire comes out like a monster. Sex I love you. I'll do anything to touch you. I've got to fuck. Don't you understand don't you have needs as much as I have needs DON'T YOU HAVE TO GET LAID?"

—Janey, close that door. What's the matter with you? Why aren't you doing what I tell you?

—I'll do whatever you tell me, nana.

—That's right. Now go into that drawer and get that checkbook for me. The Chase Manhattan one, not the other one. Give me both of them. I'll show you which one.

—I can find it, nana. No, it's not this one.

—Give me both of them. I'll do it.

—Here you are, nana. This is the one you want, isn't it?

—Now sit yourself down and write yourself out a check for $10,000. It doesn't matter which check you write it on.

—Ten thousand dollars! Are you sure about this, nana?

—Do what I tell you. Write yourself out a check for ten thousand dollars.

—Uh O.K. What's the date?

—It doesn't matter. Put any date you want. Now, hand me my glasses. They're over there.

—I'm just going to clean them. They're dirty.

—You can clean them for me later. Give them to me.

—Are . . . you sure you want to do this?

—Now I'm going to tell you something, Janey. Invest this. Buy yourself 100 shares of AT&T. You can fritter it away if you want. Good riddance to you. If your mother had invested the 800 shares of IBM I gave her, she would have had a steady income and wouldn't have had to commit suicide. Well, she needed the money. If you invest in AT&T, you'll always have an income.

—I don't know what to say. I've never seen so much money before. I've never seen so much money before.

—You do what I tell you to. Buy AT&T.

—I'll put the money in a bank, nana, and as soon as it clears I'll buy AT&T.

At ten o'clock the next morning Nana is still asleep. A rich salesman who was spending his winter in New York had installed her in a huge apartment on Park Avenue for six months. The apartment's rooms are tremendous, too big for her tiny body, and are still partly unfurnished. Thick silk daybed spreads ivory-handled white feather fans hanging above contrast the black-and-red 'naturalistic' clown portraits in the 'study' that give an air of culture rather than of call-girl. A call-girl or mistress, as soon as her first man is gone, is no longer innocent. No one to help her, constantly harassed by rent and food bills, in need of elegant clothing and cosmetics to keep surviving, she has to use her sex to get money.

Nana's sleeping on her stomach, her bare arms hugging instead of a man a pillow into which she's buried a face soft with sleep. The bedroom and the small adjoining dressingroom are the only two properly furnished rooms. A ray of light filtered through the gray richly-laced curtain focuses a rosewood bedstead covered by carved Chinese figures; the bedstead covered by white linen sheets; covered by a pale blue silk quilt; covered by a pale white silk quilt; Chinese pictures composed of five to seven layers of carved ivory, almost sculptures rather than pictures, surround these gleaming layers.

She feels around and, finding no one, calls her maid.

"Paul left ten minutes ago," the girl says as she walks into the room. "He didn't want to wake you. I asked him if he wanted coffee but he said he was in a rush. He'll see you his usual time tomorrow."

"Tomorrow tomorrow," the prositute can never get anything straight, "can he come tomorrow?"

"Wednesday's Paul's day. Today you see the furrier."

"I remember," she says, sitting up, "the old furrier told me he's coming Wednesday and I can't go against him. Paul'll have to come another day."

"You didn't tell me. If you don't tell me what's going on, I'm going to get things confused and your Johns'll be running into each other."

Nana stretches her fatty arms over her head and yawns. Two bunches of short brown hairs are sticking out of her armpits. "I'll call Paul tell him to come back tonight. No. I won't sleep with anyone tonight. Can I afford it? I'll tell Paul to come on Tuesdays after this and I'll have tonight to myself!" Her nightgown slips down her nipples surrounded by one long brown hair and the rest of her hair, loose and tousled, flows over her still-wet sheets.

Bet—I think feminism is the only thing that matters.

Janey (yawning)—I'm so tired all I can do is sleep all day (only she doesn't fall asleep cause she's suddenly attracted to Michael who's like every other guy she's attracted to married to a friend of hers.)

Bet—First of all feminism is only possible in a socialist state.

Janey—But Russia stinks as much as the United States these days. What has this got to do with your film?

Bet—Cause feminism depends on four factors: (1.) First of all, women have to have economic independence. If they don't have that they don't have anything. Second, free daycare centers. Abortions. (counting on her fingers) Fourth, decent housing.

Janey—I mean these are just material considerations. You're accepting the materialism this society teaches. I mean look I've had lots of abortions I can fuck anyone I want—well, I could— I'm still in prison. I'm not talking about myself.

Bet—Are you against abortions?

Janey—How could I be against abortions? I've had fucking five of them. I can't be against abortions. I just think all that stuff is back in the 1920's. It doesn't apply to this world. This world is different than all that socialism: those multi-national corporations control everything.

Louie—You just don't know how things are cause the feminist

movement here is nothing compared to the feminist movements in Italy, England, and Australia. That's where women really stick together.

Janey—That's not true! Feminism here, sure it's not the old feminism the groups Gloria Steinem and Ti-Grace, but they were *so* straight. It's much better now: it's just underground it's not so public.

Louie—The only women in Abercombie's and Fitch's films are those traditionally male defined types.

The women are always whores or bitches. They have no power.

Janey—Women are whores now. I think women every time they fuck no matter who they fuck they should get paid. When they fuck their boyfriends their husbands. That's the way things are only the women don't get paid.

Louie—Look at Carter's film. There are no women's roles. The only two women in the film who aren't bit players are France who's a bitch and England who's a whore.

Janey—But that's how things were in the Rome of that time.

Bet—But, Jane, we're saying things have to be different. Our friends can't keep upholding the sexist state of women in their work.

Janey—You know about Abercombie and Fitch. I don't even bother saying anything to them. But Carter's film: you've got to look at why an artist does what he does. Otherwise you're not being fair. In ROME Carter's saying the decadent Roman society was like this one.

Louie—The one that a certain small group of artists in New York lives in.

Janey—Yeah.

Louie—He's saying the men we know treat women only as whores and bitches.

Janey—So what are you complaining about?

Bet—Before you were saying you have no one to talk to about your work. That's what I'm saying. We've got to tell Abercombie and Fitch what they're doing. We've got to start portraying women as strong showing women as the power of this society.

Janey—But we're not.

Bet—But how else are we going to be? In Italy there was this women's art festival. A friend of ours who does performances dressed as a woman and did a performance. Then he revealed he was a man. The women in the festival beat him up and called the police.

Michael—The police?

Janey—Was he good?

Bet—He was the best performer there.

Louie—I think calling the police is weird. They should have just beaten him up.

Janey—I don't like the police.

I want all the above to be the sun.

INTENSE SEXUAL DESIRE IS THE GREATEST THING IN THE WORLD

Janey dreams of cocks. Janey sees cocks instead of objects.

Janey has to fuck.

This is the way Sex drives Janey crazy:

Before Janey fucks, she keeps her wants in cells. As soon as Janey's fucking she wants to be adored as much as possible at the same time as, its other extreme, ignored as much as possible. More than this: Janey can no longer perceive herself wanting. Janey is Want.

It's worse than this: If Janey gets sexually rejected her body becomes sick. If she doesn't get who she wants she naturally revolts.

This is the nature of reality. No rationality possible. Only this is true. The world in which there is no feeling, the robot world, doesn't exist. This world is a very dangerous place to live in.

Old women just cause they're old and no man'll fuck them don't stop wanting sex.

The old actress isn't good anymore. But she keeps on acting even though she knows all the audiences mock her hideousness and lack of context cause she adores acting. Her legs are grotesque: FLABBY. Above, hidden within folds of skin, there's an ugly cunt.

Two long flaps of white thin spreckled by black hairs like a pig's cock flesh hang down to the knees. There's no feeling in them. Between these two flaps of skin the meat is red folds and drips a white slime that poisons whatever it touches. Just one drop burns a hole into anything. An odor of garbage infested by maggots floats out of this cunt. One wants to vomit. The meat is so red it looks like someone hacked a body to bits with a cleaver or like the bright red lines under the purple lines on the translucent skin of a woman's body found dead three days ago. This red leads to a hole, a hole of redness, round and round, black nausea. The old actress is black nausea because she reminds us of death. Yet she keeps plying her trade and that makes her trade weird. Glory be to those humans who care absolutely NOTHING for the opinions of other humans: they are the true owners of illusions, transformations, and themselves.

Old people are supposed to be smarter than young people.

Old people in this country the United States of America are treated like total shit. Since most people spend their lives mentally dwelling on the material, they have no mental freedom, when they grow old and their skin rots and their bodies turn to putrefying sand and they can't do physical exercise and they can't indulge in bodily pleasure and they're all ugly anyway; suddenly they got nothing. Having nothing, you think they could at least be shut up in opiated dens so maybe they have a chance to develop dreams or at least they could warn their kids to do something else besides being materialistic. But the way this country's set up, there's not even opiated homes to hide the feelinglessness: old people have to go either to children's or most often into rest homes where they're shunted into wheelchairs and made as fast as possible into zombies cause it's easier to handle a zombie, if you have to handle anything, than a human. So an old person has a big empty hollow space with nothing in it, just ugh, and that's life: nothing else is going to happen, there's just ugh stop.

ANYTHING THAT *DESTROYS* LIMITS.

Afterwards Janey and Johnny went to an all-night movie. All during the first movie Janey's sort of leaning against Johnny cause she's unsure he's attracted to her and she doesn't want to embarass him (her) in case he ain't. She kinda scrunches against him. One point Johnny is pressing his knee against her knee but she still ain't sure.

SOME LIKE IT HOT ends. All the rest of the painters are gonna leave the movie house cause they've seen THE MISFITS. Separately Janey and Johnny say they're going to stay. The painters are walking out. The movie theater is black.

Janey still doesn't know what Johnny's feelings are.

A third way through the second movie Johnny's hand grabs her knee. Her whole body becomes crazy. She puts her right hand into his hand but he doesn't want the hand.

Johnny's hand, rubbing her tan leg, is inching closer to her cunt. The hand is moving roughly, grabbing handfuls of flesh, the flesh and blood is crawling. He's not responding to anything she's doing.

Finally she's tentatively touching his leg. His hand is pouncing on her right hand setting it an inch below his cock. Her body's becoming even crazier and she's more content.

His other hand is inching slower toward her open slimy hole. Cause the theater is small, not very dark, and the seats aren't too steep, everyone sitting around them is watching exactly what they're doing: Her black dress is shoved up around her young thighs. His hand is almost curving around her dark-pantied cunt. Her and his legs are intertwined. Despite fear she's sure to be arrested just like in a porn book because fear she's wanting him to stick his cock up her right now.

His hand is roughly travelling around her cunt, never touching nothing, smaller and smaller circles.

Morning. The movie house lights go on. Johnny looks at Janey like she's a business acquaintance. From now on everything Janey does is for the purpose of getting Johnny's dick into her:

Johnny: "Let's get out of here."

New York City at six in the morning is beautiful. Empty streets except for a few bums. No garbage. A slight shudder of air down the long long streets. Pale gray prevails. Janey's going to kill Johnny if he doesn't give her his cock instantaneously. She's thinking ways to get him to give her his cock. Her body becomes even crazier. Her body takes over. Turn on him. Throw arms around his neck. Back him against car. Shove clothed cunt against clothed cock. Lick ear because that's what there is.

Lick your ear.

Lick your ear.

Well?

I don't know.

Why don't you know? You don't know if you want to?

Turn him on. Throw arms around his neck. Back him against car. Shove clothed cunt against clothed cunt. Lick ear because that's what there is.

Obviously I want to.

I don't care what you do. You can come home with me; you can take a rain check; you cannot take a rain check.

I have to see my lawyer tomorrow. Then I have lunch with Ray.

Turn him on. Throw arms around his neck. Back him against car. Shove clothed cunt against clothed cock. Lick ear because that's what there is.

You're not helping me much.

You're not helping me much.

Through this morning they walk to her apartment. Johnny and Janey don't touch. Johnny and Janey don't talk to each other.

Johnny is saying that Janey's going to invite him up for a few minutes.

Janey is pouring Johnny a glass of Scotch. Janey is sitting in her bedroom on her bed. Johnny is untying the string holding up her black sheath. Johnny's saliva-wettened fingers are pinching her nipple. Johnny is lifting her body over his prostrate body. Johnny's making her cunt rub very roughly through the clothes against his huge cock. Johnny's taking her off him and lifting her dress over her body. Janey's saying, "Your cock is huge." Janey's placing her lips around Johnny's huge cock. Janey's easing her black underpants over her feet.

Johnny's moaning like he's about to come. Janey's lips are letting go his cock. Johnny's lifting Janey's body over his body so the top of his cock is just touching her lips. His hands on her thighs are pulling her down fast and hard. His cock is so huge it is entering her cunt painfully. His body is immediately moving quickly violently shudders. The cock is entering the bottom of Janey's cunt.

Janey is coming. Johnny's hands are not holding Janey's thighs firmly enough and Johnny's moving too quickly to keep Janey coming. Johnny is building up to coming.

That's all right yes yes I that's all right. I'm coming again smooth of you oh oh smooth, goes on and on, am I coming am I not coming.

Janey's rolling off of Johnny. Johnny's pulling the black pants he's still wearing over his thighs because he has to go home. Janey's telling him she also has to sleep alone even though she isn't knowing what she's feeling. At the door to Janey's apartment Johnny's telling Janey he's going to call her. Johnny walks out the door and doesn't see Janey again.

🔥 🔥 🔥

ECLIPSE

fiction by DAVID LONG

from FICTION INTERNATIONAL

nominated by Sara Vogan and FICTION INTERNATIONAL

I CAME HOME on borrowed rides, east across the sun-blinded distances of Nevada and Utah, north into the forests of Montana, slouched on the cracked seats of pickups, remembering indistinctly what had taken me away and more vividly what I had found. In the back of my mind was the idea that being home would put an end to it. The green-painted man was dead in the bathtub, over-dosed beyond bliss. The shower head had dripped all night on his startled face, rivulets of poster paint streaking the porcelain, as if the life inside him had putrified and drained itself. He was nobody I knew. None of them were. So I had stepped into the early morning glare, made my way out of San Pedro's dockyards, squinting at the furious

413

light, fighting off the stink of casualties. The curiosity had burned off me like a dusting of black powder. It was nothing religious after all, only rumors and attractions, an itch in the bloodstream I had taken with full seriousness. The Indian dropped me on the corner by the Western-wear store. "Hey, you take care of yourself," he yelled, pulling away, the beer cans rattling in the empty bed of his truck.

The wind blew dust in my eyes. I recognized nobody on the streets. I found that the wave which had carried off so many of us who grew up here had left only the most stubborn and in my absence they had made families and leaned into their work as if they were born to it. I felt born to no work in particular and had long ago been absolved of kin, having no brothers or sisters, a father who had filled his veins with a substance used to euthanize household pets, and a mother who had found religion in an Arizona retirement community. Though I figured it was as much mine as anyone else's, I was not carefully remembered in this town and I thought I could use this fact to begin a normal, unobtrusive life for myself. Within a year I married Johanna, a big, pleasant girl whose red curls hung thick and guileless around her shoulders, whose skin smelled of salt and flour, who tended to simple jokes and loose clothes of khaki and checked flannel. If she was on a quest it was for nothing ethereal or terribly hard to locate. I must have seemed like a survivor of distant wickedness, a man in need of good intentions. It was true and I was grateful for the real affection she lavished on me, never understanding it clearly, always fearful she loved the mothering more than its damaged object. I ate her carob cookies, her hardly-risen soybean breads, her breakfast rolls suffocating in honey. I never yelled, I never threatened. After suppers on late summer nights, after the thunderstorms had cleared the air, we would walk along the bank of the low-running river, the swifts darting around our heads, the silence between us comfortable enough. I would watch her sit in the debris of washed-up stones, her soft chin lifted to the light as she studied the familiar pattern of mountains which surrounded us, her eyes unable to hide their satisfaction. Saturday nights we drank Lucky Lager at the Amvets and danced around and round to the soothing tunes of Jan Dell and her band, Johanna's favorite. Home again in the insulated darkness of the trailer's bedroom, she would clutch me, so full and earnest I thought I had succumbed—to her, to every bit of it.

Johanna's father, Darrell, was the district Petrolane distributor, and though he took me with suspicion, he was persuaded to give me a job driving one of his gas trucks. Every day I followed a lazy loop of junctions and wheat towns, contemplating the horizon— stubbled or rich-tasselled, depending on the season. Sometimes the sheer size of the panorama gave me a taste of the planet's curvature, a glimpse of the big picture, but I couldn't hold it. When I stopped I would stand by the truck and listen to the troubles of the ranchers, nodding as if I truly sympathized. Every night I came home and kicked my boots off and stretched out on the recliner by the TV like a thousand other husbands in town.

Johanna had a son the next year and when he had grown past earliest infancy he looked so much like her I saw none of myself in him. She named him Eric after her father's father who had died some months before. He was solid and cheerful, everything I was not. Johanna grew less tolerant. When she wanted to lighten my mood she would come and tell me, "You have a boy you can be proud of." It was not pride but panic I felt. I would often wake and see his round clear-eyed face inches from mine as though he had stood for hours waiting for me to wake. I knew there was something that should flow between us, as unasked for as spring water or moonlight. At night I would lay him in the bottom of the bunkbed he, so far, shared with only the dark room. I would try to make up stories to send him off to a good sleep. Nothing came.

"Tell him what it was like when you were a boy," Johanna said. "He'd like anything from you."

"It's a blur," I told her.

"What is it with you?" she said.

"If I knew I'd fix it," I said.

"Would you?"

I turned away from her and went out and started the pickup and backed it out as far as the mailboxes and couldn't decide which way to turn. I shut off the engine and in a moment lay down on the bench seat and tried to clear my head. I fell asleep hugging myself in the cool November air. When I woke there was a skim of snow on the hood of the truck. I walked back to the trailer. She had left a message on the refrigerator door, spelled out in Eric's magnetic letters. *Give or Go.* I went to the bedroom. A brittle ballad was coming from the clock radio. "Listen," I said, shaking her shoulder, but she was deep asleep.

One Friday afternoon, after the long wasting winter had gone, I came home from my route, later than normal since I'd stopped along the way for two Happy Hours, and found Johanna and Eric gone. In fact, it was all gone, the trailer house and everything. I climbed out of the truck, dumbstruck, a fine rain soaking my hair. Deep tracks curled through the shoots of pale grass I'd finally made grow. The muddy plywood skirts were strewn like a busted poker hand. I was wiped clean. The only thing left on the lot was the empty dog house, canted and streaked after a bad season.

In his office the next morning Darrell handed me my last paycheck in a licked-shut envelope and went back to what he was doing, punching the digits on his pocket calculator as if they were bugs.

"That all you're going to tell me?" I asked him.

"That's about got it," Darrell said.

"What'd I do? Tell me that?"

Darrell's eyes disappeared in a squinty smile. He slid the snoose around inside his mouth.

"Near as I can tell," Darrell said, "you didn't do a goddamn thing."

I took a third story room at the Frontier Hotel and sat on the cold radiator and watched the spavined old horse-breakers limp in and out of the cafe across the street, their straw hats like barnacles stuck to their heads. I quietly considered the loss of my wife and child and felt nothing sharp—except surprise and when I focused on that I realized that the breakup had been a sure thing all along. Her letter came without a return address. Don't worry, she said, she wouldn't be hounding me for money, Darrell had taken care of her. About Eric she said: *He won't remember you. I believe it's just as well.* About her reasons she said only: *I'm sorry, I won't be your rest cure.*

The sun finally took control of the valley. Lilacs flowered outside the dentist's office, road crews patched chuck holes up and down Main Street, the foothills shone in a green mist above the roof of the abandoned Opera House. Strangers nodded *howdy* on the sidewalks. Everything was repairing itself and I was out of time with it. Years before, I had felt myself choking in this town and blamed its narrow imagination and gone off looking for something Bigger Than Life. Now I didn't have the heart to move nor any trace of destination.

I found work at a small outfit south of town which manufactured camper shells for pickups. There I met Clevinger, a scrawny, tiny-eyed man my age, a twice-wounded survivor of Vietnam patrols. He'd worn the others out with his chatter and fixed on me as soon as I arrived. I listened as long as I could. Clevinger's idea of heaven was twenty acres up the North Fork, heavily timbered and remote, a place to disappear. Every afternoon after work he drove out and looked at parcels of land that only a few years earlier he might have afforded, and every morning he jabbered about the bastards who owned the money. As he talked he flexed the muscles in his arms which were white and hard as if they had grown underground. He was a man who'd changed, so certainly I didn't need to know how he'd been before. It showed as visibly as cracks running across his face. Seeing him like that made me know that I was not so different, though I had nothing like jungle warfare to blame it on.

It was a hot rainless summer. The wilderness areas flared with fire time and again, and one afternoon in early September a burn started in a tinder-dry draw near town and crept over the close-by foothills. Clevinger and I left the shop and stood in the parking lot watching the black smoke billow above the fireline. A team of helicopters swooped in from all sides, spraying bright reddish streams of fire retardant, through which the sunlight came streaked and bloody. Clevinger said nothing, his arms hugged tight against his skinny chest, the pale skin around his eyes jerking as the smoke drifted over us. It was the next day Clevinger exploded in the shop. All of a sudden he was down in a fiery-eyed crouch, strafing the room with his pneumatic nailing gun. I was caught in the open, carrying a half-built assemblage with a boy named Buster. Clevinger hit us both. The first cleat took Buster above the wrist; he yipped and let go his end, the weight of it falling to me. My back snapped like a pop bead. As I went down a second cleat shot through my mouth, taking with it slivers of jawbone.

I lay flat on the concrete, choking on pain, staring up at the moldering light coming through the quonset's skylight, hearing shouts and grunts and finally the sound of metal striking Clevinger's skull. For weeks afterwards I could see the dark luster of Clevinger's eyes, the look that said it didn't matter who we were. It was nothing personal.

My back was badly torn but would heal if I behaved myself. My jaw had to be wired. When they let me out of the hospital I returned to my room at the Frontier and ate broth and Instant Breakfasts and anything else I could get to seep through my closed teeth. I called Workman's Comp and discovered I was the victim of a policy called The Coordination of Benefits. My caseworker, Wayne, treated me like I was both child-like and dangerous. It was months before I saw a dollar. In the meantime there wasn't much to do but stay put. My body began to mend itself, but my imagination had time to dwell on things in earnest.

One night I woke from a late afternoon sleep, got out of bed, took two or three steps across the room and halted in momentary amnesia. I had no idea who I was. I stood there in my underwear, becalmed, entranced by the blue prayer-like light filling my window, and then a few heartbeats later it all came back: the pain in my back, the peculiar tingle of mortality, shards of waking dreams that added up to nothing but the sense of being orphaned. I turned back to the bed, half expecting to see a woman's body curled in the sheets, but there was no one at all.

I wandered across the hall to the bathroom, a narrow slot of a room with only a lidless commode. When I hit the light switch the bulb flared and died. I sat on the can with only the last smudge of light in the dusty glass high over head. When I was done I discovered that my key was twisted in the lock in such a way that the door would not open. I rattled the handle. Nothing. A strong cry might've summoned one of the other tenants of that dim corridor, but their ears were old and tuned a lot out, and besides that, the hardware in my mouth let me only growl, like a groggy yard dog.

I sat down.

The darkness was complete. Minutes went by and I didn't move, didn't holler, didn't lift my head. I felt perfectly severed, as though I had waked into a world I had always known would be there, a silent starless place where the species began and died in utter solitude, one by one by one. I thought of Johanna and Eric, saw their faces floating like reflections, the blackness shining through them. I knew I had not been brave in losing them, only stiff and sullen. I hadn't understood until now the truth of it: that I had not loved her, that I wasn't able to. I had wanted a family for comfort and retreat. All the times I had mumbled love in the dark were counterfeit. And she had known it first, known it pure and simple.

I had gone on and made a son and covered my lack of father feeling with an impatient, tin-faced act. Maybe it was true and good he would not remember me, maybe he would grow toward his own adulthood with only a strange hulking shadow lurking in the backwaters of his memory. Or maybe Johanna would turn up a big-hearted man who could believe a small boy's love was worth the world and Eric would grow into such a man himself.

The sadness oozed around me like a primeval silt. I was stuck in a closet stinking of mold and old men's urine and didn't care to free myself. I could blame myself, or not. I could curse the luck of the draw or the God I never knew. None of it mattered. The world takes it from you, regardless—even the thrill, even the energy to complain. There was nothing holy and nothing magical and no point believing it was a quest of any kind.

Shivering, in my Jockey shorts and faded Grateful Dead T-shirt, I started to cry, so hard it was more like a convulsion, every beat of it wincing up and down by backbone. Some time later I became aware of a pounding on the door and then the clicking of a key. It was then, for the first time, I saw Mr. Tornelli, his great head haloed by the red light of the EXIT sign across the hall.

"What's this?" Mr. Tornelli said.

I could say that Mr. Tornelli saved my life, but it wasn't right then, nor did the man seem a likely redeemer.

"Listen, Jack," he said, squinting into the cubicle, "You move your belly-aching out to the hall a minute, OK? I need the shitter."

In a moment I was in the world again, suddenly quieted. I didn't go back to my room but stood on the strip of balding carpet, waiting. Mr. Tornelli emerged after awhile, his eighty-year-old back a little straighter, his suspenders fastened, his collarless white shirt glowing in the weak light. His head seemed too big for the wickery body it rested on, and his moustaches—there were clearly two of them—were folded down over his mouth like wind-ruffled ptarmigan wings. Composed now, he studied me like a puzzle.

"You got pants?" Mr. Tornelli said.

I didn't answer.

He shook his head gravely. "Listen," he said, "you put your pants on and come down to my room. I'll wait right here."

A moment sometimes arrives when you see the different people you are and have been all at once. It happens without warning, the

way a sudden shift of light will show depths in water. Before I'd
gone into the bathroom I would have shirked the old man's offer,
made a note to shun him in the halls. But I stood nodding at him,
found myself pulling on my jeans and accompanying him to his
room, the last one on the floor, the one next to the fire escape.

"You know this vertigo?" Mr. Tornelli said.

He walked slowly, both hands a little elevated as if holding
imaginary canes.

"Afraid of heights?" I said.

He bent to hear my muffled voice. "No, no," he said. "Not afraid
of high places. It's. . ." He stopped and swivelled his head toward
me and twirled his fingers in the air. "Feels like everything
whirls."

"Bad," I said.

Mr. Tornelli smiled. "You get used to it."

Rooms at the Frontier were stark, unremitting. Out of superstition I had refrained from making mine any more attractive. Just
passing through, the bare walls said. It was immediately clear that
Mr. Tornelli didn't see it that way. His was bright and well-
appointed: the bed was neatly made, covered with a star-pattern
quilt; succulents and African Violets and Wandering Jews crowded
on the desk by the southwest window; the walls obscured by maps
and star charts and color blow-ups. A giant photo-illustration of the
full moon hung directly over his pillow.

Mr. Tornelli urged me to make myself comfortable. That wasn't
possible, of course, but I eased into his straight-backed chair and
looked at his little kingdom. He nodded matter-of-factly and sank
into his white wicker rocker and folded his hands.

"So," Mr. Tornelli said, widening his great sapphire eyes. "You
are a troubled boy and not in a good position to talk about it."

I tried to push the words forward with my tongue, a futile effort.
Mr. Tornelli waved me off.

"Don't bother," he said. "You'll just swim around in it." He
made an extravagant two-handed pulling motion. "Then you'll
want a rope. Forgive me, but I'm not up to it any more." He
laughed with a kind of brittle pleasure. "When you get it down to
one sentence, then I'll listen. Would that be all right?"

He rousted himself from the chair and went to the dresser.

"But then you won't need me, will you? No, for tonight's trouble there's brandy," he said. "Perhaps I should shoot it into your mouth with a syringe. Would you like that?"

So Mr. Tornelli and I drank the brandy. It worked on me as it does in high timber, back to the wind—I stopped shivering. The cipher of ice in the middle of me began to melt under its heat.

I noticed after awhile that right above the chair where he sat there was a brilliant photograph of a total eclipse: a golden ring shining around a black disk. Mr. Tornelli admitted having taken it.

"Kenya, 1973. Extraordinarily clear, no?"

I nodded.

"It was a good turnout that year, but blistering. Some of these young watchers are very zealous. I spent most of my time under a beach umbrella—and there was some kind of flying ant that laid eggs in your hair." He threw open his hands. "Ah, but I wouldn't have missed it. Over seven minutes dark. I had planned that it would be my last one, but maybe I was wrong." He smiled broadly. "I might live until February and see the one here."

"Too many clouds," I managed to say.

"I know," Mr. Tornelli said. "A bad season for the sun. But I think we might be fortunate that day."

He stood, momentarily fighting the spinning in his head, then began giving me the guided tour: Caroline Islands, 1934; Boise, 1945; Manila, 1955; the Aleutians, 1963. A trajectory of blotted suns progressing across his wall.

"I hope you forgive me my fascinations," he said. "Let me tell you a secret. I was born during the eclipse of 1900. My mother was crossing Louisiana on the train and stopped long enough in New Orleans to have me. Do you think I am a marked man?"

He laughed again and for the first time in a long while I smiled.

"Do you know," he began again, "*eclipse* means *abandonment*? It does. Abandonment. Can you imagine what it would be like if you didn't know? Everything's going along just like always, then *poof*, no sun. *Imagine*. You'd have some fancy explaining to do.

"The Ojibaways thought the sun was going out so they shot burning arrows at it to get it going again. Another tribe thought all the fire in the world was going to be sucked up by the darkness so they hid their torches inside their huts. People have come up with a number of stories. . . ."

In the coming months the local papers would have a bonanza

with the eclipse, playing science off legend. They told about Hsi and Ho, two luckless Chinese astronomers so drunk on rice wine they blew their prediction and were executed, and about coronas and shadow boxes and irreparable damage to the eye. In all I read I felt a strange longing for an ignorance that could make it crucial and magical. I thought about Mr. Tornelli's attraction and it seemed that some of the raw amazement survived in him.

"We had a great friendship in those days," Mr. Tornelli said in a while. "We would meet every few years, take in the spectacle and then go back where we came from. Never saw each other in between. All unspoken. Well, many of them are surely dead by now."

"Why are you here?" I asked him finally. It was the only important question I had.

"Why this fleabag? That's very good," Mr. Tornelli said, stroking the feathers of his moustache. "Where do you go when you can go anywhere? You think it matters? I guess. To tell the truth, I knew a woman in this town once. A married lady, I'm afraid." He drifted off for a moment. "Well, I remember how it was to be here and love somebody. Amazing, isn't it? Sometimes I ask myself if this was all the same life."

A few minutes past three, Mr. Tornelli finally stood again and insisted on walking me to my room. A comic, paternal gesture, it seemed to me. He said goodnight. Neither drunk nor sober, I lay in bed listening to the silence of the old hotel, the place the old man and I had come to. I imagined what it was made of: dentures soaking in a water glass, an old woman's dotted Swiss hanging in a closet with a lavender sachet, dreams beginning and ending in some rooms and in others only the silence that follows the departure of one of our number. It was a powerful chord. I realized that Mr. Tornelli had done nothing except come between me and myself. Alone again, the trouble was with me. In the moments before sleep I tried to say its name in the simple sentence he wanted but I could not.

Autumns here aren't the fiery poignant seasons they have in country with hardwoods and rolling hills. They are as abrupt here as the terrain. Indian summer vanishes overnight, clouds pour in from the northwest and smother the valley like dirty insulation. The rain comes quickly and strips the few maples and elms in a day, leaving the slick leaves puddled around their trunks like fool's gold. I woke late that next morning and a single look at the color of light in my window told the story. My back had seized up overnight. It took many minutes to get upright, shuffle to the sink and rinse the scum from my mouth with hydrogen peroxide. Mr. Tornelli seemed like a figment of last night's gloom.

I dressed and went down carefully to the pay phone and called Wayne at Workman's Comp. He sounded edgy. The computer in Helena had spit out my claim again. "Of course," Wayne said, "You know that *personally* I feel you're qualified. You know that, don't you?" I hung up on him and walked two blocks to the bank where the story was no better. Coming out I saw my ex-father-in-law heading toward the cafe. He speeded up to avoid me, then apparently thought better of it. He stopped and took me by the shoulders and gave me a good American once-over.

"You look like shit, you know that?" Darrell said.

"That's good news."

A logging truck rumbled past us, downshifting at the intersection, snorting black smoke in a long vibrant blast.

"How's that now?" Darrell said, leaning in a little.

"I'd kick you down to the Feed & Grain," I said.

"No, you wouldn't," Darrell said. "You wouldn't do nothing. Boy, let me tell you, she had the angle on you all right."

He let go and shook his big pinkish head at me and walked off.

For weeks nothing seemed to change but the tiresome thaw and freeze in my back. When I could walk any distance I scuffed through the town park, the sad remains of the founding family's estate, watching the ducks and Canadian honkers gather in the safety of the brackish pond. Mothers knelt in the cold grass behind their kids as they tossed wads of stale bread at the birds. I never had anything to give. Back at the hotel I would sit on the edge of the mattress and feel the tightening set in.

I saw almost no one, except old Mr. Tornelli. Days he didn't answer his door I went away undernourished, aimless and vaguely dizzy. But most often he was there and ushered me in with a bright courtesy, as if he'd waited all day for me. He took my silence for granted. He talked freely, sprinkling the air with different voices. Sometimes I truly thought there was more than one of him. He had stared through the giant telescope at Mount Palomar; he had ridden boxcars from San Diego to the Midwest, once delivering a baby of a homeless woman in the light of a mesquite fire near the tracks; he had been an optics engineer at Polaroid. He had once been fired from a teaching position in Wisconsin for being a Communist, which he wasn't, and later asked to guest-lecture as a blackballed scientist, which he declined. He had once shaken hands with Neils Bohr, the physicist, outside a hotel in Stockholm. He had taken peyote with Indians in a stone hogan in the mountains of New Mexico. In his vision he had become water, felt himself evaporating from the leaves of the cottonwood and rushing into the upper air and being blown high over the mountains with others like himself, then the great sense of weight and falling at terrific speed through the darkness.

"*Outstanding,*" Mr. Tornelli said. "One of a kind."

I listened patiently. I came to suspect that his talks were something more than reminiscence, that they were aimed at me as if he knew the dimension and velocity of my mood. He always seemed to stop short of conclusions: the stories hung unresolved, in the air.

"Puzzling, isn't it?" he would say with a quick opening of the hands, as if he were releasing a dove, or maybe releasing his grip on all that his mind had tried to bring together. I was entertained, I was diverted, I was moved.

Eight weeks to the day after Clevinger's outburst, the wires were removed from my jaw.

"So," Mr. Tornelli said. "Your tongue is out of its cage. A drink, to celebrate?"

"Thank you."

He handed me a gold-rimmed glass and retired to his chair.

"Now maybe you can tell me about all this gloomy stuff," he said.

"I think you know about it," I said.

Mr. Tornelli leaned forward on his elbows, the light glowing on the waxy skin of his forehead. He looked at me a long time before speaking.

"There was a time," he said finally. "I was at sea, on a freighter in the North Atlantic." He paused, as if squinting the memory into focus. "I couldn't sleep and there wasn't a soul to talk to. I went out and stood at the railing and stared at the ship's wake. My mind was empty except for the picture of my feet disappearing, then my shirt, my head, no brighter in the moonlight than a trace of the ship's foam. Let me tell you, I was right there, a little drunk. . . ."

"What was it?"

"Who knows? A bad time, a bad year. I was sick to death of my failures. I thought the world was a hopeless place. I stayed there all night, and then the horizon lightened a little, the wind came up, and I realized. . . ."

"What?"

He smiled lightly. "I was freezing. Freezing."

Then there were times he just let me in and returned to his chair and said nothing. As winter descended on us these occasions seemed more frequent. The silences weren't painful, but it was those times I could see him without distraction. Surrounded as he was by the battery of eclipses, the piles of spine-cracked books, *Scientific Americans,* flip-top steno pads filled with his faint ciphering, he seemed little and doomed. As he breathed his ribs creaked like a ship's rigging. Sometimes he closed his eyes, battling the vertigo that spun fiercely in his head, fingering the gold medallion he wore around his neck. I finally understood that I had seen a man in his last brilliance. If my affliction was elusive and hard to name, his was as common as birth.

January was a menace. Days of cold froze the ground many feet deep and left anything exposed to the air brittle. Great clouds of exhaust drifted down the rows of pickups idling on the side streets, so thick they would hide a man. Steam rose to the ventricles of the top-floor radiators and we kept warm, the air in our rooms so humid we might have been in a sanitarium. Mr. Tornelli's plants flourished but he seemed more and more unwell. His cheeks were smudged with shadows. I remembered how Johanna bent to the bedroom mirror smearing rouge on her face to invoke the same illusion. Mr. Tornelli was coming by it with a swiftness that prickled the darker chambers of my imagination. He had shown himself to be a man who took care of himself—with grace and dignity—but now I realized there were whole days when he failed to eat.

I began escorting him around the block to a small restaurant which served steamed vegetables with its dinners. It catered to the nearby old folks home crowd, and there, in the midst of his peers, Mr. Tornelli nursed languid bits of Swiss steak and seemed to me for the first time, no eccentric, no quaint loner. Sometimes I would catch him staring at the others and blinking.

"I don't know, Jack," he said softly. "Who are they?"

Midway through February the cold broke and in the space of ten days the temperature rose fifty degrees. We could scarcely look at things for the sheen of the melting everywhere. As the date of the eclipse came nearer I expected Mr. Tornelli's enthusiasm to rekindle. Surely he would muster some sort of celebration. He said nothing. I told him I could get a car and drive up to the National Park, just the two of us. I told him I would help him get his cameras out again. He didn't want to talk about it. He was as short with me as I'd ever heard him. I backed off and waited.

The night of the 25th, Sunday, I went to his door convinced some excitement would show in him. There was no answer to my knocks. He had been sleeping irregularly then, so I swallowed my worry and left the hotel. The sky was streaked, but when I entered the darkness of the alley across the street, I could see a few stars. Months ago he had known the sun would shine. I leaned on a dumpster behind one of the bars and stared up through a film of tears. A police car flashed its spot down the alley and I recovered myself and went in and had a few glasses of beer, though the liveliness of the bar seemed desperate and stupid to me. It was almost midnight when I came out. From the sidewalk I could see the lights blazing in Mr. Tornelli's window.

I ran upstairs and knocked again and this time the silence was terrifying. I shook the doorknob hard against the deadbolt. I thought I was already too late. Finally I heard his voice, high and boyish.

"Are you all right?"

"Good enough," Mr. Tornelli said through the locked door.

"Could I come in?"

There was a long silence.

"Mr. Tornelli?"

"Jack."

"Right here."

"Could you let me be alone tonight? Would that be all right?"

"I want to be sure you're OK."

"Goodnight, Jack," Mr. Tornelli said with a queer force. I turned and went back to my room. I left all the lights on, thinking I'd get up in a while and check on him. When I woke the sun was up, blasting gold off the windows of the abandoned Opera House.

It was after eight. The moon was already nearing the face of the sun. Still in last night's clothes, I ran down the hall and found Mr. Tornelli's door ajar. I walked in but he wasn't there. The walls and bed and desk were stripped. A black steamer trunk sat in the middle of the floor, heavy and padlocked. Even the plants were gone.

I ran down to the desk and asked what was going on with Mr. Tornelli but nobody'd seen him. I ran to the restaurant and stood at the end of the counter scanning the old heads bent over their poached eggs, but Mr. Tornelli's wasn't among them. Back at the Frontier I was desperate. I went up and down the corridor knocking on doors. He wasn't in the can. Mrs. Bache hadn't seen him. No one answered at 312. Mr. Karpowicz in 309 offered to break my jaw again. It was just after his door slammed that I saw what I'd missed.

The door to the fire escape was propped open with one of Mr. Tornelli's African Violets. The other plants huddled together on the metal slats of the landing. I turned and saw Mr. Tornelli's little medallion looped through the bottom rung of the old ladder that led eight steps to the roof. My heart pounded.

As I poked my head over the edge of the roof, the sunlight was growing gently dimmer on Mr. Tornelli. He was seated on a half a hotel blanket laid over the moist tar and pea-stones, cross-legged and tiny. This old man who knew the science of light, who had followed the shadow of the sun around the world, was at this moment sitting there staring naked-eyed into the eclipse.

He patted the empty spot next to him.

"Just in time, my boy," Mr. Tornelli said. "Sit please, keep me company."

I joined him on the blanket.

"Keep your eyes down now—don't ruin them," he said.

Darkness came over our part of the world in waves, stronger and faster now. The sparrows fell silent, the sound of tires faded from the streets below. The corona emerged brilliant from the black disc of the moon.

I took Mr. Tornelli's hand and held it in both of mine.

"I didn't know where you were," I said.

"Yes," Mr. Tornelli said. "You had to find me."

"I didn't know."

"So," he said, whispering, though in the stillness his words were bright and clear. "You see how it is with trouble and happiness. There are some good moments, aren't there. Were you asking for more than that?"

All at once the stars were everywhere, pelting their grace down on us.

"This is, ah, what can I say. . . .We come this far and you and I change places. It's good."

He shut his eyes, smiling still. I leaned over and drew his head down to my shoulder and stroked it as the breath labored in and out of him. The darkness began to ease, the slightest lightening visible at the edge of things.

LITERATURE AND LUCRE: A MEDITATION

by LESLIE A. FIEDLER

from GENRE

nominated by Louis Gallo and Richard Kostelanetz

IT SEEMS TO ME ODD that I have never before, in my long life as a maker and teacher of fictions, talked from a public platform or written for publication about literature and lucre; and even odder that I feel so ill at ease attempting it for the first time. I am not suggesting that I do not ordinarily associate money with the arts I practice and for which I am these days more often than not paid. Indeed, I can scarcely separate the one from the other; since from the moment I was possessed (at age six or seven) by the desire to become a writer, I have been aware that the process—in our society at least—is inextricably involved with making money. Please understand. By "becoming a writer" I do not mean just getting out on to paper what I could no longer contain in my bursting heart and head, which is to fully consummated writing mere masturbation or *ejaculatio praecox*. What I yearned for was to be published, to be read, "to be great, to be known" (in the words of a poem by Stephen Spender which I have never forgotten), to open communication with an audience, to exist for others: utterly alien others, bound to me—unlike family or friends—only after the fact of having read me.

How hypothetical that audience, those alien others might remain, and consequently how unreal, impalpable the recognition, honor and love, I did not at first realize. To be sure, there are occasional letters of response, reviews in the press, even—if one lives long enough—testimonials and ceremonies. But for a long time, money (that one fiction of universal currency) is the only, and indeed always remains the most reliable, token that one has in fact touched, moved, shared one's most private fantasies with the faceless, nameless "you" to whom the writer's all-too-familiar "I" longs to be joined in mutual pleasure. "I stop somewhere waiting for you," is a sentence not just from Walt Whitman's but every writer's love letter to the world. It is only when the first royalty check arrives in the mail (an answer as palpable as a poem) that the writer begins to suspect that the "you" he has had to invent in his lonely chamber, in order to begin writing at all, is real; and that therefore his "I" (not the "I" to which like everyone else he is born, but the fictive "I" which he, in order to be a writer, must create simultaneously with the "you") is real, too.

But this means, as all writers know, though most of us (including me) find it hard to confess, that literature, the literary work, remains incomplete until it has passed from the desk to the market place; which is to say, until it has been packaged, huckstered, hyped and sold. Moreover, writers themselves (as they are also aware) remain reluctant virgins, crying to the world. "Love me! Love me!", until, as the revealing phrase of the trade has it, they have "sold their first piece." What scorn, therefore, the truly published, fully consummated writer has for those *demi-vierges* who publish themselves—turning in spinsterish despair to (again the customary phrase is significant) "Vanity Presses."

The fully published writer, however, feels not just scorn for the half-published and pity for the unpublished, but a kind of guilt, rather like the guilt of those who live by tourism or selling their own bodies. In his case as in theirs, that guilt breeds a kind of resentment against the intermediaries and accomplices who have made possible what he himself has desired. Just as the Western organizers of Rodeo Days hate dudes, or whores and gigolos their pimps, johns and aging benefactors, the commercially successful writer hates agents, editors, publishers, reviewers and the M.C.'s of T.V. Talk Shows—hates finally the poor audience itself for buying what has been offered for sale. That guilt and resentment I must admit I share, though by admitting it I compound my plight. But this surely is one of the reasons why, as I began by confessing, I feel ill at ease in approaching the subject so innocently proposed by the organizers of this symposium. I spoke the general version of this meditation in a setting which both symbolized and aggravated that guilt and resentment, since I had been paid to attend and testify; and I was present therefore, perhaps, not *just* for the sake of the lucre involved, but for that reason among others.

Indeed, I should like to think that the subject which I am treating is one so important to me and the community to which I belong that sooner or later I would have felt obliged to deal with it, even if somebody paid me *not* to do so. But this has not been my fate, so how can I be sure? In any case, here I am taking it up once more in print and for further payment, continuing communication much as I began it: not as one talks (or writes) to an old friend, or even to some one he sits beside on a plane, at a bar; but because there is a contract between us, because we are joined briefly by a cash nexus. In some sense, this, if not quite falsifies, at least uncomfortably modifies the nature of our discourse, creating real possibilities of distrust and misunderstanding. I have been paid to talk and write, while you have paid to listen and read. You, therefore, as you should, feel free, if I do not keep up my end of the bargain, neither entertain nor enlighten you, let's say, to grumble and complain: but *not,* in any case, to get your money back—not from me. It is a strange business, in which I am an entrepreneur, or rather a non-entrepreneur, guaranteed against risk.

But this is precisely the situation in which I have written and spoken for all of my professional life: as a novelist, poet, teacher, scholar and critic-pedagogue. Like other critic-pedagogues, I am not only paid for public performance; but I get free books for which other people pay hard cash, and am invited to attend without paying admission plays and movies for which others must buy tickets at the box-office. Moreover, I and my peers, or at least those among us who have access to commercial journals, are rewarded for a second time by being paid for registering in print our opinions of those books, movies and plays: opinions which *must* be (I sometimes uncomfortable suspect) radically different from the responses of those we address, precisely because having paid their way into the theatre, they have an investment to protect.

Even scholar-pedagogues who, out of a snobbishness desire to remain "pure," refuse to publish in paying journals like *The New York Times Book Review*, *The Times Literary Supplement* or, God forbid, *Esquire* and *Playboy* (in all of which, I must confess, I have appeared), cannot really escape the commercial trap. Unless willing to perish, they must publish *somewhere*; if only in subsidized journals of high prestige and low readability, like the PMLA, to which I have never contributed. But the readership of such journals consists not just of specialists in certain fields (unlike the readers of popular magazines, more inclined to disapprove than approve what they have paid for), but also the Promotion and Tenure committees of the Universities to which the contributors belong. Such committees will, on the basis of such articles, grant them tenure or promotion: thus guaranteeing that they will be paid more for repeating in the classroom what they have already published, or rehearsing what they hope to publish next. Eventually, moreover, such articles are gathered together, revised and expanded to make scholarly books, which have to be subsidized either by their authors or the schools in which they teach, since they are bought only by University Libraries, from whose shelves (a recent study has discovered) some seventy percent of them are *never* taken out.

Nonetheless, when these already over-subsidized pedagogues have persisted long enough in producing goods for which there is a reward but no market, they are likely to receive Grants and Fellowships, the most prestigious funded from carefully invested money, originally accumulated by Robber Barons like the Rockefellers, the Guggenheims and the Fords—which is to say, the filthiest American lucre of all. Furthermore, when they have attained seniority and prestige (or sometimes long before, while they are still only needy and promising) they may be asked to compile, collaborate in or merely lend their names to Freshman Texts. Carefully tailored to maximum classroom demand as determined by market analysts, such texts are the academic equivalents of block-busting best-sellers by Jacqueline Susann, or Harold Robbins, Think, for instance, of Brooks' and Warren's inordinately successful *Understanding Poetry*, at once smugly elitist and happily profitable.

But this is not better, after all, than "selling out to Hollywood" like that backsliding Ivy League Professor, Erich Segal; or leaving the respectable sponsorship of Princeton University Press for the fleshpots of Simon and Schuster, who are not only the publishers of my own most recent book, but (I reassure myself) of Joseph Heller's *Catch-22*, a novel "taught" by some of my anti-commercial colleagues. Indeed, many, perhaps the great majority of the books taught by even the most snobbish and genteel among us were written by men shamelessly involved with the marketplace: Shakespeare, Richardson, Balzac, Dickens, Mark Twain, Scott Fitzgerald, Faulkner, Hemingway, and Arthur Miller, Norman Mailer and Saul Bellow, to name only the first that come to mind. Morever, in the last three or four decades, many writers we "require" in class have compounded their complicity by themselves becoming teachers, i.e., secondary as well as primary hucksters.

But, I remind myself, only a generation or two ago "serious" creative writers (the heirs of Modernist elitism and Marxist politics) considered employment in the university—that front for what our own students were still calling in the sixties "the industrial-military complex"—a kind of "selling-out" comparable to taking a job with an advertising agency or MGM or Henry Luce: a search for low-level security in place of high-risk ventures in the arena of High Culture. Not in Grub Street, be it understood, but in Bohemia; that anti-Market Place, in which, after the invention of the Avant Garde and the raising of the slogan "*Epatez la bourgeoisie*," "true artists" were imagined as starving, while pseudoartists flourished.

Even in the hey-day of Modernism, the legend of *la vie de Bohème* did not deceive everyone. Sigmund Freud, for instance, remained faithful enough to the Reality Principle to argue that *all* artists were driven by fantasies of becoming beloved, famous and rich. And George Bernard Shaw, always the enemy of pious hypocrisy, ironically made the same point in his famous argument with Samuel Goldwyn over the filming of *My Fair Lady*, a musical based on his *Pygmalion*. "The trouble," he is reputed to have said, "is that you, Mr. Goldwyn, think about nothing but art, while all I think of is money." He is less likely to have been influenced by Freud, however, than by his true-blue English predecessor, Dr. Samuel Johnson, who is on record as believing that money is the "purest" of all motives for writing; by which I presume he meant it is the truest, the least likely to be mere cant and self-deceit. In any case, I remember both Shaw and Johnson each time I enter a group of strangers engaged in passionate debate, and discover that if they are discussing literature, nine times out of ten they turn out to be business men, but if they are talking about money, they are likely to be writers.

In America, however—perhaps precisely because among us commerce is offically more honored than art—our eminent writers have not typically spoken with equal candor on the subject of literature and lucre. Certainly, the great novelists of the mid-nineteenth century, celebrated in F. O. Matthiessen's *The American Renaissance* and D. H. Lawrence's *Studies in Classic American Literature*, have chosen self-pity over irony or frankness in talking about their relationship to the marketplace. The classic statement is Melville's, "Dollars damn me . . . all my books are botches. . . ." And implicit in this melancholy cry from the heart is a belief, as strong and pertinacious as any myth by which we live, that the authentic writer is neither drawn to nor confirmed in his vocation by the hope of marketplace success, the dream of becoming rich and famous; but can only be seduced by lucre, led to betray or prostitute his talent.

Paradoxically, American culture came of age at the very moment when old aristocratic sponsors of the arts were being replaced by the mass audience and the masters of the new media, who profit by responding to its taste. The first of these media was print, and the first truly popular genre, the Novel. But this is also the American form *par excellence*, invented even as we were inventing our Republic; and in it, the first American authors achieved fame for themselves and the culture which nurtured them. A commodity, mass produced and mass distributed, it offered its practitioners the possibility of growing rich as well as famous. But from the start, that possibility remained more promise than fact, at least for writers like Charles Brockden Brown, Edgar Allan Poe, Nathaniel

Hawthorne and Herman Melville, who thought of themselves as producing "literature."

Before the first of these sophisticated novelists (all male) had begun to write, "best sellers" were already being turned out by other more naive, less pretentious authors (largely female), whose taste and fantasy coincided with that of the popular audience, itself largely female. Even over the long haul, the books loved by most Americans who read anything between covers at all have not been *Moby Dick* and *The Scarlet Letter* nor even *Huckleberry Finn*, which live now chiefly as assigned reading in classrooms, but a series of deeply moving though stylistically undistinguished fictions, which begins with Susanna Rowson's *Charlotte Temple*, reaches a nineteenth-century high-point with Harriet Beecher Stowe's *Uncle Tom's Cabin* and a twentieth-century climax with Margaret Mitchell's *Gone With the Wind.* The last, though never approved by "serious" critics and seldom required in "serious" courses in literature, is still sold in paperback reprints; and, translated into the newer, more popular post-Gutenburg media of film and T.V., is probably known to a larger world-wide audience than any other American fiction.

For a century and a half, those writers among us who aspire to critical acclaim and an eternal place in libraries, have therefore felt compelled to struggle not just for their livelihood but for their very existence against the authors of "best sellers," whom they secretly envy and publicly despise. This cultural warfare may seem at first glance a struggle of the poor against the rich, the failed against the successful. But the situation is more complex than this since in terms of culture rather than economics, art novelists and their audience "fit though few" constitute a privileged, educationally-advantaged minority; while popular novelists and their mass readership remain a despised *lumpen* minority, whose cultural insecurity is further shaken when their kids learn in school to question their taste.

The struggle of High Art and Low is, moreover, a battle of the sexes. Referring to the writers who had preempted the paying audience before he ever entered the scene, Nathaniel Hawthorne called them a "damn'd mob of scribbling women." And, indeed, from Mrs. Rowson to Jacqueline Susann, the authors of monumental, long-lasting popular successes have continued to come from the sex which thinks of itself as otherwise exploited, oppressed, dominated in a patriarchal society. Unlike other oppressive minorities, however (white slave owners, for example), it is possible for both males and the cultural elite to contend, with a certain superficial plausibility, that they are victims rather than victimizers. And, indeed, both primary and secondary literature in the United States, the novels and poems of which we are most proud and the critical autobiographical works written on them, reflect the myth of the "serious" writer as an alienated male, condemned to neglect and poverty by a culture simultaneously commercialized and feminized.

There are prototypes of this myth in remotest antiquity: the legend of Euripides, for instance, first avant-garde artist in the West, having been hunted to death by a pack of angry women (or, alternatively, dogs); while behind even that is the primal image of Dionysus, torn to pieces by Bacchantes, eager to still his singing and exact revenge for their slighted sex. It is Poe, however, who first embodies that image for the American imagination, at least as he has been re-interpreted for us by French poets of the *déca-dence*, Baudelaire and Mallarmé, who celebrated him as a *poète maudit*, "*un Byron egaré dans le nouveau monde.*" But even earlier, Poe had collaborated, as it were, with his friend-enemy Rufus Griswold to create a demi-fictional portrait of himself as a dope-ridden alcoholic, dying in the streets of Baltimore after a long starvation and neglect in an environment hostile to art.

That image of the true artist destroyed by a money-grubbing society, though originally the hybrid offspring of Southern American self-hated and the French contempt for everything in our culture except its presumed victims, throve in the New World. Reembodied generation after generation, it is most notably exemplified after Poe by Herman Melville, whom we rejoice to imagine drudging away his last unhappy years in the Custom House, unpublished, unhonored, forgotten; and Scott Fitzgerald, dying in shabby surroundings in a Hollywood which preferred Mammon to literature, and had no sense that this failed alcoholic scriptwriter was destined to outlive in glory the most celebrated producers, directors and actors of his time. That Poe and Melville and Fitzgerald failed not because they despised lucre and shunned the marketplace, but precisely because they were so desperately committed to the American dream of "making it," the legend does not permit us to remember.

We really know that Fitzgerald began by producing best-selling novels and peddling hastily written short stories to family magazines at prices which mounted with his fame; and that he ended by squandering away a larger fortune than ordinary Americans can imagine earning in a lifetime of backbreaking work. Poe, too, though never as successful, even momentarily, spent his brief career as a hack-writer and editor of commercial literary journals in pursuit of the common reader and the quick buck. Indeed, the fantasies which drove them both are betrayed in stories like Poe's "The Goldbug" and Fitzgerald's "A Diamond as Big as the Ritz"— the dream of innocently acquiring guilty treasure, and the nightmare of losing everything.

Similarly, the mad, metaphysical quest of Melville's *Moby Dick* begins as a carefully planned commercial venture, with Ishmael bargaining for his fair share of the profits. And why not—in light of the fact that Melville's mad, metaphysical career began with the best seller, *Typee*. Indeed, he never ceased trying to recapture his initial rapport with the popular audience. Even *Pierre*, whose underlying theme is the plight of the alienated artist in America, he assured his publisher (and perhaps believed himself) was "a rural bowl of milk," i.e., a domestic romance as palatable to the large female audience as to the somewhat smaller male one who had admired his adventure stories.

The pathos of such writers, whether they ended in insanity and withdrawal like Melville or in premature death like Poe and Fitzgerald, is not that they nobly refused to provide what the marketplace demanded, but that they tried to do so and failed. But this is not the story which the American mass audience likes to be told, since they need to be assured that the writers they choose only posthumously to honor (if not read) in some sense died for their sins: their lack of sensibility, mindless pursuit of profit, indifference to art—but not to artists, particularly failed ones, after they are dead. Realizing how in our world nothing succeeds like failure—certain lesser writers, from Rufus Griswold to Budd Schulberg, have produced parasitic best sellers about the tragic fates of Poe and Fitzgerald.

It may have been booze that destroyed Poe or Fitzgerald, but

the great public prefers to believe they did it with their little
hatchets—thus feeling at once powerful and guilty: a potent emotional mix for all true Americans. Certainly, we do not seem to
derive as much satisfaction from contemplating the careers of
eminent writers who have made it, dying, like Harriet Beecher
Stowe, honored and rich—though cheerfully batty. It is, for instance, Mark Twain's final loneliness and melancholia we prefer to
dwell on, or his many failures along the way. Yet though Twain
went bankrupt as often as any other capitalist entrepreneur of the
Gilded Age, at the end he was able to support a splendiferous
house, and a set of bad habits which compelled him to smoke forty
Havana cigars a day and to drink enough Old Grandad to send him
to bed insensible night after night. He had finally grown so
wealthy, indeed, that the only people he felt he could talk to as
equals were Henry Rogers, Vice President of Standard Oil, and
Andrew Carnegie, whom he addressed as "St. Andrew" in letters
signed "St. Mark."

Ironically, his fortune was based on the continuing success of
Huckleberry Finn, which is to say, the classic version of the
American antisuccess story. We are asked to love Huck (and to
prove our love by buying the book in which he appears) for running
away, not just from school, church and family, but money as well:
that guilty-innocent treasure which he and Tom had stumbled on at
the end of *Tom Sawyer,* but which he, unlike Tom and the hero of
Poe's "The Gold Bug," ultimately rejects. What Twain never wrote
was a fictional account of a boy like himself, who, instead of
"lighting out for the territory ahead of the rest," stayed home, grew
up (as he would not let Tom grow up), permitted himself to be
"civilized" by his wife and daughter; and at last got rich by writing
about another eternal child who made all the opposite choices.
Before the middle of the twentieth century, in fact, there is no
respectable American book which portrays sympathetically an
author who made good. Even Horatio Alger's disreputable
juveniles, though they portray striking it rich as a truly Happy
Ending, deal with boys who rose from rags to riches by becoming
not writers but merchants or bankers.

Only in the last decade of this century did it become possible,
first in fact, then in fiction, for a novelist highly regarded by critics
(Norman Mailer is an example) to become wealthy long before his

death by having his books chosen as major Book Club Selections; then signing million dollar paperback contracts; and finally appearing on T.V. Talk Shows, where (becoming, as it were, his own Griswold or Schulberg) he played the mythological role of the writer for the benefit of an audience which had not read, never would read his work. Even novelists who shun all publicity, like J. D. Salinger and Thomas Pynchon, accumulate royalties comparable to those earned by such critically despised darlings of the populace as Harold Robbins and Jacqueline Susan. Only Saul Bellow, however, Nobel Prize Winner and Laureate of the New Conservatism, has thus far dared translate this new-style Happy Ending from life to literature. And this is perhaps why his *Humboldt's Gift* has been universally (willfully, I suspect) misunderstood by its critics.

It seems, at first, a rather conventional elegy for a *poète maudit:* the last, somewhat improbable heir to the tradition of Poe, Melville and Fitzgerald, reborn this time as a failed New York Jewish intellectual—a super-articulate, self-defeating *luftmensch,* who has died abandoned and penniless before the action of the novel begins. It has been suggested by many, including Bellow himself, that the model for Humboldt was the poet, Delmore Schwartz, who had indeed come to such a shabby end. But while there is a great deal of Schwartz in Humboldt, he is finally the portrait not of any single individual but of a whole generation of Jewish-American losers: including, surely, Bellow's one-time guru and life-long friend, Issac Rosenfeld, also dead before reaching forty, his handful of stories and essays remembered by a shrinking handful of aging admirers; and perhaps Lenny Bruce as well, that hipster and stand-up comedian who O.D.'d in 1966. Reading of Humboldt's fate, I cannot, in any case, help thinking of *all* those mad, bright young Jewish Americans, still caught up in the obsolescent myth of the Artist as Victim, and dead before they had lived long enough to realize, like Bellow, that in prosperous America it was no longer necessary to end as a Beautiful Loser.

In any case, Bellow's book is called not *Humboldt* but *Humboldt's Gift;* and the recipient of that gift, that not-so-beautiful Winner, Charlie Citrine, is its real hero. For a little while, Citrine (who at times seems scarcely distinguishable from his author) finds in Humboldt's death and his own survival, an occasion for guilt—the guilt we have long been trained to think of as the inevitable accompaniment of making it. But in the end, he succeeds in convincing himself that Humboldt has died for him, that all such losers die for all winners; leaving us as a heritage not empty regrets but a saleable story: his story once, our story now, the book we are reading. Properly exploited, that story can (in the fiction we read) be sold to the movies, or (in the larger world outside) clinch for its author the Nobel Prize; make us survivors, in short, rich enough to meet the obligations of the prosperous living: alimony, mortgage payments, credit card debits, fifty percent income taxes. And if we weep a little, remembering those others whom we loved and betrayed and by whose death we profited, we can (as the old saying has it) cry all the way to the bank.

🔥 🔥 🔥

THE RIVER AGAIN AND AGAIN

by LINDA GREGG

from IRONWOOD

nominated by IRONWOOD, *Raymond Carver, Norman Dubie, Tess Gallagher, David Madden, Gerald Stern, Pamela Stewart, and Barbara Watkins*

If I could show you how repetition
helps us to understand the truth.
If we stayed with each other long enough
to see the seasons return, to see the young animals
and the opening of peonies and summer heat.
Then we could make sense of the hawk's calm
or the deer all lowering their heads
again and continuing to eat.
And we would know each other sometimes
with a love that touches indifference.

FOR ELIZABETH BISHOP

by SANDRA MCPHERSON

from THE AMERICAN POETRY REVIEW

nominated by Jorie Graham and Rhoda Schwartz

The child I left your class to have
Later had a habit of sleeping
With her arms around a globe
She'd unscrewed, dropped, and dented.
I always felt she *could* possess it,
The pink countries and the mauve
And the ocean which got to keep its blue.
Coming from the Southern Hemisphere to teach,
Which you had never had to do, you took
A bare-walled room, alone, its northern
Windowscapes as gray as walls.
To decorate, you'd only brought a black madonna.
I thought you must have skipped summer that year,
Southern winter, southern spring, then north
For winter over again. Still, it pleased you
To take credit for introducing us,
And later to bring our daughter a small flipbook
Of partners dancing, and a ring
With a secret whistle.—All are
Broken now like her globe, but she remembers
Them as I recall the black madonna
Facing you across the room so that
In a way you had the dark fertile life
You were always giving gifts to.
Your smaller admirer off to school,
I take the globe and roll it away: where
On it now is someone like you?

AFTER THE INTERROGATION

by LAWRENCE KEARNEY

from SHANKPAINTER

nominated by SHANKPAINTER *and Jane Flanders*

There is the sack of skin, dark
or light, ready to give out
under small cunningly-applied pressures
its passage of blood
from the heart to the tongue.
There is firefall & gangrene,
there are 43 days of interrogation
& a 15-year sentence in the works.
Plenty of time to dream in your cell
of a young woman's breasts:
the purple areolas deepening to black
at the nipples, of burying your head
between them & never coming up.
Death would be like that, you say —
something that makes you ache inside
the way a woman can make you ache.
Or a few sad fragments of speech
from *The Cherry Orchard* come back to you,
& you remember the first time you read it
how you wanted to cry, because it was true,
that sadness. Russia dying
into the 20th century—what could have been
further from your life?—& yet Chekhov
was speaking only to you: telling you
he was once as scared as you were
of blank paper, of its stare, but just wrote
& wrote because all he wanted

443

was someone to talk to, that what was
writing anyway but someone talking
to someone he couldn't see.
How it came to you later, one morning
on Hoedjes Bay, up-coast from Capetown,
the wind driving the sand off the dunes
into your nostrils, your hair,
a few thick-necked Cumulus
skudding inward toward land & no rain,
the waves crashing four abreast,
each one a mouth
talking & talking, slab after slab of language
heaved up from the sea—
& for the first time you knew
you were born to this life to write
in the open, to read the braille
surface of things & give emptiness
a face.
                    Pigeons
scratching the cement in the cell-yard
wake you, but in your mind
you're back in Johannesburg,
that tree on State Street: the pigeons
underneath clucking like grandmas
as they devour the pink clusters of fruit
they imagine have fallen only for them.
How they remind you of the guards—
all appetite & affability.
And yet, nothing like the guards
at all. Who are not birds, but only men
doing a job, & you
are the job.
                    And it's only now, finally
awake from this morning's beating,
that you see it: the window.
The guards have left the window open.
But not out of carelessness, & not for the air.
So. All that blather about power
& how much of it the State can wield
over a person, when any child

could have told you—pain.
A 10-penny hose artfully employed,
a glass rod worked from the tip
of the penis to its root & then broken,
bending the arm past the elbow's
ability . . . Enough pain
that they won't have to kill you, you'll
do it for them, *that* kind of power.
And that once dead, you are theirs.
Public. Molecular. Stripped of thought,
of its privacy, which terrifies them
as it once terrified you—the solitude
& particulars of moving through time.
Time, which goes only as far
as the window, which is 4 feet away
& is open & is 7 flights down.
That everything you've written
since that morning by the ocean
is there, just past the window, pleading
don't do it!—though something
in your body is moving anyway, & no one,
not even you, has a right to stop it.
But your arms are too mangled to pull.
You'll have to help. You'll have to make it
on words alone this time, drag yourself
by the tongue to the window,
lean far enough out
& let go . . .
                    into a rush
of women's breasts, your wife, her breasts
sagging against her blouse as she bends
over the well in the courtyard at home
looking at her hair in the water. And in her hair
a pale-green comb of Malagasy tortoise-shell,
& you think, of all things, why that?
A comb. Something trivial & exquisite
your last thought on earth
as the cement shoves into you
so suddenly & so hard
it doesn't hurt—just the momentary

nausea, a few miserable syllables
coughed up with the blood, & then silence.
Silence by the well in Soweto. Silence
under the tree on State Street. Silence
with its boot in the door of your voice.

6 6 6

WODEN'S DAY

fiction by JEAN STAFFORD

from SHENANDOAH

nominated by SHENANDOAH, *Robert Phillips, Teo Savory and Stephanie Vaughn*

A Note about "Woden's Day"

"Woden's Day" will apparently stand as Jean Stafford's last story. With her consent I extracted it and "An Influx of Poets," published in The New Yorker *last year, from her unfinished novel,* The Parliament of Women, *on which she had started work in June 1968, when the publishing firm in which I am a partner signed a contract for it. Despite her aphasia, the cruel illness with which she was stricken in her last years, Jean was able to go over both stories with me in the summer of 1978. On rereading the manuscript of her novel, I had realized that these two sections could, with minor emendations, stand alone as stories.*

"My roots remain in the semi-fictitious town of Adams, Colorado," Jean revealed in the preface to her Collected Stories, *and while Adams is not exactly the setting of "Woden's Day" it is in a sense the subject of the story, the destination towards which the Savage family is headed. Cora Savage, Jean's persona in her autobiographical fiction and the intended heroine of* The Parliament of Women, *is still a child in "Woden's Day," which is mainly about her parents and grandparents. It records, so to speak, the pre-history of Adams.*

From what she told me of him, I had always hoped that Jean would one day write a novel about her father. While he was still living, she sometimes read parts of his letters to me, and they were extraordinary. One sentence in particular I've never forgotten. It began, "The trouble with Lyndon Johnson and those people in Washington, Jean,–" and she laughed uproariously before completing it–"is that they have not read their Tacitus." As far as I know, there are only two pieces of writing about him. One is the preface to her Collected Stories, *from which we learn that he was a writer of Westerns, one of which was a novel entitled* When Cattle Kingdom Fell. *The other is "Woden's Day," with Jean's unforgettable portrait of the young Savage on the occasion of the acceptance of his first story by a magazine.*

—Robert Giroux

447

The Savages had come from Graymoor, Missouri, to Adams, Colorado, in 1925, when Cora was ten. Both parents had known the town at different times and in different ways: Maud, then Miss McKinnon, upon her graduation from Willowbrook Female Seminary—ten miles from Graymoor, where she boarded but at her father's command went home on Sundays lest she stray beyond the United Presbyterian pale and lie abed on the Sabbath or read Zola's brazen novels—had accepted the position of assistant mistress in a small private school in Adams named, remarkably, Summerlid. "What kind was it?" her children, doubled up with laughter, wanted to know. "A leghorn? A Panama? Was it a sunbonnet, Mama? Did it have a mosquito net on it to keep the horseflies off?" Mrs. Savage, who had taken her year-long academic career seriously, was vexed and wounded and tried to put them down by saying, "I have told you and told you that Mr. Summerlid of Grosse Pointe founded it for unfortunate tubercular children. Now stop fashing me." But the rotten children, especially Randall and Cora, helplessly seized with giggles, ran off howling, "Missy Maud McKinnon pounded fractions into the wallydrag noggins of head chiggers in a lousy limey sailor hat!" They'd one time heard Dan (as they called their father) say this as part of one of his long ridiculing, affectionate litanies. They did not know that it had made their mother cry and, if they had, probably would not have cared. Why Dan and Mama did not run away from each other and quit their endless insults, they could not imagine. (Once when they discussed the matter in a tentative and half-fearful way, they ended up by shrugging their shoulders and saying, "Ishkabibble. One of these sunshiny days we'll run away from them.") Miss McKinnon had loved her experience of being away from home out in the wilds that way, and while she was devoted to her family and her friends and sometimes was homesick enough to cry, it had been so nice to meet new people, to be taken into the Sororsis which had supper meetings at a different house each week (oh, those treats of Mexican chili con carne and of creamed sage-hen!). And riding burros! "We called them 'Rocky Mountain canaries,' you know. What pesky scamps they were! They'd find an appetizing bush and you couldn't budge them till they'd had their fill. We'd whip and kick and scold but it was *no ma'am* as far as they were concerned, and they were so comical about it we nearly fell off laughing. The big its!" She had loved to go on picnics beside waterfalls; they'd sing and gather wildflowers and sometimes pretend they were oreads and go prancing and weaving through the lodgepole pines. During the Easter holiday she had gone to Manitou Springs with some other young ladies from Summerlid and they had had a real lark, but, to tell the truth, they had found the mineral waters disagreeable beyond words: "Pew!" said Mama and held her nose.

Some years before Dan Savage's future wife had wended her slow way west on the Denver & Rio Grande with her truck and her foulard parasol and her travelling tailormaid of grey De'Beige cloth, Dan had taken it into his quixotic head to go prospecting for gold in the Rockies. Throughout the summer of 1892, he had panned the rivers from the lower canyons to the tundra of the Wilson range and had found long tons of pyrites and his placer pan had brimmed with fool's gold. No, he hadn't made his fortune, but he had had a larruping good time; that had been far and away a summer better than all summers before when he and his older brother, Uncle Jonathan—a year ahead of him at college—had had to drive their father's herd up from the Panhandle to Dodge City through dust storms so bad that when you took a drink of water you had a mouthful of mud. He had graduated from Amity College that spring, *summa cum laude,* and this holiday had been his reward. Mind you, if he had wanted to go to sea or go to New York City to explore the music halls and free-lunch saloons and Turkish baths, his father wouldn't have put up a red cent for a fandango such as that; but while he was a cattle man and a crop man, he had an understanding of gold-fever and he staked his son to fare on the cars to Denver, the price of a horse to ride and a horse to pack with gear and grub. Dan had a companion, a college classmate, Thad McPherson, a fellow so brilliant at Hebrew that to the other students, all Methodist or Presbyterian, he was known as The Jew, and then, because he was so often lost in thought that, strolling by himself, he sometimes got lost in the woods by the river and missed classes and examinations, he came to be called The Wandering Jew. And to top it all off, he played a Jew's harp and played it like a professional, sometimes as rowdy-dowdy as a showboat skalawag, sometimes as sweet as a Muse. He was a pretty solemn man, and silent. Yet he had been a good friend to have along that summer to speculate on matters of geology, to wonder ("By the Lord Harry!") at the beaver's practicality and genius, to come, amazed, upon a solid acre of glacier lilies, to hack away with pick-axes (and find pyrites shining like pure gold), to pan in the ice-cold amber streams and, along with the fool's gold, get a mess of caddis worms. Often of an evening when they were full of trout, fresh-caught, and fried mush with bacon gravy, they would talk well past moonlight beside their camp fire about what they had learned at Amity of history and the literatures of ancient languages: they had learned little else—some mathematics, some chemistry and physics, some biology. Thad had a leaning toward The Almighty but Dan was an up-to-the-minute Darwinian and they had debated on this ticklish subject until the moon went pale, "I'd try my level best to rile him, but old Thad was as mild as mother's milk. *His* theology had no more brimstone in it than a daisy. I think that old Wandering Jew was a B.C. pagan, believed in the wee people, believed in Santy Claus." About once every two years, Dan got a letter from him, from a different state each time, for he had turned into a salesman for the Watkins Company that sold spices and condiments and soap and such like from door to door. One time he had turned up in Adams, a tall, gaunt awkward man, as red and yellow as a summer sunset. Mama saw his sample case and said, as she always said to peddlers, that the lady of the house was not at home; but he only asked, gently, to see Dan. The two of them with Oddfellow, the dog, a border collie, went off towards the mountains and Dan didn't come home until long after dark. "I declare," Mama was later and often to say to each child individually and in confidence as if she had never uttered this dread fear before, "that man looked like a *ghost* to me! I don't care about that carrot-top or that red face of his, he *felt* like a ghost, and when he went off with your father that way, I thought the pair of them would vanish. Just vanish."

The summer in Adams had been Dan's Wanderjahr, her nine months there at Summerlid had been Mama's debutante season, and when their life in Graymoor came crashing down upon them in disgrace, they picked this distant hiding place. Cora's last memory of Graymoor was of going to say goodbye to Albert and Heinie, the children of the chicken farmer next door. It was in the morning and Mrs. Himmel was busy with the wash so there was no Kinder Kaffeeklatsch (in the morning, of course, it would have been called Zweites Frühstück, which the Savage children pronounced "Fruit-stick"), but the little boys had taken them into the parlor and ritualistically had wound up the seven music boxes and when the nightingale, *Der Liebling Vogel,* sang to her for the very last time, huge golden globes of tears blinded Cora, but she managed not to let them burst and spill. They all shook hands then and, unsmiling, contrapuntally, the Scotch-Irish children said, "Auf Wiedersehen," and the German children said, "Ta-ta. See you in church."

Grandfather Brian Savage had died of dengue fever in Coffeyville, Kansas, when he and his youngest daughter were almost within hailing distance of home after having gone half way around the world to visit kinsmen in Australia. Aunt Caroline, her father's darling, his blooming emerald-eyed and raven-locked colleen, had been as quirky and as saucy as he and when she was seventeen the two of them took ship at San Francisco to go have a look at kangaroos and stranger, albeit technically human, beasts in the outback. And on the very day that they set sail for that outlandish continent, Granny and Aunt Elizabeth who was twenty, as spirited as the other two but brainier and more domesticated, embarked at New Orleans for a stylish and conventional tour of London and Paris, Vienna and Rome. They all went off at the end of June, the same June that Dan had gone to Colorado.

He would push his hat back, take off his glasses, close his eyes and, remembering, say, "Thad and I would have been about at Loveland when the tugs were toting their ships out to the bounding main, one east, one west; Loveland or a short piece beyond. We'd paid handsomely for those horses in Denver and we treated them like little Lords and Ladies Fauntleroy, not working them hard, keeping them in fettle. Besides, we weren't in any hurry and the weather was fine to mosey through." Then he would laugh his infernal laugh. "I'd lie there under the stars and think about Brother Jonathan with his mouth full of dust and his eyes full of the sweat of his brow, punching cows in Paris, Texas, while our sweet Sister Lizzie was buying kid gloves in Paris, France." But Jonathan had had his summer off the year before when he had gone to Crete to be Sir Arthur Evans' third water-boy's sixth water-boy. And then, almost to himself, with contempt, with pity, with disappointment, Dan mused, "If he wanted to be an archaeologist, why didn't he turn in and be one? Look at him now, tied to the Tammany lion's tail with all the rest of the rag-tag-bobtail tinhorns of New York City." Uncle Jonathan was a lawyer and Dan, despising the profession, looked on his success and his wealth as ill-got;

moreover, Jonathan had political ambitions and Dan, schooled by his father and mother, had looked on politicians as scum.

The travellers had been gone for half a year. In the autumn, Uncle Jonathan had entered his second year of law school at the University of Missouri and Dan Savage was left alone in Kavanagh to study over what he wanted to do with the rest of his life. Should he be a scholar? Teach Greek at some high-falutin Eastern college? He read Herodotus, Thucydides, he read Xenophon and Arrian, Hesiod and Homer, Sophocles and Aeschylus. But then, languid in a hammock on an amber day, he'd be seduced by Vergil and he would meditate on vineyards and bees and growing melons under glass in a pastoral, green land like this thrice-blessed Missouri. He'd had his fill of Longhorn beeves and the crude company of drovers.

He had enjoyed being the boss of the Kavanagh house, being alone. Once in a while, he would invite Thad or some other of his Amity classmates to come and visit for a while and his mother's cook, accustomed to feeding a flock—for when the elder Savages were in residence they and their daughters had guests to dinner four or five times each week—was pleased to serve her Louisiana French specialities to these easy-going young men and to be praised by them. The trouble was that most of them weren't easy-going; they had found jobs and some of them had already married, or, like Jonathan, they had gone on to universities to prepare themselves for medicine or the law. "What's the hurry, boys?" he'd say to them. But their fathers were not rich as Brian Savage's was and their expectations, if there were any, were far in the future. For a few days they would ride and hoot, revel at table, play billiards after dinner ("Most of the poor coots had never seen a billiard table in a private house and, my! how they would carry on") and act the role of carefree young squires but then they would itch to be back in their harnesses: "For what? For *gain*! Aye, God, they were no better than my father's hands, shackled to the land. Pawns in the hands of nature. I recollect the way those bozos used to loaf around the kitchen stove before the sun was up and before the *women* were up to make their breakfast, just purely and simply waiting in their dumb animal way for the sunrise. Like apes. They'd been raised on the precept that a man must get up when the Lord gets up, and out of their abounding self-conceit, they reckoned to do the Lord one better, but it never got them anywhere. And then they took their pay and spent it all on Jamaica rum and the doxies who just *happened* to be ambling by the horse-troughs in town when they were watering their nags before they themselves went into the saloons to wallow. Yes sir, with the exception of Thad, that moon-struck old Wandering Jew, my college classmates were not different by a whit from Pa's help. The early bird catches the worm and it don't matter if the worm sticks in his craw."

One time Randall said to his father, "Sir, why do you get up before the sun?" and Dan replied, "I emulate Frederick the Great." His tone was final; the reminiscence and the metaphor were finished; he was through talking. Randall and Cora had looked up Frederick the Great in the Encyclopedia Britannica, but they could find no mention of his being an early riser. Just as on another occasion, when Dan had bragged for the seven hundred and nineteenth time that his pulse rate was 59, the same as Napoleon's, they had tried and failed to check this arresting detail. If they had persevered in their research and tried to pin Dan down, they would have got nowhere. Instead, they would have got rods and acres, *miles*, of the Seven Year's War and the French Revolution; once Dan started he would never stop. He knew too much for a child, for anybody, to bear.

It was along about Thanksgiving time when Dan had got his sister Caroline's telegram from Coffeyville, saying that his father was gravely ill. The ship bringing them back from Australia had docked at Galveston, and they had made their way up through Texas and Oklahoma, changing trains a dozen times and travelling often by stage from one depot town to the next. They had been headed for Wichita, whence they could get a through train to St. Louis, when the fever had laid the old man so low that they could not go on another mile. He was out of his head for a week before he died and he died in the evening of the day Dan got to his bedside in the one antigodlin hotel—the floors were so slanty that when a man walked through a door he thought he might pitch right through the window opposite. It was a hell of a note to meet your maker in that one-horse burg on the plains where the wind whipped along steady at a mile a minute and your handkerchief froze to your nose if you had to blow it. The irony, the almighty irony, of perishing of tropical breakbone fever in November in Coffeyville, Kansas! "Your mother's father's Father which art in Heaven every so often takes it into his cerebellum to play a practical joke and when he does, lo and behold and *mirabile dictu*, he does it up to a fare-thee-well. No holds barred when he wants to pull off a real dandy."

Granny Savage and Aunt Lizzie got to Kavanagh two days after Dan and Aunt Caroline came back with the coffin from Coffeyville. (Cora had made up a shameful rhyme, so shameful she never even told it to Randall: "When they brought the coffin from Coffeyville/I poured me coffee and drank my fill.") And so, instead of a grand family reunion with tales to tell of Europe's wonders and the marvels of the Antipodes, there was a funeral. "My mother and I mourned the man," said Dan. "The others . . ." He shooed off his sisters and his brothers with the back of his hand. Grandfather Savage's will was no surprise to Dan, his second son and second child: the burden of the estate was left to the widow and the rest was divided equally among the four children, but while Jonathan, Caroline and Elizabeth would receive their share in trust, Dan was given his in capital since he, according to the flowery testament, was the only one of the heirs who would know how to manage his money. The Texas holdings and the Missouri holdings (which Brian Savage had greatly extended after the War between the States by buying up bounty grants for next to nothing from veterans who wanted to join the westward push) and a ninety-thousand-acre tract in Arizona, not stocked or farmed but bought for speculation, were also parcelled out equally.

Dan, in those months alone in Kavanagh, pondering the route he wished to take, had concluded finally against school-mastering; he would be Vergil rather than Aristotle and when he was not upon his rural rides, overseeing his flocks and grain, his apiary and his vineyards, he would write: not idylls, not epic poetry but fiction and meditative essays. In time he would take a wife because he wanted sons, sons to teach, thereby combining all his talents, agrarian, literary, academic. But he was in no hurry.

Jonathan quit Missouri for New York City as soon as he had his law degree; Caroline went back to Australia to marry a sheep-rancher she had fallen in love with when her father had taken her to see the wallabies and kangaroos and her Irish uncles and cousins. You may be sure that one of the early kings of cattledom, Brian Savage, mightily shifted in his grave when this mésalliance took place. He couldn't have known what had been taking place behind his back: else he would have outwitted the Lord and risen from his bed in Coffeyville at least until he'd seen his darling girl-child wedded to a decent man. Sheep! And Lizzie, sap-sweet, sap-silly Lizzie took up with a sap-*sucker* she met during Mardi Gras in New Orleans and with him went off to California to grow oranges. With her money. He was a Lothario was Lizzie's pretty Cajun and after a year and a baby, he vanished, sank plumb out of sight. She married again and married this time sensibly: Uncle Frank Boatright was an engineer, a bridge-builder, a dull, good man and Lizzie had two more children by him. After the birth of the second, Cora's Cousin Lucian, poor headlong Lizzie, feeling her oats, was out riding by herself in wild country beyond the orange grove when her horse was spooked to frenzy by a side-winder and threw her, breaking her leg so intricately and mangling it so grievously that it had to be amputated just above her knee.

("You recollect that your Dan was thrown from a horse when he was a chap," said Dan and reached for his blackthorn walking stick to illustrate. Usually the stick was not in the room and he would go to look for it; by the time he had come back, his audience had dispersed. They knew what came afterward: the children's mother's father's Lord had, for once in His life, been just—well, hardly just, but not as ornery as usual—it had been a cruelty to separate a woman from her leg but it would have been a sin crying to Heaven for vengeance if the victim had been a man.)

Dan stayed on in Missouri, lord of the manor, master of the hounds and the hinds, his mother's manager and playmate, her host when she was hostess. And, faithful to his promise to himself, he was a writer. There was a photograph of him sitting at his writing table beside an open and uncurtained window: some flowering tree is in bloom just outside and through its white, enclouded branches, the sun lies full upon a huge dictionary held closed by flanges on a stand; he has only to turn a little to the right to open the book which will lie flat, cleverly supported by the flexible brackets as he looks up a word. The table is square and its narrow aprons are carved with interlocking garlands and they are edged with egg-and-dart. The table is strewn with papers, on one of which Dan is writing with a long-stemmed pen; his other hand is relaxed, the fingers (how filled with ease they seem!) touching another sheet. He is in profile and because his sharply aquiline nose is in shadow, his face looks delicate and young. How young, unlined, how cleanly his high forehead reaches up to meet the dense curls of his dark hair. He has taken off his collar—you can see it lying on top of the bookcase just behind him—and the sleeves of his shirt look uncommonly full, they look as full as bishop sleeves, and the starched cuffs are closed with oval links; his galluses are wide. In the foreground, on the floor or perhaps on some low stool, there is a jardinière of branches bearing flowers. It is a portrait of youth in the youth of a year. You read his mortal vulnerability in his lowered eyes (he does not yet wear thick glasses) and in his bent, clean-shaven neck.

The photograph had been taken to commemorate the sale of his first short story to *Century* magazine and Granny Savage, who prided herself on her lack of pride, had had a man come over from Jefferson City to take it. Ostensibly he was there to photograph the new outbuildings, the new milkhouse and the new silo. At the same time, she and Dan had posed in the lounge where they sat playing war with their lead soldiers, smiling, both of them, Granny's white hair piled up in a pompadour with a coquettish bow above one ear. And there was another picture of them on their horses, Dan on his father's favorite, a strawberry roan named Jack, and Granny on her much smaller Betsy Ross: Dan wore a hard hat and an ascot and a jacket belted across the back, and Granny, in a broad-brimmed hat with an ostrich feather curling down against her cheek, wore a divided skirt and a pin-tucked shirtwaist beneath her tailored jacket with a perky peplum.

None of the children ever knew certainly how this loving son and mother had come to their violent and unconditional parting. It was not until they were grown that Cora and Randall understood how weak a man their father was for all his tempests and his brutality; and, seeing that, saw to their incredulity how strong their mother was, that often weepy, often quaking goose. They had been born in Graymoor, they deduced, in the shadow of the McKinnon house, rather than in Kavanagh near Granny Savage because Grandfather McKinnon had so willed. But why? They were only seven miles apart and if Mama had been dead set on being an obedient Sabbitarian daughter and bringing up her children in her own image, why could they not have made the weekly trip by buggy or, a year or so later by auto, to hear The Word and learn the topography of Hell? Had the McKinnon clan feared the snows of winter or summer thunderstorms? But, that aside, why had Dan knuckled under?

Kavanagh was not a town; it was a place, having two blocks of buildings that housed the barest essentials: a bank, a feed store, a general store for buttons and baking powder, the sheriff's office behind which was the jail and above which the doctor and the lawyer practiced (the doctor was also the dentist, and the lawyer was also the Justice of the Peace and the Notary Public and every second election or so, the Mayor), the saloon and over that the hotel; the post-office and the telegraph office were combined and so were the livery and the undertaking parlor. There was a single church, Methodist, and beside it stood the Manse. There was a barber chair in the pool-hall and the blacksmith and his sons were also the carpenters, the chimney-sweeps, the veterinarians and the well-diggers. On Saturday night, the one-room schoolhouse was the grange hall. From this small, trim and modest hub narrow roads radiated out to a baker's dozen or so of large, rich homesteads like the Savage's.

But Graymoor was a town with a Main Street a quarter of a mile long and dozens of other streets named Front Street, Elm, Maple, Miller's Lane, Plainview, Bluff, First, Second, Third and (why on earth?) Lusanne. The McKinnons lived solitary on a hill that rose up from Aberdeen Avenue, and while the Savages were out of town a way so that their address was RFD, their road was known as The High Street. Dan, used to thinking of land in terms of miles, had a mere ten acres. And these adjoining a poultry farm run by a limberger who, never seeing the ring-tailed farce of it, had named one of his kids Heinie!

Graymoor was on the railroad, on a spur of the Missouri Pacific and Santa Fe, and at four o'clock each Monday morning, Grandfather McKinnon swung aboard and from then until late Friday evening he was a conductor, punching tickets and calling "All aboard!" from St. Louis to Los Angeles and back again. By his wife and his sister and his daughters and, until they learned the truth, his grandchildren, he was known as being "in railroads." At one time, thrilled, Cora thought he was the locomotive engineer; later, even more infatuated, she thought he travelled in a private car similar to Theodore Roosevelt's of which she had seen photographs in an old copy of the *National Geographic*.

Despite the fact that they no longer shared the same roof and nightly dined together, the devotion between Dan and Granny did not falter. And then, when Cora was nine years old, they quarreled and quarreled for keeps. Dan had gone to Jefferson City and had stayed there for two nights and when he got back to Graymoor, he came home in the jitney; this in itself had been unusual, for after a visit to the stock exchange, he liked to walk home in his important city clothes, his gray fur fedora at a rakish angle but maintaining its dignity the while, carrying his blackthorn in his suede-gloved hand, smoking a cigar. But on this day, he was in such a tearing rush that he got out of the snorting jitney and straight into the Franklin. Cora and Randall were playing mumblety-peg under the black walnut tree and they heard him call out, "To Kavanagh!" in answer, they supposed, to their mother who must have seen him from the kitchen door. It had been some time in the early spring, for Cora remembered that grape-hyacinths had come up in the lawn.

Afterward, they began to be poor. And never again, not once, did they see Granny Savage, although at Christmastime she always sent them presents, clothes, usually, from Marshall Field's, so grand they made the rest of their duds look like something the cat had dragged in. Their poorness showed itself gradually, so gradually, indeed, that they misconstrued it for something else: WHEN THEIR OLDER SISTERS Abigail and Evangeline, had to give up their fancy-dancing class, they thought Dan was only being cranky. For their friends, who were in their second year of ballet and were beginning round-dancing with boys, they invented a yarn that eventually they believed: they said they had no time for they were learning French because they were going to be sent to boarding school in Paris. (Who in all of Graymoor could say more than "Parlez-vous"?) Dan's bilious moods came oftener, his "spells" were terrifying: one time we went into Hubbard's Dry, where both Aunt Jane and Aunt Amy clerked, and inveighed against his father-in-law with such blood-curdling invective, such heart-splitting blasphemy that Mr. Hubbard himself ushered him out of the store like a hobo. And he looked a hobo: barefoot, his long underdrawers showing beneath his unlaced cavalry britches; his hair was as long as William Jennings Bryan's and he hadn't shaved in a week; tobacco juice oozed down his chin from the quid he held in his cheek. Mr. Hubbard sent the mortified McKinnon twin sisters home for the rest of the day, and they sent word to Mama by their hired girl to come right over. The town was appalled and off its head with delight; the school-children imitated Dan's limp and spat imaginary tobacco juice at the Savages' feet and made up tirades with nonsense words to scream at them until Abigail, with mysterious and quietly theatrical power, one day at recess stood on the top step of the stairs leading to the main door and commanded silence. "My father is a genius," she said. "My father is poetically licensed by President Wilson to do anything he likes. Hark to my words and from now on cease and desist this persiflage." It worked, as everything always worked for her when she let out those wondrous words and phrases, as harmless as fireflies but seeming, to her bowed audience, like red-hot buckshot. She must have been as shamed as the others but though she might be put on the rack or pinioned to the Catherine wheel, she was Dan's unflinching martyr.

When he was himself—that other self, the reader of Mommsen and Shakespeare and of Victor Hugh, the writer, the kindly spouse and papa—he would be barbered and shaved; he would whistle arias from *Madame Butterfly* and dance his little jig in front of Mama, sportively untie her apron strings and with it pretend to be a toreador and he would carol, "There's always the land, me bonny! There's always the star in the Lone Star State! The amber waves of grain wave o'er the Show-Me! And my ship, she is a-comin' in, lass o' the braes."

The children could not make head or tail of this impromptu spiel. Later on, they would learn that on those two days in Jefferson City, he had been wiped clean of all his capital and had, as well, made ducks and drakes of Granny's. Granny did not feel the pinch—the money he had hurled to the four winds had been her own, and Grandfather Savage's trust fund allowed her to go on being nearly as rich as she had always been. And he was far from destitute himself because he still shared the revenue from the productive Texas cattle ranches and the Missouri farms scattered all over the state. It was Granny's disgust at Dan's reckless, know-it-all prodigality that had made her send him packing. And there was something else: Granny, that smart, witty, well-read, sure-footed little woman had fallen hook, line and sinker for Mary Baker Eddy, led down the garden path by her daughter Lizzie who, in southern California, was prey to all diseases of the mind. And

Granny, indignant over the encroachments of age (her hearing in one ear was much diminished, she had several times felt dizzy when she dismounted Betsy Ross after riding in the sun) was easily persuaded that she could handle her flesh with her mind. In the beginning, she had been skeptical when in the copy of *Science and Health* that Aunt Lizzie had sent her, she had read among the testimonials printed at the back the unequivocal claim of a man that while chopping wood, he had swung his hatchet too high and had deeply gashed his temple, an injury that would most certainly have been fatal had he not immediately requested his wife to read to him from Mrs. Eddy. Within half an hour the Mortal Error was corrected, and where the wound and rushing blood had been there was nothing but a white painless swelling. But while she knew this to be bosh and while some of Mrs. Eddy's God-talk affronted her, she was converted and believed that she could heal her servants and her livestock *in absentia.*

Sometimes, at winter dusk before the open fire in the living room, Dan, reflecting as he peeled an apple with his Bowie ("I declare to goodness you're going to cut your fingers off with that desperado weapon!" cried Mama. "For land's sake, use your *pen* knife!" Dan went right on and finally let the whole unbroken dark red spiral skin fall into the kindling hod) would say to whoever was within earshot—Cora was sure that if there were no one in the room, he would address the stuffed golden pheasant on the mantel—"I mourned to see my Ma go daft. I lamented the degeration of that fine intellect. It riddled her like ergot through a stand of oats. You see there yonder that fair crop shimmering? Now close your eyes and look again and what do you see? Black blight."

Then he would throw his naked apple into the fire and listen to its juices hiss. "But for all of that, it was a joke. A joke! A high larruping opera comique and not unlike the one the Great Lord put on for Job." His laughter strangled him; his eyes screwed up like a bawling baby's and the veins on his forehead swelled and pulsed, a dreadful blue.

Mama no longer had her chafing-dish suppers. Nobody came to call except the aunts. Now and then Aunt Rowena came with the first cousins, Fannie, Faith and Florence, with whom the Savages were instructed to play although the mothers knew that their children hated one another and even such a peaceable game as Statues could end in a nosebleed or a broken collar bone. Florence, the oldest and the biggest, had once clapped a pail on Evangeline's head, jamming it down so hard that it wouldn't come off and Dan had had to cut it with his tin-shears; there wasn't even enough room in there for Evangeline to scream but she hopped around like somebody with St. Vitus dance while Dan crooned softly to her.

"Whoa, there, girl. Hold on there, girl. Your old Dan ain't going to cut your ear off." This reassurance sent her hurtling blindly into a cherry tree which she hugged for dear life and while she was thus occupied, Dan got the bucket off.

"It was all her fault," said Florence. "She double-dared me to."

"I never!" sobbed Evangeline, holding her ears. The tin-shears had cut clean through one of her pigtails and about an inch of it was gone. Abigail picked it up from the grass, its blue bow still tightly tied.

"You lie, Florence Sinclair," she said in her coldest, her most authoritative voice. "You like like a rug. The Savages hate the Sinclairs and will forever and a day. Avaunt, you three witches! Graymalkin calls!" Evangeline was calmed. The Sinclair sisters gingerly backed away. But Dan broke the spell by clapping his hands and crying out, "Bravissima! It'll soon be time for your first buskins, Mamsell Bernhardt!"

Wholly baffled, the three sisters ran into the house. After that, when Aunt Rowena came, the children were put into the dining room to play Twenty Questions or I Spy, and the door to the small parlor was left open so that the mothers could hear if a ruckus broke out. It never did, for the seven children were as quite as mice, trying to hear what the ladies were saying.

This life in Graymoor might have gone on for years and years, gone on until the last embattled tribesman was six feet under, if Grandfather McKinnon had not died. Or, as for some months afterward, Grandmother, Great Aunt Flora, Aunt Rowena and Mama were to say, been *murdered* by Jane and Amy, always known as "the girls." They ran away from home.

Who did they know in St. Louis high society to get them invitations to the Veiled Prophet's Ball? There were no kinsmen in St. Louis, no collaterals. A drummer came to Hubbard's Dry to sell a bill of goods and, by the way, to vamp those pretty twins with their mournful violet eyes and their perfect laughing lips? Of course not: Drummers were not connected to high echelons. The store was closed on Wednesday afternoons as was every other place of business, a practice carried over from New England whence the founding fathers had come. One Wednesday, Jane telephone home a little after eleven and there was no answer; Grandma and Great Aunt Flora were outside making sure that the men were transplanting that big old box elder to just the place they wanted it, and the hired girl was making soap and was at that tricky point of putting in the lye. But Central (Jessie Lovelady; after five o'clock Belle Bruce came on) said she'd keep on ringing and give the message which was, "Tell her we're going to have ourselves a picnic and won't be home for dinner." Well, Grandma was put out when Jessie Lovelady finally reached her, but she got over her pet—it *was* an awfully bonny autumn day, smelling of nuts. She always liked to have a little treat for dinner on the girls' day off and that day she had planned banana fritters, but never mind, she'd have them for supper instead. It didn't worry her until twilight came and they didn't come home and night came and they didn't come home. About nine o'clock she called Mama and Mama said she knew in her bones that something was *very* rottin in the state of Denmark. If they'd been abducted, they couldn't have telephoned. The picnic sounded to her like a fish-story, because from the year one the girls had been hemstitching linens and painting Haviland for thir hope-chests on their free afternoons. (They couldn't let Grandfather know what they were doing so they couldn't sew their dreams on Saturday night. On Saturday night they hemmed didies for the Heathen Chinee.) Mama told Grandma that she'd better call the police and she did. She got the Marshal himself, Mr. Doff, who told her to look in their rooms and see if they had taken any clothes and then to call him back. I say! Their closets and their bureau drawers were as clean as a whistle! She looked in the attic and gone was the trunk Mama had taken to Colorado when she went to teach at Summerlid! Gone were both hat-boxes! And the only umbrellas left in the umbrella stand were Mama's and Aunt Flora's, and the spare one in case it rained as an afternoon caller was saying goodbye. As soon as Marshal Doff heard this, he called Frank Ferguson, the jitney driver. Frank Ferguson knew every bit of everybody's business because he eavesdropped while he drove his high maroon Hupmobile and at the same time spied on pedestrians: if you wanted to know who had stopped using the jakes and moved indoors, ask Frank Ferguson and he would tell you that he had seen Mrs. Cobbett come out of Hubbard's on Tuesday at 11:22 a.m. carrying a sack that unmistakably contained a roll of bathroom paper.

Frank was asleep but he snapped to attention when the police chief called and he was overjoyed to say that why, yes, he had taken the McKinnon twins to the depot for the 1:45 inter-urban to Jeff City. Were they carrying any baggage? No, they weren't but one week ago that day, they had come up to him when he was parked in front of the P.O. and had asked him to come to their house at 7 p.m. to take a trunk and two hat-boxes and check them through to St. Louis. They gave him their tickets and he returned them the next day at Hubbard's Dry. All they had with them today was just their pocketbooks and umbrellas and a book apiece. They didn't do much talking; mainly they giggled, but they said enough to let him understand that they were going to the Veiled Prophet's Ball: he had wondered at the time, pardon him please, how they had managed to get their father's permission to go. Last Wednesday night at seven. The pieces were beginning to fit together. That was why those perfidious minxes, looking as if butter would melt in their mouths, had said they were so absolutely, pos*itively* fagged out from unpacking a shipment of winter coats at the store that morning that they could *not,* absolutely, pos*itively* could *not* go to Prayer Meeting. Grandma and Aunt Flora and the girls always had supper with the Widow Bird on Wednesday night at her house (she came to them for "high tea" after Christian Endeavor on Saturday afternoon) at five o'clock and this gave them ample time to be leisurely at table and do the washing up and even crochet for a little while until they went to the church just across the road on the dot of seven. It was then that Frank Ferguson had come to pick up their traps. How did he manage that big trunk all by himself? He didn't. Chub Jackson, Judge McIntyre's yard man and strong as an ox, had brought it down the steep brick steps cut into the lawn and he and it and the hat-boxes and the girls were rowed up there right on Aberdeen Avenue. Chub was ready with a couple of ropes and he strapped the trunk on the running board and then rode in the back seat down to the depot and took it off and put it on the St. Louis through baggage wagon. One of the twins, it might have been Jane, it might have been Amy, you couldn't tell them apart, had given him what Frank was pretty certain was four bits. (And he himself only charged two bits for the run. Life is like that.)

Mama and Grandma and Great Aunt Flora were terrified out of their wits. Aunt Rowena, basically a carnal woman, shrugged her shoulders and laughing meanly said, "I hope they get themselves some Good-time Charleys. I could put one to use myself." She despised Uncle Hugh who was despicable. And while she was motified to be Dan's in-law (Catch Hugh Sinclair chewing: Never!), in her heart of hearts she admired his eccentricity. This was a fact known to the children because after school one day, Randall was lying under the bandstand in the Lincoln Park, thinking. All of a sudden he heard Aunt Rowen's voice coming, he thought, from a ringside bench on the northeast side. "My brother-in-law, you know who he is, Dan Savage?" she said to someone.

"The writer. He got word yesterday that his novel has been accepted by Dodge and Company, the publishing concern in New York City." Her companion said, "Sakes! My, Maud must be proud." "She is," said Aunt Rowena. And she was. Only, at that time, the jealous sister's statement was not true because her sister had not told *her* the truth. The only one in Graymoor who knew the truth was Dan.

In those dreadful days (The Ordeal as it came to be known) between the twins' disappearance and Grandfather McKinnon's return for the Sabbath bonfire, so much simmered under so many kettle-lids that everybody walked on tippy-toe, including Dan, The Great.

That Sunday, the diminished McKinnon congregation sat in Grandfather's parlor, erect of spine and apparently alert, although a look of languid disease showed forth now and again in all the captives. It seemed to Cora that Grandfather had never read with so much righteous rage as he did this afternoon: his voice rocked the house, its walls were going to tumble down like Jericho. How had Grandma broken the news to him? Poor little tea-cosy of a woman, she must have been scared silly. The clock in the hall chimed four and, at the last sonorous boom, something happened.

Cora and Abigail were sitting side by side on an uncushioned ottoman. Cora was demented with discipline, distempered with swallowed screams and swallowed yawns. Silently she kicked her Mary Janes together; woefully, in the absence of anything else to do, she crossed her eyes. Suddenly, and she did not know why, she turned rogue and tried to tickle Abigail who wrenched away in surprise, almost toppling off the slippery seat. Although they were to one side of Grandfather's ken, he saw the quiet scuffle out of the corner of his eye and he wheeled on them like Wrath.

"Wantons!" and he would have impaled them on his pointing finger if they had not been across the room from him. "Is a man to be made a gowk of in his own castle by the blethering of females?"

Blethering! They had not made a sound.

Abigail hotly declared that Cora was solely to blame for this outrageous impudence, this dangerous breach of decorum on the Good Lord's day. But Grandfather ordered her to be silent and he gave a familiar lecture on the wages of sin, the high price of defiance of authority, the destiny of mockers who misconducted themselves on Sunday. He raved of the cauldrons and the griddles. Weeping, his sister, Great Aunt Flora, hysterically cried, "Don't faunch yourself into a lather! Duncan! Duncan!" and he gored her with a look.

By no means finished with his diatribe, he said, "Hark!" and flicking *The Book of Martyrs* to, he opened the Old Testament to Isaiah and read of the Fall of Babylon. Red in the face with rectitude, veins standing out, dark and vermicular in his neck and on his forehead, as Dan's did when he sneered, he read:

"Therefore the Lord will smite with a scab the crown of the head of the daughters of Zion, and the Lord will discover their secret parts. In that day the Lord will take away the bravery of their tinkling ornaments about their feet, and their cauls, and their round tires like the moon, the chains and the bracelets, and the mufflers, the bonnets and the ornaments of the legs, and the headbands, and the tablets, and the earrings, the rings, and nose jewels, the changeable suits of apparel and the mantles, and the wimples, and the crisping pins, the glasses, the fine linen, and the hoods and the veils. And it shall come to pass that instead of sweet smell, there shall be stink; and instead of a girdle, a tent; and instead of well-set hair, baldness; and instead of a stomacher, a girding of sackcloth; and burning instead of beauty. Thy men . . ."

It was probably the violent, accusing voice (which was really directed at his twins) more than the words that made Cora finally cry out with terror and she ran to hide her face in Mama's lap. She knelt there shuddering and hoarsely babbling, "I don't want to be bald! I don't! I don't!"

Her uproar was contagious and all the other Savage children and the Sinclairs, in their different ways, turned mutinous.

Abigail cried, "It isn't fair, Grandfather! It was all Cora's fault!"

Evangeline giggled and squeaked, "Oracay illway avehay otay earway anay igway!" and Faith Sinclair, a precocious little snit, said, "Cora Savage is the Whore of Babylon."

"Grandfather McKinnon," said Randall solemnly, standing up as if he were in school, "is it true that we are descended from monkeys?"

"Children, children, that's enough!" said Grandma, shaking her head and clapping for order.

"Monkeys!" little Fannie Sinclair was fascinated. "How come, Randy? How come *monkeys?*"

The pandemonium lasted only a minute or two and then the children, realizing what they had done—had headed for the seething pits and locked themselves on the wrong side of the pearly gates—froze in their attitudes. But brief as the revolution had been, it had had a remarkable effect on their grandfather. He seemed to shrivel and his skin was as gray as the trunk of a tree. He pounded his craggy fists on the table. "What is the meaning of this sacrilege and insubordination?" he demanded, but he was so choked with passion that his voice lost its body and it came out thick and pallid. "Absconding and tricks and pranks and now *evolution!*"

Gasping for breath, coughing, alarmingly red again, he railed like a stark staring crazy man, called them all backsliders, apostates, iconoclasts, the gall and wormwood of his life. His storm was long but his thunder was a squawk and this thunderbolts were duds. He had lost his women and he had lost his only lad.

Holy cow! His face was bleeding. A fast red flood was coming from his beak; bewildered, he did nothing about it. His arms, too long for his coatsleeves so that his big wrists showed below the cuffs, hung slack at his sides and he relaxed his hands so that they were no longer fists. Everyone watched, astonished, as that red eruption continued to ride down his face. An age went by.

Then Grandma, galvanized at last, went to him, gently pushed him back into his chair and tried to stanch the nosebleed with a foolish little handkerchief.

"Send away the bairns," she said. "Maud, get me some ice." But Mama did not move. No one moved. They sat motionless, witless with astonishment and with a strange, inadmissable embarrassment; the crumbling of the tyrant made them shy.

Grandfather, accepting his wife's ministrations like a dog or a child, put his hand to his forehead. "Giddy," he said. His voice was as far away as if he were in another room. The forehead that he touched above his heavy, raven eyebrows glistened with a morbid sweat. Cora ran from the room, ran from the earthquake, and outdoors hurled herself into a pile of fresh raked maple leaves. But dreadful curiosity drove her back into the house and as she stood in the doorway, she saw Grandfather collapse, fall from the chair dragging the Bible with him. He lay there like a tree hewn down, his branches every whichway; his loud, jerky breathing was a funny wind and his nose kept copiously bleeding, spilling over his beard, staining the pages of the Bible where it had broken open.

"Maud!" said Grandma. "Will you let your father bleed to death for the want of a whang of ice?"

Mama got up then and seeing Cora said sharply, "Scat! You may have killed my father, you bad girl!"

He did not die that day. Dr. Grimes said that he had had a stroke and that he might live for long years yet, but on the other hand, he might go in a second apoplexy or a third, a fourth, a twenty-fifth. He wanted to know what had brought this on and when he heard about Jane and Amy, he, a sour elder of the U.P. church, was scandalized to bits.

The next Wednesday (three momentous Wednesdays in a row!) a postal came from the twins: they had had a tintype made of themselves, probably at an amusement park, posed in a cardboard Pierce Arrow and on the back of it they had written, "Having a wonderful time and never coming back to Graymoor. Love to all." There was a row of hugs and kisses and they had made a grinning face in the last hug.

And they never did come back to Graymoor, never in their lives. The next time they were heard from, more than a year later, they were both in New South Wales and both of them were married. No one ever knew whom they had gone to visit in St. Louis; they never were sure that the girls really had gone to the Veiled Prophet's Ball or had just said that to impress Frank Ferguson.

Grandfather had three more strokes within a month, and each one left him with a fresh derangement. He spent his time in the parlor in his black leather sermonizing chair, his great shoulders hunched together as he hugged Grandma's Paisley shawl to him, for he was always cold. His eyes were bloodshot; they looked sore.

He seemed half asleep—his whole life was one long doze and when the grandchildren went to visit him, a different child each day, he paid no heed to them for the five minutes they stood before him. He said nothing but his stomach querulously growled. He withered and dried; sometimes his five wits were altogether lost to him and then he fought and sought tenaciously until he collected them.

He died in his sleep the night before Thanksgiving. Wednesday again. Woden's day. "Woden was the Norsemen's Jehovah," said Dan matter-of-factly. "His familiars were two black ravens named Hugin and Munin." And then, funereally he intoned, "There were twa corbies/Sat in a tree." And laughed his laugh.

Granny Savage had lost her mind; Grandfather McKinnon could no longer shackle Mama and, as soon as school was over in May, the Savages moved west.

ODE

by PHILIP SCHULTZ

from THE KENYON REVIEW

nominated by THE KENYON REVIEW *and Marvin Bell*

Grandma stuffed her fur coat into the icebox.
God Himself couldn't convince her it wasn't a closet.
"God take me away this minute!" was her favorite Friday night
    prayer.
Nothing made sense, she said. Expect heartburn & bad teeth, not
    sense.
Leave a meat fork in a dairy dish & she'd break the dish & bury
    the fork.
"I spit on this house, on this earth & on God for putting me
in this life that spits on me night & day," she cried, forgetting the
    barley
in barley soup. It wasn't age. She believed she was put here to
    make
one unforgivable mistake after another. Thou shalt be
    disappointed
was God's first law. Her last words were: "Turn off the stove
before the house blows up." Listen, I'm thirty-four already
& nothing I do is done well enough. But what if disappointment
is faith & not fate? What if we never wanted anything enough to
    hurt over?
All I can say is spring came this year with such a wallop
the trees are still shaking. Grandma, what do we want from them?
What do we want?

THREE STUDIES
FOR A HEAD
OF JOHN THE BAPTIST

by CHANA BLOCH

from FIELD

nominated by FIELD

> *In memory of*
> *Daphne Andronikou*

1

His beard spreads in front of him
as if in the bath, the little
hairs crinkled.

It's a copper tray, embossed
with palm trees and turtledoves,
polished to a high gloss.

The head sits off-center,
a beaker among
the heaped oranges.
So this is what it feels like.
Coolness; oriental spices. His eyes
look around, curious,

as the flutes tune up.

2

At the corner, as the sun cut,
I held my head in my hands.

It was heavy,
like a bag of groceries
I shift from one hip to the other.

I wanted to set it down somewhere,
a windowsill,
a doorway, a low brick step
where it could flash its carved grin all day for the children.

3

The elegance
of the sharpened knife—it's not
the head that imagines it

but the back of the neck
that must carry such a stone
on its bent stalk,

that cannot speak,

gray-green, unbelieving.

THE GENTLEMEN IN THE U-BOATS

by SHARON OLDS

from NEW LETTERS

nominated by Carolyn Forché and Bruce Weigl

Yes, this is what they wanted—
to be underneath the surface of the sea
at night, in the blackness, green light of the
instruments glaring up at their chins,
gathering in the stubble on their jaws,
glittering over the curved mantle of their
eyeballs. This is the place. The smell is of
diesel oil, toilets, bilge, mildew,
sweat. It's a hundred and twenty degrees,
the black bread is white with fur,
they haven't been above water for days,
the lights are always burning, bilge-pumps whirring,
diesels throbbing, toilets overflowing,
they will probably be killed, and it is all worth it
to be here, now, in the depths, in the dark,
coming up in the path of a convoy—
sixty ships. Their pupils sharpen to
tiny points, like black dogs
running in circles faster and faster.
In the reek of feces, jism, bile,
their elegant hands hovering over the
levers, they rise and break the surface on a
starry night, the sea glistens,
there is nothing on their minds but beauty as they fire.

THE GENERAL
AND THE SMALL TOWN

fiction by CHEN SHIXU

from OCTOBER

nominated by Barbara Ma and Frank Taylor

(EDITOR'S NOTE: *after decades of repression, literature in China was allowed some freedom in 1979 and 1980. Much of the new fiction—often critical of the authorities—was published by Chinese versions of the small press. Here is one such story from China's October Press.*)

IN A SMALL TOWN like ours, miles from anywhere, the slightest change attracted great attention.

"Hey! Does anyone know why they're putting up a new house near the prison at the foot of Ringworm Hill? Who does it belong to? Are they enlarging the jail again?"

Ringworm Hill, about two *li* from the town centre, was actually a large rocky mound.

"You're all so dim!" The owner of this mocking tone popped his head out from behind the door of a shop. He was the barber. He was bald on top, though a few remaining hairs at the sides were carefully oiled and combed.

473

Known as a newsmonger, he was an important figure in the small town. Though confined to his shop, he seemed to have his fingers on the pulse of the town and was the first to know of any new development. When passing on news, people often started with, "According to the barber. . . ." The barber liked to add a touch of drama to the news. If he heard something important, he never announced it in his small shop. He would, like now, step out and go to the crossroads where there were all kinds of stalls.

"I bet you've no idea. The house is for a general who will soon come here to live."

"What? A general? Come to live with us?"

The news caused quite a stir. In a backwater like ours, the coming of a general was sensational news. It was indeed a great honour bestowed on us.

The barber cleared his throat and warned, damping their enthusiasm, "But don't raise your hopes! In fact, it's nothing special." The listeners craned forward, their curiosity aroused, asking why.

"Why? Humph! Listen, but this is for your ears only. Don't let on. Strictly confidential! The general's been dismissed! He's been exiled here!"

"Exiled? Why?"

"He was a renegade."

People gaped in astonishment. Like a bolt from the blue it struck at their vanity. They were disappointed and downcast.

"In name he's a retired officer." An ingenious propagandist, the barber regained the listener's waning attention. "He still keeps his rank of general."

Then he continued in a low voice, "He was allowed to keep either his army rank or his Party membership. I may as well tell you all about it. People like us are just ordinary citizens, that's all. But he was an officer and a Party member. Now why do you think he chose to remain in the army?" He stopped abruptly, letting them ponder over this question. Holding their breath, they looked at one another, not knowing what to say.

Then a young porter from the transportation team, having put aside his barrow and elbowed into the crowd, broke the silence.

"In my view, he should have kept his Party membership. It's an honour!" Quite a few people seconded him.

The barber pursed his lips disapprovingly.

"No, it's better to remain in the army," an old tailor observed prudently. "A man has to eat. Where can he get money from if he is demobbed? What can he live on if he's no income? He's probably no skills and you can't expect an old man like him to till the land, can you?"

"Right, you've got a good financial brain," remarked the barber, patting him hard on his shoulder. Excited, the tailor grew red, feeling greatly flattered.

"That's just what the higher-ups thought too, so they pensioned him off, allowing him to wear his army uniform." He paused to glance at the young porter and went on, "Don't you know, as a high-ranking officer he gets a fat pay?"

People exclaimed in admiration. But talking of money reminded the barber that he hadn't started work yet and he hurried back to his shop.

But someone caught his coat tail, asking, "Tell us, when will he come?"

"Haven't you anything in that thick head of yours?" He was obviously impatient. "Don't you see that house? When it's completed, he'll certainly move in there."

Reluctantly, people scattered, murmuring their guesses and predictions of sighing over the ill-fated general, taking the news to all the corners of the town.

Now, with the listeners departing, let's have a look at this lovely little town.

The town had two streets only wide enough to allow the passage of one jeep. Six hundred metres long altogether, they crossed at the centre of the town. The streets were paved with flagstones here and there, while paint peeled from the jutting-out buildings. All these showed its antiquity.

A stream, only ankle-deep, meandered around the town. Unfortunately, on its banks were heaped piles of rubbish and debris.

It was really surprising! People gaped when they first set eyes on the general. Everybody thought the same, "No wonder he was dismissed. An old duffer like him doesn't deserve to be called a general!"

What should a general look like then? Though we'd never met one before, he didn't fool us. A general should have grey hair, straight eyebrows, and perhaps a paunch. He must be tall and strong, looking impressive and awe-inspiring like in the films. But this man was small, wizened and wrinkled. Moreover, he was slightly hunched and lame in one leg.

Far from being broken by his unlucky circumstances, he paid great attention to his appearance as if to make up for his poor physique. Whenever he walked in the streets, his uniform was always well ironed without any creases, and he held himself straight like a soldier. The red star on his cap and his two red collar insignia stood out brightly. No matter how stifling the weather, he kept his jacket collar buttoned. Though lame in one leg from an old war wound, he walked steadily. However, all this unfortunately reminded us of his disgrace.

We often watched him, not in awe or contempt, but out of curiosity. He didn't seem to mind at all. On the contrary, he walked about, though with some difficulty, the second day after his arrival.

Leaning on his shining wooden stick, he limped from one end of the street to the other. Or sometimes, he strolled along the dry stream bed strewn with litter. Someone said, tongue in cheek, that the old man kept moving habitually because he had walked all over China!

After a short period, he began to make some unfavourable comments about our small town, in which we had lived happily for a long time. He asked, for instance, "Why don't you spend some money on putting a tarmac surface on the two streets?" or "Why don't you dig a large pit on the other side of the stream for your rubbish so that it can be made into compost?" Our sophisticated and clever local cadres would excuse themselves saying, "Where can we get the money for it? Our salaries are pretty low!" or "We're simply too busy!" Their listeners would chuckle, catching the dig at the general.

Our feelings towards this queer general were rather mixed. Though disgraced, he still got a decent pay. We all felt his criticisms and suggestions were well meant, yet no one was willing to befriend him.

Apparently, he soon noticed our mood, for he stopped making any more embarrassing criticisms. Instead, he found himself a place at the crossroads. There under an old camphor tree, whose top had once been struck by lightning, just opposite the barber's shop, he stood upright sometimes for hours, supported by his stick. Blinking his bleary eyes, he stood musing silently. No one knew what was in his mind.

His posture was really amusing. Vendors nearby raised their heads to glance at him from time to time, and even passers-by lingered to look at him before continuing on their way. Behind the glass windows of his shop, the barber gazed at him standing in the dusty street and joked cheerfully, "What do you think he looks like?"

"A sentry," someone said.

The barber shook his head.

"A traffic policeman then," said another.

He shook his head again. After some further exchanges, the barber said matter-of-factly, "Have you ever been to Hankou? At one end of Sanmin Road, there's a bronze statue of a figure standing erect and holding a walking stick. Just like him. Exactly!"

Gradually, people got used to seeing the general standing there, like a bronze statue. He became like the coppersmiths, cobblers and tinkers at corners of the crossroads. If you didn't see one of them for a couple of days, you would feel there was something missing.

But he was not a statue, he was a man, and one with a shrewd mind moreover. And one day people would discover that he was also possessed of a hot temper.

One Sunday, there was a great commotion in front of the butcher's, as some young rascals with their baskets on their backs fooled around, enjoying making a racket.

The general stood as usual viewing the scene, while his hand holding the stick trembled slightly and the veins in his temples swelled in anger. Suddenly he limped across, raised his stick and tapped a soldier on the back. Wet with sweat, he was squeezing his way through the crowds and shouting boisterously. Turning his head abruptly, he met the old man's blood-shot gaze. He withdrew from the throng at once and asked, "Anything I can do for you, sir?" Though a new recruit, he decided that the old man must be a high-ranking officer.

"Tidy yourself up before speaking to me!"

Darting a timid, worried glance at the general, the cherubic-

faced soldier quickly righted his cap, did up his collar buttons
rolled down his sleeves, and finally lowered his head, staring down
at his shoes.

"Which unit are you from? What's your job?"

"I'm a cook in the mess of the garrison stationed here."

A few brief seconds of silence followed.

"Attention!" the general suddenly shouted. This professional
harsh order immediately silenced the noisy crowd. Heads turned
to look at the two soldiers, who seemed oblivious of everything
around them.

Panting, the old man gave a second order, "Turn left! At the
double! Quick march!"

Still holding himself erect, the general breathed heavily, gazing
at the retreating figure.

All was very quiet now at the crossroads. As though checked by
some stranger power, the jostling, noisy crowd automatically fell
into line. At that moment, they felt the might of the old man, who
had once commanded thousands of troops.

Not long after, another incident shocked the small town, making
those who were inclined to side with the weak realize that something was wrong with their present situation.

It was inevitable that the old general, who had been through
hard times, had had his health impaired. Apart from the care of his
wife, once a head nurse in a large hospital, the general was
permitted regular check-ups in an army hospital some fify li away.
A sign of charity perhaps. He could also go to the town's hospital in
an emergency.

One day, he became pale and ill, breaking out in a cold sweat. As
he was entering the local hospital, supported by his wife, a country
woman who had been sitting on a bench by the consulting room
suddenly tugged at his coat, begging, "Please save my child! I
hurried over thirty li to get here before dawn, hoping to see the
doctor as soon as possible, but. . . ."

Inside it was so dim that they could hardly see each other. The
general felt the boy's forehead, then started. "Hurry up!" he
shouted. "Take him to the doctor at once!" Then he tore into the
consulting room and said to the doctor seated at a desk, "Doctor!
Here's an urgent case!"

Sitting behind the desk was the doctor, the wife of the town mayor and head of the hospital. Her occupation, social position and the way she carried herself served to demonstrate that she was the most important woman in the town. At that moment, she was listening to the heart of one of her distant relatives and chatting with the patient about her daughter's dowry. She was so engrossed that she forgot to remove the stethoscope. Interrupted by the general's cry, she glared at him and said, "Register first." Then she turned back to her relative, all smiles.

"He registered ages ago!"

"Then you'll have to wait. . . . Yes, it's worth having a daughter."

"But he was registered first."

She turned abruptly and asked, "Little Wang, did you call number one?"

"Of course!" replied a young nurse bent over giving an injection.

"See," said the doctor and, turning to the peasant woman, she added, "you weren't here when your number was called. You'll have to join the queue again."

"But I was here! Our village doctor told me that my boy was suffering from acute pneumonia. . . ." The woman, carrying her child in her arms, broke off, out of either nervousness or disappointment.

"She probably didn't hear you clearly," said the general.

"Then she can learn a thing or two about our regulations. A country has its laws and a hospital its rules. If we don't stick to the rules, there'll be chaos, won't there?" Throwing her stethoscope on the desk, she shot the general a reproachful glance.

"But this is an urgent case! You can't be so rigid! Now, what number was this patient?" asked the old man, pointing to the relative.

"H'm! So you've come to make trouble today, eh? Are you the kid's father or grandfather?"

"You should be ashamed of yourself!"

"What? Ashamed? You old fool! Why should I be ashamed? Am I anti-Party or a renegade?"

The general raised his stick.

The cocky woman screamed, protecting her head with her arms.

It was so quiet that you could hear a pin drop in the room. Her relative was flabbergasted. Nobody came out to grab the general's stick. It remained quivering in mid air. People hoped it would strike the doctor's snub nose.

But the stick did not fall. Instead, the old man stretched to grab the other end and snapped it in two.

Turning with difficulty, he asked his wife, "Is there any medicine at home?"

She nodded, knowing that he meant medicine for pheumonia.

In a trembling voice, he asked the peasant woman, "Do you trust me? Then follow us!"

The news of this incident soon got around. Now even timid people dared to show their dissatisfaction.

It was true that we were rather cut off from the world and, as a result, we were rather easily cowed. But it was precisely this that made us rely on our own judgements. If a "renegade" helped others in difficulty while a "Communist" bullied the people, shouldn't their titles be exchanged?

For a couple of days, there was no sign of the general under the camphor tree. People began to anxiously whisper about him. It was said that his condition had taken a turn for the worse. And since the incident in the consulting room, he had been deprived of the right to use the town government jeep to go to the military hospital.

Late one night, some fine young men led by the porter came to the general's house. They put the old man on a stretcher and hurried him off to the military hospital.

1976 began terribly. It was bitterly cold. Overhead the clouds were hanging thick and heavy, while the ground was muddy and slippery. Our little town looked more desolate than ever.

As if favoured by fate, despite the bad weather, the people in the town had the monotony broken by some encouraging news.

Just after the New Year, the barber came to the crossroads with an air of importance. No doubt, he had something vital to announce. People gathered around him at once. Having cleared his throat, he began, "You know what, the general's no longer a renegade! His case has been cleared!"

"Are you sure? How do you know?"

"You don't believe me?" chided the barber, glowering at the questioner. He never tolerated any doubts about his information. However, he went on, "If you don't believe me, ask him."

"I told him," admitted the porter, elbowing his way forward. Not used to speaking in public, he blushed. "When we were in the hospital, two men from the general's original army came and said that the general's record before he joined the Red Army had been cleared. He never betrayed the revolution."

"Humph! Ridiculous to have wronged a veteran revolutionary for such a long time," the barber butted in with his comment. "I said long ago that the general was every inch a damn good man! Indeed. . . ."

"Indeed, sufferings test a man." People sighed, sympathizing with the general.

"Then he'll soon leave us, won't he?" the tailor raised his question hesitatingly.

A far-sighted man! When the inevitability of this was forced into their minds, the townsfolk again became depressed.

"Well," the barber said after a sigh, scratching his bald head. "It's only natural. Ours is a small town. How can a little temple house a big Buddha?"

People felt sad. It was always the same: you realized a thing's worth only when you had to part with it.

"What a mean lot you are!" the porter snapped in anger. "The Party and the state need him badly. You always wished him good luck. Now it's come, you're miserable. Isn't that selfish?"

Yes, it was. The general had his work to do, which was of vital importance. After all, we couldn't ask him to be our mayor, could we? So his leaving would be something worth celebrating.

People looked expectantly in the direction of the hill, hoping that the general would come and stand under the camphor tree as before. They longed to see him, if possible, have a chat with him.

The desire to see the general grew stronger. Then someone suggested that everyone should go to call on him, since he had come back the previous day and was still unable to walk about.

Why not? So the crowds headed for Ringworm Hill.

The desolate, rocky hill became a lively spot. Normally people steered clear of it if they could. There was neither wood to collect nor grass to graze cattle. Moreover, for centuries, it was where those executed had been buried. If you had to pass this ominous hill, you'd certainly give it a wide berth.

But now, the house beside the prison was like a sacred place for pilgrims.

As they were swarming around the door, they saw the general inside, hunched over and looking thinner. They halted, not daring to cross the threshold, filled with shyness and awe. Even a wag like the barber was lost for words. Only when people nudged him, he muttered in a fluster, "General!" But it was inaudible, even to himself.

For some time, the general did not know what to say either, his eyes wide open in surprise. But when he soon realized their intention, tears brimmed over and streamed down his lined face.

Although Ringworm Hill was not far from the town, this was the first time that people had seen it joyfully. They were also astonished to find rows of pits for planting trees on the slope behind the general's house.

"Are you going to plant so many trees, general?"

"Yes. I hope to change the colour of this mound before meeting Marx in the nether world. It's a pity that fruit trees won't grow here. Still, we'll make do with pine trees."

"Do you mean to live here as a hermit?"

"Hermit?"

"Yes."

"What an idea! Ha! Ha! . . ." The general laughed heartily until he was seized by a fit of coughing. Then he went on, "My aim is to safeguard the small trees until they've grown big enough. When you've some time, we'll divert the stream too, build some irrigation canals and a reservoir. This will help your fields. The hills will be green and the stream will retain water all year round. If we plant some flowers, and keep some birds and animals, we'll have a fine park. I'd like to be the park keeper. And you, young man," he patted the porter on his shoulder, "can bring your beautiful wife there and have fun. I assure you I won't close the gate ahead of time!"

"Then promise not to hit them with your stick if you catch them kissing each other behind your house," the barber teased, as the people roared with laughter.

"How shall we say goodbye to him? What shall we give him as a keepsake? How can we keep in touch with him?" Those were the questions everyone in the town thought and discussed. Some even quarrelled over the order of inviting the general to dinners.

But all of a sudden, the town was overshadowed by the death of Premier Zhou. He died at a time when he was most needed. The morning that his death was announced, the general, supported by his wife, suddenly appeared under the camphor tree at the crossroads.

The sun was up, pale and dull. It was extremely cold. The small town looked more bleak and gloomy, silent as death, as if frozen numb by cold and sorrow.

The general, standing in the cutting wind, looked very pale and sallow, his deep-set eyes circled by dark shadows, his face grim. He stood erect, as solid as a bronze statue.

"Comrades. . . ." he shouted in his hoarse voice. It sounded so unfamiliar that many stopped to listen to him. The old man bent and unzipped his bag with an effort, revealing black mourning arm-bands. Raising his head, he uttered, swallowing hard, "Please. . . ."

There was no need to say any more. People, one by one, took the bands and put them on their arms.

"Whose idea was this?" A hand, its fingers brown from too much smoking, suddenly touched the shoulder of the general. It was the mayor.

The general was silent.

"We've already told you that no one is going to hold any mourning ceremony. What are you up to?"

The general did not even raise his eyes.

Turning around, the furious mayor bellowed at the crowd, "Don't move, any of you! Take off your arm-bands!"

But no one complied.

"Disobeying, eh? Old tailor, you take it off first!"

The tailor was stunned. Looking at the mourning arm-band and then at the mayor's angry face, he trembled for a second. Before dawn, the general had knocked at his door and given him a roll of black cloth. The bad news had upset him dreadfully, but he had realized at once what his visitor wanted him to do. Together, they sat down to work grief-stricken.

Now this indignant petty official was trying to force him to throw his band on the ground in shame. But it was not merely a matter of an arm-band, but of a heart loyal to the late premier. Could anything be more insulting? Clever, scrupulous and lawabiding, he never did anything harmful to others. Though he had bitter memories of being insulted and humiliated, none was worse than this. He would not swallow it.

He looked up and met the general's burning eyes, which scorched his heart. With quivering lips, he said slowly, "Is it against the law to mourn Premier Zhou? Do what you like to me. I'm a tailor. I won't die of hunger wherever I go. Sorry, I won't take the arm-band off."

"To mourn Premier Zhou isn't against the law!"

"We won't take our arm-bands off!"

Those docile, unambitious people had gone mad! They stood united in rebellion! The sense of justice, buried in their hearts, had been aroused by a general in exile, shattering their traditional timidness and humility.

Nonplussed, the mayor turned to the general.

But the old man did not even glance at him. Calm and concentrating, he seemed to be commanding a battle.

Only his wife knew the mental and physical pain racking his frail body. Despite his strained nerves and aching muscles, he stood erect. She dared not say anything, though her heart was torn.

"You'll pay for this!" snarled the mayor, his face distorted by rage. Then he took to his heels and disappeared round a corner.

Suddenly, the general gasped, short of breath, and collapsed.

A few days later, the barber heard the shocking news that the general would live in the town for the rest of his life as an "honorary" general, because of his new "mistake". This was the first time that the barber kept a piece of news to himself. He had no heart to pass it on.

Just like the changeable weather in early spring, the people became depressed once more after their few days of happiness.

Ringworm Hill was again silent. Crowds came to see the general every day, their faces showing no trace of joy.

The general never again left his bed after his collapse. In and out of a coma, he sometimes ran a high temperature, staring at the ceiling with glazed eyes, raving deliriously or muttering away.

One day, suddenly his mind cleared. Scanning each anxious face, which showed momentary delight and surprise, he said with difficulty yet distinctly, "I . . . I will not leave you. I'll look after the park and . . . you must plant trees . . . repair the roads . . . dig a canal. You won't drive me away, will you? Good. . . ."

The general died. But his noble character had left an indelible impression on the people.

Then came an order from the authorities: the body of the general was to be cremated on the spot. No notice was to be given to his relatives or friends and there was to be no obituary, no mourning ceremony. It was a stupid decision, but they wanted to have everything under their control. In fact, no one complied with it.

The people were calm, yet stubborn, and did it their way. A mourning committee was elected, and it decided at once to hold a traditional, grand funeral. Quickly, the townsfolk went into action.

The oldest citizen contributed his cypress coffin, the only one still remaining in the town; the tailor made the shroud that night; the barber spent a long time giving the general a face-lift. When the corpse was put into the coffin, incense and an oil lamp were lit. The boy, whose life the general had saved, and his parents had tramped thirty *li* to join the funeral. Dressed in mourning, he served as a filial son. People not only from the town but also from the surrounding villages came to present their wreaths and mourning streamers. The huge wreath sent by the nearby garrison, whose cook had once been scolded by the general, was particularly eye-catching.

The dawn sky was overcast on the day the funeral took place. Heavy clouds hung low over the town and open country. According to his will, the deceased wanted his ashes to be scattered over the hillside. However, the long funeral procession first headed for the town. With the bier at the head, carried by sixteen stalwart young men, people marched through both short streets, which nevertheless took them the whole morning. Finally they stopped under the camphor tree, and many people made memorial speeches expressing their grief, regrets and vows.

But two people were strongly against such a funeral. One was the general's wife. She argued that her husband had been a Communist and a revolutionary soldier and had asked in his will to be cremated. Before she could finish, people pleaded with tears in their eyes, "The general would understand. He wouldn't complain. We've no objection to his being cremated later. But please let us have our way for the time being." She closed her eyes with an effort, fighting back her tears. The other was the mayor, but he could do nothing except peep through his screened window. Furiously, he vowed through clenched teeth, "Wait till I deal with you!"

One year later, the "gang of four" fell. It was not the barber or the old tailor, but the mayor and his followers, who were disgraced at last.

When the people began to modernize their small town, they first put the general's wishes into practice.

In the last three months of that year, pits for tree-planting were dug all over Ringworm Hill and some other hills near by; the rubbish dump by the stream was removed; and the two streets given a tarmac surface. Diverting the stream was already included in the town's water conservancy plan, and the first phase of the project worked on by several thousand people was completed before the Spring Festival.

Everything went well and smoothly but, of course, there were occasional quarrels too. Once, however, there was a bitter one which shook the whole town.

It was about whether or not they should build a monument in memory of the general under the camphor tree. The porter and his mates were all for it, while the barber was in two minds. As people argued heatedly, the tailor picked his way into the crowd. Raising his hand, he pointed to the tree and said in choked voice, "Look here, what's better than this tree in memory of him? It's old and its bark has peeled, but its roots are still alive. Look at the new twigs and the lush leaves. . . ." He faltered, swallowing hard.

Suddenly the townsfolk felt as if the tree had turned into the general wearing his green uniform buttoned at the collar, with a bright red star on his cap and red insignia on his collar. Leaning on his stick, he stood erect and blinked his eyes from time to time, silently watching the changes in the small town.

Imagining this, they forgot all about their disagreement.

—translated by various translators

DYING

by ROBERT PINSKY

from POETRY

nominated by Sherod Santos and Teo Savory

Nothing to be said about it, and everything—
The change of changes, closer or further away:
The Golden Retriever next door, Gussie, is dead,

Like Sandy, the Cocker Spaniel from three doors down
Who died when I was small; and every day
Things that were in my memory fade and die.

Phrases die out: first, everyone forgets
What doornails are; then after certain decades
As a dead metaphor, *"dead as a doornail"* flickers

And fades away. But someone I know is dying—
And though one might say glibly, "everyone is,"
The different pace makes the difference absolute.

The tiny invisible spores in the air we breathe,
That settle harmlessly on our drinking water
And on our skin, happen to come together

With certain conditions on the forest floor,
Or even a shady corner of the lawn—
And overnight the fleshy, pale stalks gather,

The colorless growth without a leaf or flower;
And around the stalks, the summer grass keeps growing
With steady pressure, like the insistent whiskers

That grow between shaves on a face, the nails
Growing and dying from the toes and fingers
At their own humble pace, oblivious

As the nerveless moths, that live their night or two—
Though like a moth a bright soul keeps on beating,
Bored and impatient in the monster's mouth.

SILO LETTER

IN THE DEAD OF

A WARM WINTER

by MICHAEL MCFEE

from THE MASSACHUSETTS REVIEW

nominated by THE MASSACHUSETTS REVIEW

Silo: almost a greeting, or a goodbye, hi,
hello, so long, aloha, all in one: *silo,* Steve,
after so long, little to tell. Still no snow's
my main plaint: what's winter without weather?
(How's that for a Swinburnian hibernian line?)
Lately my mind's been turning, windmillish
tilting in the Piedmont, seriously, to silos:
a sevenfold interpretation, in fact, to pass
the time while internally combusting with wife
here and there, a Neo-Agrarian, Demi-Southern
Digression in the Modern Kind. To wit:

1. ARCHITECTURAL

Somewhere, I swear, old Walt Gropius, dean
(as they say) of the boxy Bauhaus, wrote: "Silos
are the unnoticed majesty of American architecture,"
one of those perverse and impressive aphorisms
I always relished but never believed. Well, one day
last fall, in *(sic)* transit *(gloria)*, sun setting
across a field combed with corn or tobacco,
farm cutout-plain on the horizon, I comprehended,
like with those photos of Chartres across a pasture
outside town: epiphany on State Road 1000
and something. It was then I realized how bliss-
fully ignorant farmers had translated millenia
of architectural history into a feed pit,
campanile to the barn's cathedral, classical
as a tin column, even domed and sectioned:
what a hybrid to hang *(true* American Gothic!)
Angus-like on the sign at the drive's mouth!

2. ASTRONOMICAL

Simply that a dry and drafty silo
makes a stellar observatory for chickens.

3. ETYMOLOGICAL

Root of silence. (Forget the *OED.*) Indo-
European *silo-,* suffixed (stative) form
*sil-e- in Latin *silere,* to be silent.
Ergo *silo* = "I am silent," "I am ceasing,"
silebo = "I shall be still as cows on a hill
chewing their quiet redundant cud,
who trot toward the dark lighthouse
when silence rises with dew on the grass."

4. LITERAL

Best of all is the full balance of vowels,
high/low, the assonant teeth, the liquid
tongue, or the rich little anagrams

of *oils, soil, lois,* or the exotic company
in the dictionary, *silex, silique, silk,*
silva, unutterably lovely *silence.* (See 3.)

5. MILITARY

Missilo? Somehow I can't imagine a silo
outside Rapid City wired and timed to rise,
fire, zip globewise and pop Basil's bulbs.
But NADS assures me South Dakota could
prickle with missiles in a minute, on attack.

6. SEXUAL

(North American Defense System, that is, though
I imagine this link isn't imaginary, this
coincidence coincidental: testy nads, storage
for the phallic silo, obligatory Freudianism—
"built as if each erection were the last." No go.)

7. THEOLOGICAL

Bet you were expecting the pool of Siloam,
a brilliant link between Jesus' muddy miracle
and Georgia's clay, or an eschatological exposition
of the SilAge (also known as the Auto Age), the silly
age in which we live and may well die: but no.
As before, a simple barnyard gloss, on the trinity
in the unity of *silo: fodder, sun,* and *holy goats.*

—Amen? Ah well: not a bad way to sidle up
to Swift, to saddle up the hack. Let me know
what you think of this madness.—And *silo.*

THIS DAY

by ROBERT CREELEY

from THE SOUTHWESTERN REVIEW

nominated by THE SOUTHWESTERN REVIEW

This day after
Thanksgiving the edge
of winter
comes closer.

This grey, dulled
morning the sky
closes down on
the horizon to make

one wonder
if a life lives more
than just looking,
knowing nothing more.

Yet such a gentle
light, faded,
domestic,
impermanent—

one will not
go farther than home
to see this world
so quietly, greyly, shrunken.

♨ ♨ ♨
CONTRIBUTORS'
NOTES

KATHY ACKER has published five novels with small presses and numerous prose works in art and literary periodicals. Her next book, *Blood and Guts in High School,* will soon appear from Stonehill publishing company.

ELEANOR ANTIN is Associate Professor of Art at the University of California, San Diego. She has recently exhibited her art and performed at Ronald Feldman Fine Arts Gallery, Franklin Furnace and elsewhere.

CHANA BLOCHs poetry collection, *The Secrets of the Tribe,* is available from Sheep Meadow Press.

JOSEPH BRODSKY is the author of *A Part of Speech* (Farrar, Straus and Giroux) and other books.

RAYMOND CARVER's *What We Talk About When We Talk About Love* has just been published by Knopf. He lives in Syracuse, New York.

DENISE CASSENS' stories have appeared in *Fiction, Northwest Review, Gallimaufry* and *Akros.*

ROBERT CREELEY is the author most recently of *Later* (New Directions, 1979) and *Mabel: A Story* (Marion Boyars, 1976).

SUSAN ENGBERG has published stories in various quarterlies and has been reprinted three times in The O'Henry collections. She lives in Milwaukee.

LESLIE FIEDLER, the noted critic, and a founding editor of *The Pushcart Prize* series, is Samuel Clemens Professor of English at The State University of New York, Buffalo.

CAROLYN FORCHÉ's book of translations of the poetry of Claribel Algeria, *Flowers From The Volcano,* is forthcoming. She teaches at the University of Arkansas, and won the Yale Series of Younger Poets Award in 1975.

ISABELLA GARDNER has served as Associate Editor of *Poetry.* She lives in New York.

JACK GILBERT is a winner of the Yale Younger Poet's Award and has published in *Esquire, Ironwood* and *American Poetry Review.* He lives in Greece.

LOUISE GLÜCK's third book of poems has just been published by Ecco Press. She lives in Plainfield, Vermont.

WILLIAM GOYEN's books include *Ghost and Flesh: Stories and Tales* (1952), *The Faces of Blood Kindred* (1960) and *Collected Stories* (1975).

LINDA GREGG's first collection, *Too Bright To See,* is forthcoming from Graywolf Press. She lives near Amherst, Massachusetts.

DANIEL HALPERN is the editor of *Antaeus* and the author of three collections of poetry published by Viking/Penguin.

LYN HEJINIAN is the editor of Tuumba Press and lives in Berkeley, California. She is the author of four books.

DAVID HELLERSTEIN is a medical student working at a New York City hospital.

JOSEPHINE JACOBSEN served two terms as Poetry Consultant to The Library of Congress. Her last collection of poems, *The Shade Seller,* was a finalist for The National Book Award.

LAWRENCE KEARNEY lives on Long Island and recently published *Kingdom Come* with Wesleyan University Press.

BENEDICT KIELY lives in Ireland. His collection of short fiction, *The State of Ireland,* was published recently by David Godine, Publisher.

GALWAY KINNELL's most recent book is *Mortal Acts, Mortal Words* (Houghton Mifflin). Previous works include *The Book of Nightmares* (1971) and *Body Rags* (1967).

MARILYN KRYSL teaches at The University of Colorado, Boulder and is the author of *More Palomino, Please, More Fuschia* (Cleveland State).

DENISE LEVERTOV's most recent books are *The Poet In The World* (1973), *Selected Early Verse* (1979), and the forthcoming nonfiction collection *Light Up The Cave* (New Directions, 1981).

DAVID LONG lives in Montana and has published stories in *Canto, North American Review* and *fiction international.*

THOMAS LUX's *Sunday* was published last year by Houghton Mifflin. He teaches at Sarah Lawrence College.

MICHAEL MCFEE was poetry editor of *Carolina Quarterly* and a winner of the 1980 *Discovery/The Nation* prize.

SANDRA MCPHERSON's book, *The Year of Our Birth,* was a 1979 National Book Award nominee. She lives in Portland, Oregon.

DOUGLAS MESSERLI is the editor of *Sun & Moon* and the author of two books of poetry, *Dinner on the Lawn* (1979) and *Some Distance* (1981).

JUDITH MOFFETT has published a volume of poetry, *Keeping Time* (Louisiana State University Press) and teaches at The University of Pennsylvania.

S. NOURBESE was born in Trinidad and presently lives in Toronto, Canada.

DAVID OHLE lives in Austin, Texas. His short story "The Boy Scout" appeared in *Pushcart Prize II*.

SHARON OLDS lives in New York. Her book, *Satan Says*, was just published by The University of Pittsburgh Press.

FRANCIS PHELAN's fiction has appeared in *The New Yorker, The Georgia Review, The Windsor Review* and elsewhere. "Four Ways of Computing Midnight" is part of a larger work he is now finishing, to be title *Impedimenta*.

ROBERT PINSKY's *An Explanation of America* (Princeton) won the 1979-80 Saxifrage Prize. He lives in Berkeley, California.

THEODORE ROSZAK is the author of *The Making of A Counter Culture* and *Person/Planet*. He is Professor of Humanities at San Francisco State University.

PHILIP SCHULTZ's *Like Wings* won an Award in Literature from the American Academy of Arts and Letters. He has recently completed a novel, *Birds of Passage*.

CHEN SHIXU is thirty-four years old and works in Jiujiang County Cultural Center, Jiangxi, China.

LESLIE SILKO's latest book is *Storyteller* (Seaver Books). She lives in the Tucson Mountains, Arizona.

CHARLES SIMIC lives and teaches in New Hampshire. His latest collection of poetry is *Classic Ballroom Dances* (Braziller).

ELIZABETH SPIRES' first book of poems, *Globe*, was published recently by Wesleyan University Press. She teaches at Washington College, Chestertown, Maryland.

JEAN STAFFORD died a few years ago. "Woden's Day" is her last published story.

WILLIAM STAFFORD's most recent collection of poetry is *Stories That Could Be True* (Harper and Row, 1977).

GEORGE STEINER is Professor of Comparative Literature at the University of Geneva and Extraordinary Fellow of Churchill College, Cambridge University. His many books include *After Babel, Language and Silence, Heidegger* and *On Difficulty*.

ELIZABETH ANN TALLENT's fiction has appeared in *The New Yorker, Appalachee Review* and elsewhere. She lives in Santa Fe.

BARRY TARGAN received the Iowa School of Letters Award in Short Fiction (1975) and the Associated Writing Programs Award in the Novel for *Kingdoms* (1980) published by the State University of New York Press.

JULIA THACKER is a second-year fellow at the Fine Arts Work Center, Provincetown, Massachusetts.

DEREK WALCOTT lives in Trinidad. His *The Fortunate Traveller* will soon be published by Farrar, Straus and Giroux.

GAYLE BANEY WHITTIER teaches at the State University of New York, Binghamton, and says she began writing recently while on sabbatical.

C. K. WILLIAMS is the author of *With Ignorance* (Houghton Mifflin, 1977), *I Am The Bitter Name* (Houghton Mifflin, 1972) and lives in Paris, France.

DAVID WOJAHN teaches in the Arizona Poets in the Schools Program and lives in Tucson.

✿ ✿ ✿
OUTSTANDING WRITERS

(The editors also wish to mention the following important works published by small presses last year. Listing is alphabetical by author's last name.)

FICTION

Vertigo of Loss—Steve Abbott (Androgyne)
The Idea of Switzerland—Walter Abish (Partisan Review)
Retribution—Woody Allen (Kenyon Review)
The Apple Orchard—Rudolfo A. Anaya (Bilingual Review)
Manny—Jimmy Santiago Baca (The Sun)
Dead Elephants—Richard X. Bailey (Chicago Review)
from Kepler: A Novel—John Banville (Ploughshares)
The Farewell Party—Donald Barthelme (Fiction)
The Conference—Jonathan Baumbach (North American Review)
The Trail to the Ledge—Janet Beeler (Southwest Review)
Riders—Ralph Beers (TriQuarterly)
Behind Schedule—James G. Bennett (Numen)
Mungo Among The Moors—T. Coraghessan Boyle (Paris Review)
At The Krungthep Plaza—Paul Bowles (Ontario Review)
The Rise and Fall of Sid Winter—Janel Brof (Kansas Quarterly)
selections from Prisoners—Dorothy Bryant (Ata Books)
As Never Before—Edward Bryant (Jelm Mountain)
K.—Jerry Bumpus (Crazyhorse)
The Right Address—Frederick Busch (Columbia)
The Adventure of A Soldier—Italo Calvino (Fiction)
The Calm—Raymond Carver (Iowa Review)
Gazebo—Raymond Carver (Missouri Review)
The Castration of Harry Bluethorn—R. V. Cassill (Epoch)
Blue Dive—Fred Chappell (New South Co.)
Two Dialogues—Marvin Cohen (Sun&Moon)

After Lazarus—Robert Coover (Bruccoli Clark)

Land of Goshen—Elizabeth Cox (Fiction International)

Crocheting—Moira Crone (Washington Review)

The Kudzu—Moira Crone (Ohio Review)

The Death of Picasso—Guy Davenport (Kenyon Review)

Traction—Nicholas Delbanco (TriQuarterly)

A Satisfactory Life—Robb Forman Dew (Virginia Quarterly Review)

Layaways—Stephen Dixon (South Carolina Review)

The Winter Father—Andre Dubus (Sewanee Review)

The Slit—Andrea Dworkin (Frog in the Well Press)

In Deutschland—Pamela Erbe (Antioch Review)

Report from The World Federation of Displaced Writers—Ray Federman (Phoebe)

The Roof—Pierrette Fleutiaux (Fiction)

"big house/Praise Shack"—Leon Forrest (Story Quarterly)

A Pure Soul—Carlos Fuentes (Ontario Review)

An Old Dance—Eugene Garber (Kenyon Review)

Summer Bees—William Gass (Paris Review)

Instant: (This Instant), dialogue—Anthony Gnazzo (Interstate)

The Heart of the Beast—Genaro Gonzales (Riversedge Press)

Augustin—Laurence Gonzales (Hers)

Baby—Ivy Goodman (Ploughshares)

Socialization—Ivy Goodman (Ark River Review)

selections from Shamp of the City Solo—Jaimy Gordon (Treacle Press)

Game Time—Alvin Greenberg (Mississippi Review)

Casus belli—Oakley Hall (TriQuarterly)

Identity Papers—Signe Hammer (New England Review)

David Kissed Me—Rolaine Hochstein (Kansas Quarterly)

The Fifth Day Robert Kennedy Is Shot—R. Hou (Quilt)

The Wedding Storm—David Huddle (Prairie Schooner)

Translation President—Kim Yong Ik (Hudson Review)

Perfect Love—Elizabeth Inness-Brown (Ascent)

Interior Space—John Irving (Fiction)

Mongolian Whiskey—Steve Katz (Seattle Review)

The Birthmark—Anna Kavan (Kesend Publishing)

Grandfather—Claude Koch (Four Quarters)

Fiction—Michael Koch (Ark River Review)

Invention of A Language—Wolfgang Kohlhaase (Pawn Review)

Seduction—Richard Kostelanetz (Benzene)

Honey You've Been Dealt A Winning Hand—Marilyn Krysl (Capra Press)

Home Cooking—Lynn Lauber (Holy Cow!)

Rumors—Norman Lavers (Missouri Review)

Masholowitz's Legacy—Curt Leviant (Midstream)

A Mixed Up Marriage—Meyer Levin (Story Quarterly)

Everything I Know—Gordon Lish (Antioch Review)

Home Fires—David Long (Canto)

Holy Annie—D. R. MacDonald (Canto)

Learn! Learn!—Hugo Martinez-Serros (Revista Chicano-Riguena)

Return to An Unknown City—Jack Matthews (Mississippi Valley Review)

Le Jardin du typo-poète—Kurt Mautz (Kaldron)

Lady of the World—Thomas McAfee (K. M. Gentile Publishing Co.)

Nobody's Angel—Thomas McGuane (TriQuarterly)

from A Waltz—Kevin McIlvoy (Lynx House Press)

Legacies—Shelia McMillen (Ontario Review)

The Blue Star—Mark Jay Mirsky (Fiction)

The Mouth Bone—Mark Mirsky (Mississippi Review)

Three Times The Same Trip—Ursula Molinaro (New Letters)

Chicory—Michael Mooney (Story Press)

Preserves—Mary Morris (Kansas Quarterly)

Gomez—John Mort (Prairie Schooner)

On A Beach Near Herzlia—Jay Neugeboren (Ploughshares)

Mutilated Woman—Joyce Carol Oates (Michigan Quarterly Review)

Fateful Mismatches—Joyce Carol Oates (Ontario Review)

How Amelia Devoted Her Life to Her Son—Sondra S. Olsen (Bloodroot)

The Man With the Pinto Bean Hair—Natalie Petesch (Slow Loris)

The Idiocy of Rural Life—Fred Pfeil (Georgia Review)

Bluegill—Jayne Anne Phillips (Ploughshares)

The Violent Inheritance—R. Pope (Crazyhorse)

Sonng O'Fles Flossen—Bern Porter (Benzene)

Her Visage Terrible to See—T. E. Porter (Numen)

The Waltz Dream—Barbara Reid (Hudson Review)

Twenty-One Days Back—Mark Richard (Shenandoah)

Sepwidjittinknul—Ernest Robson (Interstate)

Addressing The Assassins—Leon Rooke (Prism)
Winter Days Are Long—Robert Roripaugh (Quarterly West)
The Baby Tooth—Carole Rosenthal (13th Moon)
Curriculum Vitae—Henry Roth (December Press)
Uncoupling—Ira Sadoff (Partisan Review)
selections from To Raise A Rainbow—Teo Savory (Unicorn Press)
Her Cup Runneth Over—Penelope Scambly Schott (Bloodroot)
The Celestial Orchestra—Howard Schwartz (Parabola)
Spring Beauty—R. D. Skillings (Apple-wood Press)
The Amorist—Ted Solotaroff (TriQuarterly)
Death of An Art Dealer—Peter Sourian (Ararat)
Guerin and the Presidential Revue—Les Standiford (Pawn Review)
In Vivo—Meredith Steinbach (Antaeus)
Aaron Makes A Match—Steve Stern (Eureka Review)
Mia—Donald Sutherland (Canto)
The Advisor—Linda Svendsen (Plum)
The Aluminium Cage—Steve Szilagyi (Quarto)
Loving Belle Starr—Robert Taylor Jr. (Agni Review)
The Selling of Quantrill's Bones—Robert Taylor Jr. (Western Humanities Review)
China Across the Bay—Sara Vogan (Willow Springs Magazine)
Looking for The Lost Eden—Gordon Weaver (Chariton Review)
Moralty Play—Gordon Weaver (Canto)
Looking Back at My First Story—Eudora Welty (Georgia Review)
Elisa Domingo and the Mayor of Oresta—Julie Westcott (Plum)
Snake Hunt—David Wagoner (Western Humanities Review)
The Crier Outside Bedlam—Gayle Whittier (South Carolina Review)
In The Garden of the North American Martyrs—Tobias Wolff (Antaeus)
Toy Trucks and Fried Rice—John Yau (Release Press)
UFO Story—Gary Youree (Long Pond Review)
Lessons: Janie and Ben—Lee Zacharias (Fiction International)
Two Roads—Harriet Zinnes (Bloodroot)

NONFICTION

Fictionalizing the Past—Daniel Aaron (Partisan Review)

My Philosophical Lecture Notes and Horses—David Adams (Interstate)

Freud, Nietzche—Lorin Anderson (Salmagundi)

Mirror in the Shadows. . .—Beth Bentley (Concerning Poetry)

The Two Stages of An Artist's Life—Robert Bly (Georgia Review)

"The Way I Love George Eliot"—Wayne Booth (Kenyon Review)

Cameras In the Quest for Meaning—J. Y. Bryan (Southwest Review)

Information Fever—Andree Conrad (Book Forum)

The Necessity of Poetry—Cid Corman (New Lazarus)

The Anthropology of Table Manners—Guy Davenport (Antaeus)

The Maypole of Merry Mount—Richard Drinnon (Massachusetts Review)

Knowledge: Why It Doesn't Get Around—Erika Duncan (Book Forum)

The Language of Marbles—George Fortenberry (Southwest Review)

An Arabian Journal—Richard Franck (Salt Lick Press)

Delmore Schwartz and The Death of the Poet—Russell Fraser (Michigan Quarterly Review)

The Myths of Roland—Eugene Goodheart (Partisan Review)

Nommo Muse—Allan Gordon (New Art Examiner)

The Pursuit of Suffering—Daniel Halpern (Antaeus)

Nietzsche's Madness—Ronald Hayman (Partisan Review)

The Birth of The Letter R—Scott Helms (Kaldron)

Public Publishing In Boston—DeWitt Henry (Antioch Review)

Guilty of Everything—Herbert Huncke (Unspeakable Visions)

Rootless Primitives Need Land Masters—Andrew Hope (Quilt)

Blind Tiger: A Meditation—Fanny Howe (Fiction)

Notes for A Study Club Paper—Carolyn Kizer (Shenandoah)

Art Autobiography (1978)—Richard Kostelanetz (Precisely)

The Life of Poetry—Stanley Kunitz (Antaeus)

Faces—Berel Lang (Yale Review)

Lewis Mumford and the Myth of the Machine—Christopher Lasch (Salmagundi)

Some Propaganda for Propaganda—Lucy Lippard (Heresies)

On Some Poems by Mona Van Duyn—Hugh Luke (Pebble)

Everyone Alive Is Incomparable: Osip Mandelstam—Greg Simon (Porch)

The World of Lawrence (selections)—Henry Miller (Capra)

Edgy on The Fringe—Tom Moore (Corona)

Words and Photographs—Wright Morris (Chelsea)

Jean: Some Fragments—Howard Moss (Shenandoah)

Franz Kafka (1883-1924)—Vladimir Nabokov (Partisan Review)

Funk After Death (A Gripe)—Darryl Pinckney (Some Other Magazine)

The Idiom of A Self—Robert Pinsky (American Poetry Review)

America's Black Novelists and the Nobel Prize—James Presley (Southwest Review)

In Memoriam—Robert Hayden—Dorothy Randal-Tsuruta (Black Scholar)

Being Alone—Ned Rorem (Ontario Review)

from Wilderness Plots—Scott Sanders (Georgia Review)

Pilgrimage Around Honshu—Paul Schmidt (Hummingbird Press)

Five Green Thoughts—Paul Shepard (Massachusetts Review)

Defictionalizing James T. Farrell—Harry Smith (The Smith)

Army Brat—William Jay Smith (Hudson Review)

The Archives of Eden—George Steiner (Salmagundi)

The Grain of Poetry—C. W. Truesdale (Milkweek Chronicle)

Arabesque—Richard Vine (Chicago Review)

Andrei Voznesensky and Allen Ginsberg: A Conversation (Paris Review)

The Paper Boy—Richard Wertime (Hudson Review)

Amazon Etymology . . .—Susan J. Wolfe (Sinister Wisdom)

Miz Chapman Tells Us the Score—Al Young (Parabola)

POETRY

The Death of Francisco Pizarro—Ai (Bennington Review)

Rapids—A. R. Ammons (Hudson Review)

A Meditation Upon Christian Science Reading Rooms—Jack Anderson (Some)

Father Fisheye—Peter Balakian (Sheep Meadow Press)

The Bear on the Delhi Road—Earle Birney (Stone Press)

Inventors—Michael Blumenthal (Water Mark Press)

Sermon of the Fallen—David Bottoms (Iowa Review)

The Rose That Desired to Shut Up—Donna Brook (Hanging Loose)

Epithalamion—Olga Broumas (Copper Canyon Press)

With Family Below Albion Basin—Sharon Bryan (Ohio Review)

Quechua—Christopher Buckley (North American Review)

Complaints—Christopher Buckley (Sonora Review)

Smoke—Christopher Buckley (Antaeus)

Mary, Mary—Kathy Callaway (Cutbank)

The Crucifixion—Jean Cocteau (New Directions)

Desire—Peter Cooley (Porch)

Keeping Up with the Signs—Madeline DeFrees (Woman Poet)

8th Avenue Sonata: For Richie Hill—Alexis DeVeaux (Hoo-Doo)

Animal Epitaphs—Donna Disch (Aspen Anthology)

The House Slave—Rita Dove (Inland Boat)

Artesian—John Engles (New England Review)

The Harbor—John Engels (Georgia Review)

Meditation That Concludes on An Atlantic Beach—Robert Farnsworth (Ohio Review)

From Dread In The Eyes of Horses—Tess Gallagher (Ironwood)

Cache la Poudre—James Galvin (Antaeus)

Michael's Room—Reginald Gibbons (Hudson Review)

The Lives of Famous Men—Jack Gilbert (American Poetry Review)

Consent—Louise Glück (Antaeus)

Hawk's Shadow—Louise Glück (Salmagundi)

Mind—Jorie Graham (Water Table)

Grisaille—Debora Greger (Crazyhorse)

This Place—Linda Gregg (Ironwood)

Whole and Without Blessing—Linda Gregg (Ironwood)

A Drive to Los Alamos—Thom Gunn (Threepenny Review)

Canzone—Marilyn Hacker (Shenandoah)

Fields at Baker, Montana—John Haines (Practices of the Wind)

Filet Crochet—Hazel Hall (Ahsahta Press)

Texas Material—Mark Halliday (Ploughshares)

Night Food—Dan Halpern (Missouri Review)

Canto Amor—Sam Hamill (Willow Springs Magazine)

Time In The Woods—William Hathaway (Cimmaron Review)

Tight Denim Jeans—Jana Harris (Quilt)

Empty—Diana O Hehir (Poetry Northwest)

Come—Edwin Honig (Poetry Now)

You Hated Spain—Ted Hughes (Ploughshares)
No One—Cynthia Huntington (Virginia Quarterly Review)
Pondicherry Blues—Josephine Jacobsen (Poetry Now)
Tenor—Laura Jensen (Ironwood)
Jacob and the Angel—Lawrence Kearney (Paris Review)
The Bat—Jane Kenyon (Ploughshares)
What Came to Me—Jane Kenyon (Ploughshares)
Shaping Possibilities—Rudy Kikel (Imaginary Press)
A Muse—Carolyn Kizer (Open Places)
Passion of Body Painting—Yusef Komunyakaa (Panache)
The Doctor of Starlight—Philip Levine (Michigan Quarterly)
Toad, Hog, Assassin, Mirror—Larry Levis (K. M. Gentile)
On The Life That Waits—Laurence Lieberman (Chariton Review)
Making Bread While You Die Next Door—Cleopatra Mathis
    (Southern Review)
Birthday Letter from Rockport—Cleopatra Mathis (Stone Country)
Averted Eyes—William Matthews (Ohio Review)
Unidentified Saints of Misperception—Mekeel McBride (Iowa Re-
    view)
The Field—Heather McHugh (MSS)
The Firefly—Sandra McPherson (Antaeus)
The Mooncalf—Sandra McPherson (Crazyhorse)
Twilight—Samuel Menashe (Maxy's Journal)
Reaching Around—Judith Moffett (Kenyon Review)
Turnhold—John Montague (Ploughshares)
Rothko—James Moore (Paris Review)
Daguerreotypie Der Niagara Falls—Herbert Morris (Shenandoah)
Into Fatahland—Greg Orfalea (Greenfield Review)
Her Patience—Steve Orlen (Sonora Review)
For Some—Linda Orr (L'Epervier Press)
from "Hours Near the Crossing"—John Peck (Pequod)
Feeding the Fire—Joyce Peseroff (Ploughshares)
Picture and Book Remain—Richard Pevear (Agni Review)
Seining The Blue—Wyatt Prunty (Inland Boat)
Waiting—David Rensberger (Bitteroot)
A Day In The Life—William Pitt Root (Bellingham Review)
selections from "Job Speaks"—David Rosenberg (Unmuzzled Ox)
News From All Directions—Carol Ann Russell (Ohio Review)
Why—Michael Ryan (Ploughshares)
Sail—David St. John (Three Sisters)

Clearsightness—Andrew Salkey (Black Scholar)

On The Last Day of The World—Sherod Santos (Poetry)

To Raymond Roseliep—Dennis Schmitz (Crazyhorse)

Singing—Dennis Schmitz (Antaeus)

Holding A Raccoon's Jaw—Gjertrud Schnackenberg (Ploughshares)

Crow King—Robert Schuler (Lame Johnny Press)

False Start—Barry Schwabsky (Some Other Magazine)

When I Remember The Advent of the Dazzling Beauty—Delmore Schwartz (Ontario Review)

On Stage—George Seferis (Georgia Review)

On A Ray of Winter Light—George Seferis (Columbia)

A Jerusalem Notebook—Harvey Shapiro (Poetry)

Anthony—Jane Shore (Ploughshares)

A Theory—Charles Simic (Antaeus)

White—Charles Simic (Logbridge-Rhodes)

History Book—Charles Simic (Durak)

Vine Valley—Jordan Smith (Agni Review)

The Vampire—Jordan Smith (Agni Review)

Thinking About Shelley—Gerald Stern (Poetry)

The Rose Warehouse—Gerald Stern (Missouri Review)

Diggers At Langley—Joan Swift (Owl Creek Press)

Ermine—Joan Swift (Chowder Review)

Oats—Stephen Tapscott (Paris Review)

Spring Was Begging to be Born—James Tate (Massachusetts Review)

The Cat—Vietnamese Folk Poetry (Unicorn)

Correspondents—Arthur Vogelsang (Ascent)

Letter From Vermont—Ellen Bryant Voigt (Antaeus)

Going to Sea—David Wagoner (Prairie Schooner)

The Cap of Darkness—Diane Wakoski (Cedar Rock Press)

The Man Who Loved Islands—Derek Walcott (American Poetry Review)

A Separate Peace—Derek Walcott (Kenyon Review)

Cold Glow: Icehouses—David Wojahn (North American Review)

New Year's Even, 1979—Charles Wright (Iowa Review)

Dog Yoga—Charles Wright (Field)

At the End of Sirmione—James Wright (Antaeus)

Venice—James Wright (Poetry)

Mid-Life Crisis: A Critical Review—Al Young (Threepenny Review)

☙ ☙ ☙
OUTSTANDING SMALL
PRESSES

(These presses made or received nominations for this edition of *The Pushcart Prize*. See the *International Directory of Little Magazines and Small Presses*, Dustbooks, Box 1056, Paradise, CA 95969, for subscription rates, manuscript requirements and a complete international listing of small presses.)

Abaxas, 2322 Rugby Row, Madison, WI 53705
Acorn Press, 185 Merriam St., Weston, MA 02193
Adastra Press, 101 Strong Street, Easthampton, MA 01030
The Agni Review, P. O. Box 349, Cambridge, MA 02138
Ahnoi, 707 90th St., North Bergen, N.J. 07047
Ahsahta Press, Dept. of English, Boise State University, Boise, Idaho 83725
Akros, 21 Cropwell Rd., Radcliffe on Trent, N6122FT England
Alcatraz, 354 Hoover Rd., Santa Cruz, CA 94107
Alcazar Press, 570 Windsor St., Westbury, N.Y. 11590
Alchemist/Light Publishing, P. O. Box 5530, San Francisco, CA 94105
Alembic Press, 1744 Slaterville Rd., Ithaca, N.Y. 14850
Allegany Mountain Press, 111 North 10th St., Orlean, N.Y. 14760
Alta Napa Press, P. O. Box 407, Calistoga, CA 94515
Alternative Publishing, 15 Harriet St., San Francisco, CA 94105
Amateur Writers Journal, P. O. Box 420, Bellaire, OH 43906
American-Canadian Publishers, Inc., Drawer 2078, Portales, NM 88130
American Literary Review, 21 Woodman St., Jamaica Plain, MA 02130
American Man, Box 693, Columbia, MO 21045
The American Poetry Review, 1616 Walnut St., Philadelphia, PA 19103

American Scholar, 1811 Q St., NW, Washington, DC 20009

American Studies Press, Inc., 13511 Palmwood La., Tampa, FL 33624

Amity Books, 1702 Magnolia, Liberty MO 64068

Androqyne Books, 930 Shields St., San Francisco, CA 94172

Anemone Press, P. O. Box 441, Howard University, Washington, D.C. 20059

Amnesty International, 304 W. 58th St., New York, NY 10019

Ansuda Publications, P. O. Box 123, Harris, IA 51345

Antaeus, 1 W. 30th St., New York, N.Y. 10001

Antaries III Ltd., P. O. Box 163, Pasadena, CA 91102

Antenna Magazine, 4353 Piedmont Dr., San Diego, CA 92104

The Antioch Review, P. O. Box 148, Yellow Springs, OH 45387

Apple-Wood Press, Box 2870, Cambridge, MA 02131

Applezaba Press, 410 St. Louis, Long Beach, CA 90814

Ararat, 628 Second Ave., New York, N.Y. 10016

The Ark River Review, Box 14 WSU, Wichita, KS 67208

Ascent, University of Illinois, Urbana, IL 61801

Ashford Press, RR1, Box 128, Ashford, CT 06278

Ashplant Press, Box 235, York, ME 03909

The Asia Mail, P. O. Box 1044, Alexandria, VA 23355

Aspect, 13 Robinson St., Somerville, MA 02145

Aspen Anthology, P. O. Box 3185, Aspen, CO 81611

Asphodel, 613 Howard Ave., Pitman, NJ 08071

Ata Books, 1920 Stuart St., Berkeley, CA 94703

Mike Balisle, Box 730, Stevens Point, WI 54421

Barat Review, Barat College, Lake Forest, IL 60045

The Barnwood Press Cooperative, River House, RR2, Box 11C, Daleville, IN 47334

Before The Rapture, P. O. Box A3604, Chicago, IL 60690

The Bellingham Review, Western Washington University, Bellingham, WA 98225

The Beloit Poetry Journal, P. O. Box 2, Beloit, WI 53511

Benzene Magazine, P. O. Box 383, Village Station, New York, NY 10014

Beyond Baroque Foundation, Old Venice City Hall, P. O. Box 806, Venice, CA 90291

Bieler Press, 4603 Shore Acres Rd., Madison, WI 53711

Big Moon, 309 Rose St., Bellingham, WA 98225

Bilingual Review, Eastern Michigan University, Ypsilanti, MI 48191

Bird Effort, 25 Mudford Ave., Easthampton, NY 11937

Bits Press, Dept. of English, Case Western Reserve, Cleveland, OH 44106

Bitterroot, Blythebourne Station, P. O. Box 51, Brooklyn, NY 11219

Black Buzzard Press, 2217 Shorefield Rd., Apt. 532, Wheaton, MD 20902

Black Cat Bone Press, 3351 Caetoni Ave., Chicago, IL 60657

Black Maria, P. O. Box 25187, Chicago, IL 60625

Black Scholar, 2658 Bridgeway, Sausalito, CA 94965

Black Sparrow Press, P. O. Box 3993, Santa Barbara, CA 93105

Black Veins, 26 Main St., Brockport, NY 14420

The Black Warrior Review, P. O. Box 2936, University, Alabama 35486

Blarney Books, 6139 Shenendoah Dr., Sacramento, CA 95841

Bloodroot Press, P. O. Box 891, Grand Forks, ND 58201

Bloomsbury Review, P. O. Box 8928, Denver, CO 80201

Blue Unicorn, 22 Avon Rd., Kensington, CA 94707

Blue Wolf Press, 1240 Pine St., Boulder, CO 80302

Blueline, Blue Mountain Lake, NY 12812

Blues 10, 1 West 72nd St., New York, NY 10023

BOA Editions, 92 Park Ave., Brockport, NY 114420

Bobbi Enterprises, 1212 South 10th St., Virginia, MN 55792

Bogg Magazine, 2010 N. 21st St., Arlington, VA 22201

Boxcar, 1001-B Guerrero, San Francisco CA 94110

Bravo Editions, 480 Greenwich St., New York, NY 10014

Breitenbush Publications, P. O. Box 02137, Portland, OR 97202

Broken Whisker Studio, P. O. Box 1303, Chicago, IL 60690

Buckles, State University College, 1300 Elmwood Buffalo, NY 14222

Burning Deck, 71 Elmgrove Ave., Providence, RI 02906

California Oranges, P. O. Box 816, Point Keyes Station, CA 94956

Calliope Magazine, Roger William College, Bristol, RI 02809

Calyx, P. O. Box B, Corvallis, OR 97330

The Cambril Press, 912 Stowbridge Dr., Huron, OH 44839

Canadian Forum, 70 The Esplanade, Toronto, Ontario, CANADA M5E1R2

Canto Review of the Arts, 9 Bartlet St., Andover, MA 01810

Canvass Publishing, 1714 Tabor, Houston, TX 77001

The Cape Rock, Southeast Missouri State University, Cape Giraideau, MO 63701

Capra Press, P. O. Box 2068, Santa Barbara, CA 93120

Carolina Quarterly, University of North Carolina, Chapel Hill, N.C. 27514

Carolina Wren Press, 300 Barclay Rd., Chapel Hill, NC 27514

Carpenter Press, Rt. 4, Pomeroy, OH 45769

Cedar Creek Press, P. O. Box 801, DeKalb, IL 60115

Cedar Rock, 1121 Madeline, New Braunfels, TX 78130

Centennial Review, Michigan State University, E. Lansing, MI 48824

Center for the Art of Living, 2203 N. Sheffield, Chicago, IL 60614

Chariton Review, Northeast Missouri State University, Kirksville, MO 73501

Chelsea, Box 5880, Grand Central Station, New York, NY 10017

Cherry Valley Editions, Box 303, Cherry Valley, NY 13320

Chicago Review, University of Chicago, Chicago, IL 60637

Choice, SUNY, Buffalo, NY 14214

Chouteau Review, Box 10016, Kansas City, MO 64111

The Chowder Review, 1720 Vilas Ave., Madison, WI 53711

Christopher's Books, 390 62nd St., Oakland, CA 94618

Cimaron Review, Oklahoma State Universtiy, Stillwater, OK 74074

Cincinnati Poetry Review, University of Cincinnati, Cincinnati, OH 45221

Clown War, P. O. Box 1093, Brooklyn, NY 11202

Columbia, 404 Dodge Hall, Columbia University, New York, NY 10027

Connecticut Quarterly, P. O. Box 68, Enfield, CT 06082

Conceptions Southwest, UNM Box 20, Albuquerque, NM 87121

Concerning Poetry, Western Washington University, Bellingham, WA 98225

Confrontation, Long Island University, Brooklyn, NY 11001

Contact II, Box 451, Bowling Green Station, New York, NY 10004

Contemporary Quarterly, P.O. 4110, Los Angeles, CA 90041

Contraband Magazine, P.O. Box 4093, Sta. A, Portland, ME 04101

Copper Beach Press, Box 1852, Brown University, Providence, RI 02912

Copper Canyon Press, P.O. Box 291, Port Townsend, WA 93368
Copula, W. 1114 Indr Spokane, Wash. 97205
Cornerstone Press, P.O. Box 28048, St. Louis, MO 63119
Cornfield Review, The Ohio State University, Marion OH 43302
Corona, Montana State University, Bozeman, MT 59713
The Countryman Press, Woodstock, VT 05091
Crawl Out Your Window, 704 Nob Ave., del Mar, CA 92014
Crazy Horse, Murray State University, Murray, KY 42071
Crazy Jane, Clark University, Worcester, MA 02170
Croissant & Company, P.O. Box 282, Athens, OH 45701
Crop Dust, Route 2, Box 392, Bealeton, VA 22712
Cross Country, P.O. Box 21081, Woodhaven, NY 11421
Croton Review, P.O. Box 277, Croton-On-Hudson, NY 10520
Cryptoc/Wildcat, P.O. Box 1427, Seminole, OK 74868
Cumberland Journal, Box 2648, Harrisburg, PA 17105
Curbstone Press, 321 Jackson St., Willimantic, CT 06220
Cut Bank, Dept. of Eng., University of Montana, Msia, MT 59801

Dacotah Territory, P.O. Box 775, Moorhead, MN 56560
Dan River Press, P.O. Box 249, Stafford, VA 22554
Dark Horse, P.O. Box 36, Newton Lower Falls, MA 52438
Dark Horse Press, Box 184, Fountain, FL 32438
Dawn Valley Press, P.O. Box 58, New Wilmington, PA 16142
December Press, 6232 N Hayne, #1C, Chicago, IL 60659
Delaware Today, 206 E. Ayre St., Wilmington, DE 19804
Denver Quarterly, University of Denver, Denver, CO 80208
Descant, Texas Christian University, Fort Worth, TX 76129
Dharma Realm Buddhist University, Talmage, CA 95481
Dialogue, Bard College, Annandale, NY 12504
Diana's Bimonthly Press, 71 Elmgrove, Providence, RI 02906
Do It Now Foundation, P.O. Box 5115, Phoenix, AZ 85010
The Dog Ear Press, Hulls Cove, ME 04644
Doggeral Press, 417 Seaview Rd., Santa Barbara, CA 93108
The Donning Company, 5041 Admiral Wright Rd., Virginia Beach,
    VA 23462
Downtown Poets Co-op, GPO Box 1720, Brooklyn, NY 11202
Dreamworks, 72 Fifth Ave., New York, NY 10011
Durak: An International Magazine of Poetry, 166 South Sycamore
    St., Los Angeles, CA 90036

Earth's Daughter's, P.O. Box 41, Central Park Station, Buffalo, NY 14215

East River Anthology, 75 Gates Ave., Montclair, NJ 07042

Elpenor Books, Box 3152, Merchandise Mart Plaza, Chicago, IL 60654

En Passant/Poetry, 4612 Sylvanus Dr., Wilmington, DE 19803

Epoch, Cornell University, Ithaca, NY 14853

ET CETERA, 2988 Wilson School La., Sinking Spring, PA 19608

Eureka Review, 90 Harrison Ave., New Canaan, CT 06840

William Z. Ewert, 167 Centre St., Concord, NH 03301

Exile, Box 546, Downsview, Ontario, Canada

Expanding Horizons, 93-05 68th Ave., Forest Hills, NY 11373

Expedition Press, 420 Davis, Kalamazoo, MI 49007

The Falcon, Mansfield State College, Mansfield, PA 16933

Feminary, P.O. Box 954, Chapel Hill, NC 27514

Feminist Studies, University of Maryland, College Park, MD 20742

Fergeson Productions, P.O. Box 1072, Pearl City, HI 96782

Fiction, c/o Dept. of English, CCNY, Convent Ave. at 138th St., New York, NY 10031

Fiction International, St. Lawrence University, Canton, NY 13617

The Fiddlehead, University of New Brunswick, Fredericton, NB E305A3, Canada

Field, Oberlin College, Oberlin, OH 44074

Firelands Arts Review, Firelands Campus, Huron, OH 44839

Firestein Books, 11959 Barrel Cooper Ct., Reston, VA 22091

Floating Island Publications, P.O. Box 516, Pt. Reyes Station, CA 94956

Fly By Night Review, P.O. Box 921, Huntington, NY 11743

Focus, 1151 Massachusetts Ave., Cambridge, MA 02138

Forest Primeval Press, California Lutheran College, Thousand Oaks, CA 91360

Forms, P.O. Box 3379, San Francisco, CA 94119

Four Corners Press, 463 West St., New York, NY 10014

Frog in the Well, 430 Oakdale Rd., E. Palo Alto, CA 94303

Front St. Trolley, 2125 Acklen Ave., Nashville, TN 37212

From Here Press, Box 219, Fanwood, NJ 07023

C. J. Frompovich Publications, RD 1, Chestnut Rd., Coopersburg, PA 18036

Fuego De Aztlon Publications, 2009 E. 28th St., Oakland, CA 94606

Gargoyle, 40 St. John St., Jamaica Plain, MA 02130
Gargoyle Magazine, P.O. Box 57206, Washington, DC 20031
Gay Community News, 22 Bromfield St., Boston, MA 02108
Gegenschein Press, 711 Third Ave., New York, NY 10003
Genre, University of Oklahoma, Norman, OK 73019
The Georgia Review, University of Georgia, Athens, GA 30602
Giddyup Press, 4812½ Del Mar, San Diego, CA 92107
Gilt Edge, P.O. Box 8081, Missoula, MT 59807
Goldermood Rainbow Press, 331 W. Bonneville, Pasco, WA 99301
Gravida, P.O. Box 118, Bayville, NY 11709
Chael Graham & Press, 415 3rd St., #3, Brooklyn, NY 11215
C. P. Graham Press, P.O. Box 5, Keswick, VA 22947
The Gramercy Review, Box 15362, Los Angeles, CA 90012
Granta Magazine, Kings College, Cambridge, England
Grapevine Weekly, 114 West State Street, Ithaca, NY 14850
Great Basin Press, Box 11162, Reno, NV 89510
The Great Lakes Review, P.O. Box 461, Hudson, OH 44236
Great River Review, P.O. Box 14805, Minneapolis, MN 55414
Great Society Press, 451 Heckman St., Phillipsburg, NJ 08865
Lorna Greene, 1240½ N. Havenhurst, Los Angeles, CA 90046
The Greenfield Review, P.O. Box 80, Greenfield Center, NY 12833
Greenhouse Review, 126 Escalona Dr., Santa Cruz, CA 95060
Greensboro Review, University of North Carolina, Greensboro, NC 274
Griffon House, P.O. Box 81, Whitestone, NY 11350
Groundwater Press, 110 Bleecker St., 18F, New York, NY 10012
Gusto Press, P.O. Box 1009, Bronx, NY 10465
Gutenberg, P.O. Box 26345, San Francisco, CA 94126

Handbook, 50 Spring St., New York, NY 10012
Hanging Loose Press, 231 Wyckoff St., Brooklyn, NY 11210
Hard Press, 340 E. 11th St., New York NY 10003
Harpoon Press, P. O. Box 2581, Anchorage, AK 99510
Harvest Publishers, 907 Santa Barbara St., Santa Barbara, CA 93101
Hearthstone Press, 708 Inglewood Dr., Broderick, CA 95605

The Helen Review, 389 Union St., Brooklyn, NY 11231
Heresies, 225 Lafayette St., New York, NY 10008
Hawaii Review, University of Hawaii, Honolulu, HI 96822
Hills Magazine, 36 Clyde St., San Francisco, CA 94107
Hiram Poetry Review, P. O. Box 162 Hiram, OH 44234
Hollow Springs Press, R.D.1, Chester, MA 01011
Holmgangers Press, 22 Ardithlane, Alamo, CA 94507
Holy Cow! Press, P. O. Box 618, Minneapolis, MN 55440
Home Planet News, P. O. Box 415, Stuyvesant Sta., New York,
    NY 10009
Hot Springs Gazette, P. O. Box 40124, Albuquerque, NM 87196
Hot Water Review, P. O. Box 8396, Philadelphia, PA 19101
The Hudson Review, 65 E. 55th St., New York, NY 10022
Hummingbird Press, 2400 Hannett NE, Albuquerque, NM 81106
The Hungry Years, P. O. Box 7213, Newport Beach, CA 92660

Icarus Press, P. O. Box 8, Baltimore, MD 21139
Images, English Dept., Wright State University, Dayton, OH
    45435
Imaginary Press, 64 Highland Ave., Cambridge, MA 02139
Imagine Magazine, P. O. Box 2715, Waterbury, CT 06720
Imp Press, P. O. Box 93, Buffalo, NY 14213
Impress, P. O. Box 93, Buffalo, NY 14213
Indiana Writes, 110 Morgan Hall, Indiana University, Blooming-
    ton, IN 47401
Inky Trails Publication, P. O. Box 345, Middleton, ID 83644
Inland Boat/Porch Publications, Arizona State University, Tempe,
    AZ 85281
Inprint, 6360 N. Gulford Ave., Indianapolis, IN 46220
Inside/Out, 9 P. O. Box 1185, New York, NY 10116
Interstate, P. O. Box 7068, University Station, Austin, TX 78712
Intro II, Old Dominion University, Norfolk, VA 23502
Invisible City, 6 San Gabriel Dr., Fairfax, CA 94930
The Iowa Review, University of Iowa, Iowa City, IA 52242
Iris Press, 27 Chestnut St., Binghampton, NY 13905
Ironwood, Box 40907, Tucson, AZ 85717
Ithaca House, 108 North Plain Street, Ithaca, NY 14850

J and J Press, 2441 Montgomery Ave., Cardiff-by-the-Sea, CA
    92007

Jackpine Press, 1878 Meadowbrook Dr., Winston-Salem, NC 27104

Jam To-day, P. O. Box 249 Northfield, VT 05663

Alice James Books, 138 Mount Auburn St., Cambridge, MA 02138

Jelm Mountain Publications, 209 Grant Ave., Suite 205, Laramie, WI 82070

Jump River Review, 819 Single Ave., Wausau, WI 54401

Kaldron, 441 N. 6th St., Grover City, GA 93433

Kalliope, Florida Junior College, 101 W. State St., Jacksonville, FL 32202

Kansas Quarterly, Kansas State University, Manhattan, KS 66506

Kayak, 325 Ocean View, Sante Cruz, CA 95062

The Kenyon Review, Kenyon College, Gambier, OH 43022

Michael Kesend Publishing Ltd., 1025 Fifth Ave., New York, NY 10028

Kickingdance Press, 16 E. 8th St., New York, NY 10003

King Publications, P. O. Box 19332, Washington, DC 20036

Konglomerati, P. O. Box 5001, Gulfport, FL 33737

Kulchur Foundation, 261 5th Ave., New York, NY 10016

Lahston Press, P. O. Box 429, Bensalem, PA 19020

Lake Street Review, Box 7188 Powerhorn St., Minneapolis, MN 55407

Lame Johnny Press, Box 66, Hermosa, SD 57744

Landscape, P. O. Box 7107, Berkeley, CA 94707

L=A=N=G=U=A=G=E, 464 Amsterdam Ave., New York, NY 10024

Laurel Review, West Virginia Wesleyan College, Buckhannon, WVA 26201

Lawton Press, 673 Pehlam Rd., New Rochelle, NY 10805

L'epervier Press, 762 Hayes #15, Seattle, WA 10809

Letters, Box 82, Stonington, ME 04681

Letters, 89 Chambers St., New York, NY 10007

Light Living Library, P.O. Box 190, Philomath, OR 97370

The Lightning Tree Inc., P. O. Box 1837, Sante Fe, NM 87501

Lintel Press, P. O. Box 34, St. George, Staten Island, NY 10301

Lions Enterprises, RR3, Box 137, Walkerton, IN 46574

The Little Balkans Press, Inc., 601 Grandieu Heights Terrace, Pittsburgh, KA 66762

Live Oak Press, P. O. Box 99444, San Francisco, CA 94109

Local Drizzle, P. O. Box 388, Carnation, WA 98104

Logbridge-Rhodes, P. O. Box 3254, Durango, CA 81301

Lone Star Review, 2800 Routh, Suite 248, Dallas, TX 75201

Long Island Poetry Collective, Inc., P. O. Box 733, Huntington, NY 11743

Long Pond Review, Suffolk, Community College, Selden, NY 11784

Lowlands Review, 6048 Perrier, New Orleans, LA 70118

Lowy Publishing, 5047 Wigton, Houston, TX 77096

Luna Bisonte Productions, 137 Leland Ave., Columbus, OH 43214

Lynx House Press, Box 800, Amherst, MA 01004

Madison Review, University of Wisconsin, Madison, WI 53706

Maelstrom Review, P. O. Box 4261, Long Beach, CA 90804

Mag City, 437 E. 12th St., (#26), New York, NY 10009

Magic Changes, 1923 Finchley Court, Schaumburg, IL 60194

Magical Blend, P. O. Box 11303, San Francisco, CA 94101

Malahat Review, P. O. Box 1700, Victoria BC V8W2YC Canada

Mango Publications, P. O. Box 28546, San Jose, CA 9515

The Manhattan Review, 304 Third Ave., 4A, New York, NY 10010

Margarine Maypole Orangoutang Express, 3209 Wellesley NE #1, Albuquerque, NM 8707

Massachusetts Review, University of Massachusetts, Amherst, MA 01003

Matrix Press, P. O. Box 327, Palo Alto, CA 94304

McBrooks Press, 106 N. Aurora St., Ithaca, NY 14850

Mela, Vic Marsela 4, Florence, Italy

Merganzer Press, 659 Northmoor Rd., Lake Forest, IL 60045

Merging Media, 59 Sandra Circle, Westfield, NJ 07090

Metis Press, P. O. Box 25187, Chicago, IL 60625

Michigan Quarterly, University of Michigan, Ann Arbor, MI 48109

Mickle Street Review, Rutgers University, Camden, NJ 08103

Midstream, 515 Park Ave., New York, NY 10022

Midwest Poetry Review, Box 359, Sheboygan, WI 53087

The Midwest Quarterly, Pittsburg State University, Pittsburg, KS 66762

Milkweed Chronicle, P. O. Box 24303, Minneapolis, MN 55424

Mill Hank Herald, 916 Middle St., Pittsburgh, PA 15212

Mississippi Mud, 3125 S.E. Van Water, Portland, OR 97222

Mississippi Review, P. O. Box 5144, Hattiesburg, MS 39401

Mississippi Valley Review, Western Illinois University, Macomb, IL 61455

Missouri Review, University of Missouri, Columbia, MO 65211

Mr. Cognito, P. O. Box 627, Pacific University, Forest Grove, OR 97116

Mixed Breed, Box 42, Delray Beach, FL 33444

Mockingbird Press, 160 Sixth Ave., New York, NY 10013

Modern Poetry Studies, 207 Delaware Ave., Buffalo, NY 14202

Moma Magazine, 8565 N. Virginia St., #31, Reno, NV 89510

Moma's Press, P. O. Box 14061, San Francisco, CA 94114

Montoya Poetry Review, California State University, Sacramento, CA 95819

Moody Street Irregulars, P. O. Box 157, Clarence Center, NY 14032

Moonshine Review, Box 488, RRI, Flowery Branch, GA 30542

Mothering Publications, P. O. Box 2046, Albuquerque, NM 87103

Mountain Review, P. O. Box 660, Whitesburg, KY 41858

Moving Out: Feminist Literary & Arts Journal, 4866 Third, Wayne State University, Detroit, MI 48202

MSS, English Department, SUNY, Binghamton, NY 13901

Mudborn Press, 209 W. DelaGuerra, Santa Barbara, CA 93101

Multifarious Press, 2548 N. Bowling, Chicago, IL 60614

Museum of New Mexico Press, P. O. Box 2087, Santa Fe, NM 87503

Naturegraph Publishers, P.O. Box 1075, Happy Camp, CA 96039

New Art Examiner, 230 East Ohio, Chicago, IL 60611

New England Review, Box 170, Hanover, NH 03755

New England Press, 45 Tudor City, New York, NY 10016

New England Sampler, RFD #1, Box M119, Brooks, ME 04921

New Lazarus Press, P.O. Box 27, Station Hill Rd., Barrytown, NY 12507

New Letters, University of Missouri, Kansas City, MO 64110

New Mexico Humanities Review, New Mexico Tech, Socorro, NM 87801

New Orleans Review, Loyola University, New Orleans, LA 70160

New Poets Series, UMBC, 5401 Wilkene Ave., Baltimore, MD 21228

New Renaissance, 9 Heath Rd., Arlington, MA 02174

New River Press, 1602 Selby Ave., St. Paul, MN 55104

The New South Company, 924 Westwood Blvd., Suite 935, Los Angeles, CA 90024

New World Press, 435 Harkness Ave., San Francisco, CA 94130

New York Quarterly, P.O. Box 2415, Grand Central Station, New York, NY 10017

New York State Waterway Project, 799 Greenwich St., New York, NY 10014

Newsletter, Hawaii Literary Arts Council, Honolulu, HI 968817

The Niagara Magazine, 195 Hicks St., 3B, Brooklyn, NY 11201

Nit and Wit, 1908 W. Oakdale, Chicago, IL 60601

Nobodaddy Press, 819 N. Cayuga St., Ithaca, NY 14850

Non Objects, 2810 Creston Rd., Walnut Creek, CA 94596

North American Review, University of Northern Iowa, Cedar Falls, IA 50613

Northeastern University Press, 360 Huntington Ave., Boston, MA 02115

Northern New England Review Press, P.O. Box 111, Amherst, MA 01002

Northwest Review, University of Oregon, Eugene OR 97403

The Not Guilty Press, Box 2563, Grand Central Station, New York, NY 10163

NRG, P.O. Box 14072, Portland, OR 97214

Numen, 3202 Ellerslie Ave., Baltimore, MD 21218

Obsidian, Wayne State University, Detroit, MI 48203

Ohio Journal, Ohio State University, Columbus, OH 43215

Ohio Review, Ohio University, Athens, OH 45701

Old Courthouse Files, Box 74, Albright College, Reading, PA 19603

Ontario Review, 9 Honeybrook Dr., Princeton, NJ 08540

Open Letter, 104 Lyndhurst Ave., Toronto, Canada M5R277

Open Places, Box 2085, Stephens College, Columbia, MO 65215

Osiris, P.O. Box 297, Deerfield, MA 01342

Out and Out Books, 476 Second St., Brooklyn, NY 11215

Outerbridge, P.O. Box 2269, Montgomery, AL 36101

Owl Creek Press, 2220 Quail, Missoula, MT 59801

Pacific Poetry & Fiction Review, San Diego State University, San Diego, CA 92093

Panjamdrum Books, Inc., 11321 Iowa Ave., #1, Los Angeles, CA 90025

Parabola, 150 Fifth Ave., New York, NY 10011

The Paris Review, 541 East 72nd St., New York, NY 10021

Partisan Review, 128 Bay State Rd., Boston, MA 02215

Paunch, 123 Woodward Ave., Buffalo, NY 14214

The Pawn Review, Inc., 1162 Lincoln #287, Walnut Creek, CA 94596

Paycock Press, P.O. Box 57206, Washington, DC 20037

Pebble, University of Nebraska, Lincoln, NB 68588

Peguod, 536 Hill St., San Francisco, CA 94114

Penmaen Press, Lincoln, MA 01745

Penstemon Press, 309 Debs Rd., Madison, WI 53704

Pentagram Press, Box 379, Markesau, WI 53946

Penumbra, P.O. Box 794, Portsmouth, NH 03801

Pequod, P.O. Box 491, Forest Knolls, CA 94933

Periodics, P.O. Box 69375, Station K, Vancouver, BC V5K4W6 Canada

Persea, 225 Lafayette St., New York, NY 10012

Petronium Press, 1255 Nuuanu Ave., #18, Honolulu, HI 96817

Michael J. Phillips Editions, 430 E. Wylie, Bloomington, IN 47401

Philosophy and The Arts, P.O. Box 431, Jerome Ave. Station, Bronx, NY 10468

Phoebe, 4400 University Dr., Fairfax, VA 22030

Piedmont Literary Review, P.O. Box 3656, Danville, VA 24541

Pig Iron Press, P.O. Box 237, Youngstown, OH 44501

Pikeville College Press, Appalachian Study Center, College P.O. Box 2, Pikeville, KY 41501

Pikestaff Publications, P.O. Box 127, Normal, IL 61761

Pin Prick Press, 3877 Meadowbrook Blvd., University Heights, OH 44118

Pittore Euforico Press, Box 1132, Peter Stuyvesant Station, New York, NY 10009

Ploughshares, P.O. Box 529, Cambridge, MA 02139

Plucked Chicken, P.O. Box 160, Morgantown, WV 26505

Plum, 4606 Debilen Circle, Baltimore, MD 21208

Poet Lore, 4000 Albemarle St., N.W., Washington, DC 20016

Poet & Critic, U. of Iowa, Ames, Iowa 50011

Poetry, P.O. Box 4348, Chicago, IL 60680

Poetry Australia, 350 Lyons Rd., Five Dock NSW, Australia 2046

Poetry Northwest, 4045 Brooklyn NE, University of Washington, Seattle, WA 98195

Poetry Now, 3118 K St., Eureka, CA 95501

Poets On, Box 255, Chaplin, CT 06237

The Poet Tree, P.O. Box 25-4502, Sacramento, CA 95825

Poly Tone Press, 16027 Sunburst St., Sepulveda, CA 91343

Pontchartrain Review, P.O. Box 1065, Chalmette, LA 70044

Porch, Arizona State University, Tempe, AZ 85281

Practices of the Wind, P.O. Box 214, Kalamazoo, MI 49005

Prairie Schooner, University of Nebraska, Lincoln, NB 68588

Prairie Sun, P.O. Box 876, Peoria, IL 61652

Precisely, 141 Wooster St., New York, NY 10012

Primary Press, P.O. Box 105A, Parker Ford, PA 19457

Printed Editions, P.O. Box 27, Barrytown, NY 12507

Printed Matter, Inc., 7 Lispenard St., New York, NY 10013

Prism, University of British Columbia, Vancouver, BC V6T1W5 Canada

Provision House, P.O. Box 4587, Austin, TX 78763

Ptolemy/The Browns Mills Review, 136 Lakeshore Dr., Browns Mills, NJ 08015

Published Poet Newsletter, P.O. Box 5658, Everett, WA 98206

Puckerbrush Press, 67 Main St., Orono, ME 04473

Pulp, 720 Greenwich Street, 4-H, New York, NY 10014

Pulse-Finger Press, P.O. Box 18105, Philadelphia, PA 19116

Pyxidium Press, Box 462, Old Chelsea Station, New York, NY 10011

Quality Publications, P.O. Box 2655, Lakewood, OH 44107

Quarry Rest, University of California, Santa Cruz, CA 95064

Quarterly Review of Literature, 26 Haslet Ave., Princeton, NJ 08540

Quarterly West, 312 Olpin Union, University of Utah, Salt Lake City, UT 84112

Quilt, 2140 Shattuck Ave., Rm. 311, Berkeley, CA 94704

Quindara, P.O. Box 5224, Kansas City, KS 66119

Quioxte, P.O. Box 70013, Allen Station, Houston, TX 74007

Raccoon, 323 Hodges St., Memphis, TN 38111

Randatemp Press, P. O. Box 33, Dobbs Ferry, NY 10522

Red Cedar Review, Michigan State University, East Lansing, MI 48823

Red Clay Books, 6366 Sharon Hills Rd., Charlotte, NC 28210

Red Herring Press, 1209 W. Oregon, Urbana, IL 61801

Red Hill Press, 6 San Gabriel Dr., Fairfax, CA 94930

Reflect, 3306 Oregon Ave., Norfolk, VA 23509

Rejection—3828 Lundholm Ave., Oakland, CA 94605

Release Press, 411 Clinton St., Brooklyn, NY 11231

Review, Center for Inter-American Relations, 680 Park Ave., New York, NY 10021

Revista Chicano—Riquena, University of Houston, Houston, TX 77001

Rhino, 77 Lakewood Place, Highland Park, IL 60035

The Richmond Quarterly, P. O. Box 12263, Richmond, VA 23241

River Styx, Big River Association, 7420 Cornell Ave., St. Louis, MO 63130

Riversedge Press, P. O. Box 1547, Edinburg, TX 78539

Rocky Ledge, Wall Street, Salina Star Route, Boulder, CO 80302

Roof Books, 300 Bowery, New York, NY 10012

Roush Books, P. O. Box 4203 Valley Village, North Hollywood, CA 91607

S&S Press, P. O. Box 5931, Austin, TX 78763

Sackbut Review, 2513 Webster Pl., Milwaukee, WI 53211

Scholia Satyrica, University of South Florida, Tampa, FL 33620

St. Andrews, St. Andrews Presbyterian College, Laurinburg, NC 28352

St. Luke's Press, 1407 Union Ave., Memphis TN 38105

Salmagundi, Skidmore College, Saratoga Springs, NY 12866

Salt Lick Magazine, P. O. Box 1064, Quincy, IL 62301

Samisdat, P. O. Box 129, Richford, VT 05976

San Fernando Poetry Journal, 18301 Halsted St., Northridge, CA 91324

San Francisco Arts & Letters, P. O. Box 99394, San Francisco, CA 94109

San Jose Studies, San Jose University, San Jose, CA 95195

San Marcos Review, P. O. Box 4368, Albuquerque, NM 87196

Sands, 17302 Club Hill Dr., Dallas, TX 75248

Santa Susana Press, California State University, Northridge, CA 91324

Saru, 110 W. Kinnear Place, Seattle, WA 98119

Scree Magazine, P. O. Box 1047, Fallon, NV 89406

The Seal Press, 533 11th Ave., East, Seattle, WA 98102

Seattle Review, University of Washington, Seattle, WA 98195

Second Coming Press, P. O. Box 31249, San Francisco, CA 94131

Seven Buffaloes Press, P. O. Box 214, Big Timber, MT 59011

Shankpainter, 24 Pearl Street, Provincetown, MA 02657

Sheep Meadow Press, c/o Persea Books, 225 Lafayette St., New York, NY 10012

Shenandoah, P. O. Box 722, Lexington, VA 24450

John Sherrill, P. O. Box 8623, Austin, TX 78712

Sibyl-Child, P. O. Box 1773, Hyattsville, MD 20788

Sing! Heavenly Muse, P. O. Box 14027, Minneapolis, MN 55414

Singing Horse Press, 825 Morris Rd., Blue Bell, PA 19421

Singing Wind Press, 4164 West Pine, St. Louis, MO 63108

Sitnalta Press, 1881 Sutter St., #103, San Francisco, CA 94115

Skiffy Thyme, 713 Paul St., Newport News, VA 23605

Skywriting, 511 Cambell Ave., Kalamazoo, MI 49007

Slow Loris Press, 923 Highview St., Pittsburgh, PA 15206

The Small Pond Magazine, P. O. Box 664, Stratford, CT 06497

The Smith, 5 Beekman St., New York, NY 10038

Smith's Journal, 2009 Pinehurst Rd., Los Angeles, CA 90068

Snapdragon, University of Idaho, Moscow, ID 83843

Snowy Egret, 205 S. Ninth St., Williamsburg, KY 40769

So & So Magazine, 2864 Folsom St., San Francisco, CA 94110

Some, 309 W. 104, New York NY 10025

Some Other Magazine, 47 Hazen Court, Wayne, NJ 07470

Sonora Review, Dept. of Eng., University of Arizona, Tuscon, AZ 85721

Soundings East, Salem State College, Salem, MA 01970

Source, 161-04 Tamaica Ave., Tamaica, NY 11432

South Carolina Review, Department of English, Clemson University, Clemson, South Carolina 29631

Southern Poetry Review, University of North Carolina, Charlotte, N.C. 28233

Southwestern Review, P. O. Box 44691, LaFayette, LA 70504

Southwest Review, Southern Methodist University, Dallas, Tx 75275

Sou'Wester, Southern Illinois University, Edwardsville, IL 62026

Space and Time, 138 W. 70th St., New York, NY 10023

Sparrow Press, 103 Waldron St., West Lafayette, IN 47906

Spearhead, P. O. Box 1212, Cathedral Station, New York, NY 10021

Speedy Through Press, 56 Clarendon Ave., West Hartford, CT 06110

Spinsters, Ink, RD I, Argyle, NY 12809

The Spirit that Moves Us Press, P. O. Box 1585, Iowa City, IA 52240

Spoon River Poetry Press, P. O. Box 1443, Peoria, IL 61655

Sproing Books, 1150 St. Paul St., Denver, CO 80206

Station Hill Press, Station Hill Rd., Barrytown, NY 12507

Stone Country, 20 Lorraine Rd., Madison, NJ 07940

Stone Press, 1970 Grand River, Okemos MI 48864

Stony Hills, Weeks Mills, New Sharon, ME 04955

Story Press, P. O. Box 10040, Chicago, IL 60610

Story Quarterly, 820 Ridge Rd., Highland Park, IL 60035

Studio S Press, 1600 Preston Lane, Morro Bay, CA 93442

Substence, University of Wisconsin, Madison, WI 53706

The Sun, 412 West Rosemary St., Chapel Hill, NC 27514

Sun & Moon, 4330 Hartwick Rd., College Park, MD 20740

Sunbury, P. O. Box 274, Jerome Sta., Bronx, NY 10468

The Sunstone Press, P. O. Box 2321, Santa Fe, NM 87501

Sun-Scape Publications, % 255 Palisade Ave., Dobbs Ferry, NY 10522

Sewanee Review, University of the South, Sewanee, TN 37375

The Swallow Press, 811 W. Junior Terrace, Chicago, IL 60613

Tales from Austin, University of Texas, Austin, TX 78712

Tanam Press, 40 White Street, New York, NY 10013

Tamarisk Barone, 319 S. Juniper St., Philadelphia, PA 19107

Tar River Poetry, East Carolina University, Greenville, NC 27834

Taugus House, 1890 San Pable Dr., San Marcos, CA 92000

Teachers and Writers Collaborative, 84 Fifth Ave., New York, NY 10011

Texas Art Press, Apt. 294K, 1000 Jackson Keller, San Antonio, TX 78213

Telephone, P. O. Box 672, Old Chelsea Sta., New York, NY 10011

Ten Mile River Poetry Cooperative, 32000 North Highway One, Fort Bragg, CA 95457

Tendril, Box 512, Green Harbor, MA 02041

Third Eye, 189 Kelvin Drive, Tonawanda, NY 14223

Third Press, 1995 Broadway, New York, NY 10023

This, Barrett Watten, 1004-5th Avenue, Oakland, CA 94606

The Threepenny Review, P. O. Box 335, Berkeley, CA 94701

Three Rivers Poetry Journal, P.O. Box 21, Carnegie-Mellon University, Pittsburgh, PA 15213

Three Sisters, P.O. Box 969-Hoya Station, Georgetown University, Washington, DC 20007

13th Moon, Drawer F, Inwood Sta., New York, NY 10034

Thunder Egg Magazine, 707 W. Waveland, Chicago, IL 60613

Thunder Mountain Review, P.O. Box 11126, Birmingham, AL 35202

Thunder's Mouth Press, 1152 S. East Ave., Oak Park, IL 60304

Tide Book Publishing, P.O. Box 268, Manchester, MN 01944

Timberline Press, P.O. Box 294, Mason, TX 76856

Toothpaste Press, P.O. Box 546, West Branch, IA 52358

Total Abandon, P.O. Box 1207, Ashland, OR 97520

Touchstone, P.O. Box 42331, Houston, TX 77042

Towers Club, USA, P.O. Box 2038, Vancouver, WA 90068

Translation Review, University of Texas, Richardson, TX 75080

Connecticut Artists, P.O. Box 131, New Haven, CT 06501

Treacle Press, P.O. Box 638, New Paltz, NY 12561

Triad Press, P.O. Box 42006, Houston, TX 77042

Tri-Quarterly, Northwestern University, Evanston, IL 60201

Truedog Press, 216 West Academy St., Lonoke, AK 72086

Truly Fine Press, P.O. Box 891, Bemidji, MO 56601

Tsá Aszí, C.P.O. Box 12, Pine Hill, NM 87721

Tundra Books, 51 Clinton St., Plattsburgh, NY 12901

Turkey Press, 6746 Sueno Rd., Isla Vista, CA 93017

Tuumba Press, 2639 Russell St., Berkeley, CA 94705

Twickenham Press, 31 Jane St., 17-B, New York, NY 10014

Umlaut, 214 E. 10th St., New York, NY 10003

Unicorn Press, P.O. Box 3307, Greensboro, NC 27402

United Artists Nine, 172 E. 4th St., #9B, New York, NY 10009

Unmuzzled Ox, 105 Hudson St., New York, NY 10013

Unspeakable Visions of The Individual, P.O. Box 439, California, PA 15419

Upland Press, P.O. Box 7390, Chicago, IL 60680

Vanity Press, 160 6th Ave., New York, NY 10003

Vegetable Box, 4142 11th NE, Seattle, WA 98105

Ventura Press, P.O. Box 1076, Guerneville, CA 95446

Violet Press, P.O. Box 398, New York, NY 10009

Virginia Quarterly Review, One West Range, Charlottesville, VA 22903

Volcano Review, P.O. Box 142, Volcano, CA 95689

Washington Review, P.O. Box 50132, Washington, DC 20004

Washington Writers' Publishing House, P.O. Box 50068, Washington, DC 20004

Water Mark, 175 East Shore Road, Huntington Bay, NY 11443

Waterside Press, P.O. Box 1298 Stuyvesant Post Office, New York, NY 10009

Webster Review, Webster College, Webster Groves, MO 63119

West Branch, Bucknell University, Lewisburg, PA 17837

West Coast Poetry Review, 1335 Dartmouth Dr., Reno, NV 89509

The Western Humanities Review, University of Utah, Salt Lake City, UT 84112

Whetstone, R.R. 1, Box 221, St. David, AZ 85630

Whipoorwill Productions, Johnson, VT 05656

Wierdbook Press, Box 35, Amherst Branch, Buffalo, NY 14236

White Ewe Press, P.O. Box 996, Adelphi, MD 20783

White Pine Press, 109 Duerstein St., Buffalo, NY 14210

Wild Horses Potted Plant, 226 Hamilton, Palo Alto, CA 94301

Willow Springs Magazine, P.O. Box 1063, E.W.U. Cheney, WA 99004

Wind, Rt. 1, Box 809K, Pikeville, KY 41501

The Windless Orchard, Indiana University, Fort Wayne, IN 46805

Windflower Press, P.O. Box 32213, Lincoln, NE 68501

Wings Press, RFD 2, Box 325, Belfast, ME 04915

Wire Press, 3448 19th St., San Francisco, CA 94110

The Wisconsin Review, University of Wisconsin, Oshkosh, WI 54901

Wittenberg Review, Ohio University, Athens, OH 45701

Womanchild Press, RFD Ware, MA 01082

Women-in-Literature Incorporated, P.O. Box 12668, Reno, NY 89510

The Word Works, P.O. Box 4054, Washington, DC 20015

Words, Markinch Center, Bowling Green Rd., Fife, Scotland

Working Press, P.O. Box 687, Livermore, CA 94550

The Wormwood Review, P.O. Box 8840, Stockton, CA 95204

Writers Center Press, 6360 N. Guilford Ave., Indianapolis, IN 46220

Writers Forum, University of Colorado, Colorado Springs, CO 80907

Yale Review, 1902A Yale Sta., New Haven, CT 06520

Yellow Moon Press, 20 Tufts St., Cambridge, MA 02139

Yellow Umbrella Press, 2 Chelmsford St., Chelmsford, MA 11018

Zero, 1090 S. La Brea, Los Angeles, CA 90019

Ziesing Brothers Publishing, 768 Main St., Willimantic, CT 06230

Zone, P.O. Box 194, Bay Station, Brooklyn, NY 11235

Zuezda, P.O. Box 9024, Berkeley, CA 94709

INDEX
TO THE FIRST SIX
PUSHCART PRIZE
VOLUMES

The following is a listing in alphabetical order by author's last name of works reprinted in the first six *Pushcart Prize* editions.

Abish, Walter — PARTING SHOT (fiction)   III, 261
Acker, Kathy — NEW YORK CITY IN 1979 (fiction)   VI, 396
Ai — ICE (poetry)   IV, 81
Aleixandre, Vicente — THE WALTZ (poetry)   III, 106
Anania, Michael — OF LIVING BELFRY AND RAMPART: ON
    AMERICAN LITERARY MAGAZINES SINCE 1950
    (nonfiction)   V, 138
Anderson, Jack — CITY JOYS (poetry)   I, 374
Anderson, Jon — LIVES OF THE SAINTS, PART I (poetry)   II, 73
Andrews, Bruce — KEY LARGO (poetry)   III, 510
Antin(ova), Eleanor(a) — A ROMANTIC INTERLUDE (fiction)   VI, 289
Ascher/Straus Collective — EVEN AFTER A MACHINE IS
    DISMANTLED IT CONTINUES TO OPERATE,
    WITH OR WITHOUT PURPOSE (fiction)   III, 402
Ashbery, John — ALL KINDS OF CARESSES (poetry)   II, 257
Atwood, Margaret — THE MAN FROM MARS (fiction)   III, 490
Baber, Asa — TRANQUILITY BASE (fiction)   V, 227
Bailey, Jane — LATE TRACK (poetry)   I, 274
Balaban, John — DOING GOOD (nonfiction)   III, 445
Ball, Bo — WISH BOOK (fiction)   V, 124
Barnes, Jim — THE CHICAGO ODYSSEY (poetry)   V, 374
Batey, Kristine — LOT'S WIFE (poetry)   IV, 129
Beauvais, John H. — AUTUMN EVENING (poetry)   I, 352

Bell, Marvin — FIVE AND TEN (nonfiction)   V, 432

Bellow, Saul — SOME QUESTIONS AND ANSWERS
    (nonfiction)   I, 295

Bennett, John — BEAUTIFUL PEOPLE (poetry)   I, 403

Berg, Stephen — VARIATIONS ON *THE MOUND OF*
    CORPSES IN THE SNOW (poetry)   I, 144

Berriault, Gina — THE INFINITE PASSION OF
    EXPECTATION (fiction)   V, 360

Blandiana, Ana — DON'T YOU EVER SEE THE
    BUTTERFLIES (poetry)   II, 256

Bloch, Chana — THREE STUDIES FOR A HEAD OF JOHN
    THE BAPTIST (poetry)   VI, 470

Blumenthal, Michael — STONES (poetry)   V, 358

Boston, Bruce — BROKEN PORTRAITURE (fiction)   I, 346

Bosworth, David — THE LITERATURE OF AWE (nonfiction)   V, 244

Bowles, Jane — THE IRON TABLE (fiction)   III, 521

Bringhurst, Robert — THE STONECUTTER'S HORSES
    (poetry)   IV, 495

Brodkey, Harold — INTRO (fiction)   I, 419

Brodsky, Joseph — LAGOON (poetry)   VI, 69

Bromige, David — ONE SPRING   V, 156

Brondoli, Michael — SHOWDOWN (fiction)   V, 458

Browne, Michael Dennis — BAD POEMS (poetry)   I, 324

Browne, Michael Dennis — "TALK TO ME BABY" (poetry)   III, 222

Brown, Wesley — GETTING FREEDOM HIGH (fiction)   III, 87

Bulatovic-Vib, Vlada — THE SHARK AND THE
    BUREAUCRAT (fiction)   V, 356

Bumpus, Jerry — LOVERS (fiction)   II, 358

Burlingame, Robert — SOME RECOGNITION OF THE
    JOSHUA LIZARD (poetry)   III, 356

Cannon, Steve (with Ishmael Reed and Quincy Troupe) — THE
    ESSENTIAL ELLISON (interview)   III, 465

Callaway, Kathy — HEART OF THE GARFISH (poetry)   V, 219

Calvino, Italo — THE NAME, THE NOSE (fiction)   II, 321

Carew, Jan — THE CARIBBEAN WRITER AND EXILE
    (nonfiction)   V, 287

Carruth, Hayden — MENDING THE ADOBE (poetry)   II, 505

Carruth, Hayden — SONG: SO OFTEN, SO LONG, I HAVE
    THOUGHT (poetry)   V, 397

Carver, Raymond — SO MUCH WATER SO CLOSE TO
    HOME (fiction)   I, 50

Carver, Raymond — WHAT WE TALK ABOUT WHEN WE
    TALK ABOUT LOVE (fiction)   VI, 88

Cassady, Carolyn — POOR GOD (nonfiction) III, 386

Cassens, Denise — GIRL TALK (fiction) VI, 325

Cervantes, Lorna Dee — MEETING MESCALITO AT OAK
HILL CEMETERY (poetry) IV, 183

Chapman, Diane — VETERAN'S HEAD (poetry) I, 305

Cherry, Kelly — WHERE THE WINGED HORSES TAKE
OFF INTO THE WILD BLUE YONDER FROM (fiction) II, 164

Clark, Naomi — THE BREAKER (poetry) III, 167

Codrescu, Andrei — ANESTHETIC (nonfiction) V, 432

Coffey, Marilyn — PRICKSONG (poetry) I, 49

Cohen, Marvin — THE HUMAN TABLE (fiction) I, 210

Collins, Kathleen — STEPPING BACK (fiction) III, 418

Cope, David — CRASH (poetry) II, 500

Cooper, Jane — CONVERSATION BY THE BODY'S LIGHT
(poetry) III, 352

Cortez, Jayne — THREE DAY NEW YORK BLUES (poetry) II, 471

Crase, Douglas — CUYLERVILLE (poetry) II, 51

Creeley, Robert — THIS DAY (poetry) VI, 492

Crumley, James — WHORES (fiction) III, 427

Cuelho, Art — LIKE A GOOD UNKNOWN POET (poetry) I, 334

Dacey, Philip — THE SLEEP (poetry) II, 369

Dauenhauer, Richard — KOYUKON RIDDLE-POEMS
(poetry) III, 308

Davis, Lydia — MOTHERS (fiction) III, 443

Davis, Thadious M. — FOR PAPA (AND MARCUS GARVEY)
(poetry) IV, 289

Day, R. C. — ANOTHER MARGOT CHAPTER (fiction) IV, 332

Deal, Susan Strayer — SOME CARRY AROUND THIS (poetry) IV, 493

De Andrade, Carlos Drummond — THE ELEPHANT (poetry) I, 342

DeLoria, Vine — CIVILIZATION AND ISOLATION
(nonfiction) IV, 389

Dickstein, Morris — FICTION HOT AND KOOL: DILEMMAS
OF THE EXPERIMENTAL WRITER (nonfiction) I, 309

Dixon, Stephen — MILK IS VERY GOOD FOR YOU (fiction) II, 179

"Domecq, H. Bustos" — MONSTERFEST (fiction) III, 152

Doty, M. R. — THE MAN WHOSE BLOOD TILTED THE
EARTH (poetry) IV, 313

Dubie, Norman — THERE IS A DREAM DREAMING US
(poetry) III, 164

Dubus, Andre — THE FAT GIRL (fiction) III, 357

Eastlake, William — THE DEATH OF THE SUN (fiction) I, 175

Edson, Russell — THE NEIGHBORHOOD DOG (fiction) II, 308

Eigner, Larry — A PUDDLE (poetry) III, 398

Engberg, Susan — IN THE LAND OF PLENTY (fiction)   VI, 219
Engels, John — THE COLD IN MIDDLE LATTITUDES
    (poetry)   V, 550
"El Huitlacoche" — THE MAN WHO INVENTED THE
    AUTOMATIC JUMPING BEAN (nonfiction)   II, 371
Essary, Loris — UNTITLED   III, 487
Federman, Raymond — THE BUICKSPECIAL (fiction)   II, 402
Feld, Ross — LOWGHOST TO LOWGHOST (nonfiction)   II, 430
Feldman, Irving — THE TORTOISE (poetry)   V, 376
Fiedler, Leslie — LITERATURE AND LUCRE (nonfiction)   VI, 429
Field, Edward — THE SAGE OF APPLE VALLEY ON LOVE
    (poetry)   II, 241
Forché, Carolyn — MIENTRAS DURE VIDA, SOBRA EL
    TIEMPO (poetry)   II, 209
Forché, Carolyn — RETURN (poetry)   VI, 75
Fowler, Gene — THE FLOWERING CACTI (poetry)   I, 97
Flanders, Jane — THE STUDENTS OF SNOW (poetry)   V, 546
Fox, Siv Cedering — THE JUGGLER (poetry)   II, 459
Francis, H. E. — A CHRONICLE OF LOVE (fiction)   I, 31
Francis, H. E. — TWO LIVES (fiction)   V, 524
Gallagher, Tess — BLACK MONEY (poetry)   I, 276
Gallagher, Tess — THE RITUAL OF MEMORIES (poetry)   IV, 178
Galvin, James — EVERYONE KNOWS WHOM THE SAVED
    ENVY (poetry)   III, 249
Garber, Eugene — THE LOVER (fiction)   II, 288
Gardner, Isabella — THE WIDOW'S YARD (poetry)   VI, 217
Gardner, John — MORAL FICTION (nonfiction)   III, 52
Gass, William — I WISH YOU WOULDN'T (fiction)   I, 98
Gilbert, Jack — HUNGER (poetry)   VI, 392
Gilchrist, Ellen — RICH (fiction)   IV, 502
Glowney, John — AT DAWN IN WINTER (poetry)   I, 216
Glück, Louise — THE DREAM OF MOURNING (poetry)   III, 169
Glück, Louise — WORLD BREAKING APART (poetry)   VI, 216
Goedicke, Patricia — THOUGH IT LOOKS LIKE A THROAT
    IT IS NOT (poetry)   II, 91
Goodman, Paul — THE TENNIS-GAME (fiction)   II, 387
Graham, Jorie — I WAS TAUGHT THREE (poetry)   V, 316
Gray, Patrick Worth — I COME HOME LATE AT NIGHT
    (poetry)   I, 214
Gusewelle, C. W. — HORST WESSEL (fiction)   III, 228
Goldensohn, Lorrie — LETTER FOR A DAUGHTER (poetry)   III, 220
Gordon, Mary — NOW I AM MARRIED (fiction)   I, 227

Gordett, Marea — THE AIR BETWEEN TWO DESSERTS
(poetry) V, 545
Goyen, William — ARTHUR BOND (fiction) VI, 242
Graff, Gerald — THE POLITICS OF ANTI-REALISM
(nonfiction) IV, 203
Gregg, Linda — THE RIVER AGAIN AND AGAIN (poetry) VI, 441
Grossman, Allen — BY THE POOL (poetry) V, 221
Grossman, Barbara — MY VEGETABLE LOVE (fiction) V, 347
Hall, James B. — MY WORK IN CALIFORNIA (fiction) IV, 267
Halpern, Daniel — DEAD FISH (poetry) VI, 334
Handsome Lake — FARMING (poetry) V, 499
Harmon, William — EIRON *EYES* (nonfiction) V, 503
Harper, Michael — MADE CONNECTIONS (poetry) IV, 352
Hartman, Yuki — CHINATOWN SONATA (poetry) III, 354
Hashim, James — THE PARTY (fiction) II, 258
Hass, Robert — LOWELL'S GRAVEYARD (nonfiction) III, 332
Heaney, Seamus — SWEENEY ASTRAY (poetry) III, 251
Heaney, Seamus — THE OTTER (poetry) V, 84
Hejinian, Lyn — SELECTIONS FROM *MY LIFE* (fiction) VI, 151
Hellerstein, David — DEATH IN THE GLITTER PALACE
(nonfiction) VI, 53
Hendrie, Jr., Don — MORAL CAKE (fiction) III, 76
Herbert, Anne — SNAKE (fiction) III, 281
Hernández, Felisberto — THE DAISY DOLLS (fiction) IV, 88
Hewat, Alan V. — THE BIG STORE (fiction) II, 95
Hillman, Brenda — ANONYMOUS COURTESAN IN A JADE
SHROUD (poetry) IV, 354
Hitchcock, George — MARATHON OF MARMALADE (poetry) V, 154
Hogan, Michael — SILENCE (poetry) I, 273
Hogan, Michael — SPRING (poetry) I, 30
Hollander, John — BLUE WINE (poetry) V, 222
Hoover, Judith — PROTEUS (fiction) IV, 368
Hugo, Richard — MEDICINE BOW (poetry) II, 145
Howell, Christopher — THE WU GENERAL WRITES
FROM FAR AWAY (poetry) III, 85
Hyde, Lewis — ALCOHOL AND POETRY: JOHN BERRYMAN
AND THE BOOZE TALKING (nonfiction) I, 71
Hyde, Lewis — SOME FOOD WE COULD NOT EAT: GIFT
EXCHANGE AND THE IMAGINATION (nonfiction) V, 165
Illyes, Gyula — WHILE THE RECORD PLAYS (poetry) III, 304
Irving, John — THE PENSION GRILLPARZER (fiction) II, 25
Jacobsen, Josephine — A MOTEL IN TORY, N.Y. (poetry) VI, 336

Jensen, Laura — THE CROW IS MISCHIEF (poetry) III, 459
Kauffman, Janet — MENNONITE FARM WIFE (poetry) V, 155
Kaufman, Shirley — LAWRENCE AT TAOS (poetry) IV, 316
Kearney, Lawrence — AFTER THE INTERROGATION VI, 443
    (poetry)
Kent, Margaret — LIVING WITH ANIMALS (poetry) IV, 547
Kermode, Frank — INSTITUTIONAL CONTROL OF
    INTERPRETATION (nonfiction) V, 107
Kiely, Benedict — FIONN IN THE VALLEY (fiction) VI, 276
Kinnell, Galway — THE SADNESS OF BROTHERS (poetry) VI, 329
Kinsella, W. P. — PRETEND DINNERS (fiction) V, 424
Kizer, Carolyn — RUNNING AWAY FROM HOME (poetry) IV, 435
Kloefkorn, William — OUT-AND-DOWN PATTERN (poetry) V, 501
Knight, Etheridge — WE FREE SINGERS BE (poetry) II, 93
Knott, Bill — MY MOTHER'S LIST OF NAMES (poetry) III, 460
Koch, Kenneth — FROM "THE DUPLICATIONS" (poetry) II, 382
Kopp, Karl — CLOE MORGAN (poetry) I, 325
Kornblum, Cinda — IN IOWA (poetry) II, 503
Kostelanetz, Richard — OLYMPIAN PROGRESS II, 456
Kumin, Maxine — ANOTHER FORM OF MARRIAGE (fiction) II, 347
Kunitz, Stanley — QUINNAPOXET (poetry) IV, 378
Kranes, David — CORDIALS (fiction) I, 3
Krysl, Marilyn — LEDA (poetry) VI, 119
Lane, Mary — HOW IT WILL BE (poetry) II, 368
Lasch, Christopher — THE FAMILY AS A HAVEN IN A
    HEARTLESS WORLD (nonfiction) II, 194
Laughlin, James — IN ANOTHER COUNTRY (poetry) IV, 83
Lazard, Naomi — THE PILOT (poetry) I, 307
Levetov, Denise — INTERWEAVINGS... (nonfiction) VI, 258
Levin, Bob — THE BEST RIDE TO NEW YORK (fiction) II, 115
Levine, Miriam — THE STATION (poetry) II, 427
Levine, Philip — A WOMAN WAKING (poetry) II, 457
Levis, Larry — THE OWNERSHIP OF THE NIGHT IV, 284
Lewisohn, James — THEODORE ROETHKE (poetry) II, 501
Linney, Romulus — HOW ST. PETER GOT BALD (fiction) V, 368
Locklin, Gerald — THE LAST ROMANTIC (fiction) II, 461
Long, David — ECLIPSE (fiction) VI, 413
Lopate, Phillip — ODE TO SENILITY (poetry) II, 131
Love, John — A VISION EXPRESSED BY A SERIES OF
    FALSE STATEMENTS (nonfiction) IV, 291
Lovell, Barbara — A WOMAN IN LOVE WITH A BOTTLE
    (nonfiction) IV, 356
Lux, Thomas — BARRETT & BROWNING (poetry) II, 463

Lux, Thomas — AT THE FAR END OF A LONG WHARF
  (poetry) VI, 275
Madden, David — ON THE BIG WIND (fiction) V, 377
Major, Clarence — FUNERAL (poetry) I, 275
Marcus, Adrianne — A LETTER HOME (poetry) II, 498
Martin, Robert K. — WHITMAN'S SONG OF MYSELF:
  HOMOSEXUAL DREAM AND VISION (nonfiction) I, 379
Masterson, Dan — THE SURVIVORS (poetry) III, 69
MacDonald, Susan — HIM & ME (poetry) II, 212
Macmillan, Ian — MESSINGHAUSEN, 1945 (fiction) II, 464
Mandell, Arnold J. — IS DON JUAN ALIVE AND WELL?
  (nonfiction) I, 199
Mathis, Cleopatra — GRANDMOTHER (1895-1928) IV, 500
Mattingly, George — NUMBER SEVENTEEN (poetry) I, 209
Mayer, Bernadette — CARLTON FISK IS MY IDEAL (poetry) III, 485
McBride, Mekeel — WHAT LIGHT THERE IS (poetry) III, 399
McFee, Michael — SILO LETTERS IN THE DEAD OF A
  WARM WINTER (poetry) VI, 489
McCann, David — DAVID (poetry) III, 260
McElroy, Colleen J. — THE GRIOTS WHO KNEW BRER FOX
  (poetry) I, 19
McGrath, Thomas — TRINC: PRAISES II (poetry) V, 268
McHugh, Heather — BREATH (poetry) V, 342
McMahon, Michael — RETARDED CHILDREN IN THE SNOW
  (poetry) I, 400
McPherson, Sandra — FOR JOHANNES BOBROWSKI (poetry) V, 456
McPherson, Sandra — FOR ELIZABETH BISHOP (poetry) VI, 442
Meek, Jay — THE WEEK THE DIRIGIBLE CAME (poetry) II, 470
Messerli, Douglas — EXPERIMENT AND TRADITIONAL
  FORMS...(nonfiction) VI, 304
Metcalf, Paul — THE HAT IN THE SWAMP (fiction) IV, 472
Miller, Henry — JIMMY PASTA (nonfiction) II, 243
Minot, Stephen — HEY, IS ANYONE LISTENING?
  (nonfiction) III, 239
Moffett, Judith — SCATSQUALL IN SPRING (poetry) VI, 273
Molesworth, Charles — CONTEMPORARY POETRY AND THE
  METAPHORS FOR THE POEM (nonfiction) IV, 319
Moss, Howard — SHORT STORIES (poetry) II, 354
Montag, Tom — LECTURING MY DAUGHTER IN HER FIRST
  FALL RAIN (poetry) I, 69
Montale, Eugenio — XENIA (poetry) I, 439 (cloth ed. only)
Mueller, Lisel — THE END OF SCIENCE FICTION (poetry) II, 49
Muravin, Victor — THE RED CROSS NIGHT (fiction) II, 78

Muske, Carol — IDOLATRY (poetry)   V, 422

Myerhoff, Barbara — THE RENEWAL OF THE WORD
(nonfiction)   IV, 48

Nations, Opal — THE U.S. CHINESE IMMIGRANT'S BOOK
OF THE ART OF SEX (fiction)   II, 310

Neville, Susan Schaefer — JOHNNY APPLESEED (fiction)   IV, 486

Nickerson, Sheila — SONG OF THE SOAPSTONE CARVER
(poetry)   I, 399

Nin, Anaïs — WASTE OF TIMELESSNESS (fiction)   III, 312

Nourbese, S. — WHEN I WAS A CHILD (poetry)   VI, 395

Oates, Joyce Carol — THE HALLUCINATION (fiction)   I, 404

O'Brien, Tim — GOING AFTER CACCIATO (fiction)   II, 53

Ohle, David — THE BOY SCOUT (fiction)   II, 464

Ohle, David — THE FLOCCULUS (fiction)   VI, 79

Olds, Sharon — THE GENTLEMEN IN
THE U-BOATS (poetry)   VI, 472

Oliver, Mary — WINTER SLEEP (poetry)   IV, 232

Olson, Charles — ENCOUNTERS WITH EZRA POUND
(nonfiction)   I, 353

Orr, Gregory — PREPARING TO SLEEP (poetry)   II, 504

Ostriker, Alicia — THE NERVES OF A MIDWIFE:
CONTEMPORARY AMERICAN WOMEN'S POETRY
(nonfiction)   IV, 451

Otto, Lon — PLOWING WITH ELEPHANTS (poetry)   IV, 181

Ozick, Cynthia — A LIBERAL'S AUSCHWITZ (nonfiction)   I, 149

Ozick, Cynthia — LEVITATION (fiction)   V, 29

Packard, Steve — STEELMILL BLUES (nonfiction)   I, 278

Payerle, George — WOLFBANE FANE (fiction)   III, 318

Paz, Octavio — HURRY (poetry)   I, 95

Paz, Octavio — LAUGHTER AND PENITENCE (nonfiction)   II, 146

Perkins, David — WRAPPED MINDS (nonfiction)   V, 212

Pershin, Laura — UNTITLED (poetry)   I, 271

Peseroff, Joyce — MAKING A NAME FOR MYSELF (poetry)   III, 400

Peterson, Mary — TO DANCE (fiction)   III, 143

Phelan, Francis — FOUR WAYS OF COMPUTING
MIDNIGHT (fiction)   VI, 338

Phillips, Jayne Anne — SWEETHEARTS (fiction)   II, 317

Phillips, Jayne Anne — HOME (fiction)   IV, 29

Phillips, Jayne Anne — LECHERY (fiction)   IV, 381

Phillips, Robert — THE STONE CRAB: A LOVE POEM
(poetry)   IV, 131

Piercy, Marge — MY MOTHER'S NOVEL (poetry)   III, 488

Pilcrow, John — TURTLE (fiction)   III, 458

Pinsky, Robert — DYING (poetry)   VI, 487

Plante, David — JEAN RHYS: A REMEMBRANCE (nonfiction)   V, 43

Planz, Allen — LIVING ON THE LOWER EAST SIDE . . .
(poetry)   II, 336

Plumly, Stanley — WILDFLOWER (poetry)   IV, 233

Popocatépetl (poetry)   I, 174

Porter, Joe Ashby — SWEETNESS, A THINKING MACHINE
(fiction)   IV, 306

Porter, T. E. — KING'S DAY (fiction)   II, 214

Puig, Manuel — FROM *KISS OF THE SPIDER WOMAN*
(fiction)   IV, 400

Pulaski, Jack — FATHER OF THE BRIDE (fiction)   I, 218

Quagliano, Tony — EXPERIMENTAL LANGUAGE (poetry)   I, 333

Quillen, Ruthellen — WEST VIRGINIA SLEEP SONG
(poetry)   III, 108

Ramsey, Jarold — RABBIT TRANCE (poetry)   II, 191

Ray, David — TAKE ME BACK TO TULSA (poetry)   I, 197

Redmond, Eugene B. — FIVE BLACK POETS: HISTORY,
CONSCIOUSNESS, LOVE AND HARSHNESS
(nonfiction)   I, 154

Reed, Ishamel (with Steve Cannon and Quincy Troupe) — THE
ESSENTIAL ELLISON (interview)   III, 465

Reed, Ishmael — AMERICAN POETRY: LOOKING FOR A
CENTER (nonfiction)   IV, 524

Reilly, Gary — THE BIOGRAPHY MAN (fiction)   IV, 441

Reyzen, Avrom — THE DOG (fiction)   I, 115

Rich, Adrienne — POWER (poetry)   I, 438

Rich, Adrienne — VESUVIUS AT HOME: THE POWER OF
EMILY DICKINSON (nonfiction)   III, 170

Root, William Pitt — MEETING COOT (poetry)   III, 227

Roszak, Theodore — ON THE CONTEMPORARY HUNGER
FOR WONDERS (nonfiction)   VI, 101

Rosenfeld, Alvin — "ARMED FOR WAR": NOTES ON THE
ANTITHETICAL CRITICISM OF HAROLD BLOOM
(nonfiction)   III, 372

Rudnik, Raphael — AMSTERDAM STREET SCENE, 1972
(poetry)   V, 318

Ryan, Margaret — PIG 311 (poetry)   IV, 522

Ryan, Michael — THE PURE LONELINESS (poetry)   II, 144

Rueckert, William — LITERATURE AND ECOLOGY: AN
EXPERIMENT IN ECOCRITICISM (nonfiction)   IV, 142

Sadeh, Pinchas — FROM A JOURNEY THROUGH THE
LAND OF ISRAEL (nonfiction)   III, 110

samizdat — THE DEATH OF YURY GALANSKOV   I, 22

samizdat — THE DEPORTATION OF SOLZHENITSYN
(nonfiction)   II, 339

samizdat — THE TRIAL OF ROZHDESTVOV (nonfiction)   IV, 549

samizdat — ON THE METROPOL ALMANAC (nonfiction)   VI, 386

Sanders, Ed — CODEX WHITE BLIZZARD (nonfiction)   V, 338

Sanders, Ed — THE MOTHER-IN-LAW (fiction)   I, 248

Saner, Reg — THEY SAID (poetry)   II, 395

Sanford, John — THE FIRE AT THE CATHOLIC CHURCH
(fiction)   II, 473

Santos, Sherod — MELANCHOLY DIVORCÉE (poetry)   V, 86

Savory, Teo — THE MONK'S CHIMERA (fiction)   II, 396

Schott, Max — EARLY WINTER (fiction)   IV, 239

Schultz, Philip — ODE (poetry)   VI, 469

Schutzman, Steve — THE BANK ROBBERY (fiction)   II, 464

Schuyler, James — SONG (poetry)   II, 429

Scruggs, Charles — "ALL DRESSED UP BUT NO PLACE
TO GO": THE BLACK WRITER AND HIS AUDIENCE
DURING THE HARLEM RENAISSANCE (nonfiction)   III, 283

Schutt, Christine — THESE WOMEN (fiction)   IV, 473

Schwartz, Lynne Sharon — ROUGH STRIFE (fiction)   III, 29

Schwartz, Rhoda — NOTHING VERY MUCH HAS HAPPENED
HERE (poetry)   I, 147

Scully, James — THE DAY OF THE NIGHT (poetry)   I, 377

Seidman, Hugh — EMBARKMENT (poetry)   III, 425

Shange, Ntozake — TOUSSAINT (poetry)   II, 332

Shannon, Beth Tashery — BONS (fiction)   III, 73

Shapiro, Harvey — MUSICAL SHUTTLE (poetry)   I, 417

Sharp, Constance — I SHOW THE DAFFODILS TO THE
RETARDED KIDS (poetry)   IV, 545

Chen Shixu — THE GENERAL AND THE SMALL TOWN
(fiction)   VI, 473

Shyne, Gerard — COLUMN BEDA (fiction)   V, 89

Silko, Leslie — DEER DANCE/FOR YOUR RETURN (poetry)   III, 49

Silko, Leslie — COYOTE HOLDS A FULL HOUSE IN HIS
HAND (fiction)   VI, 142

Silliman, Ron — SITTING UP, STANDING, TAKING STEPS   IV, 346

Silverman, Maxine — A COMFORT SPELL (poetry)   III, 423

Simic, Charles — A SUITCASE STRAPPED WITH A ROPE
(poetry)   V, 198

Simic, Charles — THE TOMB OF STÉPHEN MALLARMÉ
(poetry)   VI, 121

Smiley, Jane — JEFFREY, BELIEVE ME (fiction)   IV, 299

Smith, Dave — SNOW OWL (poetry)   IV, 127

Smyth, Gjertrud Schnackenberg — FROM LAUGHING WITH
ONE EYE (poetry)   IV, 43

Spencer, Elizabeth — THE GIRL WHO LOVED HORSES
(fiction)   V, 320

Spicer, Jack — A POSTSCRIPT TO THE BERKELEY
RENAISSANCE (poetry)   I, 436

Spires, Elizabeth — BLAME (poetry)   VI, 393

Sprunt, William — A SACRIFICE OF DOGS (poetry)   III, 84

Stafford, Jean — WODEN'S DAY (fiction)   VI, 447

Stafford, William — THINGS THAT HAPPEN WHERE THERE
AREN'T ANY PEOPLE (poetry)   IV, 380

Stafford, William — WAITING IN LINE (poetry)   VI, 73

Stahl, Jerry — RETURN OF THE GENERAL (fiction)   II, 485

Stanton, Maura — BATHROOM WALLS (poetry)   III, 421

Stefanile, Felix — THE NEW CONSCIOUSNESS, THE
NEA AND POETRY TODAY (nonfiction)   II, 491

Steinbach, Meredith — VESTIGES (fiction)   II, 133

Steiner, George — THE ARCHIVES OF EDEN (nonfiction)   VI, 177

Stern, Gerald — PEACE IN THE NEAR EAST (poetry)   I, 146

Stern, Gerald — I REMEMBER GALILEO (poetry)   V, 88

Sternberg, Ricardo — THE ANGEL AND THE MERMAID
(poetry)   III, 307

Stewart, Pamela — THE PEARS (poetry)   V, 435

St. John, David — ELEGY (poetry)   IV, 176

Sukenick, Ronald — THE MONSTER (fiction)   I, 255

Szerlip, Barbara — THE GARMENT OF SADNESS (poetry)   II, 400

Taggart, John — GIANT STEPS (poetry)   V, 343

Taggart, Shirley Ann — GHOSTS LIKE THEM (fiction)   IV, 161

Tallent, Elizabeth Ann — WHY I LOVE COUNTRY MUSIC
(fiction)   VI, 247

Targan, Barry — DOMINION (fiction)   VI, 154

Terrill, Kathryn — TO MY DAUGHTER (poetry)   II, 162

Thacker, Julia — IN GLORY LAND (fiction)   VI, 126

Theroux, Alexander — LYNDA VAN CATS (fiction)   I, 139

Troupe, Quincy (with Steven Cannon and Ismael Reed) — THE
ESSENTIAL ELLISON (interview)   III, 465

Tyler, Anne — THE ARTIFICIAL FAMILY (fiction)   I, 11

Updike, John — TO ED SISSMAN (poetry)   IV, 311

Vallejo, Cesar — THE SPANISH IMAGE OF DEATH (poetry)   IV, 287

Van Brunt, H. L. — THE SPRING (poetry)   I, 195

Van Duyn, Mona — LETTERS FROM A FATHER (poetry)   IV, 235

Van Walleghen, Michael — ARIZONA MOVIES (poetry)   II, 279

Vaughn, Stephanie — SWEET TALK (fiction) V, 201

Venn, George — FORGIVE US. . . (poetry) IV, 470

Vine, Richard — FROM THE DEATH OF LOVE: A SATANIC
    ESSAY IN MOBIUS FORM (nonfiction) V, 405

Vishniac, Roman — THE LIFE THAT DISAPPEARED
    (photographs) III, 512 (cloth only)

Vogan, Sara — SCENES FROM THE HOMEFRONT (fiction) V, 437

Walcott, Derek — CANTINA MUSIC (poetry) VI, 50

Wantling, William — STYLE THREE AND STYLE FOUR
    (nonfiction) I, 328

Warren, Robert Penn — THE ONLY POEM (poetry) V, 548

Watkins, Barbara — JOSEFA KANKOVSKA (poetry) V, 403

Wagoner, David — MISSING THE TRAIL (poetry) I, 10

Wagoner, David — WHISPER SONG (poetry) V, 523

Walser, Robert — TWO STRANGE STORIES (fiction) III, 441

Walsh, Marnie — VICKIE LOANS-ARROW, FORT YATES, NO.
    DAK. 1970 (poetry) II, 284

Weaver, Marvin — LOST COLONY (poetry) I, 376

Weigl, Bruce — TEMPLE NEAR QUANG TRI, NOT ON THE
    MAP (poetry) V, 199

Weinstein, Jeff — A JEAN-MARIE COOKBOOK (fiction) IV, 185

Weissmann, David — FALLING TOWARD THANKSGIVING
    (poetry) I, 401

Weizenbaum, Joseph — SCIENCE AND THE COMPULSIVE
    PROGRAMMER (nonfiction) I, 122

Whittier, Gayle — LOST TIME ACCIDENT (fiction) VI, 29

Wiebe, Dallas — NIGHT FLIGHT TO STOCKHOLM (fiction) IV, 133

Wilbur, Ellen — FAITH (fiction) V, 275

Willard, Nancy — HOW THE HEN SOLD HER EGGS TO
    THE STINGY PRIEST (poetry) III, 306

Williams, C. K. — FLOOR (poetry) VI, 213

Willson, John — DREAM (poetry) IV, 546

Wilson, Jr., Robley — THE UNITED STATES (fiction) III, 197

Witt, Harold — STATIONERY, CARDS, NOTIONS, BOOKS
    (poetry) I, 418

"Workers University" — THE OTHER FACE OF BREAD
    (nonfiction) III, 208

Wojahn, David — WELDON KEES IN MEXICO (poetry) VI, 124

Wright, Charles — PORTRAIT OF THE ARTIST WITH LI PO
    (poetry) V, 315

Wright, James — YOUNG WOMEN AT CHARTRES (poetry) V, 136

Wuori, G. K. — AFRIKAAN BOTTLES (fiction) I, 336

Young, Al — MICHAEL AT SIXTEEN MONTHS (poetry)   V, 346
Yvonne — THE TEARING OF THE SKIN (poetry)   III, 462
Zawadiwsky, Christine — WITH THE REST OF MY BODY
    (poetry)   II, 192
Zelver, Patricia — STORY (fiction)   V, 399
Zimmer, Max — UTAH DIED FOR YOUR SINS (fiction)   III, 135
Zimmer, Paul — ZIMMER DRUNK AND ALONE, DREAM-
    ING OF OLD FOOTBALL GAMES (poetry)   II, 72
Zimmon, Howard — GRANDPARENTS (poetry)   I, 245

CALEDONIA, the type in which this book was set is one of those referred to by printers, as a "modern face". It was designed around 1939 by W.A. Dwiggins (1880–1956) and it has been called "the most popular all-purpose typeface in U.S. history".

It is an original design, but, as from the beginning, fresh and exciting designs have often evolved from variations on the old, done by competent and disciplined hands. Caledonia shows marks of the long admired Scotch roman type-letters cut by Alexander Wilson in Glasgow in the 19th century. It also shows a trace from the types that W. Bulmer & Company used, cut in London, around 1790 by William Martin.

That Dwiggins was aware of the particular needs of our time is soundly attested to in the enduring good reception his "hard working, feet-on-the-ground" type has received from countless printers, authors and readers alike.

This book was designed and produced for the publisher, by RAY FREIMAN & COMPANY, Stamford, Connecticut.